PRAISE FOR F. SIONIL JOSÉ

"The foremost Filipino novelist in English, his novels deserve a much wider readership than the Philippines can offer. His major work, the Rosales Saga, can be read as an allegory for the Filipino in search of an identity."
—IAN BURUMA, *The New York Review of Books*

"One of the [Philippines'] most distinguished men of letters."
—*Time*

"America has no counterpart . . . no one who is simultaneously a prolific novelist, a social and political organizer, an editor and journalist, and a small-scale entrepreneur. . . . As a writer, José is famous for two bodies of work. One is the Rosales sequence, a set of five novels published over a twenty-year span which has become a kind of national saga."
—JAMES FALLOWS, *The Atlantic*

"Impressive is José's ability to tell important stories in a lucid, but never merely simple prose. . . . It's refreshing to see a politically engaged writer who dares to reach for a broader audience."
—LAURA MILLER, *San Francisco Weekly*

"Tolstoy himself, not to mention Italo Svevo, would envy the author of this story. . . . This short . . . scorching work whets our appetite for Sionil José's masterpiece, the five-novel Rosales Saga."
—JOSEPH COATES, *Chicago Tribune*

"[José is] an outstanding writer. If ever a Nobel Prize in literature will be awarded to a Southeast Asian writer, it will be to F. Sionil José."
—*The Mainichi Shimbun* (Tokyo)

"Considered by many to be Asia's most likely candidate for the Nobel Prize for literature."
—*The Singapore Straits Times*

Also by F. Sionil José

Short Stories
The God Stealer and Other Stories
Waywaya: Eleven Filipino Short Stories
Platinum: Ten Filipino Stories
Olvidon and Other Short Stories
Puppy Love and Other Stories

Novellas
Three Filipino Women

Novels
Ermita
Gagamba
Viajero
Sins

The Rosales Saga
Published in the United States as:
Don Vicente, comprising *Tree* and *My Brother, My Executioner*
Dusk
The Samsons, comprising *The Pretenders* and *Mass*

Verse
Questions

Nonfiction
In Search of the Word
We Filipinos: Our Moral Malaise, Our Heroic Heritage
A Memoir of Japan
Hindsight Perceptions on Nation and Culture

The Samsons

The Samsons

TWO NOVELS IN THE ROSALES SAGA

THE PRETENDERS

and

MASS

F. Sionil José

THE MODERN LIBRARY
NEW YORK

2000 Modern Library Paperback Original

Copyright © 2000 by F. Sionil José

All rights reserved under International and Pan-American
Copyright Conventions. Published in the United States by
Random House, Inc., New York, and simultaneously in Canada
by Random House of Canada Limited, Toronto.

Modern Library and colophon are registered trademarks of Random House, Inc.

The novels in this work were originally published separately as *The Pretenders*
(copyright © 1962 by F. Sionil José) and *Mass* (copyright © 1982, 1983 by
F. Sionil José) by Solidaridad Publishing House, Manila, Philippines.

LIBRARY OF CONGRESS CATALOGING-IN-PUBLICATION DATA
José, F. Sionil (Francisco Sionil).
The Samsons: The pretenders; and, Mass / F. Sionil José.
p.   cm.
"Originally published in English as The pretenders, and Mass"—T.p. verso.
ISBN 0-375-75244-7
1. Philippines—History—1898—Fiction. I. José, F. Sionil (Francisco Sionil),
1924– Pretenders. II. José, F. Sionil (Francisco Sionil), 1924– Mass. III. Title.
PR9550.9.J67 S26 2000
823—dc21
99-087896

Printed in the United States of America

Modern Library website address: www.modernlibrary.com

2 4 6 8 9 7 5 3

First Edition

CONTENTS

The Pretenders

1

Mass

245

Afterword: Notes on the Writing of a Saga

535

The Pretenders

For Teresita

. . . They were bright young men who knew what money meant. But though they were rich and were educated in the best schools of Europe, their horizons were limited and they knew they could never belong to the alien aristocracy which determined the future. . . . They cried for reforms, for wider opportunities, for equality. Did they plead for freedom, too? And dignity for all Indios—and not only for themselves who owed their fortunes and their status to the whims of the aristocracy? Could it be that they wanted not freedom or dignity but the key to the restricted enclaves of the rulers?

—ANTONIO SAMSON, *The Ilustrados*

CHORAGUS

O N T H E N I G H T her husband left her, Mrs. Antonio Samson
could not sleep. It was not the first time she had committed an
indiscretion. In the past few weeks she had lied to him and acted as
if she had always been the faithful wife, and she had easily gone to
sleep feeling sure that, even if her husband found out, he would not
be able to do anything about it except, perhaps, make a nasty little
scene. She was sure of him and of his reactions, just as she had long
grown accustomed to the taste of his mouth, his smell, and the contours of his body. It was a comforting knowledge, and it gave her a
sense of power and security which grew out of an intimacy that tran-
scended the clasping of bodies and the living together. She had always been very intuitive, and when she occasionally looked back,
she knew that everything fell neatly into place—her meeting Antonio
Samson in Washington, his diffidence, and her final acceptance of
him springing not out of human necessity but out of curiosity and
the need to be possessed by someone who did not care if she was
Carmen Villa.

But tonight, alone in the big room that had been their sanctum
all their married life, she was nagged for the first time by a pang of

regret and remorse so sharp and intense it actually hurt. All her life she had been pampered, had everything she desired. The things she valued were never those that could be bought, but those small tokens of truth and dogged fidelity that she, herself, could not give to anyone. It was not the first time that she would sleep alone; there were the times her husband had gone on business trips, and she had gotten used to such absences knowing that they were not permanent, that he would be back. Tonight, however, she was not sure. She had tried reading the books from the shelf by their bed—some anthologies, journals, and pocketbooks that her husband always had close by, but her mind could not latch on to anything she could retain. She stood up and, noticing the torn bits of paper with which her husband had littered the floor, started picking them up out of curiosity more than anything, and read the old, yellowed pages of the book that they had brought back from the Ilocos. It was in Latin and, of course, she did not understand. Then, as if she remembered that these bits of paper were important, she scooped them up and placed them in the shoe boxes that lined one of the closets in the room. The work tired her a little but still sleep would not come. For the first time, she was afraid that Tony Samson would never return, that when he said good-bye the parting was permanent, as final as death itself.

When she did fall asleep it was almost light and the east was already gray. She slept briefly but well, and when she woke up she immediately missed the arm that was usually flung across her breast, the warm nearness of a body she had known. She was angry at herself without quite knowing why, and when she drew the curtains, the sunlight that flooded the room hurt her eyes; she looked at herself in the mirror and, without her makeup and lipstick, she told herself that she was becoming a hag; the dark lines around her eyes, the beginning of a double chin, the start of wrinkles around her neck—these brought to her the presence of time, the enemy. She had once told her husband: I won't mind growing old, I won't mind really, as long as I have you always beside me and doing what would make me happy.

But he was not by her side, and shortly afterward her father knocked on the door and told her in a flat, toneless voice that her husband was dead—a horrible accident at the tracks in Antipolo

Street—and remembering this later on, she marveled at her presence of mind, how she took the news calmly as if it was the most natural thing to have happened. Her first reaction was of disbelief; it was not true, he had just gone off somewhere, to sulk, to let his jealousy pass; he was not dead, he was coming back, and not only because with her he had finally been freed of that dreary place where he had come from. This would be just one reason for his return, of course; the real reason would be because he loved her and would take her for all that she was—good and bad, sinner and saint.

But the past is irreversible; the funeral she attended together with her parents was nothing but a blur; she did not want to believe that the man she had loved, who had possessed her and lived with her for more than a year, was in that beautiful, sealed mahogany casket, never again to talk with her, to share her gossip. And somehow, aware of this at last, of the finality of it all, she felt that she could not bear the loneliness, not so much of being alone but of knowing that she had perhaps driven him to his death.

When the funeral was over she decided for the first time to visit the place where he had lived; she had extracted the address from Tony's sister, who was clear-eyed and stony-faced throughout the funeral service, and she had driven the sister and her husband back to Antipolo Street. They showed her that portion of the tracks where they had picked up the mangled pieces of his body, and she stopped and touched the earth and the rockbed of the tracks, which were still stained with blood, and as she did something within her snapped. The last time she saw his blood was in the winter past; they had gone out for a walk in the fresh snow in Central Park and he had sneezed violently; he had a nosebleed, not a cold, and the blood speckled the snow, brilliant crimson against angel white, and even in that awful moment he had paused before the pattern and exclaimed, "How beautiful!"

They took her up the narrow alley, lined with people and children who stared at her, to their clapboard house and up the narrow flight to the small room where Tony had lived. His two suitcases were placed on one side and she asked if she could bring them back to their home, but they did not want her to; they wanted to keep something that belonged to him, to remember him by; she offered them money but they would not take it. There must be something he left behind, they said; and she said, yes, there were many things, but mostly memories. She looked around her; she had never been cooped up in a place as small as this, and yet, somehow, it did not depress her as she was sometimes depressed at home. She looked down the window, at the tracks again, and along the tracks more shacks fronted by patches of camote and greens, and suddenly she could not stand another moment in this place, in this Antipolo where Tony had lived. She went down, trembling and sweating in the morning heat, and to each of the youngsters in the living room she thrust paper bills. They took her to the car she had parked at the other end of the alley, and to their mumbled apologies about their inability to entertain her in the best way possible, she whispered a listless thank-you and then drove off, a thousand accusations tormenting her. The whole wretched city now seemed one vast prison closing in on her and she would no longer be someone apart, with an identity all her own, but a member of the nameless mass, an insignificant fragment of the crowd. It was different when Tony was alive, for he had given her not just love and devotion but, in a real sense, a personality that she had not known was there: he had been very honest with her, sometimes too damning in his criticism, but always, in the end, ever lavish in his praise. Her virtues stood out—her capacity to see her role as a woman, her indifference to the vulgar tastes of her crowd, her own rebelliousness not so much against her family but against what her family had stood for: the vaunted privilege, the snobbery, when these were never real in a society as wide open as Manila's.

In her own room she pondered these, for she now understood them. But there was something that never quite got itself spelled out clearly, and this was how she had given herself to him. She had always valued chastity not so much as a prize to be won but as a gift of love to be given in complete abandon to him whom she could trust, to a man with whom she would not mind a life of captivity.

This was the sole mystery that she could not solve. Maybe it was his fluent conversation—she always admired men who could express themselves clearly, who could argue themselves out of nooses, and Tony seemed capable of that without being boorish or pedantic. Maybe, as he had told her once too often, it was the tedium of being alone in a foreign land, unable to draw the cloying attention that she had always been used to.

Or maybe she was drawn to him as evil is drawn to virtue and all that is good—as Tony was. What he had told her was true, after all—that she was hopeless, and her family, too, and all of them, her father's friends, her friends who vacationed in Spain to polish their accents and, perhaps, to bring home some peasant they could afterward pass off as an impoverished member of the aristocracy.

Was it also true that they were all beyond redemption? She had laughed when he first told her this; it had seemed so funny then, for she had understood corruption to mean committing malfeasances in public office, in pocketing government money, accepting bribes, and that sort of thing. Even if she did commit an indiscretion, it was not really that bad; she had not, after all, left him the way Conchita Reyes, the daughter of Senator Reyes, had left her husband and gone to Italy chasing a bogus count. She had returned to Pobres Park and to her husband, who took her back as if nothing had happened, and they had rejoined the same cocktail-cum-dinner circuit as impeccably gracious as ever. In her own way, Mrs. Antonio Samson considered herself faithful. While most of the women in the Park, particularly those in her circle, changed husbands more often than their monthly visitations, she had done no such thing. She had played around only with Ben de Jesus, who, after all, had proposed marriage to her earlier. She had acceded, yes, but with a feeling of guilt not only toward her husband but toward Ben's wife, who was her best friend.

She could, of course, justify what she had done with her modern, "liberated" background. Besides, her husband was the sporting kind; in bed, when they were going through the habits of conjugal love, he would often think aloud about how it would be if he went to bed with any of her friends, and she would egg him on and tell him what her friends thought of their own husbands, how they told her of their extramarital experiences, and he had been delighted, of course, listening to her stories. It took some time, but she did realize later that he was really no more than a *provinciano*, charming in his own barrio way, who must be protected from his own simplicity.

SHE VISITED her husband's office the day after the funeral; she had become curious about what he might have left there, the mementos that were to be recovered and permanently treasured. Tony had a way of putting down on paper his ideas and all the minutiae that he came across; this was part of his training as a scholar, and the habit had been deeply ingrained. If she had not bothered herself before with knowing about what he wrote or the thoughts that often went unsaid between them, now she wanted to know all that she could about him, the wellsprings of his strengths and weaknesses, the visions he had of himself and the future. Perhaps, in the process of learning and even discovery, she would stumble upon the primordial reasons for life and death.

Her husband's secretary had been most efficient; she had filed all his papers with skill and precision and told her where everything was, even the bills that had to be paid. She was stunned by the tragedy, and she told the widow that she had never worked for a man as dedicated to his job and as understanding of people as Tony. She was handsome in an antiseptic sort of way, and Carmen wondered momentarily if her husband had ever flirted with her or had appreciated the fact that she had broad hips.

"I want to be alone," the widow said. "I would like to go over all his things, so please do not let anyone disturb me."

The secretary delivered to her all the keys to the drawers and the filing cabinets and Carmen riffled through them. She examined the expense vouchers and the receipts that Tony had assiduously kept and smiled, remembering again how Tony had lived as honestly and as frugally as always, within the limitations her father had mentioned, although such limitations had never been defined.

Then, at the bottom drawer of his desk, she found them—the ledgers in which he had written in his clear, precise longhand a sort of diary. Five of them, and four were filled up; the fifth was half full, and the last entry was three months ago. He had not written anything for a long time, although in the others he had something—a paragraph, or even just a line—every day. The entries in the last ledger were about things she knew very well—her family, her husband's work, his impressions of people he met. Here was Antonio Samson at last—raw, honest, and without pretensions. And yet, he could have told her everything he had written down, if she had just shown an interest, even the slightest. He had even brought his journal home—she remembered this clearly now—and had started to write one evening, but she told him to attend to her rather than to his memoirs. And now that he was gone, these ideas, these thoughts were suddenly alive; she could hear his voice as she read what he had written about himself; his most secret thoughts. The last entry, however, was what interested Carmen most, for it pertained to her, and in a way, it was prophetic.

Antonio Samson wrote:

I must now ask myself the purpose, the meaning of my life. Once, long ago, this was never clear to me. If I thought about life's purpose at all, I did not think of it as something beyond crassness, of which I was terribly ashamed. I did not have the means to think otherwise; I did not enjoy the luxury of contemplation, although I must admit that even in my youth I could be capable of questioning, for instance, the presence of God and the grand design wherein some are exploiters and the rest are the exploited. In those days, my only thoughts were of survival—the stern, physical kind that occupies the soldier when he is on the battlefield. Then, all that occupied me were how to finish school, get a job so that I could earn something to keep myself alive; and keeping alive meant three meals a day, a roof over my head that did not leak, a pair of shoes, clean clothes. It is all changed now and these objectives to which I addressed myself in the past are no longer my objectives. Does this mean then that I have gone very far? Economically, yes. My earliest desires were all economic, the most elementary of needs. Now, I have raised my objectives a little higher. This again is natural. No one really needs six meals a day, or two dozen pairs of shoes; to be crude about it, a man can eat only so much, wear so much. To be dross about it, a man—unless he is a superman or a sex maniac—can have only one sexual intercourse a day, or at the most, two. So what do I want out of life? I want to be justified. Whatever I do, in my heart, I want it to be right, I want to say I did it because it had to be done. I may be proved wrong, but it does not matter; at least, to my own self, I must be true. No Hamlet here, just the simple fact of a human being wanting for himself the integrity that everyone desires in his deepest thoughts, in his fondest dreams. This should be clearest to her who is my wife, who knows me now as no mortal has ever known me, for it is to her that I have voiced my understanding and, most of all, respect. God knows how much I have tried to earn her respect, to have her see that I am a person and not a thing, to have her feel the importance of the ideas, the ends that I have set for myself in the past; they are still valid even if no longer within my grasp. I have tried to define for myself what honor should be, but now it has become vague and formless. I clutch at the air, hoping to hold on to something real, but there is nothing there. And every day seems to be push-ing me farther and farther away from what I want, which is not my wife's body, which is not her family's regard for me, but the justification that I am doing what should be done in this wretched and despicable land. I see the estrangement although I will not say that it is inevitable. I will not say it is written in the stars, for fate is not as constricted, as unswerving, as all that. I only wish that someday I will be capable of doing something heroic, a deed that would ennoble me not only to myself but, most of all, to her who has accepted me for what I am. If I could be sure, however, even just for one instant, that she chose me be-cause she loved and respected me, then I would know that there is at least one human being to whom I have some value. Other-wise, it is a bleak world indeed where I have paused, and the sooner I leave it, the better.

SHE WENT over the last journal as avidly as she did the first dirty book Conchita Reyes gave her, and when she was through it seemed as if some heavy burden had been lifted from her shoulders. It was as if she knew not only her husband but the whole mystery of life; she was alive, she could pass her palms over tabletops and feel the smoothness; she could feel a dry martini scorch her throat, smell the fumes of traffic, hear the minutest tick of the clock, the scampering of some lonely cockroach across the bedroom floor. She was alive, she could explain herself, her father and mother, all her friends; she could understand why they breathed the same foul air every day, but she could not understand why Tony was dead.

Then she remembered the torn manuscripts that she had packed in the shoe boxes, and she fell to sorting them out, arranging them page by page. For days, she worked at it feverishly, barely eating any-thing while she was at it, not accepting condolences or telephone calls. But when everything was ready, taped, and arranged, she was as much in the dark as ever.

One evening, during a dinner at which she had not spoken a word, her father asked if she was feeling well. Her mother had been concerned about how little she had been eating and had ordered the cook to stock her room with fruits so that she could nibble on something if she were hungry.

"I am all right, Papa," she said, turning to her father. She noticed at once that he looked tired, that there were deepening lines in his lean, handsome face.

"I just don't have the appetite I used to have."

"We were all under strain, *hija*," Manuel Villa said languidly. "I hope you realize that. Oh, it's not money problems—how wonderful it would be if all our problems were about money! They wouldn't be difficult to solve, you know. But you and I, we understand each other clearly."

She smiled at him and continued toying with the broiled tuna before her.

Don Manuel Villa brightened up. "I am tired of fish. The sauce is not good, and tonight I feel like having a good piece of steak." He turned to his wife for approval. "I have a suggestion. Let us go to Alba's. I hear there's a new flamenco singer, too."

She did not really want to go out; she would have preferred to go up to her room and reread the ledgers her husband had left, to know him better now that it was impossible to know him in the flesh; but there was a hint of pleading in her father's voice, and her mother, too, had looked at her as if her very life depended on going out. She stood up and went to her room to dress.

They had, as usual, the best table in the supper club. The floor show had already started, a mimic from Europe who did imitations of Charlie Chaplin, Charles Boyer, and Humphrey Bogart. Their drinks came when the Spanish singer appeared on the stage—a short, olive-skinned woman accompanied by a lean, dark guitarist. She did not start with the flamencos for which she was famous, as spelled out in neon on the marquee. Her voice was metallic and yet there was a polish and mellowness to it, particularly when she lingered on the upper notes. She was not a trouper; she did not play with the microphone or emote with her hands; she just stood upright and pronounced the words clear as parchment. Her first number was inconsequential—unrequited love, death without end, God's reward to those who have suffered. Applause was polite, but even then, Carmen knew she was listening to an artist, perhaps not a showman and an egoist, but one who could carry a message of love or grief straight to the heart. The guitar spoke again, and this time the singer's words were meant only for her and for no other; these were the words Tony had uttered to her, the only Spanish song he had known and sung to her long, long ago, and it all came back— the memories of summer, the quiet walks under the elms, the unspoken acquiescence, the almost sacred tenderness, and all the love that now seemed wasted. There is no time, there is only eternity and the implacable reality that even life can be ephemeral, nothing more than a season, another summer grown cold. And with the sunlight gone, night is here.

> *Yo sin su amor no soy nada*
> *Deten el tiempo en tus manos*
> *Haz esta noche perpetua*
> *Para que nunca se vaya de mi . . .*

The words were like the ringing of a bell, then they faded, slowly, very slowly; the singer's lips moved but no sound came forth; the guitar was muted although the fingers still strummed; there came this silence, vast and sepulchral and so frightening, she could feel her arms and legs become clammy, her whole body taut. She strained her ears. This is not true, this is not real, she told herself, but the club was dead, and the whole world, too. She opened her mouth and she knew she was speaking but she could not hear herself. She turned to her father, shouted "Papa!," and her father bolted up. But there was no sound. She screamed again, twice, but nothing, nothing but this silence. Her father rushed to her and slapped her hard across the face and she fell into his arms, sobbing, while her mother went to her and they took her out.

At home her father gave her a couple of pills and warm milk to drink. She fell asleep shortly after. She woke up in the morning, afraid and cold: the world, for the first time, was deathly quiet and still. The room had suddenly become alien; the clutter of magazines on the writing desk, the line of cosmetics at her table, her open cabinets and her clothes spilling out assured her she was indeed in her room, but she missed the old, familiar feeling of security, of being safe, as in the past when her husband was here, padding around in his shorts or snoring in bed. No living sound came from the life beyond the glass windows or the locked door.

The maid came in with a glass of warm milk and, shortly after, her parents, as solicitous as ever, came inquiring about how she felt. She cupped her ears and shook her head. She was not hearing anything, not a whisper, not a stir in this big and empty room.

Her mother helped her dress while her father made some hurried telephone calls. They drove to Ermita, to Dr. Clavecilla, an EENT specialist who was a friend of the family. He was very charming; he had traveled extensively in Europe and he greeted them affably, even made a joke as was his style, for her father and mother, as she could see, were laughing. She must now learn how to read lips if she wanted to understand or, at least, be part of the human race. But the effort that she must make would be great, and as she dwelled on the thought, it repelled her. The doctor led them all to his clinic—a room with all sorts of impressive-looking equipment—and in the background two nurses stood at ease ever ready to jump at the doctor's bidding. She was led to a chair, much like a dentist's, and the doctor probed into her ears, poked something cool and smooth into them. He talked desultorily with her parents and they shook their heads at each question. Then the doctor wrote on a pad and showed it to her: Have you had streptomycin injections recently, in huge quantities?

She smiled and shook her head.

The doctor called in the receptionist, who took down notes in shorthand, and after a short while the receptionist returned with the note neatly typed.

She read it slowly: "Deafness can be caused by a hundred reasons, almost all of them having to do with the eardrum and the auditory nerve, which relays sound to the brain. Sound that is received by the external ear and relayed via the middle ear to the internal ear may be blocked by wax. Many who complain that they are deaf usually have too much wax in their ear canal. The eardrum may be perforated and, therefore, can no longer record sound. Perforation may be remedied. There may be infection, too. Neither of these affects both your ears. The auditory nerve may be destroyed by an overdose of streptomycin or a severe disease. This is not so with your case. I can have X-rays made but I do not think this is necessary. I am quite convinced that your sense of hearing is normal but that there is something—perhaps in your mind, I am not sure—that is blocking your sense of hearing. People can be deaf because, in their subconscious, they do not want to hear."

She read the note twice, then she asked for a pen and a pad. The nurse took her to the doctor's table and she sat down and wrote with deliberation: "I know now why this happened and I also know what else will happen soon. I will lose my sense of smell, and after that, my sense of touch. Then I will lose my sight, I will be alive but only because I will still be breathing. I realize there is no cure for what ails me."

She paused and wondered if she should put down the monstrous thought: I wish I were dead! But it was better not to state it. She turned to her dear father, who waited patiently before her, and the bleary eyes that met her gaze were beseeching. She could see the same troubled expression on her mother's face and she wondered how deeply worried she was about her. Her mother had always seemed too detached from human travail; her tragedies were parties that did not turn out dazzling enough, the extra folds of fat on her stomach, thighs, and arms that she could not get rid of. Once, Carmen herself was nagged by the thought that she, too, would develop into the tub of lard that her mother was. Now, both her parents seemed like two ordinary people—familiar, yes, but without any special attachment to her, without any niche in her heart.

She handed the note to Dr. Clavecilla, and as the three started to read it, she wondered what they would do now that they knew what had truly ailed her all these years. If only—the thought crossed her mind briefly—if only they, too, could realize what was wrong with them!

CHAPTER

1

I T WAS NOT the visit that bothered Tony, because it was as inevitable as the genuflection of the faithful and was the first thing to do once he was home. The visit was more than a duty. But he also knew that it was just a gesture; he had been honest with himself and what he was going to see was an old man who had been given up, forgotten, and denied. It appalled him, of course, to think of his father this way, yet there was no denying the reality; the past was, after all, not a pool of total darkness but a clear spring. In it he often saw his reflection, and what he saw sometimes frightened him. To recall those incidents that had battered the soul was like flagellating oneself and yielding to phantoms. There was, after all, warmth and friendship in this world, and all the niggling sins committed against him and his father might now be ignored. There were alternatives open to those who recognized them. A man could still fashion his life to his specifications. As for the poor, there would always be a lot of them, in varying degrees of destitution and corruption.

The stone highway to the penitentiary was flanked by flat, brown fields with huge blobs of black, for at this time of year the straw from last year's harvest that had been left in the fields was burned, and the patches of black were thickest where grain had been most abundant the previous year. It was much easier to plow the soil when there was no straw to obstruct the plowshare. Also, the farmer considered the ashes fertilizer. In the distance, from the speeding bus, he could make out the dried water holes near the irrigation ditches. The fields were no different from those in Rosales, where he had hunted for frogs in the fissures of the earth, baked and cracked by the sun. In the late afternoons he brought home a string of frogs, and his mother always said he would not starve anywhere in the world because he knew how to look for food. But Rosales and its fields and Cabugawan where he was born were but a memory now; he had left the town forever, and the old house and the farm were no longer there.

And yet, the thought of going back was always in his mind; it stirred the old aches, brought back to the inner eye the images of dew-washed mornings and fields lavished with green after the first rain of May; now came a loneliness that gnawed at the heart and made Antipolo and all the remembered places—Cambridge and Barcelona—alien and spiritless. He loved his beginnings, but the boy was no more, for he had been vanquished by the man.

It was this same man who felt superior to his father; it was a sinful thought, but Tony felt he could live contentedly, even smugly, with his limitations. He knew, however, that his father was his moral superior, and as a son, he could never aspire to the heroism the old man had shown.

He had regarded his father with awe and even fear in his younger days—a fear that pushed between them a silence that was torn away only after his father went to prison. He recoiled with dread and self-pity every time he remembered how he had gone to the Rich Man's house for the first time. One of his grade school classmates was the Rich Man's son. There was no school that afternoon, for it was the start of the Christmas season, and they had spent the whole morning cleaning their classroom and setting up a Christmas tree of agoho pine that they had cut from the Rich Man's yard. They were friends—the Rich Man's son and he. They ate in the Rich Man's kitchen and, after lunch, played in the dark caverns of the bodega where sacks of grain were stored, piled high to the very rafters. He had never before seen so much grain all in one place, and the abundance had overwhelmed him. When he returned home late that afternoon, he gushed about what he had seen, and then mentioned that he had eaten in the Rich Man's kitchen. He had never seen his father angry before; the old man did not talk much but neither did he seem to be remiss in his affection. But now his father dragged him down the house to the yard and shoved him to the sled. He lay still, his feet dangling on one end, his stomach pressed to the bamboo floor of the sled. The first lash of the horsewhip cut across his back with a sharp, cruel pain, followed by another and still another until it didn't hurt any more. His mother had cried helplessly, "Kill him, kill him, your own flesh and blood, kill him if you cannot kill your mortal enemy."

It took more than a month for the wounds to heal, and during all this time that he could not lie on his back, he learned to sleep lying on his stomach. When the wounds finally healed, his mother often looked at them and broke into tears again and again.

Not once, however, did he see a sign that the old man was sorry; not once—and it was only years afterward that he realized why his father had whipped him. Then he understood the tortured emotions that had propelled his father to anger and violence. Then, too, were all his suspicions about his father's incapacity for warmth and understanding dispelled.

The last time he saw the old man seemed ages ago, but the pain that past meetings evoked always seemed raw. When he and his sister first moved to Manila from Rosales after his mother had died, he visited his father frequently—once a week, if he had fare money. Those occasions were planned, and because of the poor provisions of the inmates he always brought something—a new handkerchief, a cake of soap, a piece of fried fish or pie—anything that would improve his life and cheer him up. It was Tony who talked then, recounting freely what was happening to him, his scholarship and the future spread out at his feet, waiting to be reaped. If the conversation turned to Rosales at all, it was with some proprietary feeling and nostalgia that he spoke of home; they would all go back someday and live again among friends and relatives. But soon his visits to Muntinlupa became less frequent, and each had to be prefaced with embarrassed explanations that were, of course, true. After all, Muntinlupa was far from Manila. There was work in the university and a scholarship that had to be maintained by diligence; he was tired, and when Sunday came he usually slept the whole day and rested for the grind that followed week after week. And then, between the uneasy silences, it was the old man who talked, not about life in prison but about what Rosales could have been, what things they could have possessed.

Tony had always avoided talking about his father. To friends, he had vaguely indicated that his father was dead. He had been greatly troubled that morning filling out his application for the university, but after a pause, he wrote that both parents were dead. He should have been proud to admit that his father was in Muntinlupa; he should have worn his old man's life sentence like a decoration on his breast: my father did what was right; he killed in righteous anger. How many people could do the same? But the time for heroism had passed; they are no more—the brave men who courted stigma, privation, and even death for their beliefs. In the end, his father did not get what he wanted and it was this, perhaps, that riled the old man most.

There were instances when he was tempted to argue with his father, to tell him that the weapons the old man had chosen were obsolete, but it embarrassed him to do so, for his father spoke from the swirling depths of passion. Perhaps it would have turned out differently if his father had acted with restraint and held back the angry hand. But then the family would not have left Rosales; it would have sunk into the implacable destiny of small towns and he would never have known the colors of autumn, the refreshing mental exercises in the apartment on Maple Street, and, most of all, he would never have met Carmen Villa.

His old man's sacrifice was not wasted then; it had exiled the family to the sullen warren of Antipolo, and from there, the vision was without limit, and for all this, Tony had his father to thank, an old man tortured with years and blinded with rage, a man who was brave when bravery was not the need, but intelligence—and cleverness.

The street to the penitentiary from the main highway had not changed in the years since he had last visited—the same fruit stalls, dilapidated shops and houses, the same bleak uniformity of small towns. His sister had not told the old man that his scholarship was over, that Tony would soon be home. There were a host of things he would talk about: the job at the university, that was the first, and then Carmen.

The fortress-like facade of the prison's main building had been whitewashed, and the hedges and well-trimmed grass that fronted the gate shone in the harsh May sun. The prison's surroundings were green compared to the dead fields below the high, whitewashed walls. The parked jeepneys and *carretelas** near the gate, the brothers and sons and daughters in their Sunday best crowded around the waiting benches in reception—the day was a fiesta even to him.

He did not wait very long. Shortly after he had filled out the visitor's form, and given it to the guard at one of the several reception desks, the iron door leading beyond the cement hall opened with a clang.

In the bright light inside the huge visiting pavilion he recognized his father at once, a short man with white hair, past sixty now, with an almost imperceptible stoop. Tony bolted up from the wooden bench and went to his father, who had walked into the airy center of the hall, scanning the faces around him, his face anxious and drawn. How he had changed! Now there was a yellowish pallor in his skin and he no longer held his head high. His orange uniform was not only faded, it was patched and needed washing, and when he moved, he dragged his wooden shoes noisily across the rough cement floor.

He went to his father, whispered hoarsely, "Father," then he grasped the horned hand and brought it to his lips. "I'm back, Father," he said thickly. "I'm back and I'm glad to see that you are healthy. . . ."

The old man turned to him; he did not speak at first, but his lips quivered and a mistiness gathered in the hollow, blinking eyes. Holding his father's hand, Tony led him to the bench at one end of the hall and they sat together. The old man was still wordless but on his face a smile started.

"I thought I would never see you again," he finally said.

"You knew I would come back."

The old man nodded. "I know—that I know. But I thought you would come back to claim a corpse." The old man shook his head. "I do not want to speak like this . . . but it is the truth. I am glad you

---

* *Carretela:* A two-wheeled horse-drawn cart.

came before I died. I am dying, son." He was stating a fact that did not need to be glossed over. "But it has been a good life. I see you tall and straight, grown up and able to stand alone. Your sister is well—how I would like to see my grandchildren! It has been a good life, and that takes out some of the sting of death."

It was the first time the old man had spoken about dying; his father had always talked of past angers or delighted in describing the truck garden he was tending, the milking cow he was pasturing. He had not expected to hear this in his first meeting with his father in six years. "You'll live to be a hundred," he said lightly, not wanting to be morbid.

The old man shook his head. "I'm not sad, my son," he said, his voice grown brittle. Soon he was coughing, a deep raspy cough. When it was over, "And your sister? And her children? She has never brought them to me. Tell her to bring the children, even just once so I can see them before I die."

"I'll do that, Father."

"You have changed." The old man drew away and looked at his son. "You have grown more stout, and your hands . . . how soft they have become. Well, what did you bring home from America? What did you do there?" The small, wrinkled eyes seemed serious.

"I studied to be a teacher, just as you said I should," Tony said.

"I have always been proud of you and your sister," the old man said, looking away, a new smile lighting up his face. "Many times I've been sorry I haven't shared your life more. I know that you are not proud of me. No one is proud of us—" he paused and swept the hall with a glance; the other inmates in orange uniforms were receiving visitors, too. "But someday you and your sister will understand."

"Please, Father," Tony said in feeble protest.

The old man sighed. He leaned against the rough adobe wall and lifted his eyes to the asbestos ceiling. Around them was the noise of people, the happy talk of relatives and children.

"I brought something for you," Tony said. He took out of his pocket the cigarette lighter he had bought in Hong Kong.

The old man fondled the lighter. "I can't use it," he said quickly. "It's much too good for me. But Bastian—one of the guards, a nice young man who calls me *Ama*—I'll give it to him and he will be grateful."

Tony wanted to say no but he nodded instead. "Is there anything

I can do, Father? I've made some friends in America who might be able to help us. It is not too late to hope that someday you will be out and . . ."

The old man reached for his son's hand and pressed it. "What is there for me to do outside? I won't live another year, son. And sometimes, if you and your Manang* Betty have time, do come and see me. If you ever go to Rosales again, don't forget to visit your mother's grave. And when you get married, try to get one who will stand by you."

Tony stood up. He had thought about this reunion, had tried to shape the words, all the proper things to say, even if his father was this sorry shadow of a man; this old, withered man who had soaked suffering into his bones and numbness from his years in this prison. "I also came to tell you something very important," Tony said. "I ask your permission that I may get married soon."

For awhile they just looked at each other. Then the old man stood up and placed an arm around his son's waist. "You know very well you don't have to ask my permission about anything you do. But thank you for honoring me still. Is she like you? Where did you meet her?"

No, she is not like us. She is a Villa and all that the name implies. I met her in Washington; I was lonely and she was kind. It may be a mistake because she is not one of us, but I'm bound to her now and not only by love.

He could not say these words, so he said instead, "She is Tagalog, Father. I met her in the United States and we took the same boat home."

The old man moved to one of the windows and Tony followed him. Beyond the iron bars, a portion of the penitentiary grounds lay before them, the well-tended grass and the whitewashed walls and, to their right, the rows and rows of *pechay*† and beans—deep green in the sunlight. Prisoners tended the truck garden, and even on this Sunday, which was a visiting day, prisoners in yellow uniforms worked the vegetable plots.

"When will the wedding be?" the old man asked.

Manang: An affectionate, respectful form of address for an older sister or woman. Ilocanos do not call older relatives by their given names alone. Masculine form: *Manong*.

†*Pechay:* A variety of cabbage, like bok choy.

"I don't know, Father," Tony said. "Maybe in a year, when I have saved enough. I just wanted you to be the first to know. I haven't told Manang Betty yet."

The old man looked thoughtful. Again, a smile turned the corners of his mouth. "Of course, you don't know how much I'd like to be present when you get married. And when you have children, I hope you will be able to understand that I'm not sorry for what I did. If I were given the chance, I'd do it again. There is no other way."

Tony did not want to argue with his father again, but the old man had started on the ancient recitation that must be listened to, to the end. "I know that you are learned, but some day I hope you can go to Cabugaw. Find your root and my root. I did not start with myself. I had a father, too, and he was a brave man."

"I know, Father," Tony said fervently. "Someday I'll go there."

"You will find," the old man continued quietly, "how even your grandfather changed his mind."

They sat on the bench again. The old man shook his head. "I'll die soon and that is why you must know what to do in case I die. This is what will happen, son. They will sell my body to a medical school in Manila and students will cut me up. They will learn all about me. But not what is in my heart—they will never find out about that. They will not know what I did in Rosales. No one will know now, no one except you and your mother in heaven and your Manang Betty and those who are in Rosales still. Are you angry that I did what had to be done?"

Tony shook his head. "It is not for me to judge, Father."

The old man leaned on the cement wall and sighed. He clasped his gnarled hands and spoke almost in a whisper: "That night, I remember. But you were very small then."

"I haven't forgotten," Tony said.

"Would you have done what I did?" the old man asked, but he didn't really care for an answer; he stared at the cement floor, at his handmade wooden clogs with rubber thongs.

Tony did not speak; he had been asked this question many times and the next would fall neatly into place.

"Yes, all those years— All those years that your grandfather and I cleaned the land, all those years . . ." the voice trembled and Tony thought it would break into a sob. But the old man steadied himself. "We found that the land we cleared and planted was not ours. The wilderness we tamed was not ours. Nor yours. It was the Rich Man's, and after all those years . . . we were his tenants."

The strong over the weak, intelligence subverting ignorance. "There was nothing you could do, Father," he said.

The old man said placidly, "Your grandfather's sweat, my sweat, my blood were mixed with every particle of soil in that land. But they were not satisfied with getting it. They emptied our granaries, too."

"It's different now, Father."

The old man smiled again, then coughed—a deep, thin cough that seemed to wrench life from within him, and he doubled up as one in pain. Tony sidled close to him and hugged the shoulders, the wasted body, until the old man straightened up again. He looked at his son and his eyes were misty.

"Let us not talk like this again, Father," Tony said.

"All right," the old man said weakly. "But grant me one last request, son. Don't let them cut me up. Just promise me that."

"I'll do all I can," Tony said with feeling.

"Take me back to Rosales when I die. Bury me beside your mother."

"I'll do that, Father," Tony said.

"I'm not working in the fields anymore. They have transferred me to the offices and I clean desks and books. My legs and arms feel numb. Pain shoots up my spine. But now that I've told you what I want most, I'm glad. And when you get married, bring her to see me. And I hope I'll see my grandchildren before I die."

"You will, Father."

The old man ran a nervous hand across his white hair. The bell above the iron door to the barracks rang. The visiting hour was over. Tony held the horned hand to his lips again. "I'll come and see you again, Father," he said as the old man turned away.

ON THE WAY back to the city, it was the heat that made his homecoming absolute. The boat had left San Francisco in April and the air was fresh and sweet with spring. After that, Hawaii and balmy weather, the informality, the white beaches, the palm trees, and the people in shorts; then Japan and Fujiyama capped with snow; Hong Kong—Victoria Peak and its houses and many-storied buildings gleaming in the sun. And finally, Manila, in early May simply unbearable. The heat claimed him back the moment they sailed into Philippine waters. The city hadn't changed really, not its dusty streets, not its Antipolo. Its houses were still unpainted and falling apart, and the children who played in the dirt had the forsaken look he had always remembered. This was the dead end, the street where dreams vanished, and this fact was stamped on the faces of the people, the jeepney drivers, the anemic government clerks, the jobless, the petty racketeers, and the con men. This despondency was etched on the face of Antipolo, and there was no escaping it unless by some miracle one happened to have gone to college, gotten a fellowship, and set his course on distant sights.

In May the body tires quickly, the brow is damp, and the mind is sluggish. The day commingles with the smell of sweat and the fumes of a thousand jeepneys; then dusk descends, and with the coolness that it brings, the fret and drudgery of the day is banished at last. The neon lights sparkle along Rizal Avenue, spewing greens, yellows, and reds at the darkening sky.

Tony felt a kinship with twilight, for it brought him an inner peace no matter how brief, and a reminder, too, that day must end and that, extending this vision, there was a terminus to all the good things that were shaping before him.

Tony got off the jeepney in Blumentritt. The sky was washed with indigo and with a lingering dye of red in the direction of Manila Bay. The walk home would be cool—a healthy excursion down a side street that was muddy during the rainy season but scraggly now with dying weeds.

Home was his sister Betty's *accesoria*.* She taught grade school in Sampaloc and her husband clerked for a Chinese flour importer in Binondo. They had three boys who slept in the living room with the maid now that Tony was back and was occupying his old room. The house stood near a narrow dirt road that seemed to have been totally forgotten by the politicians because it was choked with garbage piles, and farther down the street it was pocked by those small sweet potato patches that squatters with untidy lean-tos tended. There were two ways by which one might reach the house:

Accesoria: An apartment; literally an "outbuilding." A word widely used until the 1950s.

the railroad tracks or the narrow alley that curved from the road. The alley was seldom empty of children and housewives and drunks with heavy talk and desperate joys, their lives made more viable and secure by steady doses of devil gin that they bought from the store at the far end of the road.

Tony followed the railroad tracks, stepping away from the little mounds of human waste that those in the vicinity had left, being too lazy to go to the public midden shed down the line.

His sister was busy in the kitchen—a small, dark corner at the other end of the living room. His nephews met him and they were all hands at the comics section of the afternoon paper and a bag of peanuts that he had bought.

"I've prepared something special for you," Betty called out from the kitchen. She turned away from the kerosene stove. She was a short, anemic-looking woman with deep-set eyes and thin lips. She had always been frail, and motherhood, as it had happened with many women, should have endowed her with more flesh, but she was thinner than ever. Her voice, however, had a certain warmth and fullness that somehow made up for her meager frame. "I remember your letters and how you used to crave for *pinakbet** with broiled mudfish. Well, the mudfish—I stopped by the market this afternoon—"

"Thank you, Manang," he said. He stood beside her, opened the earthen pot, and the heady smell of eggplants, bitter melons, onions, tomatoes, and mudfish in stew whorled up to him. For a while he let the luxurious aroma engulf him, then he placed the lid back on the bubbling pot.

"I do wish you'd eat more," Tony said, looking at his sister. She was indeed thin, and now, in the yellow light, she seemed even thinner. But Betty was not pallid in body or spirit, for each muscle in her taut frame was toughened by hard physical work—washing and housecleaning—and by the work in the fields when she was younger.

"How is Father?" Betty asked after a while.

"He is all right, but he thinks he hasn't long to live," Tony said. "When was it that you saw him last? He wants to see the children."

"The children," Betty sighed. "Tony, you know the children can't know about their grandfather—it is for the best."

---

* *Pinakbet:* A vegetable dish made with fermented fish.

"Yes," Tony said quietly.

"They will not understand. No one in this street will understand."

Tony didn't speak.

"I wish Father would understand," Betty was saying, "but he seems unchangeable. I can't do much for him. I never did much for him. Six years you were away, maybe I saw him only twice a year."

Tony quickly veered away from the nettlesome subject. "Where is Manong?" he asked.

"Upstairs. Go ask him to come down," Betty said, laying the chipped china on the table beyond the stove. "He likes *pinakbet*, too."

Tony climbed the narrow stairs dusty with afternoon, to the room that faced the street. Bert, his brother-in-law, was there, plucking hair from his armpits and grimacing properly before the cracked glass of the *aparador.**

"We are having *pinakbet* this evening," Tony said.

Bert grunted. He was short like his wife, but massively built, and his short-cropped hair accentuated the shortness of his neck and the squareness of his chin. He was Ilocano, too, with thick lips and deep brown skin. While he clerked for a Chinese flour importer in Binondo district, he studied law at night. He followed Tony down the darkened stairway, his steps heavy.

Betty's boys were already at the table, noisy as pigs, and the maid darted about, attending to their every whim.

Tony had never discussed the subject of marriage before with his sister, although they had touched on its fringes in the past, bantering about the girls in Rosales who had shown him inordinate attention. And remembering Rosales, thoughts of his cousin Emy thrust themselves once more on his consciousness. She had been with him in this very house, studying to be a teacher because that seemed to be the cheapest course for her to take, although it was not the limit of her talent.

He wondered how his sister would react to what he had to say. No, he was not shirking his responsibility of sending her children to school in gratitude for the assistance she had given him. There would

Aparador: A wooden cabinet for clothing.

be no shirking—the duty was his, he being a younger brother, and it was as natural as birth itself.

"Manang," he started, searching Betty's face for a sign of reproach or approval, but Betty was attending to the food. "I'm getting married."

Even the boys stopped eating and turned to him.

"To whom?" Betty asked, leaning forward, her spoon motionless in her hand.

It was Bert's turn. "Carmen Villa? The girl in the pictures you sent us from Washington?"

Tony nodded.

"This is wonderful!" Bert was enthusiastic. "Isn't she the daughter of the Villas? Do they already know and have they accepted you?"

"Carmen has. As for her parents, I don't think there will be any trouble."

"When will you get married?" Betty asked.

"In a year—maybe even less."

Bert stirred in his chair. "There has to be more time. Preparations. After all, the Villas . . . you know what I mean."

"That's why I'm telling you now."

"This is foolish," Betty said, aghast and overjoyed at the same time. "Tony, what can we do?"

"You don't have to do anything. Don't worry."

"How easy it is for you to say that!" Betty said. "You know we have to think of the sponsors."

Tony had never given the embellishments of the wedding serious thought, and to his sister he said simply, "You'll be one, Manang."

"Me? Me?" Betty objected shrilly. "Let's get the governor. After all, he is from our town and he knows you. We have to show we know someone important, have influential acquaintances. I'm not saying that we can ever equal the Villas, but we can put on an appearance."

Tony laughed hollowly. "There is no sense in that," he said. "Carmen knows everything about me. My income. I've told her everything."

"So what if she knows." Betty was insistent. "There are her parents, her relatives—people who don't know. It's for them that we will put on an appearance."

"There will be no people. Just us—and the members of her family. It's already settled. It's going to be very quiet. Besides, I don't want us to spend. You know I have no money."

"But we can get the investment back. Oh yes, Tony, we can," Betty said. "Just don't forget us when you are there. The Villas . . . I haven't really stopped hoping. Maybe, someday, I'll go back to college and get a master's degree or something, and then I'll be able to get a better job. But so much will have to depend on you."

"Even I, someday, may come to you for assistance," Bert said. "But this does not have to be said. I will—particularly when I'm through with law. It's so hard to get a position these days, even when you are a lawyer. You know what I mean."

"But how can I be of help?" Tony asked. "I am not even sure if I'll be able to live on my salary. Certainly I'm not going to live on Carmen's money. Oh no."

"Throw *delicadeza** out of the window," Betty said. "Maybe I will yet be able to leave that public school. Ten years—can you imagine that? Ten years and not a single raise."

Tony ate in silence.

"Well, you can do something," Betty insisted.

"I don't know," Tony said sullenly. "It all seems confusing now."

"The Villas are rich, aren't they? I'm not saying that you should be grasping, but look at how we have suffered. Don't you remember any more?"

"I don't want to sound ungrateful," Tony said, his appetite gone.

"It's not your fault that she is rich," Betty was determined. "After all, not every girl can have a prize like you. Do you remember how those girls back home vied for your attention? You can write to Emy and she'll tell you about all those who are there waiting. She knows, and here you are worrying about what people, particularly the Villas, would say. They wouldn't ask questions, my dear."

Emy—and the caverns of the past were lighted up again; memories, sharp and shining as if they were minted only yesterday, lingered in his mind, and briefly he wondered where his cousin was, what she was doing, and if she still cared. But the wondering was quickly pushed aside by his sister's insistent, "The Villas are rich . . . rich . . ."

**Delicadeza:* Delicacy, refinement, scrupulousness (Sp.).

"I just want to show them that we don't need their money," Tony said. "We have to keep a little of what face we have."

"Face? Face?" Betty was grim. "Do the poor have any face or the right to it? It's too late now to think of that. A hundred years ago maybe—then it would have been different. There were opportunities then for people to succeed with industry, honesty, and pride. Not anymore, Tony. In school I repeat all these things, but I know I'm lying to those children, and they themselves see what's happening. The poor cannot be proud."

"They can at least have self-respect. They don't have to be so ingratiating," Tony said faintly. He saw how useless it was to argue. His nephews, too, had lost all interest in the squabble, and they now tackled their food with happy noises.

"It would be different," Betty continued, "if we didn't lose everything—and most of it went to you."

"It's not for you to say that," Bert came to Tony's defense.

"It's true," Betty glared at her husband. "When he was in college he never had to worry about his fees. I helped."

Betty turned to Tony. "I'm not saying that you didn't deserve to be helped. You have always been bright. That's why it's up to you to help us." The edge was gone from her voice, but she impressed upon him now the fact that he was no longer a part of the family, that he had grown far beyond their conception of him. Now he was salvation, a symbol of the elusive dream they never could attain.

"Do not forget," Betty measured her words. "The land—it was precious, but your career was more important."

"You went to college, too, Manang," he said sullenly. "And Mother slaved for you, too."

"But I'm a woman, Tony, and I'm not as bright as you. Don't think of repaying me. Think of Mother. Think of how we all came to Manila because there was nothing left in the province for us. Nothing but old people and tenant relatives who couldn't help us."

"I know, I know," he said dully. "But it's still wrong."

"Go ahead then," Betty said, "be righteous, because you have never suffered. Can't you see that you are our only hope?"

Tony shook his head. "What you are trying to tell me is probably the same thing that bothers Carmen's parents. Where's your pride?"

"Talk to me about pride," Betty raised her voice again. "You didn't talk to me about it when I was giving you my pay."

"That's not the way to talk," Bert said.

"Now you accuse me of ingratitude," Tony said bitterly. "You know I'm aware of my debts and that I'll pay—not all of them, but I'll pay."

He could have said more, but he was the younger. A silence laden with remonstrances descended upon them, broken only by the boys slurping their food. There was no sense in staying at the table longer. "I'm full," Tony said, not turning to his sister, and rose.

He went up to his room. It was stuffy. Its wooden sidings were bare but for a calendar with the picture of a man happily guzzling a bottle of beer. His iron cot was on one side along with the writing table, which was piled with books and his old typewriter.

Tony went to the only window that opened on the railroad tracks, four bands shining in the afterglow.

Now loneliness welled within him and magnified the words he had just heard. Pride, poverty—they trashed at the chest and emptied it of other feelings; they dulled the mind after one had heard them over and over again. Yet in this ugly room they seemed to belong like beckonings he could not ignore. It was as if the words evoked an ancient world where he had gotten lost, and now he must go and find the place where he had started, the small town, the rain-washed field, and the muddied river; find the locusts on the wing, the farmer boy calling the stray calf home, the brass bands in the early morning, and the acacia leaves closing.

Tony left the window and sat on his cot. The sounds of evening were around him, and he could hear from downstairs his sister's continued arguing with her husband. Why did they have to be so craven in their needs? If only they could see the hopeless limits of this street and accept this as the fate they must endure and not moan over.

The door opened and Bert stepped in. "You have to stuff your ears with cotton every time your sister speaks," he said in an affected, jovial tone. "It's the heat, and she's tired. What's more, there's the summer vacation and no teaching, therefore no money. You know, the kids are already going to school." He laughed lightly. "You know what I mean."

"I understand, Manong," Tony said.

Bert continued, "You shouldn't think badly of her. As Betty said, when you are poor, you can't have pride. Only the rich have pride. And we . . . we are stubborn, that's all."

"I know, I know," Tony said, but his words were drowned as a freight train thundered by. For an instant, a yellow glare flooded the room and everything in it shook.

Bert moved to the chair and sat like an impassive Buddha. As the train moved on and its noise died away, he spoke again: "There is no sense troubling you, particularly now that you are about to be married. It's just that your sister worries so much. You know what I mean?"

Tony nodded. "I am not angry with her. She will always be Manang Betty."

"Yes," Bert said with another shaky laugh. "And I'll always be your Manong Bert."

Tony nodded again.

Folding his stubby hands, Bert said, "I hope you have made the proper choice. Still, I always feel that a man should know women. Your sister— I'm not being unfaithful to her, remember this," he spoke with some hesitation, and Tony felt uncomfortable because his brother-in-law was about to confide in him, and he never liked confidences. They served like heavy fetters that drew the confidant and the confessor cumbersomely together. There was no common ground between him and this fat, bumbling man who knew nothing better than clerking and dreaming of being a lawyer. But there was no way out; he couldn't run away from this room; he must listen now to the drab tale. "There were three others before Betty came," a slight, nervous laugh. "I had to make a decision. So here I am."

"And here I am," Tony said without emotion.

"You are making the right choice," Bert said, "marrying into that family. But I hope just the same that you got some experience in the United States. Not just book learning and that sort of thing. Experience with women, you know what I mean."

"Yes," Tony said.

The older man's eyes gleamed lecherously. "American girls are really hot, aren't they, Tony?"

Tony could almost anticipate the next question, and watching his brother-in-law working up to it, watching the smile broadening on his rotund face, Tony felt uneasy and almost angry at having to answer such asinine questions.

"Everyone says that," Bert went on, making sounds with his tongue. "Do tell me about them . . . not now, I know you are tired, but some afternoon when you aren't too tired and when your sister isn't around. You know what I mean?"

Tony smiled. "Yes, when she is not around." Relief came over him; he didn't have to talk about American women now. It wasn't that they were unpleasant to talk about, but talking about them involved deception. He had always found it difficult to talk about sex. He had never, for instance, talked about Emy. And now, even while he faced this inquisitive man, his mind wandered to thoughts of Emy—Emy as he had known her, chiding him, telling him he would be someone to look up to, and when one is respected, said Emy, can one possibly hope for more?

The sentiment was pedestrian and tritely put, but it had seemed so meaningful—the whole world was in it—when she had expressed it to him, in this very room, the evening before he was to leave. And now, if Emy knew what was going to happen to him, would she approve? What she thought of him meant so much, even now, and within him he could feel a flickering tenderness, tenderness for the girl who was the first, an indefinable feeling that was both sorrow and joy, for Emy now belonged to the past. This was not final—it could never be final. He was faithful to her—if not to her person at least to her memory. He had long wanted to ask Bert how she was. He couldn't tell Bert that he had written to her and she had never answered; he just wanted to find out what she was doing, if she was well and happy or if she had married.

But the question as he would have worded it wouldn't take shape, and the guilt that he had felt about her fed his anxiety instead. "I wonder how Rosales is. And Emy, too. Is she already teaching?" Just like that, matter-of-factly, as if she were someone who had merely touched the edges of his life.

"Well, not much has happened to Rosales," Bert said. "I've never been there—you know that. And as for Emy . . ."

"I hope she has already found a job."

"She is not teaching." Bert spoke with some difficulty, as if he did not want to talk about her.

"Why not? She should have approached some politician—"

"It's not that way," Bert said. "That girl—Your Manang and I, we were disappointed with her. Something . . . something happened to her. Well, she had it coming, and you wouldn't think it possible. She was such an intelligent girl. She has a child and she's not married. You know what I mean?"

Fear, sadness, and a hundred other feelings engulfed him. Not this, not the magnitude of this tragedy could befall Emy.

"She wouldn't say who he was," Bert continued. "But that girl did change a lot. You wouldn't recognize her afterward. Remember how she used to be very well mannered? Well, she often went out alone. At night, too. After school, God knows where she went. This was after you had gone. We tried to talk to her, and we told her that nothing good would come out of her habits, but she refused to listen. There must have been a man she had been meeting some place all those nights that she stayed out late—sometimes past midnight. We warned her. But that girl— Why didn't she have the man come to the house? Your Manang Betty said we would like to meet him. A wild one she turned out to be."

Tony couldn't believe what he was hearing, but somehow the truth of it seeped slowly in, and the pity that he felt for her vanished and in its place was something akin to loathing, not only for what had happened but for this city, which had destroyed her. In his heart there rose a helpless hatred for the street and all that it was—the repository of everything ugly and dark.

"She went home that Christmas for the vacation," Bert continued, "and she never returned. She didn't even write to your *manang*. We just learned afterward that she had this baby."

"What's she doing now?" Tony asked.

"Nothing. Tending the house and looking after her son and Bettina, the younger sister. Remember her? I hope nothing similar will happen to her. Since their father died . . ."

"Yes," Tony said, "Manang Betty wrote to me about it."

"Didn't Emy write to you about it?"

"No," he said. "I did write to her, then . . . I stopped."

"I came upon her reading your letter," Bert said with a smile. "She seemed absorbed in it. I tried to ask her what was in it, but she didn't even answer. Well, fate is fate. Nothing can be done now." Bert stood up and idled at the door, his bulk filling the frame. "I overestimated Emy. I always thought she was smarter than most girls. But when a woman is titillated, her mind becomes useless. You know what I mean?"

"Yes," Tony said, walking to the window. Across the tracks the night was pocked with the lights of shabby wooden *accesorias*. Farther beyond, where the city blazed with neon, the night was pale orange. The four lines of black steel below him shone in the uncertain night.

Bert went on in a sonorous voice: "Tell me, Tony. As I said, you don't have to be ashamed. I'm your brother-in-law. Are American girls really different? You know what I mean."

Tony did not speak; the revulsion had always lain fallow in his mind and now it burgeoned fully, a disgust for this talkative slob whose only interest in America centered around its women.

He had a mind to lie, to tell him of satisfied hungers and nymphomaniacs ravishing the campuses, but Tony said instead, "They are the most incomprehensible and frigid women I've ever seen."

"You must be fooling," Bert laughed.

"I'm not," Tony said, his words rimmed with sarcasm.

"I don't believe you," Bert said. "You are trying to fool me."

"Maybe I am."

"But you'll tell me? You know what I mean?"

"Maybe I will."

Bert left him, making clucking noises with his tongue as he went down.

Alone again, Tony despaired at the thought of having to be confronted with the same question, by other people in other places. And what could he say? It would perhaps be simple if Emy were still here and he could tell her the truth; she would then tell him how to go about elaborating on his American experience and saying the right things, the true things, because, as Emy said, the truth always mattered. Emy—she would make a good wife for any man.

They had shared this room, this single window, too. Between them, as a halfhearted concession to privacy, they had hung a curtain, an old Igorot-woven blanket, blue with stripes of black and red. He had gotten the blanket in the mountain province of Bontoc during an excursion there to do research on indigenous Igorot culture. It was slung across the room, and it shielded her from him when she was asleep or when she was dressing. There were times, however, when the blanket was ignored because it was warm or because they had something interesting to talk or argue about, and they would face each other without shame. No one would have suspected that what happened would ever have happened, because they were first cousins. But it did, and remembering it, a twinge of pleasure compounded with sadness touched him. The first possession is bound to wedge deep in the mind—this seed, this wisdom, and this hurt that would never be blown away and be lost to the wandering wind.

It was the month before he left for America. It had rained that evening—one of those brief but heavy August showers—and he had tried to avoid the soggy ruts in the street. He had stepped into one instead and suddenly had wet his shoes, his only pair. Emy was asleep, and in the dark he took off his clothes silently, hoping not to make a sound, but he sneezed. Knowing that he would soon catch cold, he groped for the blanket on his cot. As he wrapped it about him, Emy stirred. She asked if he was drenched. Go on and sleep, he had told her, but she ignored him. As she lifted the blanket that hung between them, he could make her out standing before him in her nightgown. It must have been quite a *despedida*,* she had said; what time is it? Past midnight, he had told her. He sneezed again, and without another word she went downstairs and made him some tea.

When she returned she switched on the small lamp on the table they shared when they studied their lessons, and she looked at him, her eyes aglow, and told him to lie on his stomach so she could rub his back with Mentholatum. He didn't object because she was full of maternal solicitude. No, she had told him clearly, he had no business catching pneumonia, particularly now that he was leaving, and then she asked how the *despedida* turned out, who was there, which girls. What he said was incoherent, for he was aware only of her soft hands on his back spreading the ointment, patting it, pressing it below his shoulder blades. How delightful, how soft her hands felt, and as she bent lower, her breath murmured in his ear and warmed his neck, her thighs pressed close to him, he turned on his side and saw her young face, traces of sleep still on it, her eyes gazing down on him, full of care. Then it was all blurred, Emy in his arms uncomplaining, the stumbling to the table to switch off the lamp, the quiet remonstrations, the final surrender. It had happened without prelude, as if the moment was something inevitable and expected. The following morning he woke while the dawn was not yet alive

* *Despedida:* A going-away party; a farewell.

upon the city to find a delicious ache in his bones, and Emy cuddled close to him in his narrow bed, still asleep; the fragrance of her hair and her breath swirled all around him.

He had kissed her, tasted her mouth, and she had wakened with a start, stared at him, frightened and confused. Then she had turned away from him when realization came to her in all its happy, terrifying completeness, and she sobbed quietly. It was the first time a woman had cried before him and he didn't know what to do except fumble and stammer and clasp her hand and tell her he loved her. And he said it with a thickness in his voice, for his cold had developed quickly and "I love you" sounded like a rusty whisper: "I love you, I love you." And he kissed her again, telling her that she would catch his cold, too, and she stopped crying then and kissed him in that shy, wary manner of women who had finally discovered this first but lasting knowledge.

Love? Was it really love, and if it was, was he old enough to have understood its consequences? Emy had always been more firm, more sure of herself, and before he left, on the last hour that they were alone, she had told him: "Tony, you have to be sure. You have to be sure."

It had sounded so dramatic and mushy afterward, and how often had he relived it, seen himself in that frustrating mirror called conscience. He was sure he loved her; he was sure that he would return to her, claim her, and take her away from the intractable damnation of Antipolo. He was so sure of all this, but time and distance conspired against him, and in the end he was no longer sure. He developed this sense of frustration about her, and in time the frustration turned to indifference. He had done what was expected of him—written to her religiously, avoiding those endearments that lovers shared, dropping but a few stray insinuations, fond recollections of the Mentholatum rub, the lamp on the table, the Igorot blanket. But to all his letters she had given but one reply, then all was silence.

He had once asked Betty where Emy was. Betty wrote briefly, told him that Emy was all right and back in the province, that her father had died. Emy was alive and she did not care.

Now he knew why Emy had not written.

Still, how could one escape the past? It had dogged him before and he had fled it only because there were other consuming interests—America and its neuroses and its preoccupation with order and new and gleaming things—and then there was Carmen, who by herself had meant all that was unattainable. Her very name created visions of the gracious life, the air-conditioning, the air-foam mattresses, the automatic refrigerators and Florsheim shoes—all that he was alien to, even now. Now all these things and the bountiful life were his for the picking. The past be damned then, for what really mattered was now. He asked himself to what infinite reaches had he staked his claims? From the depths of him he heard his own voice saying: Accept, accept! The words ticked in his head like the strikings of a pendulum, measured, persistent, confirming loudly the fact that he was still possessed of a conscience and a capacity to study himself, a capacity for humility, too, and with the humility, a readiness to search the wild, unending landscape of his vision for that single and vivid spark that would tell him he was a success. In all ways he was, and there was more coming. America had not been miserly after all with its benevolence, nor had it spoiled him. No, America had not defiled his perspective and his innocence.

How was it then? How had it been in the old boardinghouse on Maple Street, the four years he spent in it with his roommate, Bitfogel? Larry Bitfogel—and he rose quickly and started a letter. Larry, who majored in agricultural economics, was now in South America as a consultant with the International Cooperation Agency.

"My dear Larry," he wrote in his slow, careful hand, "I am now back home and safely under the yoke at the university.

> I hope you will soon be able to visit Asia, where your services are urgently needed. If you come, please let me know so I can show you around.
>
> I haven't gone around very much as yet. I don't know how I'll be thinking in a few more days, but at the moment, while the impressions are still sharp and clear, let me tell you that I'm pleased as well as disappointed by the things I see.
>
> There are new buildings, a lot of traffic on the streets, but this progress, as you know, is deceptive. The slums are still here, the poverty, the filth. I told you once that poverty is a way of life with us.
>
> Remember how we used to work in the summers—you in the construction gang where there was always more money and I in those greasy restaurants? That was honorable and we saved a

lot. It's not so here. It's still a disgrace to be poor and to work with one's hands. But the situation seems to be improving. The waiters look neater now—they wear white and they even have caps. Poverty now wears a starched uniform.

I do hope you'll come to Manila soon. Of course, only third-rate Americans come to the Philippines to make a living exploiting us yokels. The first-rate Americans stay home to reap the milk and the honey. And you, my dear Larry [he paused and beamed at his patronizing attitude], you are first-rate. . . .

I miss the old room, the bull sessions, and your coffeepot. [He cast his eyes about his room.] I miss your electric typewriter, too.

You used to insist—after I had told you of our problems and our history—that only a revolution could change the stink in our social order. I still disagree with you and that is why I do hope I can have a revolution against revolution. Do come so that we can start livening up this place.

He closed the letter with that little nicety, then lay on his hard, old cot, deaf to the noises of the world and finally immune to the heat of the early May night. He was home; a very secure position at the university awaited him, and there was, as a bonus, Carmen Villa. So this was Antipolo—and this was not the end. It was the beginning, and before him the opportunities were limitless. He could no longer be bothered by nightmares, for a man sure of himself, sure of his achievements and of what the morrow would bring could not be shaken by such trifles as the omnipresent past, or social responsibility. Knowledge always brings comfort, and before he went to sleep, Tony Samson felt like the most comfortable man on earth.

WHEN TONY awoke the sunlight had already splashed the room, a dazzling white on the mosquito net and on the starched doily that adorned his reading table. It was not the sun that woke him, though; it was the freight train that thundered by and shook the wooden house as if it were a flimsy packing crate. The train was the final reminder that he was in Antipolo. Another train had passed in the night, but after its clangor had gone he drifted quickly back to sleep. He remembered the times he looked out of the window right into the coaches as the trains sang by. The pleasure of being home was intense, and could have been more so if he had returned not to Antipolo but to Rosales, whose images lingered longest in the years that he was away. But home was Antipolo now, and it would only be by the sheerest of accidents that he would ever return to Rosales.

Tony stood up. Beyond the iron grill of the window lay the city—a jumble of wooden houses and rooftops, of rusty tin and gleaming aluminum. No breeze stirred on this muggy morning, but nevertheless the warm odor of dried fish frying in the kitchen below wafted up to him. And he heard his sister shushing her boys because their uncle was still asleep.

Listening to these domestic sounds, Tony felt at peace. He looked around him at his luggage, at the bookcase with its paint peeled off, at the lightbulb that hung above him, and, finally, at the bent, rusty nail that stuck out from the post at the other end of the room. The nail that had held an Igorot blanket a long time ago—the thought came languidly. I must not think of Emy now, he told himself, it's enough that I'm back in this room and it is not as forlorn or as empty as I expected it to be.

After breakfast he went to the corner drugstore to make a call. The number Carmen had given him rang at once and he was pleased to hear her voice, vibrant and clear, at the other end of the line. A tingling sensation raced through him at the sound of her laughter. Yes, she missed him terribly and she wasn't able to sleep at all. Yes, what a horrible night it had been, even with the air-conditioning. *Oye,* she was thinking of him always and the night reminded her of Washington, too, and that August when it was practically suffocating and, remember (another happy gurgling sound), they both went to sleep with nothing on (a peal of laughter). But that wasn't important really; it was her missing him, his nearness, that mattered. And he tried to tell her, you shouldn't be saying these things over the phone, darling. Isn't anyone within earshot? And remember, all Manila phones are party lines.

But she wouldn't stop teasing him. Then: Damnit, her anger came over the line like a jolt. Damnit, so what if the whole world is listening in. Tony, darn you, I miss you very much, your arms, your lips, the way you kissed me. I miss you and you should be glad to hear that. . . .

IN THE BUS, on his way to the university, Tony beheld the completeness with which the dry season made its conquest. It had licked each blade of grass until the greenness was wiped clean from the landscape and what was once living patches as he remembered them had become huge brown scars. The season seemed to have infected the air, and from this infection it had moved on, crept into the pores and under the cranium until it lodged itself in the folds of the mind.

It was on a season like this that he had met Carmen, and deftly he brought to mind that August in Washington when he lived in a dingy room on Massachusetts Avenue near the Philippine embassy.

No breeze could drift even accidentally to his room, even after he had moved his bed next to the window that opened onto the street lined with elms. He had gone that morning to the embassy to talk with the cultural officer—an old acquaintance—about some of his research problems, and he had chanced upon her asking for the latest Manila papers because she did not know what was happening to her friends and she had not read a Filipino paper in days.

Yes, she was studying in the area, public relations and interior decoration, and tomorrow (she had gotten the paper she was looking for and she was headed for the door) she said she hoped she would see him again at the ambassador's cocktail party. He was leaving, too, and was walking out with her, and he had said, "I really want to see you again, but tomorrow, I don't think I'll be there. . . ." It could have ended on the spot and he would not have known anything more about her, but he saw her again, because in Washington, Filipino students often saw one another. He had no time for parties—he did not have the money—because he was busy finishing his doctoral thesis on the *ilustrados** and the Philippine Revolution; yes, he would like to show her the town if she would care to have him for company. And one afternoon she even went to his boardinghouse, because he knew people at the International Center and she wanted to visit the place, and some day the Library of Congress, too—if he would take her there. It had seemed as if love could not sprout from such a prosaic beginning, and thinking now of all this, Tony Samson wished that his conquest had encountered more difficulties and was not as easy as it turned out to be.

HE WAS GLAD to find Dean Lopez in. His office was still on the ground floor of the main building and its frosted-glass windows were open to a faint breeze. The ceiling fans were unchanged and squeaky. When he was a graduate assistant he used to work in this office, and he remembered, with a sense of lightness, bringing the dean his lunch in an aluminum *fiambrera*† when the dean worked overtime. He ate his lunch here, too, after all the doors were closed

---

* *Ilustrados:* The first Filipinos, usually of means, who studied in Europe (beginning in the 1880s) in order to become "enlightened"; literally, "learned" or "well informed" (Sp.).

† *Fiambrera:* A lunch basket or nest of pots use for keeping food hot.

and he was alone. His lunch often consisted of nothing but three pieces of *pan de sal** with Spanish sardines or a slice of native cheese, and these he downed with a bottle of Coke that he got from the vending machine down the hall. After lunch he often stole a nap on the bench reserved for visitors until the one o'clock bell jarred him back to his chores.

The old man seemed genuinely pleased to see him. "Tony, you don't look like an Ilocano anymore!" The dean leaned back in his swivel chair and looked at him. "Your complexion has become fairer. And you have been overfed—look at your waistline!"

The old man's tone, his fraternal remarks, touched Tony. He had finally established rapport with the dean.

"I brought something for you, sir," he said. "I bought it in Frankfurt over a year ago on my way back to Boston and kept it so that I could give it to you personally."

It was a meerschaum pipe. Dean Lopez, stout and past sixty, stood up and held it in the light, his eyes crinkling. "It must have cost you a fortune. . . . How much did you pay for it?"

Tony felt uneasy; he had saved the money scrimping on meals in Madrid and taking buses instead of planes on his return from Madrid to Hamburg, where he took a freighter back to Boston. "It isn't really expensive, sir. But I knew you smoked pipes, so I thought I'd get you one."

"Come on, I want to know how much," the dean sounded stern.

"Well, it was only eight dollars, sir. . . ."

"Eight dollars, ha! Listen, Tony," he took him by the arm. "I'm grateful for this. But don't mention it to anyone, ha? I'll go around showing it to other pipe-smokers and I'll say it cost me a hundred and fifty pesos. That's how much it costs at the Escolta. Here's one Ilocano smoking a meerschaum pipe. We'll play a joke on everyone, ha?"

Tony smiled. "Yes, sir, we will play a joke on everyone."

Tony wanted to leave, but Lopez kept him. He was again talking to himself and Tony listened to the old, familiar tune. "Everything in this school is going to the dogs. I'll never get to be university president as long as the politicians interfere. They are even trying to ap-

* *Pan de sal:* A salted bun.

point protégés as professors. But not in my college; I'll not permit that sort of thing. So be at my side, Tony, and you will go places. We will teach these interlopers what we Ilocanos can do. Remember that."

Tony smiled politely. In a while the other professors started filtering in—Dr. Santos, who taught Oriental history; Dr. Gomez, who taught government—and after more amenities, they started talking spiritedly about what Dean Lopez had started. The summer session was almost over. A new board of regents would soon take over the university administration and new promotions were being contemplated. Sometimes, almost in condescension, they directed a word or two in his direction. The full professors, his seniors by twenty years, had about them an aura of intellectual impregnability.

"Well, what we lack is national discipline and nothing else," Dean Lopez said. "We are apt to blame our leaders for the mess we are in, but if we had discipline as a people such a mess would never have happened."

"I think we don't really know how to make democracy work," Dr. Gomez said. He wore his gray hair long and he took pride in having served as technical assistant to no less than the president of the republic. "We are all fond of elections, but we don't put the result of the ballot to work once elections are over."

"You are thinking like an American adviser," Dean Lopez said. "The American definition of democracy cannot work in benighted areas of Asia. Why, that's a fact. Now listen, when I was in Germany . . ."

Tony knew what would come next. Listen now to Lopez bluff and bully his colleagues around, listen to him boast that only he, because he happened to have taken one summer course in a German university, could have the final word.

Now the talk became unbearable as the old men spewed big words about the mess at the university and in the whole country. They ranted about the challenges to the academic life that the school could not meet because the young teachers were cowardly or were not imbued with enough wisdom—ah, how they took liberties with words like academic freedom. And truth. And obligation. Tony knew all along, of course, that what they were trying to say with their abominable half-truths was that they were important, that age mattered because it meant wisdom and experience. They did not say that they were frustrated and embittered with their small pay, their bleak future, and the fact that, in the university, with no other strength to boast of, they were prisoners of their own meager talents. What he heard now was not different from what he remembered about them six years ago.

"Am I not right, Dr. Samson"—he was being addressed as "doctor" by no less than the dean himself—"when I say that we are debased in spirit because we have not yet properly exorcised our colonial past?"

"Of course, sir," he was saying, not quite sure that he was in pious agreement. He would have said more but Lopez had already returned to the other professors.

He must get used to that title, doctor, professor—associate professor, which the dean had conferred on him. After the other professors had left, the blustery voice was once more directed to him. "Hell, Tony, you'll be a full professor before you are forty, and if you play your cards right you'll be president of the university before you know it. And as a starter, you should be a member of the Socrates Club—I'll see to that. Hell, not every Ph.D. can be a member of the club, but you are an exception. You are Ilocano. . . ." He roared good-naturedly.

Dean Lopez was short, but he made up for his lack of stature with a brusqueness in manner and speech. He was supposed to be an authority on English literature, too, but his diction was coarse and his speech full of clichés. In the two years that Tony had served him before going abroad, he knew that the dean was displeased with his writing popular articles for the magazines. Now the subject came up again: "You've got to make up your mind now, whether you want to be a pulp writer or a scholar."

He had wanted to disagree, but he did not want to fall into the rut of an argument or antagonize his true benefactor. They were both Ilocanos—that was the finality to consider. The dean had, in fact, filled his faculty with Ilocanos so he would perhaps be assured of obedience and the comforting sense that none of his hirelings would ever revolt or intrigue against him.

Tony appreciated Dean Lopez's interests in his welfare, but he knew that someday the dean would want to collect. The old man would not ask for a case of beer, as he often did with the graduate students, nor would he ask for something as vulgar as a loan. It would have to be in kind, in loyalty—unquestioning fealty.

And loyalty, gratitude could take on many subtle forms in the university. It would mean speaking in favor of Lopez when the dean was discussed, as he always was in the faculty coffee sessions. It would mean putting in a good word for him when he was lampooned by the graduate students who had grown too big for the dean's bullying. It would mean a line or two of flattery in articles on the university or on the disciplines or research projects the dean championed or sponsored. Wasn't he an expert in linguistics? Wasn't he the only authority on Ilocano culture and the Ilocano migration? There could be no work on these subjects without mentioning him in the introduction, without having him copiously represented in the bibliography and footnotes. He must now help sustain the myth that Dean Lopez was the scholar who had studied the Ilocanos more than any other man, a myth that had disintegrated before his very eyes long ago but which he had no choice but to recognize, to nurture. This myth was one of those mysterious and inexplicable assertions that made the university a vast riddle. He came upon the myth in Boston, when he went to the Widener Library looking for materials on the Ilocano migration and the Philippine Revolution. Sure enough, he came upon Dean Lopez's "immortal book," *An Examination of the Symbolic Pattern of the Ilocano Language.* But beside the book was an American scholar's manuscript, ten years older than Dean Lopez's. He took them both and started reading. The discovery was complete; the myth was built on sordid plagiarism.

He recalled how the graduate assistants in Dean Lopez's department had grumbled when the dean collated their papers and affixed his name to their collective work. That was it—that was scholarship at the university. But while he loathed it, he couldn't quite bring himself to hate the old man; it was he, after all, who had sent him to America and the beginning of wisdom.

AMERICA—and again there flashed in his mind that continent laved by ozone and smog; in his mind's eye flashed the vast reaches of its green timberlands and frothy oceans, its still vaster space where the soul could wander and search. And so it happened in that wide and tumultuous land, to him who was lonely—this one honest moment of self-scrutiny and self-seeking. Sometimes you look at yourself in the mirror and wonder why that nose looks as it does, or those eyes—what is behind them, what depths can they reach? Your flesh, your skin, your lips—you know the face you behold is not yours alone but is already something that belongs to those who love it, to your family and all those who esteem you. But a person is more than a face or a bundle of nerves and a spigot of blood; a person is more than talking and feeling and being sensitive to the changes in the weather, to the opinions of people. A person is part of a clan, a race. And knowing this, you wonder where you came from and who preceded you; you wonder if you are strong, as you know those who lived before you were strong, and then you realize that there is a durable thread that ties you to a past you did not create but which created you. Then you know you have to be sure who you are, and if you are not sure or if you do not know, you have to go back to those who hold the secret to your past. And the search may not be fruitful. From this moment of awareness there is nothing more frustrating than the belief that you have been meaningless. A man who knows himself can live with his imperfections; he knows instinctively that he is part of a wave that started from great, unnavigable expanses.

There was such a wave and a man who was a part of that wave. And this man, this grandfather who was part of that wave, was the personification of courage and intellect, because it was he who brought all of the Samsons from the ravaged hills of the Ilocos to the new land—to Pangasinan. Someday he would go to the old country to find out more about him. To Carmen he had confided: I'll come across my grandfather's name in the things he did. She had, in turn, told him bluntly, this Carmen who was a rich man's daughter, this Carmen who squandered dollars on a sports car, clothes, and beauty aids that had all grown scarce in Manila: "*Esto*, you'll end up thinking you are so good you can do no wrong. There are no supermen in this world, Tony, except in comic books. Look at what they did to the supermen in Germany. The Americans transformed them into peddlers and shopkeepers. And the Ilocanos—you think they can be supermen? Wait till you see Papa—there's the superman for you. He can influence almost everyone—labor leaders, politicians, good-for-nothing daughters, and, I have a feeling, even errant teachers."

• • •

HE WENT OUT of the college cafeteria, the senseless palaver still in his head: Who are these tyrant regents dictating who shall get promotions this year? Politicians were hounding the deans who did not pass out appointments to their protégés—all the damnation that had long been embedded in the matrix of the university was out in the open again. And he was glad that he leaned on no less a personage than Dean Lopez; that blustery old man had given him a full load in the coming school year, plus that imposing title, associate professor, and the invitation to join the Socrates Club.

From the bus Tony surveyed the scene fondly, the white antiseptic buildings, the grass grown mangy and tan under the sun. In the afternoon the campus slept. Now the conductress, a short plump girl with flat-heeled shoes, screeched again: Quiapo *derecho!** The driver idled the motor, and as the bus stood in the sun, Tony could feel waves of heat lapping the interior of the vehicle. Only a handful of summer students were in the bus, and when the conductress saw no more prospective passengers coming, she thumped on the side of the vehicle and shouted, "Roll!"

Beyond the campus, suburbia bloomed: the new California bungalows, the well-tended gardens, the bougainvillea, the TV antennas; then the city flowed by: the wooden buildings, the gasoline stations, the atrocious billboards—how depressing they all were! And yet, one must accept these cheapnesses that America had inflicted upon his hapless country. Hapless—he had to define his country as such and insinuate, too, the gutlessness of his people and of himself.

In a while, Quiapo—the mass of jeepneys, the burning asphalt, and the smell of the living city. The heat coagulated again like an elemental fluid that submerged all—the nondescript crowds, Quiapo Church impiously painted cream against the pale, smoky sky.

He hurried across the plaza to the shaded sidewalk, where the sun was not as raw. It would be hot anywhere and it would be hottest now in the newspaper office where he was going. Godo's last letter cursed this heat and at the same time lyrically reminisced about the New England he had known in his brief visit to America.

Godo Solar and Charlie worked on a magazine. They were his

* *Derecho:* Right (direction).

friends, members of that undefined fraternity he had been drawn to when he was in college. The two had chosen newspapering and had lavish hopes, both of them, of writing the Great Filipino Novel, while he elected to be a history teacher because teaching was far more creative and challenging than newspaper journalism.

You could see at once—Tony had explained—the effect of your ideas upon young, pliable minds. It isn't so with newspapering; you cannot know if your message gets across. The only praise you might receive would be from crazy letter-writers or from friends who won't hurt your feelings. You have no way of finding out whether or not you are understood.

It was, however, Dean Lopez who made up his mind for him. To be in the periphery of newsmakers, to be hounded by deadlines, the dean had said, is to acquire some dubious glamour. Maybe Tony would have enjoyed the work, but he had had a taste of newspapers in college and he could not stomach the merciless dictation of deadlines and the very act of writing, which, though it meant a liberal education, was drudgery in itself.

The choice had not bothered him, and once or twice he had speculated on what would have happened if he had heeded the beckonings of Newspaper Row. He could turn to Charlie and Godo now for the answer, but it had been six years since he saw them last. How well off were they? Had marriage sobered Godo? Did they own their houses or cars now? Such questions were shallow and yet there seemed to be no other way by which success could be measured.

He had never done this before, measure success in such gross, material terms, not in those years when he had little to eat and but one pair of shoes, when the three of them were in college and bound together by a friendship that seemed enduring. And now that he remembered, this knowledge disturbed him.

They all contributed to the university paper, for which Godo also wrote an angry column that always damned the equal rights granted to Americans, the disparity between the rich and the poor, the corruption of high government officials, and the abdication of responsibility by the middle class—the little there was of it. The highest accolade they could hope for then was a word of approval from Miss Josephine Tinio, that fabulous woman, the epitome of understanding and tutorial genius, who conducted a class in creative writing. Under her wing they had found sympathy and knowledge for more than two semesters after they went on to higher grades and could only wedge into their schedules a course or two in the humanities under her. She had understood their problems and had inspired them, and they often visited her at her home in Pandacan, the three of them, or as it sometimes happened with two other student-writers who were drawn to them. One was Angel, a soft-spoken engineering student from Iloilo who wrote poetry, the other was Jacinto, a sturdy peasant from Nueva Ecija whose one obsession in life was to get back the five hectares his father had pawned so that he might go on to college.

After a visit to Miss Tinio, and a *merienda* of tea and *galletas*,* they often walked to Quiapo, and while waiting for a ride to their homes, they would talk on and on about Jefferson, Marx, Kierkegaard, and Del Pilar.† If it was at the university where they met, it was usually in the dimly lighted cafeteria in one of the old World War II Quonset huts; they would sit there toying with their empty ten-centavo cups of coffee till the owner closed for the night. If the weather was good and their stomachs could hold, they would go on talking at the bus stop, or sprawl on the grass, and they would agree always on the bleakness of the future, of the terrible challenge that was handed down to them by their fathers who were either betrayed or beguiled by destiny. They felt deeply about duty and responsibility and were convinced that the salvation of the race could only be earned by sacrifice. Then, toward the end of their junior year, Jacinto came with a proposal that tested their conscience as well as their dedication. He had stated it simply one evening in March: he was leaving school, he was going to the hills to join the Huks‡ because he was convinced there was no other way. Did they want to join him? They need not bring anything except the clothes on their backs. . . .

Tony had balked at the idea because in the back of his mind he had always held in reserve the final acquiescence to revolt. He knew what it meant; his father was ever in his thoughts as the final and painful proof of that failure.

When Angel and Jacinto did not show up the following school

---

* *Merienda:* An afternoon snack; *galletas:* cookielike biscuits.

† Marcelo H. Del Pilar: Filipino writer in the 1880s.

‡ Huks: A Communist-led revolutionary group that fought for agrarian reform in the Philippines after World War II; it grew out of an anti-Japanese resistance movement in Luzon during the war.

year, he knew what had happened, and much later, the three who had remained received identical letters written "in the field." The letters were not hortatory; they were, as a matter of fact, even apologetic. They asked for help, and if this was not possible, "then we ask that you do not lose hope." He never heard from them again and he was quite sure, after all these years, that they were dead, or if they were alive, they could not now return to the life they had left.

Remembering all this afterward, Tony sometimes loathed himself for having been such a coward. But then, Charlie and Godo did not flee to the hills, either; like him, they had elected to conform, to glean the ravaged land of whatever token of grace and beneficence was left in it after the dinosaurs had trampled everything.

AT RIZAL AVENUE he turned away from the crowds to a narrow asphalted side street dusty with horse manure, its sidewalks reminiscent of the Walled City and composed of the ballast stones of galleons that returned centuries ago from Acapulco in Mexico.

The newspaper office was in a bleak, gray building, a gothic edifice that had somehow escaped destruction during the war. He went up three oily flights to the sanctum, a room alive with the whirr of electric fans and the racket of typewriters and teletypes.

The magazine section had not changed—it was still the same dusty corner with drab, unpainted walls, mahogany-varnished tables, and antique typewriters. His friends were at their desks. Charlie saw him first and yelled, "Tony! How's the Oriental American?" Then it was all noise, Godo standing and slapping him on the back, the usual greetings and the handshakes and ribald remarks about American girls and the inevitable invitation to the squalid Chinese coffee shop downstairs.

They hustled down the cracked stairway, Tony in the middle, Godo—fat, wobbly with flesh and talk—at his right, and at his left Charlie, lean and quiet. The coffee shop had not changed, either. Its red-tile floor was as dirty as ever, and the corners reeked with the implacable smell of cockroaches and ammonia and were as dark as secrets. The shop was called Newsmen's Corner and it lived up to its name, a nook as greasy-looking as some of the characters who frequented it.

They found an empty table still sodden with spilled Coke and cigarette ash. A waitress, short and dowdy, her lips flaring red, took their orders (soda for Godo, who said coffee made him nervous).

"You are going back to the university?" Godo asked. The exuberance of greeting had subsided and they spoke in even tones. They seemed to soak in impressions, alert, taking in all words as if they were truths to live by.

"There's no place like home," Tony said.

"The profound comment of the afternoon," Charlie said. It was his favorite joke—"profound comment"—and Godo, jocular and looking more like a landlord than a writer, laughed loudly.

"Well, the university is an easy life," Godo said.

"It is a rat race," Tony said lightly, but he meant every word.

"Doing any writing?" Charlie asked.

"I never stopped," Tony said. "Right now I'm on a very ambitious project. A cultural history of the Ilocos. It's something that has never been attempted before. Someday I'm going there to trace my ancestry. Find out things about my grandfather. The great Ilocano migration, you know. Saw a lot of my people in California, Chicago, New York."

"Wonderful project," Godo said. "Show us some chapters when you are through. We may run them in a series."

Then the talk turned to a familiar theme. "Now, about American women," Charlie said, a leer spreading across his dark, pimply face. "I haven't been abroad so I'd like to listen to your wonderful lies." Nudging Godo, Charlie said, "Tell him about your pickups in that staid, puritan city of Boston. Compare notes."

Godo had gone to Boston two years back on a fellowship of sorts and had not stopped talking about the trip. But this afternoon he seemed rather reticent. "It's not necessary," Godo said. "I'd rather Tony tell us of his experiences. As for America, I still have hopes for its people. Otherwise I feel they are wrong, trying to buy friendship with dollars and scholarships. But we shouldn't object too much—beggars can't be choosers, you know. Cliché, but hell, it's true."

Tony wanted to steer the talk away from the forthrightness of Godo, which had always exasperated him. "If I only knew you were coming to Boston," he said, "I could have entertained you."

"Did you get my card?" Godo asked. "I left one, you know. You were out in Vermont, enjoying the New England scenery no doubt"—another gale of laughter.

"It was a summer job really and I had no choice," Tony said. "My fellowship was never enough."

"Be on the lookout now," Godo said. "Anyone who was in the United States as a freeloader is suspect or is an apologist for American policy."

"And that includes you," Charlie said, grinning at his colleague.

"Of course!" Godo said. "Have I ever said I don't like freeloading? But I'm an ingrate and you know that I accept all that I can and I suffer no compunctions about being ungrateful afterward. I wasn't born yesterday."

"I can't understand," Tony said gravely, "this new nationalism. Haven't we always been Filipinos? In the university the talk is confusing. And I am suspicious of anything that's worn on the sleeve."

"There you go again, mouthing platitudes," Godo said with a hint of irritation. "When will you and your kind—the bright boys who loudly proclaim themselves intellectuals—stop talking and start working?"

"I have written articles for you," Tony said. "That's action within my limitations."

"Oh yes," Godo said. He loved speeches and in his formalistic style was ready to perorate again. "I appreciated your last one—the uses of the past. The writers in the universities, the teachers—I am bowled over by their nationalistic talk. You have everything tagged and placed in a compartment. Go ahead, and while you write facetiously about high and ghostly matters, I go out and meet the people. Ah, the people! And what do I find? Something you never knew and will never understand because you have never been a part of them. Here you are, cooped up in Manila, in your sewing circles, in your coffee clubs, while the people seethe. I know because it's my job to know. And some day the whole country will blow up before your eyes. It won't be nationalism and you won't even realize it, because you have lost touch."

Godo had not changed, nor had his speeches. Tony felt a touch of superiority not only because of his new doctorate but because he could look at things more dispassionately now than either of them. And so the talk dropped again to the hoary and angry themes that he had long discarded. Oh yes, they tried to be trivial about it, but the distinction between sarcasm and wit became thin and, hearing them talk about culture, the economic chaos, and their insecurity, he couldn't help pitying them. Look at them, grasping at ideals long outdated because these were what they understood, because it was with such ideals that they could justify their lives. They held on to beliefs that were bigger than they: once it was the Common Man, pervasive and purposeful because the Common Man was salvation. Then it was the Barrios, and now Nationalism, because they had finally gotten down to essentials, groping for identities they all had lost.

"But damnit," Tony said, "I've never doubted my identity. I've never lost sight of the fact that I'm Asiatic."

"Filthy word. It's Asian, not Asiatic," Godo reprimanded him.

"Semantics—that's for gutless aesthetes," Charlie said. He spoke seldom, but when he did his opinions were strong and his words had a sure, unrelenting sharpness.

"I do hope all this noise will die down," Tony said. "Then maybe we will be less conscious about being Filipinos. I wish I could write on that. Could you use it if I did?"

"You are always welcome to our pages," Charlie said. "And more so now that we can attach a Ph.D. to your byline. It's good for the magazine. Gives us snob appeal."

"I liked your last piece," Godo said, "about the uses of the past. But I doubt if you believe all you said. You are always trying to pull someone's leg, and sometimes it is your own. I gather that the piece constituted your doctoral thesis."

"Yes," Tony said proudly. "The *ilustrados* had much to contribute to the Revolution of 1896, you know. They knew the past and its meaning."

"It's not the complete truth," Godo said firmly. "I disagree with you when you say it's the whole truth. The *ilustrados* were not the heroes, nor were they brave. It was the masses who were brave. They were the heroes. Not your Rizal,* who wanted to help the Spaniards frustrate the Cuban revolutionists. Not your Rizal, who loathed rev-

---

*José Protasio Rizal (1861–1896): Filipino physician, poet, novelist, and national hero, considered to be a founder of Filipino nationalism.

olution. He and his kind—they were not the real heroes. It's always the small men who are. Bonifacio* and the farmers at Balintawak. The people—you call them contemptible, don't you?"

"That is not true," Tony said. "I'm poor, too."

"Yeah, but you have the attitudes of the rich. Well, the people, the ones you suggest are the rabble, they are the ones who rise to great heights when the time comes. Revolutions for a better life are never made by the rich or the intellectuals. They have everything to lose. Revolutions are made by small men, poor men—they are the ones who suffer most. They care the least about the status quo."

"But revolution is so outmoded now," Tony Samson said, thinking of his father and his grandfather. He was thinking, too, of Lawrence Bitfogel, his roommate for four years in Cambridge, who had told him bluntly the very things Godo was saying. "The *ilustrados*," Tony tried to defend his thesis, "you must remember, had the minds to plan, the money, and, most important, the capacity to administer government."

"Yes," Godo said, "they also had the mind and the capacity to accept the bribes the Spaniards gave them at the Pact of Biak-na-bato. Paterno—all the merchants and shopkeepers you worship now—they were all bribed. . . . I'm sorry you wasted so much time on that thesis. Yes, it's interesting, it's well done—your article on the past—but it's not the whole truth. Slash away at the myths. That America gave us democracy, that MacArthur ordered us to fight the Japs as guerrillas. Our job is to destroy myth, not build them."

It was useless arguing—they would not understand, they did not have his training and his background. "I'll try to do that," Tony said, affecting a tone of humility; then he changed the subject abruptly: "But I'll not be able to write for you in the near future. As a matter of fact, I'm getting married."

The maneuver worked and Godo turned to him: "To whom?"

"Don't ask because I won't tell. It's a surprise. But don't worry, I'll invite you to the wedding. Next week or next year."

"Charlie has to get married soon, too," Godo said. "It is a wonderful institution, but never marry for any reason except love. Then you won't have regrets. Somehow every problem seems easy to

* Andres Bonifacio (1863–1897): Philippine patriot and founder and leader of the nationalist Katipunan society; instigated the revolt against the Spanish in August 1896.

solve. Money, I've come to realize, is one of the easiest problems to overcome. It's when something happens to your inner self—that's something money can't solve."

"Another profound comment of the afternoon," Charlie said lightly.

But Godo was dead serious. "That's the truth and you better think about it."

"How is your wife?" Tony asked solicitously, recalling the frail and lovely freshman whom Godo had met when they were in their senior year and with whom Godo had eloped. Tony still had a clear image of Linda—her quiet, soft features and her long, flowing hair, which she wore in a tight bun.

"That's what I mean," Godo's bluster was gone. "When you marry for love, every problem seems easy to solve. Well, she has not been doing very well. After two children— It would have been easier for her if she were healthy, but you remember Linda, Tony, she was always sickly. She has to have an operation soon. I don't worry about that. You can always steal or sell your soul to the devil and rationalize such an act with a clear conscience."

"I'm sorry," Tony said.

"Thanks for the sentiment," Godo said, smiling. "I really don't ask for much. Just a chance to have my wife and children go through life with the least physical pain. That isn't much to ask, is it? But in this bloody country, when a millionaire has a cold he goes right away to a fancy clinic in New York. And me, I can't even afford to have my head examined. Hell, there's justification in the old class struggle—I don't care what you call it—but does a rich man have more right to live simply because he has more money?"

"You could have married for money," Charlie said.

A smile spread across Godo's flabby face. "I like that," he said. "But, as I have always said, I have no regrets." He turned amiably to Tony. "So don't commit that mistake, chum. Don't marry for any reason other than love. And who is she? Your cousin? She is pretty, and I recall, too, that you were more than cousinly with her the last time I visited you in Antipolo."

"No," Tony said, a flush creeping over his face. He was instantly reminded of Emy, of how once she had been a part of his life. Godo and Charlie had met and had come to know her during the times they dropped by to borrow books or to talk, for it was she who usually prepared the coffee. Perhaps all along they had suspected.

"That's too bad," Charlie said. "Did you fall out of love or something?"

Tony smiled wryly. "It wasn't that, really. But you know how it is; we are cousins."

"Oh now, this isn't the eighteenth century," Godo laughed. He had fully regained his humor. "Don't tell me you are still bothered by taboos. Write a letter to the pope and he will give you a quick dispensation."

Tony tried to laugh the joke away, but the old hurt was back, and above his personal anguish he heard Godo cackle: "Well, if you are not interested in her you can give me her phone number. If she won't object to a married man . . . or Charlie here, he may yet change his mind. Why, I was envying you, Tony boy, that setup you had in Antipolo."

"I haven't been in touch," Tony said, "and she is not in Antipolo anymore."

The talk glided on and Tony tried to be casual, tried to steer away from all reminiscences that gravitated to Antipolo and Emy, but no matter how hard he tried, his thoughts always swept back to her, to those precious bits of the past embedded in his mind. She was once more with him, the memory, the feel of her, and the day would never be the same again.

Strange how thoughts of her didn't bother him very much anymore, particularly in the past few months. This might have been because of his involvement with Carmen—or could love wither like maple leaves in the fall? But the withering away was not complete; her name always brought an undefinable pain to his chest—a sharp, sweet pain that came quietly with all the silent urgings of that thing called conscience.

No, he could not forget Emy, not only because she was the first but because she was the past—his dear, dead past, without which he had no currency. No, he could not brush her memory away as he would dust from a book. Emy was in him, as real as his breathing and for as long as he lived.

THE DRUGSTORE, Boie's, was on the ground floor of a pink
building, a refreshing pink in the dazzling heat. Tony hurried to
the mezzanine coffee shop where Carmen was to meet him and
scanned the crowd. Carmen would stand out in any gathering—fair
skin, pretty face, shapely figure—she could easily draw all eyes once
she walked into a room. Tony often wondered why she had accepted
him at all. But Carmen was different from her sisters; she took up
philosophy and letters instead of the usual liberal arts courses. She
was open, too, in her preferences and outspoken in her views. She
could be what she desired because she had money to shield her from
all forms of noise, to enable her to damn all that did not agree with
her.

She was not in the coffee shop, so Tony returned to the ground
floor, to the stacks of paperbacks there, and was soon browsing.

How would it be if his mother were still alive and he took Carmen to her? How would his father have reacted—the stern, broken
man who was incapable of repentance? It was in Washington that he
told her about Rosales and his family. The student party they had attended had become a bore, and in the warm Washington dusk they

had decided to walk home, loaded as they were with canapes and wine. Yes, that was it; it was the vermouth that had loosened their tongues, and under the elms, as they walked hand in hand, feeling alive, he told her why he was in Washington searching in the archives for papers on the revolution. Oh yes, his father had been so right about learning and college, but he, Antonio Samson, went to college not merely because the idea was propitious, but because he wanted to find out if he was made of the same stuff as his father. With wine in his head he had felt compelled: "Let me tell you about my father and about our town. It was never a haven for those who were weak. It was only for those who were strong. And my father was strong in his own, silent way. Do you know that he was not afraid to die?" But she didn't want to hear about death and suffering, not then anyway, because she wanted perhaps to be noble or was in no mood to have the evening spoiled. "I'm afraid to die," she had said plaintively, "and I'm a coward and I'm mean. I haven't any virtue, and what's more I think I am already drunk." She had laughed gaily and so he would not tell her more about his old man, whom he loved and hated because he was so simple in a world that had grown terrible and complex. "Let me tell you then," he had insisted, "about myself when I was young." And under the elms, keeping in step with her, he spoke of the creek where he had bathed, of the old man who horsewhipped him. But he did not tell her, though he wanted to, of what his father had done—the *hacendero** he had killed, the municipal building he had burned; he did not tell her how he saw a squad of Pampango soldiers slap his father again and again until his mouth bled. His father no longer fought then, for his hands were cuffed; he merely spat the blood out at their faces and said, "You will not be masters forever." That was the image he treasured most of his old man, bloodied but defiant. "I've known the vehemence of his anger," Tony told Carmen, but there was no sorrow in his voice, only the placidity of remembrance. "I have long since known what I must do. No, I'm not going to fight another useless revolt as my father and my grandfather before him did. What happened to both of them? They lost all of their land to the thieves who called themselves leaders. No, I'll do the fighting in my own way and live while I can. The weapons have changed."

---

* *Hacendero:* A landlord or owner of a hacienda or big tract of land.

Their footfalls on the sidewalk were slow and soft, and in a while they were inside an apartment building and going up in an elevator. They paused before the door, still holding hands, and because this was Washington and not Manila, and because his head was still brimming with happiness and confession, he held her, and that was the funny part about it, the delicious part: she did not object one bit. He held her, felt the rustling of her dress, the softness of her body, her shoulders, and then he kissed her gently on the lips and murmured, "Thank you for a very pleasant evening," and she laughed softly and said, "Thank you, too, and I hope we'll get around to see each other again."

When he was in the foyer and out in the street the traffic had suddenly become alive. Wonder of wonders, he had kissed Carmen Villa! Who the hell in Manila would believe him even if he shouted this news until his lungs burst? Fool, he had thought, smashing his fist into the trunk of an elm. And with feet that seemed to float on air, he had danced on aimlessly in the magic summer twilight, bubbling to himself: fool, fool, fool!

FOOL—and the self-inflicted stigma was forgotten, for into this May afternoon, into this rendezvous, Carmen walked gracefully. He turned to her as she entered and forgot everything; he was intensely aware only of this girl who had come at his bidding. She came to him like a lissome goddess and a great happiness welled in his chest. She wore an apple-green dress that accentuated her freshness, and smiled that knowing smile of lovers, then sidled close to him, taking care, however, that their arms merely brushed, for she had said, in anticipation of times such as now, when, back in Manila, she would be seen with him: "I have many friends, Tony, and I don't want them to talk too much."

"I'm not late, darling," she said breathlessly as he guided her up the flight of stairs to a table.

A waiter hovered and took their orders—two cups of coffee. Then the crowd disappeared and they were alone. It was just the other day that he last saw her, walking down the gangplank arm in arm with her father. The hunger for her, for the honeyed tang of her lips, her talk, had been whetted; they had taken the ship together and had tried their best to be strangers to each other (it was impossible, of course) because she did not want the Filipinos on the boat to be oversuspicious. Moreover, she had a cabin to herself while he had a tourist berth. The effort at distance had strained the voyage, more so when it ended and she did not even introduce her father to him at the pier when the boat finally docked.

Her cheeks were flushed and her dark eyes mirrored an inner anxiety as they sought his. She leaned forward and spoke softly as if in secret: "Tony, I hate to bring this up again. You forget many things. I'm supposed to have some pride. Tell me now, when are we going to get married?"

He smiled, "I've told you, baby. I have to save a little first." She lowered her gaze and bit her lower lip. She did that every time she was distressed. He leaned forward, "Is something the matter?"

"We should get married now. This week. Tomorrow. Isn't it important to you?"

"Of course, it is."

"I don't want to do this. It's supposed to be blackmail, but you have to know."

"A secret?"

"In a few weeks it won't be. Tony, it's that important. This month. It was due two weeks ago, but I wasn't too sure. I thought I was just seasick. On the boat, remember? Well, this morning, I threw up again. And green mangoes . . ."

Tony reached out and held her hand and all of a sudden he had an urge to pick her up and fondle her. "Baby," he said, his voice shaky, "I didn't know. Yes, this month. Don't worry. Don't worry . . ."

He had expected something like this, but the thought that he would soon be a father had never occurred to him so bluntly as it did now. One riddle had resolved itself into something exhilarating and, at the same time, frightening, but he felt no twinge of guilt— only a feeling akin to joy. It was another summer in a place called Washington; it was another place—Carmen's apartment, its sensual attractions and, most of all, her welcome. Yes, that was it, the lavish welcome—that was what he treasured most.

Bending forward, he whispered, "Baby, I love you"—meaning: Baby, I love your welcome, your warmth. And this was what he shared with her, for Carmen loved her body, too, she loved her skin and her patrician features, more than the ordinary woman. He had, at first, taken her beauty for granted, just as he had taken for granted the generous attributes of other girls. And certainly Carmen was not fairer than some Mediterranean types he had seen on the Boston campus and in his Spanish summer study tour later on. On their first night she brought to him the attention and pride that she lavished on herself. "Touch me gently," she had told him while the lamp in the corner bathed her with a soft, even light. He had made a move to switch the light off, thinking she might be embarrassed. But she stopped him and said, "You can turn on all the lights if you want to." The suggestion had pleased him and he did turn them on—the twin fluorescent lamps above flooded her bedroom, and in their cool, bluish scrutiny he marveled at the luster of her skin, the velvety yielding of her breast to his touch. She stood there, basking in the light and smiling.

His throat was parched and his voice, which he heard only dimly, rasped, "You are so beautiful!" And as he thought of this and lived it all over again, the welcome and the abandon, sin no longer was sin but fulfillment.

"We will get married soon," he said. "Even if we have to elope. I can't stand it—meeting you like this, missing you and unable to do anything."

Creases appeared quickly on her brow as she pouted. "My folks, Tony, you have to meet them. I've told them about us."

"Everything?"

"Don't be a fool," she said, smiling.

THEY AGREED to meet at Boie's again at three. He toyed with a cup of coffee without cream and sugar—a sophistication he had acquired in Cambridge—and wished that the ordeal would soon be over. He knew he would meet Carmen's parents someday, but in the past this expectation had not bothered him or filled him with foreboding as it did now, with the meeting so near.

It would have been vastly simpler if her parents were ordinary people and not mestizos. In the beginning, his awareness of this fact had been conveniently ignored, only to be resuscitated now that he was home. But before a host of equally depressing images could shape in his mind, Carmen arrived. She was prompt and Tony had not finished his cup.

She refused to sit down—no, they must leave right away. Her mother was home at the moment, and Don Manuel would be home before five—he was scheduled to play a round of golf before sunset. They sailed out, Carmen filled with banter, Tony uneasy and serious, into the sparkling sunlight.

Her Thunderbird, which had arrived with them on the ship, had been unloaded and serviced and was parked at the riverside lot. "The traffic is awful," she said as they got into the low-slung thing, flaming red and a beauty among the old cars parked alongside it. "It's like learning how to drive again."

In a while they were free from the knot of traffic and the car hummed evenly on the asphalt. She had always been a careful driver and she was more so now because her car was new. There was no disconcerting shift of gears, no jerky stops. As the coupe hummed up the Santa Mesa incline, she placed a hand on his thigh.

"*Oye*, remember now," she said with a slight, knowing pressure, "Mama always goes by first impressions. It's not that what she thinks matters. But, you see, she is my mother and yours, too, now. You may just as well get used to that fact. My family isn't so bad, Tony, not half as bad as some people may have already made you think."

He had not been attentive to her chatter, for he had been engrossed in what was ahead, in the scene that would probably be created, and he did not realize that, at last, a cool wind had swooped down upon them, clean and fresh, now that they had risen above the level of Manila and ascended the hilly suburb.

"Yes," Carmen repeated with emphasis. "We aren't the monsters some people think."

"Who said that?" Tony asked, moving closer to her. The drift of her talk caught up with him.

She said seriously, "We are always supposed to have more malice and wickedness simply because we have money. That's the proletarian way of thinking, isn't it?"

"Don't be too free with such words," he chided. "This isn't Washington anymore."

Her hand went back to the wheel and she turned onto a road that branched from the wide street. Both sides of it were flanked by tall and leafy acacias that curtained the sun from the houses. They were all surrounded with high stone fences, with gates of wrought iron, and some even boasted guard houses. No jeepneys blundered into this street.

"Here we are," Carmen sighed. They had stopped before a massive iron gate that stood at the end of a high adobe wall. Carmen blew the horn once and a servant ran up the driveway and opened the gate.

It was the first time he would see her home and his future in-laws—if they would accept him as a son. They would subject him to scrutiny and ask, perhaps, who is this servant that Carmen brings home? Is he after the money of the Villas or is he simply a lonely student to whom Carmen took a fancy while in Washington?

It was neither; he was here because it was the honorable thing to do, and besides, there was no sense in arguing with Carmen, who always had her way. She got out of her car below the wide sweep of the creamy marquee. The stairway was black Italian marble. From there Carmen led him into the wide hall, with its parquet floor. The hugeness of the house was now evident. The lamps were all huge and the sunburst at one end of the hall was massive; the hall was amply stocked with heavy, cream-colored upholstered chairs, and it had none of the antique and *bejuco** furniture that many of the elegant houses he remembered had. In almost every panel, on every table or gleaming lattice, there was some memento of a country the Villas had visited: a Swiss cuckoo clock, Scandinavian earthenware, Venetian glass, African carvings, and even an Ifugao god from the Mountain Province—Tony recognized it immediately—in one corner of the room.

A maid in white appeared at one of the doors that opened to the hall and Carmen asked where her mother was. Holding Tony's hand, she led him to the terrace and, cutting through a break in the hedge, they went down to the garden, an invigorating flood of Bermuda grass.

Tony took one of the iron garden chairs and gazed at the scene—the tile roof, the grand sweep of the rear wing of the house—while Carmen called, "Julia, Julia!," and when the maid appeared again ordered her to bring cold drinks and cookies.

"This damned heat," Carmen said. "I can feel it again—the nausea. It's back. The sooner I get over this, the better. For a full week now, ever since we arrived. Tony, I miss spring most. And here we are, in midsummer. We should have stayed in San Francisco until June."

"Please," Tony sounded a little peeved. "Let's not go into that again. I've obligations, you know that. I have to be here before the school prospectus is made. My classes . . ."

"*Esto*, your classes," Carmen said hotly. "And look at me. It's been my death and God knows how long it will last."

* *Bejuco:* Rattan.

Tony was sympathetic. "It won't be long, baby. My sister, when she had her first baby, she said the feeling lasted only until the third month."

"My God," Carmen said. "Just hope that I won't feel this rotten at our wedding, Tony."

He suppressed a desire to laugh at what was now a ridiculous situation. Here he was in her house to ask for her hand in marriage and he was already assured of fatherhood. Briefly, in his mind's eye, he saw again her apartment in Washington, the tap that pelted like thunder in the dead of night, the wide handsome bed that squeaked.

With a sense of discovery, he also recalled the *ulog* of the Bontoc Igorots, which he had visited in one of his excursions to the north years before, remembered the smell of pine splinters burning in the chill dark, the young Igorot girls huddled around the flame and the frisky youths talking with them quietly. The *ulog* was not big; it was no more than a thatched granary sitting on a shelf overlooking a creek, and that evening it seemed even smaller. In the morning, when he revisited with his guide, he saw its dim interior—the cold ashes in the hearth at one end of the hut, the flat broad stones that were laid in some sort of mosaic as a floor, and the years of soot that clung to the walls and covered the floor, marking all those who visited it with a badge of black just as his khaki had already been marked. The *ulog* where the Bontoc youths met for trial marriage had one entrance and no window at all, but even in the dim light he could see it shorn of the exotic sensuality that had pervaded it the evening before.

And finally, sweetly, there was Washington again, and Carmen on that frozen Sunday morning preparing breakfast in the kitchenette, her lipstick all gone, her hair mussed, and her face oily and flat with the wash of sleep. She smelled more strongly than ever of woman and fulfillment, acutely so, and seeing her thus and smelling her thus, he dragged her back to the bedroom. What was the difference? This, this thing that had happened, was nothing but a sophisticated copy of the custom of those sturdy hill people in Bontoc, whose life he had tried to understand; the same, the same—they who practiced trial marriage and who made the union binding only when the woman was finally with child were no different from him and Carmen. Civilization simply had more refinements—the apartment on Massachusetts Avenue, this girl, twenty-four years old, with her Spanish ancestry glowing in her clear skin, her exquisite nose and imperious chin, the rich endowments in her limbs.

"This heat," Carmen interrupted his thoughts again. She took the seat beside him. "I hope the air-conditioning in my room, our room, is doubled soon. That cannot wait, can it? Lovemaking in this heat. It's just like being pigs, no?"

He leaned over, pressed her hand, and laughed at her little obscenity.

The maid returned with a tray of drinks. "Tell Mama and Papa we are here."

"Your papa is not yet in, señorita." The girl returned to the grilled door of the terrace.

"Mama is a character," Carmen said. "You'll adore her."

His drink, relaxing and complete, sank down his burning throat. "Should I worry about her?"

"No," she whispered. "You have nothing to worry about now."

It was not different—his being here was like the Igorot ritual a thousand years old. A young man expressing suit went to the house of the girl and cast his spear at her stairway. If the girl's father came down and brought the spear up, he was welcome; if, however, the father grabbed the lance and hurled it away or, as sometimes happened, flung it at the young man himself, that meant his rejection. He was here now with a primeval want, to see if the spear would be picked up and brought into the house, or if he would feel its blade upon his flesh.

In a while the sliding door of the terrace opened again and a woman in a short red playsuit, pudgy-looking and in her early fifties, padded out, an ice bag on her head. She was swinging a palm fan languidly across her face.

"Carmen, this damned heat. Did you see the invitation to the fashion show this Sunday?"

"No, Mama."

"You never are a help," the older woman pouted and kept swinging the fan as she waddled down. She flopped into the chair opposite Tony, who had risen and said, "Good afternoon, Mrs. Villa." The chair creaked and sagged under her weight. She was not really enormous, but she was solid and she struck a ridiculous picture in her briefs, her thighs bulging out in folds like those of a chubby child.

Her eyes glanced off Tony and in that brief encounter he knew she had probed through him.

"Good afternoon, Mrs. Villa," he repeated.

She looked again at Tony indifferently.

"This is Tony, Mama," Carmen said.

"Of course," she said, swinging the fan. "Oh, it's warm, really warm. Where do you stay?"

"In Antipolo, Mrs. Villa."

"There?" incredulously. "Why, how can all those people ever live in that place. I remember passing that way last All Souls' Day. It was warm then. It must be broiling there now."

"One gets used to the heat."

"Don't tell me," Carmen's mother apparently did not brook dissent. "Our bedroom is air-conditioned and it's still warm. Heaven knows how I can ever live without air-conditioning."

"The old houses, Mrs. Villa," Tony said, trying to make conversation, "were built to be cool. The old architects, they did something about the weather. The houses they made had wide windows and high ceilings . . ."

"Air-conditioning is unbeatable. I hope the air-conditioning in Mr. Villa's car is repaired soon. Then he wouldn't want the driver to drive fast. Come to think of it, don't drive fast, young man. Simply because it's hot is no reason for you to drive fast."

Carmen threw an uneasy glance at Tony. Then, to her mother: "Tony doesn't drive, Mama."

"I don't have a car," Tony said flatly.

The older woman sat back. "What did you say your name was?"

Carmen answered for him. "Mama, I told you already. Tony Samson."

"Ah, yes, I remember. You must be a relative of Dr. Alfonso Samson, no? That man! He certainly gets around. Remember, Carmen? Have I told you how we met him—your pa and I—in New York last summer? And then on the boat to France? There he was on the *America*—and I could have sworn he followed us. And did I delight in your father's show of jealousy!" Turning to Tony, she went on with amazing lightness: "Do you know where he is now?"

Tony Samson looked at his shoes. "No, Mrs. Villa," he said hopelessly. "He isn't a relative. I just know him from what I read in the papers."

"Aren't you from Negros?"

Carmen's voice was desperate. "No, Mama. From Pangasinan."

"Oh well, names really mislead."

Tony felt his mouth drying up again; one more question, he thought, and I'll melt. Oh, this terrible heat.

Mrs. Villa rose. "What do you do, young man? I should know because, after all, Carmen is very keen about marrying you. I want to make sure you can support a wife."

"Mama!"

"I'm through with college," Tony said bravely.

"At Harvard, as you already know," Carmen helped him.

"I am going to teach," he said, turning to Carmen as if to say, I can take care of myself. "I'm also doing a little writing."

"Writing? Now, that's really good. I read in the papers about an American writer who sold a sexy book for a million dollars."

"It's different here, Mrs. Villa," Tony said.

"You mean you don't earn enough? Romulo is a writer, isn't he?"

"Yes, Mama," Carmen hurried to Tony's defense again, "but—"

"I'll make enough to live on, Mrs. Villa," Tony said grimly.

"They all say that," the older woman said with a hint of boredom.

"Carmen," she faced her daughter, "if only Nena de Jesus didn't grab Ben. He is back in your father's office. You left on the same boat for Frisco, didn't you?"

Carmen glared at her mother. "He is my best friend's husband, Mama," she said with striking stiffness. "He is dumb, no good," she touched Tony's hand. "I have made my choice."

"You are insolent," Mrs. Villa chided her. She dismissed her revolt with another languid swing of the fan. "I give up," she said, rising, her flabby thighs and her chin quivering. Then she waddled back into the house.

They didn't speak for a while. He looked at the white wall lined with bougainvillea. Beyond the garden wall, a piano tinkled. A car whined up the road and the afternoon steamed on.

Carmen spoke first: "I'm sorry, darling. But I told you Mama is a character."

"She wasn't a bother, really," he lied.

"She was, too," Carmen insisted. "But she's always like that. Just like a child." She laughed mirthlessly and her eyes as they slid to him were supplicating.

"It's all right," he said. "I'm not from Negros and I'm not related to this Samson doctor. Damn it, America was fine on a scholarship, but life would be better if I were a *hacendero* from Negros, wouldn't it? Maybe we should elope and then we would have nothing but ourselves—"

"That's being impractical, darling, but I'll give it a thought. Besides, it's just Mama and she can't do anything. And Papa . . ."

"He won't like me, either."

"He's different," she said. "He's more understanding, less of a scatterbrain than Mama."

SHE HAD BARELY finished her sentence when a car was heard crunching up the driveway. Carmen's Thunderbird hogged the way and the new arrival had to park near the gate.

A man in white trousers and white barong Tagalog* stepped out.

"Wait," Carmen said, leaving Tony. She ran to the driveway, took the man by the arm and kissed him on the cheek. Don Manuel Villa was displeased with his daughter's bad parking but she did not seem to mind him; she dragged him up the flagstone walk to the garden where Tony had risen and had come forward to meet them.

"Good afternoon, sir," he greeted Carmen's father politely.

"Go on, be seated," Don Manuel grinned, the displeasure now banished from his face.

His skin, like Carmen's, was fair and his nose was high and straight. His teeth were good and his hair was neatly combed. They shook hands. Don Manuel's palm was soft and moist. He thrust his chin at his daughter. "Go get me my drink." He spoke again with authority, but Carmen did not seem to mind the tone.

"Your favorite, Papa?"

"Yes."

To Tony, before she departed, she gave one look, meaning this is it, be a good boy now because you are on your own.

Manuel Villa spoke lightly. "I hope Carmen didn't wrap you

---

* Barong Tagalog: A loose-fitting, long-sleeved shirt—the national dress of the Philippines for men—made from gauzy pineapple-fiber fabric, often embroidered on the collar and facing.

completely around her little finger. She does that even to me." He flung himself on the iron chair. "This time I know it's going to be the last. You are going to be a part of the family."

Before Tony could speak, Don Manuel droned on. "I know it's going to be you. Not only because Carmen told me so but because she never acted this way before. I hope you don't find her very stupid, as I sometimes do. I hear you are a professor."

"Just an instructor, sir," Tony said quietly.

"It's always wise to start from somewhere. My grandfather, do you know how he started? I like telling this to everyone—how the old man went about repairing furniture in Intramuros. But he was a good businessman, mind you. And when the revolution came, the stakes became bigger. And my father . . . it's a long story and someday I'm going to tell you."

"I'll be very happy to hear it, sir."

Don Manuel did not seem to care about what Tony said, for he interrupted him. "Are you in love with her?"

Before Tony could answer, Don Manuel bent forward, placed a hand on Tony's knee. "What a foolish question. I'm sure you are."

An uneasy silence, then Carmen returned with a tray. She gave her father a glass of fresh orange juice.

"Thank you, my dear. Now go over to the car and sort out my mail in the briefcase while I talk things over with your young man."

Carmen smiled, patted her father's hand, and, before leaving, looked at Tony meaningfully again. Don Manuel turned to Tony. "I don't like hard drinks. Never did." He was expansive. "Of all my daughters, Carmen is the most practical. With a good business mind, I might say, if she will only put her heart to it. Before she left last year, for instance, she convinced me to invest in Philippine Oil. Just thirty thousand. She was visiting the daughter of the firm's president and she came upon him excitedly answering a radiophone call about a strike in Palawan. The following day the stocks shot up and I made a hundred thousand."

"I would say, sir," Tony said affably, "that Carmen uses her ears properly."

Don Manuel slapped the tabletop and laughed. "You have a sense of humor," but somehow, his voice failed to relay his blitheness and he sounded hurt instead.

He sat back and sipped his drink. His nails were carefully manicured and on one finger was a simple wedding band. "Have you met her mother already?" he asked and when Tony said, "Yes," Don Manuel had another question: "I have forgotten, but where do you come from?"

"From the North, sir."

"Yes, you are Ilocano, aren't you?"

"Yes, sir. From Pangasinan. My grandfather migrated there about a hundred years ago. He came from Ilocos Sur, walked all the way. I'd like to follow his trail someday to see if I still have relatives in the North."

"And what do you expect to find?"

"I'm not sure," Tony said. "You see, my grandfather left with his whole clan. He was a teacher when teachers were few."

"Some sort of aristocrat, eh?"

Tony measured his words. "Not in the sense that some people today are aristocrats, sir."

"Why should you be doing such a thing?"

"A personal dream," Tony said with a tinge of embarrassment. "I think the past is necessary, particularly to one like me who is rootless now."

"Ah, yes, I've heard of that," Manuel Villa became pensive. "Tradition—it's another name for nationalism, isn't it?"

"If you choose to call it that, sir."

"Are you aware of my background?"

"Carmen has told me a little."

"I'm not saying I'm proud of it," he said, emptying his glass of orange juice. "Less than a hundred years ago my grandfather . . . I've told you he was poor. . . ."

Tony nodded.

"I might just as well admit it: he and all the rest, they were opportunists. They are called heroes now, but actually they sold their services to the highest bidder—to the revolutionists, to the Spaniards. It didn't matter to whom, as long as they made money."

"Sir, I don't want to pry . . ."

"Now, don't try to stop me. I don't know what you young people are thinking of, although sometimes you amaze me. But this is one thing I know: all this rot about tradition—no, I don't mean you, my boy, I mean the professional patriots—how can I believe them? I feel just as they feel. There's too much hypocrisy around. Frankly, I know which side my bread is buttered on. Only two years ago, for instance, I was entertaining a Japanese contractor. He had his eyes on my construction facilities. We and some local boys, including Senator Reyes and Alfred Dangmount, were planning an integrated steel mill in Bataan. The Japanese approached me. Now he is in on the deal."

"If it's a business deal . . ."

"That's what I mean! For us, where does patriotism begin and where does business end?"

Manuel Villa slapped the tabletop again as if to emphasize his point. Then, settling back in his chair, his aggressive and cynical tone changed and he spoke as if in a whisper: "I'm always a practical man." He spoke without taking his eyes off Tony. "You must excuse me now if I am frank. I know Carmen has made up her mind."

"I hope you don't object."

"And if I object, what can I do? Disown her? You have to admit it, we are not like those Negros *hacenderos*. Cousins marrying cousins. Incest! That's what it is—and do you know why?"

Tony nodded.

"Because they don't want their wealth to be shared by strangers. And look what has happened to their children. Nitwits—that's what has become of them. Have you anything to say?"

Tony shook his head.

"Well, I have a lot to say. I've made inquiries. Tried to know as much as I could about you."

Tony stammered senselessly.

"You are not a businessman yet, but I'll make you one. I don't know if you love Carmen for herself or for her money. Excuse the bluntness," Don Manuel spoke blandly. "But if we are going to be friends we must have frankness. The less secrets in the family, the better."

"I'm poor, sir," Tony said, his temper starting to rise. "Perhaps you also know how much I'll make. I intend to live on that. And Carmen, too, if she's willing. And as for your money . . ."

Don Manuel stood up, a grin on his face, and placed an arm on Tony's shoulder. "I like one who fights back," he said, pleased with himself. "At least my son-in-law is going to stand up and fight."

Before Tony could speak again, Don Manuel boomed: "You wonder why I can talk freely? I have influence and, more important, money. These give me a sense of true freedom. I see nothing wrong in appreciating money. Even priests appreciate money."

Manuel Villa, the satisfied look still on his lean, handsome face, patted Tony paternally on the shoulder. "If the wedding will be next month—or any time you two decide—we can talk again. We may yet become very good friends."

Speechless, Tony watched him disappear behind the sliding glass door of the terrace. A hundred things crowded his mind, a hundred important things that he could have said. The candor of Don Manuel both repelled and fascinated him, and yet the businessman had strength of conviction. Was Tony *never* interested in Carmen's money, was he right in sounding so self-righteous and proud? The wedding, Don Manuel had said, would be next month and that was not far away.

Carmen appeared on the terrace, and when she drew near, her eyes were shining. "How did you like him, darling?" she asked, caressing the hair on the nape of his neck.

He stood up and smiled. They walked slowly to the driveway. He held her hand, squeezed it at the gate, and replying to her insistent "*Oye*, tell me," he gazed at her radiant face, and because he loved her and because she would be the mother of his child, he replied, "An admirable man. A most unusual father, too.

"Of course I like him, baby."

CHAPTER

TONY CAME to know what a headstrong girl Carmen was the afternoon she picked him up at the university. She had parked under the acacias that fronted the main building and had apparently waited there, watching those coming out of the hall. The moment he stepped down the main stairway she drove up to him, opened the door of her car, and beckoned him to get in. A student had impudently whistled; blood spread warmly over his face and she was flippant about it: "At your age, darling, you shouldn't blush when a wicked female like me picks you up."

She shifted into first gear and they were off.

"You should have told me you were coming," Tony objected weakly.

"It wouldn't have been fun," she said. They were slipping out of the campus into the broad avenue lined with acacia saplings. "I wanted to surprise you."

They drove quietly. After having known each other for so long, there did not seem to be much to talk about.

In a while the ancient obsession returned. "I wish I really could take a breather from school," he said. "Not a long breather, just a month or so, so I could go to the Ilocos. You with your excellent Spanish—you know how poor I am in the language . . ."

"Oh, no, not again," she said in mock disappointment. "No more of that crazy old man who walked to Pangasinan."

He placed an arm on her shoulder. "Yes, that old man," he said.

She turned to him briefly and he saw the cool, laughing eyes, the patrician nose, and the full lips parted in a smile.

"I wish you'd believe me when I say it's important," he said softly.

But she was Carmen Villa, self-centered and secure; she would never understand his inner tumult, and there was no way by which he could impress upon her the tenacity of his dream.

THE AFTERNOON shed a pleasant warmth and a light that was spread like tinfoil on the bay. At the right, etched white against the blue waters, was the naval base of Cavite. She had stopped talking and he saw a secret smile crinkling her eyes. Then she laughed—that quiet, contented laughter of women used to having their way, as if she did not have a care, although she had told him there was one, the life embedded in her belly that would someday betray her sin.

She turned at a corner to a church and stopped on the asphalt churchyard before the entrance to the sacristy. She pressed his hand: "Darling, you won't run away, will you? You wanted to elope—you said so—and I have shanghaied you."

He had, at first, thought of the whole thing as a joke; he had already given his word that they would be married in a month's time at the most, after routine had settled in at the university and he had found them a house.

A flush colored her cheeks; her white pumps, her white lace dress, the happiness written all over her face—all these marked her, indeed, as a bride. "You are all roped and branded, darling," she said.

As they stepped out of the car, a matronly mestiza was upon them, gushing: "Carmen, how really romantic! I was talking with Mr. Soler in the sacristy, and with Father Brown. I've never seen anything like this. Darling, you have imagination."

The introductions were hurried; the stout woman was Nena de Jesus, a friend of Carmen's from convent school, who was married to one of Don Manuel's junior partners. She was of Carmen's age, but the leisurely life or a surfeit of sweets had spoiled her and she was now twice Carmen's weight. "You look the pretty bride—slim and fair. Oh, Carmen, keep your figure that way. Look at me." And then there was Godo, too, shaking a finger at Tony and grinning, and Carmen telling him, "I'm glad you are on time," but he was not listening for he was pumping Tony's hand and exclaiming, "Tony, I didn't know you would do it, but boy, you are doing it."

"Who brought you here?" Tony asked and Godo turned to Carmen. "I couldn't say no to her."

They all fell to laughing. "I wanted Charlie to come, too, but only Godo was in the office when I went there," Carmen said. The two women left them in the churchyard and went to the parochial office where the priest was waiting.

Godo was pleased. Everything had been taken care of. Carmen had been very thoughtful and precise, and had polished off the smallest detail. "I had to take this barong Tagalog out of mothballs," Godo said, explaining his clothes. "I never thought I'd see a wedding like this. She is some girl, Tony. A lot of spunk—that's what she has. She came to the office five days ago and swore me to secrecy. How can you say no to a girl like her? Boy, you sure got yourself a classy female."

Tony laughed inwardly and slapped his friend on the belly. "I'm glad you like her," he said. I like her, too, he reassured himself. But the surprise had waned and for a moment he had a chance to think soberly. How would his sister take the news? She would surely be disappointed; she had long ago taken on the role of guardian angel, and now she was being left out of this most significant event in his life. She would not understand what Carmen did; in spite of her having stayed in the city for a long time she was provincial and still had all the peasant attitudes of Rosales. She would never believe that a woman like Carmen Villa would literally drag a man to church. But he could take care of his sister—they were blood relations and, in the end, he would appeal to this infrangible fact. But where would they go after the wedding? He could not take Carmen to Antipolo to share that narrow, unpainted room and to awaken in the night when the trains roared by. They could not possibly live in a hotel, not on his meager savings of one hundred and fifty dollars (that would bring more than five hundred pesos in the black market—the thought was of little solace). And her parents, particularly her mother, they would never let him step into their house, and worse,

Don Manuel might yet disown her. But Don Manuel seemed to be a reasonable man and, besides, this was Carmen's doing, not his. You silly girl, you unpredictable, impulsive woman, look at what you have done to me, but I love every hair, every single pore of you. Carmen, I worship you. . . .

"You happy?"

The question caught him off-guard. Even when he said warmly "Of course," he was already wondering if he really was happy, if this was the zenith he had sought, for there was no overflowing joy in his heart, no strange warmth spreading to his fingertips, to the roots of his hair, no pleasure as that which suffused him on that drizzly evening when he finally found out how it was to have Emy cuddling up to him, to feel her body melt with his own feverish being because communion was complete.

But time changes so many things in a man—his attitudes and even his ideas about this strange amalgam called happiness. What has happened to me? Have I no longer the sensitivity and perception to understand the significance of this hour? This was what he had always wanted—this marriage, this belonging to an ethereal world that would forever be untouched by the damning frustrations he had known.

Godo gave the last word, a gentle nudge and that raspy, ingratiating voice: "A real catch, Tony. Remember what we proletarians used to say about licking the *hacenderos*? If you cannot destroy them, marry their daughters."

Tony laughed good-naturedly, but afterward, Godo's remark angered him, and the decent thing for him to have done was to shove the filthy words down Godo's throat. He loved Carmen, and that made all the difference.

In a while the girls called them to the church office. Father Brown was there waiting, his big frame shaking with mirth as he said, "I can't imagine Carmen doing this." He had been Carmen's father confessor since she was in grade school and he knew the Villas very well. He had been in the Philippines too long and had acquired a taste for Filipino food, he said jokingly, which also explained his girth and his broad, ruddy looks. They talked some more about San Francisco, his native city, about the ocean fog and Tony's trip to Sacramento Valley, where he had met many Filipinos and the writers and artists in Carmel-by-the-Sea, whom Tony visited one summer

while he washed dishes there. Then it was time for the priest to perform his duties and he beckoned Tony to go to the confessional.

He knelt, feeling warm in the collar; gone was his belligerence
against the act of confessing. Now he was just another penitent, de-
sirous to get the ritual and the penance over with. The strangely intimate questions that were asked did not sink into his consciousness,
and he answered them with mechanical swiftness: Yes, I have done It
with her—don't you know there's a baby coming? And It wasn't
once or twice but many times. I did not seduce her. In a way it was
by common consent. Sure, there were other times. In Barcelona
there was this girl who clerked in a photography store. And in
Boston there was this coed from Radcliffe. I did not marry them,
mind you. It's this girl I'm marrying, so let there be no argument
about that. Of course I'm in love with her. And it's not her money,
either, because I can support her with what I make. Nothing fancy,
but I can support her. Yes, we will have as many children as God
pleases. A dozen maybe, because I like children. . . .

ONE SHOULD get married in church for the experience. It all
seemed hazy—the ordeal before the altar, the coins and the holy
water, Godo smiling through it all and this Nena de Jesus, whom he
had not met until now, misty-eyed and actually crying when it was
all over. Just like that they were man and wife, and they held hands
and looked into each other's eyes, a brief kiss, then the hugs and the
handshakes and Father Brown smiling benignly at them.

They could not all fit in Carmen's car, so Carmen left it at the
churchyard. Taking, instead, Nena's car, they drove off to one of the
Chinese restaurants near Pasay.

By eight they had finished dining and, for the occasion, Carmen
asked the headwaiter to bring some brandy. Tony objected. "Let's
have that some other time," he said. But Godo nudged him: "Can't
you think of a better time than now? I have brandy very rarely. Don't
be Ilocano. Not on your wedding day, anyway."

He had learned long ago that gallantry and poverty did not go
together—this lesson had long been etched in his mind. He turned
to Godo in that meaningful way only friends understood and said
simply, "I'm picking up the tab, Godo."

"And the Villa millions?" Godo had always been brash.

"It's not the Villa millions," Tony said firmly, unmoving in his chair. "It's the Samson centavos and there aren't many of those around."

Carmen laughed gaily. "I admire this smart talk. You really can jump at each other's throats. But I doubt, darling," she turned coyly to Tony, "if you have heard of conjugal property." She thrust her silver-lined handbag to him.

She had flaunted her wealth, but he must be civilized, he must now show his displeasure; he must be able to live with grace and equanimity in this new and glittering circle. He smiled wanly.

"That's a blessing I didn't know about," he said and went back to his coffee.

Nena must have noticed his discomfiture; she came to his aid. "How many children do you intend to have, Carmen?" she asked, her gaze shifting to the newlyweds.

Carmen laughed. "Well, now that I'm a respectable woman I would like to have a dozen."

Nena seemed appalled. "You are not serious, are you?"

"Ask my husband," Carmen said.

"If a dozen she wants, she'll have them," Tony said. His good humor had returned.

"You don't know what you are talking about," Nena said, pouting. "That's all wrong"—and the words poured out. "Look at me: in five years I had six children. I look like a tub of lard now, don't I? I don't think it is fair at all. I was once slim like you, and full of grace—no, Carmen? I don't walk anymore. I roll. And six kids. I'm going to have my fallopian tubes tied this year. No more children for me. I'm going to enjoy life while I'm young. God, I'm only twenty-five and everyone calls me 'Missus.' There are some married women who are forty years old and they are called 'Miss' in beauty parlors and department stores. With me no one ever makes that mistake. It's all over my figure."

Her truthfulness was pathetic, and Carmen tried to dismiss the topic, to assuage Nena's grief over her lost youth: "But six darling children, isn't that enough compensation? You should be happy, Nena. Alice, you know her, poor Alice, married ten years and not even one miscarriage!"

Tony could see Nena de Jesus at home, her six children tended by a dozen *yayas*, the rearing of her children rendered an impersonal chore. Wealth does this—removes the warmth and the closeness that parents can have with their children—and he felt sorry for her misery and for her lost youth.

"No matter what you say," Nena insisted. "Six is too much. And in the meantime, what happens? You know my dear, dear husband of course, my darling Ben."

"They are both friends," Carmen said, turning to Tony.

"Well, he is now gallivanting around. He takes off for Nueva Ecija to visit the tenants. Ha!" Nena apparently relished her story. "Do you know where he really goes? I wish he knew something other than real estate. You should tell your papa to shift him to another department."

"He works in the office—top man," Carmen explained to Tony again.

"Perhaps if he worked in the plywood factory, or in Mindanao, that would diminish his libido somewhat," Nena rattled on.

Godo leaned forward, grinning. The story had piqued his interest and the brandy glass before him was empty.

"Nena, that's what a man's for," Carmen said lightly.

"I know, dear," Nena tapped Carmen's hand patronizingly. "But there can be too much of it, you know. And what happens? Six children! And where has that taken me? Of course I love him, dear. But does he love me still in this condition? I want to apologize to Tony," and she nodded to Godo, "but most men can't differentiate love from sex. I feel that I repel Ben now. I can feel it—this sagging bust, these flabby arms, this tub of lard. I'm not one to arouse the romantic instincts anymore. This year I'm going to have my fallopian tubes tied. That's final . . . and I've already seen a doctor. A good one. If I'd only seen him earlier then I wouldn't be looking like this today. I was very slim, remember, Carmen?"

Carmen nodded.

"You still want a dozen children?" Nena asked.

"Well, we are off to a good start," she said, winking at Tony.

They had finished their coffee and the waiter started clearing their table.

"What do we do now?" Tony asked after their table was cleared.

"What do newlyweds do?" Godo asked. They all laughed.

Carmen turned to Godo. "I hope you won't mind if I ask you to take Nena home. Her husband might beat her up—"

"It's all right, darling," Nena said, rising. Her flabby face was sad. "Ben never gets jealous. Not with a figure like mine."

"Please, it's a pleasure," Godo said gallantly. "I may yet prove that your husband has no right taking you for granted."

Nena de Jesus smiled and Tony knew that she had not been flattered in a long, long time. The restaurant foyer was lighted by a soft flow of *capiz** lamps that dangled from the mahogany ceiling. Godo turned to the couple behind him. "I'm sure you are in a hurry to be left alone."

"Of course," Carmen said gaily.

They drove to the church where Carmen's car was parked, and before Tony got out, Godo held his arm. "Be good to her, old boy. You will not find another girl like Carmen. Not in a million. And that goes for her millions, too."

Laughter again, but this time Tony didn't laugh.

Alone at last, they drove quietly to the boulevard.

Carmen parked on the sandy shoulder just behind the seawall, and night rushed about them, alive with the shudder of waves against the rocks, the swish of cars speeding on the boulevard behind them. Above, through the windshield, the stars shone, and before them was the seawall, the sea flat and quiet. Beyond the dark expanse the lights of Cavite gleamed and a beacon flashed green and red above the lights.

"I wish Godo had more sense than that. As if your money meant everything to me," he said after a while. "He makes me feel so cheap, the way he talks. He had never learned refinement."

"You are sore," she said with alarm. She moved closer to him. "Not all our money is filthy, honey. And those crooked deals—they can't be helped nowadays. Besides, have you forgotten that money isn't corrupt, that it's the people who are?"

"You don't know what you are saying," he said glumly. "I don't think anyone in your family ever knows what money really means—

Capiz: Translucent, squarish inner shell of small marine bivalve common in Philippine coastal waters; used to make lamps and decorative objects.

the immense responsibility that goes with it. That includes your father.

"*Esto,* there is one important thing you don't know," she said hotly. "This quiet, simple wedding about which you had second thoughts—I didn't want to go ahead with it at first. But Papa, he was thinking of you, your pride, and he said it was best this way. You should at least give him credit for thinking of you. And don't let anyone know I've told you."

He couldn't believe what he heard. "The wedding, everything . . . everything was your father's idea?"

"Yes," she snorted.

Now that he had drawn from her this confession, he did not know whether he should be angry or grateful. Above the confusion in his own mind he realized that, henceforth, none of his waking hours would be spared the businessman's attention. He should be grateful for having been relieved of considerable expense and embarrassment, but gratitude to Don Manuel Villa would now take the form of soft, comfortable chains that would never be shattered.

"He must think a lot of you to have consented to this," he said.

She moved away from him and sat back. On the rocks below the seawall the waves were a whisper, and in the night, somewhere among the grass and in the stunted palms, cicadas found their voice. She spoke softly, as though talking only to herself: "Yes, Papa thinks he loves me, but I know he doesn't really care. And if I got pregnant and had an illegitimate child, he couldn't care less. He would simply ask that I be well taken care of and the child, too. That goes for Mama and all my dear brothers and sisters. And they'd worry about me only because what I might have done would give the family a bad name. I've known that and money has nothing to do with it. Do you know Papa has three mistresses and I've never heard Mama complain? Papa once brought one of them to a party at the house. Everyone knew, even Mother, and we all acted as if nothing was unusual. So you see, I'm really alone—just like you. And that's why I want something I can call my own."

"It is not true," he said, feeling sorry for having been so direct. "You are dramatizing things again."

"It's true," Carmen insisted. "So don't think I'm being nasty this way. If I had told Papa that I'd already gotten married to you, he couldn't have cared less."

She sidled closer to him, her face beseeching. He touched her cheek and kissed her gently. "We shouldn't be mad at each other on this day—of all days," he whispered. "I shouldn't tell you these things; they are what I should keep to myself."

"And I . . . I have no pride when I am with you."

"Listen, so you think you know what my father did when I was young? I told you, he bound me to a sled and horsewhipped me. Do you know what a horsewhip is? Well, my old man was careful not to strike my eyes. Just my back. You saw the scars."

"It's just a few marks—not really scars, just white marks," Carmen said. "Mama, well, you know who she is, how her tongue works. She was poor until Father met her."

He had wanted then to tell her how he had lied, that his father was in prison, not dead.

But his courage did not come. So tonight he decided that the problem would never surface again; he must live the lie now and talk of his father as belonging to the past, irrevocably there and pertinent only as a memory. He caressed her hair and told her how his mother had always been an angel, how she had slaved without a word of complaint.

"Perhaps you will be like her," he said.

And she kissed him. "That's the best compliment you've given me, darling."

A balut* vendor approached them. After refusing, Carmen started the car and they slid back to the boulevard.

She wanted to drive him to Antipolo, but it was late and they parted instead at her gate. He waited until she was safely within the high, white-washed walls, then he walked to the corner and got a cab.

Tony did not wake his sister, choosing, instead, to go to bed immediately. But sleep was a long time coming, maybe because of the coffee and the brandy. It was long past midnight and he wondered if Carmen was awake, too. She always had an agile mind; in Washington they would sit up talking, cozily snuggled together. But he could not recall anything searing that they had talked about, nothing that had bared her soul, although he had told her much about himself.

---

*Balut: A snack made from fertilized duck eggs incubated almost to the point of hatching and then boiled.

All that he could remember was the coffeepot bubbling somewhere in the kitchen, the late-night TV shows they watched together, her eagerness. Why had it been that way? Was it true after all that Carmen never knew how it was to be really loved, and that because she did not know, she had tried to find the meaning of surrender? There would be no secret meetings anymore; her most important problem was solved.

Below the house, in the slimy ditch half-covered with grass, the frogs started to croak, for the rains had finally come.

CHAPTER

6

D ON MANUEL went to the railroad station at noon to see them off. Just as Carmen had said, he did not seem ruffled at all. "Your mama is angry," he told Tony as they stepped out of the car.

Tony had not expected him to come, and in Don Manuel's presence his composure left him. "Thank you, sir," he stammered. "I knew you wouldn't approve of what we had done." He tried to sound sincere. "But Carmen and I . . . we thought there was no other way."

"You should have seen the rumpus at the breakfast table this morning when I broke the news," Carmen said gaily. "You should have seen Mother cry. She was just putting on an act, of course. Mother was glad, too, that I'm already married. Now she won't have to worry about me being seduced."

"I had other plans, of course. I thought we would get to know more of each other," Don Manuel said evenly.

Carmen sidled to her father. "Thanks, Papa," she said. "But I'm sure you'll like Tony just the same."

"Now, Tony," Don Manuel turned to him. "When you get back you proceed directly to the house. No 'buts' about it. It's so wide and empty, what with all the children already married and living on their own. . . ."

Tony looked at Carmen. He had hoped that when they returned, Carmen would stay with her folks until he found a small place to rent. But now that Don Manuel had spoken, his predicament seemed solved. He could not think of bringing Carmen to Antipolo—no, that was farthest from his mind. He turned to Carmen, and by the look in her eyes he knew that this, too, was what she desired.

"I thank you for your offer, sir," he said humbly, "but—"

Don Manuel leaned back on the couch: "I know what you are thinking—of Mama and her displeasure. You don't know her well enough. I'll take care of her, you'll see."

Don Manuel stood up, and because they were the only people in the waiting room, he spoke freely: "I believe that you should live independently, but that should be when you really have settled a few important details—after you have found a place. Give us a chance. We won't keep you forever."

Don Manuel's driver entered the room with their tickets.

"I wired the Pines Hotel this morning and have already arranged the bridal suite for you," Don Manuel said at the door. "It's a wedding present to my favorite daughter and to you."

BUT FOR THE SCENERY the trip was uneventful. The city's fringes marched by—the same ugly houses huddled along the tracks, the muddied water and filth was a moat between him and the houses and their squalid yards. Then the train broke out into the open country, into sodden fields that were now starting to be tinged with green. The houses were no different in their smallness from those on the edges of the city. Why had the country not changed at all? Why were people like Don Manuel hoarding their money in Manila and cutting themselves off from the land that was the beginning and the repository of all wealth?

The sun poured down in a steady stream, saturating the landscape and burnishing the fields and the mountains with dusty blue and streaks of gold. The thatched houses bobbed out of the brown earth and the singing grass. But in this air-conditioned coach Tony could not drink in the air, could not listen to the wind, could only be

aware of the nearness of his wife and her domestic talk, her reminiscences of New England and Washington, of the changing colors of
autumn, and the reds and golds of the maples and the sycamores.

"Have you ever tried swimming naked in a muddy brook?" he
asked as the train sang over a creek, rich brown with mud. "In that
dirt?" she exclaimed, a little aghast, and he explained to her that
there was a world of difference between the mud in the fields and the
mud in the *esteros** in Manila. There is, he told her impatiently and
with conviction, such a thing as clean mud. "Yes, yes, darling," she
said, "there is clean mud." And she nudged him in that insinuating
manner with which he had become familiar. She was referring to
him as clean, wholesome mud, and for a moment anger crossed his
mind—but only for a moment, for he had looked out the window
then, into the flood of late afternoon, and rising on the horizon was
this hump of a mountain streaked with veins of gold, and beyond
this familiar blue was Rosales and home. He could not imagine himself being born in another place or growing up in another town, and
nostalgia lashed at him, whipped away the anger that had started
and stirred that old and nameless longing to see the town again, its
crooked and dusty streets, and the neighborhood—the cogon
shanties, the bamboo trees creaking in the wind, the carabao dung
on the narrow trail that led to the river, and the papayas blooming
in the morning. But he was not going home now, just passing
through, just winging and dreaming through—and there would be
no way by which he could find how it was with Rosales, if it had
changed, and Emy, too, if she was all right and healthy and not completely blighted by a past that had made her fair game to the devil.
He himself could feel his voice sandpapery and hoarse: "Beyond that
mountain is home. . . ."

She glanced out of the window and smiled that quick, meaningless smile which meant that she understood but was not particularly
interested, then went back to the picture magazine she had bought
at Tutuban. He sat back beside her, wondering at the way his life had
changed, wondering how he ever got here, in this air-conditioned
coach beside this fair-skinned and lovely woman. The great distances
he had traveled, the bitter winters of New England, the summer in

---

* *Esteros:* Land adjoining an estuary inundated by the tide; estuary; pool or
pond; marshy land.

Spain, and the searching among the archives in Barcelona and Seville—all these now seemed shriveled into this hollow moment, this certitude of Carmen and the honeymoon. He sought her hand silently and held it, pressed it, his mind lazily meandering back to re- membered images—not to those great distances he had crossed but to those places where he had seen the seed become a plant, to the house he had left, the home with its leaking roof, with plows and harrows rusting below the bamboo stairs, and the chicken roosting under the kitchen, the fence that had fallen apart. The house no longer stood, of course, for it had been dismantled long ago when his father went to jail and the family left Rosales for the uncertain beneficence of Manila. There was no Samson left in Rosales; there was nothing left for him to go back to or to claim but Emy, who lived on the other side of the broken-down fence. And if he did see her again, how would she take him? Would she loathe him for having left her or would she look up to him in wonder and say, Tony, you've gone so far, you've changed. And deep within his heart, he could feel that overwhelming sense of helplessness, that awful incapacity to hold back what had already happened. If he had stayed behind, if he had not gone to America, perhaps things would have been different for Emy, and that ignominy that had overcome her might not have touched her at all. The coolness of this coach, the softness of the girl beside him, and the racing of this train toward its destination were the realities he could not now ignore. They were the solid shackles around his ankles and his wrists, reminding him of what could no longer be changed.

It was when they had already arrived in Baguio that he recalled that they had not acted like newlyweds at all, that they had gone through the trip as if they were an old married couple.

They arrived at the hotel at dusk and were immediately taken to their room. Now that they were alone an awkwardness commingled with relief came over Tony. It was a strange feeling, both pleasant and unreal, for it was something new. Not that he had never been alone with Carmen before this union was sanctified, but now the pleasure of being together was no longer the delirious thrill that he had expected it to be, for all that he expected of it was the posses- sion and not the discovery of that possession. For a while he lingered by the door, holding her hand, and he would have asked her what she was thinking had not the bellhop come at that moment with their luggage and switched on the fluorescent lamp in the ceiling.

Tony surveyed the suite, the well-ordered sofa and chairs done in rich, red upholstery, the fresh calla lilies and the dahlias as big as saucers in the slim, metallic vases. The paneling of red dao shone in the cold, blue light. No trace of pine scent lingered in the room, which, in fact, smelled faintly of floor wax. Then they were alone again. Night was falling swiftly outside, a phone jangled somewhere in the quiet corridors, and the cold of Baguio finally touched them, told them that the time to make love had come.

Carmen sat on the wide, cream-colored bed and watched him open the lock of the suitcase.

"I think we should do it as we have planned," Tony said. "About entering this room, I mean." She shrugged. "You can keep the illusion at least, baby," he said, grinning. "You shouldn't wear a Good Friday look—my God, not on your wedding day!"

He went to her, lifted her, and kissed her. The lips on which his mouth fell were warm but unresponsive, and Tony quickly attributed this to Baguio, to the slivers of cold that stole into this rich, intimate room. Or could it be more than the cold? Remembering her condition and the life that was developing within her, he felt an abiding warmth for this girl who had accepted him.

"*Esto*, we should not have bothered coming here," she said with an air of boredom. "I didn't like the look of that bellhop when we came in—and the clerk at the desk. They were practically undressing me. Me, of all people! Now, if we had gone to the summer house, as Papa had suggested earlier, we would be alone just the same."

"Honeymoons are meant to be spent in hotels, baby," he said, trying to humor her.

She sighed and placed her clothes on the bed. "It seems foolish, doesn't it?" she asked but expected no answer. "A two-day honeymoon. A weekend actually, then you rush back to that miserable university for the good of this country's future, for the benefit of the downtrodden Ilocano race."

It was her way of showing displeasure and he brushed aside her sarcasm. "You married a teacher," he said.

"An associate professor," she corrected him. Her blitheness had returned with a quickness that pleased him.

She rose and hugged him. "If we were now living in that hick town of yours I would be called *Maestra*, wouldn't I? Or is it *Profesora*?"

She laughed and he was glad that he did not have to bend backward again and try to please her, play up to her whims, humor her, because she was this way and women were supposed to be pampered and cuddled until the uneasy days of conception were over.

Outside, beyond the polished glass windows, the pines were already shrouded with the oncoming night, and mist wrapped the darkening trees and the whole landscape in white motionless suds. She moved away from him and idled at the window. She was every inch a bride, lissome and beautiful as he once dreamed his wife should appear to him on his wedding night. Then she turned to him and demanded, almost shrilly, "But must we return so soon? You need a vacation. All the past days you did nothing but work and prepare your papers and your program. You need a vacation. Look at yourself—all bones, and you want to get back to that salt mine."

"It's Monday and classes," Tony said, "and more than that, baby, I've already told you—the Socrates Club. Not every teacher in the university . . ."

". . . is a member of this club," she said coyly. "And all the members are brilliant minds who have gone to Harvard and Oxford."

She had found her nightgown in the suitcase—a shimmering black, which contrasted with her light, rosy skin. She held it to her bosom, preened before him and, smiling again, said, "Now, will I qualify?" Before he could answer, she dropped the negligee on the bed and continued: "The things that interest men are so trite. God, they bore me. Let's throw the university out of the window and concentrate on sex."

He cupped her chin and kissed her. "I'm sorry if I am such a bore," he said, burying his face in the fragrant curve of her neck.

She detached herself from his embrace and, turning around, asked him to undo the zipper at the back of her dress. He did this carefully, remembering how once, in his haste to undress her, he had brought the zipper down quickly and it had bitten into her skin. Having finished with the zipper, he kissed her nape.

"I love you," he whispered.

Matter-of-factly she asked, "Even when I get fat and dowdy like Mama?"

He bit her ear again and whispered, "Yes, even when you are as fat as a circus freak."

She opened her eyes and looked reproachfully at him. "When the children start coming my breasts will sag. My belly, too. Will you still love me then?"

He laughed and hugged her.

She drew away and started undressing in that casual manner that often amazed him, for it seemed as if she were on a stage, showing off to an admiring audience. She had done it before, undressed before him, and the act had almost become a ritual. She walked to the bed and picked up the negligee again, then stood before him, her fair skin gleaming, the smooth, white flanks shining in the cool blue light; her legs tawny and clean.

"Have I changed, darling?" she asked, letting his gaze caress her.

"No," he said, holding his head a little backward. "You are beautiful." And his blood singing, he went to her.

TONY WOKE UP with the sun in his eyes. It was chalky white on everything in the room. Carmen was still asleep, bundled against the Baguio cold in the pale blue woolen blanket they had shared. He watched her for a while—her easy, rhythmic breathing—then kissed her, pressing his tongue through her lips to her teeth and tasting the honey saltiness of her mouth. She stirred, opened her eyes, and embraced him, making happy gurgling sounds.

"I just wish we never had to return to Manila," she said, yawning. It was their weekend honeymoon all right, and though the thrill of first possession had waned, she had acted like the perfect bride, demanding love.

It was Sunday, and in the afternoon they would have to go back to Manila. The phone rang and Carmen reached for it, muttering in her breath, "Who is it?" The pleasantness was gone and she sounded sulky and injured. Then her face brightened. "It's Papa," she said. "He is at the golf club with friends. He came in this morning in Dangmount's plane and we will have supper with him. What do you say, honey? We can go back to Manila with him in the plane."

"Yes, Papa," she said without waiting for Tony's reply. She gave the phone to her husband.

Tony sat up: "Good morning, sir."

"Don't 'sir' me now. It's Papa, Tony." Don Manuel sounded a bit displeased at the other end of the line.

"I'm sorry, Papa," Tony repeated, trying out the word with little confidence, and he was pleased to find that "Papa" was not awkward at all.

"That's better," Don Manuel chuckled. "The course at Wack Wack was a bit crowded so Dangmount and I decided to fly in just now." After the hurried explanation for his presence in Baguio he went on: "You don't have to take the train this afternoon. We can all go home tomorrow by plane."

"My classes start at nine, Papa," Tony said, "and it's rather important that I be there."

"There's a lot of time. We fly at daybreak."

It was pointless to argue. "If you say so, Papa," Tony said. "And thank you very much."

"Now, may I have that daughter of mine again?"

Tony handed the phone to Carmen.

"Yes, Papa," she said. "Yes, right here at the Pines."

She placed the phone on its hook, turned complacently to Tony, and, as if she were speaking to a secretary, said, "Don't forget to remind me, darling, I'll call Manila tonight, so that my car will be at the airport and I'll drive you straight to the university. That will make you happy?"

"There's a lot of time," Tony said.

"I'm glad you accepted Papa's invitation. He will come here tonight and have dinner with us."

Tony Samson, unable to say anything that might spoil Carmen's plans, lay on the bed. But sleep had left him. Even Carmen, soft to the touch, now appeared to him as no more than any other woman. It would have been vastly different if this were Washington, although Washington was now a year past. He recalled again the apartment Carmen had in Massachusetts Avenue, its comforts. Her family—did they really accept him as Carmen had wanted him to be accepted? Why did her father now come to Baguio? Was it to play golf as he had told her or could there be a more significant reason?

"Get up, darling," Carmen said, pulling the woolen blanket away from him. In another instant she was over him, all arms and kisses and warmth and woman scent.

"Food is what I need," he said, biting her ear.

• • •

THE BOY who brought in their breakfast was silently efficient and he left as quickly as he could. Sipping her coffee and still in her negligee, Carmen became thoughtful as she returned to the clear glass window. The pines outside were covered with mist. "Once, I dreamed of this day. In college we read a lot of books, most of them things you wouldn't think *colegialas** would be capable of taking a glimpse of. But there we were, reading and looking at pictures when the nuns weren't looking. You know, the kind of stuff that gets discreetly shown under false covers in the shadow of the Eiffel Tower . . ."

"Monsieur, feelthy pictures," Tony blandly imitated the French vendor.

Carmen laughed heartily. "*Oye,* do you know that in the last week of our high school the nuns asked a priest to lecture to us about the facts of life? It was funny. We were all giggling in the rear. Here was this priest, fat and kindly looking—a German or a Belgian, I don't remember—rattling off the facts about the sperm meeting the ovum. It was funny, I tell you."

"What I want to know . . ." Tony stretched his hand across the table and held her hands, "is it someone other than me who made you really aware of these basic facts?"

She pouted: "You know damn well that you were the first. *Esto,* what more proof do you need?"

"I'm satisfied," Tony said. "But then I was away for a summer in Europe and I heard when I was away that you were dating this fellow who works for your father—Nena's husband, this Ben—"

He wasn't able to finish. A piece of bread struck him in the face, and before he could recover, Carmen had rushed to their bedroom and slammed the door after her. Only after some mushy explanations did Carmen open the door.

Thinking about the incident later, Tony was vaguely amused, yet at the same time surprised that he had asked the question at all. Through those years when he was exposed to the morality of the American campus, he no longer attached value to chastity, and he believed that he would not care about a woman's past as long as he loved her. He brought to mind that dilapidated room in Antipolo

* *Colegialas:* Female college students.

and again, that sharp, sweet pain of remembrance stabbed at him. He had changed; yes, he had changed so much that now he could afford to say, Carmen, I don't care how many men you have had. I love you, that is all that matters.

AT EIGHT Don Manuel was in the lobby. In the crackling glow of the fireplace where a pine log burned, he looked young, almost like an older brother to Carmen. He smiled. "Just the three of us," he said. "I have so many things to tell you and I can hardly wait." Explanations: how the summer house where the newlyweds should have stayed needed a greenhouse, how badly he fared in golf the whole day. They walked with Carmen in the middle, holding their arms, to the dining room, where they were seated at a corner table. Carmen bantered about Tony learning golf, and just before the coffee and the dessert came, Don Manuel dropped the amiable air and became serious.

"I'm not satisfied with the service we are getting from our advertising agency," he said with a hint of impatience. "Look, we give them more than fifteen percent commission on the ads they prepare. They also charge us a retainer—five thousand a month—and that is not peanuts. And you know what they do? They can't even cook up a sensible reply to all the accusations against this steel mill we are putting up. It will be the only one of its kind in the country. So what if the Japanese get a sizable chunk of the profit? After all, they are helping put it up. And what difference does that make? If it isn't the Japanese who make the killing, it's the Americans—as if we have no surfeit of Americans here telling us what to do. They just want us to be hewers of wood and drawers of water for as long as they can manage."

"What do you want me to do, Papa?" Tony asked. He already sensed that Don Manuel did not come to dinner to talk about golf.

"Nothing much as far as your talents are concerned. I've read some of the stuff you have written, Tony. That article on the uses of the past, for instance, your thesis on the Philippine Revolution—I've glanced through them. I know how you teachers regard businessmen as nothing more than money-mad people. You'd be surprised if you went around more with some of my friends. I'm money-mad, all right, but that doesn't stop me from honing on new ideas. And you have many bright ideas, Tony, brilliant ideas . . ."

"Thank you, Papa," Tony said. Under the table Carmen pressed his hand.

"It will not be difficult. I want you to work for me, to be in places where I need you, to talk in places where I want you, to talk and write what I want you to write. My interest is Carmen's interest and her interest is yours—and your children's. . . ."

A pause, then Don Manuel turned to Carmen and then to Tony again: "Isn't that logical, son?"

This was the trap with all its embellishments, but Tony nodded nevertheless.

"Don't think of it as inevitable. When a man marries, the decisions he makes are not for him alone but for his wife and his family. I want you to leave the university. Start working for yourself, for Carmen."

IN THE EARLY morning Tony knew that he would never be able to visit Baguio again and wander through its emerald hills with a sense of freedom. As they drove to the airport on this chilly morning, an undefinable feeling almost akin to sorrow riled him. There could be no rationalization now of his defeat—for what else could it be but a defeat?—and yet, if he must look for one, he could always say, as did Don Manuel, that he must think of Carmen and the child she bore.

The landscape was sun-washed, white with the mist that floated down the hills, engulfed the city, and then drifted away. The drive to the airport was smooth, and as they looped down the hills, the wind singing and the cold biting, Tony wished that he had stayed longer, savored the illusion longer, before going down to the lowlands. And yet he could not hate his father-in-law, for Don Manuel was a gentleman. The businessman saw to it that his feelings were spared. Dale Carnegie—he must have been Don Manuel's favorite author. Not Malraux, or Mabini,* or Ortega y Gasset—these men exuded not light and goodwill but depressing truths. Tony must know how

*Apolinario Mabini (1864–1903): Theoretician and spokesman of the Philippine Revolution.

to parry with words, to hide under the clean, happy jargon of public relations. Don Manuel had been very kind: "I'm not hurrying you up. If you think you have a future at the university, by all means stick it out there. Give yourself two months to think it over, then let's talk shop. Two months is no water under the bridge. That was how long it took me to decide on the steel mill—just passing it around among friends. Then it came clearly: we had to start somewhere; if we didn't, someone else would—the Japanese or the Americans or, in some future time, the Chinese. And where would that leave us? It's always best to be out there first. You may not know it, but if you are first you will not fail. The first zipper maker, the first rubber shoe manufacturer—they can afford to retire. They were the first and that was how they made a profit. And if you don't make a success out of it, there's still the distinction of being first. No one can take that from you."

WHEN HE WALKED into the department, most of his colleagues were already waiting for the first bell.

"You old dog, we never knew you'd marry—and so soon. And the Villas. Now there's another man gone wrong correctly. You should have told us so we could have given you a *despedida*." The words sang in his ears and they sounded sincere. He let the ribbing go on until the bell rang and he had to hurry off to his first class.

His students were but a handful—only twenty-two—and he always had a notion that they could have been brighter if they only tried. He was prepared as usual for an interesting Monday morning and was greeted by smiling faces. Then a girl out front, who was majoring in political science, stood up, "Congratulations, sir. It is all over the campus."

In the afternoon the ribald jokes became less frequent and he accepted the fact that his marriage was public knowledge. It gave him peace of mind to know that the marriage had been viewed matter-of-factly and was even something he could be proud of. There was none of the knowing looks and the sharp double talk at which his colleagues were agile, none of the little thrusts that would tell him that they suspected he married Carmen Villa only for her money.

The dean's office was on the ground floor and he was halfway there when this awful sense of having been remiss came to him: he hadn't told the old man at all about his wedding. He could easily rationalize that now by explaining that it was a surprise even to himself. But that was not easy to believe and, besides, the first decent thing he should have done this Monday was to go to the dean.

The dean was a small, dark man, and sitting behind his huge narra-wood desk with its small Filipino flag and his name carved in gothic on black hardwood, he looked more like a schoolboy, with his chubby cheeks and pugnacious chin.

He acknowledged Tony's presence with a quick smile, then he went back to the stapled sheaf of papers he was reading.

It went on like this for about three minutes. Tony started shuffling in his seat. He was now growing aware of the Lopez "treatment." In the past the old man had used it to put his subordinates and the professors under him in their proper places. Dean Lopez, however, exercised the utmost care in inflicting this kind of punishment. He meted it out only to those he could officially order around, or those who stood to gain from him some benevolence, those tokens of official largesse that he passed out—a good word at the faculty meeting, the promise of a raise or a promotion, an invitation to his house for *merienda*. I'll give him two minutes, Tony thought, glancing at his watch. Beyond the open window the afternoon was bright. Students idled under the leafy acacias. In a soft, firm voice he said, "I still have to prepare some papers, Dean, and since you seem very busy, I'll return and see you after five."

Dean Lopez slowly lowered the sheaf he was holding and looked at him. "My time is important, too, Samson," he said. The old man had always called him by his first name, but now he was calling him by his family name. "So," the dean continued, "I hope you don't mind while I finish this. It won't take but another five minutes."

Dean Lopez finally dropped the sheaf.

"Yes," he said, standing up and, without looking at the young man, turning to the window. "I want to talk to you about your paper on the Ilocos. It is a waste of time and you should not continue it. Work on something more useful, something that has never been touched before. You know I have already done some work on the subject. Do you think you can dredge up something on it on which I haven't already dwelt? That's presumptuous of you, you know. . . ."

Tony Samson studied the stout, motionless figure and tried to surmise what had come upon him.

"I'm sorry that you should think of it that way, sir," he said. "You see, I'm doing it on my own. On my own time, too."

Dean Lopez wheeled and his mouth curled. "You are wrong, Samson," he said. "Your time is not your own. It's the university's. Or didn't you know that?" His voice was sheathed with bluster.

"I didn't think it was like that, sir," Tony said.

"Well, you had better start thinking now the way I want you to think," Dean Lopez said. "Do you want to be a full professor in five years or do you want to be a mere associate all your life? I decide on that, too, or have you forgotten?"

"No, sir," Tony said simply. The old man was bared to him in all his rawness. "Is that all you wanted to tell me, sir?"

"No, that's not all. I will talk to you for as long as I please. About the Socrates Club—you are not qualified for it. Simply because you have a doctorate doesn't mean you are in. I drafted the rules of the club, you know. And don't think that I don't know— There's such a thing as a Chinese B in Harvard."

"I don't know what you are driving at, sir," Tony said sullenly.

"Well, if you don't know, let me tell you that Orientals in Harvard get a passing grade as a charitable gesture. After all, they won't degrade Harvard by staying in the States. It's that simple, Samson. In other words, we don't want Chinese B's in the Socrates Club."

"I hadn't expected it to be this way, sir," Tony said icily. "I don't think I deserve to be crucified for something I did not really aspire to."

"Don't be coy with me and say you didn't aspire for membership in the club. That's a lie, Samson, and you know it."

The blood left Tony's face and a clamminess came over him.

"That's the trouble with you," Dean Lopez said serenely. He went back to his desk. The afternoon sun stole in from the glass windows and fell on its glass top, reflecting onto his ruddy face, his peasant hands, and his shock of white hair. "You presume too many things. Look, I've been here for more than two decades and that's why I am the dean. And look at you, you have just started and you already want to be a regent or the dean. Over my dead body, Samson. Understand that? Over my dead body. You cannot be dean of this college, not while I am alive. You may have married well and you may have political influence, but you cannot be the dean while I am alive. And all the politicians you know can go to hell for all I care."

"Whoever gave you the idea I wanted to be dean and that I'm taking over your post?" he stammered.

Dean Lopez was smiling now. "I know, I know," he said sarcastically. "That's just the problem with people who get too big for their breeches and who want to go up fast. Did America do these things to you? And you can't even qualify for the Socrates Club."

Tony Samson felt like slapping the old man's face. "I don't like to disagree with you, sir," he said faintly, "but you said you submitted my name. And I didn't even know it until you told me before I left for Baguio."

"Now, now," Dean Lopez said. "Let us not be like women. Everyone knows of the honor that goes with joining the club. Think of it: in the country there are only forty members and in the university there are only ten. Do not tell me that you aren't interested. . . ."

"I am, sir," Tony said. "I'd be a hypocrite if I said I was not. It's just that I did not apply."

Dean Lopez exploded. "Damn you!" he said, his eyes darting fire. "If the club does not want you, you should take it with grace."

He had never expected that a moment as rife with anger as now would come, for he had never made an allowance for the time when he would glare back at his benefactor and damn him. But in a voice that was hoarse and almost a whisper: "Don't ever talk to me about grace. Or scholarship! You have no right—you plagiarist!" And trembling with unspoken rage, he wheeled out of the dean's office into the raw, sun-flooded afternoon.

That evening Tony wrote to Lawrence Bitfogel again. He did not say, however, that he had quit the university. That would have been too painful to relate and Larry would never understand. He had worked so hard for the chance to be a teacher, and now all the anguish, all the privation, six years, six long years of starving, of wandering and despairing—all this had gone to waste.

Dear Larry, he started, I would have invited you to my wedding, but it caught even me by surprise. We eloped and up to now I'm still in a daze. No, it's not someone you know or someone I've told you about. I met her in Washington and, of course, she's Filipina. You know very well my views on mixed marriages and you know I'm too much of a coward to attempt something as radical as a mixed marriage. But at least you can grant me some imagination—I eloped, didn't I? This isn't the only reason I'm writing this letter, though. I must tell you, too, that I have acquired new interests. Perhaps these interests have to go with marriage and my new status. I do wish very much that you were here now, so that we could talk things over. It's not the marriage that has me all dazed and confused, far from it. It's the university and the host of problems that it has dumped upon my lap. At any rate, I am doing all right, and don't . . . don't ever loathe me if someday I mellow or change into an arch-conservative. Come to Manila soon.

The letter was the last he mailed to Lawrence Bitfogel.

There were other letters, of course, wherein he expressed his thoughts candidly, and this he could do easily, objectively, because he had always been analytical and even ruthless with himself when he sought the bedrock of truth, the soft shale of emotion, of egoism having been eroded by his own relentless questioning. But when all these letters were written, he could not mail them and he placed them all in that folder where he had compiled personal notes—not to be read by anyone, he told himself wryly, until I am dead.

IT WAS CARMEN who announced it a week afterward at the breakfast table. "Well, Papa," she said airily. "Tony has quit the university. I think we should celebrate."

Tony raised a hand to stop her, but she ignored him. "Papa, don't you think it's about time Tony started learning how you operate, too?"

"I don't think my quitting the university is something to be taken lightly," Tony said petulantly. "You must understand, Papa," he turned to Don Manuel, who had set his glass of orange juice down and was now looking at him, "that the university was what I had prepared for. Teaching is in my system. It wasn't an easy decision."

"We all have to make decisions." Don Manuel sounded sympathetic. He picked up his glass. "The decisions are sometimes difficult, but it's better that we choose to make them rather than be forced to make them. A good soldier, I always say, selects his fights."

"I wish I could say that, Papa," Tony said. "I was forced and that's what I hate."

"Well," Carmen said, "there's always a silver lining even in the darkest cloud. Or at least silver-plated."

"Of course, of course," Don Manuel said equably. "And I must tell you that this development pleases me. One man's loss, after all, is another man's gain. I've told you, Tony. I need someone I can trust, someone with perception and talent."

The flattery was pleasant to his ears. How pat, how neatly everything was falling into place.

After breakfast Don Manuel beckoned Tony to the terrace. In the shade of the green canvas awning, looking down on the rain-drenched city, Tony listened to his father-in-law speak with almost childlike simplicity. "Today, Tony, I'd like you to see the office, get the feel of the place." He discoursed further on such mundane topics as knowing how to get along with people, praising them when praise was needed, and showing a firm hand when this, too, was necessary. They parted on such platitudes. It was too late to retrace his steps; he was trapped in a maze where the Villas were the minotaurs, and somehow, though he should have detested the entrapment, it was not as distasteful as he once thought it would be.

The morning wore on in a drizzle. Beyond the patio glazed with rain the bougainvillea drooped and a murkiness cloaked the acacias, the garden, and, in fact, the whole world. Somewhere in the caverns of the house Tony could hear Mrs. Villa ordering someone in her brisk manner to do the marketing early. The very sound of her voice, the thought of having to sit with her at lunch again, riled him. And yet Tony did not really hate her. He was aware of this the first time he met her and the incapacity to loathe her came about not because she was Carmen's mother but because Mrs. Villa, in spite of her grossness, was herself.

He went to their room, where Carmen was reading the papers in bed, and he sat down beside her. He kissed her lightly on the cheek. "Baby," he said, "when I start working for Papa, don't you think we should start living alone? Not that I don't like it here, but we should be able to live our own lives."

She looked up. "All right, darling. Promise me we will not talk about this subject anymore, because if you do I'm going to say yes."

He bent over and bit her ear.

"Papa is going to build a cottage at the end of the lot beyond the pool. It will be for us."

He shook his head. "I mean, if we leave this house we should live away from here."

"You give me a good reason, darling. If it's mother you don't want to see, well, you don't have to see her at all once the cottage is finished. *Esto,* the entrance will be from the rear, from the other side of the street . . ."

IT WAS STILL raining when he reached the boulevard, and the asphalt glistened like a mirror through the dreary, slanting rain. The Villa Building stood alone on a wide lot planted to grass and aroma trees. Its five stories were shielded from the sun, for the building was one of the first in Manila to use horizontal sun-breakers. It was painted in soft cream, was fully air-conditioned, and could have easily passed for a box—well-proportioned and neat—if it did not have an unusual facade that featured a long, sweeping cantilever marquee flanked by two columns of gray Romblon marble. The foyer, too, with its floor and walls of marble, was quietly elegant.

Don Manuel's office was on the fifth floor or "executive country," and there was an express elevator to it. Tony was quickly ushered in by the efficient matronly secretary, who often came to the house with Don Manuel's homework.

A Japanese, whom Don Manuel introduced as a steel expert, and Senator Reyes were getting ready to leave when he went in; they were already at the door, engaged in parting niceties. The senator and his Japanese companion had one thing in common: the porcine face of a man well-fed and contented. The senator's cheeks were white with talc and he grinned meaninglessly when Don Manuel introduced Tony.

"Ah—" Senator Reyes sighed. His eyes were pouched and flinty. "It's a pleasure meeting you, Dr. Samson. I respect Ph.D.'s, you know. Well," he turned to Don Manuel and slapped the entrepreneur on the back, "I hope everything at the university turns out fine. I was there last Monday as you requested. Dr. Samson will surely be a regent next month. Two regents will vacate their posts. Their terms have expired."

Senator Reyes faced Tony with an expansive mien. "You'll be big there, son. You have the qualifications and, most important, the best connections . . ." His laughter was like the crack of splitting bamboo. "And you can even be the dean of your college if you like, let me see to that. And if you have complaints . . ."

Don Manuel shook hands with the Japanese and then with Senator Reyes. The door was open. "My son, *Compadre,* I'm sorry to tell you, has already left the university. He will start working with me."

Senator Reyes paused. He looked disappointed. After a pause, "Well, that's a lot better. At any rate," he turned to Don Manuel again, "don't tell me I didn't try."

"Thank you, sir," Tony said automatically. Now it was all clear why Dean Lopez hated him. But it was beyond explaining now and no thought could shape in his mind, no thought, only revulsion.

He followed Don Manuel, who had returned to his wide steel desk. "I didn't know, Papa," Tony said, "that you had asked Senator Reyes to intercede for me."

Don Manuel avoided him. "Wouldn't you like being a regent? Or dean? Don't you like the fact that I'm interested in your welfare?"

"I appreciate it, Papa," he said, the fight ebbing out of him. "But I wish you would understand. I can go up on my own . . . it may take longer, but I can go up."

Don Manuel stopped arranging the papers on his desk and faced Tony. "That's what I like about you," he said paternally. "You have pride. But remember, you are now in the family. And if I can help you get ahead I'll do it."

Then Don Manuel drifted back to the visitors who had gone and his tone became jovial again. "Politicians," he said, "are a species you have to understand. No, they aren't difficult at all. All that you must remember is that they are after one thing—money. Once you know that, you can't be wrong. They are very brassy about it. Gentleman's language—don't waste this on politicians. They name their price and it's up to you to haggle."

Tony did not speak.

"That's distasteful to you, isn't it?" Don Manuel laughed slightly. "Well, that's how it is. These are the realities. Maybe when this country has become industrialized these politicians will give jobs to their constituents. And if they can't give jobs, they must help in another way. That's where a little of their money goes."

"Just like one big happy family," Tony said.

"Don't be so sarcastic about the family," Don Manuel said. "In this organization, for instance, all the employees are related to one another. The family system—oh yes, I've heard young punks in the business underrating it. And they are right, too. I am all for effi-ciency. That's why I'm going all out for this mill. But as long as there's no substitute for the family, it stays. Besides, what substitute have you for loyalty? You can't expect loyalty from the politicians. Not even at the price you pay them."

"So money isn't everything then," Tony said happily, as if one last pinnacle of his own beliefs had stood up to the rich man's bat-tering reason.

"Of course money isn't everything." Don Manuel leaned back on his chair and beamed. "The price is not always money. But if you want to know what the price of a man is, or his services, you must be wise." Don Manuel brought his forefinger to his right temple and tapped twice. "It's all a matter of understanding what a man wants most. If you can give him that, then he is yours to command. Don't expect that he will be eternally grateful, because all men hate to be indebted. Every man wants to be independent. As for the price, some men want friendship. If you can give them that, well and good. Money cannot buy friendship but it can *create* friendship. See? It can create the atmosphere. It can create the conditions for all the reasons you need. But, as I said, don't expect gratitude. You'll be terribly dis-appointed. All men act in self-interest. Even the conduct of nations is guided by this unerring rule. It was George Washington who said that, no?"

Tony nodded.

Don Manuel went back to his monologue. "It's the truth. Every-one has a price. Christ had a price—the Cross and the salvation of mankind. I have a price—the future of the Villas and of everyone in the family. You have a price—and don't feel that I'm insulting you. Your self-respect. I'm just stating a fact. You are vulnerable where you are most sincere. And I think that is why Carmen likes you. You have self-respect. As long as you know these vulnerable points you will know also how to deal with people. Even our highly touted press has its price. I know. I get my way around business editors. Everyone in this racket can be bought. I have yet to see one who cannot be bought."

Tony looked at the ceiling and a thought crossed his mind. Godo—he had always been insufferable, but Godo was someone who would not bend to something as crass as money. He had gotten into trouble because of this single virtue—integrity—and he brimmed with it. He was cynical and brassy, vulgar, loud-mouthed. He was a peasant in manners and attitudes, but he was an aristocrat when it came to honor. Tony shook his head.

"You don't agree, huh?" Don Manuel asked.

Tony nodded. Godo would yet be his redeemer, the one who could prove to Don Manuel that the price tag does not apply to all human beings. Godo would be his final proof that a man's reward is in heaven. "I'm not very sure, Papa," Tony said. "But if there's anyone I can trust it's Godo Soler, an editor and an old friend. He may have faults, but one thing I know, you can't buy him."

Don Manuel became silent. "Godo," he said, twiddling his thumbs. "Well, I'll remember that. Bring him to me someday. Next time there's a party in the house, ask him to come. No, bring him to lunch—or dinner. I'll yet find his price, and because he is your friend, I'll be extra generous with him. It's not that I want to prove you wrong, Tony. It's simply I've never been wrong."

One of the office boys came in apparently at the ring of a buzzer, and Don Manuel said, "Bring me a Coke—and Tony, is it coffee?"

Tony nodded. As the boy disappeared at the other end of the room, Don Manuel continued in the same serious vein: "I cannot find it in me to dispute the usefulness of the family system. For the moment it's doing wonders. You get loyalty because of it—and efficiency. I have heard it said that with industrialization the family system will have to go."

"I think that's true, Papa," Tony Samson said. "In the United States family corporations are a thing of the past."

"In the United States," Don Manuel repeated in an annoyed tone. "Must you always bring the United States into the conversation? The conditions in this country are different—that is the first thing you should know, Tony. This isn't America; this is Asia."

"I know, Papa," Tony said, "but the family has to go if there must be industrialization. I remember in college we had a discussion along this line . . ."

"This isn't college anymore, son," Don Manuel said softly.

"I know that, too, Papa."

"I hope I am not being a bore," Don Manuel said apologetically.

"No, I don't think it's wrong for people to be idealistic. I just ask that people like you be realistic enough to know that the real world is full of compromise."

Tony loved Don Manuel's clichés. His father-in-law was being emphatic.

"What I'm trying to say," Don Manuel said, "is that poverty has its place, but what would happen if poverty were to become a symbol of the elite? Then there would be no more reason for people to want to work harder."

"I know, Papa," Tony said. "Poverty is degrading."

Don Manuel stood up and paced the floor. "I knew poverty. I'll tell you how it was when my father was just starting to build his furniture factory. He had to wake up at dawn to count the lumber that came in. We had to walk to school, all the way from Ermita to Intramuros. That's a good long walk, even now. I've known how it is to be hungry, to be broke, and to be unhappy. Father would give us no more than five centavos a day. Five centavos! And one pair of shoes until they were worn out and our toes and soles stuck out."

The rich man cracked his knuckles. "He was a tyrant, but he taught us well." A long pause, then the talk veered quietly to what Tony had to do. The simplicity of his job amazed him; he was to be the official spokesman of the Villas. Henceforth, there would be no business negotiations unless he had spoken on the plausibility of having these negotiations exploited for the good name of the Villas. He was to be a troubleshooter and a member of the brain trust. He was to be a public relations man, he was to be a facade-builder.

"I don't want to sound ungrateful, Papa," Tony said, latching on to every word, "but there must be some other thing I can do."

"That's honest of you," Don Manuel said kindly. "Not many people can say that, Tony. Well, there aren't many like you. But you are different. We are all crude moneymakers, but you, you are different. And you can start making yourself useful right now by telling me if there's anything wrong with teaming up with the Chinese, Japanese, and Americans. I want an honest opinion, Tony. You can give me the answer next week."

Don Manuel led Tony to the door at the left side of the room. It led to a room with cream-colored drapes and a thick rug. The businessman tugged at a line and the draperies opened to a rain-shrouded view of the bay and the boulevard.

The desk was not as modern as Don Manuel's, but it was huge. One side of the room was lined with empty, glass-fronted shelves. And on a low table beside the desk was the latest electric typewriter—its soft red color glowing handsomely in the light.

"You'll love working here," Don Manuel stated proudly. "All this is yours. Your secretary will be outside. Look for one right away—that's your decision. When I need you I'll just buzz you, and son, do please jump when I do."

"Yes, Papa," Tony said.

ALONE IN THIS comfortable room, Tony felt lost for a moment. He sat in his upholstered swivel chair and turned around. Those shelves—they would soon be filled with his books. His hand caressed the electric machine. It did not seem real, his being in a place as comfortable, as conducive to easeful thinking as this. How supremely convenient it was for him simply to accept the fact that now he was no longer a Samson but someone drawn into the magnetic circle of the Villas and therefore a nonentity without a mind all his own.

He could see his personal landscape and in it there was nothing extraneous. Everything fitted handsomely. He would probably build a house in Pobres Park like Ben de Jesus, Senator Reyes, Alfred Dangmount, and all the rest, and see how well Carmen had learned interior decorating in the United States. He would not interfere with her plans; all he would require would be a small room, a study where he would be able to work. And someday he would grow a paunch in his job and learn to play golf. He would have money stashed away somewhere—that was most certain because he had married Carmen Villa. He would have an affair, too, probably a dozen at that, not because such affairs were necessary but because they were inevitable concomitants of his status. A beautiful secretary, perhaps? Or one of Carmen's close friends? Or the wife of one of his associates in the office? These were the handsome possibilities. As for children, there would be at least five—and several more who would naturally be illegitimate. Carmen would send the girls to the Assumption Convent, where they would learn French—or to Madrid, where they would polish their Spanish and acquire a European accent. As for the boys, they would go to La Salle, of course, or to the American School, or to San Beda. Not Ateneo—my God! That school had become too common and too crowded with plebeian characters. And after La Salle there would be trips to Europe, not America. Going to America—that was also now too common. Everyone, absolutely everyone, had gone there. And then when the children had grown up they would have to take their pick from the Villa crowd. That was the only way to perpetuate the system that he had joined. There was no fighting against it because the system, which afforded him such delicious comforts as he had never known before, was bigger and more formidable than Antonio Samson.

He stood up and went to the window. The sea again, the rain, memories rushing in and stirring up and about, inchoate and yet alive. When he was in Antipolo, or when he was in the States, wandering in the gilded wilderness of that continent, he seldom looked at the sea. And at night, if there was no rain, there would be stars. How long had it been since he last looked at the stars? He knew them when he was in Rosales, going home in the dark or playing in the dusty street where the lamps were not strong enough to banish the vast attraction of the sky. How was Rosales now? And Emy?

A dull ache passed through him and he assured himself that this was what he had always wanted—this progress, this change. The world was changing and if in the process he was changed, too, well, he could not stop the inevitable any more than he could stop time. I'll be all right. Tony Samson repeated the words carefully in his mind. I'll be all right—and he wished to God that he would be.

W HEN SENATOR REYES invited Tony to lunch, it had never occurred to Tony that there would be a measure of rapport between him and the politician who had made a career of nationalism.

Don Manuel bantered with them in the foyer. "Be careful, Tony. He might take you to one of those joints where they serve nothing but peasant food."

"I'll take him to a place where they sprinkle cyanide on those who don't know what Filipinism means," Senator Reyes chortled.

"Ahhh . . ." grunted Alfred Dangmount. He was on his way to his car, too; the board meeting had just ended and the directors were filing out of the elevator. "Take him to that place where they spike the drinks with *cantaritas*," the American said, grunting again.

The American's sally raised more remarks, but Tony didn't catch them; by this time he had already gotten into Senator Reyes's air-conditioned Cadillac. Within, the scent of cologne was a refreshing change from the antiseptic smell of his office.

Senator Reyes was a master politician. "It is seldom that I have a scholar, a Ph.D., with me. So don't be alarmed if I ask too many questions and pick your brains," he said, flashing what seemed to be a genuine smile. The senator's eyes crinkled. His teeth were yellowish from cigar-smoking.

"The pleasure is all mine, Senator," Tony said.

They went to one of the new Spanish restaurants on the boulevard—a low, adobe building that was air-conditioned. Its interior was dim, and although it was high noon, the cartwheel lamp that dangled from the low ceiling was lit. Senator Reyes guided his guest to a corner table, but before reaching the place he had to stop at a table to slap an anonymous back.

They sat down without ceremony, and as the headwaiter rushed to them, Senator Reyes ordered two dry sherries. "I shouldn't have any complaints," he turned to Tony, shaking his head. "And I don't want to sound hypocritical, but I do have troubles and I sometimes wish I could earn a living without having to pay too heavy a price."

"Whatever the price," Tony said, "I am sure that you can afford it."

Senator Reyes became somber and again he shook his head. "I suppose that I should be envied then? People are blaming us for the mess in this country, but people should blame themselves occasionally. Who is to blame? Politicians for giving the people what they want? They expect us to do the impossible, to cast aside all morals, all concepts of justice. And when we do, we are pounced upon. A man comes to me and says, Senator, please see to it that my boy gets accommodated in the Foreign Service. That's where I want him, because there his views will be broadened and he will be able to travel free. I want someone in my family to be an ambassador someday! I ask this man if his son is qualified, if he has passed the Foreign Service examinations. And this man—one of my trusted friends and leaders—says to me angrily: Senator, if my son were qualified, I would not have to come to you for assistance!"

Tony knew the rest and he could have told the senator why the road to power was often covered with slime. But the owner of the restaurant came to their table; he was a swarthy, pot-bellied Spaniard, and he greeted the senator effusively in Spanish, then started talking about his difficulty in getting dollar licenses that would enable him to import the senator's favorite sherry. To this, Senator Reyes said, also in Spanish, "You can save the sherry for me; as for your other customers, you can serve them goat urine—they wouldn't know the difference."

Tony Samson laughed and was joined heartily by the Spaniard, who, after more pleasantries, moved away from his most important customer of the day.

"You speak Spanish?" Senator Reyes turned to his guest.

"Not really, sir," Tony said. "Crammed for three months, that's all—and then, of course, there's the two years in the university, which no one can escape."

"Tell me about the cram course," the senator said. "I am interested about attitudes toward the Spanish language."

"It was a matter of urgent necessity," Tony said. "Before I left the country on this scholarship, I knew that the basic documents I would have to go through would be in Spanish. I taught myself. Then, at Harvard, well, the three-month cramming did help. But I have to think first when I speak, although I can say without being immodest that I do read Spanish very well and, perhaps, write a little, too. Of course, I cannot hope to approximate your skills."

The senator thrust his hands at Tony in protest. "No flatteries, no flatteries, please, or else it's you who will have to pay for this lunch!"

While they sipped their sherry, Senator Reyes reminisced. "I am supposed to be a Spanish scholar—that is to say one of my interests is Spanish literature. Did a little writing in the language. Were you ever in Spain?"

"Yes, Senator," Tony said. Now there drifted to his mind the remembered places: Barcelona and its Gothic quarter, the narrow streets and the bars of Barrio Chino, the painted tiles in the doorways.

"Wonderful country," Senator Reyes said. "And Sevilla—were you ever there?"

"Yes, sir," Tony said. "I did some research in the Sevilla archives."

The waiter came and took their orders—paella for both—and Senator Reyes made desultory remarks about the bad paella in Barcelona. From there the politician guided the talk to where he deemed it should go. "Politicians have no time to think," he said, and Tony could sense real regret in the senator's voice. "What I'm trying to say is that I have ideas, but I have no time to thresh them out. For instance," the senator leaned over and tried to sound like a conspirator, "how I would like to make a speech on nationalism as a cultural instrument, as an ideology creating a oneness in this country. But what materials can I cite? What antecedents will support me? It's easy to speak, but I must have historical authority. Even one in my position must have that."

Tony Samson sat back and above the clatter of silver at the next table, above the sensuous guitar-strumming near the bar, he could make out the sound of the flute, the wide ring of young Catalans dancing the saldana before the cathedral in Barcelona.

After a long pause, he said he had come across the problem many times and had found partial answers in Barcelona when he was there tracing the footsteps of Rizal, Del Pilar, Lopez-Jaena, and all the *ilustrados* who propagandized for reforms. "There must be some merit in the Spanish people," he said with feeling. He almost said, there must be some merit in tyrants. "After all, Rizal and his friends worked for reforms not in Manila but in Barcelona and Madrid."

"Yes," Senator Reyes said excitedly; "this is an aspect of our history that is not quite understood. And what else did you find? Did Rizal and Del Pilar have anything special to say about what I'm thinking of?"

"The *ilustrados*," Tony Samson brightened up. "I think I can speak about them with authority. I studied them—what they did, what they wrote. They created a national unity, Senator. Without them, there would perhaps be no Filipinas as we know it today. But they made errors, of course—and it was a matter of attitude, more than anything. Let me tell you how they tried to define the limits of freedom, how desperately they tried to prove that there was a true and indigenous Filipino culture so they could claim equality with the Spaniards. That was it—all they wanted was equality. Oh no, I'm not saying that they were not sincere, that they did not love their country, but you must realize that in those days they were second-class citizens even though they had studied in the best schools in Europe. You see, they were not Spaniards, their skins were not white, their noses were not high, and because of these shortcomings, they could never be rulers."

"But you could be barking up the wrong tree," Senator Reyes said. "My dear fellow, look at my skin. It is as dark as the bottom of a pot, my nose is like that of a prizefighter." He laughed raucously.

"You are missing the whole point, Senator," Tony said. "Equality could be won on paper. But once it was won, that was the end of it.

Freedom and the fight for it must be constant. It must never cease. And do not forget that men can be enslaved by their own people, by their own prejudices, by their own rulers. . . . What I am saying is that the *ilustrados* were not the real patriots. They wanted nothing more than equality. They didn't want freedom. It was enough that they could dine with their rulers, could argue with them. But it is another thing to be free. And that is why I do not consider Rizal a hero. He was great in his way, but Marcelo H. del Pilar was a greater man. He died a pauper in Spain. In the end, none of the *ilustrados* could approximate the stature, the heroism of Bonifacio. There was a man—he was far more heroic than Rizal. He was a laborer, he was illiterate compared to Rizal. But he fought for freedom. Rizal merely wanted equality. Perhaps the new nationalism can address itself to this, create a new sense of values."

Senator Reyes was pensive and, for a while, an expression of seriousness came over his flabby face. "I do not want to be old-fashioned," he finally said. "Revolutionaries are a dime a dozen now. You get them everywhere. And what happens—revolutionists do not live; they are eaten up, just as Bonifacio was eaten up."

"How right you are!" Tony exclaimed. "But that is what I have always said. A revolution does not have to eat its children. In fact, it is those who are in power who could very well initiate revolutions— oh, let us not be old-fashioned and think only of armed uprisings of minorities as revolutions. Any movement that seeks to overhaul established attitudes is, I think, revolutionary. I'd hate to listen to another address extolling Rizal's virtues; I'd hate to read the inanities written about how many women he had, how he frequented this bar or this toilet."

They laughed. "I see, I see," Senator Reyes said, grinning.

"Now, when we escalate Bonifacio's greatness—after all, he really started the revolution against Spain—that is revolutionary. People think of Rizal always as the greatest merely because he was martyred and Bonifacio was killed by his own people," Tony said. He remembered again the protracted discussions on Maple Street, Larry Bitfogel's intellectual argot and his own deft reasoning piercing the maze of contradictions. He continued: "How can one be a revolutionary in an age when revolutions have become commonplace? There is only one way, and that's by creating an entirely new definition of revolution itself and knowing your position once you have made your definition. If we talked about cultural revolution, we would be giving both culture and revolution an entirely new emphasis."

"Good!" Senator Reyes exclaimed. He sat back and rubbed his stomach with his chubby hand. Supreme contentment spread over his dark, corpulent face. "You are the man, then, who can help me—the only man, Tony." It was the first time the senator called him by his nickname. "This will be a favor, something I can never repay. Write me a speech for next Sunday. I am going to speak before the Socrates Club at the university. Nationalism is going haywire and I want its proper cultural definition. Only you can do that."

They parted on that nicety.

Back at his office Tony sat before his typewriter, pondered his quarrel with Dean Lopez and how he would have been a member of the Socrates Club. It was ironic that he should now be writing Senator Reyes's speech before the club. He felt no regret, no gnawing feeling of being left out; he did not really care about being a member of the club now that he was here in the comfortable confines of the Villa Building. He dwelt again on the old theme, the bedraggled subject that he had not quite really resolved: Were the *ilustrados* really patriots? Or was the real hero of the revolution that almost illiterate laborer, Andres Bonifacio, who grew up in Tondo?

His own past reached out to him in this uncluttered room and it seemed as if his father were beside him again, saying that courage was not enough. There was no way by which they could rise from the dung heap. It was easy to sharpen a bolo until its blade could split a hair, but without a mind sharper than a blade. . . . And so, when his father went to jail, his mother slaved and sent him and his sister to school and college. She took in laundry and worked herself to a hopeless case of consumption and a slow, sure death. This was the sacrifice she had made, and in Barcelona, recalling what she had done, he had wept that morning when he went to the bleak, gloomy cathedral to place a candle at the altar of the Virgin on the anniversary of her death. From the cathedral he had meandered to the Ramblas and sat on one of the wooden benches there, watching the people pass. He had mused about the young Filipinos in Barcelona in another time, and he envied them for the good they had done, although he did not see the monuments of tyranny against which they had flung their young bodies. And then he saw the impossibility of it all: the revolution the young men in Spain had inspired did not end as a true revolution should.

He finished Senator Reyes's speech on time and it was printed in full in the newspapers and even editorialized for giving new proportions to nationalism. And when Don Manuel learned that it was his son-in-law who wrote the speech, he did not hide his pleasure from his wife and Carmen.

"Today," Don Manuel said that morning at breakfast, "you will be with us during the board meeting. Everyone must profit from what you know."

On the way to the office Don Manuel became more open and he impressed upon Tony how the Villa fortune was not built overnight. Don Manuel's grandfather had a furniture shop in Intramuros and it started everything. Don Manuel's grandfather was, of course, Spanish; and in the last days of the Spanish regime and the early days of the American occupation, the narra *aparadors,* the sala sets embossed with mother-of-pearl, and the ornate *kamagong* chests of the Villa furniture shop acquired an appeal with the *ilustrados.* No aristocratic home was complete without Villa furniture. After the illustrious grandfather died, Don Manuel's father built up the business. In time it expanded to include lumber. Then the Villas branched out into construction and were soon building magnificent residences in Malate and Ermita and in the new posh suburb of Santa Mesa. And as they built and decorated these homes they also moved into a wider and more affluent circle.

When Don Manuel was old enough to help his father, the Santa Mesa residence of the Villas was already finished, but the family did not move into it. The Villas still lived in Intramuros and kept the new Villa house as a showcase. By then, too, the business had already spread out to include transportation and shipping. It was only when Don Manuel's father died of a heart attack while in the bedroom of his mistress in Malate that the whole family decided to move over to Santa Mesa—a change from their antique and cramped appointments in the Walled City—and discovered the handsome refinements of suburban living. This was, of course, when Santa Mesa was still considered a suburb and the fast-growing city had not encroached upon its rusticity yet. As the eldest, Don Manuel became manager of the bigger and more profitable branches of the Villa interests. The business was not damaged much by the war. In fact, the war was a blessing to the Villas and to Don Manuel in particular. He had readily foreseen the construction needs of the country and the shortages that would be difficult to fill. He did not slip in his planning nor did he fail to see the importance of developing the friendship and the loyalty of political leaders like professed nationalists of the caliber of Senator Reyes. Now Don Manuel's eldest son managed a new plywood factory and lumber concessions in Mindanao. Another son became interested in textiles and Don Manuel set up a mill in Marikina. The mill produced fishing nets, cotton fabrics, and upholstery material for the furniture factory that had expanded and was attended to by Don Manuel himself, since it was the progenitor of the Villa fortune. The husbands of two daughters managed the construction branch of the Villa Development Corporation. As for Carmen, she had gone to the United States to study interior decoration, public relations, and advertising, so that she would be able to assist in the family business.

All the Villa children had married according to their choices, and Don Manuel took immense pride in this fact. There were enough executive jobs for his sons-in-law and there was nothing he asked from them except loyalty.

The board met on Wednesdays from nine in the morning until lunchtime. The boardroom was on the fifth floor, in the executive country—a handsome dao-paneled hall with a long table made of one solid piece of narra and surrounded by high-backed swivel chairs upholstered in genuine cowhide. All the furniture in the Villa Building and in the homes of most of the Villa employees and executives was, of course, produced by the Villa furniture factory. At one end of the boardroom was a special panel that included, among other things, a well-stocked bar, a kitchenette, a high-fidelity set, and several tape-recording machines. Don Manuel did not have extraneous interests other than golf and high-fidelity record-changers, and the electronic equipment of the conference room was his idea. On his desk in the boardroom was a series of switches that enabled him to pipe high-fidelity music to the room or to record what was said— to the consternation and delight of the other members when the recording was played. He did not drink—he didn't even touch beer, and during social functions he always asked for ginger ale because it looked like Scotch. The bar in the boardroom was his concession to his brothers and to Senator Reyes, in particular, for the senator was an excessive drinker.

The directors started arriving at nine-thirty. The first was Johnny Lee, an ascetic-looking, fiftyish Chinese who spoke pidgin English. He was born in Amoy, China, and talk had it that he started as a junk peddler. He had built up his business well, and during the Occupation he collaborated with the Japanese by providing them with gasoline and diesel engines. He had been a most astute businessman. So well did he manage that after the war his junkyard became a huge automotive shop. He bought American surplus equipment, particularly heavy machinery, by the thousands and then resold these to the government and raked in huge profits by being friendly with government officials. Now his hands were in every kind of moneymaking enterprise. He kept a respectable front, of course, by managing an automotive assembly plant and a chemical factory in Mandaluyong. It was also said that he owned a chain of motels in Pasay City, and these motels were actually classy prostitution dens that catered to politicians, newspapermen, and visiting firemen. Lee knew that he would live and die in the Philippines, and even before World War II he had himself naturalized. He had married his former help—an unlettered Cebuana—and raised a dozen children. His wife was never seen in public and that was to his advantage, because she was reportedly homely and no one would understand why a millionaire like Lee had an ugly wife. She served him more than a wife should serve her husband. Lee registered many of his properties in her name. The fact that Lee was naturalized and had a Cebuana wife and a dozen children rendered him immune to the deportation laws. When the Manila nationalists became vehement with their nationalism, Lee provided them with money. The ads he placed in the newspapers sold not only his automobiles and chemicals, but also decried how aliens were exploiting Filipinos.

The last director to arrive was Senator Reyes. He explained his breathless entrance: there was an important bill on tobacco, which would affect the businesses of Johnny Lee and Alfred Dangmount, and he did not want to be absent from the deliberations of his special committee until he had the bill safely pigeonholed to oblivion for "further study."

All eight of the board members were present. Lee was complaining about the surveillance that the Bureau of Internal Revenue was placing on his cigarette factory in Pasay. It was simply unthinkable. Did he not contribute more than three hundred thousand pesos to the party so that Senator Reyes and all their friends would win?

"I'll look into that," Senator Reyes said, making notes on the pad before him. Johnny Lee settled back on his swivel chair, a grin spreading across his boyish face. "Thank you, *Senador*," he said. That was the only English he spoke during the meeting and "thank you" seemed to be the only words he spoke with a smile. Always, when he spoke, an inscrutable expression clouded his face and his even tone somehow gave the impression that beneath his blandness was cunning and determination.

"Include me, too," Dangmount groaned from the other end of the table. A southerner, he had come to the Philippines during the Liberation and married into a wealthy family from Negros. With the initial capital he thus acquired and some financial sleight of hand, he built an octopuslike business.

"I'm having a helluva lot of trouble with the bank," Dangmount snapped at Senator Reyes. "Look, *Compadre*," he turned to Don Manuel with a knowing wink, "I'm getting a lot of questions about that plywood machinery we're buying for increased operations in Mindanao. Now, if we don't get that license soon . . ."

It became clear to Tony that the interests of each were enmeshed in those of the others. The distinction between government, business, and politics was demolished. The controls on dollar exchange were meaningless; Dangmount had worked out a convenient system. The machinery, for instance, was highly overpriced through collusion with the American supplier, in this way the dollars saved from the transaction could be stashed away in Switzerland. It was the same with Johnny Lee and the other board members. The brilliant senator and nationalist was their legal counsel.

Tony tried to justify himself; the capitalists were creating many new jobs. Dangmount, for instance, had started another tile factory and Lee had gone into the manufacture of electronics equipment with transistors imported from Japan and Hong Kong. And there was no one in Congress, of course, more vociferous in his nationalist protestations than Senator Reyes. "I'm doing this for my country and people" was his favorite battle cry.

• • •

"HOW DID YOU LIKE the members of the board?" Don Manuel asked Tony that same gloomy afternoon in July. "Come on, be honest with me."

Inside the cool sterility of executive country, inside Don Manuel's regal office, the mind could be free. The fluorescent lamp burned like liquid silver and the new rug of abaca gleamed like soft gold. Tony said, "Dinosaurs, prehistoric monsters feeding on the weak."

Don Manuel's lean, handsome face was emotionless, but his voice was rimmed with disdain: "Well, you should have spoken up at the meeting, Tony. You were free, no one was holding you back."

"I did not mean to be impolite, Papa," he said with apprehension for having spoken thus. "But you asked me what I thought."

Don Manuel shook his head. "Should I be glad now that you kept your trap shut? Just the same, let me remind you, Tony, that you are part of the family now. Don't you ever, ever forget that."

"I won't, Papa," Tony said solemnly. "I knew that on the day you first talked with me."

"We understand each other then," Don Manuel said, smiling. "But when there's something on your mind, tell me. You know I like discussions . . ." He was about to say more, but the phone jangled. When Tony left the room Don Manuel was still busy at the phone, emphatically telling Saito San at the other end of the line that the installation of the machinery for the mill should be speeded up even if bottoms had to be chartered to dispatch the machinery from Japan.

Back in his own office Tony gazed through the glass window. Yes, the rainy season had finally come.

The rain was no longer just a brief afternoon shower but part of the seasonal downpour. It would last nine days. The bay churned with white caps and waves leaped up and sprayed the seawall. The boulevard was no longer the ebony black it was when the sun drenched the city. The rain had washed the oil away and the asphalt had lost its sheen. The grass on the boulevard islands, on the hotel fronts, no longer had a bedraggled look. It had turned green. The banaba trees bloomed and their clusters of purple brought throbbing color to the green. His first rainy season after six years evoked many images and odors, the smell of grass, of carabao dung, and of the earth being broken for the seed. These came to him in remembered whiffs whenever he strolled along the boulevard and the scent of the new grass under the feet of other strollers reached his nostrils. But the rain and the seed were no longer within his vision; in this land of dinosaurs nothing would grow.

THE JOB Don Manuel gave Tony did not require technical training or an exemplary business sense. It was, as the entrepreneur had said, public relations. He bought a dozen books on the subject to augment Carmen's books and he went through them earnestly. The books were all loaded with unblushing seriousness on the necessity of not telling everything and of practicing Dale Carnegie's approach to life.

He had hired a secretary, too—a pretty Ilocana his sister Betty had recommended. She was twenty-one and was taking political science at the university but had to stop schooling because her parents in La Union could no longer pay her tuition.

Tony visited Antipolo almost every week but was not quite successful at reconciliation with his sister. He usually went there in a cab, and on the way, he would stop at a supermarket and buy groceries—sugar, rice, vegetable oil, candy for the boys, and a lot of canned goods because his sister could not afford a refrigerator. His income was, of course, more than what he thought his father-in-law would give him. In addition, he had a representation allowance and could obtain even more cash from the cashier anytime he needed some. His signature on the voucher was as good as cash, and the feeling that he had ready money brought to with it a higher sense of responsibility. He did not want his father-in-law to think that he was taking advantage of the Villa coffers. He meticulously kept the receipts of his expenses until the auditor told him that it was absolutely unnecessary. One of the office cars was also assigned to him, but he used it sparingly, taking a cab when he was on his own. Carmen did not bother him for money, for she had her own bank account plus a generous monthly allowance from her father. To this Tony added his monthly pay, which he gave to her with the simple statement that this was a matter of custom and Carmen accepted it with good humor.

The first public relations survey that Don Manuel assigned to Tony was not difficult. Tony had had experience in public-opinion sampling. In his undergraduate days he had worked on a paper on the non-Christian tribes of Mountain Province. He used the same technique and gathered a fairly representative sample of opinions from varying levels; he talked with taxi drivers, business acquaintances of Don Manuel, students and professors, and salesgirls. He was amazed at what he found. The pervasive resentment against the Japanese had dwindled. Only a few—those with extremely bitter memories of the Occupation—were pathologically opposed to more business contact with the Japanese. As for the steel mill, it hardly mattered that the Japanese had a big hand in it. As Don Manuel had said, if the Japanese were not in it, the Chinese or the Americans would be there and the result, the economic tentacles with which these aliens would encompass the country, would be just as stringent.

It was this observation that Tony wrote in his report and handed to the board. It seemed that the last war was relegated to some forgotten eon. The men around him brimmed with goodwill. His report was actually no more than a confirmation of what Don Manuel and the other directors expected.

Don Manuel was kind, even gallant. He did not gloat over what he had expected all along. But even if Don Manuel did not do this, Tony began to feel that there was little justification for his presence in the Villa organization. He often brooded, and this uneasy feeling disturbed his placid routine. He would then ask Fely, his secretary, to bring out his press releases, measure the clippings, and calculate how much they would have cost Don Manuel if the clippings were paid advertisements. To make his job important, he had an order relayed to all the departments that there would be no press story released—not even a story on a marriage or a baptism of anyone connected with the Villa organization—unless he had put his imprimatur on it.

Mrs. Villa took advantage of Tony's new function and she always had a story about her in the society pages. Neither writing Mrs. Villa's press releases nor ghosting occasionally for Senator Reyes, however, gave Tony the justification he sought. Somehow he had to achieve something dramatic and spectacular, to make not only Don Manuel but everyone in the organization look up to him and say: That's Antonio Samson, and he is earning his money as Antonio Samson and not as Manuel Villa's son-in-law.

To do this he would have to ask his close friends to assist him.

Someday he would have a good story not only on Don Manuel but on his operations as well, and he would have this story featured in Godo's magazine. He weighed the possibility, the arguments to buttress the soundness of his proposition. Name any five leading entrepreneurs in the country today and you will have Don Manuel among them. Isn't that enough reason?

Maybe Godo would write the story himself, but if Godo would do that the credit would be Godo's, and he hesitated, for he remembered that Godo had a set of values that could not be easily eroded. In the end, Godo might even loathe him for having broached the idea at all. Godo had not camouflaged his loathing for the Villas and all those "filthy merchants" who were not creating new industries for the country. An approach to Godo was, indeed, compounded with the subtlest of problems. Still, Tony would have to make the pitch sooner or later, and he would naturally lean on the good old college days and all that mushy sentimentalism as the basis for the favor. He justified the strategy with Don Manuel's definition of friends: they were not friends if they could not help.

To Tony, a friend was someone who could offer sanctuary. To Don Manuel, a friend was someone useful. But values change as the social stratum rises. Now Tony must look at friends, too, in this utilitarian fashion. They must no longer be the ones to whom he was emotionally tied by youthful references, by common problems, and, perhaps, a common past.

There was Ben de Jesus, for instance, who could be useful to him. He seemed likable enough, maybe because he was in the employ of Don Manuel. He seemed to be a regular fellow and not the stuffed shirt Tony had presumed him to be. And this afternoon Ben had tried to be amiable.

He was, of course, a mestizo like Don Manuel, but his skin was darker and his arms were hirsute. His thick eyebrows gave him a rugged look, but his cleft chin, which needed a shave twice a day, imparted to his very masculine face a certain softness.

Ben had sounded patronizing: "I've been married longer than you, so that makes me an authority. Let Carmen come home late once in a while. Like tonight. My wife called up—she is with Carmen. They are in a beauty parlor or clinic or something and they will have supper together. If I were you, Tony, I'd step out occasionally, too, and vary the menu. Carmen wouldn't mind—if she doesn't know."

Ben had laughed, but in his attempt at casualness Tony noticed a tinge of nervousness. Ben's comment was an attempt to ingratiate himself into Tony's personal domain, and Tony understood that; understood, too, the gamble Ben had taken. If his wife was a good friend of Ben's wife, did that mean he must develop Ben's personal friendship, too? Quickly he decided that it would not be bad to know Ben better, to appear friendly. He was a part of the organization; this was now the primary consideration.

"That's a good idea," Tony had said, smiling. "I'm sure Carmen wouldn't, but I'm so out of touch that I need someone like you to show me around, to help me with the window-shopping."

"That shouldn't be difficult for someone who has lived for some time abroad." Ben flattered him. "You have taste and there's a lot of class around this establishment or down the boulevard."

"Having taste can be different from having an acquisitive talent," he said.

"You tell me that after you got Carmen?" Ben had laughed. "You should be teaching me tricks."

They parted on this light note and Tony, feeling kind of wonderful, told Fely, his secretary, to finish typing the article on steel and have the clean copy ready on his desk the following morning.

IT WAS ALMOST midnight when Carmen came home. Tony was still at work when her car stopped in the driveway below their room, and he paused at the desk and rearranged the research materials he had been collating.

The moment she came in she started to gripe about her busy day. "Sometimes I envy you," she said in a strained voice. "You just sit in the office and never worry about tomorrow." She planted a dutiful peck on his forehead and went straight to the bathroom.

Tony went on with his work. His notes were voluminous and Fely had not been very good in her transcription. The Ilocano communities on the west coast, the areas where they converged—Salinas Valley, Stockton, and Lodi—and the cycle of their movement from California to Oregon and then to Alaska during the canning season . . . the notes were not properly arranged. The shower in the bathroom sounded and in a few more moments Carmen would begin her evening ritual, the cream on her face, the ointment on her skin. It was, as usual, half an hour, and when she came out she went straight to bed.

"I'm very tired, darling," she said.

"After the beauty parlor?" Tony asked, closing the folder on the Salinas community. "You were supposed to relax there."

She grumbled something inaudible. He was growing sleepy, too, and in a while he quietly slipped into the bed with her. It was late and he was not particularly stimulated tonight, but out of habit he cuddled close to her and ran an inquisitive hand quickly up her satiny thighs. He had expected the familiar tuft of pubic hair, soft and furry under her silken underwear.

He drew back, amazed and incredulous all at once. She had suddenly come to life and the answer she gave to his unspoken question was an angry push and a retort: "You think of nothing but that. You are getting to be a shameful bore."

"Baby," he sat up and was looking at her face, at the frown. "So, you aren't going to have a baby after all. Why didn't you tell me right away? When did it come?"

"Do I have to tell you everything?"

"Yes," he said, "you must tell me everything." He stood up and held her hands and he was surprised to find them cold. "When did it happen? Don't tell me it was delayed three months. Is that possible? Has this happened to you before? No, you said it never happened before. I remember it—that afternoon we were at the Boie and you were so worried . . ."

"Of course it's possible," she said, shaking away his hold. "Accidents can happen and they do happen. You have to be a woman to understand these things. *Esto*, there was a time Nena de Jesus didn't have it for three months—and then it came. Well, you have to understand these things. Do I have to be so goddam clinical about it?" She had raised her voice, but even in her anger Tony could sense something wrong, something missing, and he knew it at once: there was not enough conviction, enough sincerity, in what she was saying.

But he was not sure of himself, either. Tolerantly, "I'd be happier, honey, if you tell me the truth. Come on, I want the truth. Nena was

with you the whole afternoon . . . was there an accident or something?"

"Oh, stop acting like a policeman," she said coldly. "I just had an
abortion, that's all. Nena took me to her doctor. There's nothing to
worry about. It was all very sterile and efficiently done. He gave me
some pills, just in case . . ."

The truth clawed at him. "Did you have to do it?"

"It was necessary," she said peevishly. "I'm young. I can have
children when I'm past thirty."

"And you don't think of me at all? Don't you think you should
have told me before you did this?" He had never been angry with
her before, but now this rage coiled within him quickly and sprang
up and he cried out, "You are a murderer, that's what you are!"

A clamminess came over his hands and in his stomach was a
sickening turn, a nausea. When he spoke again his voice was hoarse
and there seemed to be a rock in his throat: "You are rotten, you are
no good. I can expect this from a tramp, but not from you . . . of all
people, you!"

The suddenness of his fury must have shocked her, for she
backed away from him. "I didn't know this would upset you, really,
darling," she said supplicatingly. "I thought I was the only one responsible, since it was in my belly anyway!"

"It was mine, too," he said.

"It was more mine than yours," she said, almost casually. "*Oye*,
I'm not trying to say that we should have no children. But I'm not
thirty yet, darling. There are many years still ahead of us. We can
have them afterward—a dozen if that's what you want."

But it was too late now and not all the honeyed words could
bring back the life that was lost. What was marriage without children? There came briefly to his mind the mist-shrouded mountains
of Bontoc, the *ulog*, and the girls who lived in it. They loved by another code and they did not have this preoccupation with creams
and diets. They worked hard in the fields, half-naked. To them a marriage was not sanctioned, it was not real, until the woman became
pregnant. And only then did the marriage become sanctified, only
then.

"You love yourself too much, you really don't care for children.
You shouldn't have gotten married at all—that would have made

you happier. Are you thinking now that we've made a mistake?" he asked, his voice rimmed with hate.

She evaded him with amazing agility. "Do you or don't you love me?" she asked.

Tony walked to his desk.

"*Oye*, I asked you a question." She was behind him.

"The time is rather late for that kind of talk, isn't it?" he asked.

"I want to know."

"I love you—and you know that," he said, facing her.

She kissed him blandly, then went back to bed. Tony sat down, leafing through all that he had written. It was useless. He could not concentrate. He took a paperback book from the shelf above the desk, a detective story, but after a few minutes he gave that up, too. He lay beside her, watched the rhythmic rise and fall of her belly and the almost childlike smile on her face as she slept. She was lovely and at this moment pure, like an angel, beyond the reproach of a constant and damning conscience. Yet it was to her own self that she had sinned, not so much to him.

She is a murderess—the thought ate at him, but it did not persist. She was his wife—this was the finality to consider. She was his wife, the key to the good life that was proffered to him and which he had gladly accepted.

10

Some unscholarly notes

I HAVE NEVER FELT the need to unburden myself as I do now. I could easily go to Godo, but I must be prudent and should not jump to conclusions. I miss my classes. They had given me pleasure, for the classroom was my forum. There I could speak freely of the history that to me is self-evident; there I could narrate my hopes and, most of all, my fears. I looked upon my students in the light of my own experience; I did not hesitate to tell them that I not only had the authority of facts, but that it was my conviction that our worst enemy was ourselves, our vanity, our pride, and our desire for honor.

‡

I marvel at my own resilience sometimes, and I am beginning to understand why it is possible for me to get along with D. I know why he is a success; he told me the other day that he follows all the Commandments, particularly the eleventh: Never get caught! But he is a peasant and a loudmouth, and these shortcomings may one day prove to be his undoing. There is no doubt about it: he gets things done, perhaps because he is a Kano, and maybe, because he knows power and he traces its very origin. From him, at least, I have learned never to trust clerks.

‡

I sometimes tell myself that if I were only someone like R I wouldn't be opening my mouth too much, particularly if I am not too seriously involved with my own statements and speeches. The final draft of the speech on steel appealed to him because I now see his vision of himself in Philippine history. More than anything, he sees himself as the champion of the new class, the entrepreneurs, although he himself belongs to the old import-export elite. It is because of his desire to be on top of the wave, on the frontline of innovation, in the phalanx of progress, that he now champions this steel mill. Of course, there is money in it for him. I will not be surprised if he cuts not a single line from the speech introducing his bill that will make the new steel industry not only tax-exempt but also the recipient of government subsidy until that time when it will be able to rise on its own feet.

And because I helped prepare it, I am both flattered and angry at myself for having been in this situation, where I no longer know how to define my own independence. And yet I find myself agreeing with what R publicly declares. Steel is the basis of industrialization. It is a part of our life, it is all around us, in the very air we breathe. We cannot move without steel; it is the basis of our transport system. The clothes we wear were woven, tailored on things made of steel. The can opener with which we open tinned goods, everything we touch has been processed by steel.

But in the end, and this I now say to myself: steel rusts.

‡

I do not know if I did right today when I faced the settlers from Cotabato; I suppose there was nothing I could have done even if I wanted to help them, for they came with nothing on their side save brave words, and an appeal to the sentiments of men like D. It is true, after all, that they were dispossessed by the Villa Development Corporation when the corporation set up its cotton plantation. They had this small-town lawyer and, if I must now recall my own experience in Pangasinan, this lawyer must have milked them dry. There was something in his manner, in the ingratiating way he talked with me, that made me sure he had taken those poor people for a ride, feeding them false hopes. What could I tell them? It is true I speak their language; it is true that my origins are no different from theirs, but I cannot dissuade Papa to act on their behalf, for I already know what he would say if I tried. He was not, after all, breaking any law. He has always been that smart. He did everything properly—the application for the land rights, the declaration of the property as public land; if he bribed his way through some government bureau in Manila or in Cotabato, that is his business. I did not want to see the entire delegation, because to do so would have been most painful. I suppose Papa did right in having me see the leaders not only because I could speak Ilocano but, perhaps, because he knew that I could explain to them in careful terms what the problems were. It is not easy to undo what has been done. Papa does not usually go around attending to details. If he had to do this, he certainly would have no time. His men out there certainly must have told him everything was going fine, that the land for expansion was taken from public lands.

‡

Papa had read my thoughts and he has spoken: You think I am the enemy? Think again, because I am not. I do not belong to the old export-import class that did nothing but live off the fat of the land. I am more than this, and you should at least credit me for some vision and, if you please, a dynamism that the old class never had. You may say, however, that perhaps I am more dangerous precisely because I have vision and I am dynamic. But it is people like us who will build the country, not the importers and exporters, not the intellectuals who mope in the universities. We are what you may call the action people. Do you want to know who your real enemies are? The vested groups, the sugar bloc. They are tightly organized, they have no dreams about creating more jobs for people, about using human energy. All they want is to export sugar to the United States, and if that market were to disappear, they would export the same sugar to China. Do you think they care about the people they do business with as long as they can sell their sugar and get their millions? They do not develop the country industrially the way we are doing. They have government leaders in their palms, and scores of American congressmen, too. How else can you explain how they get those quotas in the United States? Every ambassador we send to Washington sooner or later is enslaved by them.

There are those among us who spend their days moaning about the past, as if the past were good. The past be damned! It was never good. It meant degradation and all the dastardly things that we associate with poverty. Some look back to the past as the source of all the good that ever happened to this country. This is not so. It was after the war that a lot of good came about. After the war we broke the old bastions of power. Opportunities were made more democratic; they went to more people other than those who were already entrenched. They call us the nouveau riche. What is so bad about that? And what about the Old Rich? They don't like us; they are jealous of us. Yes, particularly the mestizos. Oh yes, I am mestizo, too, but we were poor. And the Old Rich? They are no better; they are scum. How do you explain their wealth today? How come they still own vast tracts of land in Quezon City, in Makati? They were smugglers turned shipping magnates, illegitimate children of friars who licked the asses of the Spanish archbishops and American governors. They do that all the time. We don't do such degrading things, now. All we do is contribute to the ruling party, or see to it that our friends stay in power!

‡

Plain mathematics. Two oxygen converters (better than both the electric arc and open hearth converters) overpriced at five million dollars each. At the going rate, that's about forty million pesos. Stashed away in a Swiss bank, this could mean a vacation for life in the Alps. I could go skiing every winter at nearby Innsbruck, and in the summer, I could drive down to San Sebastian where I would also have a villa tucked somewhere in a cove. I will at least be self-sufficient (and comfortable) if and when the Communists come, as G has often foretold. And I will only be doing what some of the people in the Park are already doing, which is providing for their family's future. Only problem here: the forty million is not mine.

‡

I saw G again today, and sometimes I cannot help but envy the man for the steadfastness of his views, for his capacity to compartmentalize all things and then explain why they have fallen neatly into place. Here is G's explanation of the origin of sin:

We all crave recognition, acceptance, entry into the restricted territory of the elite, not quite realizing that we who think, we who write, we who are artists are also members of the elite, except, perhaps, that the only difference between us and the social and economic elite is that we are immobilized. Does joining them mobilize us? Does this mean we are finally accepted by them? It is not so, because these people always will have contempt for us, just as we should have nothing but contempt for them. This is the world and only in one fell swoop can it be changed.

G tells me about Ching Valdez, who was society editor till she resigned three years ago when she got married. She got the most Christmas presents, and her table was one big pile during the Christmas season. She got invited to the most lavish parties in Pobres Park. And then, when she left, you know what happened? They no longer knew her.

G also relates stories of President Quirino's retirement in Novaliches. He went there shortly before Quirino died, and who do you think was there? Ma Mon Luk, the noodle king, and he brought with him a basket of pears and, of course, his famous *siopao*. Quirino said, What a wonderful thing to have a man like Ma Mon Luk visit you whether you are a president or not!

G says it's the same with all of them up there, but the most pathetic is this woman, this big politician's wife, who goes around the Park lapping it up, thinking that because she is with the mestizas and the wives of millionaires she has become a member of their exclusive circle, too. Ah, the tragedy of it! They are laughing at her behind her back; they are amused by her, by her trying to be one of them, aping their mannerisms, when she is actually, insofar as her manners are concerned, nothing but a barrio woman.

‡

I have tried to understand self-delusion and I must be honest with myself in saying that I do not want to be poor. No one wants to be poor. The poor are not respectable simply because they are poor. When I have basic desires that cannot be satisfied, I am this earth's most frustrated human being. I'd like to think I have brains and, therefore, I am superior to those who have more money than I. But how can I call myself really smart? As D often tells off those bright boys in his advertising agency, If you are smart, why aren't you rich?

I cannot but agree with G that I have already lost a bit of myself, I don't know where—maybe in the United States, maybe right here in this city of dinosaurs. I would have wanted very much to speak out loud, to be heard, because I have something to say about the young who are being pawned away. But my voice is no longer strong and firm. I have aged, not with years but with the sullen wisdom of experience. I have seen how the innocents have been slaughtered and how the hapless victims were herded to their final ignominy with praises ringing in their ears. Thus we are destroyed, not with hate but with kindness. And the foul deed is never realized for what it is. We suffer most who are blind to it, who do not recognize it or who justify it as part of the social fabric, as part of living itself. We give legitimacy to a crime and are, in turn, the worst of criminals for this act. But prisons can be wonderful if they are air-conditioned, if they are mansions in the Park!

CHAPTER

11

I N N O V E M B E R the first unit of the mill was ready to operate and the new pier was completed. The tracks from the pier for the diesel trolleys that would carry the ore and the scrap iron to the furnaces had also been laid, and in the scrap yard, mountains of junk were ready for cutting before they were fed to the furnaces.

A covey of newspapermen including Godo and Charlie had visited the mill and the visit itself had climaxed Tony's work of a month, preparing background materials, photographs, and related data on the country's steel needs.

The first cool winds of the Christmas season were already upon the city. The air was electric and the sun lay pure on the wooden panels and on the marble floor, glinted on the glass windows, and danced on the grass beyond.

Don Manuel had suggested a vacation for him, and the opportunity to visit the Ilocos had come. Carmen had some reservations about the trip; for her, there were only two places to go to for the weekend: Baguio and Hong Kong. The idea of slumming in some benighted village did not appeal to her, and she would not have gone if her father had not prodded her to go along.

And so, on this cool, wind-washed Saturday in November, Tony and Carmen were in the Ilocos, marveling at the well-preserved houses of brick and stone in the old capital of Vigan. They had gotten out of the car several times to take photographs of the old stone churches with their impressive baroque facades. The sturdy houses, the well-tended farms, the sunburned women, and the fruit trees in the yards—all these impressed upon him the kind of people his ancestors were.

They had started from Manila in the early morning and passed fields of ripening grain and small towns that were immobile in their lethargy and impersonal in their destitution. Now they were at the source of the pioneers who had settled in the towns they had passed. This was where they had started—the praetorian guard, the brave men who uprooted the old posts of their homes and transported them to the plains and the new towns of Central Luzon and Cagayan Valley and across the sea to Mindanao.

They reached Po-on in the late afternoon. The day still washed the squat, thatched houses, embossed them all faint gray against the massive deep blue of the nearby foothills. The dirt road, just wide enough to admit the Thunderbird, had broadened—disappeared, rather—into what seemed to be the village plaza, which was actually a wide yard in disarray, cluttered with half-naked children playing marbles and ill-clothed women nursing babies and chatting beneath the grass marquee of the barrio store at the far end.

Tony breathed deeply. The earth smelled rich, its aroma compounded with the sun's rage upon the ripe November fields and the dung of work animals. The air was brilliant, and a cool wind that came from the direction of the sea creaked in the small grove of bamboo that formed a natural arbor, a gateway to the village.

Carmen had taken over the wheel since they passed the town of Cabugaw, because she did not trust his judgment on the quality of the road. She had driven so slowly that he was at first unaware that she had stopped. His eyes roamed about—to the huddle of houses, to the children who paused in their raucous game and were now looking at them with awe.

So this is Po-on, he mused. So this is where my grandfather, the illustrious Eustaquio, lived. What did he look like? If he was a learned man, as the old people said he was, could he have left here a few sprouts of his wisdom for me to glean?

"Well, aren't you going to get out?" his wife asked. "Now, I hope you'll find that you have not descended from an ape."

Some of the women at the store approached them, as did two men who were spinning cotton spindles, which they held at arm's length. The women were dark-skinned and the men, like most Ilocano men, were heavy-jowled. Their narrow foreheads and flat, broad noses conformed with the common anthropological concept of the Ilocano.

They stepped out of the car, and to the crowd Tony extended a greeting. They answered as one and without hesitation.

Carmen held on to his arm as if afraid she would melt away and become a part of the mass. She had told him at the start of the trip that there was no sense in it, in looking up members of his family two generations back, because they couldn't matter anymore or alter the present.

"Why don't you ask them if we are in the right place?" Carmen asked.

"This is Po-on?" he asked the nearest woman, who was smoking a black cigarette with the lighted end imprisoned in her mouth.

"Ay, it is so, *Apo*,"* the woman answered. "What can we do for you?"

"We came from Manila," he spoke to no one in particular in their own tongue, which was also his. He turned briefly to his wife, who was contemplating the crowd. "My wife and I . . ." he paused. "You see, it may surprise you, but I am here to seek my relatives. Our root, my grandfather—he was from here."

In the many peasant faces he could immediately discern the bright, new kinship that he had established and he knew that they had accepted him.

"Samson—that was his family name, and mine."

The crowd murmured and the woman with the cigarette spoke again: "But there's no Samson here, *Apo*. I don't remember a Samson here at all and I'm now thirty-five."

"I was thinking," he tried again, "if you could point to me the oldest man here. Maybe he knows."

The crowd started a discussion.

"What are they talking about now?" Carmen nudged him.

* *Apo:* A respectful form of address.

"They are deciding who the oldest man is," he explained, catching their every word.

The woman with the cigarette stepped forward. "My grandfather, *Apo*," she said brightly, "he can help you find your root."

The man they sought, it turned out, was not in the village but in a *sitio* across the fields. "It's not a long walk," the woman explained. "And, besides, the sun can't hurt you now."

HE WAS GLAD that his wife had worn comfortable pumps instead of high heels. Once, in Washington, during a humid and burning summer, they took a long walk. They had met barely a week before, and he remembered it now with the objectivity that marriage makes a mockery of. He was in the Library of Congress and she had gone there that afternoon to have him show her the efficiency with which the library operated. It was five when they left and the sun hung over the gleaming city in a gray haze, glinting in the elms and on the ebony pavement, empty of buses and streetcars because the city's whole transportation system was on strike. He had told her earlier that they would walk home to Dupont Circle across the city to where she lived, and she had acceded. They had not gone ten blocks when she decided to rest in one of the city's main parks. And there, while she watched the squirrels nibble at the crumbs an old lady had tossed, he realized that he had been unaware of her suffering. She had worn high heels, and there lay before them a long stretch of pavement yet. He was making every penny count, knowing as he did the bitterness of a niggardly winter the year past. He desisted from calling a cab. It was she, when they started out again, who hailed one, and inside, while his cheeks burned, he confessed that he did not have enough money for the fare. "It's all right, Tony," she had said. "I can pay the fare and, if you care, may I treat you to dinner, too?" He refused, of course, but he had never been able to live the incident down, and afterward, even though they were married, his inner self cringed in embarrassment every time he thought of her so calm and poised, listening to his stammered apology.

But she was walking beside him now doggedly as a wife should. He wondered if she still recalled Washington and he took her hand. "Remember our first hike?" he asked.

There was no humor in her answer. "Of course," she said. "I just hope all this is well worth the trouble."

He did not reply, for he himself was not yet sure. Why was he here among the new hay and what force was it that propelled him beyond the precious confines of the Villa executive country, that made him break out of the full life into this past that was anonymous and dead?

He could not recall when it all started. Maybe, when he was working on his research papers on the Philippine Revolution, or when he was young and his father told him of barren hills and wicked fields and the churning sea, carried him on his shoulder and told him in a pious whisper of still another man, his grandfather, who led them away from the wasteland to the plains, a learned man who could read Latin and speak it like a monastic scholar, who wrote about death and life and the suffering in between. Istak—that was what he was called—and Eustaquio was his Christian name. "Mark him," his father had said, "for you are descended from a big root."

"LOOK," SHE SAID edgily, holding his hand as they went down the margin of the village with their guide ahead of them. "Will we really get something from this? I doubt if this old man has the qualities of a chronicler."

He smiled inwardly at her prediction. "It's a quality of the rich," he said evenly, "to be skeptical, but not of us, we who were made to choose between the sea and the bald hills." With his hand he made a sweep of the hills at their left—barren and dying. "We always expect the worst and still we are able to laugh."

"You are talking in poetry again," she said sourly. "Can't you stop being so pretty about your tribe?"

The path dipped down a newly harvested field with the bundled grain spread out in the sun. It curved through the field and disappeared into a cluster of *marunggay** trees. Within the cluster stood a house.

The man they sought was perched on one of the rungs of the

Marunggay: A tree whose leaves and young fruit are cooked as vegetables.

bamboo ladder. He, too, like many of the men they had seen in the region, was spinning cotton. He was barefoot and his trousers of blue Ilocano cloth were frayed at the knees. His toes, unused to shoes, were spread out. He was probably seventy, but his short, white hair made him appear too venerable to have something as trivial as age. He stopped spinning and peered at the faces of his three visitors.

"It's I, Simang, Grandfather," the woman who accompanied them said. She took the patriarch's wrinkled hand and pressed it to her lips. "We have visitors from Manila and they would like to talk to you because you are the oldest here and you know many things."

Tony greeted the old man amiably, but the eyes that regarded him were cold.

"Yes, I know many things," the old fellow coughed. "And everything is here, stored in my mind." He brought his forefinger to his temple and gestured. "Everything there is to know I know." His beady eyes closed, the old man turned and climbed up.

Tony stood dumbly before the crude ladder, waiting for him to reappear, and when the old man did not return, Carmen nudged Tony. "Perhaps we'd better go."

Their guide, aware of their discomfiture, mumbled an apology, then went up into the house. In a while she returned and behind her hobbled the old man, looking at them dourly.

"I hope I'm not a bother, *Apo*," he started suavely again.

"Of course you are," the old man said.

"Don't mind him, please," their guide told them and, to the old man, raised her voice. "They were from this place once, Grandfather, and they want to know if some of their relatives are still in our midst."

The angry countenance vanished. "Who were they, my children?" he bent forward, eager to know. The arrogant chin had dropped and the cracked voice had become warm.

"They left about a hundred years ago," Tony Samson said simply.

The old man picked up the talk. "A hundred years! I'm not that old, but I know there were many who left in search of better land. I was one of the few who stayed and now I'm alone. I could have gone, too, but my place was destined to be here."

Tony groped for the proper words. "He was an acolyte, *Apo*," he said, searching the crumpled face for a sign of recognition. "The family name was Samson. My grandfather . . . he migrated to Rosales. That's in Pangasinan. He had wanted to go to Cagayan Valley but the land in Pangasinan tempted him. He couldn't resist."

"Yes, Pangasinan," the old man eased his back against the rung. "All of them wanted to go there, where they said rice grew taller than a man. Fate shackled me to this land. Maybe I was not strong enough to cut the umbilical cord that tied me to this place. But there's no cause for regret. God willing, this land still produces and its kindness still suffices."

The talk was drifting away and Tony quickly salvaged it. "The family name was Samson, *Apo.* Surely you know of some people who bear it."

The old man faced him again. "Samson?" His brow crinkled. "There's not one Samson in all Cabugaw whom I know. So your grandfather went to Pangasinan, eh? The first trips were difficult, or so I was told, and some were killed by the Igorots. A few drowned in crossing the bloated rivers. I knew of their problems in the new land. I would have joined them, too, but I didn't feel the need. It's only now that my days are numbered that I do."

"You never heard of him, *Apo?*" Tony leaned forward and smelled the old man's sour breath. His voice was impatient, demanding. "He was a scholar, a teacher. All Cabugaw knew him. He started as an acolyte and wrote in Latin, too. That's what my father remembers."

"Oh yes," the old farmer continued. "There were some learned men among those who left."

"You didn't know of a Samson among them? Or if there is a Samson left behind?"

The venerable head shook.

"WE SHOULD have gone to the church first when we passed through the town," Carmen said sharply as they drove out of the village. He nodded and gazed fondly at the scene once more, the yellow fields, the *catuday* trees with their edible white flowers, and Po-on itself unchanged and everlasting.

Dusk fell slowly as if it had lengthened the day for him to sum up all—the quiet trees, the blurred shapes of houses. I must find him, press my feet upon his footprints and feel the solid, permanent things his hands shaped. What am I? he had once asked Carmen in a moment of self-scrutiny. Impossible, that's what you are, she had told him. They had gotten married after some misgivings, but she had always reassured him of his own competence. "Every time I introduce you to my friends I say, I've married a man whose wealth does not jingle." What a condescending cliché! But she believed in it, even before she met him at that cocktail party. She had gone to America ostensibly to take up interior decoration and public relations, but actually, she admitted to him sheepishly later, "to hook a man, since the best hunting ground is no longer Manila or Hong Kong, but America. Look at all my friends or look at the men my sisters bagged—oafs and loafers," she often told him, "that's what they are. Why, they can't even use the word *eclectic;* to them, all Marxists are people who should be lined up against a wall."

SHE SWUNG the car out of the gravel road and now, on the stone highway, the engine purred steadily. The landscape was flat again and to the right, in the direction of the sea, the sky was a purple ribbon stretched along the far horizon.

"*Oye,* just hope now," she said above the steady thrum of the car, "that there's a priest who knows what you are looking for. Records. They keep all sorts of papers there."

He grunted in reply. The night covered the land completely and the yellow blobs of the headlights showed the white road, the edges of the fields, and some farmers trudging home with neat bundles of grain balanced with poles on their shoulders.

Cabugaw, like most Ilocano towns, was shabby, and it did not have the bold pretensions to progress, the profusion of soft-drink signs, and the brash architecture that the municipalities of Central Luzon had. The church was not difficult to locate. They had passed it earlier in the afternoon—a huge stone building with a tin roof, set on a green, weedy yard. In the darkness it loomed black and secret, with squares of yellow light framed in the windows of the adjoining convent.

She drove into the yard. Together they went to the door—an unwieldy mass of wood that towered above them, solid like the walls of the convent itself. He lifted the iron knocker and rapped twice.

"You'd better finish the interview as quickly as possible," she said. "Remember, we still have a long drive to Vigan."

He grunted more in displeasure than assent. Footsteps echoed within the convent and dispelled from his mind what he wanted to say. In a while the low second door opened and a beefy man in a white soutane stood before them, a candle in his hand.

"Good evening. We would like to see the parish priest," Tony said.

The priest peered at the darkness behind them—to see the car perhaps. "Yes, yes," he said. "I'm the parish priest. Come in and sit down." He was past middle age. The candle flickered, but it was bright enough to show the priest's features, his rimless glasses, the smudges on his soutane, and its frayed cuffs. He smelled faintly of tobacco.

"This is my wife, Padre," Tony Samson said leading Carmen forward.

The priest raised the candle higher to get a better look at her. "Yes, yes," he repeated. "Do come in and sit down."

They entered what looked like a medieval cavern, a high-ceilinged room with a well-scuffed tile floor. The priest stood the candle on a circular table in the middle of the room and bade his guests sit on the wooden bench before it.

"I came here now," Tony apologized, "because I may not find another convenient time."

"Yes, yes?" the priest clasped his hands and nodded as if wanting to prod his visitors into talking more.

"The drive has been very difficult," his wife said, contributing her bit. "And my car hasn't been broken in really. The roads are not uniform—gravel here, asphalt there, and then cement . . ."

"Yes, yes," the priest spoke mechanically.

"I was a teacher," he said as if nettled into admitting it. "I taught history in the university and did some writing. But I'm now in business."

"Where there's definitely a lot more money," Carmen added hastily.

"Ah yes, yes," the priest agreed in his toneless manner. "But have you eaten supper?" He called out a name and a boy emerged from the shadows. "Prepare two more plates," he shouted, and the boy disappeared beyond the door. "Now, what can I do for you?"

"It may seem foolish to you," Tony said self-consciously. To his wife he turned for encouragement but she was not looking at him. She had turned away, her eyes on the walls and the narrow grilled windows.

"Why, why?" the priest asked, throwing his head back.

"I'm Ilocano," he said, naturalness settling back in his voice. "And my grandfather came from here. I've come to see if I have relatives left."

The priest rose. What he heard obviously impressed him. "I've never seen one like you, returning to where his ancestors were born—I mean, one going on a pilgrimage, sort of." He spoke with enthusiasm. "Of course I know that Ilocanos—"

"They are all over the country," Carmen joined him. "The country is crawling with Ilocanos."

"Ah yes, yes," the priest went on after a short, brittle laugh. He cracked his knuckles and peered at the woman. "Indeed you'll find them saying that our root is in this or that town, but do they know what the Ilocos really looks like? I've been here all my life and I know that it hasn't changed much. The houses are still small, the rice is still the same hard variety. They are planting Virginia tobacco now, too much of it—and that's the only difference. And, of course, a few new houses with galvanized iron roofs . . ."

The boy who had set the table returned and told them supper was ready. They padded through a dimly lit corridor and up a wide stairway into another wide room as shabby as the first.

The boy hovered, a paper wand in his hand. As Tony had expected, the convent larder was well-stocked. They had fried rice, broiled pork, chicken broth, and an omelet.

The priest made the sign of the cross. "Eat, eat," he said amiably.

Tony did not want to waste time. They had barely started with the soup when he spoke again: "You may have heard of my ancestor. You see, about a hundred years ago he used to be in this very church, serving as an acolyte."

The priest dropped his spoon. "No, no," he said. "I cannot really say. A hundred years ago? But I wasn't even born then. And Samson? I have met none of your relatives. There's not one Samson in the whole town—that's what I know."

"Surely, Padre," Tony didn't want to give up, "there must be something here that will be conclusive." His appetite had dwindled.

"Church records, baptismal notices. They could hold his name. You see, he migrated to Pangasinan with his whole clan. But this may not be true. And he was a scholar—that's what my father always said. He wrote in Latin . . ." He felt proud.

WHEN THEY FINISHED the dessert of preserved *nangca,** the priest took them down again, explaining that they might find something among the records. They walked silently through corridors. The taper threw their shadows against the crumbling masonry and etched the thick, rotting posts and the red brick. They stopped before an appallingly large wooden cabinet, which seemed to sag into the very floor—an elaborately carved relic with iron handles rusty and immovable on their hinges.

"We might be able to see something here," the priest said. "Most of the old records are here—from 1800 up."

He gripped the rusty bar and, with a violent tug, opened it. "You'll have to forgive the sorry state of the papers," the priest said gravely. "I have no time to look after them."

The layer of age that covered the rooms assailed them, and Carmen instinctively held her palm to her nose. The priest picked one of the ledgers at random. Its cover was clearly marked *Registro de Defunciones, 1840.* He leafed perfunctorily through the pages of the death registry. The line marks, which may have been straight and black once, were all smudged, and the pages themselves threatened to break apart like flakes if they were flipped. In the sallow light, however, Tony Samson could trace the fine scrawl, the elaborate crosses of the *t*'s and the flourishes at the beginning of all the capital letters. The priest read aloud some of the names and, after two pages, stopped.

The boy who had served upstairs at the table joined them with a Coleman lamp, and the shimmering light identified everything in the giant room—the old tile floor and the battered chairs. "Now we can see better," the priest said. He reached for the top shelf and, at random again, got two ledgers and handed them to Tony.

Tony read the inscriptions on the covers of the registries of marriages and births. One was marked *Registro de Casamientos,*

* *Nangca:* The jackfruit tree or its fruit.

1860–1865. The other bore the equally elaborately written title *Registro de Nacimientos, 1865–1867.*

"You'll see that the names of the priest and his secretary who wrote these down are on the first page," the priest told him, "What else do you know about your grandfather?"

"He was a learned man," Tony repeated with emphasis, "and he wrote in Latin as if the language were his."

"We will see," the priest said, rubbing his hands. "There's another batch of ledgers here." He stopped and opened the lowest panel. "These are records of jobs, important decisions, some diaries. . . ." He held the ledger to his face, then turned thoughtfully to the young man. "What was his name again?"

"Eustaquio Samson."

"I once saw a manuscript in Latin, a philosophical one, written by a Eustaquio. It should be somewhere here." His pudgy fingers went through the ledgers, then he brought it out—a tattered black book. The priest glancing at the cover, read aloud: "Eustaquio Salvador."

Tony knew the name vaguely. Salvador, Salvatero, Sabado— many family names in Cabugaw used to start with the letter *S,* a convenient arrangement initiated by the friars. By knowing a man's family name it would be easy to deduce what town he came from.

Salvador!

Then it struck him with its full and magic force and he remembered how once his father had told him that their name was not really Samson. Clasping the battered book, his heart now a wildly pounding valve, Tony turned to his wife and cried, "This is it, baby! Written in his own hand!"

Carmen hedged closer: "It's Salvador, not Samson."

"But didn't I tell you once that his real name was Salvador and that he had to change it because of a fight with the Spaniards?"

She laughed. "It's an alias then. I wonder what the Spaniards did when they found out."

"I wouldn't know," the priest said, handing the manuscript to her husband.

Tony read the title again. It was legibly written in block letters: *Philosophia Vitae, Ab* Eustaquio Salvador. "A Philosophy of Life," he translated aloud and turned questioningly to the priest for confirmation.

He nodded. "You know Latin?"

"I had a year of it in college," Tony said, "but that wasn't enough." He handed the book back to the priest. "Please read to me some lines."

The priest moved toward the light and opened the book to its first page. He mumbled the phrases and then recited haltingly: "*Cum magna pretentione*—it is with great pretension—*est ut hunc librum scribere incipio—sed cum aliquis veginti unum annos tingit, est illa temptatio desiderandi ad somnia ascribienda quae asperat . . .*"

He paused and glanced at the author's grandson. "Well, I must admit that his Latin was not bad."

"What does it mean?" Carmen bent forward, trying to follow the reading.

The priest went back to the first phrase: "*Cum magna pretentione*— It is with great pretensions that I start this book, but when one is twenty-one there is that temptation of wanting to record the dreams to which he aspires . . ."

The priest stopped again.

"Dreams," Tony mused aloud and quoted the Spanish poet: "All of life is a dream and all those dreams are dreams . . ."

"Yes, yes," the priest intoned dully, "but, you see, he apologizes for that. He was but twenty-one."

"Please," Tony repeated. "Do go on—one paragraph more."

The priest opened the book to the pages he had left. ". . . *quia veginti anno annis majorem aetatem finaliter attingit* . . . for at the age of twenty-one he finally comes of age." His drab fleshy face brightened up. "Listen to this now," he enthused. "*Mundus viro no sperat. Eo tempus non habet*— The world does not wait for a man. It has no time for him." He returned the book to Tony and his voice was tinged with emotion: "He had the sensibility of a poet—and humility, too. This is the virtue of all those who create and who are great, no matter how obscure they may have been. Why, I believe that God, even in His greatness, was humble. Your forefather had this quality and more. He was restless, too, and now I know why he left Cabugaw."

Tony flipped the pages of the book and his whole being flamed and the vacuity within him seemed suddenly filled with something burbling and glowing that lifted him beyond the common touch. "Now I leave you to your discovery," the priest sounded remote behind him. "And, of course, you have to sleep here. I'll have the cots prepared upstairs. Come up when you are sleepy."

"Thank you, Padre," he said happily without lifting his eyes from the engulfing maze, the fancy script, and the words he couldn't read and understand. And, holding on to the ledger, he felt a kinship at last, tangible and alive, with this thing called the past. Maybe there is wisdom buried in this, or romance, or just a diurnal account of a young man's fancy, his pride and his hurt. The transcription will not be important, he decided quickly. It was this solid memento that mattered, because it was the root on which he stood.

"You can ask him for it. It is but a scrap of paper that he has no use for anyway," Carmen said.

He lifted the Coleman lamp, which had been left atop the wooden pedestal beside the cabinet. At the door the boy waited for them, his eyes heavy with sleep, and showed them to their room.

AS THEY LAY on two cots that had been brought together, they held hands—a soothing domestic habit—and were motionless but for their measured breathing. Beyond the heavy sill and sash shutters, which were flung to the remotest edge, the stars shone clear and tremulous in the cloudless sky. A silky breeze floated in, laden with the scent of the warm earth. A dog barked in the unknown recesses of the dark, and in the rotting eaves Tony heard the soft scurrying of mice and the snap of house lizards.

"It's just like Washington," she said after some time.

"Why Washington?" he asked, pressing her hand.

"The Library of Congress," she said. "The first printed Bible. The American Constitution. They were all nicely framed and lighted in special containers, heated to keep out the frost and the humidity. It must have cost some money to install those devices . . ." He had taken her there because "when you are in Washington you just can't miss the biggest library in the world," and she had valiantly tried deciphering the scrawls.

"You are way off the track," he said, divining her thoughts.

She turned on her cot and tweaked his nose. She smelled clean and, in the faint light of the other rooms, he could make out her face. "Oh, now, I'm not saying that we will have to go to so much expense trying to preserve your grandfather's manuscripts."

"What then?"

"But you can do it, maybe have an Augustinian friar in Manila transcribe it, and then, who knows, it may be an important document in literature—or ecclesiastical history."

"That's not funny," he chided her.

"But I'm not trying to be funny," Carmen said. "I'm merely carrying to a logical end what you have started. If you won't have it translated, then at least we can bring it with us—not just the book, mind you, but all the other papers that were written in his hand: *Oye*, think what wonderful conversation pieces they will make!"

"Is that all you think of? Conversation pieces to show off to your illiterate friends and relatives?"

"Now it's you who are being silly," she reproached him. "We drove over horrible roads, ate in that filthy restaurant in Vigan, and now we are sleeping in this convent—on smelly cots. Five hundred kilometers—and the gas, I spent good money for it . . ."

The situation had suddenly become ridiculous and he did not know whether to laugh or to curse. But the feeling subsided quickly and gave way to his old understanding of the unchangeable dung heap that surrounded him. He brought to mind once more the American lady in her sixties on the boat crossing the Atlantic. He had met her on his way to Europe during his summer study tour. She was on an almost religious mission to a Sussex hamlet in England to seek the wellsprings of her ancestry, which were, she was told, still intact. A genealogical research agency had promised to do the job for a few dollars. "It's dirt cheap," she had said of the deal with the patent exuberance of an American who had accidentally stumbled upon a bargain. Tony recalled, too, the rapt crowds in the National Art Gallery in Washington, in the Louvre and the Prado, the hordes gaping at the old pictures, searching for beginnings in the cemeteries of art as if they were afraid to drift into the limbo of their own making, and these paintings, these revered pictures and stone images, were the anchors that would make them and the future secure. Their faces were all indistinct yet vaguely familiar, exuding as they did an enthusiasm and a longing. He had now struck an infallible identity with them, because he, too, had gone to great lengths to find but a book and a vanished name in a small town. And yet everything could have been simplified: a gilded museum, an efficient gravedigger with an encyclopedic memory—these were all that would have been necessary to find the clues to that unalterable pattern that he did not shape but which shaped him. And his wife was all this because she had the money and he . . . he had only the dream.

"You, your money . . ." he said.

She turned and pressed close to him. He could not see her face clearly, but he could define the glaring dark eyes.

"You have too much of it," he said with conviction.

"All right," she said, lying on her back again. "But remember, it's what makes the world go—not an old, rotting book that may not even sell as a collector's item. You know that very well. You've seen all those first editions in the secondhand-book stores, the one near Dupont Circle. In Greenwich Village . . ."

"Let's not start this again," he said hotly.

"You started it," she said, her voice betraying a hurt. "You wear those big chips and dare everyone—even me—to knock them off."

"Is that what you found here?"

"You could have asked me a long time ago and I would have told you."

"And yet you married me?" Tony pressed on.

She did not speak.

"At least," he said, "you can be kind and say that you made a mistake."

She turned to him again. "I was in love with you. What is it that you want? Have you forgotten that I can always ask Papa?"

To her it all seemed so simple: I can always ask Papa—omnipresent, omnipotent.

"I want only one thing: to be myself," he told her.

"Aren't you?" she flung at him. "Really, now you are asking for blood. *Esto,* even coming here is asking too much. The past is past and no one can alter it."

But the past still demanded attention, and that was not all— there was need for continuity, too, and belonging to a huge and primeval wave. He knew all this now and the knowing evoked transcendental joy. He was, after all, not a drifter in the vast ocean of want. Now, if he could only return to his teaching and once in a while write, maybe about the urgencies he believed in. . . . If he could only forsake the drudgery of his commerce, maybe he could do more for some future searcher to covet and, maybe, the self-justification that had eluded him for so long might yet take shape under his very hands. There flashed again, vivid and taunting, the face of the old man he had talked with in Po-on earlier in the day, and finally the faceless vision of the gentleman, the ancestor, who, perhaps, could have been in this very room with a pen in his hand. How did they in their listless youth face the chasms between fact and fancy? One refused to pioneer, to forsake the barren land, and the other wrote a book and then, on his puny legs, led a whole clan on a journey to a strange, new land.

But what happened to them? And what happened to his father, who had tried to be brave in his own, narrow way when the times demanded another form of courage? He could look back now to Cabugawan, his birthplace and his stigma, and he would find the answers there.

"Baby?" He spoke tentatively.

"Please," she still sounded angry, "I've already told you that I'll buy it. I will buy everything you need if the priest won't give it for free."

He stood up and walked to the window. Beyond the wide, vacant churchyard the whole town lay quiet and asleep. They would most probably leave in the morning and she would surely be glum. To her this was not a vacation—it was a meaningless jaunt into some benighted towns. But he would not mind. What was important now was getting back to the city to glean the small parts of himself that he had scattered to the shiftless wind. If he could only teach and write again—he must teach and write again.

Standing there, pondering the implications of Cabugaw, he wondered how soon morning would come sneaking into this musty room.

CHAPTER
12

IT WAS TOO EASY to be true, and looking at the lean, handsome face of Don Manuel on the cover of the *Sunday Herald*, Tony felt achievement glow all over him. Godo had been very thoughtful; he had sent this advance copy on a Wednesday when the board was to meet, so that Tony could show the magazine to everyone. Below the smooth, angular face of Don Manuel was the title in bold type: Man of Steel.

He immediately delved into the magazine and was even more amazed. Godo had given Don Manuel a six-page spread with the fewest ads, and the story included the latest photographs of the steel mill and statistical graphs on the steel needs of the country.

The article brimmed with authority and prestige because it sported Godo's byline. Tony read it, tried to ferret out any of Godo's barbed cynicisms that would easily nullify the story, but after going through the article twice he found not a single line in it that went sour. Don Manuel was right after all—friendships were important. He had invited Godo to the house only twice, and on the third visit he had made the pitch. Godo had not acted smart-alecky. He had said, I've done it for people less significant, and now, sell me Don Manuel. It had not been easy, of course, for by then Don Manuel's many transactions, particularly the timber concessions in Mindanao, were under fire. But the mill was significant; it symbolized national aspirations and dignity. Steel was the foundation of modern society. The barrio could not rise from the dung heap unless it was energized by domestic steel mills that would cut down the huge imports of steel. That was it: steel was the bedrock of progress.

But it was not so simple. Tony had boned up on steel, and after the many board meetings he had attended and the conversations with Don Manuel, he had stored up a vast amount of knowledge. He had told Godo: we have limitless iron-ore deposits, and only the fringes of these deposits—in Mindanao, the Visayas, and Luzon—have been tapped. The figures are merely illustrative, but here they are: we export iron ore to Japan for processing at a mere thirty centavos a ton, and when we get this back in pig iron or elementary steel materials, do you know how much we have to pay? Three hundred pesos a ton. The opponents of Philippine steel are, of course, the American importers in Manila. Once a steel mill in this country is set up they will lose a very profitable market. And their arguments are downright silly. So what if our coal is bad and low grade and we don't have coke! That is cheap and we can import it. Japan imports coke. And that is not all—hydroelectricity is becoming cheaper and our hydroelectric projects continue to be built. I've seen them in Mountain Province, and the Bontoc Igorots have been transferred from their ancestral homes because many new dams are being built there. Two are already finished. And there is this new Swiss process that is going to be very cheap. We can adopt it here. We don't have to cling always to America's apron strings. It's not only being patriotic or nationalistic to ask that we support a local steel industry now, it's also good business. It will absorb the surplus agricultural workers of the lethargic barrios. It's nationalism—and Godo took the bait.

DON MANUEL was in his office. Without a word Tony laid the magazine before the entrepreneur. The older man stood up, looked at the magazine, then went to his son-in-law and slapped him expansively on the shoulder. "I don't have to tell you how happy I am about this, son." His eyes were shining.

The board meeting that followed was short. Not much was discussed except the prospects of speeding up the work. Senator Reyes announced that the latest applications for dollar licenses by Dangmount and Johnny Lee were approved. Don Manuel had a word or two to give Dangmount—he should use his influence with the American community to get more contracts for the firm. The same appeal went to Johnny Lee, who took down notes in Chinese and bared his teeth in futile attempts to smile.

With the business for the day wrapped up, Tony hurried down to Newspaper Row to thank Godo and Charlie.

But the two refused to go out. They had work to do, so they went to the crummy shop below the newspaper office and sat in a sullen corner, smelling the accumulated mustiness of the years. They drank tasteless coffee and ate the same old *siopao* and *mami*.*

They started lightly enough with Godo trying to match Charlie with one or another of Carmen's friends.

"I'm not getting married," Charlie said solemnly. "It's too much of a risk and, as far as I'm concerned, there's no future in it. I will not marry and bring to this world children who will be as insecure as I am."

"But it's so easy to live," Godo said brightly. "All you have to do is breathe and slave your guts out. And when you die your body will be taken to the Press Club. Just think of it—those mountains of flowers and all those fine speeches. Even your employer will be there. And as for your widow . . ." the cheery note had left Godo's voice, "she will go on living in the stale rooms you've never freed yourself from."

Charlie nodded and did not speak.

"Do you understand, Tony?" Godo asked. "There's nothing that can enliven me now. I'm aging and I have nothing for my children."

"We are all insecure," Tony said. "There's no one who is secure in this life. We all die—and that is the root of our insecurity."

"Yes," Godo said, "but security for me does not mean immortality. All I want is for my wife and children to be healthy and well provided for. But you can't have security in this bloody country

*Mami: Noodle soup.

anymore. The rich won't let you have it. They wouldn't even let me have a battered Ford."

"In America," Tony said evenly, "everyone has a car. It doesn't mean a damn thing."

"In America," Godo sighed. "But here, what do your American friends do? They won't permit us to industrialize. And what happens? You have the same old bastards at the top. A few years back, when they stole, they justified themselves by saying 'What are we in power for?' They have changed the tune. Now they say 'What's wrong with providing for your family's future?' Visit Congress. Listen to our good friend Senator Reyes. He commits everything now in the name of nationalism."

"Scoundrels always use patriotism as a last resort."

"But that's not the point," Godo said. "What is important is this. We are all committing suicide. And we can't stop it because of the uncertainty that hovers above us all. Listen," he leaned close to Tony. "There is a village in your native Pangasinan. It's near the sea, and the people there earn a living diving for the bombs that were dumped at the bottom of the gulf in 1945 by the American navy. They extract the powder from these bombs and use it for dynamite fishing. Three months ago a bomb they were opening blew up. Thirty-seven were killed, including women and children. Last week I sent Charlie there for a story. Tell him, Charlie."

His dark, thin face empty of emotion, Charlie leaned over and spoke softly: "I came across them, near the ruins made by the first blast. And they were opening another bomb. I asked why they were still at it after what happened to the others. And they said there was no other way. Life must go on."

"I refuse to believe it," Tony said. "No man, unless he is sick, takes his own life. There must be a sickness, an incurable one. And it must have been there since his birth, secretly growing until that time when it has consumed the love for life and then becomes nothing else but hate. Then the man takes his own life because he has been drained of love. Because there is nothing else in the body but that disease, that cancer of hate. I cannot think of any man wanting to die. Even in pain there is knowledge—and therefore joy."

Godo was in his best form again. "But, you see, there is no alternative really. They have to live. We have to live. So we raze our forests, we dynamite our fishing grounds. We export all our ore and our best logs to Japan. And businessmen like your father-in-law say that life must go on. Or if Don Manuel sets up a steel mill he ends up being a dummy."

Tony leaned back. "You don't mean what you say; you're pulling my leg again."

Godo's forehead knitted. "Do you mean to tell me that you weren't able to read between the lines?"

"What do you mean?" Tony sounded incredulous.

"Tell him," Godo nudged his assistant.

"Well, I did research on the cover story, you know," Charlie said. "I even talked with some people from Mindanao—just to find out about your father-in-law's investments there."

"Well?"

Charlie leaned over. "Your grandfather, how was he dispossessed? How did he and all other Ilocano settlers in your town lose their farms?"

"I've told you," Tony said wearily. "But it was different then. My grandfather . . . he was learned, but he was alone. The landmarks that they had—the mounds, the trees, the creeks—were swallowed up by the landlords when they had the land surveyed for Torrens titles. But I'm not bitter about that anymore."

"You have a short memory," Godo said bluntly, "and, of course, that's understandable. You are living it up, you are a landlord now."

"I resent that," Tony said hotly.

"But it is true," Charlie said evenly. "Why don't you go to Mindanao as I have? There are hundreds of Ilocano settlers there now. And they are being dispossessed right and left. By learned men like Don Manuel Villa. Ask your father-in-law about his lumber concessions. Check up on the haciendas under his name. You want land reform, don't you? You said in your thesis that the revolution had agrarian undercurrents, didn't you?"

"I do not deny that."

"Well, the beginnings of another revolution are around us again. The Huks may have failed, but there is another uprising coming clearly and surely, and this time there is one unmistakable ideology behind it. The poor against the rich. And it will be a revolution that may wipe out this stinking society from its false moorings. And with the cataclysm, you may have to go," Godo said.

"You are not frightening me," Tony said without emotion. "The

circumstances do not support you. Besides, we know better now—
all of us. Power does not reside in the poor and it takes more than
anger to move the world."

"Yes, it takes more than anger. But how did the revolution start?
What makes you so sure that, right now, there aren't poor men like
me who are plotting, thinking, devising ways for the time when all
this rottenness will explode?" Godo asked.

"I will be prepared when that time comes," Tony said evenly.

"There will also come a time when we will be face-to-face with
ourselves not as we want ourselves to be regarded by others but as
we really are. When that time comes, I'd sympathize with you,"
Godo said.

"I regret nothing," Tony said.

"Stop being so smug," Godo told him.

"Stop being angry."

"We cannot stop being angry," Charlie said calmly. "We go about
our dull routine, we get drunk on a bottle of beer, we look forward
to the pleasures of fornication. And when all this is over, we are
angry again. We who are trying to write, Tony—you know this, we
talked about it in the good old days. We are the real revolutionists
not only because we hate this quagmire but because in essence we
reject all reality."

"We must start from there," Tony said.

"Yes, but just the same, we reject it," Charlie said. "No, we don't
reject life, we love it. But we do not love hunger and illness and the
despair they breed all around us. Hunger is real, Tony. You can see it
in the villages, in my own neighborhood. You do not see it in Pobres
Park—it is an academic thing to be discussed in the Villa Building
and you do not feel it there. It takes the poor to understand poverty,
you said that yourself. And whatever you say now, your friends in the
Park would not understand, for if they do, they wouldn't have gone
there."

"They are our people, too," Tony said. "You know that ours is an
open society. You can go up and down, right or left, to any distance
or height you may want to reach. Everyone has a chance . . ."

"You are wrong," Charlie said. "Not everyone has a chance. We . . .
we are lucky in a way. How many artists, how many geniuses, how
many great minds are aborted in the nameless villages and slums of
this country because children don't go on to college? Do you know,

ninety percent of our children don't go past the fourth grade because they cannot afford to? Universal education—that is one of the biggest jokes."

"Maybe so," Tony said. "But still, there are millionaires today who didn't have a centavo to their name after the war."

"But what happened after they got to the top?" Charlie asked. "They forgot those at the bottom of the heap. Perhaps we shouldn't ask them to have a conscience. Perhaps all we need ask of them is vision."

"Manuel Villa has vision," Tony said.

"He does not have it anymore than Dangmount and his friends," Charlie said sadly. "A chicken in every pot, a Ford in every garage. These are meaningless slogans, but the men who fashioned them had vision. America had her share of robber barons, but these same robber barons dreamed big dreams, empires, progress."

"Pax Filipina," Tony said.

"No, I don't mean that," Charlie said. "I am for Filipino entrepreneurs who can think of progress for this country, and not just of vacations in Europe, marble swimming pools, and a dozen mistresses."

"I assure you," Tony said, "there are men in the Park who think of progress for this country, too, because it means progress for them first. The poor do not have a monopoly on virtue, you know."

Godo picked up the talk in anger again. "Are you trying to be comfortable in a place where you will never have real peace of mind?"

"What do you want me to do?" Tony said desperately. "Go home and run amok? Bring a hand grenade to the next board meeting of the Villa Development Corporation? Is that what you want?"

"Now you are talking sense," Godo said in mock seriousness. "No, Sonny Boy, I don't expect such heroics from you. I just want you to know how things stand. I have no illusions. My publisher is no different. Like your Don Manuel, as long as the money keeps pouring in, that's okay with him. And us? He doesn't even know I have a dying wife, that I live in an *accesoria* that stinks to high heaven. That's the social order, Sonny Boy, and don't you ever forget it!"

"I have enough problems," Tony said lamely. "I try to be useful in the best way I can."

"That's nice to know," Godo snorted. "It's nice to hear that you are comfortable being a dummy."

Tony was in no mood to argue; Godo and Charlie could still be useful to him, and they could help to publicize the steel mill again in another year or two. He held his tongue and said simply, "You are being nasty again."

Charlie smiled. "There are many things that were left out in that write-up, Tony. And you know just what I mean."

"No, I don't." Tony tried to be vehement.

Godo grinned. "You mean to tell me that you don't know that the Villa steel mill is owned by Japanese, Americans, and Chinese? Do you mean to tell me that you never knew the firms list Senator Reyes as their counsel? Or that Senator Reyes is a member of your board?"

"I know," Tony said morosely.

Godo rattled off the names. "Dangmount, Saito, and the Chinese millionaire Johnny Lee."

"They are on the board, but what difference does that make?" he asked, feigning ignorance, remembering what Don Manuel had said about his being in the family now.

"They control the stocks, son," Godo leveled a finger at him. "And your father-in-law is a dummy in spite of his wealth. Don't let Senator Reyes and his talk of nationalism fool you as he has fooled almost everyone else. He is in the employ of the monopolists and the sugar people—another vested group. Aside, of course, from working for your father-in-law."

Tony sneered. "Why didn't you print the story as you saw it, then?" He leaned over and spoke softly for a moment. "Look, I had thought that perhaps you would do just that. Deep inside I always believed you were brave, Godo, that you wouldn't pull your punches." Then, his voice rising, "I'm tired of polemics and excuses. And you're just giving me one more lousy excuse."

Charlie smiled laconically again. "Ah, Tony, the things we can't print. The publisher has to make money and we have to live on the ads your father-in-law and his friends place in the magazine."

"In other words, you are not pure."

"I have never claimed purity," Godo said, "but I'm honest with myself. I hope you can say the same, Tony."

"Look," Tony said solemnly. "What is it that you want? My skin?

In college— Let me tell you about my old roommate, Lawrence Bit-fogel. The three of you would make excellent bedfellows. He believed in revolution as an alternative. But it is too late for us to engage in that. You know what happened to my grandfather and my father? The Huks. The weapons have changed, but I don't think you realize that."

"Yeah," Godo snickered. "Sex is the weapon. Marry the landlord's daughter—or Don Manuel's."

The blood warmed in Tony's temples.

"The Ilocano settlers in Mindanao . . . the pattern is clear," Charlie repeated.

"I can't comment on that," Tony shot back. "Don Manuel has reasons, and everything—I'm sure of that—must be legal."

"Legal!" Godo exploded. "Yes, corruption is now legal. And tyranny, too. And deception. Everything is legal."

"I don't care anymore," Tony said wearily. "There's no sense in going against the wave, against all of you. I want to run away." He checked himself, for Godo was looking at him intently.

"Where will you go? Back to America and its comforts?"

"I just don't know," Tony said weakly. "But another revolution is so cheap, so commonplace. Perhaps if we killed ourselves instead . . ."

THEY PARTED on that note. It was not yet eleven and Tony decided to return to his office and try to shake off the malaise of the encounter. He did not want to remember what Charlie had said about Mindanao and the settlers. He tried to place the subject in a hidden corner of his mind and ignore it. He decided to return to his grandfather's journal. The labor would dispel the anguish of the day and all the discomforts he felt from meeting with Godo and Charlie.

Before noon someone came to see him—a relative from Pangasinan, according to his secretary. No one had visited him in the past few days, no one from the old crowd at the university, least of all someone from home.

Bettina.

He remembered Bettina as a lanky kid with pigtails, climbing guava trees in the backyard of the old house in Rosales, and as a visitor to Manang Betty's *accesoria* one dry season. An inquisitive youngster who had wanted to see all of the city during those two vacation months, she was always out the whole day visiting places like Tondo and San Nicolas, which he had never bothered to see, until her older sister Emy became concerned and put a stop to her wanderings.

Now Tony studied the neat, girlish scrawl on the visiting card. A pang of homesickness possessed him, and in this cool, anesthetized room, a host of remembered images bloomed in the recesses of his mind—the Cabugawan of yesteryears; the small, thatched houses; the broken-down fences; and beyond these the eternal fields of gold and green. He rose and strode out. She saw him first and she stood up, smiled shyly, and reminded him at once of his own youth, of the things that were, of Rosales. She was a young woman now in her early twenties or late teens. Somehow, the *provinciana** character was discernible in her, in her lips, which were not painted; her shoes, which were cheap pumps; her cheap printed dress; and her bare arms browned by the sun.

"Bettina, I'm so happy to see you," was all he could say and he took her hand as he used to, then led her away from the curious gaze of the other visitors.

Alone in his office, Tony looked at her closely. "I never thought you'd come and see me," he said. "You don't know how nice it is to see someone from home."

They sat together on the sofa. "Do you want anything to drink? Coffee? I know, stay for a while and I'll treat you to lunch. We can eat in one of the restaurants near here and then you can tell me everything about what's happening in Rosales. And Emy— I'm starved for news about her. How is she?"

For the first time she looked at him fully. "She's well," she said simply.

"I'm happy to know that," he said, meaning every word. "Tell me, what can I do for you? I haven't seen anyone from Rosales for a very long time. I miss the place, but I can't seem to get away from here so I can have a breath of fresh air."

Bettina clasped her hands. "I know you are always busy and that's why I came here myself. Manang Betty said that I shouldn't bother you like this. Am I bothering you, Manong?"

He laughed. "Of course not," he said. "When could Bettina

* *Provinciana:* Provincial; masculine form: *provinciano.*

bother her cousin? Remember, it's been years since I saw you. And look at you now, so grown-up. It's about time you get married."

"That's not an easy thing to do," she said, blushing. Then her eyes crinkled in a smile. "A man must first love you and be faithful to you, no matter what happens."

"Don't be too choosy," Tony said, laughing. "You'll end up being an old maid."

Bettina turned away.

"If it's a job you need," Tony said, "I can help you get one. . . ."

"No," she said hurriedly and faced him again. "It's not a job, Manong. You can help me when I am ready. Now . . . now, I . . . I had to stop schooling—after Father died. There wasn't enough money. . . ."

"I'm sorry," Tony said softly. "I was in Europe when I learned about it. But still, if you want me to, I can help send you to school. I'm helping Manang Betty's children now. I can really help," he said eagerly.

"I know, but . . ."

He leaned over, the better to catch every word, for now he realized that she had come to tell him something important, much more important than a job or the need to go to school.

"Manang Emy— she will never forgive me for this," she said. "Promise me that you won't tell her that it was I who came and told you. She will kill me if she learns."

Tony did not speak. He nodded dumbly.

"I'm returning home right away, this afternoon. I saved enough money for this trip. I told her I was going to Dagupan, not to Manila. I'm going home and what I will tell you, please, let this stay with you, only you."

Tony leaned forward. A moistness was gathering in the girl's eyes and in a while she was crying softly, the stifled sobs shaking her.

"She did not want you to know," she said, "but she couldn't hide it from me any longer. Six years she hid it from everyone. All your letters, all you wrote from America—she kept them all. She reads them and sometimes cries over them. And that's how I found out. She couldn't hide anything from me. We have grown so close to each other, particularly after Father died and there was no one in the house but us and her little son."

"Yes?" he asked in a voice that was not his. "Do you mean to tell me that the boy is mine?" But even when Bettina had given him the answer he both expected and dreaded, he was being lifted away from this air-conditioned office to that drab, old room in Antipolo that he had shared with Emy. A wistfulness commingled with remorse, filled him.

"She should have told me. Why didn't she tell me this?" he asked desperately. "If I had only known. Why didn't she tell me?"

Bettina spoke huskily. "You know the answer to that." After a brief silence: "I hope you don't misunderstand. Emy did not send me here—that is something she would never do. It's just that Rosales, well, you know what the town has always been. Things haven't changed. If only there was work to do, Manong. You must understand."

Tony did not speak.

"I'm not blaming Manang Emy," Bettina said. "Nor am I blaming you. But the boy, it's him I'm worried about. He often asks me now who his father is, because the children—his classmates and the kids in the neighborhood—you know how Cabugawan is. It is so small that you cannot hide anything. What will happen when the boy finds out?"

"And what am I expected to do?" Tony rose and spoke sharply. "It's all her fault. She never told me. I wrote and wrote to her and she never answered—only once and she didn't tell me."

For the first time Bettina flared up. "You don't understand. She was thinking of you. Can't you see? If she had written, if she had told you . . . can you imagine what would have happened? You were studying. Here was your chance to make something of yourself. Here was your chance to get out of Rosales and get something more than what Rosales could offer. It is that clear, Manong, and you haven't even realized it."

It didn't sink into his consciousness at once and when it finally did, Tony knew what a fool he had been. Her faith—how beautiful it was! It could not be anything else but that—and the beauty of it sustained him through the years. The memory of Emy had made it easy for him to stave off his shameful physical hunger in those days when his allowance did not come on time and he had nothing to eat but stale bread and tea. And in the evenings, after he was through with his lessons and his papers, he would lie awake thinking of her, of the narrow room in Antipolo and the bittersweet memories it evoked, of the Igorot blanket strung across the room, and Emy behind the blanket, the trains whistling and thundering by, shaking the room, the whole house, and rattling them both. He brought to mind the old hometown, and how he and Emy had grown up together as only cousins in small towns did, and with a great ache welling inside him, he remembered how he once told her that someday, if he would ever marry, he would look for someone rich, so that he wouldn't have to slave anymore, skin his knuckles, have a premature ache in his bones. He was in a jovial mood when he told her this. They were in Rosales, and beyond the coconut trees, the moon sailed in a velvet sky and they could hear the shouts of children playing *patintero** down the dusty street. In two months they would both leave Rosales with his sister Betty. He was in a jovial and expectant mood, but Emy must have taken him seriously, for after he had spoken she became silent and sullen.

Now that his halfhearted wish had come true, what did Emy think of him? Did she loathe him for having married Carmen Villa? The doubt that assailed him, the feeling that somehow Emy did not approve of what he had done, hurt him deeply.

I am not to blame, he said to himself, and besides, I'm not in love with her anymore. Emy belongs to the past. It's Carmen I married and it's Carmen I love.

But somehow the reiteration seemed hollow. He could cheat anyone, all of the professors in the university, all his friends, and even Carmen, but there was someone he could never lie to successfully—and that was himself.

* *Patintero:* A game usually played in the moonlight.

13

IT WAS an ordinary town whose life was shaped by the seasons, the planting and the harvesting of rice, and the drudgery and the idleness between. Years ago, when it was a mere *sitio* of ten or a dozen cogon huts, a Spanish Dominican friar on his way to Cagayan Valley passed it. June—and he came upon those bushes crowned with white, fragrant flowers. The bush was called rosal, and the town, which had an abundance of them, was baptized Rosales.

Many of the bushes were still in the churchyard, in the cemetery, and along the streets when Tony left Rosales. Their flowering marked the coming of the rains, the advent of the planting season, and the town fiesta. Tony always associated the town fiesta with rain because it was held in June—on the feast day of San Antonio de Padua—and June was always a rainy month. He liked the fiesta, with its rice-planting and flooded paddies; it was the paddies, of all the things he had left behind, that he remembered best, the brown mud, the growing rice, the frogs and the freshwater crabs, and the smell of earth touched by rain. But the paddies also brought to mind things that had nothing to do with grain and growth—his father, an embittered rebel, and his grandfather, who took a whole clan from the wretched narrowness and persecution of the Ilocos to the broad plains of Rosales, who joined the revolution and fell in some nameless battlefield.

Homecoming could be pleasant if it did not stir, as it did now, an ancient sorrow and that sense of utter inability to undo what had been done. When he stepped down from the air-conditioned coach in Paniqui an urge to rush back to the train or catch the next bus to Manila took hold of him. The helplessness was now compounded with a sense of guilt.

The train connection was waiting on the tracks beyond the cement platform, a battered diesel trolley with peeling orange paint, the black hump of its exhaust shaking and spewing thin wisps of gray smoke.

Tony went to it. The day was unusually humid and the fumes from the engine stung his nostrils. The wooden benches were wobbly and decrepit. Bamboo baskets, most of them empty, a few still filled with greens and bars of soap, lay on the well-scuffed wooden floor. Farm women talked in quiet tones around him. Their faces were dark with sun and work, and he could tell at a glance that they were homely, with sagging breasts and horned hands. They smoked cheap, hand-rolled tobacco-leaf cigars, and the smoke from their constant puffing and their earthy smell were all around him.

In a while the train started. It quavered along the rails, and as its whistle blew, choked and discordant, a sense of urgency filled him. He was going to Rosales after seven years, years that seemed no longer than a week or a month. In that time he had established himself in a precinct much more comfortable and secure than he had ever dreamed of. There, in that new domain, the past could not reach out and claim him. But it did hound him. How could he ever escape the tenacious grasp of conscience? He glanced about him and saw again the tired, deathless face of endurance of the common people. Day as bright as glass lay on the fields. Years ago, when he left Rosales, he was on this train and beside him was a girl named Emy, barely eighteen. It was April and the sun was a brown flood upon the land. She was beside him, fragrant of skin and breath. Years ago . . . and now he was returning to Cabugawan, to Emy, and to an uncertainty.

The fields that slipped by were a shimmering monotony. The trolley picked up speed, slid noisily along the rails, and the wind that whipped into the coach blew the dust up from the wooden floor. Every so often he could predict the approach of a whistle stop, for the trolley would screech and the rhythm of its engine would diminish. Then they would be upon the small sheds marked by rusting steel posts with painted names.

They drew into the town of Nampicuan, and beyond it loomed a bald, cogon-covered hill. Cuyapo was next, and after the foothills through whose shallow valleys the trolley sang, he finally saw the plain. At right rose the hump of Balungao Mountain, and at left Rosales declared itself—a patchwork of tin rooftops, rice mills framed in the white heat, and the shapeless houses of all small towns.

The trip from Paniqui took barely an hour, but it seemed less. I'm going to my son—he turned the words over in his mind—my son, for it was really to his son he was going, and Emy, whose stoic silence he could not fully understand even now. My son—he savored the words again, hoping they would pry from him some new or unusual response, an identifying sentiment perhaps. But no such feeling was evoked, because he had not seen the boy, he had not watched him grow or smelled his sweet baby breath.

My son—and a huge wave of remorse swept over him again, a living sadness reminding him that, maybe, it was not too late to learn to love this child who was his very own. How would the boy receive him? Would the boy rush up to him to be swept up in his arms? Now it was no longer sadness that bridled him but a feeling that was almost fear. He did not want to be hated, not even by a boy who was, after all, no common lad—and who was Emy's, too.

HE WENT DOWN to the broad cement platform. The station had not changed—it was the same old stone building with galvanized iron roof painted dirty cream. The chicken fence still enclosed a yard planted to rows of *gumamela** and papaya that never bore fruit. He went to the ticket window and asked the clerk when the train would start back for Manila. The clerk peered at him through cracked bifocals. The train would leave at three in the afternoon.

In the palisaded yard at the other end of the platform he boarded a *carretela*. The rig driver took him across the bridge and

---

* *Gumamela:* Hibiscus.

through the mounds of rice husks that the mills had spewed out. Then they were in the town, the old skinny mare jogging evenly.

How compact the town appeared—and how small. He saw it once more: the municipal building surrounded by *banaba** trees, the tin roof shining in the sun. It was, of course, not the building that he knew when he was a boy—not the wooden edifice his father and his friends had burned in an evening of senseless, futile fury. The ruins had been quickly cleared away, a new building of stone had been erected, and the saplings that were planted had become these trees, these *banaba* with their purple blossoms, these broad acacia, and these agoho that soared as gracefully as the cypress.

But beyond the *municipio,†* in the wide vacant yard, the ruins of the *Apo's* house still stood, the broken brick walls covered with *cadena de amor.‡* No one had cleared the wide yard, and it was completely shrouded with weeds. The Rich Man's relatives had never visited Rosales, not after what had happened, and it was just as well that the old brick mansion was never rebuilt, for now these very ruins were here to speak a stern language, a warning and a vicious reminder of a past that could be conjured still. What an arrangement it was then—the municipal building, the Rich Man's house, the whitewashed monument of Rizal, the stone schoolhouse, and the Catholic church. These were the ageless constructions that made up the Filipino plaza. Now the *hacendero's* mansion was gone. What would disappear next and what unknown force would demolish the next marker in this ancient grouping?

He did not stay long. His destination was beyond—Cabugawan, the *sitio* his grandfather founded, the corner wherein his father had raised him and told him of other places, of the Ilocos and the frothy sea and of the town of Cabugaw where they all came from. It was after this town in the far-off Ilocos, this ancestral home, that Cabugawan was named. The first settlers had not intended to stop here. They had hoped to cross the Cordillera range to Cagayan Valley, but in Rosales they came across these cogon wastes and still-virgin forest, so they unhitched their bull-carts, unloaded the *sagat§* posts of

* *Banaba:* A tree with medicinal leaves and flowers.

† *Municipio:* The town hall.

‡ *Cadena de amor:* A climbing vine with small pink flowers (literally "chain of love," Sp.).

§ *Sagat:* The hardest Philippine wood; it is used for house posts and railroad ties.

the houses they had uprooted in the Ilocos, and decided to try their luck in Rosales. The land was kind and the creek that ran through Cabugawan seldom ran dry. In time more Ilocanos came to Rosales. At first they came to help in the cutting of the grain and to glean the already harvested fields, but there was plenty of room for those who wanted to work, and so they lingered to build their own homes and risk the future. Like his grandfather, they did not reckon with the greed of the *ilustrados*. In another generation the settlers had become tenants. The families broke up. Some continued the long march to Cagayan Valley, others dared to cross the sea to the malarial jungles of Mindanao, still others were herded like cattle into cargo ships that took them to the pineapple and sugar plantations of Hawaii and the orange groves of California. But wherever they went they brought with them their traditional industry, thrift, and perseverance, and wherever they sank their posts their communities grew, linking them all with that clannishness they themselves could not explain. Those who stayed behind in Cabugawan were the least fortunate. They were born as tenants and they would die as such, unless they managed to get a little schooling and, with this initial strength, escape the lethargy of Cabugawan, to strike out for the uncertainty of tedious jobs in Manila, to live in dingy *accesorias*, such as those that cluttered Antipolo.

Beyond the houses were clumps of bamboo, and beyond the bamboo were the fields his grandfather had cleared.

Cabugawan was the past and the present, never the future. The immensity of this fact was all around him—the cluster of thatched houses, the smell of slow decay under the kitchens, the manure of pigs and work animals, the broken-down fences.

The house where Emy lived was bigger than most of the houses in the *sitio*. It was roofed with cogon like the rest, but its posts were broad and solid *parunapin;** and the bamboo for the floor had been carefully selected and dried. Emy's father, who was his father's brother, had boasted once that not even termites as big as cockroaches could bite into it. Now, to him whose mind was inured to the broad, soaring dimensions of the city, the house appeared pathetically small, and smaller yet were the houses around it.

The lone dirt road of Cabugawan was quiet. A few pigs grunted

---

* *Parunapin:* A type of hardwood tree.

and wallowed in a side ditch. The sun played on the *marunggay* trees and the *gumamela* hedges. Nearing Emy's house at the far end of the road, his legs became wobbly and his heart thumped so loud he could hear it.

He pushed the bamboo gate and walked up the gravel path. The San Francisco hedge that lined it was taller now. Within the house a figure scurried to the door.

"Manong, come up," Bettina said happily, going down two rungs of the ladder.

"It's good to be here," he said lightly.

He went up with her and at the top of the flight, his eyes still unused to the dimness of corners, he looked around him. At one end of the house, in the kitchen, were the earthen drinking jars, the sooty cubicle where the stoves slumped, and to his right was the living room, its door bright with cotton curtains. Across the shiny bamboo floor two wide sash windows framed dangling pots of begonia. The wall clock on the bare post was no longer ticking. Its pendulum was still. On the sawali* wall that separated the living room from the single bedroom of the house hung Emy's high school diploma. The whole house smelled clean and lived-in.

Bettina led him to the living room and bade him sit on the rattan sofa by the window. Before him was a glass-topped table with a crocheted doily, an album of pictures, and tattered magazines.

"And Emy?" he asked.

"She's not at home right now, and I'm glad." The girl sat beside him. "I'm sorry I ever went to Manila to see you. I shouldn't have gone at all."

"It was best that you did."

Bettina drew away. "No," she said. "I had to tell her that I saw you. It would change things, I hoped. I doubt it now."

From the direction of the stairs: "Tina, did Mrs. Salcedo come for her dress? I'm so tired. I couldn't finish it today."

Bettina stood up. He followed her to the door but didn't go beyond the curtains. Emy stood there, big as life, grown older now and slimmer, and on her face were the cares of motherhood that had come too soon.

---

*Sawali: A coarse twilled matting of flattened bamboo strips used in the Philippines for partitions, walls, and baskets.

"Tony, you haven't changed at all," she said almost in a whisper, the recognition in her voice dull and empty, as if she did not want to utter his name. She stood there, her hands limp at her sides, her fragile face a shadow of her youth. And in that instant, as the truth clawed at him, he wanted to hold her, to touch her face and trace the lines on it with his fingers, and tilt her chin to feel the warmth of her lips. But it would not be right anymore; he had become another man and was not who he had once been. He had come looking for what he had lost in another time and another land or, perhaps, in his own mind. He could not be sure now. He was sure only of this woman before him, not the girl he had known but a woman who had suffered alone. It was not my fault, it was not my fault, he thought, attempting to exculpate himself.

"Tony," she repeated, "you didn't have to come—or believe Bettina." To her sister, who hovered wordless nearby, she said, serenely: "And you, what is cooking in the kitchen? Oh, you should prepare something, something . . ."

"I'm not staying for lunch." Tony wanted to be polite, but Emy would have none of it. She did not even let him finish. She turned, saying, "I must go down and get something for you—a soft drink and, yes, you must have lunch with us."

She ran down the stairs, her handkerchief pressed to her mouth.

Tony sat back amid the noiseless whirl of welcome. Bettina was enthusiastic again: "I have been reading the things you wrote and, of course, Manang Emy has clipped them all. You should see the scrapbook she made. Ask her when she returns. She locks it in there," she said, pointing to the *aparador* with a glass door at one end of the living room. "But you haven't written anything for a long time."

"A year," he told her.

"What's the matter? You don't have the time anymore?"

"It isn't that," he said. Gathering courage, he asked, "How is he?"

"Who?"

"The boy."

"Pepe? He is fine. But he won't be here until lunch time. School, you know."

"What grade is he in?"

"First. A very smart boy. You are not going to teach again?"

"Not anymore," he said dully.

She betrayed her disappointment. "Manong," Bettina said, "you should keep on writing." A hissing sound came from the kitchen and the girl stood up. "It's the rice I'm cooking," she said.

She did not join them when Emy returned with a bottle of Coca-Cola. It was warm and it was only out of politeness that he accepted the drink. She sat on the chair opposite him—dear Emy—and her eyes were lustrous.

She spoke naturally and with ease. "Tell me about yourself. What have you been doing? Bettina tells me that you are no longer at the university. And you worked so hard for that job. What are you doing now?" She piled the questions one on top of the other and did not give him much of a chance to talk.

"I'm working in an office," he said, looking at her, thinking of her as he knew her, and his answers were too concise, but she did not seem to care.

"How long ago did you return? You've stopped writing, I heard. No, it's not your fault. I understand. You said that you wanted to go to Spain. Tell me about Spain. Oh, Tony, you have so many things to tell me. And I'm so eager to hear. Remember all the plans you had, the places you wanted to visit? How you would go sailing up the Volga and the Yangtze if you had your way? How many great rivers did you cross?"

"Not many," he said. "Yes, I remember all that I told you in Antipolo."

Then silence came between them, a heavy and meaningful silence.

When she spoke again her voice was wistful. "I'm happy for you. Don't feel sorry for me. Life is difficult—that's to be expected. But you know how life in Rosales always is."

"I had difficult times, too," Tony said. "There was a winter I almost starved. I had to walk great distances. It was not easy living in America. The fellowship was not enough. I had to work in the summers. It was hard work."

"I wish I could have helped you," Emy said with sympathy. "But I couldn't, Tony. I couldn't . . ." and her voice trailed off into silence again.

"I thought of you a lot of times. Many times," Tony said after a while, and, speaking thus, he could not look at this woman who had borne his child, who had loved him and cherished his memory. "I couldn't understand why it turned out this way. I should have come to you right away when I got back. But Manong Bert . . . when I got home," he paused and the words knotted in his throat, "he said many things. Manang Betty, too. That you had gone wild. You never wrote to me and it was so easy to believe all that I heard. . . ."

"Oh, Tony! How could you believe such things?" she said softly and tears filled her eyes. "How could you think of me that way?"

He turned away, unable to look at her. "Forgive me," he stammered. "Emy, please forgive me."

She was sobbing quietly now. "Those days," she said after a while, "I was so alone. I couldn't tell anyone—no one." She turned to him, the tears glistening in her eyes. "At first I wanted to have the baby removed. I wanted that desperately. I thought about it. I stayed out late, even hoping that some accident would happen to me. Then I thought of you and how you would feel. And somehow it wasn't so dark anymore. I knew that someday you would find out, someday you would return. That was why I went home, not caring anymore about what people would think."

"Believe me," he said tremulously, "I'm sorry. I prayed for you. I thought of you. I was lonely and frightened many times. But when I thought of you . . ."

Her hand slid into his, but she did not clasp it. Her touch was not a caress. It was just a gesture that she understood. "I always knew that you'd be somebody and that you'd come back important, someone we could all look up to."

This was Emy—the Emy he knew. She had not quite freed herself from the embrace of an old, banished dream.

"What do the neighbors say?" he asked after a while.

"About you? They all know that you have become important. But they . . . they are what they will always be, Tony. You can't move away from this place. You have known that all along—you and I."

THAT WAS IT—both of them understood the great and staggering distance he had finally spanned. "Son," his father had told him once, "it takes those who have suffered to understand and be kind to the suffering." Those were the days his father had carried him on his shoulders and they had gone to the caving banks of the creek. There they had caught shrimps and, beyond the creek, in the delta, they had planted watermelons. It was there that his father had cleared the land and there, too, the sky was kind and the field bountiful. But the *ilustrados* came armed with cadastres and Torrens titles. The *ilustrados* dispossessed his father and his grandfather, and in time the land became anonymous and cramped. Beyond the plain even the infertile hills were plowed, the grass was burned, and at night the hills glowed as flames licked the skies. But even when the hills were bald at last, the grain that was planted there was not enough. False lawyers came to their house and promised aid. Flushed and happy, his mother had busted her bamboo bank open and handed the lawyers her savings—coins grown greenish with mold. The lawyers left and afterward he heard the hollow laughter of his father. They had all been cheated. And then there was more: the Rich Man came and demanded the grain in the granaries. This was when his father had said, "This time, it will be my way." His father went away for days and when he returned he wore this red band across his chest. He had become a *colorum*, a rebel. It was that way with his father, it was that way with his grandfather, and it would be that way with all men who lose hope.

But it would be different with him. While the old rage was quiet now it still pulsed faintly within him—to remind him that here in Cabugawan was the beginning of perception, and here he should be true. But even Cabugawan had been conveniently forgotten. He did not want to dwell on empty phrases, but he could not bring himself to be blunt, not to Emy. "I could have come here last May when I arrived. . . ."

"You didn't," she said simply.

"There were many things I had to do. The university . . . well, I told you that education means so much nowadays. I had to make sure of my position there. And then I got into trouble with Dean Lopez. But I haven't lost the interest I've always had. Remember how I used to tell you about going back to the Ilocos to trace our grandfather's past?"

She leaned toward him, her face alight with expectation. "Yes— and what did you find?"

"A book written by him. He was a wise man, all right—and a brave man, just as Father said."

He stood up and looked out the window, to the now vacant lot where their old house once stood. He could see it now—the pitched grass roof, the buri* sidings, and the granary behind it. Where the well used to be was a shallow indention now. Beyond the vacant yard was the alley that dipped down to the banks of the creek where he and the children of Cabugawan used to swim.

"What is the book like?" she asked.

"It's in Latin and I can't understand all of it. I'll show it to you when you come to Manila. Would you like to go to Cabugaw one of these days? It's not a big town, Emy, but it is well-preserved."

"I can't," she said. "I'd like to see places—visit Antipolo, too, and Manang Betty, but I can't. I'm not like you, Tony. Here," she became apologetic, "here, every centavo means much. You understand . . ."

He nodded and sat back. He picked up the glass of warm Coca-Cola and drank all of it.

"What have you been doing with yourself?" he asked.

"What else? Making a living," she pointed to the sewing machine—an old Singer—by the window. Beside it was a glass case with a few folded dresses. "You don't know how fortunate I have been. Almost all the important people here are my customers, even the mayor's wife. I didn't know that it was easy to sew."

That was not what he wanted to know, so he told her, "I want to help. Please let me."

"Help me? I don't need any help."

"Please don't speak to me like this. I've suffered, it's true."

"And I? Father— Before he died he beat me as if I were a beast of burden. But I did not tell him. Or anyone. I kept it all to myself, until Bettina . . ."

"Oh, Emy . . ."

"There was no other way."

"You could have written to me and told me and I would have hurried home. If you had only answered my letters!"

"Oh, God," she said, her voice almost a moan. "We are cousins, have you forgotten that? How could I tell you? And besides—"

"It wouldn't have mattered."

She went on, not minding him: "Both of us— We are older now, we can look back. I would have been a weight on your shoulders."

* Buri: Talipot palm; a showy fan palm of the Philippines.

"And how did I feel?"

"That isn't all," she said, bending forward. "You were alone in America, and it was your studies that mattered most. Then I learned about you and Carmen Villa. . . ."

Even as she spoke, even as she sat beside him, who had now grown thin and ravaged by work, he could still trace the fine contour of her face and, hearing her, he sank back to another time.

"I did not want to stand in your way," she said softly.

"How is the boy?" he asked, not caring to talk about his wife.

She was filled with pride. "He's a fine boy—and think, he is in grade one now! He is bright. I don't help him with his homework."

"How does he look?"

"He has your eyes. And his family name is Samson."

The old anguish lashed at him. "Emy, why didn't you tell me? It would have been so simple and everything would have been all right."

"What are you complaining about?" she asked. "You are doing well. And look at us, at Bettina—she can't even go to college."

"Emy . . ." his voice trailed of into silence. Then he straightened and faced her again. "There must be something I can do."

"There's always something you can do."

"Let me take him with me. Let me bring him to the city."

Her answer was quick. "And what will your wife say?"

"I'll find a way."

She smiled wryly. "And when you have children, what then?"

Tony spoke slowly, as if he was ashamed of what he had to say. "Carmen— She does not want a baby. She could have had one, but last July . . . she aborted."

A complaint was stifled in her throat. "And it has to be my child. You can adopt one—it's so easy nowadays."

"I am thinking of the boy. It would mean a load off your back." He swept the room with one knowing glance. "And besides, I can give him a better education, so many things in life you won't be able to give. He will go to the best schools—even to the United States afterward. He will not know hunger and want. This is for the best, Emy, I'll tell Carmen the boy is mine—"

She cut him off. "It's all very clear." Bitterness tinged her voice. "Now money is everything—everything. You came here not because you want to. Tony, what has happened to you? You did not talk like this before. You did not mention hunger and money before as if these were all that mattered." Then she asked, "What has happened to you? What has changed you?"

He could not shut off from his ears the words that implied his destruction. "You don't have to hurt me further," he said humbly. "Isn't it enough that I am here, unable to look after the boy and see him grow?"

"He will grow up properly," she said.

"You are strong," he said. "I would like to say that I'm weak, but I don't want to make excuses."

"Stop talking like that! Look at me, at my hands. What do you see? Years. What have I done? Look at him when he comes. I haven't complained."

"What do you want me to do then, for you and the boy?"

"Nothing," she said, the pride shining again in her eyes like jewels. Her hands were on the windowsill. Beyond the window the sun dripped white. She wanted nothing and she was right. She had always been able to take care of herself anywhere, even here in Cabugawan, where dreaming had stopped and the only certitude was the bondage of the fields beyond.

"Be honest with me," he asked her.

"I have never lied to you," she said. "Have I ever? You were everything. I looked up to you. This place cannot produce another like you. It just won't happen anymore. Father, before he died, said this, too. We all know this."

"Tell me then where I have failed."

"It's too late," she murmured, looking away.

"Do you still believe in me?"

"Yes . . . yes." She was alive again. "Why shouldn't I believe in you?"

"Will you do what I will ask of you?"

"Anything," she said with alacrity. "I'll do anything, but please, Tony, don't ask me to give up the boy. He is all that I have. Please believe that."

"Even if it would be for the best?"

"You are not the one to decide that," she said. "Look at you, the years that you were away. I slaved for the boy. I want him to grow up like you, Tony. And someday he will leave Cabugawan, too. And when he does I'll see to it that he doesn't forget where he came from."

"I haven't forgotten anyone," Tony said lamely.

"I'm sure of that," she said, but there was no conviction in her voice.

Tony glanced at his watch. It was almost twelve and in a while the shrill blast of the rice-mill whistle near the railroad station came to them.

"He will be here soon," Emy said. "It's a short walk from the school—if he hasn't stopped to play."

His legs felt watery again and his heart thumped. "What will I tell him?" he asked, hoping that she would help him.

Emy did not answer. She clasped her hands and looked away.

"Tell me that I'm useless," he stumbled on the words.

"You aren't," she said.

He got up and stood by the window, remembering the school-house, the stone porch, and the *gumamela* hedges, the mango tree in the yard, Emy in pigtails when she was young and in bare feet, cleaning the schoolroom with coconut husk.

"There he is now," Emy said behind him. He turned to see at the far end of the street the boy walking toward the house, a bundle of books under his arm. He asked in a strangled voice, "Tell me, what should I tell him?" He turned to her and her face was calm.

"The truth," she said. "Someday he will find out, and when he does I want him to know it from you. He has asked me and I've told him what there is to tell."

"And what is that?"

"I used to hope that when you returned you would remember. So I told him that his father was in some distant land. That was what I could honestly say. And then . . ." she stopped and looked away, her lips trembling, "and then I found out that you had gotten married. I wished you well, Tony. But the boy— When he asked me again I said that I did not know where his father was. I hadn't heard and perhaps I would never hear from his father again. I told him to get used to that, growing up without having his father around."

As the footsteps sounded on the gravel path, as the rungs of the bamboo ladder creaked under his puny weight, in Tony's mind the words formed: I am your father. I am your father. . . .

But he did not speak aloud when the boy was finally before him, slender of build, with soft hair and eyes as dark and lustrous as his mother's; any man would have been proud to have someone like this young thing, barefoot and brown from the sun, with a firm chin. Yes, anyone would have been proud to claim this boy as his son.

Tony was proud, but only for an instant, for his pride turned quickly into confusion and even despair as the boy turned to his mother and kissed her lightly on the cheek. To the boy Emy said quietly, "Go to him, Pepe, and kiss his hand."

Their eyes met and there could have been recognition and that spark of genuine affinity that comes only between a father and his son, but when their eyes met he only felt that he was a stranger to this boy and that he no longer belonged to this small, stifling room.

To him the boy went, but Tony did not extend his right hand as Emy had wanted. Kneeling down, he held the boy instead, held him close to his chest, felt the boy's quick breathing upon his face and smelled the sun upon his son's skin. Much as he wanted to proclaim to this boy that he had found his father, the words in his mind would not take shape, and he could only say, in a voice filled with emotion and tenderness, "Son, son," and this boy, this six-year-old innocent, escaped from his clumsy embrace and rushed back to his mother. Then, wordless, the young eyes still questioning. What is in his young mind now? What does he think of me? Is it time to tell him everything or must he find out the truth in his own time and in his own way?

The question was like thunder in the narrow room: "Is he my father, Mama?"

An eternity slipped by, and in this eternity Antonio Samson died. He did not speak, and when the silence was broken it was Emy who said, "No, Pepe. He is not your father. He is a dear, old friend, a relative, someone from this place who thinks he loves all of us."

CHAPTER

14

I⁣T WAS early evening when Tony reached home. Carmen was out and the maid simply said that Ben had picked her up at sundown. He brought his manuscripts out and went through them again, but the urge to work escaped him. At suppertime, when Carmen was not yet back, he went down to dinner without her.

"Ah, Tony," Don Manuel looked up from a batch of papers beside his soup. "I thought you wouldn't return tonight. Remind me to show you something tomorrow."

"There wasn't much to do in the old hometown, Papa." He had lied about the trip and said that he would stand as sponsor at a baptism. "I think I wasted my time. You know how baptisms are."

Mrs. Villa, her hair done up in pins, her flabby face oily with cleansing cream, nudged her husband. "Better tell Tony that, with the factory almost finished, there's got to be something social about it. A big party. I'll think up one. And this means that there will be more work for him. And the opening celebration—that's the most important thing. Let's get the President and the First Lady."

"I think that's your department, Tony," Don Manuel said. "To-morrow we will have the last transformer installed and then in the afternoon we hope to have a trial run of all units. I leave it all to you—the plans for the opening, all the ballyhoo you can cook up."

"The plans will be tentative, Papa . . ."

"It's all yours as long as you show me your plans tomorrow and we can talk them over."

Tony idled through the meal, and when it was over he rushed back to the room and took a warm shower. The shower should have relaxed him, but it didn't. If Carmen were only here now, perhaps she would understand and be sympathetic, tell him to do what was right.

He tried once more to attend to the manuscripts on which he had been working, but the words would not take shape, and the cohesion that would string his thoughts in an orderly fashion just would not come. The notes on the migration to Mindanao, for instance, did not jell and he found himself repeating the same tired phrases about the courage of the Ilocanos, their adventurous nature and their capacity to retain their identity even when they were surrounded by a polyglot of Muslim and Visayan farmers.

He went to bed with a detective story, but that was useless, too. He was already asleep when Carmen switched on the chandelier, which flooded the room with its bright, pinkish glow.

"Where have you been?" he asked, blinking in the light. He glanced at the clock near the bed. It was two o'clock in the morning.

"Stop it," she said hotly. "Do you have to know everything I do, examine everything I tell you to see if I'm lying? I've been with Ben. He had to take me to the rehearsal because you weren't in—you were in that hick town of yours."

He rose and found his slippers. He walked to her. "I'm not cross-examining you. I just want to know where you have been. I'm your husband, am I not?"

There was no belligerence in his voice and he laid a hand softly on her shoulders. She shook the hand off and faced him. "I have to be frank with you, Tony," she said, frowning. "You know damn well I've a life to live, too, and I'm not to be cooped up here. I have to have interests. If they keep me out the whole night, you have to be understanding. I understood you enough to have gone with you to look up your crummy ancestors."

Her manner defied explanation. It annoyed him but only for an instant, because he had something much more important to tell her.

He held her and looked into her eyes and said, "Baby, listen now. I meant to tell you this earlier, but I wasn't sure. I'm sure now because . . . well, I have been there."

"You are talking in riddles," she said, unmindful of what he was saying. She took off her earrings and laid them on the dresser, then started undressing.

"This is important, baby."

"All right," she said, unbuttoning her dress with a hint of annoyance. "Is it something you have already done or something you are planning to do?"

"It has been done. . . ."

"Water under the bridge. *Esto,* if it's done, then what's the use telling me about it?"

"This is important—this thing I have to tell you. Listen, there was something in the past that I never told you. Seven years ago, before we met, when I was just a mere graduate assistant at the university, there was a girl . . ."

Carmen didn't even look up. She had started brushing her hair.

"This doesn't interest you?" he said.

"Of course it does, darling," she said. "Everything you do interests me. Now go on with your delightful little story. *Esto,* I was beginning to think you had lived a puritanical life."

"This girl, you must understand— I didn't even know you then. And I didn't expect it to happen, either. . . ."

"Those are famous last words."

"It's the truth. But that isn't as bad as the fact that this girl is my cousin."

Carmen turned to him and laughed merrily. "You need not feel so guilty about it, honey. It's done all the time. Have you met Nora Lardizabal? Well, she's married to her first cousin. *Oye,* you told me once about this being done by the *hacenderos* in your part of the country. . . . Well, it just happens that Nora's parents are sugar planters. She isn't a social outcast. She is very respectable."

"You don't understand, baby," he said, shaking his head. "You don't understand at all."

"But I do, honey."

"Would you still be smug if I told you there's a child?"

She bolted up.

"There's a boy," he said, as if he were again at the confessional, and the confession was a growing flame in his throat. He waited for her to speak, but she did not. She merely looked at him, the beginning of a smirk playing on her face. Then she sat back and was silent.

"You don't even want to know what happened? You don't care about children and this particular child, my child?"

"Is there anything you want me to say—or do?"

"You can be angry with me, you can do something," he said in quiet desperation. "After all, I had gone to Rosales to see for myself. It is true, honey. I saw Emy again and this child—this son of mine."

"Well, can you change that?" she asked with hint of impatience. "If it's your son, well, let him be your son. You are not going to turn away from him, are you?"

"No," he said, amazed at her indifference.

"I'm not angry," she said with a yawn, "and I'm sleepy now. Maybe we can talk more about it in the morning."

HE LET it go at that, but, somehow, he could not quite banish the thought that Carmen did not care about his son, about children, or even about him. She had sounded so uninvolved and there was something about her attitude that now recalled to him the girl he had met in Washington, the young dreamy-eyed girl who was warm, not this woman who was now with him. Or had she simply camouflaged her feelings so well that he was unable to recognize them? Could there be some depth in her that he could not reach? He was telling her about his son; he was being truthful to her; he was conceding to her his fallibility, and all she did was say that she was sleepy. Her attitude baffled him. Still, Carmen was human—not a cold, unfeeling hunk of stone.

Much later, when she was quietly snoring, he watched her, the softness of her features, the easy peace upon her face.

Somewhere in the nameless reaches of the night a cock crowed. It would soon be morning and that morning would be unwanted. The sky would still be the same cerulean blue and the wind wandering among the agoho pines in the garden would still be the same wind that cooled Antipolo and all the ancient rooms he had stayed in. But one great change had, at last, caught up with him, and it was not the kind of change he wanted. During those bleak years that he was in college, during those days when he had but one pair of army boots, and *pan de sal* with margarine for lunch, he had nourished in the quiet core of his mind a dream of peace and abundance. The dream did not include a girl like Carmen or a job such as the one her father had given him, a job writing anemic press releases. Carmen's aspirations were not his. If he had understood this before, the knowledge would have helped him and he would have been able to look at her, her father, and the whole Villa clan in a less opaque perspective. Almost his whole life he had lived in the gravest of want, amid the most vicious uncertainties. It was different with Carmen. Her aspirations were directed toward people and objects that could be possessed. How happy she had been to know that she could tell him to do things, that she was listened to and believed, that she was desired and loved. These were the measure of her needs.

What am I to do? He should have answered this upon meeting Carmen. But he had chosen to ignore this question, not because he did not want to find out if he were merely vacillating, but because in time, the question might resolve itself without much pain.

THE NEXT MORNING Tony rose before Carmen. He had many things to do. The stories he would write on the inauguration of the mill and on the party Mrs. Villa would give—these must be finished within the week. It was better that Carmen slept on. It would be torture to face her this morning and suffer the silent lash of her scorn.

Don Manuel was at the breakfast table very early, too, and on this particular morning seemed ebullient. "Tony, I have been waiting for you. I have something to tell you."

He sat down before his father-in-law. The news must be good enough to warrant the glow on Don Manuel's face.

Don Manuel's portfolio was on the breakfast table. "I wanted to speak with you last night, but I didn't want to spoil your sleep. You see, I like to think that I am a very considerate man. That is why I am starting the day right by making you think."

Tony could not get the drift. "What is it, Papa?"

"Let me get this clear," the older man said. The maid brought in his orange juice and he took a sip. "I am very glad for what you did in the *Sunday Herald*. I knew you tried your best and sometimes it's really the intention that counts."

"I'm glad you feel that way, Papa," Tony said.

"What I am trying to say, Tony, is that I have my ways of persuasion, too. Now don't get me wrong again, but, you see, I could have very well done that on my own."

"What are you trying to say, Papa?"

"Am I being too abstract?" Don Manuel laughed. He unzippered the portfolio and brought out a canceled check. "Here," he pushed the check across the glass top to him.

Tony looked at the check and read Godo's signature on it. The sum was two thousand pesos.

"I thought you said this friend of yours could not be bought. Well, his price is two thousand," Don Manuel said, smiling.

The coffee had no taste in Tony's mouth. He laid the check back on the table.

"I don't gloat, Tony," the entrepreneur said. "But look—" he waved the check, "you see what my method can do."

"It isn't fair, Papa," he cracked his knuckles. "You shouldn't have drawn Godo into a situation like this in the first place."

"That's the point." Don Manuel laughed with great triumph. "A man's character comes out only in a crisis, when temptation is before him. We are all weaklings, son. No man is expected to be of steel—and even steel melts. There isn't much choice for a man once he is born. There is no certainty except death. One has to live the best way he can. I believe that. Your friend apparently believes that, too. That's why I don't hold anything against him. I only wish he were made of sterner stuff."

WE ARE ALL WEAKLINGS. These words were now wedged deep in Tony's mind. He was saddened yet at the same time angered that Godo had not been the heroic figure he had expected him to be. It was Godo alone who could have stood up to Don Manuel, it was he alone who could have shown that, at least, there was some essence of purity left in a country where filth overflowed not only in garbage dumps but also in the most aristocratic of appointments.

How long ago had it been when he had ceased thinking that, somehow, there must be an inner strength in himself? Now he looked back and wondered if it was not some miracle instead that had uprooted him from Rosales and blew him away to Antipolo, then across the ocean to America and Spain, and finally to Sta. Mesa.

Was it weakness? How pleasant even now was the memory of distant places, of Maple Street, the old brick house, the doorbell that had to be twisted so that it would ring, the screened door that kept out the summer flies, and good old Larry, wherever he was now.

Why did they stick together? Was it because they both had but a nominal faith in God, was it because he seldom went to church and Larry himself had never been inside a synagogue? It was Larry who helped to shape the dream, out there in that spartan room on Maple Street. Larry, with his ambition to go forth and wipe poverty and prejudice from the earth. But Tony had said: Let poverty be erased from my lot first. The dream had long since become real and he would never know the nagging damnation of insecurity again. But this newfound security was not what he wanted. It was self-justification that he had been chasing blindly. Was it not the flame that drew him, as flame draws a moth inexorably to that searing and most glorious death?

We are all weaklings, Don Manuel had said.

HE WAS ABOUT TO LEAVE his office at noon when his secretary announced that his Manang Betty was waiting outside. He had not seen her for weeks and a twinge of guilt now bothered him. He had not visited her or brought her the usual things, canned food and a little money to help tide her over.

"You should come and see me more often, Manang," he said, trying to be blithe when she came in, but he himself realized there was a lameness in his effort.

Her face was ashen and grave. "I have never come to you for help," she said. "I'm not asking for help now, but this is something that we must share."

She did not cry when she finally told him the news. She had long been beyond the rapacious reach of grief, and she told him what there was to tell with the casualness of a neighbor passing on the latest gossip. Only the tightness of her lips and the sorrow in her eyes showed the grief that she wanted to share.

The promise he had made to the old man flashed through his mind.

"He wanted to be buried beside Mother," Tony said. "What did Manong Bert say?"

His brother-in-law did not know yet. A man had simply gone to the school where she taught and relayed the news to her. "What shall we do, Tony?" she asked in a squeaky, frightened voice. "I don't know what I must do."

"You must understand, Manang," he said hesitantly. "Carmen— She never knew about Father. You know what I'm trying to say?"

Betty sat on the upholstered sofa beside his desk. How plain his sister looked, and now, in her grief, she wore that pinched, wasted mien of old maids. But she held her head up with dignity, this woman who had helped send him through college and to whom he would always be grateful. "I know, I know," she said, almost in a moan. "You don't have to tell me that. The children . . . the lies I had to tell. Will Father ever forgive us?"

He could not answer. After a while, he assured her that their father would be buried with proper Christian rites, and that someday, perhaps, the two of them would be able to go to the penitentiary and get the old man's remains and transfer them to Rosales, to a plot beside their mother's grave, just as the old man had desired.

Much later, after Betty had gone, he pondered the finality of what he had done, and in his mind intruded the specter of dissecting rooms, of his father's body ready to be butchered by unfeeling, unknowing hands. He wanted to banish the thought, but it persisted. Henceforth, he would have to live with it for as long as he was Antonio Samson.

On his way home that evening he passed the church where Carmen and he were married. It was open and he went in. The scent of calla lilies on the altar wafted around him. He had visited scores of churches in Europe, particularly in Spain, and had planted candles in his mother's memory in the cathedral in Barcelona, but he had never believed in the potency of prayer. Still, there were tears in his eyes when he whispered, "Father, please forgive me."

CHAPTER

15

O N THE DAY Mrs. Villa was to give the most lavish party in her career as hostess, Tony had a problem. Charlie had gone to his hometown in Sorsogon—his first visit since he finished college—on a two-week vacation. He had returned to Manila with the startling news that he would end his gallivanting days and return to Sorsogon to get married.

Charlie was the last in Tony's circle of college friends who had remained single. He had warded off the idea of marriage not because the thought was unattractive but simply because the very prospect of having to support a family on his meager pay as staff writer of the *Sunday Herald* discouraged him. He had found pleasure in a some-what profligate life that took him to the Ermita bars, cabarets, and disreputable places in Pasay and Caloocan. Now he had found someone in his hometown, a charming girl whose morals and vir-ginity—these he was most emphatic about—he was sure of. He had known the girl when she was still in high school and she had bloomed, according to Charlie, in those years that he had not been home. As for the bleakness with which Charlie always regarded the future, even this seemed to have been blown away. "There are clerks,"

he said, "who make less than I do and they manage to live with honesty and with fortitude. Besides, if the worst comes, the hell with it;
we can always return to Sorsogon, to her father's little farm, and live
on coconuts and camote." The morning after Mrs. Villa's party Charlie would take the Bicol Express to Sorsogon; his last night in Manila
as a bachelor was to be spent with his closest friends, Godo and
Tony.

"I'll explain it to your mama," Don Manuel had said when Tony
informed his father-in-law of his inability to attend Mrs. Villa's dinner party. He had gone to sleep wondering what useful gift he could
give Charlie, who would live in Manila with his bride. Carmen had
decided that for him. It would be a book on sexual hygiene and a
matrimonial bed with a rubberfoam mattress.

When he woke up the sun was streaming through the blue voile
curtains and was splashed on the cool beige of the panels and the
polished parquet floor. Tony turned on his side. He was now wide
awake. His wife lay on her stomach—her usual sleeping position,
her pink nightgown flowing over the edge of the bed, exposing her
thighs. She snored slightly—a domestic sound that assured him in
the quietness of this air-conditioned room that all was well with Carmen Villa and, therefore, with the world. He stood up, shivered
lightly, and, having groped for his slippers, padded to the bathroom
and readied his shaving kit.

He thrust his chin at the mirror and looked at his face—a young
face, the lips a trifle thin, the brow a bit wide. There was nothing impressive about the face. The nose, the cheeks were sallow now although once they were darker, almost like a peasant's. Nothing
impressive, nothing striking except the eyes. What did Carmen once
say about them? Soulful? Meditative? Melancholy?

He passed the blade steadily across his jaw. It's made of glass,
he thought—and that's another joke on me. With another arc he was
through.

Back in the bedroom he let his wife sleep on. It was when he
was dressing that the thought whittled at him again: Emy. He was
not surprised anymore that he thought of her with more frequency
now, particularly in this room, where he had known completeness—
not the bootleg kind he had shared with Emy, but the completeness
that was public, that sometimes had a touch of achievement.

He speculated about how his life would have turned out if it had

been Emy he had married and not this lovely woman. He would perhaps still be at the university, taking breakfast that Emy herself
would have prepared, or he would be in some anonymous corner of
the city, escaping from the strictures of convention.

Tony opened the door and went down to the dining room. It
was one of those days when the morning was dazzling and pure and
the conspiracy of heat and dust had not yet started its insidious dom-
inance over everything. Beyond the sliding doors and the marble terrace, the garlic vine and the *calachuchi* bloomed. The pool was filled
and opaque blue in the crystal sunlight. Beyond the pool, four carpenters were busy setting up rough planks for the tables that would
be covered with Mrs. Villa's finest linen, then loaded with food only
her fastidious mind could conjure. Across the wide lawn, near the
rear entrance to the garden, bunches of rattan chairs were piled,
ready to be set in place.

Tony sat alone at the breakfast table, drank coffee, and regarded
the work that would transform the garden, the lawn, and even the
terrace into another one of those gaudy "dreamlands" that Mrs. Villa
always fashioned when she gave a party. "Gaudy" was the word—a
bit unkind, perhaps, to his mother-in-law but the truth nonetheless.
Inwardly Tony recoiled again at the prospect of having to be here
tonight, to go from table to table with Carmen and live the happy
notion that he was now a Villa.

Carmen would probably not awaken until noon. Tony wondered
where she had been the evening before, perhaps with Ben de Jesus
again, for he now seemed to be always around when Carmen was
working on her favorite charity. Carmen's relationship with Ben had
been more than friendly once. She had explained Ben to him, and
because he did not want to appear prudish or possessive, he accepted her explanation at face value and tried to forget all about
Ben. Although, thinking of it now, Ben's name drew a nagging
thought of those brief, casual meetings with him in the office or at
the parties he had to attend with Carmen.

It had been several weeks now since Carmen had started to
come home late, and sometimes she would arrive after midnight
while he was still at his desk. She would sidle up to him and plant a
simple kiss on his cheek. Sometimes she smelled faintly of liquor.
She always came home with someone, though. Sometimes it was

Ben and Nena or Ben and her friend Carmita. He did not ask for explanations. They were not necessary. She would tell him, nevertheless, that she had been to Cora's or Annie's—friends who were still single and were doing a lot of charitable work.

Now their latest venture was a fashion show, and Carmen's assistance, as she herself had told him, was indispensable because she had seen several fashion shows in New York and in Paris. Her attendance at these foreign shows was an achievement in itself. With such a background she could contribute some splendid suggestions about how the parade of models should be conducted.

What should happen tonight was no fashion show, although in this very house such a display had been held several times before; the last was called Oriental Night—a party given by Carmen's mother on her birthday. He had mixed with the guests to please Carmen and for no other reason, and tonight he had to be here again, because this would mark one of the most important events in Don Manuel's life.

The Villa Steel Mill was now fully established after years of skulduggery and greasing palms.

DON MANUEL came down in golfing shorts, which he preferred when he was at home because they were comfortable. His legs were lean and hairless and he walked briskly to the table. Tony greeted him.

Don Manuel smiled and sat down to his glass of orange juice and the morning papers, which were neatly arranged for him.

The scraping of slippers along the staircase that followed was familiar. Mrs. Villa was also up early. She wore her graying hair in curlers again and, like her husband, had on shorts.

She did not return Tony's greeting. She plopped down beside her husband, then rang the small table bell before her. She pulled out a newspaper from those before Don Manuel; her eyes were alert. In a moment she turned to Tony. "I thought you knew the society editor of this paper. Look at this—look at it—just a tiny, tiny photograph. Do the society editors have anything against me? And to think that last Christmas I sent all of them Christmas gifts—Swiss lace. Do you know that you can't get Swiss lace even at the Escolta?"

"I'm sorry, Mama," Tony said. "I hope it will be better tomorrow. It's good, though, that it came out."

"Well, this is going to be an important party. The first mill of its kind in the country. Don't you think that's important? And look at the motif that I designed. Steel Party—don't you think that's novel enough?"

Don Manuel looked up from his paper. His tone was paternal: "The mill is important, *hija,* but its place is in the construction or industrial pages of the newspapers. You should thank Tony that he was able to do something about it."

Mrs. Villa dropped the paper and said to Tony, "I don't have to thank you. You know that I'm grateful—if what you do is right."

Tony smiled. "I know, Mama," he said.

Mrs. Villa stirred the cup of chocolate the maid had placed before her. "I wish you'd invite those friends of yours in the newspapers. And your sister in Antipolo, too. What's her name again?"

"Betty, Mama."

"Don't forget now. I asked you to invite them. They may think you have forgotten them. And did you tell them that they are welcome in this house? I want you to know that your friends are welcome here."

"I've told them that, too, Mama, but I don't think they will come."

Mrs. Villa lowered her cup and turned back to Tony severely. "Isn't this house, isn't this party good enough for them?"

Tony grinned. "One of them, Charlie—you remember him, I hope, the thin fellow—well, he is getting married and tonight we are giving him a party."

"So you won't come to the party, either?"

"I will, Mama, of course. But it will be later in the evening. I hope you understand . . ."

"No, I don't," Mrs. Villa said crisply. "Aren't you proud of your papa's work?"

Manuel Villa tapped his wife lightly on the hand. "Tony has already told me. And if it would make you feel better, he has taken no chances with the press photographers. They will be here, won't they, Tony?"

He had given them fifty pesos each for "taxi fare." "Yes, Papa," he said simply.

"Well, bring your friends just the same. Even if it's late. Do you understand me?"

"Yes, Mama."

Mrs. Villa sipped her chocolate gingerly. With the vitamin pill in a cup before her, the chocolate was her only breakfast. She had long been trying to lose weight. She even attended sessions in a reducing salon and consulted a hypnotist who had been, for a few months, the rage among the flabby women in her circle, but she did not seem capable of losing a single ounce, and she looked stouter now than she did when Tony first met her.

When she finished her cup she stood up. "Your friends, don't forget, they may think we have forgotten them simply because this party is for your papa's friends." She turned and waddled out to the garden.

Don Manuel laid the papers aside and looked at Tony, who had finished breakfast and was reading the paper Mrs. Villa had not finished.

"Try to be here," Don Manuel reminded him. "And the press release—I hope you'll use real influence this time. You know how your mama is. The society page is her life. You must do something to make tonight memorable."

"I'll try my best, Papa," he said.

The older man stood up and beckoned to him. They walked to the terrace and down the lawn. "I wonder if the kind of décor your mama has selected can be made." Don Manuel paused and gave the balcony above the terrace and the massive rear of the house a careful look, followed by a little head shaking.

Two men were up on the tile roof, stringing lines of colored lightbulbs from there to a bough of the acacia tree, on which another worker had nimbly perched himself. The acacia would blaze tonight—like a foundry, as Mrs. Villa described it.

Apparently pleased with the work, Don Manuel sighed. Then, turning to Tony, he put an arm around his son-in-law's shoulder: "I know," he said in a jocund voice, "the mill never got your whole-hearted approval." A slight laugh. "I know that for a fact although you never said it aloud."

Tony felt embarrassed. "That is not fair, Papa," he said.

"Don't apologize. I know you are capable of swearing, and tonight—since there will be a lot of foreigners around—I hope you'll stop being so educated and polite. I'd like to hear a few swear words for a change. Don't think of them as people. Just think of them as business partners."

"The term is rather misleading, Papa."

"See what I mean? You don't approve," Don Manuel said with a hint of annoyance. "Didn't we settle this long ago when I asked you to stop teaching? At the salary they were giving you, you were being exploited. I'm glad you changed your mind. I admit that with your connections with the papers and with your own capabilities as a writer . . ."

"A writer of press releases, Papa."

"Hell," the older man laughed, "you can call it what you wish, but I must thank you for the good that you have done. The opposition was terrific but, somehow, you helped allay all the misgivings. In the meantime, just think of tomorrow. The new factory will mean just that: more employment, cheaper goods."

"Papa," he said, realizing again how alien, how strange the word sounded every time he disagreed with Don Manuel, "there are other things you can do. Perhaps—this is just a suggestion . . ."

"Tony, you know very well that you can speak your mind. After all, once my mind is made up, no one—not even your mama—can change it."

"Well, since you are already in a position to do as you please . . ."

"Correction, Tony. I'm not in a position to do as I please. A man cannot be a builder and be free. A builder always has to compromise. He has to be friendly with senators and banking officials. That is obvious. Even in America many builders have to depend on government contracts. And government means politicians."

"There are other ways," Tony insisted. "Compromise means slavery. If it is not the politicians—the bad ones, I mean—who will control this country, then it will be the Chinese or the Japanese. The Americans already do."

"Can we escape that?" Don Manuel asked. "Talk to the others who are less fortunate than we. We would all like to be straight, Tony. Would you rather close shop and throw to the streets the many workers who remained loyal to you in the black years when you were not doing well?"

"Still, with courage . . ."

Don Manuel flopped down on one of the stone benches that

stood on the side of the pathway that led away from the pool. He shook a manicured forefinger at Tony. "Listen to me," he said sadly. "When you are in business you can't borrow without collateral. Courage and a good heart—what are these when banks demand figures? Ask Dangmount and Johnny Lee. Why are we partners?"

"Life would be empty if there was no courage in it," Tony said.

"Yes," Don Manuel said. "Life and the world would be empty. But think, hasn't it always been empty since the world began? And do not tell me, as Godo and some of your newspaper friends are insinuating, that our cold-bloodedness was brought here by the Americans and their materialism. Or by the last war and its wantonness. It's been here since time began. The original sin is as menacing as ever. We are all beasts. There is no man who can claim he isn't. He can't have integrity for breakfast. Progress comes not because there are people who are free but because there are people who are happily enslaved by their desire to own Cadillacs."

"After one has satisfied the baser instincts, one can try to be human," Tony said with conviction. "But here you'll be—" the words were difficult in coming, "a dummy. . . ."

"Is there anything wrong with that?" Don Manuel asked in a voice more surprised than hurt. "I'm after money, am I not?"

"Yes. And Senator Reyes and Lee?"

"They are after money, too, aren't they? Although, of course, they won't make as much as I will."

"And what about Dangmount and the Japanese?"

"The Japanese must expand or die. Do you want another war? With us the losers?"

The older man smiled gravely, then turned and walked back to the terrace. The brief encounter, like others he had had with Don Manuel, was over.

"Is there anything you want in the press release about tonight, Papa?" Tony asked as they mounted the marble steps.

Don Manuel seemed lost in thought. "Just say it's your mama's party—and no one else's. This is purely social."

BY MID-AFTERNOON the whole lawn of the Villa mansion had changed. A minor miracle had transformed the terrace into a stage that was part forge and foundry. Beyond the swimming pool, gleaming posts of aluminum shone in the sunlight, and along the paths and at the base of the acacia trees were bundles of tinsel-covered lamps. The members of the household staff—all of them—were on the lawn, arranging the tables and the drinking glasses. In a shed, at the far end of the garden, coolers were stationed, and beside them were piled cases of Coca-Cola and San Miguel Beer.

Carmen was not in when he returned from the office. And, somehow, he did not miss her. Mrs. Villa was at home and she had lunch with him—a quiet lunch—then she went to her beauty shop where she would spend the whole afternoon until she was ready for the evening's show.

Tony wanted a nap, but the air-conditioning would not let him. The coolness sharpened his mind, and he welcomed this sharp edge, which had long been denied him. It was here, in the solitude of this room, that he must recapture the discipline he had abjured. He strode to his desk and lifted the cover of the electric typewriter. He switched it on, then started to work on the manuscript he had left the night before.

On the paper he had already written: "There is something in the future of the Ilocano that renders him capable of sacrifice. Of all the ethnic groups in the country, he is endowed with the most protestant ethos. This has been superbly illustrated, of course, in the heroic figures of Isabelo de los Reyes and Gregorio Aglipay, who founded the Philippine Independent Church. With this capacity for sacrifice the Ilocano has thus given himself a vision of life, and it is generally a tragic vision.

"The Ilocano has two alternatives: survival or suicide. Almost always he chooses the former. The latter comes only after he has pondered all the constrictions that enfeeble him and learned that there is no other way. If, however, he finds a small hole—even though it is no bigger than the eye of the needle—he will still try . . ."

He sat back and turned the thought over in his mind: sacrifice, sacrifice. How did his grandfather come to live in Rosales, how did the family flee the barren land of the Ilocos after they were persecuted by the Spaniards? They ended up being enslaved by the very hungers and the oppressors they had sought to flee from—the mestizos, the *ilustrados* who knew the arts of government and deception.

This was what he had always wanted to write about—the fleeing, the struggling away from a beginning that somehow always caught up with the runaways in the end. These are the truths, but what can a man do? The limitations are everywhere and a man has but two puny hands and a brain that sometimes cannot function well because it has been fouled up by the excesses of the heart itself.

Tony did not add anything to what he had already written. He studied the page, then got up and lay down on the wide bed. The pink chandelier reflected bits of the afternoon sun. Above the low, steady hum of the air-conditioner the pounding of the carpenters still at work below came to him, reminded him that tonight would be the most important event in the life of Don Manuel. This was the beginning, "the dawn of a new era." Tony dwelt on the cliché, but he knew, too, that as far as he was concerned, the new factory of the Villas was neither beginning nor end. It was a form of bondage, and the factory would continue to be such as long as he stayed in this wonderful prison cushioned with Carmen's love.

Love—the thought rode on his mind. Was it really love? When they met in Washington, was it not loneliness for him and rebellion for her that had brought them together?

HE FINALLY dropped off to sleep, and when he woke up the room was already darkening and the sounds of working carpenters had ceased. He went to the washroom and freshened up, then changed into a gray polo shirt with red printed flowers.

Out in the hall the flowers had arrived—mountains of them— dahlias, gladioli, orchids, bunches of roses, and Benguet lilies in wicker baskets, all of them with ribbons and cards. A sickening fragrance, almost funereal, clogged his nose. He picked up one of the envelopes. It was from one of his father-in-law's poker cronies, a former cabinet man, and it said, "*Compadre*, may the smelting be good."

A maid came down and started hauling the flowers out to the tables, which were now draped with red linen. He asked if Carmen had already arrived. No, the señorita had not shown up yet.

"Well, when she comes," Tony said, "tell her that I'm going downtown and that I'll probably call her from there later. She knows where I'm going."

• • •

THE NEWSPAPER OFFICE pulsed with life. It was always in a state of frenzy at seven in the evening, for by this time the reporters had started filtering in with their stories. All the typewriters clacked and there was more alacrity and more tension in the movement of all the people at the desk. A few greetings, a few remarks about the heat of the office, then he shuffled out of the newsroom to an equally warm cubicle beyond it, where Godo and Charlie worked.

They were waiting for him and were apparently getting bored, for the moment he showed up, Godo greeted him in his usual boisterous manner. "Hell, how can we see the girls at their cleanest when you come in after every damned son-of-a-bitch with twenty bucks has visited them?"

He laughed Godo off: "I really don't see why we have to go out when we can go to my in-laws' place." He always regarded home with guarded distance—my in-laws' place.

"I know that the drinks there will be superior. No imitation Scotch. The food will be from the best caterer in town, too, and the women—why, they are also the best bitches in town. But I'm a snob, Tony, a reverse kind of a snob." Godo was perorating again. "You can have all your Scotch and your rich, clutching women, but this is one time we have to pay for the fun. It's more satisfying. It doesn't make you feel obligated to anyone, be they society matrons or racketeering tycoons."

"Cut the speech," Charlie said, rising from his swivel chair. "This is my execution."

The bantering continued for a while, then Tony remembered Carmen and he picked up the telephone and dialed the private line to their room. Carmen answered. She sounded matter-of-fact and wanted to know if he would return in time to catch the tail-end of the party.

"I'm not sure," he said. "You know how it is. Charlie's last night as a bachelor . . ."

She grumbled about his bad manners, then he said, feeling a little peeved himself, that he would be home as soon as his party was over.

He returned the telephone to its cradle. "Well, that's that," he turned to his friends with a look of triumph. "Now the evening is all ours."

Godo looked at Tony thoughtfully. His balding head shone in

the light and the creases on his brow deepened. "That's the example you are setting before one who is about to join the herd? Sometimes I wonder if you are really happy, Tony. You get ordered around, writing releases for your in-laws. You don't believe all that rot, do you?"

Tony turned away and the air suddenly felt watery. The words gouged at him until it seemed impossible for him to retain a secret thought, and his innermost cerebrations were in the open, raw and exposed. He balled his fists and under his breath he said, "Damn you and damn your pretensions! You'd give your right arm to be in my place."

And then he regretted every word the moment all had tumbled out.

An uncomfortable silence, and Charlie, his small voice sharp as a blade, said, "Now, both of you, this is supposed to be my evening, so let's get moving."

THEY STOOD UP and morosely went down the flight of stairs to the dusty street, where they got into a cab. Conversation was bare. In Ermita they entered the first bar they saw.

Godo, toying with his glass of beer, started it again. "You should have married your cousin Emy, Tony. That was your mistake. You should have carried her off, then lived—just the two of you."

"You are dreaming," Tony said curtly. "This country is so small that you can't hide a needle in it."

"I'm sure it would have turned out better for you," Godo insisted.

"Don't talk like that," Tony said, shaking his head. "It's bad enough as it is."

The name, loved and lingering yet, stirred the imperishable hurt. His head slightly dizzy with drink, he drifted again to another place and time, to that high noon in Rosales when, after seven long years, he finally saw Emy and the boy, her son, his son—Emy braving everything, the world, because these were her real treasures: faith and courage and this boy who might someday grow to loathe him, to spit at the very mention of his name. He did not tell them what had happened long ago in that small wooden house by the railroad tracks in Antipolo, the Igorot blanket that was flung across the room that he and Emy shared.

"So what if you are cousins," Godo pursued the subject. "You should have gone right ahead and gotten a dispensation from the pope. Those Negros *hacenderos* would marry their sisters just to keep their haciendas from breaking apart. Now I'm not saying it's incest. If it were love . . ."

"It's not incest," Tony said, breathing deeply, hoping that Godo would stop. Then he could not dam the words anymore, and, looking away, he spoke barely above a whisper, "I saw Emy only last week. Emy has a child. And the child . . ."

"Oh, well," Godo said expansively, and bluntly, "I was just saying how much better it would have been if Emy were already married, then there'd be no more problem. But Carmen, hell, Tony, you are worlds apart. Art, truth, beauty—these are never in the world of the Villas, and you . . . you had so much promise. You still could fulfill that promise if—"

Tony glared at his inquisitor and said aloud, almost for everyone in the bar to hear, "Emy's son is six years old—the time I was in America, all the time I was there. . . . Can't you see? The child is mine! And that's not all." The words flowed freely now and he could not stop. "My father— I never told you about him. I never told anyone about him, not even you whom I call my closest friends. He had rotted in jail and I let him die there. I didn't even claim his body. And do you know who he was and what he did? Listen, he was a brave man, braver than all of us. He burned down our town hall; he killed a *hacendero* and three soldiers. He was as brave as no one among us will ever be. And I . . . I'm a coward because I'll never be able to whisper my father's name without recoiling at my own shame. Now do you know what I really am?"

Silence, the hum of an air-conditioning unit, the clinking of glasses at the counter, and the squeaky laughter of a girl somewhere in the shadowed cubicles.

Then Charlie spoke. "Life is always sad. That's what makes suicide so tempting, because life is all that we really have and haven't. Death makes us equals, too, because the foul and the good all die. The past, the present, and the future—what escape is there from these? None. And yet sometimes we are life's happy victims."

"What are you trying to say?" Godo asked with a smirk. "That we should all commit suicide?"

"No," Charlie said resolutely, "that we should accept life and live it. Life is to be lived. It's that simple."

Godo turned to Tony. "Does Carmen know?"

Tony nodded without looking up. "She had a right to know. I told her the moment I returned from Rosales."

"How did she take it?" Charlie asked.

"Civilized," Tony said. "Carmen is always like that. It's her passion to have people act civilized."

Silence again, then Charlie tried to salvage what little exuberant mood was left. He called a waitress who was seated on one of the stools near the bar and asked her to join them.

She was pert and young and talkative, a Cebuana, according to her, who had finished home economics in one of the exclusive convent schools in the city and would have gone places had she not become too trusting with men. Now, look where she was, talking with slobs who did not care about her feelings, who considered her no more than someone who could be pawed all over in one evening and forgotten the next.

Tony ignored her prattle. The night was suddenly a senseless void. What he had hidden in his private consciousness had finally been exposed. The long skein had been unraveled and in the end was this: people knew, and no amount of protestation could prove how sincerely he had loved Carmen, that he would have willingly hied back to the university, to the hopeless drudgery of it all if only to show that he did not care for her money but only for her.

He did not care for Carmen's money?

He lingered on the thought and found that it was not as absolute as he had wanted it. All his life he had known that dead end called Antipolo, he had known hunger—and not just the spiritual kind but also that merciless and embarrassing physical hunger, not just for food but also for all the things he could not possess.

After trying to caress the obstinate waitress, Godo suggested that they go find someplace where the women were more reasonable if not cooperative. But the brief encounter could not be forgotten, and shortly before midnight, after more senseless palaver in an Ermita bar called Surrender, Tony stood up. Holding his wallet, he said, "I feel guilty. You know how it is. It's my in-laws' big day. Carmen's father—you understand, don't you, Charlie?"

Charlie nodded. Tony motioned to the waiter, but Godo stopped him. "You don't have to pick up the tab every time you are with us just because you are an ersatz Villa now," he said with a boisterous laugh. "We still have some money and self-respect."

He could not hold his contempt for Godo any longer. He had always been nice to him, particularly after his marriage, because Godo could be useful to the Villas and to himself, but tonight the insult must not pass.

"Don't talk to me about self-respect," he said with quiet fury. "You haven't got any. You accept bribes just like the people you condemn—and don't say that you didn't get two thousand from Don Manuel for that lousy story you wrote about him. I have the canceled check and I can hang it on your neck anytime I want."

He had said what he wanted most to say for the last few days, and a great and solemn peace filled him.

Godo jabbed a finger at him. Charlie's glass of beer in the middle of the table toppled, but no one moved to escape the spreading blot.

"Is that your view of corruption?" Godo asked with a sneer. "You really have come a long way, Tony. You identify yourself with the Villas now. I'm sorry for you, I'm sorry for your children, and I'm sorry for this goddam country that permits people like you to go to college and then go about speaking as you do. Hell, you haven't been educated at all. Nor have you grown up. I pity you."

"The truth hurts," Tony said quietly.

"The truth! Listen to my part of the truth. I am poor. There are thousands of poor jerks like me. Big men like Don Manuel, Dangmount, Lee, your nationalist Senator Reyes—this pack has robbed me of my rightful share in life. These sons of bitches band together. They have one thing in common: greed. And that's what you have now. And the thousands like me? We scrounge around, we don't live. Our children starve, our wives get sick and die. My wife is dying—and that's where the two thousand went, you damn fool!" There were tears in Godo's eyes and his voice trembled. "And you call me immoral? What right have you to make such a judgment? I was only getting back a little of what I could from the thieves and scum who call themselves nationalists and philanthropists. Two thousand lousy pesos. That is not even a fraction of what your father-in-law has stolen from the settlers in Mindanao. Want me to tell you how he got that steel mill set up? The dollars salted away in Switzerland? No, you don't want to hear what I have to say because the truth hurts—just as you said. Me and my kind, I don't owe you any favor. It's you who owe us your comforts, your very lives."

"I— We don't owe you anything. You have been paid, Godo. You are now answerable only to your conscience and to God."

"Look, I believed in God once." Godo paused and his voice, which had been rimmed with venom, was now calm and soft. "I once thought that there was goodness and virtue, and nice wonderful presents awaited those who were virtuous. But not anymore. I see around me nothing but the work of an unjust and merciless God. There is too much suffering in my world not because men have caused it but because God has created men like the vultures of Pobres Park. And so I don't believe in God anymore." Godo's voice became a whisper. "Someday, Tony . . . you know how it was when we were in college. You know how some of our friends disappeared and how they went to the hills to join the Huks. Wasn't it wonderful then?" A smile played briefly on his face as he reminisced. "Oh, how we talked in those grubby restaurants about the meaning of life, about being committed to duty, creating a new order for the future, for our children . . . not for us—I'm moving on to forty, Tony, and I'm not as healthy as I was then. I get rheumatic pains. I have poor vision. But if I get called again, I will join them. I shall not hesitate as I did before. I do not care anymore who they will be. Colorums, Huks, anarchists—Satan himself—whoever they are who believe that only with violence and blood can we wipe out the terrible injustice around us. Yes," Godo raised his voice, "I will go with them and may God have mercy on you, for one of the first things I will do when I have the power to do so will be to tear down your high walls and set afire that garbage dump you call Pobres Park! And I will not be sorry for you, I will not have one single regret. You have deserted us, Tony. You are a traitor now to your class and to your past. You have become one of them!"

For an instant Tony felt like picking up the table and smashing it on Godo's corpulent face, but he smiled tolerantly instead, then rose and walked out into the night.

ON THE WAY BACK to Santa Mesa, Tony vowed never again to have anything to do with Godo and Charlie. He loathed himself for having let them trample on him—Godo, in particular, who had taken him for granted.

The big house came into view. Cars were parked all over the road and the traffic barely moved. As his cab neared the entrance, Carmen's red Thunderbird was slipping out. She was at the wheel and beside her sat Ben, composed and grinning. Tony saw nothing wrong. Carmen and Ben were good friends. In a moment, however, the old suspicion, never completely banished, returned. There was something in Carmen's face as the headlight of his cab struck it.

To the cabdriver he said, "Back out and follow that car with the girl driving. Don't lose them."

He trailed them down Santa Mesa Boulevard, then to Highway 54, Carmen drove leisurely. Once, as they neared the intersection in Cubao, he saw them kiss and his first impulse was to tell the driver to go alongside them. But his anger quickly subsided and gave way to a perverted curiosity. He brimmed with anxiety to find out what they would do, although in his mind there had already formed an inexorable image. The driver slowed beyond Cubao and asked in a rather apologetic tone who were the two they were following.

Tony had no immediate answer, for he had presumed all along that the driver knew. In spite of the tightening in his chest, he replied, "The man is a very good friend of mine. I just want to know how successful he is this time."

The driver seemed satisfied with the explanation and all the way, past Makati and the approaches to Pasay, he did not speak.

At the junction in Pasay, Carmen turned right and headed toward Taft Avenue. She turned at a corner into an open gate. Tony felt faint. He glanced up at the sign spelled in neon—the shining name of the motel—and in that one glance all the sordid things that the name implied mocked him. It happened so quickly, as if everything had been planned. Now a hundred visions flashed in the tortured cavities of his mind. Nothing else mattered but this discovery, and above the growing din of his anger, the driver's voice came clear. "Do you want to follow them in?"

"Drive on," Tony said in a voice that was not his. "Drive on," and his voice trembled. The cab picked up speed, and in Vito Cruz, Tony said he would like to go to Surrender, the bar where he had left Godo and Charlie.

He stumbled out of the cab and did not wait for his change. He peeked inside each cubicle, even went to the men's room, but Godo and Charlie had gone and the bartender did not know where. The anger was no longer just the anger of a man betrayed. It was compounded with an engulfing, nameless loathing for his wife.

Betrayal—but had he really lost anything except his pride? That was it, his pride. It had been afflicted before and he had outgrown the pain, because he was mature and sensible, because he was "civilized"—Carmen's hateful word.

Why should he complain? He had known the good life and its beneficence could continue. He could go on making believe that Carmen still esteemed him and that this abominable thing that he had witnessed could be scraped off the mind as one would wipe the mess off a festive table.

He could still make-believe—another obnoxious word, an evil word—and he hastily repudiated the thought. Had he become so callous, so drained of self-respect that he would now think of disillusionment and the withering away of a once impregnable trust as nothing more than an inconsequential variation of living? Had he been so naive or so blind as not to see that around him worms had worked fast, eating away at the strong buttress which the past and all that was true and good had built? Or did he not see early enough that below him, underneath his very feet and pushing him up, was a dark force that no one could reckon—the greed and folly all men want to cast aside but cannot, because all this greed and folly are woven into the finest threads of their minds and their flesh, inseparable and eternal as original sin?

He prayed for an inner voice to redeem him, to tell him that he had done no wrong, but what he heard did not relieve him. It was the swish of a knife that sliced his heart, struck the finest tissues, and exposed their tender nerves to the faintest breeze. He had sinned, not against any single, identifiable man but against someone much more important—himself.

CHAPTER

16

AFTER THE FOURTH BAR Tony gave up looking for Godo and Charlie, and simply raced away from the shadows of Mabini.

It was almost three o'clock when he returned to Santa Mesa. On the lawn of the big house the orchestra still played languorously. Most of the cars that lined the street leading to the house were still there, a formidable phalanx of shiny machines, their drivers gathered in groups, talking and waiting for their plate numbers to be called by a loudspeaker at the gate.

He avoided the lawn and the people. He hurried to the driveway, past the terrace to the rear entrance, and up the main stairway to the room where he and Carmen had lived the past year. The air conditioner hummed, and through the closed windows the music from the garden below stole into the room. He flicked the switch by the door and the chandelier exploded into dazzling pink.

From the closet in the adjoining room he brought out his old suitcase of battered leather, well-scuffed at the corners, its tattered stickers stubbornly clinging—Hotel Colon, Barcelona. He laid the suitcase on the bed and opened the cabinet at the foot of the bed. Most of his things were there. He had never acquired a collection of either clothes or knickknacks—just five suits, half a dozen barong Tagalogs, photographs of college life, and an assortment of paper-weights. He took these to the suitcase, then he went to his books, to the typewriter he had bought in Rome, now rusty with disuse. Near it were the manuscripts he had been working on, his own thesis and his grandfather's *Philosophia Vitae*.

Should he take these, too? These materials that marked his be-ginning and his perdition? He viewed them, these fragments of the past whereon he stood. And in this cool, quiet room lavished with comfort, the futility, the smallness, and the terrifying finality of his failure reached out to him, clutched at him. It was of no more use, it was of no importance now for him to go on working with this sham—he who had been corrupt from the start, when he did not be-lieve in what his father and even his grandfather had believed in. He was heaping blasphemy on the past and on what his grandfather had done. If he were honorable (to this question he steeled himself) . . . but there was nothing firm left to prop him up. What remained was this corroded frame that could not stand up to this one fearful gust of discovery: he had defeated himself.

He looked at what he had hoped to finish, at his grandfather's work, and the meaningless sorrow that swept over him became a strength that surged to his hands. There were no tears in his eyes. He felt his breath strangling him as he bent down. With a firm hand he grabbed his manuscript and tore it apart. He did not hear the sound of paper being rent. Inside him was only emptiness. His heart began to be torn to shreds when he finally took hold of his grandfather's *Philosophia Vitae*. It was so fragile, so easy to destroy that he did not even have to try.

When he was through, the papers were all about him, the mean-ingless scraps, the work, the heritage that had lasted a hundred years and had lain undisturbed in an Ilocos convent until he had stumbled upon it. A weariness came over him. It seemed as if he had been me-andering in a desert or a swamp only to find that there was no bear-ing, no end to the wandering. The desert was sand without horizon, and the swamp was muck and slime forever. He had journeyed far, he had learned much, but he needed to go still farther, to the moun-tains of Bontoc, to the *ulogs* and eyries that were almost forgotten, only to be recalled again now. He would not find them in the desert or swamp of Santa Mesa. The beginning of knowledge, after all, lay not in the land that he had traveled but in the dark and anonymous folds of his own mind. He must hurry now, he must hurry. But where?

Carmen came in then, looking fresh and sinless. Seeing his things on the floor, the manuscripts and the old book for which she had paid good money now nothing but torn scraps, she stepped back and asked, "You did this? You must be out of your mind!"

Before he could speak she saw the suitcase and confronted him. "Are you going somewhere without even telling me?"

That was all the interest she showed. She was not eager to know his answer and she walked across the room, stepped on the litter covering the floor and sat at her dresser. She studied her makeup. She was not going to change her clothes. She merely primped, then stood up.

The weariness still clotted his mind, but he watched her attentively.

"I asked if you are going anywhere," she said, turning around, satisfied with the reflection in the mirror. "My God, Tony, you don't expect me to clean up this mess, do you?" She glared at him, her eyes lovely as ever.

"I don't expect you to do anything," he said. How strange. No anger welled within him and neither the curiosity nor the grief that had gripped him earlier returned. He turned his back on her, went to the suitcase, and brought the lid down. But the suitcase would not close. "And as for my going away," he said, almost mumbling, "I don't think it matters to you, so there's no need for you to know where I'm going or what I'm going to do."

Casually, she asked, "Where are you going?"

He removed one of his summer dacron suits, then pushed the lid again. This time it clicked shut.

"I'm leaving. It's best for both of us."

His mind was clear, as clear as on those mornings when the sunlight was pure. But the words, tainted with hatred, took shape: "You should take a bath and change your clothes. That way you'll be cleaner. I'm sure you must be full of dirt—lying on a strange bed. God knows who was there before you." He spoke evenly, as if he were stating a simple fact.

Carmen did not speak.

"I hope you understood what I just said," Tony said. "I just said: you are a whore."

Carmen did not move. "Tony, you don't know what you are saying," she said, aghast.

Tony turned to her and smiled grimly. "I know," he said. He studied her face. God, she was pretty—the nose, the questioning eyes, the lips, those full, red lips. "Tonight," he went on, measuring every word, "I followed you to the motel. I waited for a while, but it took you so long. Ben must be losing his virility."

"It's not true," Carmen said desperately, backing away from him.

Tony followed her to her dresser where she slumped down. "I told you once that I'd kill you if you ever did this, remember? It was in Washington. It was freezing and there was no coffee in the pot, remember? And after I had gotten up and made you a cup I said, 'I'll do anything for you, be your servant, as long as you are true.' Remember?"

In the quiet glare of the chandelier above them, her face was frightened and pale.

"You're scared," Tony said, enjoying himself, standing before her.

"Tony, don't hurt me."

Tony smiled in spite of himself. "How can I do that? Haven't you always said that I should be civilized like you? Well, I'll be civilized. If I touched you I'd soil my hands."

"What can I say?" Carmen choked on the words.

"Nothing," Tony said.

"Please be more understanding . . ."

"What more do you want? I am leaving without touching a hair on you." He strode to the tall narra cabinet and opened it. When she followed, he barked at her, "Leave me alone. I have a lot to pack."

Carmen lingered. Strange, there was no high drama, no passionate remonstrances. This was the Big Scene in his life and he was, like her, acting "civilized." This was what she wanted and he was acting according to her script.

"Will it matter if I explain, if I tell you how it happened? You must know at least how I feel—there were so many things we did together, told each other. . . ." Her voice suddenly had the warmth and tenderness he had missed all these months.

"Well," he said, looking briefly at her, "I suppose I shouldn't mind the background music. Go ahead, shoot your mouth off."

"Tony," she was imploring him. "Listen and do not hate me for what I am going to tell you."

"I can't hate you enough," he said.

Her voice was quivering. "Once upon a time, I knew I would do anything for you. I'd do what you would command me to do. If you had wanted, we could have gone together wherever you wanted to go, lived where you wanted to live. I would have missed many things and I would have objected strongly. But I would have gone with you just the same . . . if you had put your mind to it, if you did not fall so easily to Father's bait—and to mine. I love the things I'm accustomed to, but I would have gone with you. . . ."

"But it's different now. Is that what you're saying?"

She turned away. "So many things have changed. Now I see nothing of value. And you, I don't blame you, because a man's ambition is different, and because Father wanted you—honestly, sincerely . . . and I . . . I pushed you . . ."

"You know damn well this wasn't what I wanted," he said hotly. "Not all this, not all—" Then he stopped, suddenly aware that he was lying. He had coveted this, this comfort, this bigness, this power.

"I pushed you, that's what I did," she said quietly.

"No, no one did," he told her. "My fate, my reasons, are mine alone. Now that you have made your excuses please leave me alone . . ."

She stood by as he carried another suitcase from the closet and laid it open on the bed.

"Believe me," her voice betrayed a real disconsolation. "It won't happen again. I'm bad. I guess I had forgotten, I've always been bad. I will never be a saint."

"It's not simply a matter of forgetting. So don't talk about sin."

"I imagine you are sorry for yourself," Carmen said. "If it were Emy you had married, it wouldn't have turned out like this. I must see her sometime and learn from her."

"She has suffered enough without your seeing her."

"But it's true," Carmen said hollowly. "She is different. She's good in spite of all that happened. Maybe that has been in the back of my mind all the time—her goodness and my rottenness."

"It happened long ago," Tony said, going back to the closet. She followed him there.

"You can forgive me," she said desperately.

"I can, but it won't be the same again." He paused. "And most of all, how can I forgive myself?"

"Are you going back to her?"

"To Emy?"

"Who else? You have always been sentimental about her."

"Even if I did she wouldn't take me. No, I'm returning to Antipolo, that's all."

"You don't have to go. Do you want me to explain how it happened?"

"You don't have to. It happens to the best people."

"Don't say that. I'm not the best. Father is not the best. You said so yourself once. You said he is a scoundrel, a patriot for convenience. Maybe that's the reason. For convenience we do so many things."

"Don't explain life," he said. "Please, I don't want to hear another word from you. I despise you."

Carmen shuffled to the door but did not close it after her.

THEN HE WAS ready. He surveyed the room, wondering if he had forgotten anything. All that he wanted to bring were in these two suitcases, bulging now with his old clothes. The rest he left behind, and if Carmen should send them to him he would write her a thank-you note. That, too, was the civilized thing to do.

He lifted the two suitcases. They were heavy and he was amazed, since they did not really hold much. He remembered that he had not done any manual labor in months and had not lifted anything heavier than a portfolio. He smiled at himself and, flexing his muscles once, carried the suitcases to the door.

Mrs. Villa stood there, her flabby form barring the way. She was still dressed in blue denim overalls, her party costume. The theme was industry and she represented a typical steelworker. Her voice sounded old and it lacked the acidity with which it always dripped. "Carmen's crying. She didn't tell me what you quarreled about and I don't think I can find out from either of you. You are both old enough to know what's right and what's wrong. Are you really leaving, Tony?"

"Yes, Mama," he said, putting down the suitcases.

"Is it because I have been mean to you?"

Tony studied the painted lips, the fleshy chin, the wide, inquiring eyes. "I've learned to like you, although I know you never liked me. You wore no mask. You were yourself."

"That was not everything, son." It was the first time she referred to him as a son and the word touched him. "I'm sorry if I made you think I didn't like you."

"It's all right, Mama," he said. "With you I didn't have to be on guard. That's the truth."

"I'm such a scatterbrain, Tony."

"But you are sincere. You didn't try to be good to me, because you didn't like me. And I didn't have to be jolted by the way you acted, because from the beginning— Remember, Mama, when I first came here?"

"That's past," she said. "We should all learn to keep the past where it should be."

"But the past is important. It's linked with the present."

"Well, I don't care about the past. Why should I?"

"I know, Mama."

"Did Carmen tell you?"

"Tell me what?"

"She never did tell you what my family was?"

"Never, but I know. I've known it for a long time now and, frankly, I never cared."

"Well, it was more by accident, but why should I tell you what you already know? And after all the things that I've done to you?"

"I understand, Mama."

"You don't," Mrs. Villa said, "for if you did, you'd unpack your things now."

"I wish what you just told me made a difference, but it doesn't. It merely explains your distaste for me. I remind you of yourself."

"Don't try to talk smart," Mrs. Villa scolded him.

"I'm sorry, Mama."

"Don't be a fool. I'm not saying that you should stay here because I like you. I'm a selfish woman, Tony. What's going to happen to Carmen? You are the first good thing that she has had, the first good thing this family ever had—if I may flatter you. Somehow, well, let's admit it, my friends often talk about you. They say you have another kind of brains, something the Villas never had—unless, of course, you mean brains for making money. . . . And your papa, he's my husband and I know—nights he'd lie awake, saying, 'Tony is right. Tony is right . . .' "

"I didn't know I had a market value or that I had some snob appeal," Tony said.

"Don't talk smart, I said. What I'm trying to say," Mrs. Villa came forward and shook a pudgy finger at him, "is: have some sense. Someday you'll find that what's good for the Villas is also good for you."

Tony could not face Mrs. Villa anymore. "I'm leaving, Mama," he said with finality. "I don't know, but if I change my mind, you'll be the first to know."

Mrs. Villa shook her head. "I know your kind," she said softly. "When you make up your mind it's made up. Once you've gone through that door you'll never return."

"Am I such an open book?"

Her hand drifted to his arm, held him tightly but her grip relaxed as Tony moved to the door.

"It will never be the same again, Tony," she said sadly. She followed him to the hall.

"I'm sorry, Mama," he said, holding the suitcases firmly. They seemed lighter now and he carried them, almost blithely, down the rear stairway and to the back entrance, where he called a cab.

THE NIGHT was quieter when he reached Antipolo. Traffic had not cluttered Blumentritt yet, and beyond the asphalt and the weeds, the street where he once lived was what it had always been—narrow, incongruous, wooden frame buildings thrusting their ugly roofs, their shapeless forms, from the black earth. A few jeepney drivers who lived in the shanties farther up the narrowings and curvings of the road were at Mang Simeon's store, drinking cheap coffee, their jeepneys parked before the store, waiting for the meager traffic that would stir when the Bicol Express arrived.

It had been weeks since he was here last and he remembered with a dull ache how he had tried to forget the street. Now he was back like some criminal returning to the scene of his crime, for it was here where he had done people wrong—his sister Betty, Emy, and, finally, himself.

He carried his suitcases across the narrow alley flanked with scraggly weeds. The door to which he went was closed, but within the house a faint light burned. He knocked twice, wondering how he would tell his sister what had happened. His knocking did not stir anyone in the house, so he rapped again, this time a little louder, calling out, "Manang Betty, Manang Betty," his voice resonant in the night.

Finally, a stirring sounded from within. A lightbulb above the door went on and, at the door, Betty's squeaky voice: "Who is it?"

"Tony," he said. The door opened and Betty stood before him, looking thinner. He had not seen her since she told him of their father's death, and the shame that nagged at him now formed an impossible barrier to all that he wanted to say, the words of entreaty and regret. He stood in the light, the suitcases on the ground. The sight of him in the night must have startled his sister and, for a while, they just stood there, wordless. Then Betty spoke, as if this was Tony coming home from school or a binge: "Come in with your things before some rascal picks them up. It's good you remembered to visit us."

Tony could glean the sarcasm. He had expected it, for had he not really forgotten them—his sister who had sent him to school and this wooden crate that was home? And yet it did not hurt as much as he had imagined it would, because it was his sister who spoke. She had a right to feel aggrieved. Never had he realized it as fully as he did now that he had really strayed away and forsaken them all the while that he was in Santa Mesa, all the while that he roamed in an ethereal region that was never meant to be his.

Wordless, he followed Betty to the living room. It had not changed, either—the battered *bejuco* furniture with the knife marks inflicted by his young nephews; the starched white doilies that Emy had left behind; the Ocampo painting that still hung by the staircase, dominating everything in the house with its splurge of color. Yes, nothing in Antipolo was altered.

"I'm not here on a visit, Manang," he said humbly. "I'm here to stay, and I hope you will take me back."

Now Betty's sarcasm was more defined: "What has happened now? Have you at last decided that you belong here and not in that palace in Santa Mesa?" Triumph tinged her voice.

"I don't know how you will take it," Tony said, not caring really about what Betty's answer would be. "Maybe I'm foolish, but I have left Carmen."

Betty sat on the rattan sofa beside the stairway and regarded her brother. She had become amiable again and she smiled. "Your Manong still snores like a hog, and so do the children. Listen to them now. They didn't even hear you knocking, although the whole neighborhood has been roused."

But Tony did not want to talk light. "Tell me, Manang," he said, "did I do right? Don't bother about the reason. Did I do right?"

"You have to tell me why you left her," Betty said.

Tony turned away. "It does not matter, really," he said. "I quarreled with Carmen, that's all." Deep within him what he wanted was confirmation, not denial. What he wanted was sympathy, not the truth.

"You were wrong," his sister said evenly. "You were wrong to leave. I was trying to tell you: your beginning is there. Not here. This is the end, Tony. You'll never get the same chance again."

"But I'm free now," he insisted, his voice faltering with emotion.

Betty laughed bitterly. "Pride is not for us, it's for the wealthy. How many times have I told you that?"

"I don't believe you."

"I mean it," Betty said. She stood and listened to the snoring from upstairs. She turned to Tony. "How long are you staying here?"

"I don't know," he said, rising, too. "Maybe I'll stay here for as long as you will let me."

"It will be crowded," Betty said, her displeasure completely banished. "You'll be needing quiet. Are you going back to teach at the university? Have you any savings?"

He shook his head. "I will not teach and, of course, I have no money."

"You will not find this neighborhood quiet anymore. And what will the neighbors say? Everyone knows how well you have married. Everyone teases me when I wear my old rags, or when we have nothing but *tuyo* for lunch."

"You are right. I'll stay here until I find a new place. And, most important, after I find a job."

"Is that what you will do in the meantime? Look for a job?"

He nodded. "I need the money not only for myself but also for my pledge to you."

"You can forget that," Betty said amiably. "As long as your Manong and I have jobs we will be able to send the children to school."

"I know my duties," Tony said. "And that's final. But, really, it's Emy who worries me most. Her son . . ."

"She shouldn't worry you. She can take care of herself and her boy."

"Yes, she can. But her son . . . he's mine, Manang. I didn't know it until last week when I went to Rosales."

Betty bent forward, not quite convinced by what she had heard.

"Yes," Tony repeated, "the boy is mine. Six years—how she has suffered!"

"But Tony, what can you do now?" she asked after a long silence.

"I don't know."

"What did she say?"

"She despises me. She didn't say so, but I felt it."

"I wouldn't be so harsh if I were you," Betty said. "If I know Emy, she would never be that harsh. . . ."

"She has a right to be harsh," Tony said.

"But what will you do now? Marry her? You know you can't do that. We don't divorce, and Carmen— Will she let you go?"

"I don't care anymore what she does. And as for Emy, I want to do right by her."

"And what is that?"

"I don't know. Give her things, perhaps—the things she never had. And more so now that there's the boy. I don't want him to grow up hating me. I'm his father and it feels so different being one."

"Still, you can't marry Emy."

"I know."

"I'd like to help you," Betty said with feeling. He had not asked for her assistance and her offer touched him. "I may have been a little impossible—that's the schoolteacher for you. But I want to help."

"The family, we . . . we will always stick together."

"You are my brother. You may steal, you may murder, but you are still my brother. I'll fix you a place to sleep." She turned and went up the wooden stairs.

Alone in the house where he had known possession and its haunting joy, it finally occurred to him that he was, after all, part of the herd—the herd with the gross instincts of self-preservation.

He stood up and walked to the window. Through the iron bars he looked into Antipolo, which was as dark and disreputable as ever.

This is corruption, this is decay of both the spirit and the body, this is home. Then, above his own musings, he heard his brother-in-law, Bert, saying thickly, "I'm sorry, Tony. I was sound asleep, I didn't know."

Bert was standing beside him in his underwear as chubby as ever. His hair was still cropped short and his face shone swarthy and full in the light.

"It's I who should be sorry, Manong. Waking you up at such an hour."

"Betty told me about your leaving Carmen. It's a big mistake. You know what I mean."

He smiled. "I don't think it's a mistake, Manong."

Betty joined them. "Go on up and sleep," she said, tugging at his sleeve.

Tony sat down on the sofa instead. All of you have a reason to go on living, he thought, but I have lost everything that is good and true. Emy, the future—I've lost all of it because there is inherent corruption in me. It's something entwined with my flesh and I can't wash it off. My God, I should have known this long ago. I should have known then that I was weak and that I hadn't suffered enough. He turned the words over in his mind, and because they were true, he pounced on them as if they were the only nuggets his soul could treasure.

"I am not really sleepy," he said, laying a hand on the old narra sofa. It had a lot of bedbugs once and he remembered how he took it out in the sun between the railroad tracks and poured boiling water on it, then left it there, exposed, the whole, hot afternoon.

"Your bed upstairs is being used by the boys now," Betty said, "but I will spread a mat for you on the floor. It's not soft—you haven't slept on the floor for years, I know. But it will be daylight soon."

"It's all right," Tony said. "I'll go out and take a walk and maybe I'll be able to think better." He lied, of course, because never before had his mind been as clear as it was now. He moved to the door.

"You need sleep," Bert said.

"It's all right, Manong," he said. "I need the walk more."

They accompanied him to the door, telling him to be careful because this was Antipolo and not Rosales, and danger lurked in the crevices and alleys. He stepped out into the night after appropriate assurances that he could really take care of himself here in Antipolo, which was the beginning. Would this also be the end?

The realization that it was swept over him and strangled all hope, all sense of enduring life. He had gone so far, trying to leave Rosales and then Antipolo. He could not return to Rosales now, not anymore, for he could not face Emy, whom he had wronged, or look into the eyes of his son, who would grow up in a world he might not want and might never be able to change. But the boy would be different. He would take after his mother, who would dote on him, teach him, and imbue him with a courage as true as blood. That was it: the boy would be rooted in the land, unlike him who had severed his roots. And while he could hope for the boy and keep him always in his thoughts, Tony could not reach out to him, hold his hand, claim kinship with him. He had sinned not only against Emy but also against this son and, from the depths of him, the agony was wrenched out: *Emy, forgive me, forgive me.*

There was no warm hand to touch him and tell him everything was going to be all right. There was no Emy to loosen the deadening grip of what he had discovered—that it was she whom he really loved; it was Emy after all who was a part of him, who could have been his salvation if he had possessed but a fraction of her faith.

He was here in this desolate and meaningless geography, this Antipolo. Yes, this would be the end, when all his life he had tried to run away from it, repudiate it, this ugly street and its clinging smell of old ammonia and foul decay. And now he was back, inexorably, it seemed, because there was nowhere else he could turn, not Rosales and Emy, who had sent him away, not the university, which he had discarded, and not Newspaper Row, either, because there his frustration would rekindle itself into that wild, consuming fire that had already burned out men of more vigor and vision than he. Would he end up like Godo and Charlie, afraid of the slightest stirring of the wind, who had sublimated their fears and their insecurity with senseless bravado? No, none of these alternatives were for him.

The knowledge that he had been rejected implicitly by everyone, that there was really no place he could turn to now for one single, saving bit of peace, of belonging, shriveled all his pride. He had never felt as lonely as he felt now—not even in America, in that iron-cold winter, nothing of this terrible loneliness had ever touched him before, for it was too huge, too engulfing to be defined. Although, of course, it was not new, for this loneliness was actually the final growth of that greater loneliness called truth or living that had corroded him from the start without him actually being aware.

Perhaps it would help if he cried just a while. Then the ache would be eased. But only a sob broke in his throat. No tears came to his eyes, and the tightening vise upon his chest seemed to choke all blood and breath.

He turned to the alley that ended in the railroad tracks, and from the distance he heard the unmistakable whistle of the train— the Bicol Express, perhaps—echoing in the early dawn.

NOW THE VISION was clear and reassuring, as if he had vaulted the last terrifying abyss of doubt. It was not so much really what Carmen had done that tortured his mind; he could forgive her easily, for he was, after all, broad-minded and capable of taking a less personal attitude to her treachery—did he not believe in the *ulog* and in the primordial faithlessness of man's urges? Perhaps they could still make something out of their marriage and he could still live with her and share with her the beneficence of the Villas, making believe that this was what he wanted, this surfeit of ease.

But it was not as simple as that; it was not so much what she did that was the gentle nudge, the flimsy straw, the last turn of the screw—it was what she had told him, what was behind the act, inconsequential in its implication but too damning, too grievous in magnitude and meaning to be ignored; the act had peeled off the last skein that had shielded him from the truth.

What he would do now was not for Carmen, that would be granting her too much value. It would be for himself more than anyone. It would be the only act by which he could illustrate to himself his own brand of courage. He was, after all, his father's son.

He brought to mind the grandfather he had never seen, the acolyte who served God and had written in Latin of ambition and humility. And he wondered how that brave and illustrious forefather had died, if in that last moment of lucidity and conscience he had believed, had no cankering doubts, as Tony now doubted—not only the wisdom but the very existence of a just and powerful God who rewarded virtue and goodness so that these might be perpetuated and spread like blessings upon the face of a land that was damned. You kill Him who doubt Him. The thought came briefly, but in this hour, surrounded by poverty's bleak conquest, by need's sorriest shapes, he could feel no piety, not the slightest twinge of regret for what he must do. It was no sin. It was no sin, and if there was sin, it was not his but those of his fellow men who had shaped him, who had molded him so that in the end he had no choice but to succumb to the illusions of his own righteousness when he was neither right nor beyond cavil. He could still atone for all this, could still wipe out the huge and shameful blot, could be contrite and win virtue again, but he could not pray. My God, he repeated in anguish, I am doing no wrong; I cannot repent, I cannot pray!

There was no shred of doubt in his mind now. He had been deluded; for he was human after all, and the desires that were stirred in him were really as ancient as life itself. He was not the first to have succumbed to them. He accepted his humanity now and, therefore, recognized his capacity for sin. With a little more striving—and courage—he would have been redeemed not from God's hell but from the endless turmoil only conscience could make. There was honor in death, and if he was a traitor, or a weakling, he would not depart as one.

How many times had he conjured it and never realized that it was the only way, the only honorable thing for one like him to do? He had been weak, he knew this fully now, and the knowledge was seared upon his breast with all the pain and wisdom a child attains when, for the first time, he reaches out to a living flame. And this . . . this would be his only act of strength and, perhaps, faith. He would do it now or he would not be able to think of it seriously on the morrow, when the sun would be true and it would deceive him again as it had already deceived him—in Boston during that bleak winter when he subsisted on nothing but stale bread, and even in his hometown, in Pangasinan, when he thought he would never be able to go to college. It was too late to write a letter, and besides, a letter would do no good. It would even be useless. In the first place, he did not want to be melodramatic about what was inevitable, for he could not blame anyone for it, not even Carmen. It would perhaps be a bad joke that she would not dare discuss in public when she found out—as surely she would.

He looked at his watch, and the luminous dial shone in the

dark. It was almost five and the morning star still blazed like a solitaire among the lesser stars winking out from the black bowl that arched above.

Antonio Samson breathed deeply. It was strange that he could not detect the usual odor redolent of human decay, of rot and blackish mud in the canals along the tracks. The air that he sucked in seemed fresh and clean instead. It could be the night, he told himself, for the night bathed everything, and he could not see the wobbly houses and all their sorry shapes.

He stooped and touched a rail. The steel was cold and unfeeling. The sentiment was again a cliché, but the wheels of the train—like Fate—would be warm.

I'll be a mess, he thought, and shuddered, but only for an instant. "I'll be a mess," he repeated, this time aloud, and for the first time in his life he really did not care how it would appear or how it would feel when Death finally came.

CHORUS

Lawrence Bitfogel, specialist in agricultural economics, arrived in Manila in early December. He was being thrown into the godforsaken dump called Vientiane, in Laos, and Manila would be his last civilized stop before proceeding there. So, for the two weeks that he would be in the Philippine capital, he had arranged for himself a full schedule that would set his perspective in better alignment. For him the Philippines was now a more interesting object of study after he had stayed in South America for two years. He had seen the influence of Spanish civilization in the continent and the far-reaching impact of that civilization upon the traditional society of the Indian peasant. He wondered if the pattern of feudal exploitation and development such as that operating in South America had been transposed to the Philippines. This scholarly interest was, of course, secondary. What he wanted most was to see Antonio again and check on the "little lies" Tony had told him about the country. The bare-breasted damsels and the trial marriages in Mountain Province—how Tony Samson had spiced his stories!

It was early dawn when the Super-Constellation flew in and the lights of the city spread out below and sparkled like jewels spilled out of a basket. It was a full two weeks before Christmas, but the small airport was already decked with Christmas lanterns and multicolored lights, and from the jukebox of the restaurant across the customs zone, "Jingle Bells" blared forth in all its raucousness. Indeed, as Tony had told him, he would not feel homesick in Manila, because the city and the Filipinos had long been hopelessly Americanized. The airport, just as Tony had described, was ramshackle and dirty. It seemed flooded with that stale odor common to all government buildings—of cuspidors and disinfectants and tobacco—and the customs officials were extraofficious. He did not mind these things too much, for, as he said, he had taken a liking to the Philippines and to that thin, smart-alecky Filipino who had shared a room with him in Cambridge for four years.

The surprise he planned never materialized, for that same afternoon Larry learned of Tony's death.

One cannot live with a fellow for four years without feeling an attachment to him. And now he was too late even for the wake.

He arrived at the campus shortly before four, and for once in his travels, the new scenery did not catch his eye. Thinking about it afterward, all he recalled of that trip from the agency to the university was the greenery flitting by, the paper lanterns, the wooden houses, and the stretches of grass. He could not quite accept the fact of Tony's death, of all people. And he recalled one of Tony's jokes, adapted from the original Scottish tale, about half of the populace of an Ilocano town committing suicide when a funeral parlor operator, as an advertising gimmick, made it known that all funeral services for a week would be free.

He thought grimly about death and the possibility of its striking him, too quickly and without a by-your-leave. There was so much promise in Tony, so much virgin hope and dogged dedication. Young men like him—and Lawrence enthused once more over those intellectual jousts in Maple Street—young men like Antonio Samson should not die before they have proven themselves.

With this, Dean Lopez readily agreed, and when the aging professor learned that this inquisitive American had been a roommate of Antonio Samson, his manner softened. "The good die young," he said, rising from his swivel chair and offering the American a bottle of Coke, which the dean's secretary had brought in.

Larry took the bottle, said thanks, and was silent again.

"I had high hopes for him," Dean Lopez said. He moved to the window and looked out at the sunny campus. "You know, I would have seen to it that he got far in the academic world, but he had other ideas. Did you know that he quit the university and forfeited everything?"

The dean had wheeled around. Larry shook his head. "That's unusual. It was the last thing he would have done."

"I thought so, too," Dean Lopez said, "but you know how young people are. They have ideas—particularly those who have gone to the United States and returned with Ph.D.'s. They think they can change the world in one sweep. I'm not saying that Antonio Samson was immature. He was very close to my heart. Why, everyone knows that it was I who helped him get that scholarship."

"I know that," Larry said. "He told me so himself. He held you in very high esteem, sir. He wanted to work under you, to follow your direction especially in this project he was working on—the Ilocano migration. I gather that you are an Ilocano, too."

Dean Lopez smiled. "Well . . ." after a long pause, "he was impatient. In this country people must have patience."

"I always had the impression that he was patient," Larry said softly. "When he was working on his doctorate, particularly, I know the research problems that he encountered. Anyone without patience would have given up."

Dean Lopez nodded. After another awkward silence he resumed talking: "His doctoral dissertation—his study on the *ilustrados* and the Philippine Revolution—is already out. His wife had it published about two months ago. And I hear that his notes on the Ilocano migration will also come out soon."

Dean Lopez strode to the bookcase behind his desk and picked out a new, shiny volume. He handed the book to the young American.

Larry opened it, the words swam before his eyes, and in the acknowledgment he saw his name together with those of the other people Tony Samson had consulted. And in his mind's eye there loomed again the old room and Tony Samson bent over the walnut table, laboring in longhand, his frail figure bundled up in his woolens, while outside snow fell and glistened on the windowpane.

He remembered, too, their long discussions about vested groups, wars, and revolutions, about the aristocracy and the bourgeoisie always banding together to protect their business interests and collaborating with whoever the victors were when the bloodletting was over. It's a pattern that will always persist in whatever climate, in whatever country, Lawrence Bitfogel had said, and Tony Samson had answered that it was not always so, not in the Philippines, anyway, because the *ilustrados* were also revolutionists.

Larry found himself smiling. "Yes," he said softly, returning the book to Dean Lopez, "we had wonderful times together."

Then Larry asked how Antonio Samson died.

"You don't know?" Dean Lopez asked. He went back to his chair, shaking his head. "It's a sad story. They say it was an accident. It happened very early in the morning and they said that he was drunk. He had just left a party or something and had gone to visit his relatives in Antipolo. The train engineer said that he tried to stop . . ."

"God!" Larry said hoarsely.

Dean Lopez nodded. "Tony Samson's back was to the train. He was trying to cross the tracks. There's a double track in Antipolo, you know. It was an accident—all that drink. You see now how he had dissipated himself? It's this thing called civilization and his hurry to get to the top."

"And his wife?"

"You don't have to worry about her," Dean Lopez said with a smile. "That's the least of the things you should worry about. I've never seen her, but they say she is very pretty—a mestiza. And that's not all. You know who her father is? Manuel Villa. The Villa Building on the boulevard. Real estate, plywood, shipping, steel . . ."

Lawrence Bitfogel sighed. "So, Tony Samson didn't have it bad after all. If he had only lived . . ."

WHEN HE CALLED Don Manuel thirty minutes later, Larry was pleased to find the entrepreneur eager to see him. "Yes, Professor Bitfogel. Tony did talk about you. Look, you don't know how happy I am to know that someone close to Tony is in town. Are you doing anything tonight?"

Larry said no.

"Good!" the voice boomed. "Don't leave your hotel. Someone

will pick you up at seven. I would be very pleased to have you join us tonight for dinner. There are a few friends who are dropping in. One of my boys got elected barrio lieutenant of Pobres Park. And a friend is leaving for Rio and this is his *despedida,* too. You may be able to take the talk away from business. It's so depressing—" Larry noticed a sudden softness, almost sorrow, in the businessman's voice. Then the lilt returned, "Say you will come, won't you? And if you get bored I'll have you taken back to your hotel right away."

"I'd be very happy to come, sir," Larry said.

He took the warning about being bored to heart—one can never tell what will happen at a dinner with businessmen, who know nothing except how to make money. Afterward, thinking of that evening in the house of Manuel Villa and in the affluent appointments of Pobres Park, he knew that he would never be able to attend a gathering as enlightening and as transcendentally provoking as that again. He never regretted having attended the party in the sense that it had revealed to him the nature of the Philippines and the mighty odds against which people like Tony and well-meaning Americans like himself must pit themselves. It came to Larry with the clarity of lightning; under such onerous pressures, there was not much that Tony could have done.

It was Ben de Jesus and his wife who picked him up, and when he went down to the lobby, they were having martinis at the bar and already had a glass waiting for him. The lobby looked pleasant and cool. The *capiz* lamps were all lighted. But for the other Caucasians who were there in their charcoal-gray suits, Larry would have felt awkward in his navy blue suit. Ben was in barong Tagalog and his wife, a lumpy woman, wore a blue cotton satin frock that made her look formidable.

After Larry had started to sip his drink, Ben said, "You sure do look like an Ivy Leaguer—three-button suit, crew cut. You are not yet thirty, are you?"

"I am," Larry said. "I'm thirty-two."

"I can't fancy an Ivy League man in this neck of the woods," Ben continued. His wife, all aglow, punctuated her husband's small talk with appropriate giggles.

"I'm in government. Agricultural economics," Larry explained briefly.

"Well, I majored in farm management," Ben said expansively.

They had finished their drink. Ben stood up. He was tall and handsome, and his wife, who was light-skinned, could have been beautiful once. "Farm management—but that doesn't mean a thing in this bloody country," Ben continued as they stood below the hotel marquee. Their car, a chauffeur-driven Lincoln, drew up and they got in. "You see, our farms aren't producing as well as they should. And that's the reason why I have to be here in Manila, working for Don Manuel. I'm not complaining, mind you."

"You're so modest," his wife said. "Everyone knows that without you Don Manuel's real estate investments wouldn't pay." She turned to the American. "He helped develop Pobres Park—that's an exclusive suburb—and that's why he was elected barrio lieutenant of Pobres Park last Sunday."

"My ever-loyal wife," Ben said, patting his wife's chubby hand.

"Congratulations," Larry said mechanically. "I understand the party tonight is for you."

Dusk had shrouded the city completely, but when they slipped into the boulevard, the dazzling mercury lamps, the afterglow above the bay, the multicolored lights and star lanterns that adorned the shops, softened the night and momentarily dispelled all the dark thoughts that crowded Larry's mind. The air, too, had a freshness sharpened with the odor of asphalt.

As they drove on, Ben became more voluble. "There's a new dance step—the off beat—you should visit our nightclubs and learn it."

"I have only two weeks here," Larry hedged.

"Now, now, remember, all work and no play . . ."

They let it go at that and the talk glided on to less nettlesome subjects—the weather, Christmas, the local color. In a while, they were going up an incline to a street flanked by tall trees; then they entered the wide lawns of the Villas.

When they joined the company on the terrace, Larry knew at once that Don Manuel had already had a lot to drink, although all the guests had not yet arrived. His eyes were bleary, and in the cool light of the lanterns on the terrace, his face was red and there was a brashness in his manner as they shook hands. He seemed frail and anemic but his grip was firm, and it somehow relayed to Larry an initial sincerity. "I'm so glad you came, Professor Bitfogel. You know, I seldom meet Americans like you. Those I meet are usually carpet-baggers."

Larry was caught off-balance and he turned around to the assemblage for some cue, for some sign that would put him at ease, but the guests—about two dozen men and women who had gathered to bid this Senator Reyes good-bye and congratulate Barrio Lieutenant de Jesus—were all grinning. He was a guest—that was the thing to consider—and he sallied on bravely, Don Manuel's grip on his arm. "Thank you for the compliment, sir," he said dryly.

There were the hurried and mumbled introductions: Senator Reyes, looking important and pleased with the world; Alfred Dangmount, the American millionaire; a couple of Chinese; a Japanese who showed his teeth; and an assortment of bejeweled matrons and their husbands, their hair slicked with pomade, fingernails carefully manicured, some of their conversation in Spanish, which he understood. He was led to the main table and placed opposite Don Manuel's wife. The drinks and the canapes came and he took a gin and tonic. He looked around him again, but when the introductions were over, no one seemed to notice his presence anymore. Only Mrs. Villa seemed to be interested. She leaned over and asked, "How long will you be staying here, Professor?"

"Just two weeks, Mrs. Villa," he said politely. "I had intended to surprise Tony. We were roommates for four years, you know, and—"

Mrs. Villa seemed to have definite ideas about what kind of conversation she should have. She interrupted him rather rudely; he could sense that. "You should stay here longer," she said. "Two weeks isn't enough for you to know the hospitality of the country."

"Mama, there's no hospitality in this country," Don Manuel said, standing up and winking at his American guest. "Come, Professor, let's have a chat. It's too noisy here."

He went to Bitfogel and held the American's arm again. "Take your drink," the businessman said amiably.

They walked slowly across the grass under the multicolored lights. He did not know what to say except that he knew he must humor Don Manuel by reminiscing and making polite noises. "Please forgive my sentimentality," he said. "I don't want to impose on you, but Tony and I were together for four years. We did a lot of things together and I just can't quite believe that he is dead."

Don Manuel paused. He was shorter than the American and he peered at his guest with bloodshot eyes. He said without emotion, "He is dead and that is that. Oh, I'm sorry that he is dead. He died so young."

The garden was indeed wide, with many rows of bougainvillea and roses, carefully tended shrubs, and an expanse of well-trimmed grass. Beyond the grass was the pool, shining bluish and placid in the light.

"It's so nice to be able to talk to a stranger who is not involved in my life. You are that stranger, Professor," Don Manuel said. He glanced up at the sky. "You can be a shadow or a ghost who can only listen and not talk back—or bother me. You get what I'm driving at?"

"No, sir," he said uneasily.

"Don't act like an innocent. You talk to yourself once in a while, don't you?"

The American nodded.

"Well, I must tell you that I am a dummy—a rather expensive dummy. Do you have dummies in the States, too, Professor Bitfogel? I'm sure you have dummies there. Now, who am I dummying for?"

He took Larry by the arm and pivoted him to the edge of the pool. Then, continuing in the sinister manner of conspirators, Don Manuel droned on: "I know what I'm saying, Professor. Just remember this. Tonight I may be drunk, but tomorrow I'll be as sober as a judge. And tomorrow I'll leave my conscience behind me. You know who I'm a dummy for?"

"Please, sir, let's not spoil the party."

"Look, I'm not spoiling it, but you are. I have to tell this to you and you must listen. You know that Dangmount over there? He came to this country with nothing but two tin bars on his shoulders. That was way back in 1945—during the Liberation. Do you know how much he is worth now? Over thirty million. He's got his money in everything—shipping, agriculture, tobacco—in everything. And I am his associate. I give him a measure of respectability."

"I am not sure I want to hear this, sir. You may regret it later," Lawrence said, trying to move away, but Don Manuel's grip was firm. "Listen, you are an economist, aren't you? Like my son, Tony Samson, you have bright ideas, haven't you? Well, let me tell you that I am surrounded by a lot of bright fellows. Dangmount is only one of them. That Chinese over there, Johnny Lee, is in the Villa bandwagon, too. He smuggles dollars to Hong Kong regularly. He takes care of some of our dollar remittances. And that toothy Japanese, ah, you will enjoy Saito San. He takes care of barter and the Japanese end of the line. He helped put the steel mill up. But these goddam Japs, they always have you where they want you. . . ."

"You shouldn't be telling me these things." Lawrence Bitfogel spoke weakly.

Don Manuel laughed. "You'll not report me to the authorities, will you?"

Don Manuel turned and headed for the terrace. "And, yes," he said, "I almost forgot. When Senator Reyes leaves tomorrow for that conference in Rio, you know what else he is going to do? He will be taking out with him pesos and dollars. He is a bright messenger boy. He salts it away for us, but of course he always takes care to salt away a lot for himself, too. No one will bother to search him, of course. Inspect a senator? That's unthinkable . . ." Another quiet laugh.

BACK IN THE company of his friends, Don Manuel spoke aloud for all to hear: "You all look happy and contented. That's what I like about you." He was addressing no one in particular. Food was already being served. "You have no time to examine your consciences. You have only time for food, for liquor. I hope these will last forever."

Senator Reyes, hefty and dark at one end of the table, laughed aloud. "That's what I like about you, *Compadre*. You have such a wonderful sense of humor. No wonder you don't grow old."

"*Coño*—Satan is ageless," Don Manuel said.

Senator Reyes changed the subject. "*Compadre*, what's this I hear about Carmen selling her Thunderbird?"

"She did," Don Manuel said. "That was three months ago. She used the money to publish a book."

"Is she a writer after all?"

"You are an optimist," Don Manuel said. "It was not her book. It was her husband's."

"Did Rivera really get the car? That would make twenty-four in his stable."

"Twenty-four cars?" Larry asked.

"Yes. Rivera—you should meet him." The senator turned to the American. "He is a sugar planter. He collects cars just as he collects fighting cocks and women."

Larry shook his head in disbelief.

"That's true," Senator Reyes said a little sadly. "You can believe that. Why, I used to have eighteen cars myself, including a 1930 Rolls-Royce. That was before I got into politics. Now I have only twelve, half of them junk. If you wish," he winked at the American, "I can give you a spin in my latest toy. It's not much really, just a Karmann Ghia . . ."

"You should sell them all for scrap, *coño*," Don Manuel said. He took another glass.

Senator Reyes laughed. "You are really funny tonight."

Mrs. Villa laid a restraining hand on her husband's arm. "Don't Papa. That's the seventh. I have been counting. . . ."

"Again?"

"Please, Papa."

But Don Manuel raised the glass just the same.

"You are drinking like a fish now," Senator Reyes said.

"I must drown my conscience," Don Manuel placed the glass down. "Oh, it's all right with you, *chico*."* He thrust his chin at Senator Reyes. "You don't have to drink at all. You have no conscience."

Again Senator Reyes laughed. "Padre, that's the best quip from you tonight. But it's true. In politics you can't afford a conscience."

A servant hovered by and asked Larry if he wanted a second helping of dessert. "I have never tasted mangoes this sweet," the American said, nodding to the waiter.

Don Manuel did not let the nicety pass. "Imported from Cebu. Everything good we have is imported. And don't you know? Many American scholars and soldiers stay here on the pretext of studying the country or loving the people. Actually, they are here to marry into our wealthy families. And that's good, because we like foreigners—even if we use them as bulls to improve the native breed."

Larry felt warm under the collar as another gale of laughter went around the table. When it subsided, unable to find something to say, he leaned over to Mrs. Villa. "I would like to extend my condolences

---

* *Chico:* Brown, golf-ball-size tropical fruit; also, a term of endearment.

to Tony's wife, Mrs. Villa," he said softly. "Is there a way I may reach her?"

Mrs. Villa looked up from her ice cream, but she did not speak.

"I'd like very much to meet her. Tell her I knew Tony. Maybe that will take a load off her mind."

Mrs. Villa looked at her husband and all conversation stopped.

"Well," Don Manuel said suavely, grinning, "don't just sit there, all of you, and pretend to be ignorant. What are we so secretive about?" He turned to the American and smiled wanly. "There's really nothing to hide, Professor. But you see, my daughter, Mrs. Antonio Samson—how she likes using that name!—is at this moment indisposed. Hell, that's one way of saying it. She is in the hospital now with a psychiatrist, whatever you call him. She is high-strung and emotional. She is going crazy. Is she to blame for the death of her husband? She thinks it was suicide. I insist that it wasn't. Still, I know that boy and I have reason to think that it was so. And Carmen—my Carmen—do you know what she did? A month—one full month, thirty days—she did nothing but piece together the things that her husband had written and torn apart. A full month. And when it was ready she had the book published. She hadn't worked that hard before and with such dedication—never before. Why then should a young man commit suicide if his wife loved him so? God, people quarrel. Mama, how many times do we quarrel in a day?"

"Papa, please," Mrs. Villa placed another restraining hand on Don Manuel's arm.

"It's all right, Mama. Everyone is talking about us anyway."

"I'm very sorry, sir," Larry said, almost choking on the words.

"I don't know what made him do it. Was it an accident? I can't believe that one hundred percent. How am I to know? When a person dies, he takes with him all his secrets. He had freedom, that Tony. That's the most important thing, isn't it?"

"I don't know what you mean by freedom, sir," Larry said. He tried to smile, but he just could not make himself do it.

"Freedom," Don Manuel said, taking another glass of scotch and raising it to his lips, "is there more than one kind?"

He hated having to explain himself, but he was cornered. "Well, sir," he said cautiously, "the word takes on other meanings when spoken by other groups."

"Ah," Don Manuel sighed, "you are like Tony, too damned technical and precise. When a man can wander to great heights—that's what I call freedom. Tony called it mobility."

"Well, sir," Lawrence Bitfogel said calmly, "that is a pretty good definition. But freedom, the one I'm thinking of now, is in the mind more than anywhere else. It enables one to dream. And there's no ceiling to those dreams."

IT WAS almost midnight when the party broke up. They had talked of many things—agriculture, the national economy, Europe, and the Common Market. On the way home, Ben de Jesus was quite excited.

"Look," he said as they slid down the highway to Santa Mesa Boulevard, "I don't quite agree with you when you say that reform and development must start with the land. Why, you are voicing what some radicals and the Huks have been saying all along."

"I am sorry if I gave that impression," Larry said, trying to sound apologetic. He was weary and did not want to argue anymore. "That is just an opinion, really. It isn't dogma. After all, I don't know much about your agrarian conditions except what I have read and heard from people like Tony."

"That's the trouble," Ben said. "I wish you would study the situation more. I told you I majored in farm management. I have a farm in Nueva Ecija and I know just how to make it produce more. I'm starting to mechanize it now. That's the only way to make the farm productive. But the tenants, they know nothing about mechanization. They are impossible. It will take them centuries to learn the value of tractors and fertilizers. They are also thieves and they are ignorant—it's useless teaching them new things."

"I can't comment on that," Lawrence Bitfogel said. "But you must be sure of what you want the land for. And as for your tenants, if they don't own the land, don't expect them to make sacrifices. It never works, you know. Besides, the transition shouldn't create dislocations. It isn't easy to shift from agriculture to industry."

"Talk about dislocations," Ben said with a hint of impatience. "Do you know what the supposed intellectuals are trying to do? They are campaigning to have the tenant get the land at our expense—and they call it the Magsaysay Revolution. I call it robbery. The tenants don't know how to work the land. They are so damned

ignorant. What do tenants know about farming and efficient pro-
duction? They have never gone to school to learn these. I know all
these things."

Ben's anger petered out as they drove along the quiet streets.
After a while of leaden silence, Ben spoke again, this time in a lighter
vein. "Look, Dr. Bitfogel, why don't you drop in at the house?
There's a cafe-espresso set that I bought in Italy last year. I'd like you
to have some really good coffee."

Bitfogel wanted desperately to return to his room and shake off
the tedium and useless talk to which he had been exposed all
evening. "I don't want to impose on you. It's so late and—"

"It won't take long," Ben said, and before Larry could say anything else the landlord ordered the driver to proceed to Pobres Park.

THE COFFEE, as Ben had said, was strong and excellent. Sitting in
the couple's cozy living room, Larry examined everything in it—the
gray marble floor; the rich, upholstered sofas; the heavy blue drapes;
the oil portraits of Filipino patriarchs and landscapes, the finely paneled walls and, beyond the living room, the gleaming crystal and silver of the dining room, the appurtenances of Filipino upper-class
living. The whole house was air-conditioned, and the air was spiked
with the refreshing scent of cologne. He remembered his own home
in Cleveland, the simplicity of its furnishings, and again there rushed
to his mind in all its vividness the room he once shared with Tony—
its two iron beds, the porcelain washbowl, the sagging wooden cabinets . . .

"I must say, your good taste shows in the way you have furnished your house," he told Nena de Jesus. She had not talked much
and now, at the compliment, she started gushing. "It was a difficult
thing to do. You must understand my problem. It was difficult ordering the furniture. It's good that I was able to go with my husband
abroad again last year. Notice the drapes—they are from Marshall
Field's—and the furniture, well, I managed to gather odds and ends
together."

He felt like a heel asking about it, but he asked nevertheless,
"Did Tony and his wife have a home of their own?"

"No," Mrs. de Jesus said with keen interest now. "That's the trouble. They never lived away from his in-laws. You don't know how ter-

rible Mrs. Villa can get sometimes. Heavens, she is close to me, she adores me, but she can get on one's nerves."

Ben finished his cup and asked the sleepy maid standing by the door of the dining room to pour another cupful. He nodded to his wife's talk.

"I always say," Nena said firmly, "that young people should be able to experience a little suffering, that they should start from the bottom. When we were married, Ben and I . . . you know what happened? Father packed us off to that horrid farm, to an old house. Imagine, we had only five servants and an old Ford. I was angry at Father, but, of course, he always knows best. That's the root of it all. Carmen and Tony—they were pampered. They never knew what it was to start from the bottom or to live alone as we did."

He drained his cup, turned to Ben de Jesus, and finally asked the question that had tightened his stomach all evening: "Is it true that Tony committed suicide?"

Ben smiled broadly and he answered with the readiness and familiarity conviction engenders. "Carmen believes it's suicide," he said. "Her father, too. But me, I don't. It was an accident, what else could it be? Why, the fellow had absolutely no reason at all. What more can a man want? His luck—it couldn't happen to just any guy, not in a million years."

"I don't follow you."

"It's pretty obvious, isn't it?" Ben said impatiently. "Why should the man commit suicide? Everything was laid out for him—the future, all the money and the comforts he wanted. And most of all, you should have seen his wife then. She's slimmer now—this breakdown business is simply sapping her vitality. But she's a knockout, a real beauty. Tell him, Nena."

Mrs. De Jesus smiled. "She had a wonderful figure. She's thin now, but she's still lovely. Why, I think she is one of the loveliest girls in the country. I never could understand how she fell for Tony Samson, his being Ilocano and all that."

He did not want the couple to accompany him to his hotel, but they insisted. There was nothing more they could talk about. Nena tried to point out some of the impressive houses in the Park, but they seemed shapeless and anonymous, and so were the names of the residents she rattled off, names she tried to impress upon him as important. To her prattle Bitfogel could only reply with polite, meaningless grunts. It was only much later that he understood why Ben had wanted very much to take him to Pobres Park. It was not only to show him the accoutrements of the De Jesus residence, but also to point out with an almost personal pride that this Park was the epitome of gracious living and could compare with the richest neighborhoods in the United States. In the two weeks that he was in the Philippines, he was to see the Park again in the daytime—its fire trees in bloom, the whitewashed fences and sprawling residences almost uniform in their ostentatious bigness, so uniform in fact that even after he had left the Philippines he could not recall what the houses in Pobres Park looked like, although he could readily bring to mind the poetry of the nipa huts and the shell-adorned windows of the frail wooden houses that lined the main streets of the small towns.

They were now driving out of the Park and were crossing an expanse of open country that separated it from the less affluent suburbs of the city, and it was on this highway, away from the cozy security of high fences and armed guards, that a rear tire of the de Jesus limousine blew out.

They got out of the car, shaken by the explosion, which had sounded ominously loud in the night, and Larry could sense the urgency in Ben's voice: "We cannot stay here at a time like this!" To the driver he said, "Hurry up. Do something!"

Larry looked at his luminous watch. It was already three o'clock and the sky above them arched immensely black and wonderful with its millions of stars. The air was sharp, and above the smell of the asphalt he could make out the familiar odor of grass and living earth. "I don't think you should worry," he said lightly. "If it's only a tire, I can help."

The driver had already opened the rear compartment of the car and was heaving the spare tire out. "Of all things," Nena could not hide her apprehension, "here on this road. Do you know, Dr. Bitfogel, that robberies have been committed here?"

"Well, you can always give the robbers what they want," Lawrence Bitfogel said lightly. "We can also walk back to the Park. It's so near. Or we can flag down a car. Do you think a car will stop?"

Ben de Jesus answered with a meaningless grumble and, with his wife, moved toward the narrow shoulder of the road. The driver fumbled in the dark, and when he could not see what he was doing, he would strike a match and the little flame would cast light on his shadowed, anonymous face and the apprehensive faces of Ben de Jesus and his wife.

In a while two bright headlights appeared and came streaking toward them. The vehicle screeched to a stop behind them. A babble of voices—young, high-pitched, and raucous—followed, and Larry soon recognized the vehicle as one of those converted jeeps that crowded the city streets. From it there poured out more than a dozen men.

It was around him, standing on the asphalt, that they crowded. "Whatsa trouble, Joe?" one of them asked.

"A flat tire," Larry said, trying to make out the faces before him. He was surprised to find that they were all youngsters. The jeep engine was running, its headlights on. Orientals always look younger than Occidentals, and he roughly placed their ages at eighteen and below. One carried a guitar and another a ukelele. All of them wore some sort of uniform—white shirts with frilled cuffs and dark pants that sank into what looked like cowboy boots.

"We can help, Joe," the fellow who held the guitar said. The guitarist gave orders to the rest of the boys, and the uniforms took the names of Rod, Clem, Roger, Sam, and what else. A flashlight materialized and Larry joined them, watching their young enthusiasm translated into swift, sure movements, into gawking at the car and its fine finish, while all the time, on the narrow shoulder of the road, Ben and his wife stood motionless and silent.

"I see that you are wearing a uniform," Larry said to no one in particular. All the bolts of the flat tire were already loosened and two of the boys were helping the driver to pull the tire off.

"Yes, Joe," the guitarist replied. "We are called the Gay Blades."

"What's that?" He did not understand.

One of the boys brought from the jeepney what looked like a bass fiddle. The only difference was that it had only one string and at the other end of the silly-looking contraption was an empty gasoline container—the rectangular kind that usually went in the rear of an old U.S. Army jeep as a reserve gas or water tank. On this container was painted in bold, unerring red, The Gay Blades.

"We do many things—play basketball, sing. We're the Gay Blades, Joe. You have something in the States like we have here, Joe?"

"My name's not Joe," Larry said, a bit annoyed.

"Sorry, Joe," the guitarist went on. "We just came from a contest, you know. Good luck for us. We won second prize. We will beat the Roving Troubadors, yet. Just watch us, Joe."

From the shadows, Ben de Jesus and his wife finally emerged and joined the group. The last bolt was being tightened and some of the boys—the one who carried the improvised bass fiddle and the one with the ukulele—went back to the jeepney.

Then the driver stood up. A look of triumph brightened his face and the faces of the youngsters who had helped him.

"Well, Joe," the guitarist said, moving toward Larry with an extended hand. Lawrence took the hand and shook it. "We better roll now."

It was only then that Ben spoke. "No, wait," he said. He went to the youth and thrust out a bill. "Here—here, take this."

They spoke in the vernacular and argued a bit and, from the drift and tone of the young men's voices, Larry knew that the payment was being refused. "It's Christmas—it's Christmas anyway," Ben was saying.

Some discussion had started in the jeep now and then they poured out—the bass fiddle and the ukuleles and a pair of bongo drums—and there in the open highway, under the stars, Larry heard the Gay Blades and the song they had adapted, the song they spiced with bongos, ukuleles, and the silly-looking bass fiddle—a medley of "White Christmas" and "Jingle Bells" and "Santa Claus Is Coming to Town"—and while the boys sang, two cars slowed down, then zoomed on, and in the glare of the headlights he saw them clearly, fully: the lean, young faces, the alert eyes, the shiny black boots and the blue pants, the immaculate white silk shirts. But most of all, he relished hearing them, the clear voices welded as one, and in the end, after the final flourish of instruments and voices, the guitarist stepped forward. And having received the money from Ben, he shook Larry's hand again.

"Merry Christmas," the Gay Blades said.

WHEN HE RETURNED to his room, Larry was amazed at himself, at how in the end he had managed to stand up to Ben de Jesus. He had never been quick to anger and he could not immediately trace the root of his vehemence, for he often prided himself on his self-control. His voice had trembled and, even now, there was the empty feeling that always sucked in his belly when he was angry. He wondered how Ben and his wife took his rudeness, particularly after they had invited him to their house and shown him their hospitality.

He did not feel sleepy, although it was almost daybreak, and an unusual freshness and clarity of mind suffused him instead. Above his anger, everything that he had heard and seen was lucid and well-defined. He decided to write down his impressions on this early dawn—a useful habit he had acquired since he started working for the agency in South America. After a few sentences, however, he gave up. The impressions were incisive, yes, but always he could hear, like some grating and endless commercial in the back of his mind, the blustery talk of Senator Reyes and Don Manuel and the cocksure assertions of Ben de Jesus.

He stood up and lingered before the window. He could not see what lay beyond the glass, for the light of the table lamp diffused all images in the room. He turned the lamp off and the images before him jumped out—the lights of the ships that sat in the bay, the acacia trees brooding over the boulevard, the glistening mercury lamps, and the star lanterns of the shops and eateries. It suddenly seemed strange that he was here, alone in this distant, tropical land now undergoing the turmoil of change. How will it end? Lawrence Bitfogel wanted to divine the answer, and what immediately formed in his mind was unpleasant. But the big men he had met tonight were not representative of the race, for there were also other people to consider—the Gay Blades, for instance—and there was the pervasive malleability of the race itself that could always absorb a shock or be relied upon in a moment of need. Yes, the Villas and the Reyeses were not representative, but unless they were changed, and made impotent, weren't they the people who controlled the country? Wealth dictates government, and in this fair Oriental land, wealth resided in a few hands, in the hands of people like Manuel Villa and Ben de Jesus.

And where were the young people like Antonio Samson, who had gone to the United States and to its fountainhead of wisdom if not of courage? They were destroyed because they were bribed. And because they were destroyed, the country and the beneficent change they would have brought were lost. The future that once seemed evocative and real when it was but an academic subject to be tossed around in a crowded room on Maple Street had been aborted in the dank bowels of the earth. Knowing the dark immensity of this fact, Larry felt all joy leave him. A tautness clutched at his heart, and in the quiet of this room he could hear his own grief welling up. He thought of Tony, fought back the tears that scalded his eyes, and when they stopped, when his hands were no longer shaking, he had one consolation left: he had told Ben de Jesus just what he thought.

He could not quite understand why the young businessman had been needlessly riled by the Gay Blades after they had helped change the tire. When they arrived at the hotel, Ben had checked the car's hubcaps. As for the youngsters with those outlandish uniforms, he had dismissed them: "Juvenile delinquents, that's what they are. They would have robbed us, too, of more than just the hubcaps if they had a chance. See what's happening to our young people? They go about in the craziest costumes and they have lost all sense of respect."

"I'm glad they came along," Lawrence Bitfogel had said.

Now that he thought about the Gay Blades some more, and of their singing on the road just outside Pobres Park, he marveled at their capacity to improvise. The bass fiddle, for instance, and that jeepney they rode in, that omnipresent carrier in the narrow streets of Manila, gaudily painted, driven by impious individualists, rakishly modern with chrome and the most atrocious-looking fins—where else could one find something like it but in a country where ingenuity thrives and where the young people are capable of almost anything?

But de Jesus had chosen not to look at it that way, and he had snorted instead. "They are thieves, and they will kill you if you don't give them what they want."

It was then that Lawrence Bitfogel could not hold back the anger coiled within him, and when it sprang, it was clear and loud: "Damn you! Those kids are not thieves. The robbers in this country, the real murderers, are people like you. All of you—you conspired, you killed Antonio Samson. Why, the poor guy didn't have a chance! You had snuffed out his life before he could fling himself on the tracks!"

He had left them speechless in the driveway, in the shadow of the acacias that fronted the hotel, and he did not even close the door of the car. He had raced up to his room and, alone at last, he had cried—something he had not done in years. Now, when was it that he had cried last? Was it when his father died? In a way he was glad that he had spoken his mind when the need for it finally came. This thought, though it all seemed so futile afterward, brought back to him that sense of peace that had eluded him all through the frantic evening. And he knew that if Tony Samson were aware of this, if Tony had seen him and heard him speak out loud, that dear old friend would have applauded.

—*Marquina, Vizcaya*
June 1, 1960

Mass

**To the memory of Eman Lacaba
and the youth who sacrificed for Filipinas,
and for
Alejo and Irwin Nicanor**

They lied to us in their newspapers, in the books they
wrote for us to memorize in school, in their honeyed
speeches when they courted our votes. They lied to us because they did not want us to rise from the dungheap to
confront them. We know the truth now; we have finally
emptied our minds of their lies, discovered their corruption and our weaknesses as well. But this truth as per-
ceived by us is not enough. Truth is, above all, justice.
With determination then, and cunning and violence, we
must destroy them for only after doing so will we really
be free. . . .

—JOSÉ SAMSON, *Memo to Youth*

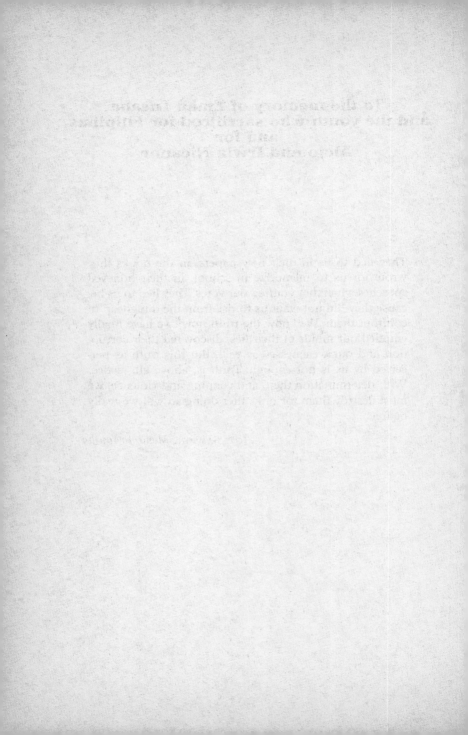

Let Water Burn

MY NAME IS SAMSON. I have long hair, but there is nothing symbolic or biblical about it; most people my age just have it as a matter of inclination, and nobody really cares. My long hair is a form of self-expression, of a desire to conform, to be with *them*. It is a measure of my indifference to remarks, even to Father Jess's, to which I had countered that Christ had long hair and if God had intended us not to have it, He would not have given the likes of me a shaggy mane. I could let it grow down to my shoulders so I could tie it in a knot and then shave most of it off, leaving just a lock, a pigtail, such as Chinese gentlemen did generations ago. And look at the Chinese now, at Chairman Mao, whom so many of us revere—but it would perhaps only set me off as a freak, and that is not what I want, for I desire to be anonymous, to be simply the me nobody knows, for this me, this José Samson, a figure of no-good plastic that should be burned or buried under tons of scum. But plastic seems to survive all sorts of punishment. Please, I have self-respect and I know my sterling potential and what I am worth (which isn't much), but this is how I was, this is what I am, how Mother knows me, and cutting my hair would not erase my stigma, my shame, or dim the glaring blunders of my past.

My name is Samson, and I have always known I was different no matter how often Mother had repeated to me, shrieked at me, or told me in soothing and dulcet words that I have an honorable name. But José Samson, Pepe, Pepito, Joe Samson is simply, honestly, irrevocably, and perhaps resolutely a bastard. It is not difficult to bear this indelible yet invisible tattoo, but not an Igorot facial emblem or a deep, keloid surgical scar can erase—thank God (do I utter His name in vain?)—the origins that have not been wrought on my face, nor deformed my physical being. Yet this is me, unerring in the devastation of the inner self.

Sometimes, I wish I were never born.

Still, I like being here, transfixed on this plain, this vast limbo without rim called living. I like being here, feeling the wind and the sun upon my skin, the fullness of my stomach, and the electric surge of an orgasm—now that I know it.

The only times I was really depressed was when I filled out those awful forms which demanded that I name my father and I would put "deceased." As far as I was concerned he died long ago because I never knew about him then, although Mother—and she is an honorable woman—loves him still, his memory. Auntie Bettina, too— she worships him though she never told me who he was no matter what wiles I used. The way they had quarreled, Mother always telling her to shut up for my sake. I knew Auntie Bettina had known him well, that something in the dark shriveled past went awry. No, as Auntie had hinted, it was not Mother's fault, nor anyone else's. It was in the stars, written with precision and clarity, infallible and inescapable, this, my damnation: to be in Cabugawan forever, a destiny that would hound me because a crime had been committed not by my mother and her sister but by my father. I need no proof of this, for I am here, wearied and rotting with self-pity and misshapen under a burden too heavy to bear.

Yet I am Sagittarius, and I am supposedly easygoing and frivolous. The planets cannot chain me to any spot for I am fated to strike out, but to where? Is Tondo any better? Here, where for a year I have lived and known this warren of tin shacks and fouled air as I knew Cabugawan, too? But I am no bastard here; no shadow hounds me, for I am Pepe the scholar, the loyal comrade who will rise to any challenge, scour faraway places, and if I choose to be a priest, I would certainly be archbishop, or if I veer the other way, I would be the czar of crime of the barrio, mightier than Roger will ever be. After all, I organized the Brotherhood here, extracted the mindless ferocity from the gang and gave it a purpose other than thievery and drinking bouts. With this Brotherhood, I showed them how they could extort gin money, contributions for the fiesta from flinty politicians in the name of charity, civic pride, and all those shibboleths that plastic nationalists swear by.

My career as a politician is assured if I so decide to become one, that is what Father Jess had said, shaking his ponderous head at the prospect. But I will never be a politician. Though interested in people, I detest being friendly to those I feel no vibes with, not because I am not hypocritical, which I easily can be, but because it takes so much effort, so much violence to one's self to attempt friendliness where there is nothing but indifference or contempt. Sagittarius—I am friendly—this is my nature; I am open to anything. I have a mind like a sponge that absorbs oil, water, muck, and dirt, a cast-iron stomach; I eat anything. They also say I am an achiever, that I can do what I set my mind to; in the two years I have been in Manila, what wonders have I done to my mind, to my body, to me? Two years— how many light years is it to the nearest galaxy, and even if we got there, in the end, will the trip be worth it? How long did it take the pterodactyl to disappear from the swamp, for the diamond to be? A baby feeds on its mother's womb for nine months and is strangled slowly after birth because it does not have milk or proteins. Does it make any difference if it dies in nine months or before the age of nine? I have long known that time is an enemy rather than a friend, a deceiver, because it lulls us into thinking it can solve everything and, therefore, nothing. So it has been two years here in Manila, and what can I show for those years? Calloused knuckles of a novice karatista, the muddled brain of an aspiring politician?

If I deprecate myself too much, then this is also my nature, for I really cannot understand myself sometimes. For instance, why was I glad to leave Cabugawan where I was born, where I knew people and where people had been good to me? I don't know why I had been unkind to Auntie Bettina and to Mother most of all, for it had never been my intention to hurt them, but that was what I did when I left.

• • •

HOME. But where is home to this free mind, to this heart that throbs and expands beyond its prison of flesh? I could very well forget this home, this blob of black upon the green side of the earth; here, where dreams are slaughtered, and having buried them, I could strike out to other reaches and lift myself away from this Cabugawan, this enclave to which I was doomed as were those before me—those stunted people from the North who first came to this village and are now but memories, their presence ever with us when we talk before our meager meals, when we unfold the buri mats and prepare for the night. They hover around us, their remembered images blurred by years—uncles and aunts and grandfathers and great-grandfathers, their names, their lineage, their ghosts drifting up the grass roof with the soot and smoke of the kerosene lamp, and out into the night. Who are they but names of old men who fought with bolos, whose blood washed this land and whose bones are now embedded in the soil, their hatreds forgotten and unresolved, their ambitions unresurrected by those they left behind, certainly not by me, least of all, who could fancy an armalite spraying the sky not in anger but in wonderment that I could ever possess a two-thousand-peso toy and, with it, perhaps rob some bank so that once and for all I would finally be away from this blob of black, this home. . . .

CABUGAWAN is a village not really far from town, so I cannot say I am a farm boy, for I did spend a lot of my time in town, in the marketplace and around the movie house. Follow the dirt road from the main street, head south, cross a wooden bridge, and you are in Cabugawan, a huddle of thatch-roofed houses, though a few are roofed with galvanized iron now, for some of our neighbors have pensions from the government and a few families have relatives on the West Coast. Mother told me once that all who lived here were tenant farmers, and the bright ones were those who left.

The village street is just wide enough for bull-carts and an occasional jeepney. During the rainy season it is churned into mud by carabaos plodding through. In some places, the village street is lined with *madre de cacao** trees—how beautiful they are when they are in

---

Madre de cacao: A shrub planted as fencing, with lovely cherrylike flowers during the dry season.

bloom. On both sides are our homes, mostly walled with buri palm leaves, surrounded by fences of split bamboo that rot and fall apart. The yards are swept clean. Fruit trees—tamarind, papaya, pomelo, *caimito**—surround the houses.

I know all the houses and their interiors—the cheap wooden furniture, the low eating tables, the kitchens sooty with years, the calendar frames and covers of *Bannawag* pasted on the walls, a cracked mirror, yellowed photographs of weddings and funerals, and on one side, the crude wooden chests where starched clothes and trinkets are stored. The village road dips down an arbor of bamboo, green and cool in the sunlight, and beyond it, the open fields. I have wandered here, swam in the irrigation ditches, gathered snails, and helped in the rice harvest.

It is difficult to explain my restlessness. I have not been hungry, as some of our neighbors had been during the planting season when they ate only twice a day. Thank God, Mother had good customers who paid her for her sewing, and Auntie Bettina is a schoolteacher. I cannot take pride in being Ilocano; I am not industrious, frugal, or serious, but I do have this desire to rush into the unknown, and I did that through books passed down to me by Mother and Auntie Bettina. I have meandered into the recesses of the imagination, wondered how it was when they first came to Rosales—those ancestors who had named the villages after the towns they came from. But I am not eager to know about them or why they came, by what means and with what infernal motivations. Perhaps it is just as well that I was born in Pangasinan, where, somehow, the Ilocano mystique has been diluted and where there is little affinity with the Ilocos, no real ties with the venerable towns that our forefathers had left; perhaps it was best that I was thrown into this cauldron called Tondo, for here, though we were still Warays, Maykenis, and etceteras, the distinctions have been muted and we are what we are, and the great equalizer is the fact that we all live here, and we live here because we cannot live in Santa Cruz or Quezon City or Makati. Still, there was no denying it, the Iglesia ni Kristo had more followers than Father Jess's Church.

As for home, I see Cabugawan as the end, a monotonous prison where people grow old yet remain the same. When the time finally

---

* *Caimito:* Star apple.

came for me to leave, I could not face Mother. So what if I did steal at school, from Auntie, from her? I just could not help myself. The last time Mother whipped me was when I was in grade six; it was also the year I flunked again. She did not have change for the five pesos of Mrs. Sison, one of her regular customers, so when she got home, she gave me a peso to return to Mrs. Sison. I never had money; I did go to town, but not to the house of Mrs. Sison. I went straight to the *panciteria* and ordered a peso's worth of noodles. I would not have been found out, but Mrs. Sison ordered another dress in a week's time, and when Mother came home, I knew at once that she knew. How could I tell her I spent the money on noodles? I told her I lost it—not a likely excuse. She grabbed her measuring stick and lashed at me. The pain in my thigh was sharp, stinging; she was about to swing again when she paused, the bamboo stick in midair, then crumpled to the floor, gasping. I went to her, frightened. "Mother! Mother!" but if she heard, she did not turn to me; her hand clutched at her chest, and after a while she got up and sat on the stool. Her face was livid and her breathing came slowly. When she spoke again, her voice trembled, almost inaudible: "Pepe," she said, "what have I done wrong? I have raised you as well as I could."

But there was only one thing in my mind: she was ill and I had made it worse by making her angry. And since then, every time she was hard of breath, I would worry that it was my doing. I am a bastard born to do wrong and could not help myself.

When I finally left, it was without recriminations. Mother had always wanted me to go and had prepared for it for so many years. She had set her mind on my going to college, perhaps to compensate for never having finished her degree. She had to stop in her second year, the year I was born.

You will be somebody, she used to say. And even after I failed thrice in grade school, she did not lose faith.

I love Mother. I only resented her wanting me catapulted to the stars when what I really wanted was just to be on solid, sordid ground, reading what I liked, eating *pancit*** and bread if I could have it every day—not vegetable stew with salted fish, rice fried without

---

* *Pancit:* Noodles.

lard, and coffee brewed from corn. I wanted more, but how could I tell her this when she worked so hard and yet made so little?

Auntie Bettina had cooked some rice cakes for me to take to Antipolo Street. All through the week, Mother had told me how to behave, to be obedient to Uncle Bert and Auntie Betty, to help in their house and do my own washing and ironing.

Unknown to Mother, Auntie and I had an argument. It was May, a month after my graduation from high school. Four years of it took me six years; and before that, nine years of grade school instead of six, so I was older and more mature than my classmates. It is not that I was dumb, as my Auntie used to say. Through it all, Mother had veiled her disappointment each time my grades were very low; her reproachful silence was enough. Auntie Bettina was right, of course. I did not try hard enough even to just pass. Arithmetic, for instance, bored me, and I was absent so many times my teachers had no alternative but to flunk me. In one particular year, Mother got to know of these absences and she followed me one afternoon to the creek where I had gone to swim. She caught me there and lashed at me with a strip of bamboo so hard, the welts were on my legs for several days. This and other forms of punishment did not deter me. In high school, it was geometry, physics, algebra, or Pilipino—that senile euphemism for Tagalog—in which I could orate but whose grammar I could never learn although there was nothing grammatically wrong with the way I spoke. I have, since then, come to believe that the real enemies of the development of the national language were the grammarians, and the sooner they were banished the better for Tagalog.

But while I loathed science and math, I loved literature and was happiest when absorbed in a novel. I saw an ever-widening world ennobled by the possibilities of eternity. I was visiting lands I would never actually see, also the bleakest and grimmest of lives, the convolutions of the libido and the subconscious. I trembled with the angst of the psychological storytellers and was chilled to the bone with spy and detective fiction. Indeed, I grew up rich with books, and they made our house different from all the houses in Cabugawan or all of Rosales even.

This interest in books was shared by Mother and my auntie. The library, one big glass-encased cabinet, was essentially their making.

Though the selection was predominantly fiction and the classics, there were also cheap paperbacks on the origins of man, history, and Asian philosophy. Ortega y Gasset and Marx were side by side with Confucius and Shakespeare, whom I did not like though I had read all of him. Most of the books were secondhand or hand-me-downs from Uncle Tony when he was in the United States. I scaled the Himalayas, dined at Maxim's, savored the new wines of Australia, safari'd in Africa; indeed, I had thrilled to the excursions of James Morris, V. S. Pritchett, Santha Rama Rau, and others. I also followed the latest shows on Broadway, the winners in international film festivals, delved deep into the human spirit with Hesse and Boll, and agreed completely with Negritude and the struggle for an African identity.

A few times each year, Auntie Bettina went to Manila, and she always returned with tattered paperbacks and copies of *Esquire, Look, The New Yorker, Encounter,* and *Harper's* or *Atlantic Monthly,* for she always forayed into the secondhand magazine and bookstands in Recto and Avenida. I kept them all in reading condition by taping or pasting them when they started falling apart.

But the life of books was plastic; it mesmerized me with the triumph of virtue, the goodness of man, the plenitude of rewards awaiting the kind and the honest when they ascend heaven, nirvana, or some such Shangri-la. Yet all around us, even in this village, it was the rapacious landlord and the omnipotent politician who amassed rewards, not in some unreachable netherland but here, where I, too, could see how far, far away from this planet was the world of the imagination where I had thrived.

This wretched geography to which I was shackled was made livable only in the mind, and to it I went all the time, so it was a full six years of high school instead of four—or three—if I tried. And I would not have passed in my senior year if Auntie Bettina had not talked with my teacher so he would not press charges against me.

I was a thief.

It started way back in grade school. I used to envy my classmates who, during recess, would go to the stores in front of the school and buy rice cakes, ice cream, or *halo-halo** while all I would have at times would be a cold ear of corn or boiled sweet potatoes, which Mother had me bring. During recess I'd steal back into the

---

* *Halo-halo:* Literally "to mix," usually sweets in crushed ice.

classroom and ransack the bags of my classmates and sometimes pil-
fer a few coins. Through all those years I was never caught—till I
was a high school senior. My teacher left his Parker pen on his table,
and as we were filing out I simply swiped it; he had asked us the following day if any of us had seen it. I did not want the pen for myself. I wanted to go to Dagupan early in the morning, have a good
meal, a movie, and come back in the evening, and I made the mistake of peddling it in the bus station to someone who knew my
teacher.

There was a confrontation in the house, Mother crying at the
dishonor I had brought her; Auntie Bettina asking why I did it. What
could I tell them?

My teacher was kind; he said he would not press charges after
Auntie Bettina had talked with him, that he would pass me, too, in
spite of my low grades, and he even had a few kind words—yes, I
was poor in many subjects, but was tops in literature and composi-
tion, and that if only I listened, was not absent most of the time, and
studied . . . studied . . . But what was there to study? At twenty-two
I felt I knew enough of the world, that Cabugawan was its asshole,
the repository of all its grief and agony, that I must flee it, even if
only for a day in Dagupan.

Dust was thick on the street. It had already rained but not
enough to bring a touch of green to the dying grass. Though it was
only mid-morning, with the heat it seemed as if it was already high
noon. I had stripped to my shorts, but it did not help. I wanted ice
cream or *halo-halo* or just iced water, but we did not have a refrigerator. Auntie was cleaning in the kitchen; Mother had gone to town
to deliver a dress. She supported me with her sewing; the sounds
that I grew up with were the snip of scissors and the whirring of the
infernal sewing machine late into the night.

I had read everything in the house, even Auntie's technical
teaching books, and I could not go to the library anymore, nor face
any of my teachers. I had even read the scrapbook on Tio Tony that
Mother kept under lock as if it were some heirloom. I had wondered
why, so I asked her once and it was then that her voice trembled and
she showed it to me—articles mostly, on nationalism, on the uses of
the past—and I sometimes thought about what Tio Tony had written
and concluded it was a waste of time. Although he had long been
dead, his memory lingered tenaciously. Of all the Samsons, he had

traveled farthest and reached the very top; I sometimes wished I were like him, if only for his travels, and when I told Mother this, she smiled wistfully as if I had made her happy.

It was *Don Quixote* that really fascinated me. I read it when I was in grade school. We were having difficult times; Mother was working very hard to help send Auntie Bettina to college. We could not afford electricity although the line had already reached our village and many of our neighbors had it. I was so fascinated by that crazy old man; the kerosene lamp I fashioned out of an old pop bottle was often empty so I used to walk to the far corner and there, under the streetlamp, with all the moths and mosquitoes about me, I would follow Don Quixote's meanderings.

I would often wander to Calanutan, too, follow the railroad tracks, wondering how long it would take if I followed them and walked to Manila, although the trains no longer came to Rosales.

In the mornings, pretending that I was going to school, I went to Carmen and watched the buses as they sped on to Manila. And when I was tired of walking, I would lie in the shade of trees and watch the clouds turn into boats and planes, palaces and faraway snow-capped mountains—all the compass points that I would someday explore.

It was all those books, their sweet poison, their untruths that beguiled me. But I could not go far. Although I was already twenty-two and earned a little polishing shoes and selling newspapers on holidays or gathering firewood and delivering it to regular customers in town, what I earned went to noodles and excursions to Dagupan.

On this particular morning I was just listless and saying again and again, "Life of a shrimp, life of a shrimp . . ."

Tia Bettina came into the living room, her printed dress quite wet as she had been washing the earthen pots. A few years back she had looked lovely, just like in her photographs, but she had become a teacher and had been assigned to a barrio in the next town. Though there were some suitors, she never paid them any attention, and now she was past forty, an old maid—but without the sour rancour of spinsters.

"What are you saying, Pepe?" she asked. "Why are you like this?"

"Why? Why? Because of this place! Everyone!"

"What wrong have I done?" she said, smiling, trying to humor me.

"You are contented," I said. "You are a teacher, you are Miss Samson, and you are happy."

"And you are young, talented. The world is before you. And next month you will go to college. You should be happy," she said.

She, too, had worked hard and saved to send me to college—no, not in Dagupan, in Manila. In another month I would leave to be the lawyer, doctor, or whatever they fancied me to be. I can understand Mother saving for my education, but Auntie Bettina need not have saved for me even out of gratitude to Mother. It seemed as if there was no meaning to all they did. I never wanted to be a lawyer or a doctor; what I really wanted was to go see a movie, devour a good meal, or tarry in Dagupan just looking at the shops, the new shoes and clothes and denims for men, and go to the dance hall, drink a little beer and hold the girls, then dinner, not the vegetable stew we had at home, but plenty of pork or fried chicken.

"Why do I have to go to college?" I asked.

"Because that is how it will be," Auntie Bettina said, still trying to humor me.

But I was not to be humored. "Why do you and Mother work so hard for me?" I asked pointedly. "I did not ask you to. I could be an ingrate. I am already a thief. You cannot be proud of me."

Auntie looked at me, more hurt than angry, then she spoke, making each word sink like stones in a quagmire, without trace or ripple in the dark, opaque surface of my thoughts: "You don't know many things because you are young. You don't know how she worked so that you can leave this place and not suffer."

"I don't want you to be disappointed," I said. "All I want is to be happy, to be . . ." I groped for words. I had never given thought to what I really wanted to be. But now, in this illuminating instant, it was laid lucidly before me, gleaming like a polished morning—the dream, the purpose. "I want to be happy so I must go away. I have known nothing here but sadness. I want to be myself," I said clearly. "I don't want to be told what I will never be. I don't want to have a single worry, and I don't care about this place. I want to leave and not come back."

She stared at me as if I were some stranger, and her voice was strained. "I don't want to hear this. Where will you go; how can you go? You have just finished high school; you don't know anything, you are not trained for anything."

"I have hands," I said defiantly, knowing I was only hurting her more. "I can sweep floors, shine shoes. And if the worst comes, I can steal."

Those thoughts, submerged for years, were being freed from their moorings.

Her countenance softened as she slumped on the chair before the sewing machine. Tears misted her eyes, rolled down her cheeks, but she made no effort to wipe them.

"Pepe," she said, "it is all wasted then, the years your mama worked for you. No, I will not talk about myself. And for what? Please think about it again. You can finish college if you only tried, if you stopped playing. There is no future here. You can see that in us. Only through education . . . if only you knew your father. . . ." She stopped, shocked at her own revelation, and wiped her tears quickly. But I did not prod her into telling me who my father was, for by then I no longer cared.

Destroy the Bridges

FIVE HUNDRED PESOS, that was what Auntie Bettina and Mother gave me—my tuition for the semester. I would still have enough left for the extras. Within the month, Auntie would come to Manila to follow up her promotion at the Department of Education and she would bring me more.

Mother embraced me before we went down the steps; then she started to cry. We walked to the bus station in the early morning, my stomach filled with fried rice, coffee, and salted fish; all my clothes—three knit shirts, three denim pants, and some underwear—in a shapeless canvas bag that belonged to Auntie Bettina.

As we crossed the creek, I looked down the wooden bridge at the sandy riverbed; it would be a long time before I would return here to swim. Some of our neighbors were up early, sweeping their yards. They asked where we were going and Mother said proudly that I was going to college, in Manila.

Before I boarded the bus, she reminded me, "My son, whatever course you take, do not forget Cabugawan. You can only leave it if you study hard."

Her printed dress was frayed at the hem and her slippers were soiled. Looking at her careworn face, her hands hardened with work, my chest tightened. I pressed her hand to my lips. I wanted to ask her for forgiveness I did not deserve, to embrace her again, but I was twenty-two and on this morning I was on the threshold of a new life and should not be sentimental. "Mother," I said, "thank you."

The bus crunched out of the dirt driveway. I looked back as we neared the highway. She still stood there, watching.

Auntie Bettina had taken me to Manila when I was thirteen—a two-day visit, all of which was now a haze. The land we passed was parched with sun, all through Central Luzon, and the towns were stirring with unrest. It was the dry season's beginning, and before the heat came and seared everything, the last lingering coolness of March brought with it, as if in some stubborn but futile protest, the burning red cascade of flowers from the fire trees.

The grass, ready to die, had started to brown. The smell of rot, of decay, the familiar odors of garlic and dried fish permeated the small restaurants in the towns. The heat had baked the mud, which the pounding of feet and the slashing of tires had ground into dust that now hovered over everything like morning mist; it was the dull glaze on rooftops, a pattern on the roadsides, the patina over trees. And with the dust came the heat that went deeper, through the skin and into the bowels, and festered there, to be released not at dusk, when the heat diminished, but with the magic of *cuatro cantos** or San Miguel, and when released turned to violence. Be wary of Filipinos who are drunk—I read once that our amiable ways are a veneer that, when peeled away, uncover the real frustrations, the dormant angers; in *vino veritas*.

I was both thirsty and famished when the bus rolled into its terminal at noon, noisy and awash with weary travelers from all over the north. The air around us was soggy with fumes and sweat. I had a quick lunch of *siopao* and noodles in the squalid restaurant within the terminal. Though I heard about how *provincianos* like myself were preyed upon by porters and taxi drivers, I was not apprehensive. As for pickpockets, I had my money, as instructed by Mother, pinned inside my shirt, and I would have to strip to take it out. I had only twenty pesos in my plastic wallet, no watch, no ring. It would be a foolish pickpocket who would consider me good picking.

---

*The beer bottle has four corners (*cuatro cantos*).

Auntie Bettina's instructions were clear. I boarded a bus for Quiapo; through the steaming, clogged streets, I kept wondering how I would be welcomed in Antipolo Street, how relatives to whom I had never been close would take in a vagabond.

MANILA—here I am at last, eager to wallow in your corrupt embrace and drink from your polluted veins. Manila, Queen City, Pearl of the Orient, Jaded Harlot, and cheap, plastic bauble—luminous with the good life, I am here to feast on your graces, admire your splendor, your longevity. Be kind as a whore is kind to a virgin man. Lead me through your dispirited streets, your dank and festering neighborhoods into the core of your warm, affectionate heart.

All of the city was warm and Quiapo was the cauldron, bubbling with people, the spillover from all over the country, spewed into Plaza Miranda like sewage from the innards beneath it. They are all here, the evacuees from the folds and recesses of the villages and the small towns, all drawn to Manila as flys are drawn to carrion.

I walked around Quiapo, crossed the burning asphalt, took in the acid breath of the city, and sought the shelter of the sidewalks filled with the swell of people, soot and grayness above me, the peeling, garish signs of stores, the pungent smell of cheap restaurants— the troughs where we would feed.

The length of Rizal Avenue was quite a walk. Although it was warm, my shirt was barely wet with sweat when I reached the Antipolo crossing. As Auntie Bettina said, the railroad tracks were the best guide, so I followed them.

The whole neighborhood smelled of urine, or refuse that had accumulated too long. On both sides were squatter homes, and the canals that lined the tracks were strangled with weeds, black with washings and the garbage of years.

The second railroad crossing—Isagani, then the house where Uncle Bert and Auntie Betty lived, a three-door apartment, reached through the street that narrowed into an alley flanked with weeds. The apartment had not been painted in years, the wooden sidings had started to fall apart and were reset by galvanized iron sheets. The fronts were festooned with hedges of *gumamela*. I remembered the apartment—it was in the middle and it bore Uncle Bert's brass sign: ATTORNEY-AT-LAW AND NOTARY PUBLIC. I knocked on the door.

No answer. It was Sunday and my relatives should be in. I rapped again, this time louder. Almost imperceptibly, the window at the right opened a little, and someone—a woman with a sharp, shrill voice—called out: "Who are you? What do you want?"

"Tia?"

"Who are you? What do you want?"

"I am Pepe, Emy's son, from Cabugawan."

"What Emy?"

I was puzzled. "She wrote to you and also told you a year ago that I would be coming."

"What Emy?"

"Your cousin, the sister of Bettina."

The window opened wider. I had not seen her in years and my memory held on to a woman past fifty with quiet but pinched features. The eyes, suspicious at first, finally glowed and she opened the door. "Yes, yes—Pepe, come in, *hijo*. Come in." And to someone upstairs, she called aloud: "Bert, your nephew is here.

"I had to be sure," she said, her voice had grown very warm. "I was in the kitchen cooking . . . we eat very late, you know, and besides, I cannot open the door at once. So many holdups, even here. What can they get from people like us? Me, a poor schoolteacher?"

"Mother wrote to you, Auntie," I said. "Last week . . ."

"Last week!" she laughed. "It will be another month before we get it."

My uncle waddled down in his long cotton shorts, fat and dark and balding, and he shook my hand firmly. He drew back and appraised me. "I hope you will like it here."

It was cramped, almost airless within. The red-tile floor had cracked in places, but it was polished to a sheen and the whole place smelled of wax and careful attention. The chairs were old narra and woven rattan, and at one end of the living room was a black-and-white television set with a crocheted cover. The center table was topped with glass and several weekly women's magazines. Potted begonias sat on pedestals in solemn corners and beyond the living room furniture, by the turn of the stairs, was the dining table. Their maid came in from the kitchen and looked me over briefly, then returned to her work, setting the noonday meal. She was dark, about my age, and pretty in a *provinciana* manner.

In a while we sat down to a lunch of fried milkfish and vegetable stew. My auntie and uncle lived by themselves; their sons had married and one had migrated to San Francisco.

Uncle Bert was talkative. "We have been expecting you to come and go to college here," he was saying between chunks of fried *bangus** and mouthfuls of rice. "And of course, the room upstairs has been vacant since the boys left. You should try to find work in the daytime and study at night like I did. So it took me eight years to finish law, but I finished it. So it is true that you can get lawyers for two pesos now, but it is always an honor to be called Attorney, to have passed the bar. You know, first time I tried, I made it! More than two thousand of us and only seven hundred passed. Ha! Seven hundred! There is always room for a good lawyer and maybe you should also take up law."

Tia Betty looked up from her cracked plastic plate. Her tired face was lined and her hair already had streaks of gray. "Do not impose your will on him," she said. "I am sure he has plans." Then to me, "Pepe, what course will it be?"

"Maybe I will just try liberal arts," I said meekly. "I don't know what I am good at—my mind still wavers. And besides, I don't really like going to school." I paused, knowing I should not have said that, but it was out, and they looked at me as if I were a freak, or worse, a heretic.

"I'm surprised," Uncle Bert said. "Your father . . ."

"My father?"

"Tony would have urged you, and Emy— I know she did. Did you know how hard your father studied so that he could go to the United States and be a success? There is nothing that hard work cannot accomplish, no matter how poor, no matter what your origins."

"My father?" I asked again.

They realized then that Mother had never told me, nor Auntie Bettina. Aunt Betty looked at her husband, then at me, and since it could not be hidden anymore, she said slowly: "Well, you are no longer a child and if Emy never told you—or Bettina—then we may just as well do it. There is nothing wrong in your knowing it! I am sad that it has to come from us, but Tony was my brother. I loved

* *Bangus:* milkfish.

him dearly and I should love you, too. And I do— That is, you are very welcome here, Pepe. You are our nephew . . . and we have no one in the house now."

"Yes, yes. Very welcome. Very welcome," Tio Bert repeated.

Tia continued. "It was so long ago, more than fifteen years, and I have forgotten that you are not supposed to know. I think Emy was ashamed, not because you were born . . ." she paused and did not quite know how to put it, "out of wedlock . . . but because she and Tony, first cousins, that is not supposed to be good."

"No, not now. Not now. It is done now," my uncle said.

"She is a very brave woman, your mother. You don't know how courageous she was," Auntie went on.

"Tell me about my father, Auntie," I said. I could not eat anymore, though the hike from Quiapo had made me hungry. "Why did Mother hide it from me? It was so . . . so unnecessary."

"Maybe she felt it was not time for you to know. That you were too young to understand."

"I am twenty-two," I said. "I am going to college." Tears were starting to scald my eyes, and my chest was heavy.

"I don't know everything," my aunt said, turning away. "Your father got married to a very rich woman. I heard she died afterward, insane—that is what I learned. Before your father died . . . on that very same early morning he told me about you. Just before he died." She stopped, looked at her plate, and toyed with her food.

"Your auntie visited Rosales afterward—after the funeral," Uncle said. "And your mother," he tried to smile, "where did she get the idea? Your father committing suicide? It was not an accident? But it was an accident! Betty?" he turned to her for confirmation, but Tia Betty did not speak.

"He was troubled, he was always thinking, forgetting things, forgetting where he was!" Uncle Bert insisted. "But the important thing . . . the important thing is that your father became successful. And we know you are talented—just like he was."

"No, Tio," I said. "My report card says I am not. I always failed."

"But what is a report card?" Tio could not be dissuaded.

"I am not interested in school," I said lamely. "I don't know what I want. But I know I do not want to stay in Cabugawan."

My auntie looked at me with pity. "You have to find a job and you cannot find a good one unless you are prepared, trained. This is so simple, I should not have to tell you."

"I will work," I said. "But I will not sweat trying to be somebody."

"Surely," Tio said, "you will want to eat well, dress well, live well. Surely, you would like to live in a place better than what you left."

Food, clothes—they are important, but not that important. Still, I must not antagonize my relatives, not on my first day in their house. "Yes, Tio," I said meekly. "I know that. I just don't know what I want to be."

Tio clapped his hands in delight. "So there. You see, Betty, Pepe will be a success. It is just that he still does not know what he wants. Give him a year, he will."

In a year. I turned the words over in my mind, but even then I was already thinking how I would be able to free myself from the clutches of the world's end, this street called Antipolo.

MONDAY, and I was left in the apartment to mark time. After a breakfast of fried rice, *tuyo,* and coffee with Tia Betty and her voluble husband, I went back to my room upstairs and lay on the old iron cot. How would I fit in this old house, in this dilapidated neighborhood, which, even in the hush-hush hours, was already noisy with the snort of jeepneys and the babble of housewives?

Downstairs, Lucy, the Bisayan *atsay* from Dumaguete, was singing softly the latest Nora Aunor song—*I once had a dear old mother who loved me tenderly—for when I was a baby, she took good care of me. . . .* My thoughts meandered to Cabugawan again. How would Mother be on this bleak June morning? At least her bastard son would not be around to annoy her, remind her of an ancient grief. I could see her now, the traces of sorrow in the somber eyes, and again, I was nagged by guilt, for here I was, with the money she had saved, to be what she wanted me to be. Tio Bert and Tia Betty, they, too, would be hounding me with fancy ideas about the lofty virtues of a college degree; only with it could I flee the deadening embrace of Cabugawan.

Just look at me, my uncle seemed to say; just look at me! He clerked for this Chinese merchant in Binondo and his morning ceremony was to polish the small brass sign beside our door: ALBERTO S. BULAN, and underneath, also in brass but in smaller letters, ATTORNEY-AT-LAW AND NOTARY PUBLIC. Having done that, sometimes with his handkerchief, sometimes with a paper napkin, he would zipper his cheap, plastic portfolio and then, puffing his chest, he would be on his way, waddling down the alley to Dimasalang for his jeepney. Moments later, Auntie Betty would leave by the same route for the elementary school in Sampaloc where she had been teaching for more than three decades—thirty years! Do people really work at the same dreary job for that long? The very thought was stupefying.

I was jolted from sleep when a train roared by, its horn blowing harshly, and the house shook like an empty crate. It was like an earthquake. I was so shaken I could not sleep anymore. But only that morning. I soon became accustomed to their roaring, clanging, shrieking—the diesel trolleys, the commuter trains, the Bicol Express, the Limited to Lucena, the baggage cars. Through their clangor I would sleep soundly on.

I walked around the neighborhood, taking in the narrow streets—Isagani, Sisa, Blumentritt—characters in Rizal's novels. The wooden houses were old and weather-lashed and their tin roofs were rusty. Along our street was the same crowdedness, the shacks of squatters farther down the railroad line, and everywhere big-bellied, hungry children and jobless men in rubber slippers idling in doorways.

Our immediate neighbors, my aunt said, were nice; most of them had lived in the area as long as they. An Ilocano clerk was to our right and the new tenant, though she had been there for almost two years, occupied the apartment to our left; I saw her once coming out of the house with her maid; she was pretty and about my age, with shapely legs and breasts that begged to be fondled. She was the mistress of a businessman, or police agent, and he often parked beyond the alley in his green Mercedes 220, the only evidence of affluence in our neighborhood. She was very quiet, very polite, and as Auntie said, she could have been anyone's ideal wife.

All through the haze of day and through the night, thoughts of Tio Tony, Antonio Samson, my father, badgered me, and though I tried to imagine how it would be to love him the way I loved Mother, I just could not. I remembered his visit long ago to Cabugawan, the way Mother would change the subject abruptly if his name came up in conversations. Mother had kept a scrapbook of his writings as if it were the most precious of documents. When she was not around Auntie Bettina sometimes talked about him in tones of the highest esteem. I resented how he never came to claim me, or tell me, and I resented, too, Auntie and Mother, not for what had happened but for their not telling me.

At supper I asked about him again and Auntie Betty said he wrote a book—it was there on the shelf—that I should read so that I would know what his thoughts were. She was proud of how he had gotten his Ph.D. through perseverance, which, damn it, they said I should also have, and yes, they would help all they could. But most of all, how well he had married into the Villas and how rich he would have been, how comfortable we would have all been, if he had only lived!

How did he die? I finally asked the question that had bothered me all through the tedious day.

"An accident, a most horrible accident," my aunt said.

Uncle Bert stood up, walked to the kitchen and pointed through the iron grills of the rear window that opened to the tracks. "There . . . there . . . that was where we picked him up. I mean, that was where we picked up the mangled pieces. It was early dawn—about five, or maybe four," he said quietly. "He perhaps did not know that the train was on this track . . ."

I joined him at the window. The rails, almost choked with weeds, were shiny with the last vestiges of day, the rock bed dirty with the garbage and dust of the dry season. I could imagine him walking there, and the train rushing at him. I could see him beyond human shape, his blood on the iron, the rocks and weeds. He must have felt trapped or rendered deaf; the trains always slowed down when they approached this bend of the tracks, for a scant two hundred meters away was not only a crossing but the station of Antipolo. Besides, the train's headlight could light up the house, my room, with the brightness of day. It was a senseless way to die.

I took his book from the shelf—*The Ilustrados*—but did not read it. I preferred literature. I felt strange handling my father's book, leafing through it as if it were a part of him inanimate in my hands. These were his thoughts, but I did not want to know them, to know him, for there was one thing I was sure of: he did not care; he forsook me and Mother. The damn train. I would look out onto the tracks every morning and imagine him there, how it was when he died, what troubled his mind, for he must have been in deep thought as Tio Bert had said, so deep he did not hear the train coming! There are no more steam engines, but I remember them from when I was a boy, spewing steam, chugging, big black monsters with bronze bells clanging. They are all diesel now, but it was not a diesel train that had killed him. Could he really have committed suicide? He had written a book; he had married well. It should be me—living off my relatives, on my mother's meager earnings. I could contemplate taking my own life, but that dastardly, foolish act, I couldn't even think about it.

I went to Diliman, convinced that I could not enroll because my grades were low. If I had to take the entrance exams, I would have to review. I did not relish that or the idea of studying there, for it became clear that I would come across people who knew my father, and meeting them, being subjected to their inquisition, would be too traumatic for me to bear. I had to make the motions, however, if only for my uncle and aunt, who would then tell Mother how it was that I was not admitted to the University of the Philippines. The real reason, however, was that I had spent my tuition money, and all that was left after two weeks of cavorting was one hundred fifty pesos, not enough for the entrance fee. It did not happen in a way that would have left me chastised and sad; I saw two movies a day, gorged myself with fried chicken, *siopao, mami,* and *pancit canton*— all the goodies I never had in Cabugawan.

We had enough to eat in Antipolo, the infernal vegetable stew with almost no meat in it, and I got easily tired of that. A TV set adorned the living room, but it was there for display and rarely did my uncle and aunt look at it; they were saving on electricity, for they always went around the house turning lights off.

With the little money I had left, and worried that Mother would know I was not enrolled, I went to Recto with just enough for a quarterly payment. What was one wrong initial? If it was not UP, it was a diploma mill. No degree in the world could improve me anyway.

"*Recto!*"—the jeepney drivers shout it, the name circumscribes and describes youth, the urban malady, and pollution; *bakya* supermarket at one end, which is Divisoria, and vision and corruption, or whatever you want to call it, at the other . . . Malacañang. It is this other end, the vision-corruption part, that would be familiar ground to me for four years.

Recto! Rectum of Manila! Here are the odors of the posterior, particularly when the sun is warm and a busted sewer is gushing yellowish froth, with flies as big as bottle caps on the garbage piles. But we are young and if we see them, we look away. It will all be swept clean when the revolution comes and this Recto . . . this will be the boulevard of great erudition; it will be the avenue of hope. It already is to thousands upon thousands like me, for it is here where I go to school. Recto has these diploma mills, about half a dozen of them, and at dusk the students pour out of the airless schoolrooms, clogging the street and the narrow, smelly sidewalks, their young voices mingling with the noxious bedlam of a thousand jeepneys. Coming out of one of the Kung Fu movies on any afternoon, the faces I see have a certain pallid gloss to them—a trick of sunlight maybe, or it may just be the kind of funereal patina that covers everyone, for in this mass of young people are the great unwashed hoping to be scrubbed clean, hoping to be someone other than their anonymous selves.

I MET Augusto Salcedo on my first day at school. Toto was as tall as I, with thick glasses that made him look like an underfed owl. He approached me in the corridor that morning and asked if the room beside me was for World Lit and it was, so he stayed and sat beside me when class started.

Our teacher, Professor Balitoc, had an M.A. in English literature from the University of California at Berkeley, and he never stopped reminding us of it. I liked him because he truly loved literature and could regale us with his own interpretations of the great novels he assigned to us.

Toto was taking liberal arts, too, but his course was heavy on science and math; World Literature was the only humanities subject he had that semester and it worried him, for he never liked works of the imagination. "Novels, they . . . they," he stammered a bit, "are so difficult to follow and I get lost in the long-winded dialogues."

"Read the comics," I said.

He smiled. "That is what I do."

I no longer had money to splurge on food, so I had to go home at noon to the vegetable stew my aunt had taught Lucy how to cook. The maid was alone most of the time, for my uncle and aunt worked the whole day. She had already finished cooking. She was dark and a little chubby, but her face was warm, friendly. She had finished high school and had wanted to study in Manila, but she did not have enough money. She had worked instead as a maid for one of Aunt Betty's fellow teachers, but the teacher no longer needed her so she passed Lucy off to my aunt who took her grudgingly although Aunt Betty often complained how difficult the housework was.

"You can eat now if you want to," Lucy said at the door. I was warm and perspiring, for though the rains had started and the brown weeds along the tracks had started greening, it was still humid.

The shower adjoined the kitchen and I started soaping myself with the laundry bar. I was a virgin. Though I knew all that should be done, the most that had happened was a brief interlude with Marie; she was in section B in my senior year and I often danced with her at our high school parties, holding her so tight her breasts were pressed close against my chest, and I could feel the smooth curve of her thighs. But there were few chances for us to be alone, and though we had some sort of understanding that we would continue the relationship when she got to college in Manila, her family could not raise the money for her tuition and board.

Anyway, I was soaping myself and had to do it again. It did not take long really and, though I enjoyed it, I looked forward to the time when it would be for real.

When I got out, Lucy was at the bathroom door, her face lighted up with mischief. I was very embarrassed when she asked in a bantering manner, "What have you been doing?"

She was slightly older than I, maybe twenty-five, and I asked angrily, "What do you do when you take a bath?"

"It depends," she said. "I didn't hear the shower for some time."

"You do not rub off the dirt or soap yourself?"

"It was not soaping or rubbing," she said, looking at me, the grin on her face telling me that she knew.

I fumbled and did not know what to say.

Then, confirmation, the laughter crinkling the corners of her mouth.

"You peeped!" and I went after her.

I did not want to hurt her, and I really was not angry, just embarrassed. I grabbed at her, but she was ready, and we were soon wrestling like two children from the kitchen on to the living room. I pinched her buttocks and she yelped aloud, then she grabbed my arm and bit it so hard, I cried at her to stop. When she let go, I held her and dragged her to the floor, then pinned her down, panting. She glared at me, her breasts heaving; I had her legs wide apart, my torso between them. Her arms were pinned down and she could not move except to try to bring her head up. Then, suddenly, I felt this stirring and, bending down but still holding her wrists so that she could not hit back, I kissed her breasts. Almost immediately her struggling ceased, and when I looked at her face, the fight was no longer there—instead, the unerring light of expectation, of wonder. Bending over, releasing her hand, I kissed her, thrust my tongue into her mouth.

I really did not care anymore if a sudden knock exploded on the door or if the windows were open, which they were not because they were always shut more as a matter of precaution against robbers than for privacy.

I thought conquest would be easy, for, by then, the compulsions that were surging in me could no longer be leashed. But Lucy started pushing me, wriggling, and was all arms and elbows and pointed knees. But these, more than anything, served only to heighten my resolve and convinced me afterward that there was a latent rapist in me. Her resistance, it turned out, was temporary; I do not know if it was just to show that she was no easy prey or that she wanted to test how determined I was. Or maybe she found out how physically strong and well beyond calming I was and that there was no further sense in lengthening the struggle.

My entry was gentle and smooth; through her gasps, she said: "Do not hurry . . . please. No one will be here . . . we have all the time."

She did a lot of housework, but her hands were not rough. They were soft, beautiful hands, exquisitely expert and strong; her breasts were firm and after a time she cautioned me, for, as she said, they began to hurt.

After we had lain for a delicious length of time on the tiles, which were cold, we went up to my room. We had become impervious to cold, sweetly unconscious of everything but the rhythm and warmth of our bodies. We took our time upstairs as she had suggested, savoring each other in the light of day, and then it was dusk, time for her to cook dinner. Exhausted, it was an act of will for us to part.

Everything was not in the script, everything was not as I had read in those paperbacks that passed through our hands in high school—explicit American guidebooks to that mysterious domain that is woman. I had thought that I would be clear-minded and would recall everything—the step-by-step preparation, the plateau, the peak, the cozy, cuddling talk and display of tenderness that would cap it all—but I had merely acted out the hasty and irrational beast. I did not forget, however, to ask her if she was happy and in reply she looked at me—those big, black eyes dreamy and half-closed—and nodded.

I HAD fulfilled a prophecy made when I was thirteen by an aging sacristan named Lakay Benito. He was the oldest acolyte in the church, a tenacious remnant of a bygone age, out of place in a church where they also played guitars and sang Ilocano and English hymns. He was, however, at his best in the novenas held in our houses when he responded in Latin, his rich, sonorous voice booming *Ora Pro Nobis*. All the way back, as far as memory could drag me, he had been to us not only an acolyte, whose knowledge of Latin opened secret vistas, omnipotent talismans beyond the comprehension of many even in Cabugawan, but was also a *brujo*, an *herbolario*,* and he looked it. A wisp of a beard dangled from his chin and his white hair framed a dark face pocked by two piercing eyes, a large black mouth, and an eggplant protruberance for a nose. His legs were spindly and bowed and he could not wear shoes except Japanese rubber sandals because his toes were splayed from walking barefoot in the muddy fields for too many years. He performed the ceremony of manhood for all the boys in the village when they reached puberty. That early January morning six of us gathered in his yard, shivering in the cold. He had built a bonfire of dry bamboo slats and coconut leaves and we had sat around it, waiting. He came down the stairs in his cotton *carzoncillo*+ and under

---

* *Brujo:* A sorcerer; *herbolario:* an herbalist or folk medicine man.

+ *Carzoncillo:* Men's shorts that are tied around the waist with a string. Usually made of cotton, often knee-length.

his arm, an old, soiled kit and a bundle of young guava leaves. Then he led us to the creek.

Strips of fog floated over the calm, still waters. He picked me to be the first, maybe because he liked me, I think, enough to teach me my first *oración*,* a charm to ward away malevolent dogs—an *oración* in Latin that I should not repeat to anyone, else it would lose its potency.

We all stripped on the bank of the creek. I squatted before him, surrounded by the other boys, my fear spiced with curiosity as I watched him unsheath the razor, slide back the foreskin with a bamboo stick and then, with one swift whack, cut it off. It hurt a little, no more than a bee sting, but then the blood started to ooze and would not stop. He did not appear worried, but my anxiety now turned to fright. He chewed the guava leaves, then spat them on the wound, mumbling words I could not understand. The blood formed a small puddle on the dry earth. After what seemed like an hour, the bleeding stopped and he looked at me, his craggy face lighted up. "You are a bleeder, and that is very good."

I went home to a special breakfast of fried eggs and adobo—a rarity in our house. Mother and Auntie Bettina were all smiles, but they never asked how it was. I had become a man.

Lakay Benito had wrapped the wound with a clean rag. I was not only a bleeder. In another day, the wound had swelled and frightened me again, I had to show it to him. "Big, overripe tomato," he chuckled, his eyes shining, "Pepe, a few more years and I predict you will make your women very happy."

---

* *Oración:* Prayer, usually in Latin (Sp.).

Paper Tiger

SO MUCH for the loss of my virginity.
At school my thoughts always meandered to the remembered feel of skin, silky motions, musky scents. I could hardly wait for the morning class to be over so I could hurry home and find out how efficient were the Masters and Johnson instructions, how true their thesis. But for all the grace of Lucy, I did not miss a day of school; a dogged sense of doing what was expected of me or perhaps a belated acceptance of duty kept me there.

One day, Toto, whom I had taken to be a serious student, asked if I wanted to join a student organization in the university, The Brotherhood. They were recruiting new members and I had seemed to him an excellent candidate.

"It is a very active organization," Toto said. "You will like it; we discuss contemporary history in our meetings. And you know so much."

I would be nice to Toto; after all, he occasionally invited me for a Coke and once or twice for *siopao* and coffee, although I had not been able to reciprocate. He was a scholar and also had a job as an acolyte for a priest in Tondo. He said he was an orphan and did not have to worry about saving money.

I had other ideas. I tried to hold off but I remembered his acts of kindness, the Coke, and the *siopao,* and he even gave me a paperback book that his priest boss gave him, a novel, *Man's Fate,* by André Malraux.

Gratitude! Why do I always have to be grateful? Why couldn't I do things because I liked to do them and not because I wanted to repay a favor? I came to Manila, to this university, not because I wanted to but because I did not want to displease Mother and Auntie Bettina. I tried to get home early, although there was no specific demand that I do so, because I wanted to be grateful to Tio Bert and Auntie Betty for the room and for the *dinengdeng.* And I did not try to impose myself on Lucy when my relatives were at home not because discretion demanded it but because I was grateful to her for being my first, grateful that she gave herself to me, and not because I was worried that she might lose her job if we were found out.

And here I was being grateful again to Toto, whose friendship I did not seek but who had nonetheless become my friend and was someone I could tell everything to, although I did not tell him about my father or Lucy.

We went to the small noodle restaurant at Recto and had *siopao espesyal,* and because Auntie Bettina had not arrived yet with my money, Toto paid again.

We walked from there to a cramped wooden apartment in Dapitan where the meeting was to be held. I had expected a big group, but there were only four of us. Five others straggled in. Perfunctory introductions were made as we came from several nearby schools— Far Eastern, Santo Tomas, PCC, National U, UM. We filled the small living room cluttered with newspapers, pamphlets, and that cheaply varnished furniture found in abundance in Misericordia. We had soft drinks without ice and an open can of chocolate cookies that was soon empty.

The meeting did not start till after two. I had become restless and told Toto that I wanted to leave, but then a man in his early thirties arrived and everyone stood up. Toto had told me a little about him, so here he was—the epitome of virtue, of intellect—a lean man with a mop of dry, uncombed hair in a cheap cotton shirt that was not properly ironed. He was a political science professor at my university and I recalled a poster in the corridor about his public lecture on nationalism and the oligarchy that was crammed to overflowing when it was held at the Student Hall. He looked undernourished and dried up, but there was this warm smile on his face as he greeted us and tried to have a word with everyone, and for Toto, a patronizing arm around the shoulder. He apologized for being late. The Brotherhood, he said, was now being put through an inquisition. The dean, he said, was particularly vexed with him, with his nonacademic activities, and had wanted him to resign. He was able to convince the dean otherwise, he said, by appealing to his sense of decency, his compassion, but at the same time, implying that the Brotherhood may do something drastic if this happened—a student strike, for instance. He must work quietly now, stay in the background, and henceforth, it was the students who must be in the forefront, doing the hard chores of organization, of demonstration, if the Brotherhood was to thrive.

I listened with amusement; the man was angling for sympathy. He started talking about the Brotherhood in tones almost sacramental. This is the answer to the problems of the young, of inequality, disunity, and corruption. If the nation had been exploited by imperialists, if the caciques were despoiling the land and making serfs of freemen, it is because the young have not banded together to spell out the future in their own terms. The Brotherhood would make war on the enemies of democracy, and the young could triumph in this war for the Brotherhood is theirs to use.

The harangue lasted for a while. I looked at the rapt faces around me and then I chanced a glance at Toto and was surprised to see him looking at me; I winked at him and he seemed ill at ease that I had caught him observing my reaction to the speech. I never liked speeches, whether by professional politicians or professors turned politicians. I had lived long enough in a village to know who exploits the little people—the landlord, yes, and the money-lenders, too. But it is the riffraff who really take advantage of their own kin. I had planted vegetables in the yard and when the eggplants were ready, who would come but our neighbors, asking for them when they could easily have planted their own.

HE was through and he looked around. I realized that we were a carefully selected group.

"Any questions?" he asked perfunctorily and was surprised

when I raised my hand. I was the only one to do so. I glanced at Toto, at his shock, as if I had just committed the worst indiscretion. But hell, I am not a robot that will go where it is pushed. The professor turned to me, his eyes expectant: "Yes, please."

I asked plainly, "What can we expect from the Brotherhood? Why should I give it loyalty? What do I get in return?"

I had caught him unaware and he fumbled for words. "Please clarify your question" he said. "Am I to understand that you expect benefits from such a membership? Is that what you want to ask?"

I nodded. "You see, sir," I said, "when a politician comes to our village and makes a pretty speech about corruption in government, about how he intends to change things when he gets elected, we know it's just words. But sometimes, particularly before the election, he gets our muddy road fixed. And of course, there is the five pesos he distributes to those who can vote."

They all laughed and even Professor Hortenso smiled. "I cannot promise you these things," he said. "As a matter of fact, you may not get anything from the Brotherhood. It is you who will give to it. As duty, perhaps, if you can look at it that way."

"You cannot ask the poor for sacrifices," I said. "We are already poor. What can we give? How do you measure the patriotism of the poor?"

The giggling had stopped and now everyone was listening.

His eyes turned upward, to the unpainted ceiling; his words were soft but clear, as if he had searched his conscience for them: "I ask," he said finally, his eyes roving around the room to each of us, "that you give faith, your presence, your little support—centavos, if they are needed—your muscle, your time, your numbers. When there is a demonstration, you should be there, leading because you are the leaders. When there are petitions, you should sign them. When there are errands, run them. What can the Brotherhood give you in return? I tell you: nothing, nothing but strength. Alone, you are nobody. The Brotherhood gives you numbers. Unity. And with the masses with whom you will be welded, for whom you will be working . . . you will be doing something for the future that is yours to shape in any way you like. It will not be for people like me; we are getting on in years. It will not be for your parents. It will be for you because you are young and the whole world is ahead of you. The Brotherhood will ask you to work till you sweat blood. And your reward is not here, now, but in the future—if you live that long." A long pause. "If you believe in yourselves then do not deny yourselves . . . this is all that I can say, and I am sorry," he turned to me, "that I cannot, myself, promise you something more substantial. But," he smiled, "you are always welcome at my house and there is always coffee and cookies."

"Thank you, sir," I said. I did not like speeches, but Professor Hortenso was honest. I clapped and the others followed.

We started to break up, and as we headed for the door Hortenso came to me, placed an arm on my shoulder. "I am glad you asked that question," he said. "It enabled me to reexamine my own premises." He was shaking his head, grinning. "I can get carried away by rhetoric, like most politicians. There's nothing like a good question to bring one back to earth." He then asked if I would join him for a cup of coffee.

Almost everyone had filed out into the street. Toto and I were the only ones left in the room. I could feel his nudge on my back.

"Yes, sir," I said. "Very much."

He disappeared into the kitchen, talked to someone there, and a woman emerged. "My wife," he said, and she smiled at us, a tiny woman in her early thirties, beauty in her full lips, thin straight nose, high cheekbones, and eyes that sparkled. She must have been listening to everything, for her eyes were on me. So this is where they really lived, this dingy apartment no better than my auntie's in Antipolo, and I wondered how much he made teaching and why he had time to serve us coffee. It must have been brewed over thrice for it was very weak. There was also a stained saucer with a few limp cookies, but the *siopao* still held. It was already four in the afternoon and Professor Hortenso was going to talk on. Toto obviously wanted to stay longer, but now my thoughts were straying to Lucy, who would be waiting and her welcome would be far better, more to my liking than this cup of stale coffee and soggy cookie.

Sheer patience and deference to Toto made me stay and listen to his prattle about the economic classes, the need for hothouse ideology and all that razzle-dazzle about the future of Filipino society. Though I had grown to like him for his forthrightness, for his hospitality, instinct told me I did not have to listen to him. I was from Cabugawan; he was not telling me anything I did not know—the exploitation, the squalid hypocrisies. And much as I appreciated his candor and honesty, the kind of activism he was proposing was not for me, it was for Toto, perhaps, quiet, introspective, his eyes always burning. I was concerned with more earthy matters, *mami espesyal* and Lucy, than in battering the bastion of Pobres Park or the high walls of Malacañang.

He finally came around to asking my name—the dreaded question that would fling me back to that harsh and brutal past I had tried to leave behind. A pain more ancient than memory, as once again: "Are you related to Antonio Samson?" He must have gleaned it from the membership form Toto had asked me to fill out. "Yes," I mumbled, expecting the next question. "I— He is an uncle, my mother's first cousin." Under my breath I cursed the lie I had to live. Toto regarded me as though I was as pure as virtue, glowing with kindness and honesty. While this turmoil raged within, Professor Hortenso went on equably: "I hope that you have read it—his classic on the *ilustrados*. What shall I call you? What do your friends call you?"

"Everyone calls me Pepe."

"Well, Pepe, there you are, your own uncle providing you many of the answers, perhaps the answers to all the questions you are asking. He explains why the revolution failed and he reminds us, and clearly, too, what mistakes to avoid. The most perceptive book on our history ever written, and it was written by your uncle. You should be proud, Pepe, the way I am proud that his nephew is now a member of the Brotherhood. He is dead and I was told it was a horrible accident. It is a shame, really, that he was only able to write one book when he could have written more. I am sure he must have manuscripts lying around. You must look into that and see if they can be brought out. He could have easily been the brains of the Second Revolution—its genuine ideologue. I have very little to contribute, really"—he sounded so humble—"except my little time and that is not enough." His eyes shone and I could not look at him straight for I was uneasy. I looked down instead at my battered shoes, at the doormat of shredded old tire that had gone awry, the rubber slippers there—probably his—the scuffed tile floor that was dirtied with the comings and goings of people. He enthused: "Antonio Samson had proven one thing—and you should know it and be proud of it: that with his background we know for sure leadership need not come from the social and economic elite, that it should spring from the masses."

In a sense he was justifying himself, but I really did not know much about him then, how he graduated from a splendid English university. I resented it, his implication that it was good to be poor, that the poor had superior virtues, qualities to be rhapsodized about *because* they were poor; there was nothing noble, nothing exalted about going hungry, about having to live in Cabugawan, and though I had not meant to be rude, I think that was how I sounded when I said, "He married a very wealthy girl. Perhaps that was what he was working for all the time."

The professor drew away; shock was splattered all over his face, and it stayed there for some time. Then, perhaps thinking I was just making light of a relative, he ignored my remark and went on: "There is nothing wrong with being wealthy—I hope you did not misunderstand. We all want to be comfortable, that is a common human aspiration. But precisely, it is not possible for as long as the ceiling to our aspirations is low. It is actually limited by our rich, by our oligarchy, and our government, which serves the upper classes but not the people."

No need for me to linger; his words bored me to my very bones and made me feel sorry for him, for he was sincere and he would die at the barricades together with Toto. I made another move to the door but Professor Hortenso held my arm. "Pepe, we need your help." I did not want to embarrass Toto, and for his sake—mustering all the light and sweetness I was capable of, although I was about to retch the putrid words of valor, of commitment—I said, "You can depend on me." He and his wife obviously believed me, for they both grabbed my arm and shook it so hard I thought they would wrench it off.

Yet I was sorry to leave them, their small, lightless apartment that probably flooded when the rains came; I was sorry that I was bored, that I had not been more attentive and was just thinking of myself, but who would do that for me? I was silent, walking with Toto on the sidewalk, avoiding the piles of garbage that had not been collected for days, remembering how he had asked me about my father and how I had lied again.

"Isn't he good?" Toto was gushing, keeping in step with me, for

I was really hurrying. We would both go to Quezon Boulevard, where he would take his ride for Quiapo, then Tondo, and I would catch the first jeepney there for Dimasalang. "He likes you. He is very sharp and he knows the bright ones, the ones who think and who care." He nudged me and I turned to him briefly and snorted, but he would not be bothered now by any snide remark I made.

"Yes," I said dully.

"Do you know," Toto spoke with wonder, "that he spends his own pay—the little he can afford—for the Brotherhood? I have known him for a long time—he and Father Jess are very good friends and each does his own thing. He is very dedicated."

"I can see that," I said glumly.

"You made a good impression," Toto hit me playfully on the arm. "I am sure you will be somebody in the Brotherhood."

"I always make a good impression," I said lightly.

"Let us go to Tondo. I want you to meet Father Jess, too."

"And impress him just as well? No, I have done enough impressing today."

But he missed the sarcasm, for he hit me lightly on the arm again. His ride came and I pushed him toward it lest he tarry. "Tomorrow," he called, but I did not look back; I had started to run toward the boulevard to catch my jeepney.

THE HOUSE was padlocked when I arrived; Lucy must have gone to market to buy vegetables for the abominable stew again. I sat on the hollow blocks lining the small greenery before the apartment and waited. Across the patch of grass, from the alley, the green Mercedes of the tenant next to us was parked and the apartment door was open. When he saw me, he gave one of those meaningless smiles that was supposed to be neighborly. We never really knew his kind of living except that he always wore brightly printed shirts, his hair slick and well-groomed, his fingernails manicured, and he sported a ring with a big sparkler. And on his hip always, if his shirt was tucked in, was the butt of a revolver. We had surmised that he must be a detective, but Uncle Bert said he must be a fixer at the Bureau of Customs or a customs broker, for he often saw him there on the several occasions my uncle followed up the papers of his Chinese boss. Obviously, neither his mistress nor her maid was in. She rarely came out of the apartment, except at night when the Mercedes was parked in the alley and he came to pick her up. She seemed to pass the hours watching television or reading the comics that a newsboy always slipped under her door.

Now he stood up, walked toward the door, and leaned on it. He was no taller than I, but he was well-built, tautly muscular, and had a bull neck that his long hair could not quite hide. He was in his early fifties but had the easygoing manner of a much younger person. "Well, you are locked out and I am locked in," he laughed. "We can talk together while waiting. No use being alone."

I did not rise from the hollow block I sat on. I was really in no mood to talk; I was eager for Lucy and nothing more.

"What college?" he glanced at my notebooks and the new pamphlet from Professor Hortenso.

I replied in the polite language.

He shook his head. "You should have gone to UP—or Ateneo, La Salle . . ."

His implication about my school's inferiority vexed me; in the short time that I was at Recto, I had grown to like my university, my crowd. "If I had the money, that is where I would have gone," I said, not looking at him. "How could anyone who lives in this alley afford those schools?"

He laughed lightly. "That is the problem with young people nowadays," he said. "You think only of difficulties. There are so many ways to make money. What I was going to say is that if you were studying there, I could even give you a job, perhaps with more than enough to pay for your tuition. After all, I feel that I already know you, your being a next-door neighbor. And more than that . . ." he shook his head and grinned, "You are really a *toro*."

I was surprised by what he had implied; we had talked about the *toro* once in school, although I had never seen one at work. He is the male performer in the sex shows that they stage in Pasay, in Caloocan, and in Ermita—for only ten pesos. I ignored his remark.

"Which is good," he continued. "You will have many chances with women and you will make a good salesman. I am really serious," he said, nudging my knee with his shoe for I was not looking at him.

"Think about it," he said as I turned. "If you can manage, you should transfer to La Salle or Ateneo next semester. I just had this idea, you know. I will pay for your tuition, but you can pay it back in a month—I assure you—and then you will be earning money. You look bright, you are good-looking—and most important, you are a *toro*!"

I stood up, irritated and not quite sure what he was really trying to say. Continuing in the polite language, I asked what a *toro* was. He smiled, took me by the arm, and drew me inside the apartment.

It was my first time inside. With the upholstered furniture in the living room, I realized immediately what a cozy, well-furnished apartment it was. The refrigerator, big, shiny, and new; the electric oven; the pictures on the wall. He took me up the flight to the two rooms upstairs, painted in cool blue, in one another set of chairs upholstered in blue velvet, a Sony color TV, a stereo set like the expensive ones displayed in Avenida, and then, to the other room, the massive, mahogany bed, a glass cabinet filled with his mistress's clothes and his suits and shirts, and on one side of the room, the air conditioner humming. How comfortable the whole place appeared compared to the drab appointments that were ours behind the wooden wall. Here then was what money can do even in Antipolo.

He shucked off his shoes and asked me to do the same, then he went up the bed and pointed to a portion of the wall just below the ceiling. He beckoned to me to look. A narrow crack in the panel showed clearly the floor of my room—just where Lucy and I had lain.

He went down the bed, chortling. "Mila discovered it," he said. "She has been comparing you with me. After all, I am a full thirty years older than you. I cannot do it twice anymore like I used to. Ah, when I was younger! Now, not even with vitamin E and KH3 and all that sort of thing—they aren't much help."

His words, every nuance, were mirror-clear. He was not telling me that he enjoyed watching, he was saying that he envied me, for his mistress was young and she must have desires he could no longer satisfy. We went down to the living room and he opened the refrigerator. It was stocked with food—enough to last a month, cheeses I had never seen, preserved meats, candies. He opened a bottle of San Miguel, but I never liked beer and told him so. He hastily opened a Coke, which I took, together with a cold leg of fried chicken. I was beginning to feel comfortable after my embarrassment when I had looked down the crack in the wall.

We went back to the door and its unchanging view of weeds and dilapidated houses. He asked me my name and when I told him, he said, "Pepe, do not *po-po** me. Just call me *kuya*† if you can't muster enough will to call me Nick."

"All right, *kuya.*"

"But don't ever tell my wife that I took you upstairs," he nudged me with his elbow and I almost dropped the glass. A burst of laughter, then he was all seriousness again. "You must really go to La Salle. I think it is easier for you to be a salesman there. And it is much easier getting them to buy, too. You can start in the next semester."

"What will I be selling?"

Another nudge and laughter. "You want to earn money, don't you? There are easy ways of making it if you know the right people, like Kuya Nick." He gave a flourish with his hand then thrust his chin toward the alley. The neighborhood kids were shouting at one another in their immemorial game of *patintero* and, beyond them, Lucy was coming but without her market basket.

He took my empty glass and closed the door, saying, "I will see you again."

One of those faultless June afternoons coming to an end. It began to get dark. When Lucy saw me, she smiled wanly as if to say she was sorry. "Where have you been?" I asked hotly. "I have been waiting here for hours."

She opened the door and we hurried in. There would be time before my aunt and uncle arrived and Lucy sensed the urgency, too. But the idea of being watched, now that I knew it, dampened my desire. Still, I wondered if I could perform knowing that someone was watching. I decided not to tell Lucy, but that I would try and put on a show that the mistress next door would not forget. Perhaps she might even end up wanting me and that would be something over Kuya Nick and his diamond ring, his manicured nails, and his Mercedes 250.

Lucy was explaining that she had gone to visit her sister—she did this once a week, no exact day—and she was sorry she had not told me.

I ignored her explanation as I put the latch on, then kissed her.

---

* *Po-po:* Tease.
† *Kuya:* Eldest brother.

Her mouth was wet and she kissed me with passion. Her arms around me were viselike and her hair smelled of sun and cigarette smoke. I wanted it right there, the door behind us, but she would not let me.

"No," she said. "It is much too late. I have to cook. I have to cook—" She quickly disengaged herself, but I followed her to the kitchen, my hands eagerly all over her, my lips on her nape. She stood still and let me do what I wanted, but when I turned her around, she kept saying, "Pepe, there is no time. Tomorrow, please, we have all the time tomorrow . . ."

It really had to be on the morrow, for in another instant there was a rap on the door. I kissed her again then went to open it. It was Tio Bert, arriving a bit earlier than usual.

I bade him good evening and he seemed surprised to see me. He switched on the light in the living room. I did not ask why, but he seemed to think it necessary to explain—"I finished early today"— then he rushed upstairs. I tried to tell him that I had to wait at the door, for Lucy had gone to visit her sister, and perhaps it was time for me to have a key but he mumbled, "Tomorrow, tomorrow, we will talk about it." But when he came down finally, shortly before my aunt arrived, and I repeated what I had said, he said perfunctorily that he would have the key made, but that I was not to mention to my aunt that Lucy had gone out and left the house. She would not understand, there would be another scolding, and it was so difficult to get a maid nowadays, they were all working in the factories for higher wages.

"So many robberies in Manila, Tio," I said. "Your TV. If Lucy plans on visiting her sister, she can go when I am here so that there will always be someone in the house."

He thought it was a good idea—yes, it should be that way—but he would give me a key nonetheless—it was so easy to have one duplicated, but again, conspiratorially whispering, "Don't tell your tia Betty. It is so difficult to get a good maid."

I could not sleep, thinking of Kuya Nick, his promise that I would earn enough to pay him back in a month. Selling what? I pressed my ear to the wooden wall to hear any sound of his mistress moving about, but there was none loud enough to penetrate the wall. I placed a chair beside the wall and stood on it; then, with the lights out, I peered into the crack, but all I could see was the ceiling.

Sleep finally came to me after midnight; the last baggage train had thundered by, shaking the house like a matchbox. When I woke up, it was already light and Lucy was on my bed, kissing me, telling me we were alone again.

She pinched me saying I had been naughty and impatient; now we had all the time. The old cot creaked so we transferred to the floor. I had an urge to turn to the crack above, to wink at it, for with all the noise we were raising she must be watching and wondering, perhaps, how it would be if it was I, and not Kuya Nick and his vitamin E and KH3, paying homage to her this beautiful day.

Now, to my mind, I was really Toro. A vulgar sense of superiority, of prowess suffused me. My self-control amazed me with its perfection; I was Toro, unflappable; Toro the terrible, endowed with vaunted willpower. I decided to put on a good exhibition and Lucy was responsive—each wave I stirred lifted her, arched her, shook her. She moaned so loud I thought the whole neighborhood would hear. Then I scaled the crest and what a dizzying, electrifying varooming dive it was; I collapsed on her limp, quivering form, a euphoric peace enveloping me like a warm, silk cocoon.

We lay thus for some time—I didn't know how long—and did not care. Outside children were playing, a vegetable vendor was shouting her wares—eggplants, string beans—and women were gossiping on their way to market. I tensed, hearing a sound in the other apartment. I could hear the hum of the air conditioner. We had been seen.

The greatest show on earth.

I WAS late for my first-period class, but it was one time I did not mind. Toto obviously did, for he rushed to me when I arrived; it was much too late to go to class so we went to the canteen and had Cokes.

He was stammering again. It was always like this when he was excited. "Pepe, listen, you should really be somebody in the Brotherhood. But first, here, in the university . . . you must be in the Student Council. That is the important thing. And to be in it you must be class president. You can do it. I can campaign for you and we can prepare posters—all that you will need."

"*Hoy,* I am not a politician. I do not like politicians."

"But you are popular, with boys and girls. Your name . . . it is easy to remember. And you have personality."

"Your words are difficult to resist," I said in high humor. "Flattery will get you somewhere."

"I am serious, Pepe," he said. "First we have to elect you class president—that will be next week—then you must run for the Student Council."

"What will it get me?" I asked the old question.

It flustered him. "I don't know, more popularity I think. But that is not the reason. I am thinking of the Brotherhood. If we can have a member of the Brotherhood in a high position, in all the high positions . . . can you not see what this means? It is so damn basic." He was exasperated. "All right, you will be invited to many parties. Meet many girls, the prettiest in school. You will even get a scholarship, I think, if you become president of the council. And you will not spend everything for your tuition."

"Those are things I like to hear," I said eagerly.

"Damn you!" he cried, the strongest expression I ever heard from him. Then he was contrite. "I wish you were not so demanding, Pepe. But I am beginning to understand. You are very . . . very pragmatic."

"Practical!"

I put my arm around his shoulder. "Toto, if it will make you happy, I will be a candidate." He did not speak, but I knew he was very pleased.

Looking back, I am surprised at the slow change that had come over me, my interest in school, my running for election, for I was not doing these for myself but for Mother and Tia Bettina. My class was crowded—sixty of us—and I could not ask questions as much as I wanted, and yet I had begun to find the atmosphere to my liking. Some of the teachers were quite repulsive; after all, most of them were there just for a living. If they were any brighter they would be at the elite colleges where the pay was better and the workload lighter.

There was, however, one exception, and that was Professor Hortenso. He had a very good reputation among the teachers, the only Ph.D. from England who was in Recto by choice. It seemed at first as if this permanent smile was plastered on his face. I saw him quite often in the corridors, for he had a full load, which meant teaching classes four hours a day.

My classmates lived in the districts—Sampaloc, Santa Cruz, Tondo—in cramped apartments, and I suspect some of the girls worked in bars and restaurants, particularly those who seemed aloof and well-dressed. The classes at night were packed with students who worked during the day. At nine, when the last classes were over, the human flood gushed out of the dimly lighted halls into the boisterous arteries of the University Belt, racing after buses and jeepneys already bursting with people. By eleven, Recto, Morayta, and Legarda were empty and silent but for the small cafes and restaurants such as those we frequented.

In the end I was left to fend for myself and hammer out my own education. I could fail, of course, for the teachers were not all that lenient, but as long as I read, attended class, and did not get my report card marked for absences, the likelihood of my failing was remote.

The election for class president came within two months of our enrollment, and after that, the election of the University Council. Our class election was no problem. When the call for nominations came, Toto was the first to raise his hand. There were three other candidates and we were allowed five minutes each to speak. I wanted to be last. The first three went beyond their limit, and they perorated on duty, freedom, all the usual stuff about the responsibility of youth and the future of the nation.

I never had stage fright, for as Toto had said, I was so outgoing and extroverted I could manage any crowd.

"I want you to know," I said, "that I have many honors to my name. In high school, for instance, I was the Ping-Pong champion. [Laughter.] But I do not expect to win this particular election, for I almost failed to make it to this university. Physical education and recess have always been my favorite subjects. [Laughter.] Many politicians, I need not tell you, are dishonest. And because I am now a politician, I should not claim exception. [Laughter.] So I am telling the truth.

"You will want to know what I can do for you. I have no money, but I have a big mouth. [There was now laughter after every sentence.] But you can do something for me. You can elect me. Then, because I have no money, I can, as my good friend here said, attend more parties, get to know more of the girls, and if forced to study, I may even end up with a scholarship.

"You are laughing. But if I lose, it will not be a laughing matter anymore. Since I am supposed to make a promise, I will make one. It will be very difficult for me to do it, but I will try to be honest. If there are funds to be collected, I promise not to spend them alone. I will spend them with the treasurer.

"But I would rather be president. Even if I have to be honest to be it."

As Toto said, I would easily make it. It was, in his words, *lutong macao*.* Fifty votes out of sixty.

Next was the Student Council, not the presidency—that was almost always reserved for the seniors who had been in the university longer, had more of a following—just membership, or the secretaryship at the most.

I still did not have money, and I wondered when Kuya Nick would really give me a job, even if only for afternoons. Perhaps I should see him next time his Mercedes was there. Thus, it was Toto again who treated me to *siopao* and Coke at our cafe in Recto. It was not yet noon, and the place was quite empty, so we had a corner to ourselves.

For all the warmth that I felt for him, I did not deserve his kindness; I had briefly suspected that he was gay, but he made no advances and we even talked of some of the students who were gay, those in the dramatics guild, how some of the more handsome ones made a living being call boys for them. It was just that Toto was raised differently—an orphan. Now, as I ate his *siopao*, I thanked him for being good to me, then sprang the question: "What have I done for you, Toto?"

"Luck, Pepe," he said. "You were the first person I met on the first day of school. That is all. I would have developed the friendship of others, but, well, they all seemed plastic. You are a real person."

"Shit," I said.

He shook his head and smiled patronizingly. "If you had grown up in an orphanage, you would look at people differently, too. You would understand what I am saying. It is so difficult to explain to someone who has parents, relatives. I never had these—friends in the orphanage, yes, but they all left and we never saw each other again. Sometimes I go there with Father Jess to see the nuns—they

---

* *Lutong macao:* A manipulated outcome or result.

are old now, the ones who took care of me. I love them but they belong to another world."

I had always been myself. Now here was one who needed a brother. "How was it inside? How does one get in?"

He bit into his *siopao*. "I should take you there sometime. On a Sunday when the kids are taken out for a breath of fresh air. A baby gets in this way: A revolving basket is at the door. The baby is placed there together with anything the mother wants to leave, maybe some clothes. She rings the bell, turns the basket around so that it faces the inside of the orphanage. Then she leaves. The bell would bring the sisters out."

"What was it like when you were small?"

"It was not a harsh life," Toto said softly, "if that is what you want to know. Children have little knowledge of what is difficult as long as their bellies are not empty. I did not mind the secondhand clothes. And I had many playmates! But from the very start I knew I was an orphan."

His eyes were misting, and I told him not to continue if the telling was too painful. "No," he said, attempting a smile. "It is just that it is a very difficult feeling, to know that you have been cast aside, that no one wanted you, not even your mother."

I wanted then to tell him that my father did not want me, either, that the world is not cruel, but both of us knew the knavery, the wretchedness around us.

"It does not matter much after you get to accept it," he said. "Besides, there were the sisters and the maids. They were mothers to us. Then there were the visits of prospective parents—couples who came to look for kids to adopt. Usually they took the very small ones, the babies. But there was always a chance that the bigger ones would be considered. And as we grew older, we knew the importance of these visits and we tried to look our best and act our best, wondering if we would be taken. But the years went on. I grew up and no one took me. The girls were taught skills and some were even chosen as brides. But boys can stay there only till a certain age, after that they must leave. They are too much of a problem, I suppose. That was when Father Jess came—good luck, I should say, for he is a very fine man. Without him, I would not be going to school; I would not be earning a little money so that I can feed you like this."

"Thank you," I repeated. I was finished with my *siopao*.

"Pepe," he said, "you are honest, even if you joke about it."

"Shit."

"You appeal to most. And you are sincere. It shows on your face when you are angry."

"Then I'll make a lousy politician."

"The old kind," he said, emphatically. "We really need good people, particularly in the Brotherhood. You have no pretensions."

"Shit."

"Yes, yes," he said. "I know psychology. With my background. And in church, I meet many people—phonies telling us problems that are not true. I can read you."

"Shit again," I said.

"But most important, Pepe, you are bright. Brighter than I. Though perhaps you don't know it."

"I should be feeding you," I said.

Leaving him, I felt this wonderful warmth suffuse me, satisfied not with the pork *siopao* but with the friendship. Toto did not want anything from me and I wasn't going to be of any help to him. He stuttered, he looked lost, he was deeply religious but was an activist. He had nobody but a priest named Father Jess and a professor, both of whom he held in awe. There was also an old woman who cooked for him named Tia Nena. Now he had a brother as well.

WHEN I got home I was surprised to find Lucy furious at me for not having arrived earlier. Toto's *siopao* had filled me and I had not realized it was past one. "Now," she said petulantly, "I cannot go and visit my sister."

"Shit," I told her. "Why did you not tell me this morning? You can go now and not blame me. After all, there is the whole afternoon if you wish."

"But you don't understand," she said. "She was waiting for me in Quiapo at lunchtime. And I did not go."

"I thought you visited her at her home," I said. "How did you know she was going to wait for you in Quiapo?"

"That is what we agreed on."

"You should have told me," I said wearily, all desire for her having ebbed.

"I forgot." She said it lamely.

I suddenly felt uneasy; intuition told me it was not her sister she was going to see.

"You are lying," I said. "It was a man you were going to meet in Quiapo."

"Now, Pepe," she said, her voice pitching. "Don't you start suspecting things. I forgot, that is all."

"Stop it then," I said, unconvinced.

It was our first quarrel. I went to her and kissed her softly on the cheek, then the lips with passion. But she was holding back; it was as if she was expecting someone anytime to knock at the door, for she would turn that way, although her hands were all over me. After a while, I looked into her eyes. "What is disturbing you? Who are you expecting?"

She blushed, and quickly her arms encircled me again. But I pushed her gently away, looked into her troubled face. "It was not your sister you were going to see, Lucy. It was your lover."

She got angry; she pushed me roughly saying it was none of my business, then she marched off to the kitchen.

I followed her. "Lucy, it's two months now. This is not something that I do as a machine. There is some feeling here," I held her hand and pressed it to my chest. "You must know that. If you do not have feelings at all, I have."

Her countenance softened. She turned to me and touched my face in a caress. "Do not ask questions," she said. "We have not known each other for more than two months, like you said. And look what we are already doing. What more do you want?"

"Honesty," I said.

"But my life is my own."

"Not anymore, not after what we have done. You are now a part of my life."

She must have realized how hurt I was, for she kissed me softly and then led me up the stairs to my room again.

I did not put on the greatest show on earth—my mind was too troubled—and when we were finished and relaxed, she said, "If you were the first I am sure that I would have been very hurt."

She was being honest finally, and though it had not occurred to me to ask, on reflection, I had known that I was not her first. There was no bleeding, and though I had read somewhere that this might not be the case if the girl was athletic, I realized that she had not expressed pain but had, instead, acted with confidence.

"Tell me who was the first," I asked, turning on my side to look at her pretty, brown face.

She faced me, "You will not be angry?"

"I can bear it. What can I do about the past?"

"I had some difficulty. Of course, I bled. Three times, and each time, I bled a little. But Pepe, he was not like you at all."

"Who is he?"

She drew away and pinched my nose. "Now, you know enough and I have been truthful. Let us not talk like this anymore." She kissed me once more, and we would have lingered but for an infernal rapping on the door below.

In fright, she bolted up, put on her clothes, and ran downstairs. I took time putting on my clothes but did not go down. I lay in my cot, turning over in my mind what she had said and was sad and yet a little comforted. Lucy had begun to be honest with me.

IT HAD BEEN MY UNCLE at the door, and his voice was angry although I could not make out what he was angry about, and Lucy was trying to tell him something, but he had rushed up the stairs, slammed the door, then, after a while, rushed out again.

I went down wondering what it was all about. "He seemed very angry," I said. Lucy was preparing the evening meal and dusk had come. Soon, the Lucena Express would thunder by.

"He forgot an important paper, I think," Lucy said. "He had been at the door a long time and we did not hear him."

"I hope he did not suspect you were upstairs with me."

Lucy tweaked my nose. Uncle Bert did not stay long at the door, even the slightest rap on it could be heard in the house, and I wondered what it really was that had made him angry at Lucy.

Remember the
Oppressor

KUYA NICK was in his green Mercedes, apparently waiting for me. He was bright as a lightbulb as I emerged from the alley, and he beckoned to me to take the seat beside him. I demurred but he was insistent. "I will take you to school," he said. "It is on my way anyway."

It would be my first ride in a Mercedes and I would be hypocritical to let the opportunity pass. Besides, there was also the promise of a job. The engine purred quietly to a start and we headed toward Dimasalang. "How is my *toro* this morning?" he asked, nudging me with his elbow.

"All right," I said. A protracted silence. He was not just giving me a lift; he had something to say. "Are your classes this morning really all that important? I am about to give you a job in the afternoons if you want it. Let us go somewhere we can talk."

Of course, I wanted it! Me, with a job at last, me with something to add to my little spending money, money that was almost gone. He stepped on the gas, and we sped toward Dimasalang, Quiapo—to the boulevard, to one of the coffee shops there.

I was not hungry but he ordered a hamburger and a cup of coffee for me anyway. The shop was almost empty and we had a corner to ourselves.

He was no longer jovial; his face was serious, with a hint of brutal coldness. He folded his hands on the table, the morning sun glinting on his diamond ring, on his polished nails. "I will speak to you frankly," he said, "and you are free to reject what I offer. But you are not free to talk about it to others. If you do, God have pity on you because you will not live long if I find out. Is that clear, Pepe?"

Goose pimples pricked my skin. "What do you want me to do?"

"First," he said, toying with his cup, "I want you to make deliveries on the appointed time, at the exact place. And no mistakes. If you cannot make it or if no one shows up, report to the same place in thirty minutes, on the dot, and after that, if no one shows up, then leave."

"What am I going to deliver?"

"Drugs," he said simply.

I had lost all appetite; the hamburger became tasteless mush in my mouth and rocks started forming in my throat.

"Speed?"

For the first time, a smile crossed his corpulent face. He shook his head. "That's for children. No, the real thing. Heroin."

My anxiety must have been etched all over my face.

"Afraid?"

I nodded.

"I am not surprised," he said, touching my hand briefly. "They are all afraid in the beginning. But it is not really all that dangerous. You don't have to worry about the police. I take care of them. It is the customers you have to worry about. But you will learn quickly. And besides, just think, it's big money, you will get ten percent of all the deliveries. Easily two hundred pesos in a week. And you will make only a few deliveries in a day. And not every day. It all depends, of course, if you can bring in new clients—but not from your school. They don't have money in Recto. That is why I said you should go to Ateneo or La Salle. That's where the money is. All those spoiled brats. And if they don't have it, they will give you their mothers' jewels, or their fathers' watches, anything they can lay their hands on. They live in Pobres Park, in those fancy places."

Two hundred pesos a week, about a thousand a month. Who cares for the Brotherhood?

"Kuya," I asked, breathing easier, "why did you pick this day? Why all of a sudden?"

Again, the fleeting smile. "You are the best candidate. You live close to my wife." I had to get used to his calling his mistress his wife, and I wondered how many women he had. "Communication would be no problem. The truth is"—he lowered his voice—"the one you are replacing got too ambitious. I think he was trying to blackmail one of his customers. He was killed yesterday. His body was taken probably in a car and abandoned in a field in Marikina. And all his stuff was stolen."

Could that happen to me? The unspoken question was answered immediately.

"Even though they are addicted, one must not deal too harshly with them. Sometimes, when they don't have the ready cash, it may be necessary to give it to them, but be sure to collect it at the following meeting. They always come through because they know that if they don't they will not be given another chance."

He could see the indecision in my face. I was going to be a pusher—that was farthest from my aspirations. I may have stolen and lied, and I may have been plastic to my mother, but now I would be putting my neck on the block.

"Try it for one week—just one week. And if you don't like it, then stop. And no hard feelings. But no talking—that is very clear, isn't it?"

I nodded.

Time was important and I had no watch. We stood up, got into the car, and drove to Makati. At the first jewelry shop he bought me my first Seiko.

I DID NOT go to school that morning, but spent time studying the code, the hazy description of each customer I was to meet. Kuya Nick had seen them from a distance, he knew where they lived, how they could be contacted, and he had a long list. He must have had in his employ at least ten pushers.

At exactly one that afternoon I walked hesitantly to a red Volkswagen 1500 parked beside the Rizal Theater. The young man inside, about eighteen, thin, with glassy eyes, was startled when I approached him. He was about to start the engine and leave when I said that Joe—that was the old pusher—would not be servicing him anymore. I gave him the numbered envelope, which he immediately recognized. He opened it, took the small packet out, and sniffed its contents; a benign smile spread over his face. He gave me an envelope in return. I opened it in his presence, expecting two hundred pesos as Kuya Nick said. I was wrong. Joe had been upping the price—it was three hundred—and I had a hundred pesos more for myself.

In a moment he was gone. I had two hours to waste before the next delivery at the supermarket. I had become hungry so I went to the Japanese restaurant across the shimmering expanse of parked cars. I had never been to a place like this, but now I had a hundred pesos and could afford it. It was almost two, but there were still people eating. I had read about Japanese cooking, the subtle taste of raw fish, seaweeds, and all that. It was fashionable for young people to be in jeans, in faded T-shirts as I was, and though I felt uncomfortable in these strange and elegant surroundings, it was the experience I wanted. "Raw fish," I told the kimono-clad waitress. "Then sukiyaki."

"And what would you like to drink, sir?"

"Sake," I said.

She brought the sake first and it was a bit warm like I read it would be, then the raw fish. It was then that she knew it was my first time in a Japanese restaurant, for I did not know the chopsticks were joined and she parted them for me while I watched with fascination.

If she had any doubt about my capacity to pay, it disappeared when I brought out the wad of bills from the boy in the Volks. Fifty-six pesos for a small dish of raw fish, squid, and sea urchin insides, sukiyaki cooked before me, and a tiny bottle of sake, but it was worth the adventure. This bastard from Cabugawan living it up at his first opportunity in this precinct of the rich. I would tell the Brotherhood not to tear down the walls of Pobres Park; we should take over the Park instead.

At three on the dot I was in the supermarket's book section, browsing over the cookbooks and paperbacks, then this girl came in not a minute late, the yellow scarf on her neck the recognition sign. She went to the magazines; there was no one close by, so I walked over and said softly, "Tessa, the two envelopes are here." She turned to me, and again the look of surprise, of fright, and she turned aside as if she had not heard. Again, I had to tell her. "Joe is not coming; I have taken over."

It was then that she turned to me, her face sunny as a flower, and she shoved the two envelopes immediately into her bag and handed me an envelope. She did not tarry; when she went out I followed her at a distance. Below the marquee, she waited briefly. Soon, a Mercedes with a uniformed driver drew up. As she went in, I could see that her legs were shapely.

My last delivery was at six at the Intercon; she sat in one of the sofas near the bar—a forlorn, emaciated creature in her late teens. She wore a series of colored bangles, the recognition sign, and I passed her once on my way to the men's room, then I hurried back, afraid that she might have gone after the appointed time. I sat opposite her. She glanced at me and watched with interest as I brought out the envelope from the folder. No one was looking, so I bent forward, "Joe is not coming, Mary. I am taking his place."

No emotion rippled on her face, no recognition lighted her eyes; she opened her notebook, threw the envelope at me, then took what I gave. I had expected her to leave, but she just sat there, looking straight ahead as if I did not exist. I felt so uncomfortable, I left after a while.

Five deliveries in one day, all within the Makati area. Inside the toilet, I counted what I had legitimately made: a hundred twenty pesos. And Joe's take which was now mine was six hundred pesos! Some poor clerk slaved for two months to earn that much and here I was raking it in in one afternoon. I could cry at the irony of it all.

Outside, I flagged a taxi. It was already dark when I got to Antipolo. The door of the apartment of Kuya Nick's mistress was open and she was there, waiting. She had been instructed, and though we had never talked before, now it was as if we were old friends. After all, she had seen me, and perhaps appreciated me more than Lucy did.

"Please come in," she said. I handed her the envelope with the money and she gave me a larger one for my deliveries the following day. She closed the door.

"We are alone," she said. The house was shadowy, but she did not switch on any of the lamps. In the soft dark I could see the mounds of her breasts thrusting through her simple sack dress, the full lips, the eyes shining like jewels. "My maid," she went on, "she went to see her sister, but will be back soon."

I did not want to poach on another man's domain; I had the envelope for the following day and I turned to leave.

"Wouldn't you like something to drink, a beer maybe?" It was an unmistakable invitation. I held her close—so close I could feel the mound pressed against my thigh. "This is what I want," I said.

I had expected her to resist, but she did not. She did not put her arms around me as I kissed her, and her lips were cool.

"Please," she said. "There will be plenty of time. Not here . . . I don't want to . . . not here. You understand."

"When?" I asked impatiently.

In a whisper, "I'm not prepared."

"When?"

"I can go to three places: my beauty parlor, my dressmaker, and church. On Friday," she was saying softly. "On Friday, in the morning, we can meet there, or any place . . ." She started to kiss me but stopped abruptly.

"I must control myself," she said. I kissed her again, and she let me plumb the crevices of her mouth.

We walked to the door, and she unlatched it slowly. There was no one outside, and I knocked immediately on ours.

I COULD NOT SLEEP that night thinking of the woman next door, of Friday and its allure and promise. And the money in my folder—how would I explain it? I even had to hide the watch that Kuya Nick bought me. Who was the fool who said one can hide wealth but not poverty? He did not know of my predicament. I had several hundred pesos for the first time in my life and I did not know where to put them; not in my old canvas bag, which had no key, not in my folders. Tomorrow I would go to a bank, open a savings account, and hide the bankbook. It would never be the same again now that I knew what it was like to have money, to be able to buy anything I wanted or to eat anywhere in this wide, wonderful city.

I woke up with a start; Lucy was in my room with my freshly ironed clothes, which she gingerly placed in the old cabinet that my father used. As we went through the morning ritual, she was unusually coy. "You did not tell me what you did the whole day yesterday. I only overheard you telling your uncle about a job. What is it?"

"Nothing for sure, Lucy," I said. "I was just interviewed. I went to

Makati, to the big companies. Even just a janitor if they will take me. But I don't know any skill—except this," I said, pumping.

"You are so good," she said, arching her back.

Slowly, we savored every movement and, as usual, I was late for school.

In the jeepney to Quiapo I wondered how Friday—two days away—would be, how Mila would take me. It was one of those humid mornings when the rains had lifted and the sun stole out, drenching the sidewalks and the sweating people as they jostled about in the plaza, the asshole of Manila. It was much worse underneath, in the cavernous underpass, the tile floor now blotched with dirt, the lightbulbs konked out, the stench of the broken urinals, but still people came to Quiapo, whorled up from the depths, borne out of despair, for here there was light and hope, and they knelt in prayer or wobbled to the altar on their knees, repeating the rosary, invoking the spirit, praying for good fortune and good health and all the handsome rewards that befell those who believed.

For me it was not belief; it was something deeper, inexplicable, recondite as sin. I entered the church and thanked them up there for the goodies that had fallen my way and for what was yet to come; then, having done my duty, I went back across the burning asphalt, to the bank and made my first deposit.

It was past eleven when I got to school. I had just one more class and when it was over, Toto was at the door. "Now," I said, "I can treat you to *siopao* and *mami*."

He asked if I had become a call boy and I said, "No, the money from my mother arrived."

Then, "Where were you yesterday?"

I did not want to lie, but how could I tell Augusto that I had become a pusher? That in a single and uneventful afternoon I had earned more than six hundred pesos? Yet I suffered no twinge of guilt about the money—it came from those rich young punks across the river, they had trunkfuls of it and they did nothing to earn it. If they went straight to perdition I would not have shed one solitary tear.

I thought quickly. "I am terribly ashamed, Toto. My mother, you know she slaves for me. And my auntie Bettina, too." I was speaking the truth, at least. "I went out the whole day looking for a job, in Makati, after reading the ads, in government offices—"

"You think it is difficult, you don't know anything. Excuse me,

Pepe. But you cannot type, you cannot take shorthand, you know no accounting. And there are thousands of filing clerks, janitors, messengers. Maybe, in a newspaper office you have a chance. But even there . . ."

We had reached our cafe and we joined the line. The usual *siopao espesyal*. We went to the second floor. As we started to eat, he noticed the watch, which I had put on when I left the house. "Hey, that is an expensive Seiko. I know the style."

Quickly again: "My auntie . . . it is a gift. Her salary for a month, or even more, and she buys a watch for me. Do you understand why I feel so guilty?"

He nodded and appeared thoughtful. "I hope you can come with me to Tondo," he said after a while. "Father Jess knows some important people. He may be able to give you a few names and you can go to them."

I thanked him, but said that I would first try it my way.

I did not go home for lunch; I had only two deliveries that day and the package also included my deliveries for the next three days. Kuya Nick was efficient and methodical, and like he said, if there were extra orders, all I had to do was put them down in writing in the envelope that I gave to Mila. However, the weekly supplies that I had already delivered seemed enough. Nor did my customers increase their requirements as Kuya Nick said they were bound to within a month. It was during the first few months that the increase becomes very marked, then it tapers off and becomes steady—and that was when the business really got booming. The problem was to keep the old customers regularly supplied and happy. As long as the stuff comes, they don't make trouble.

I was in blue jeans and a brown T-shirt, the brown envelope and my books under my arm. I tarried before the appointed time at the entrance of the supermarket again, and though it was not raining, she brought the red parasol by which I would recognize her. She was a fair-skinned mestiza with a sculpted nose, dimples, and black eyebrows. She wore faded jeans and a cheap *katsa** blouse. She went straight to the dry goods section and I followed her there. I turned around once more and there being so few people at this time, I said, "Doris—"

---

* *Katsa:* Coarse cream-colored fabric, like sacking.

She turned tentatively to me and smiled; her clean, even teeth could have been used for a toothpaste ad. "Yes?"

"Joe is not making deliveries anymore," I said. "I am taking his place."

Her face grew taut, relaxed, then the surprise: "I hope you have time . . . why don't we go somewhere for a cup of coffee or something?"

"Something," I said.

She smiled brightly.

We walked out of the cash counter and found a corner table in the supermarket cafeteria. I brought out the numbered envelope, and she slipped a bundle of bills under the table to me. I did not bother counting it; I stuffed it into my pocket. The next delivery was at four, and I had time.

I asked her what she wanted, but she had just had lunch; a cup of coffee would do. I ordered a hamburger. She wanted to talk and I was eager to listen. Then I remembered what Kuya Nick had told me, that I was not to fraternize with my customers for I may be telling them things I shouldn't, but more than that, they might find out ways by which they could put one over on me. Remember, Kuya Nick had said, they are dependent on their pushers, whom they hate. It is a loathsome but necessary relationship. But it was too late now, she was just too pretty to be ignored, and I was just, as Toto had said, too much of an extrovert, and a Sagittarian, to keep away from people even though they might spell danger or doom.

"What is your name?"

"Toto," I said.

"I see that you are a student."

I had no special bookcover and my notebooks were not bought from the university store. She did not know, and she was trying to find out, where I was studying. "Not in the school where your friends go," I said.

"You are evasive," she quickly got the point.

"Is Doris your real name?"

She nodded. Then, the other surprise. "Do not get me wrong. I don't use it. It's for my friend. I would like to help her stop, but I don't know how I can make her. It is not the money. She has lots of it. But she has been at it for six months now, and she is growing thinner."

"Then why are you giving her this?"

She was quiet for a moment. "Because I understand," she said finally. "I tried it once, twice, and liked it, but I had more self-control."

"You can go to a hospital, or this foundation I have heard about," I suggested.

"Her parents would die of shock. They wouldn't believe that their daughter—and I, a pusher. I used to accompany her when she got the stuff from Joe. But she hated him." She smiled at me again. "You are not repulsive at all. How did you get started on this?"

"Money," I said simply.

"That's three hundred fifty I gave you. How much is yours?"

"Only thirty-five," I lied, realizing I had made more again. "And I am not rich like you and your friends." I thrust at her my battered, brown leather shoes. "That's the only pair I have."

Her face was downcast. She sipped her coffee and her hand trembled. Her arms bore no telltale injection marks. She had none of the glassy, sleepy look of the boy in the Volks, the girl at the Intercon.

"You are so unlike Joe," she said. "Joe is always trying to increase the price, saying it is more and more difficult to get the stuff. The supplier in Cavite, that was what he said, was demanding more and more, too. Is it true?"

"I am new," I said. "I don't know many things. I just follow instructions."

"Where is Joe?"

I told her. She blanched and her cup almost spilled.

"I am not sorry," she shook her head. "Will you stay in this job long? You are not afraid? After what has happened?"

"I have no choice," I said. "Jobs are hard to find and I am not through with college. Besides, I said I would try it for a week." Bending over to her, I said: "Don't judge me too harshly. I am not rich like you or your friends, the whole lot of you who have no better use for your money than this. I don't want this job, knowing what it does to people. But if I did not take it, someone else would. It pays well; something I never dreamed I would get when I was in the province. Maybe I will hang on to it, if my tastes do not interfere, and make a little pile, then I will retire. Ha, that is what every prostitute says, but they all end up old and wrinkled and penniless."

"You really know," she said, her eyes crinkling in a smile.

"Of course," I shot back. "You think wisdom is the monopoly of those who go to exclusive schools?"

She shook her head. "You really have a chip on your shoulder."

"A block," I said.

"What is it you really want to do?"

I looked at the intense face, the dimple that had disappeared, the down on her arms. "You are very pretty," I said.

She blushed. "I asked you a question," she prodded.

"I would like to eat well," I said. "I ate at a Japanese restaurant for the first time yesterday. And I do not like to go to school."

"Same here," she said.

"But I like campus popularity—and my friends in school."

"Same here," she laughed.

We were now both laughing.

"Hey," I said. "We are both pushers, you know. Except that I get paid and you don't." Then, seriously: "You must tell the parents of your friend even if she ends up hating you. And take her to a doctor . . . only a doctor can help her, and you can, by refusing to give all this to her, by reducing her intake. By talking her into disciplining herself."

"You will be losing one good customer."

"I'll make two new friends."

"You are no pusher."

"Not yet, but given time . . ."

We had sat there for almost an hour. "I enjoyed talking with you," she said as we stood up.

"The pleasure is mine," I said leaving a big tip for the waiter. She noticed it. "My—" she shook her head.

"It's not my money, it's your friend's," I said.

We walked to the door and shook hands. "Next week," I said.

She turned and walked across the small plaza to the parking lot. She had a mustard-colored Beetle, and as she passed me on her way to the exit, she smiled and waved.

At four, the Medical Center. I sat in the lobby, a few minutes early, but I noticed him at once, a man in his forties, very patrician, with a black leather portfolio on the floor at his feet. He was impeccably dressed in a gray double-knit suit as if he was an executive, which I was sure he was. I walked over to him with the usual, "Joe is not going to make the deliveries anymore." He quickly stood up and told me to follow him. He walked fast ahead of me as if he did not want to be seen with me, and I followed him to his car in the parking lot, a huge, black Lincoln. He motioned me inside. It was air-conditioned. We drove out without talking. He was soon driving very fast, and he seemed tense. This was all wrong, but there was no way I could tell him to stop. I had already gotten the envelope out and laid it beside him, saying it was all there, and may I please have the payment? But he grunted angrily, and we sped on. We were on the highway now. I began to panic. Then, at the intersection, at a red light, I tried to open the door so I could rush out, but it wouldn't budge. He turned to me with that kind of laughter that chills. "Only I can open the doors," he said. "They are all automatically locked."

I could break the windows and squirm through. This was one time I should have been armed or known karate.

"I am not going to harm you," he said softly. "I just want to ask a few questions. You know what happened to Joe? I am sure you suspect. No, I am not a policeman—it is useless going to the police. The sonofabitch was blackmailing me, was upping the price, too. . . . He had it coming . . . and you will, too . . . if you don't talk."

There was something frantic about him, and I knew that there was a gun under his jacket, for the bulge showed.

"What do you want to know, sir? You know I am new at the job," I said. "I just follow instructions."

"Well, I want to know who your boss is—the top man—because I want more, and no blackmailing, no stories. I have been on this for two years now, and I need it as I need food and air. I will kill if I have to. Or I will have to get it from other sources. Why are you doing this to me? Am I not paying enough? Why do you want my family to know . . . and my friends? Don't you know this will destroy me? Each man has his private passion. Can you not understand that?"

He was shaking and beads of sweat glistened on his forehead. We were now in Cubao, and he drove toward Marikina. He was no longer talking sense: "You are greedy; you cannot be satisfied. You want everything and only because I have this passion that only you can fill. Why can it not be a simple business transaction? The supply is there, abundant, and so is the money, so why ask for more?"

"I don't know what you are talking about, sir," I said. His eyes were not on the road and, once or twice, I thought we would crash head-on into trucks.

"Please, sir," I said, "your driving."

"Hell," he said, then laughed. "You only live once."

His gaunt face was now really wet with perspiration even though the air-conditioning was working. We had reached Katipunan, and to the right was the huge Ateneo compound. He swerved left, his tires screeching, but he was not fast enough—the car crashed over the embankment. He stepped on the brakes in time to avoid hitting the acacia tree by the side of the road. The automatic lock of the car door clicked and I rammed my shoulder against the door. It opened, and to his curses, I jumped out and ran. At the corner, I looked back. He was sitting in his car like a statue.

I boarded the first jeepney that came by—all I wanted was distance from him and from this job.

Kuya Nick answered the number I was to call in an emergency. Yes, he would be in Cubao where I had stopped, in thirty minutes. "Just go to the Chinese restaurant by the Nation Theater and wait."

When he arrived, we drove together to Katipunan. The car was gone. "It is one of those things," he said. "I told you there are certain risks. When he asked you to follow him to his car, you should have resisted. Never fraternize. You don't know them, you did not get them originally—"

I had made up my mind. "Kuya," I said as we drove back to Manila, "this job is not for me. I am too cowardly for it. I like the money but . . ."

He was silent.

I had to tell him about Joe. I asked what he was like, how old he was.

"About thirty; small, a little bit on the fat and balding side. He looked unkempt but he was always clean."

"He was extorting money from them," I said. We should part as friends, I should go with his trust. "I did not make only so much yesterday," I said. "Even today, the girl gave me a hundred fifty pesos more. I would like to give it all back to you. And the watch, too."

Kuya Nick turned to me, a broad smile on his face. "Pepe, that is what I like about you. You can be trusted. No, you can keep them— you earned them. My problem now is to find someone who will do the job tomorrow. If the worst comes, I may have to do it myself."

I gave him the money and the notebook with the codes and time tables. He placed them on the console beside the gearshift.

"Next semester," he still tried, "think about La Salle. You really have to work in those schools, not in Recto. Like I said, that is where the money is. And those girls, if they will not give you their mothers' jewels, you can have all the cunts you want. My *toro*, you will have the time of your life!"

It was all so appealing, but I had to turn it down.

"Think about it, Pepe," he repeated as he dropped me off in front of the university.

PROFESSOR HORTENSO was not in; I had more than a hundred fifty pesos so I decided to see a movie.

It was seven in the evening when I got to the apartment, and Mila's door was ajar. She sat in the dimly lighted living room, and when I walked in, she bade me put on the latch.

"I was wondering why it took you so long," she said coyly. And then, as if to reassure me, she said she had sent her maid out to see a movie. There was a lot of time for us before she would return.

But I was not going to be unkind to Kuya Nick; he had, after all, given me a chance and, in his own perverse way, he had practiced some form of ethics. I did not even hold her or kiss her when she stood up and came to me, her breath warm and sweet on my face, her body pressed against mine. "I am sorry," I said, "but I will not be able to see you on Friday."

She held my hand to her breast. "Then now," she whispered. "We have a little time. Nick . . . we really don't do it, not even once a month . . . and I need it so much."

I pulled away. "They are waiting for me," I said, "and besides, I was just with him and he may be on his way here, now."

Her arms dropped. I headed for the door, trembling and angry at myself as I walked out.

Our Hope Is the People

T HE FOLLOWING DAY I enrolled at the International Karate
School two blocks down Recto from my university. My decision
to take karate was preordained not just by the experience with the
psycho but by Lakay Benito of my boyhood, who had taken me on
a journey to a subterranean world that imbued those who belonged
to it with inexplicable powers. He had taught me an effective *oración*
against unfriendly dogs and I wanted more. He was inclined to pass
on to me and to those with whom he felt vibrations the knowledge
he had accumulated; he was long past middle age and the *comedia*
he directed and acted in was no longer being shown in our town fiesta. Cheap penicillin, too, had diminished his clientele, and only
the gullible or fanatic went to him for his miracle cures. Even in
church, he was no longer an imposing presence, as a new priest had
taken over and gathered around him young people to "humanize"
and make the Church ever present and relevant.

You are on the way to manhood, he said; so it is time for your
perseverance and your courage to be tested. It was possible—he said
this, his face as somber as if it were Judgment Day—to achieve the
kind of power that would make you more agile than the fly, more

sensitive than the weed whose leaves fold at the slightest stirring of the breeze, and run faster than a horse. When the banana flowers, just as the heart of the flower dips, there would drop from its tip a jewel that you must be prepared to swallow instantly. You should, therefore, be before the plant, with mouth wide open, your hands clasped behind your back, and once the jewel is in your mouth, let no force take it away. All this would happen in all probability at night and there would be unspeakable and powerful forces that would strangle me and pry my mouth open. This was the hour of judgment and I would either end up as just another weakling or a man possessed with mind and muscle of incredible strength.

I remember my initiation into that secret domain Lakay Benito knew. We had this *aritondal* species in our backyard that had survived both typhoon and drought. It was a popular native variety, bitter when green but deep yellow and very sweet when ripe, not pulpy and tasteless like those bananas grown in the south for export to Japan. That dry season one of the plants had started to flower. I had waited for the heart to rise then dip, a process that took almost a week. I watched the whole time, wondering how much longer it would take before the heart would drop to point earthward.

On the fifth day I knew that the time had come, and after Mother and Auntie had gone to sleep, I stole down to our backyard and stood breathless beneath the banana plant. It was one of those April nights when not a breeze stirred, yet all around the night was alive with the chirp of crickets, the distant barking of dogs, wisps of talk from the neighbors, and the mooing of carabaos in their corral. Above, the stars studded the black cloudless sky, and I wondered if the jewel that I coveted would be just as bright. I was not afraid, standing there alone, the bananas like a dark canopy before me, while around were the huddled shapes of houses, some still distinct with yellow frames of light; even the earth seemed to heave and listen to the steady pounding of my heart. Vivid imaginings swooped through my mind, my eyes transfixed upon the pointed end of the banana heart above me. How would it be when the jewel finally fell? What powers would it give me? Would I be able to walk a single wire or ascend any wall like a fly? Would I be dexterous enough to pick any pocket without being caught? Standing there, for how long I did not know, my neck had started to cramp. I turned to ease the discomfort and the pain then arched skyward again; it was then that

I noticed a glow on the ground and felt the earth breathe; the glow started up the banana trunk, rose slowly, filling the trunk with an eerie light that pulsed slowly up the trunk and then to the heart itself. And I stood beneath it, my feet planted apart, my hands clasped behind me, my mouth wide open waiting for this white and dazzling pearl or jewel or king's ransom, paused uncertainly at the tip of the heart, to drop into my mouth. I felt it warm and smooth, but hardly had I closed my mouth when I felt huge and hairy arms clasp my neck in a grip so tight I could not breathe, while more slimy hands tried to pry my mouth open. I could smell the damp foulness of age, of decay, warm and final upon my face. I would choke if I did not free myself; if I opened my mouth to scream, however, everything would be lost. No, I must not yield. I must summon all the nerve and bone that this puny body could muster, I must not give up this vaunted treasure. With one final surge, I twisted around to evade those grasping, coiling hands and crashed to the ground.

That was where I woke up, in the chill dawn, the east already amber, the other houses already stirring with the womenfolk who must cook the morning meal. When I looked at the banana heart, indeed, it had already dipped.

I rose and walked to the house hoping that my steps would be light and some unfamiliar strength would suffuse me, but I felt instead cramped and feverish and when I sneezed, I knew that I had caught, not an incredible talisman, but a cold.

THE STAIRWAY that led to the karate school wound through floors occupied by nondescript law offices and companies that must have survived through sheer tenacity. Past doors tarnished with age and secured with three or four padlocks, I finally got to the top—the karate school—and the beginning of a new wisdom if ever I was to survive in a deformed physical world. So here I was, ready for another kind of school, not just to build my stamina but to discipline my body. My lessons were to be twice a week, but I could come every afternoon if I wanted to for the karatistas liked having people around. Various schools of self-defense had proliferated in the area— tae kwan do, kung fu, and judo—and the competition was very keen. It was eighty pesos a month, plus thirty pesos for my very rough cotton uniform. I was not aiming for a black belt or to smash bricks and planks of wood. I was just interested in self-defense. I did not have a gun, not even a knife. My instructors were all young, and they enjoyed their work, for when they were not teaching they were always practicing. They lived in the school itself to save on rent. Cups they had won from various tournaments adorned the shelves. When I went for my first lesson I was amused at the ritual of bowing to the instructor before the actual exercises started. Rading, who was the best, took me under his wing, although he was available for instruction anytime. He asked where I went to school, and when I told him he said he went there, too, but was just taking a few credits in accounting, for he wanted to be a karatista. He was about twenty-one, slightly taller than I, and his taut frame was all muscle.

I wanted to tell Toto what I did during my disappearances in the afternoons or early evenings, or sometimes in the mornings, but he would not understand. Though he was all talk about violence and revolution, these were mere ideas; I suspect he would not pull the trigger or stick a knife in someone else's belly when the time came.

There was no day that the name of Father Jess did not obtrude into our conversation; Toto really looked up to the priest. He was the father he never had. And as for a mother, in their *kumbento** was an old woman—Tia Nena, he called her—who was once deranged or had come from the Psychopathic Hospital at Mandaluyong. She did the cooking and the laundry for Father Jess. It was, to my mind, a weird household, set up from driftwood.

As the election for the Student Council was soon, Toto made plans for my candidacy. I was pestered by doubts. Though I was popular in my own class and in the other sections where I was enrolled, I did not have a university following. Furthermore, I did not want to spend my money on handbills or for those simple posters made from newspapers that we would plaster on walls and bulletin boards. That money would be a hedge for something more urgent.

"I will ask Father Jess for money," Toto assured me. "And the Brotherhood will help. You must not forget that."

I finally got to meet him. We went to San Beda where he was going to address the senior class in social studies and history. Just as he started with the usual greetings, the platitudes, we took seats in the empty front-row seats because I wanted to hear what this minor

---

**Kumbento:* The part of the sacristy where the priest lives.

god said. Toto was too shy to walk down the aisle and sit there with all the students, teachers, and priests on the stage looking at us late-comers, but I did not care—the Sagittarius in me again—so he followed me reluctantly.

Father Jess glanced at us, then went on. He was really huge, with thick bristly hair, thick lips, wide forehead, a jutting jaw, and eyes crinkled into two slits. He could have been an overfed Japanese or Chinese were it not for his dark complexion. He was not in a soutane, but instead wore denims and sandals, which I learned from him afterward were JC boots (Jesus Christ boots), and as a concession perhaps to his vocation, he had a gray close-necked jacket, a tiny silver cross on the collar.

There were more than three hundred in the auditorium—the entire senior class—and the lecture was one of six that the students would receive every week as part of their final orientation course. The air-conditioned hall was chilly, for it was not even half full. Father Jess had finished with the niceties and now his tone turned serious. Even without the loudspeaker, he could carry on like any *bomba* politician. His vocabulary was without bombast, earthy English spiced with Tagalog that had a very strong Visayan accent. Benedictine seminarians in white cassocks were in the front rows, and his first remarks were addressed to them. He spoke about the change that had come to the Church—a change that had been a long time in coming. He dredged up the encyclicals that were not believed in, about rituals that had become meaningless because they were not part of our lives. And finally, he spoke about the new role of priests: going to the masses, the poor, to prepare them for the liberation that was sanctioned by Christ.

Cliché stuff.

Then he spoke of the elite schools, how they had produced graduates who became the Establishment and how it might be necessary in the future to close these schools, for they were only perpetuating a decadent elite and the corruption in society.

This raised some questioning looks from the priests behind him on the stage.

The priest smiled at the *bomba* he had tossed. "I will tell you about this Establishment to which you—and I—belong," he said. "It is a word so often used, it has lost its meaning. But it is real, like syphilis. We have it and, like syphilis, we don't know it. We have to know it first before we can cure ourselves."

Fuck yourselves, I thought, but listened intently just the same. We had a neighbor in Cabugawan who worked in the railroad station; he had gone to the whorehouse near the rice mill and the day after he could not urinate except in terrible pain. And later there were sores all over his body. They said that not only did he have the sickness given by a woman, but the worst case one could get. He had to go somewhere for treatment, both he and his wife, whom he had also infected.

Father Jess described how big men made the laws, how these laws enriched them, how poverty became the way of life of the masses because they were made poor on purpose. And the poor—he lashed at us—we did not know any better, we did not organize, we did not define our purpose and mark our enemies so we would know whom to fight if only so we could get what was ours by right because it was we who worked the land, the factories.

He may have been telling something new to the students, but not to me. Though I had scant knowledge of what went on in Congress or the life that throbbed in Pobres Park and in other places where the rich slop it up, I always knew that it was the strong, the powerful who ruled, who drank the sweet juice of life. I could see that in the children of the landlords, who were my classmates in grade school, who then went to Manila for high school; how the rich women of the town always haggled with Mother no matter how hard she worked. Years bent before that damn machine and what had she to show for it? Not a big house, not jewels, just me going to Manila, to listen to this drivel.

I did not resent Father Jess, though. I was just sad that he could narrate these so clearly, so neatly. Cabugawan was in my mind, and leaving it, though it had not seemed that way then, was a painful wrenching away. I saw myself playing again in the dirt road that was never widened or asphalted. How would Cabugawan look in this year's rainy season? That dirt road would be churned by carabaos as they went to the fields beyond. The houses would be lashed by winds, their cogon roofs disheveled, their buri walls rotting and dripping; the bananas all tattered. And after the rains, the dry season—in April the wind lifted our kites, brought music to the bamboos as they bent, sounds I would not hear, sights I would not see. And I left them so I could be like the wind, meandering where it pleased.

The applause brought me back. It was loud and long, as if the auditorium was full, as if they had just heard the most exhortatory of speeches. Toto had this dazed, rapt look and he was applauding madly, too. Reluctantly I started to clap. There were questions, a whole hour for them, and I thought they would never stop. I could have easily disposed of the questions with words like "shit," or "drop dead," and when I could not stand the aridity of the questioning any-more I stood up with Toto hissing under his breath about how im-polite I was.

"We came to listen to the speech, not to those questions," I said.

We waited for Father Jess outside. It was dusk and the girls from Holy Spirit and Centro were filing out; they were in white-and-pink uniforms that hid their legs and obscured their good-looks. A short time later Father Jess appeared: "*Hoy,* you should have waited inside. There was *merienda—pancit* and sandwiches."

Toto introduced me. Father Jess was six feet tall, as swarthy as Idi Amin, and his grip was very tight.

"He tells me you are a very good politician," Father Jess said af-fably.

"I don't like being one, Father."

"What do you want to be then?"

"I'd like to be the country's karate champion," I smiled.

He gave my arm a playful chop. "You should visit us in the bar-rio. Where do you come from?"

I told him.

"I know the place," he said. "That is in eastern Pangasinan, isn't it? You know, they have a lot of faith healers there. And there was an uprising once and some tenants were killed. Are the Colorums still strong?"

It quickly brought to mind my grandfather, who had gone to jail for that uprising. "No, the Colorums are not there anymore," I said. "But the landlords still are."

We walked to the corner where they boarded a jeepney. I de-cided to walk to Quiapo. Even in that crowded evening, in that ooz-ing human flood which Recto's sidewalks become at this time of day, I was alone and back in Cabugawan again, stoking long-dead memories and giving shape to limpid ghosts of people I never saw, whose names we utter in reverence commingled with shame—grandfather, granduncle, and who else from our village—all the brave and angry men who marched into town a long time ago, burned the *municipio* and the Rich Man's house, then killed him, his wife, and children. The Colorums are gone, but the landlords are still with us, leeches beyond satiety. But the landlords are no longer the mestizos of yesteryear—imperious, fair-skinned, and loud of speech. Now they were brown like us, their origins not from Spain but from the village, farmers' children who had gone to school to be lawyers, had grown fat with the spoils of the land, the children of farmers who had forgotten what their fathers were and therefore were no different from the landlords they had replaced.

Around me, the milling mass of students, puny people loaded with speed dreams, here in Recto to slave for their diplomas from the mills so they could get jobs and eat three times a day. Nothing edifying, nothing lofty. And who knows, some day they would be landlords, too. But to think about the future now was to daydream. We were concerned with jeepney fare, *mami* and *siopao*, an occasional movie, clothes. Many of my classmates did not even wear shoes but cheap Japanese rubber slippers. Their blemished skins, their thin bodies showed only too well how badly undernourished they were.

I would have continued in Kuya Nick's employ. But the niggardly pleasures as I knew them, being able to see, feel, and appreciate the whorl and whirl around me could end in a job such as Kuya Nick's. I loved being alive, being here in Recto.

I survey the rubble of my past, the excesses I have committed without even really knowing why, and Mother comes to mind again and a sharp pang of regret, of sorrow, courses through me.

What is it that I really want? Certainly not to live in Cabugawan, although I miss the friends with whom I swam the flooded irrigation ditches and caught the silver fish in the shallows; the schoolhouse whose wooden floors I had scrubbed, and those high school dances when I held them close—Letty, whose breasts were small, whose thighs were silky; Marie, whom I often kissed when the boys, on purpose, switched off the lights. All the wonderful confections that are kept stored in the mind to tide one over when there are no coins jingling in the pocket, when the stomach is a yawning pit that contains nothing, none of the rice cakes that Auntie Bettina made, and those things Mother saved, a piece of fried pork, bread with margarine.

What is it that I really wanted? The whole world but no sweating for it, opportunities for which all I would have to do is to appraise them and refuse them. But it was not that way, it would never be that way. I'm walking on a one-way street to perdition.

Excitement, affluence—I craved these. I've spent time in thought but not for any ennobling cause, least of all my own betterment. So here I am by myself, alone. I could be blown down by one chill wind, and it is perhaps for the best then that I sleep through it all, the season of thunder and lightning. I had listened to an old lullaby that shut my eyes and dulled my brain, for this, too, was what I wanted: to be lulled into forgetting. But how can I forget that young bird I had picked up, fallen from its nest in the buri palm, unable to fly because it was too young?

I have asked myself how far I should go, what it is that should make me happy, urge me on, and always it has been a full stomach, a sound sleep. Now, I am not too sure anymore of these desires, though they still command my waking hours. All I know is that there should be wings on my feet and light in my mind where once all was darkness and mustiness and age.

What have I really done with my years? I am older than almost all of my classmates. Perhaps I have held on foolishly to the bliss of youth, that there need be no justification for this breathing. Yet in the depths of me I had been perhaps in love with death, not life, because I have not cared for anyone but myself and the self dies as surely as flesh rots, and death, after all, is the boundary. And this selfish, unthinking self had failed to give, not even to Mother and Auntie Bettina, a little of itself.

I would like now to be different?

Will I be permitted this? Will I be strong? I know it will be difficult, for it is the strong who write the laws, make the prisons. Will I be like them? Will I also feed the weak with lies, just as I fed the hogs in Cabugawan with mush so they would fatten easily?

I CROSSED the underpass to Quezon and headed for Plaza Miranda. My stomach was beginning to churn and I was sorry we had not waited for Father Jess in the auditorium so we could have eaten.

The thought of hurrying back to Lucy's *dinengdeng* was depressing. It was too late now for the other pleasure, for my aunt and uncle would already be home and Lucy absolutely, resolutely refused once they were there. One night I had gone down on the pretext of going to the toilet, but had detoured to her cot under the stairs. She woke up, and when she realized it was me who was kissing her, she hit me in the stomach so hard I almost screamed. Then she whispered sweetly, softly: "Pepe, they are here."

I paused before a crummy noodle restaurant, then went in. Nothing like a bowl of steaming noodles. These tasted soapy and the *siopao espesyal,* God knows what meats were in it. When I was through, I decided on a double feature, a war picture and a *bomba*— at Life.

I really like movies; I even kept a listing of the films I had seen since I got to Manila and rated them. I was partial to science fiction. They propelled me into another world, real in the mind, plausible to reckon with.

It was drizzling when I got out, that soft, malevolent rain that one expects to pass but instead goes on interminably. There were a few jeepneys and I could easily clamber into one, but I decided to walk home. Auntie Bettina would be coming soon; she said she would be in Manila in a month, but two months now had gone by.

I should not be walking this late; there were robberies and people did not bother reporting them to the police anymore. I knew a little karate and felt a bit safe; besides, what could they possibly extort from a student like me, walking in the rain perhaps to save jeepney fare? When I got to Recto, however, as if by some heavenly signal, the rain abruptly stopped. It was not a long walk to Dimasalang and Antipolo, and I recalled Mother telling me that she and Father walked this distance when they were students to save on jeepney fare.

It all came to me, hazy and cobwebbed like some disordered dream, his visit to Cabugawan, the few things he had written that I had read, fragments of ideas, and through it all, I could not quite understand why Mother kept it away from me, this one truth that would have meant so much, particularly when I was young and would be asked who my father was. It became clearer now, Auntie Bettina and Mother, they both wanted me to be like him, a university professor maybe, so that I could also marry properly—an heiress perhaps.

I could do that, of course, look for a rich girl with a face like a hot cake, with pimples as big as tomatoes, but girls like her were not in Recto; they were in the exclusive colleges, and it would never be my luck or inclination to meet any of them because I considered them beyond my reach.

I was surprised when I arrived in Antipolo to find Lucy waiting in the unlighted *sala;* after a first light knock so Tia Betty and Tio Bert would not waken she was there and whispering, "Pepe, is that you?"

In the darkness, I sought her, but she drew away and asked if I had eaten, and curiously, I was hungry again. She switched on the light; there was food on the table; it was cold, but I did not mind. The abominable vegetable stew that we were fated to eat every day tasted unusually good. She hovered by asking where I had been, what kept me so late, and I beckoned her to come close and when she did, thinking perhaps that I would whisper to her, I fondled her thighs instead. She let me, but her hand went quickly to my side and her pinch was a shock of sharp pain.

She would not let me wash the dishes; she would do it in the morning. I tried to kiss her good night but she eluded me, shaking her head and whispering, "I told you . . . I told you . . . ," so I went up the stairs on bare feet; my only pair of shoes were wet and I wondered if they would be dry in the morning.

I WAS AWAKENED by happy voices downstairs and I recognized the voice of Auntie Bettina. I rushed down in my shorts. When she saw me, she let go of the bundle she was holding, rushed to me, and kissed me. "Now, Pepe, help me with these—" She had brought with her those infernal vegetables, camote tops, eggplants, and bitter melons, a bottle of salted fish, coconut candy, half a sack of rice, mudfish squirming in a buri bag, and, at the bottom, snails—the small kind that I used to gather in the irrigation ditches and in the flooded fields. Tia Betty and Tio Bert were full of admonition: "Bettina, you should not have brought all these . . . and the taxi fare from the station . . . I hope you found a taxi with an honest meter. Bettina, we can get all these here, and you know, it may even be cheaper."

They had to rush off to their jobs and Auntie Bettina, too, had to go to the Department of Education to follow up on her raise, which had not come for eight years. But I did not have to hurry, and when Lucy had put away everything and even roasted a mudfish, we were all by ourselves again, alive to the promise that had not been fulfilled the evening before.

MY FIRST CLASS was World Lit, and when I got there Toto said Professor Hortenso wanted to see me. It was very important. I must not fail to see him before the end of the morning period.

I did not have to go to the Faculty Room after World Lit; Professor Hortenso was waiting for us at the door as we filed out. I had Philippine History next, but he said my teacher would not mind if I was ten minutes late. We went to a corner where the boisterous shuffling of students was muted. He asked if I had ever thought of becoming a writer like my uncle.

"Farthest thing from my thoughts, sir," I said.

"You can start becoming one then. It is not difficult. What is important is for you to arrange your ideas properly, logically. Then just put them down. Toto told me that you can write."

I looked at him, puzzled.

"Toto said that your report on Manuel Arguilla was held up as a good example of literary criticism by your teacher."

I did not realize Toto had taken such an interest in me. "Pepe," Professor Hortenso was saying, "I am the moderator of the student paper. I am also one of the three judges. The examination will be held at seven in the evening, at the small auditorium. There will be about a hundred participants, maybe more. Take it. It could mean a minor post . . . and it will make you stand out in school. A scholarship, too. And most important, it would mean a little pocket money."

Money. Now I could explain my watch, my bankbook even.

I did not go home for lunch. At noon when I told him I'd go home, Toto said I should stay in school and do some research in the library on newspapering so I would be ready for the exam. I had always been honest with him and when he asked why I did not want to stay, I said simply I had to go home to eat. Again, he treated me to lunch and despite my protests shoved a five-peso bill into my pocket. "Return it when you get your pay," he said.

The exam that afternoon was not difficult, mostly commonsense stuff about headlines, what to present in news stories, things that one should know by instinct after a casual perusal of any newspaper. The essay-writing part was even easier—a nonsense piece about the role of youth in a changing society. I was perhaps the first to finish, but even so, it was already past nine when I got home.

Auntie Bettina and Lucy were watching Nora Aunor on TV when I arrived. Lucy set the table for me and though I had eaten at six I was hungry. What a wonderful change—vegetable stew with mudfish and the snails cooked in coconut milk. While I gorged Auntie Bettina plied me with questions; she was disappointed that I was not in the state university, but I told her that, with my low grades, to aspire for that was futile. She was happy with just the thought that I was going to school. And Cabugawan and Mother? I was anxious to know about her health, for she never mentioned it in her letters though I always asked. She was all right, she was sewing and saving, and I should not worry because Auntie Bettina was there to look after her.

I told her about my taking the editorial exams and this pleased her. I said that I would sleep on the sofa downstairs, and she could take my bed, but no, she would have none of that. As a compromise, she agreed to take my bed—she would be in Manila for a couple of days—and I could sleep on the floor beside her.

With the raucous sounds of Antipolo finally stilled, I decided to ask her. "Every time I look out of that window, Auntie, I see the spot where Father was killed. Why did you not tell me? Why did Mother not tell me?"

She stirred, then sat on the edge of the bed; her face, in the soft light, was troubled. She bit her lip and when she finally spoke, she was almost pleading. "You have to forgive and forget many things, Pepe. So, they told you—we should have expected it. But your mama and I— We had quite forgotten that they knew. In the beginning, your mother wanted to tell you, but so many things held her back. He was always in our minds, Pepe. I remember how you used to ask me, but when you grew older, you stopped. And remember how I used to tell you, you have a good head? Just like your father. And you look so much like him!"

"Why did you not tell me?"

"I do not know," she said. "When you were small, Manang and

I— We believed it was best that you did not know. They were first cousins, you know, and that was not good. Your uncle being your father. Do you understand, Pepe?"

"I don't," I said, although it did not matter anymore. "They do it all the time now. It would not have made any difference."

"Then your father got married," Tia Bettina said. "It was not your mother's fault, or his. He did not know you were born. Your mother— She wanted his marriage to succeed. His wife was very wealthy. And someday, when you are through with college, I hope you will marry just as well."

So this was the purpose of my education: to marry well. It was all so clear and simple.

"Why was I not told?" I insisted.

"Does it matter now? What is important for you to remember is that your mother did everything to make life easy for you, to provide for you, and that she did it alone."

She did not have to tell me this, and I was humbled by it. "Stay in my place, Auntie, just one moment."

She was silent. I had to know so I asked again: "Whose fault was it? What did Mother do wrong?"

She answered quickly, "Your mother is an honorable woman. Be proud of her. I do not know anyone else who would do what she did, not just with honor but with pride. So you see us quarreling sometimes, but that is just between sisters. I know what she has done, not just for you but also for your father. She would rather suffer."

"Why didn't he come and see her? When he visited us long ago, did he know? Why didn't he take care of her? And if Mother did no wrong, then it was he. It was he!"

She shushed me; I would wake up my relatives. She got off the bed and sat beside me. "Pepe," she said, "it was not his fault either. No one else's. They were not fated from the beginning. You will grow older and you will understand. He was a good man; do not hate him."

I shook my head. "Whatever you say cannot change my feelings toward him."

"He tried," she said. "I know. But he died."

"He was a liar," I said. "His book—all those principles . . . he could not even face the simplest responsibility. How could he have written such things?"

"Believe me, Pepe," she was now distraught. "He was the best Cabugawan could produce. He was good, honest. You should be proud of him, now that you know."

"I will always remember him in shame," I said.

She went back to bed after patting me on the shoulder. A baggage train thundered by, throwing its light on the walls, shaking the house. From down the alley, a balut vendor called out, then the faulty silence of Antipolo once more.

I could not sleep; questions crowded my mind. "Auntie?"

She stirred. "Yes, Pepe?"

"How did it start?"

"Your mother and he— They were both here, in this house, but they knew each other in Cabugawan."

"What was he like? His picture in his book . . ."

"He was good-looking," her voice quiet with remembering. "And he was very good in school. A full scholar. That was how he managed to study in the United States. The best university there. He also went to Spain—and yes, he spoke Spanish. Imagine someone in our family speaking Spanish! He looked just like— Look in the mirror. Same eyes, same wide brow. And he also read a lot."

"I don't want to be a teacher," I said.

"Not like me, but like him."

"I will not marry into a rich family."

"It is too early to tell," she said, smiling.

"And I am sure I will not dishonor any girl or bring into this world an illegitimate child."

The July night was cool, frogs announced themselves noisily in the ditch below, and the raucous talk of late passersby walking on the tracks drifted to us, broken and incessant. Far away, the siren of a police car or an ambulance wailed, the snort of jeepneys making their last rounds. It was long past midnight, but I could not sleep. There was this last question that ached to be asked, the answer to which could, perhaps, unravel a skein without end. Finally: "Did he really commit suicide?"

My aunt was silent for a time then, almost in a whisper: "I had hoped your mother would tell you everything. After your father died, she visited Carmen Villa. It was a very difficult meeting. She was in a sanitarium, she was deaf and very thin. Your mama, she never believed Manong Tony was killed in an accident. They had lived for years here, and he knew the tracks. Carmen Villa confirmed what your mama thought. Carmen told her it was to show his integrity, when he did not have to, when she never doubted it. There were no letters saying good-bye. Your mama— She agreed with Carmen Villa. But how can we tell you this? It was bad enough that you are a—"

"Bastard!" I finished it for her.

She was silent again. "To tell you that your father killed himself, no . . . you will not understand."

A cock crowed, and after some time Auntie began to snore softly. The world was asleep, and I was still awake, my mind open to the stirring wind, my ears alert to the sounds of my own torment, which had hounded me since I learned who I was. But now they filled me with a loathing beyond words, made me want to flee not just Cabugawan but even this Antipolo where my father had lived and died.

AUNTIE BETTINA returned to Rosales Sunday afternoon, but before she left she admonished: "Whatever you think, just remember one thing: We love you. You will have many problems, but we will always be there. And your mother—please, do not hurt her anymore."

"I will not steal again," I said. "But I am not too sure that I can keep the promise."

"It was a youthful mistake," she said.

"I wanted the money," I said flatly.

"You will get it someday, like your father."

"Don't remind me of him."

"You will also write," she said, leaving me at the gate, for her bus was getting ready to move. She waved at me before going in, and I stood at the railing till the bus had pulled away.

SHE WAS RIGHT, of course, about my writing, for on that day Professor Hortenso left a message with Toto, and Toto was all smiles as he went with me and the professor to his apartment in Dapitan. It was not a long walk. And for Toto, it was an honor to be invited with me to Professor Hortenso's house for lunch.

His wife had prepared the meal just for the two of them and though she welcomed us good-naturedly, I was quite sure she was displeased at our unannounced presence. Still, she must have gotten used to many an unexpected guest. She asked to be excused while she worked in the kitchen.

We had talked of nothing but the Brotherhood all the way through P. Noval, although I knew, of course, that he had something important to say, but there was time for that. We were almost through with the sour shrimp soup and Mrs. Hortenso was preparing the coffee. Professor Hortenso got up from the dining table, walked over to his desk in one dingy corner, and brought out a bottle of Fundador. I had sipped whiskey once but never brandy, and to my protests he said, "There is always the first time. Just don't drink it too fast. It is stronger than rum or *cuatro cantos*. Sip it."

He passed the glasses with a flourish, his eyes crinkling in pleasure: "We have to celebrate. Pepe, you are the new literary editor. One of the judges wanted you immediately to be the managing editor, but you are a freshman."

Toto was looking at me, wonder in his eyes.

"Thank you, sir," I said, "I know you said good things about me. I cannot thank you enough."

He took off his glasses; he looked younger without them. "But that is it! I was the last to go over the papers. You were one of the ten newcomers. I did not say a single word about you. The three other judges did all the talking—they were all for you, the way you wrote your essay, 'The Role of Youth.' They simply loved it, the probity, the freshness."

"I wrote as simply as I could, like you said."

"Simplicity," the professor was expansive. "Not simple. You know the difference."

I nodded.

"It was unanimous. You will be the literary editor, which means you are third in line. And next year, you can be managing, like I said, or even the editor. You have no one to be grateful to but yourself. You don't owe me anything."

"You told me, sir, to take the exam. Toto gave me hints. No, I am grateful just the same."

The brandy burned my throat. Toto must have been drinking in the sacristy for he emptied his glass without wincing.

Mrs. Hortenso joined us for the same weak coffee in the living room, her handsome face streaked with perspiration, which she wiped with her apron. The living room was shabby and cluttered with magazines and pamphlets, the old rattan furniture covered with crocheted doilies. But if the house was threadbare, it was certainly rich with books. One wall was lined with shelves and the books were even laid atop one another so that no space was wasted.

Mrs. Hortenso saw me looking at the titles. "That's where his salary goes," she said. "Why, if he could, he would also pay for the publication of the articles of Juan Puneta."

Professor Hortenso scowled at her, but she did not mind him. I had heard of Puneta—a man of great wealth, a champion of nationalist causes, a graduate of one of the English universities; he also had the reputation of being unabashedly on the side of virtue.

Mrs. Hortenso must have noted my questioning look. "If you'll be with the organization long enough, you will surely meet him. And you will be able to know what he has between his ears. He thinks he is a writer, too."

Professor Hortenso looked at her again, and I could see he was not pleased with the revelations his wife was making. Mrs. Hortenso continued blithely: "I wonder who reads all the things my husband writes. I do, of course, because I have to proofread them."

The professor's countenance changed and he smiled at her.

"I hope you will not be a writer," Mrs. Hortenso said, appraising me, "even if you are urged to be one. I hope in the end you will do something else. Otherwise, I will have nothing but pity for whoever your wife will be."

"I will not get married, ma'am," I said.

"He will be a priest," Toto added.

She laughed then left us to do the dishes, for they had no maid. By ourselves, Professor Hortenso became serious. "Tell me, Pepe," he asked, "what are your plans?"

"I don't know, sir," I said. "I told you I need money."

"I understand that," he said. "But what will you write? What will you do after school? What can you do for the Brotherhood? You are a member, you know—an important member. And most of all, you can write. How will you use your time?"

I was tempted to brag about my karate lessons, how good I had become with the flying kick, but Toto would probably not understand. "I don't really like writing, sir," I said, "unless I have to. It is easy for me, stringing words together, but my thoughts sometimes come faster than I can write them."

"What do you like to do then?"

"Eat," I said quickly. I would have added "fuck," but that would have shocked Toto.

They laughed and I joined them. "He is always making jokes," Toto said, thinking perhaps I was being funny and did not realize how honestly, how truly I liked to eat. I always look back, for instance, to my first week in Manila—the *comida China,* the steak, the whole fried chicken, the pig innard *halo-halo,* and that exotic lunch at the Japanese restaurant. To have the stomach full, to savor all new and wonderful tastes—how I longed for these. I wanted to tell them that the Brotherhood bored me, that I joined only because I did not want to say no to Toto, that if I had to be a writer so that I could make a little money, I would do that—it would certainly be safer, perhaps more mentally exacting, but I would not have to deal with psychos and those poor addicts. I would write for money, be a politician, be a member of the Student Council only because these positions meant money, scholarship, the things that would make life comfortable and worth all the sweat and the saliva.

Professor Hortenso was saying, "Your essay was easily the best and it should be in the first issue of the paper. We will offprint about a thousand, distribute them within the organization, to other schools, paste them on bulletin boards. Then the Student Council, and afterward, maybe secretary, and, finally, president. With this essay, you will be very popular on the campus. Your election is almost assured."

We would have stayed longer talking about politics and the Brotherhood, but he had a class at three and I was eager to rush home to Lucy.

As we walked toward the boulevard for the ride to Dimasalang, Toto was all questions: "What did you put in that essay? You made such an impression on Professor Hortenso, he even told me you could easily be the best editorial writer the paper ever had. I always knew you could write, ever since that paper you wrote on *Don Quixote.*"

"I read Cervantes three times. And not in comic books."

"What did you say in the essay?" he was insistent.

"What they wanted to hear," I said with some disgust. "What else would I say? I can dance to any tune they play, I anticipate their moods, their desires. I was not being honest, the way I am honest with you. Those blasted judges—sorry, Toto, but I suppose this includes Professor Hortenso—they are full of shit. They expect us to be full of shit, too. I just wrote what they wanted. It was so damn easy to fool them."

"Pepe!" he sounded aghast. "You are joking again."

"I am not," I said. "What do you think the role of the youth is?"

We paused and he turned to me, his eyes afire with purpose, with vision and all the blather that the Brotherhood had pounded into him. "To look toward the future," he said in a tone almost exalting. "To see to it that the mistakes of the past will not be committed again. To create a society that is egalitarian, that is dedicated to the upliftment of the masses. To serve the people, that is what!"

"Bullshit!" I shouted at him. "Now listen, my friend. The youth have no role. They have no jobs. They have no money. They are not in power and they do not make decisions. If there is going to be a war, they will all be dumped into the army. And they will be killed like young men everywhere have been killed—whether or not they believe in the war. Having no role is their role."

He stared at me, unbelieving. "You really think that?"

I nodded.

"And still wrote differently?"

I nodded again.

He took a deep breath, then it came, "Son of a whore! Cheat, liar!"

"Son of a whore yourself," I flung back. "I did it for something. Can you not see that? How can I pay back the five pesos you loaned me? The *siopao* you stuffed into my stomach? Get it into your simple head that I need the money, the scholarship. I am honest with myself, Toto, and with you. So, damn you, don't you ever call me a liar. You are my friend so I am telling you this. Now—" I poked a finger at his face. I had become really angry with him, and we had stopped on the sidewalk. "Now, shall we go on being friends, or is this the last time I will talk with you?"

Toto bowed and shook his head; when he turned to me again and we started walking, his eyes, even with his eyeglasses on, were misty. "I understand, Pepe," his voice quavered. "Yes, we will always be friends. But can you not see?" His face was taut and pale. "It is so clear. You had to do this, to lie, to cheat—things you really don't like to do—and only because you—" his voice was now hoarse, "you . . . we, Pepe . . . we are poor. The *Wretched of the Earth*—read it some time. We—the poor—have no choice."

His voice faltered and he turned away; he was crying, so I placed an arm around his shoulder. We had reached the boulevard.

A jeepney to Dimasalang had come. "But we are not alone now, Toto," I said, then broke hastily away from him. What he had said skewered me, lanced me, hurt me so grievously it was almost physical.

LUCY did not help ease my depression. By now she was used to my erratic schedule and took my late arrivals with grace. Without my telling her, she lighted the kerosene stove and heated a lunch of snail and mudfish, but the food at Professor Hortenso's had sufficed. Perhaps she was surprised that I gave her but a perfunctory kiss when I arrived, and when I called from upstairs that I was not hungry, she came up to my room and lay beside me.

For some time now, I had been thinking about our relationship—extremely convenient and pleasurable—but there were aspects of it that were hazy. Too many questions had begun to form in my mind that needed to be answered. What, for instance, if she got pregnant.

"You don't have to worry about that," she assured me, pressing her belly to my side. "I am taking pills."

"Where did you get them?"

"Do you need to know?"

"I would like to."

"Come with me to the Family Planning Center in Dimasalang—that is where I sometimes go when I say I am going to my sister's."

"You had to fill out forms?"

She laughed. "Do I have to tell the truth?"

"Did he start you on pills?"

She was silent.

"We cannot get married, you know that."

"Because I am just a servant?"

That never entered my mind as the reason. "No," I protested. "I cannot feed you."

"I can feed myself," she said with a laugh.

But her relationship with the other man irritated me. "Do you still see him?" I asked, hoping she would not avoid the question.

She stood up. "I thought this is something we will not talk about," she said pointedly. "If I see him now and then, it's not important to you."

"It is," I said, rising and confronting her. "I don't want to share you with anyone."

"I am not your wife."

"You prostitute!" I lashed at her.

She looked at me aghast, then turned and ran down the stairs.

I did not follow her; I had uttered *the* word and quickly realized my mistake. Remorse filled me. I had no money to give Lucy. How about him, whoever he was? And why was she not faithful to him if she loved him?

She was in the living room when I went down, lying on the sofa; her eyes were red from crying, but there were no more tears. I sat beside her, and she turned on her back. "Lucy," I said, "forgive me. I love you."

I surprised myself, telling her I loved her, holding her hand, kissing her hair. "I cannot bear the thought that another man . . ."

She remained immobile; she did not push my hand or turn away as I kissed her cheek. Words were not enough, but still . . . "Be honest with me. I love you, can you not see that? Who is he? What has he that I don't have, that you still have to go to him making all those pretenses that it is your sister you are seeing? Why can't you leave him? Does he give you a lot of money—and I cannot even give you a centavo . . ."

She turned on her side and hugged me. "Pepe," she said in a voice husky with sorrow, "we cannot change things now. Yes, your uncle gives me money."

Litany of Slavery

I T WAS just a matter of time before I would lose Lucy—this I knew not as instinct but as implacable fate, and the knowledge seared. She was the first; she was, like myself, a victim of this vicious condition, this living. Could we have avoided not just this entanglement but this very station into which we were flung? Always, there is something conspiratorial about circumstances that merge and fit, about feelings that ravage, showing how human and fickle we all are.

I always remember what Mother told me when I was about nine or ten: all those we love we will eventually lose, all those we hate we will eventually face. This is the inevitable sequence, the deafening roll that follows the lightning flash, the drab brown of the fields after the living green of the rainy season.

My first loss that Mother had described came the year the harvest had been niggardly. I thought I would never be able to continue schooling, which would not have mattered, except that, for Mother, this would have meant the end of the world.

I was fond of animals as if they were friends with whom I talked—stray dogs, cats, carabaos, hens and the roosters that chased and mounted them. I understand now the refusal of Buddhists to kill animals although they may not hesitate to dispose of their fellow men who cross them. They would eat meat as long as they did not do the actual butchering. I read somewhere that the cows roaming the streets of India are holy not because they are anointed but because, in rural India, they provide milk for the people and fire for their stoves. They may just be a pack of old, rickety bones held together by tough, dried-up skin, but an Indian writer said he could not endure to see them killed for meat because he had grown up with them, slept with them on the same earthen floor.

I understand this feeling.

The space below our house was walled with split bamboo, and there we stored battered furniture that could no longer be salvaged but were still precious enough not to be dispatched as firewood. Under the house, too, were four solid hardwood posts uprooted from the Ilocos. A huge bamboo basket sat in the center, circular and tall as a man and wide enough to contain a calf. During the harvest season it was half filled with the grain some of Mother's customers used to pay her. But in June, July, and August, the basket was empty, for we had either eaten all the grain or Mother had sold it for my school expenses.

I often slept inside this basket, curled at the bottom with my dog, Pugot. An earlier pet, also named Pugot, a big, fat pig, was much too heavy for me to bring inside. We had no farm, so the underhouse was not to house work animals except when the pig Pugot, which we had gotten from one of Mother's customers as a piglet, grew into a beautiful beast. When it was big enough to sell, the money would be shared by Mother and the owner. Pugot was a "mestizo," with pink skin, white bristles, a very short snout, elephant ears, a tail that curled, rosy hooves, and the bluest eyes. In the mornings before the dew had vanished, I went to the fields beyond the arbor of bamboo and gathered leafy weeds, which, together with leftovers and bran, I cooked for him. He recognized his name; when I called he would rush to the gate grunting, then lie on his side as I stooped to scratch his stomach. I sometimes slept under the house with him on frayed jute sacks laid on the ground, and more than once I had rested my head on his belly. I had feared for his life when he was castrated and felt it a gross injustice to this handsome animal to have been treated thus and made to grow unlike a normal being, but grow up he did, into a huge and lumbering thing—so heavy that once, in his eagerness to meet me as I was coming home from school, he threw me to the ground.

By then, Mother and I were tired. There were not enough leftovers from the neighbors who also had pigs of their own, nor enough edible weeds in the field or free bran from the mill. The dry season came, then it was June and always, in June, there was this harried scrounging for money for the school opening.

The day before school opened I returned from the fields where I had gone to catch grasshoppers for our evening pot. For the first time, there was no white behemoth rushing to me. A chill came to my heart as I raced up the bamboo ladder to where Mother was at work, taking advantage of the last vestiges of afternoon light. She turned to me, her face pained and drawn. I had always anticipated Pugot's fate, but I cried just the same when she confirmed it. She told me how much we got for Pugot, that I could go on to school, although I did not care for it. She told me then—and this I will never forget—that we will lose all those dear to us, and those we hate, we must face.

Then Auntie Bettina gave me a black puppy. I came to love him like I did Pugot. The dog was a mongrel, but a beautiful animal nonetheless, with sad, luminous eyes and soft glossy fur. It had belonged to a fellow teacher who was migrating to the United States. There was no one to take care of the puppy. Auntie Bettina happened to be in Manila for one of those interminable bouts with the bureaucracy, and her friend asked if she would please take the puppy. He grew up, not big and cumbersome like Pugot, but just as handsome and well admired by the women who came to the house.

One of them was the mayor's wife, a stick of a woman with a dozen children, who loved loud colors, dazzling reds and deep blues, so that when she flapped down the street, one knew it was she even at a distance. She had a demanding, grating voice, and if she did not order a dress almost every week, Mother would not have put up with her as a customer. When she first saw Pugot, her face was immediately agleam with the same acquisitive expression she had when she saw a gaudy piece of cloth.

Pugot may have sensed the evil in her, for he would cower and whimper no matter how she tried to coax him in the kitchen or under the house. She was asthmatic, her breath coming in gusts that plumed out of her flaring nostrils and her gaping, painted mouth.

When she had attacks, so we learned, she would hug the pillows and wet them with her frothing, her wheezing tormenting her household. Her husband took the frustrations of sleepless nights out on the luckless people in the *municipio*, lashing out at the underpaid clerks and policemen, his bleary eyes and listless mien transforming him from a mild and gregarious politician into a ranting devil—a state that lasted the whole morning but disappeared when he had slouched on his sofa and gotten a drink of gin and the sleep he had missed.

It was he who came to the house one day and said that he wanted Pugot for his wife. He was offering a lot of money only because Pugot was all black with not a single patch of white on him.

Mother told him I should be consulted, although I had listened to the whole transaction from the kitchen, where I cuddled Pugot. The mayor told Mother about her working without a license, that she was not paying income tax, also contrary to law. And finally, his wife would take her business to another dressmaker, but—some hesitant laughter here—all these would be "conveniently forgotten" and never dredged up again if Mother was willing to part with an insignificant little dog. He would also give her thirty pesos for it, which was just too much.

"And what have you to say, Pepe?" Mother asked.

"Why do you want Pugot, *Apo*?" I asked. He smiled beatifically; he had not yet had his gin or his nap, for his eyes were bleary and the smile became one gurgling laughter that tapered into a sigh. "Ah, my boy, you should come and see!" He brought out a wad of bills and started counting. Mother received the money glumly.

After he had gone, the whimpering dog in his arm, I followed him. He was just going up to his house when I reached their gate. I called out and he turned to me, his blob of a head shaking in disbelief.

"You really want to know?" he asked.

I nodded.

In their living room, the mayor's wife was seated on a rattan chair; she was fanning herself, and when she saw Pugot she stood up, came to me, and hugged me like a leech saying in a breath that stank how grateful she was that I would give up my pet. Yes, it would not be in vain for now her asthma would be cured.

With her was Lakay Benito; we went to the *batalan*—the open space behind the kitchen where the earthen jars and the wash were hung and where, in most provincial houses, the artesian well also stood. I pitied Pugot and was disgusted at myself, the mayor, and the people around us. Reciting some incomprehensible phrases, Lakay Benito went to the table where Pugot lay, his paws now bound together. The mayor held the dog up while Lakay Benito, now finished with his mumbling, raised a small gleaming knife, searched for the vein in my dog's throat and with one swift stroke, slashed into it. Pugot started to thrash but to no avail, and as blood spurted out, the mayor raised the dog higher. His wife now stood before him, her cavernous mouth open, her eyes closed. The blood splattered into that cavern, and down her neck, onto the front of her dress. She lapped it, making happy throaty sounds while Pugot thrashed and quivered, then stopped moving altogether.

They said I could wait for some dogmeat to bring home, but I did not linger; they laid my dead Pugot on the table and the mayor's wife glanced at me, her eyes glistening with gratitude. She came to the house the following day and ordered three new dresses, but she never had a chance to wear them, for that same week she died in her sleep.

HOW WOULD it be when Lucy left? Would we part with recriminations that would scar us both? I could no longer bear staying in Antipolo. Hearing the trains rumble by, smelling the fetid decay along the weed-choked tracks, repelled me, angered me.

Mila next door had become a sweet nuisance as well, for her invitations had now become indiscreet. She seemed to know just when I would leave for school, and once, on the pretext that she was going to Quiapo, she walked with me to Dimasalang.

I was really taken aback that same evening when Kuya Nick was at our door, apparently waiting for me. He asked me to walk with him to Avenida, to one of the new air-conditioned restaurants near the railroad crossing. On the way he had remained matter-of-fact, his face serene and quiet. He wanted me to order dinner, but hunger had left me, and I asked instead for coffee. He, too, had a cup—nothing more, and with the first sip, he shook his head with displeasure. "Now," he said, "there's really nothing like coffee from Benguet. Better than Batangas. You should learn to patronize your own, you know."

I was no coffee connoisseur; in Cabugawan, our morning coffee was really corn roasted black, then brewed and flavored with milk and raw cane sugar, and the brew was far more exhilarating than what I now had. I was apprehensive; I thought he had learned of Mila's efforts to seduce me. I did not expect him to start with a nationalist spiel and had, somehow, never connected him with such interests, so when he asked if I was an activist, I was not sure why he asked.

"Not all the way," I said. "It is one way of getting something—a scholarship, money."

"Just as I thought," he sighed. A waitress with high wooden clogs and a flat chest asked if he needed another cup, but he waved her away. "It's all right," he continued, "as long as you know what you want. But be careful, you may start believing what you say—and then you forget the important things."

"Important things?"

He sat back, his brow creased. "It is important that you know the nature of man, of the society in which we live." He sounded like a college instructor, his English impeccable though interspersed with Tagalog.

"Would you believe it, Pepe?" he enthused. "I was a working student, went to Ateneo, and finished with a B.A. in sociology. The first thing you must understand is that we are status-conscious; we easily believe in appearances. At night, I was a waiter and a pimp in Dewey Boulevard. I often fell asleep during the lectures. You would not think, looking at me now—my cars, these clothes—that I did not wear shoes until I reached high school."

"You have climbed very high," I said.

"Ha!" he leaned over, his eyes alight with pleasure, his mouth drawn across his fleshy face in a grin. "School helped a lot—the friends I made there, the contacts, the entry into the homes of the genteel upper class. Upper class!" he snorted contemptuously.

His tone became tense, conspiratorial: "I worked very hard, saved all I could, and started pushing early. I had only three shirts in college, a couple of dark pants, a pair of black shoes—Ang Tibay. But I kept them clean. And when I had saved enough, I bought a car—a secondhand Ford, but I kept it running. Then I looked around for the fortune to be made. It was not difficult, the girls, the boys who were spendthrifts, who never knew the likes of me, slaving to make it to their level. And I did it and here I am, still making money off the bastards!"

He emptied his cup. "One thing you must remember," he said, easing himself back into his chair, "everyone can be corrupted because everyone is human. Give me an hour—maybe that is too long—with your student leaders, with your nationalist idols in Congress, and I will have their price."

As I pondered what he said, he asked: "What is your price, Pepe?"

His question did not surprise me. "I don't know," I said.

"What is it you want most?"

It was as if I had known the answer to this question all along; I wanted to live well, to be rich, but now that it was put to me in its utterest simplicity, I had no ready, unequivocal reply.

"To be truly alive," I said tentatively, wondering if those were the right words, and then it came to me in all its morning clarity. Indeed, this was what I desired, to be fully alive, to have a real meaning to my waking and sleeping, that I was no vegetable in a simple photosynthetic relationship with the sun, that every pore in me exuded not just animal sweat but the essence of me. "To be honestly, truly alive," I repeated.

He sat back as if stupefied by my reply. "That is very tricky of you," he said somberly. "What is it then that makes you alive? Money? Food? Women? Reading—ah, I noticed you are fond of books."

"Those and more," I said.

"Money," he mused, "can buy everything."

I shook my head. "Not friends," I said. "Because if money can buy them then they are not friends. Not loyalty. Not love."

Kuya Nick toyed with his empty cup. His hair was thick, but at the crown it had started to thin. It was deep black as the dye was fresh.

I had come up with a good definition of my wants, but I did not want to make him feel I had confounded him. "You act as if you have planned everything. Did you ever plan on being in love?" I asked.

He glanced at me and again, a smile crossed his rotund face. He gazed at the bright *capiz* globe dangling from the paneled ceiling. "Yes, Pepe, I have been in love. Still am. No, it's not Mila, whom I like very much. Do you know where she came from? Rather, where I salvaged her? I don't want to boast about what I do. I have a wife and three children—the oldest is now in his teens—and I love them and shield them from what I am, from what I know." His voice became stern. "I have told you more than I should," he said, his eyes piercing into me. "But only because I think you are honest. You must never do this: get people to know you, be really close to you, to read you like a book."

"I will remember that."

"There, up there in the enclaves of privilege, they know me as Nick, efficient, trustworthy, dependable. I come across with the goods, the contacts, and the contracts—at the time agreed upon. They don't need to sign stacks of paper with me. My word is enough. Real estate dealer, customs broker—everything. My office is small, but it is up there, too. The other things I do, they don't know. My family, where I live—these I keep away. These are mine alone. And elsewhere, I am Nick the avenger, the merciless harbinger of my law."

"I don't want to be on any side other than yours," I said. "I am scared. Besides, it will not be decent."

"Do not think about decency, Pepe," his voice rose again. "This is an indecent world. All those people dressed up, attending those concerts, those fancy parties splashed in the society pages—they are all indecent. Each has his little scheme and in the end, they all use people."

"You use people, too," I reminded him.

He balled his fists. "Listen, I will not deny that, but when I use you, you will know it and you will get what is your due, just as it has already been so. And you will get more, if you are smart. That makes the difference!"

We stood up and walked back to Antipolo, through the shuttered stalls of the market, the leaves, and the garbage thick as shingles on the asphalt and on the sidewalk, and the stench of rotting vegetables around us. Then Kuya Nick told me why he had waited for me; he was a master politician, he had really worked me over, molded me to the form he could handle best, and he did this with his homilies, his ingratiating confidences that could have been lies but sounded sincere.

This was one of those emergencies and he would not have thought of me were I not dependable. Indeed, I was the man for it, with my capabilities and endowments.

"You will enjoy it," he said, pausing in our walk, his eyes narrowed into serious slits. "I would not bother you, Pepe, you know that, unless it was really serious. I am compromised."

The job was vague at first, but now it became unmistakably clear, and I should have been revolted by it, but I was not.

"You can do it—you have done it," he said, breaking into a nervous laugh, and of course, he was right. "It will not be different. It will be in an apartment, with privacy, and you won't even know who will be watching. No cracks in the wall. A one-way mirror."

I had one last argument and it would have sufficed, but he had a ready answer for that, too.

"You will be with someone familiar. As a matter-of-fact, she is quite good-looking if I may say so."

WE HURRIED to Makati. It was an unhealthy August evening, a break from the nine-day rain, with this strangling humidity that permeated everything, enervated the senses, and fogged the mind. We banged away through rutted streets, and in his air-conditioned Mercedes we were free from the gummy clutches of the hour, free from the warm glue of traffic, free from the urinal odor of neighborhoods. Then Quiapo, Taft, and the new highway to Makati, the center embankments screaming with the posters of revolution, *Ibagsak ang Pasismo, Marcos Diktador** . . .

But there will be no revolution, no change in this rimless bog of creation; the poor have always been with us, Cabugawan, Tondo, and everywhere, the hovels and the scum. Bonifacio and Sulaiman— where are they now? What have they really left behind except a Tondo that will be there for another millennium? There will be no revolution, not while the only honest thing we can perceive is in our gonads.

Ibagsak ang Pasismo, Marcos Diktador: Down with Marcos!

We stopped before one of those spindly apartment buildings in Makati. At the far end of the lobby, aglow with *capiz* shell lamps, across the shimmering expanse of Romblon marble, Mila was waiting. She walked to us, her high heels a rhythm on the stone. As she passed below the *capis* chandeliers she looked beautiful, the contours of her breasts thrust against her blue jersey blouse, her legs creamy and well formed below the mini-skirt. She went to Kuya Nick and planted a dutiful peck on his cheek, then turned to me, eagerness aglow on her face. We got off the elevator on the fourteenth floor and walked an additional flight up. We were at the penthouse terrace, lined with palmettos and shrubs. Beyond the grill and greenery Manila was ablaze in the last furnace reds of sunset and, to our left, the neons of Makati burned against a heavy, clouded sky. The boy who opened the door greeted Kuya Nick with cloying obsequiousness, which Nick did not acknowledge. If the apartment was not his, he had seen a lot of it, for he took us directly across the parquet-floored living room, furnished with overstuffed leatherette sofas, to a wide room with a massive, circular bed, a wall lined with bric-a-brac, and a corner dominated by an Ifugao grotesquerie—the headhunter with a severed head, the hunter's face in an immemorial pose of calm victory.

Mila followed Kuya Nick and I behind them, wondering how it would be when the moment came. He patted his mistress softly on the cheek and cast an assuring look in my direction: "Pepe," he told her, "will know what to do."

I don't know how I rated with my audience behind that wide mirror, which occupied almost half of the wall beside the bed. I was sure, however, that Mila had long been denied her needs by her lover, whose mind, if not his values, was beyond my comprehension.

Kuya Nick had been extra kind to us—he did not let us meet our audience, which, he later told me, included a couple of senators, some millionaires, and other assorted members of the upper class. They left immediately when the show was over and, by ourselves, over bottles of beer and cold kimchi, he talked casually about what had happened, how his regular *toro* had been incapacitated. The *toro*'s wife—not his performing partner—had gotten jealous and angry because he was unable to perform in his own bedroom. As a consequence, his wife brought physical logic to the matter; while he was asleep, she simply snipped off that part of him which was denied her.

Serve the People

MY ONE-NIGHT STAND may have been a smash—I could deduce that from Mila's exalted and adroit performance, her whispering that she wanted it again and again—but it left me in a state of depression. It simply revealed how detached and cynical I could be. My mind had shut out everyone and everything, and knowing this reinforced my suspicion that though I considered myself human and warm, I was also a gross animal creature. This saddened and disturbed me, for I had considered Kuya Nick as such and I realized that I was cast in the same ugly mold.

By now, too, he had become bothersome, for he was intent on recruiting me, and many a morning he would be parked by the alley, and many a morning, too, he would give me a lift to school with the usual spiel that soon it would be November, the semester was about to end and I should transfer to Ateneo since "that would be closer to Maryknoll—and think of the variety, Pepe, that a young *toro* like you would get there."

Damn him and his vitamin E; he could not even satisfy his mistress! But I did not covet Mila, for to do so would be to live dangerously; she was, after all, his property, and what had transpired in Makati was with his consent.

One morning he was peeved, for I had moved the bulky narra cabinet to the wall where the crack was and no longer could they see Lucy and me. I had a plausible excuse: the cabinet was heavy and, where it had been, the beam had started to sag.

"No more shows then," Kuya Nick shook his head with a smirk.

It was not he and his mistress, however, who made Antipolo so oppressive I could no longer endure being there. Everytime I looked out of my window, I would imagine Father lying there on the tracks. I was in the same room, with the same bed, where he had slept. His memory often dominated the conversations at the table—how good he was, how full of promise, how well he had married, and what a waste it had all been.

But it was Lucy who really pushed me away. At first I tried to stay in Recto the whole afternoon, sweat through karate, read in the library, or devote time to the college paper and the Brotherhood. The Student Council did not require much effort. I was a representative of the freshman class and we had few talky sessions.

Lucy was quick to notice the changes. Maybe she did not expect the pleasant arrangement to end, but it was difficult for me to accept my uncle as the man who made love to her and paid for it. The most I did was buy her a cheap cotton dress at the Central Market and an inexpensive bottle of Intimate, the first perfume she ever had, and for which she was so pleased and grateful, her eyes shone.

From the moment that she revealed my uncle's perfidy, I had tried to understand, to cast aside the discordant demands of ego and see ourselves as victims. The effort was futile. I had become too enmeshed with her, wanted her for myself alone, or not at all.

By now, Toto and I had also become inseparable; he had helped me much more than I ever could repay him. I did not, however, tell him the real reason why I wanted to leave Antipolo Street—that since I was already making a little money, a hundred and forty pesos a month as literary editor, I should be independent so that I could go home in the late hours if I chose to.

He had suggested that I move in with him. He would talk with Father Jess and I could help in church and have free board and lodging, but we might no longer go to school together in the next semester because if I stayed in the *kumbento,* I would have to assist in the mass, clean the chapel, list births, marriages, deaths, and do other chores.

The idea of living in a *kumbento* as an acolyte repelled and fascinated me, but whatever my feelings, they had to be subdued for the more practical purpose of acquiring distance from relatives whose concerns were not mine no matter how well-intentioned they have been. Besides, there was always that lingering belief that priests, like policemen, were never hungry; I would finally be free from the infernal vegetable stew!

I had never been religious, although I liked the religious holidays, the solemnity of Holy Week and its somber processions, the gaiety of Christmas, the dawn mass and the biting cold. God was a personal experience and belief; He fitted in my hierarchy of authority only as a last resort, the ultimate explanation of all the things too recondite for me to grasp. But He was no arbiter of right or wrong; it would seem that He did not care. He did not reward virtue; it was the scheming and the dastardly strong who lived happily ever after. Babies without sin die and so do mothers who are poor and cannot afford medicine or expensive doctors.

But I would work in a church just as unquestioningly as I would work in an abatoir. Besides, I had had experience in the sacristy, although that was long ago and traumatic.

LAKAY BENITO, the ancient sacristan and dispenser of talismans, had ushered me into this job as acolyte after I was circumcised and my voice had started to change. Much earlier, like most of the children in my village, I had gone through catechism and knew all about the body of Christ and His holy blood. I had tasted the communion wafer but had never had a sip of wine till that afternoon, the second day of my short-lived career as sacristan. I had just finished cleaning the sacristy when I noticed that the cabinet where the vestments and the wine were kept was open, and there it was—the blood of Christ—a half bottle of it, waiting. I was determined to take just one tiny sip, no more, but one tiny sip became two, then three, and before long the whole sweet bottle was empty. With a prayer of thanksgiving on my lips, I fell into a dreamless sleep.

It was already evening, time to toll the Angelus, when I woke up and realized the immensity of what I had done. The bottle had to be refilled for the morning mass and I must do that quickly. I searched the other cabinets, but there were no bottles there. I hurried to the market and, with my hard-earned money, bought half a bottle of cane wine—at least that was what I thought it was. It would be a different wine in the same bottle and, perhaps, it would not have done so much harm had I been more careful. Alas, the bottle I bought was filled with a similarly colored liquid and from the same cane, only the *basi** had fermented and had turned to vinegar. I need not recount the high drama that transpired the following morning; needless to say, it ended my brief career in the service of the Lord.

Now, among the few, I was being called again, and this time, if only for the fact that I knew priests eat very well, I heeded the call.

My relatives did not like the idea at first, but Uncle Bert saw its necessity. Lucy was restrained in her objections. We no longer made it frequently and she accepted that, too, with little questioning. As my departure drew near, she exacted a promise that I would visit her during lunchtime as always.

I did not know if I had made the right choice; Antipolo Street could be limbo or purgatory, but the barrio was purely and simply Hell. Yet, as Roger and all its denizens would tell me later, it was much better than the penury, the deadening monotony, and the slow death in the villages in the Visayas that they had left.

There was not much for me to take that could not fit into the old canvas bag; my only new acquisitions were half a dozen books scrounged from the bargain counters on the sidewalks of Avenida, dog-eared rejects from Clark Air Base and some library in the United States, and a couple of books that opened new vistas of Mexico and the civilization of the Andes Indians.

Toto and I walked over to Avenida and took a jeepney to that huge emporium, Divisoria, then transferred from there to a jeepney to Bangkusay, the end of the line. We got off on a narrow street, for the moment expropriated by a covey of children, many of them emaciated and soiled, playing in the dirt, while in front of the battered apartments and houses idle men gathered in small groups, talking away the tepid afternoon.

We entered a narrow street, half submerged in slime, more chil-

---

* *Basi:* Sugarcane wine.

dren playing, screaming, fighting around us, past tables with cooked food and swarms of flies, and more tables with wilted vegetables and dried fish, more men talking, and still more packing-crate houses, sorrier-looking than the ones in Antipolo.

We were in the Barrio.

I had read somewhere that to get into it was to enter a demented world where perspectives changed, as if one saw through cracked lenses or glass smeared with mud.

Years ago, shortly after the war, this whole area was a putrefied expanse of mudflats, the bay foreshore. In one of those rare, foresighted moves of government, this was filled up, and for some seasons weeds and other green things sprouted here, bearing plumes of white. Then the hordes from the provinces came and built shanties from packing crates, bamboo, cardboard, burnt tin, construction debris, anything that would shield them from the rain and the sun.

Not all the Barrio people were poor or from the lowest castes. There were politicians who enriched themselves with their pickings in the slums, and they built houses of stone with high walls, incongruous structures surrounded by dismal shapes and dismal lives. Policemen also built houses, which they rented out, promising protection to their tenants and their neighbors, for here the policeman was not just a man in uniform or a figure of authority, he was also the arbiter of justice.

There were no sewers; if government were more humane, sewerage would be the first thing it would have provided for the Barrio. And because there were no sewers, around us was the pervasive smell of rot, heavy and powerful in the rainy season and much more so when the sun shone. In spots, the waters never drained and planks were laid where the water was deep; otherwise, we would have to take off our shoes and walk in blackish mud.

They came from all over the country—farmers running from the Huk rebellion in Central Luzon, the ravages of typhoons in Samar, the poverty of Bicol, the laziness and inertia of the Visayas. They lived together because they were relatives or because they came from the same benighted place, and it was here in the Barrio where relationships became stronger as, perhaps, they had never been elsewhere. Relationships were a bulwark against disease, unemployment, hunger, and, in some instances, a safe haven from the gangs that preyed on people in the dark and convoluted recesses of the Barrio.

There was religion, too; the folksy kind with its symbols and rituals. Religion was their last hope, and I was not going to deny it to them. With Toto, I was their pusher.

The chapel Father Jess built was at one end of an alley, close to the man-made creek that flowed to the sea. It was fronted by a small, multipurpose plaza, no bigger than the basketball court into which it was often transformed. The plaza was covered with gravel and was actually a street that was not yet filled up and opened.

The chapel was no different from the tawdry shapes that surrounded it. Its uneven sidings were made of salvaged construction materials. A *kumbento* just as decrepit as the church itself was an extension of the church rear. It was divided into quarters, for Father Jess on the second floor and for the two of us as well as Tia Nena, who was the cook and *lavandera,** on the ground. Apart from the church was another building, also made of the same castaway material, and it served as a kindergarten and meeting place for the parish.

Father Jess was in the multipurpose center when we arrived; he was talking before a huddle of young people, most of them with rubber slippers and T-shirts. He himself was in blue T-shirt, sandals, and blue denims, looking more like an overaged bum than a priest. His big hands were gesturing and when he saw us, he beckoned to me: "Children," he said, "this is Pepe; he will stay with us so that he will be out of harm. Now, remember, he is a *provinciano,* so you should not immediately convert him to your spoiled city ways."

They responded with that self-conscious, shy laughter of young village people.

FATHER JESS ate by himself and Toto and I served him. Between mouthfuls of Tia Nena's excellent ox tongue at lunch he asked, "Did you notice how those kids this morning seemed so distant? And I have been here seven years! Do you know what that means? I knew most of them when they had bare bottoms, and yet they still cannot feel at ease with me. Is it because I am a priest? Is it because I really do not belong here?"

I could have told him a few truths, but I was going to live with him for some time, share his food, laugh at his jokes, so I said, "I do

___
* *Lavandera:* Laundress.

not know, Father. Honestly, I do not know. But I do know priests are not poor."

"I know what you mean," he said sadly. "It had occurred to me many times, and it is true, I was not poor. Even now, I am not poor. I eat better than they and I have choices. I do not have to be here."

A long gap of silence. "What can I do to be accepted by them?" he asked.

"I just don't know, Father," I said.

IN ANOTHER WEEK, I still did not know. There are many things I will never know, and a lifetime in the Barrio would not suffice. There is no ready script I could follow in my relationships with people, in my journey through Tondo. All that I sought was to survive, and to find no difficult answers to the questions that I dared to ask.

The Barrio was not easy to know—this is what all those researchers and scholars believed; they came with their tired questions, their long-winded interviews. I soon realized we were overstudied, with all that fancy data stored in libraries and in computers. Still, nothing changed.

They came—those do-gooder sociologists, those slumming foreigners—maybe because they wanted their troubled consciences salved a bit, that by "studying" us, they would be able to unlock the gates of our hell and welcome us to their paradise.

But they never reached the pith, the core, the heart—it is beyond their perception because they don't live here, because they are not poor, because there is always a way out for them. Look at this artist, Malang, how prettily, how daintily he pictures our homes. If only he had lived here, even just for a week—I wonder how all his pictures would turn out then!

All they will know will be gathered, concluded from comfortable positions they would not lose no matter how sincere or close they will be to us. Not us; we could not say the many things that strained to be said, that were coiled and seething within.

But not all of us in the Barrio were the flotsam of the country, nor were our houses of lowly shape and material. There were also those whose tables were laden, whose roofs did not leak, and even among the riffraff, some had power and influence that were real, though subterranean, because here were enclaves ruled by terror, by laws that applied only to us.

And among these men was Roger, Toto's friend, although that did not seem possible at the time, considering how Roger teased and ridiculed him. Roger, Toto explained, was the leader of the Tayo-Tayo gang, one of the biggest and most powerful of the slum gangs. He was always around with his young toughs, most of them half-naked in the morning heat, their tattoos neatly etched on their gleaming brown bodies. He was fat and short and, that first morning, as we passed him on the way to Bangkusay for our jeepney, he stopped us.

"He will live with me in the *kumbento*, Roger," Toto said in his usual halting manner.

Roger appraised me, then shook my hand in a viselike grip he thought would hurt. "You must bring us Father Jess's wine one evening, and we will have a drinking party," he said.

But though he did not warm up to me, he was not taciturn or menacing. And not once did he milk me for anything the way he did the strangers—the researchers, the journalists, the assorted do-gooders. He always extracted from them gin money, cigarettes, pens—anything that could be considered as tax for their working or just passing through his well-defined territory. I could very well get to like Roger, to understand him better than Toto, although Toto and I by then were like brothers. With Roger, it was easy to find out what he wanted, and what he wanted was not, in a sense, different from what I also desired.

It was Toto who confounded me—his seriousness of purpose, his narrow compass that was disturbing because of its rigidity.

At night, before we went to sleep, he would muse about his vision of the future. It evolved out of the Tondo that we knew, the Tondo that bothered him so much, not because we lived here but because it seemed so permanent and unchangeable.

And so, once bored by his quiet musings, I said that perhaps it was best if we just let people be, that we should just eat and run. This was what everyone was doing, and look at how comfortable and obese those who were good at it had become.

He raised his voice then. "We will bother," he said, "because we are people, because we believe there is a just and merciful God."

"Don't bring religion into this," I told him. "The God that you speak of is not merciful but cruel. And He is vengeful, too."

I had read the Bible that Mother kept, a thick book with colored illustrations of bearded prophets, of Moses smashing the tablets, Jesus on a donkey, the Resurrection. I had loved the Old Testament because it was so tantalizing with all its gore and sex. I could look at Jesus as a historical man, a guerrilla leader who threatened the Roman empire and, when caught, must necessarily be executed by the Romans, not for his messianic preaching but for his subversive activities. But how could I explain this to Toto who was weaned on holy water and had breakfasted so long on communion wafers? How can I tell him that the God he worshiped admonished men to sell their garments to buy swords? Toto would need them, of course, to destroy the money changers at the temple, if not the temple itself; he would need them to tear down the shacks that were all around us so that this Tondo, this ugly scab upon the face of the land, would be banished forever.

So here I was, surrounded by the debris of the city. I had often thought how trivial was my life and the lives of those around me, how transitory this station. But Toto's despair, this Tondo, had been here for years, for generations. My history book says so. It was here where Bonifacio started his Katipunan, that ill-fated secret society that he hoped would wrench from the Spaniards the freedom they had taken from us. Here, too, was where the organized labor movement began, only to be subverted and exploited by future generations of rapacious labor leaders. What had happened to those men, those professed paragons of righteousness who came from Tondo? Some reached the highest niches of government, and when they had gotten what they wanted, they fled Tondo to wallow in the perfumed precincts of Makati.

Still, a limbo like Tondo has its uses—it is a cause, a symbol people can cling to. It is a sordid reality that Father Jess and all those stodgy missionaries with big, fat cigars, those salivating messiahs oozing with human kindness, want to change. It is the wellspring for all those politicians who want to proclaim that their beginnings are lowly, who want some vestigial identity with the masses. It is the essence of which dreams are made, particularly by those who want to grow rich writing about the poor. No place in the country has been as religiously studied, surveyed, plotted, and discussed in seminars. How many doctoral dissertations have been written on its problems without those problems ever being attended to?

So we delight in saying that those who don't look back to where they came from cannot go far, but some have gone far indeed while the rest stayed to rot where they are, to be visited again and again by the sins of their fathers.

Could anything be done? I have always looked with some envy at those romantics, Father Jess and Toto, for instance, who think that the human cussedness of which Tondo seems to have a surfeit can be tempered with good deeds and lofty thoughts. But I knew that the way was not through the pulpit, nor could it be lighted up by such slogans as those the Brotherhood had made.

I could take a kindlier view toward people like Father Jess, maybe, because I got to know the difficulties he had to live with, the condemnation of family, the sneering of friends, and the skepticism of most, including myself. There are so many imitators of Christ and some of them come in jeans, with long hair, but they refuse to raise the sword, to fire the armalite when the moment comes. Still, I must work with them, live with them, for they are allies and protectors at the moment. Would I protect them, too, if and when they need us?

There was one creature in Tondo who, I felt, needed me: Tia Nena. She could have been seventy or more, but after a time, age does not matter when it demands nothing but affection and respect. Though she was Father Jess's servant, she was much more than that to Toto and me; she was a godmother from whom blessings flowed, for there was, in her silences and in her sweet forbearance, that quality of ageless compassion. Her face was lined, but her eyes were alert. There was something, in the way she was often bent at her chores, in how she spoke, that told me she had borne well and with fortitude a tragic burden. She spoke a little English and, I later found out, better Spanish. She had welcomed me quickly and took to washing my clothes as she did Toto's and, on occasion, cooked especially for Toto and me. She smoked long black cigarettes sparingly, the lighted end in her mouth, and I always bought her a pack afterward. She knew almost everyone in the parish and even Roger, the gang leader, respected her. Toto and I were not spared an occasional sermon on punctuality, on thrift, the way she said she had lectured her two sons whose names came up again and again, as if she were measuring us against their images. Tia Nena opened up the neighborhood for me, saying to the people that the new sacristan was an Ilocano who could be trusted, unlike some Ilocano leaders.

It was not difficult getting to know the neighbors, particularly those close to the church, for, as in a village, we jostled one another like relatives and a secret did not seem possible among us.

Just across from our window was Lily and her mother and brothers and sisters. They lived in a two-story shanty; on the ground-floor living room–kitchen were her brothers. She stayed in the room upstairs with her mother, who was suffering from TB. Lily had a baby who died, whose father was a Peace Corps volunteer. He had worked in the village school as a teacher's aide.

Ka Lucio, an ex-Huk commander, and his nieces lived next to Lily's house. Farther down the alley was the house of Roger, the leader of the Tayo-Tayo gang.

Tia Nena was disgusted with Roger. "So young, so capable— and what does he do all day? Just sits in that *tienda*,* drinking gin and seeing to it that no one ever crosses his path."

Tia Nena moved about the *kumbento* quietly. When I arrived, she acknowledged my presence with a mere nod, and I felt that I had to win her approval. It was Roger's gang, she said, that blocked the organization of the young people in the Barrio. At Father Jess's suggestion, the youth had organized to keep away from trouble and to find out how they could be trained for work outside of the village.

Once, because Toto and I had to pass the *tienda* every day whenever we went to the city, Roger, who was there with his usual coterie, asked us to drink with them. Toto had always excused himself. Given his eyeglasses and weak eyes, they did not consider it manly to tangle with him. But here I was. I said, "Thank you, Roger, but please, not more than one small sip. Father Jess would not want me drunk."

They laughed and Roger gave me his glass. He did not have a shirt on; he was pimply, fat, and on his chest a tattoo of a cobra with bared fangs, and on his arm a red heart impaled with a blue dagger.

Toto tried to drag me away, but it was better to know them, and this was an opportunity through which I could get closer to them. I raised the glass and downed the gin in one gulp. The boys looked at me in amazement, then they all broke into laughter. Even Roger

* *Tienda:* A shop, store, covered stall (Sp.).

laughed, his small eyes disappearing into narrow slits, his mouth studded with buckteeth yellow with nicotine.

"Next time," I said, "it will be my turn to invite you."

We hurried to the *kumbento*, Toto behind me, and when we got there, I rushed to our room. I never drank gin, and now I was drunk.

THEN THE RAINS stopped, but mud puddles scarred the alleys; nothing changed in Tondo except at night, when darkness brought a little quiet. But the darkness did not eclipse the life—the radios, the babble of children. Then the morning would drift in, heightening the putrefaction, the smell of feces that was thrown in the pathways at night, in the knee-deep waters between the houses, along the canals. The voices of children all around, the laughter of mothers who had no milk in their breasts, no rice in their kitchens. The day came brilliant and harsh, bouncing off the rooftops like silver.

Toward Christmas the sky was often cloudless and blue. At times the winds were rough. They churned the sea and brought to us the rancid smell of the bay. The clouds would boil, then darken, and waves would batter the sea wall. The fishermen could not sail out of the channel and they sat in the *tiendas* instead, drinking gin and wishing for the sea to calm. But even on days when they had a good catch of crabs and fish, it was never enough and they would always return to this island as poor as before.

It was better at night not only because there were dreams. I had read once that there was this man in a concentration camp having a nightmare, but his fellow inmates did not wake him because they knew no nightmare could be more horrible than the reality to which he would wake up.

NOW I WENT to school in the afternoons and on toward evening. I was in the church the whole morning, and Father Jess had more time to go around, looking for jobs for the young people in the Barrio who had finished college. He was also trying to set up a vocational school. In the afternoons, he was at the archbishopric, where he assisted in the work of Catholic Charities. Sometimes he would return with a sack of powdered milk, which we then transferred into smaller plastic packets and distributed to nursing mothers. I always slipped a few to Lily across the alley; she needed them for her mother and brothers and sisters, and it pleased me to give her whatever I could.

Father Jess permitted me to work with the youth group and the first thing I did was to call a meeting. I asked them individually and they all agreed we could do a lot. But Roger's gang stood in the way. His boys called me and Toto homosexuals. Still, we had to be together. I asked Roger and his boys if they wanted to affiliate with the Brotherhood, which was rapidly growing in the city and all over the country. They said they did not oppose it, but there was no hearty approval, either. In the end, I simply assumed that they would not object to our first project—to cement the basketball court so that we could play there even during the rainy season or use it for dances. I also planned for us to raise money for paint so we could beautify the multipurpose building and grade school, and transform the rusty brown sidings into something colorful.

There was plenty of skepticism at first; even Toto thought I was starting out wrong, with more imagination than was practical.

Yet something was missing; all through my first days in the Barrio, I kept thinking of Cabugawan, how very much the people in my village and in Tondo were alike, how they had come to this place, too, with nothing. The government had reclaimed this land from the sea and it was not meant to be a warren of squatter homes. But no one could turn away the hordes of jobless who had taken over the railroad flanks of Antipolo, the vacant lots in Quezon City, and this huge scab of idle land that was meant for commerce.

Ennui hounded me no matter how hard I worked on the school paper, in church. I swept the tile floors and scrubbed them where the mud of many rainy seasons had caked.

I swept the ceiling, too, of cobwebs and helped in the kitchen, although Tia Nena did not want me there. She was often quiet when the three of us ate at the small table in the kitchen. It came bit by bit that she was once in Mandaluyong—the mental hospital.

I tried not to worry about Mother and Auntie Bettina, and I did write to them, saying that I had moved to Tondo, that I had a job, and Mother had answered—it took so long, almost a month—saying how glad she was. She was proud of me, she hoped for me to be somebody, when all I wanted really was to see movies and eat Tia

Nena's wonderful cooking, something she learned when she worked for a Spanish family in her younger days.

I had reveries of Lucy and our first encounter, how we had wrestled and done it on the floor. Memory burned bright; I could not blot her from my mind or diminish my sense of loyalty even when I recalled her affair with my uncle. As she had explained, it was business. Auntie Betty and he were no longer sleeping together—she was in her menopause and sex repelled her. At first Lucy felt that she should leave, but Uncle Bert had not made any physical demands at home, for there Lucy was always a servant. Lucy was helping a sister in college who was "brighter" and could make a future for the farming family in Dumaguete. At first, Tio Bert's offer was just fifty pesos, but Lucy told him she was a virgin, so he increased it to a hundred—the most he could afford. They would meet during lunchtime, maybe three times a month, near his Binondo office, then they'd trot over to a small hotel with a side entrance in an alley off Juan Luna, and they would spend an hour or two together. It was fifty pesos each visit, fifty pesos that went a long way in helping out the father in Dumaguete and the sister in Manila, who was their only hope.

I did not see her for two months, but toward January I had a terrible longing for her. I went to Antipolo; I had done her wrong and I wanted to tell her so, that someday, if things turned out all right, I would help her.

I boarded the jeepney, what I would say formed clearly in my mind—words of entreaty, of endearment. I was hungry and hoped to have lunch in Antipolo. Even the vegetable stew seemed appetizing. But when I got to the house, the lock was on. Mila came and said they had all gone out. She invited me into her apartment, said she could send her maid on an errand, but I refused. I waited for maybe half an hour at the door talking with her. I returned the following day, around lunchtime, to find the house locked again.

After mass that Sunday I went to Antipolo with one whole fried chicken, which I bought in Avenida. Tia Betty and Tio Bert were very happy to see me, but Lucy was not around; they had a new maid, a middle-aged Ilocana from Tayug who smoked hand-rolled cigars. I had difficulty bringing the subject up, but finally, when we were having lunch, I asked where Lucy was.

Tia Betty explained; Lucy was summoned home by her ailing father. It was a very pleasant parting, there were no recriminations. My aunt talked about her in glowing terms—maybe to impress her new maid—how industrious Lucy was, how clean the house had been, how polite, how little she ate, almost like a mouse, and how wonderful her vegetable stew was. To all of these, my uncle nodded, grunting approval.

At the university where her sister was supposed to be studying, I pored over the student roster, but her sister's name was not there. I wrote to Dumaguete. Two months later my letter was returned unopened. I decided that if and when I could afford it, I would be a pilgrim to Dumaguete. I should have understood, I know that now. Lucy would always be in my mind, tormenting me, for I had judged her unfairly when I was not any better.

Unite, Don't Be Afraid

I T WAS NOT difficult setting up the Brotherhood in the Barrio, but it was a paper organization and would not be able to do much, not until the cooperation of Roger was assured. I did not think he was all that tough; what he wanted from me, I surmised, was recognition. Spending years in Muntinlupa prison was a stigma he could not wash away. He was an "outsider" and he knew it.

Every time I passed his house I always greeted him. I also inquired about his likes and studied his movements. Thus, one afternoon, I followed him to Divisoria where he went to collect protection money. He was alone, and when he got off at Juan Luna, I overtook him before he could cross Recto.

"Roger," I called.

He turned and, as I suspected, he was no bully when alone. Out of the Barrio, he had no swagger.

"Pepe, where are you going?" He even sounded pleasant.

"I was going to invite you for *mami*," I said. "Let's go to Avenida—there is plenty of time."

He tensed with indecision and I put him at ease. "Roger, I really want to talk to you. I'd like to be a Tayo-Tayo member even if I am not Bisaya."

He relaxed immediately and sounded superior again: "Well, it is not easy, you know."

"Not even after *siopao* and *mami*?" I asked with an ingratiating nudge. "Please come with me—there are many things you really don't know about me."

I put an arm around him in a brotherly gesture; it would also give him an opportunity to make body contact and assure him that I was not armed. The gesture was not necessary, I think; they all knew that though we were in Tondo, Father Jess did not want us to carry weapons.

We boarded the jeepney to Recto, sitting together in the front. I asked him what it was like when he was in Muntinlupa. At first he was reticent, but then I told him that he had this reputation in the Barrio as being the toughest. He nodded, pleased with himself, and slowly he described a bit of the life within prison, the hardships that sadistic guards imposed on them. It was because of these conditions that the Tayo-Tayo gang existed, grew, and spread out from the penitentiary, and because of its rigid code, some were killed in prison riots. The noise and the traffic of Manila eddied around us and his voice turned soft and quiet; now it was easy to understand why he was so aggressive, as if the whole Barrio, his domain, was a kind of prison, too.

There was such a jam at the Avenida corner, we decided to walk over to my karate school, two blocks away. We pitched up a dimly lighted stairway. On the cement floor, the caked mud of years, scraps of paper and cigarette butts; so, too, that stale smell of tobacco, dried sputum, and perspiration that had drenched these surroundings and impregnated them with that unmistakable odor of a humanity gone sour.

"My school is upstairs," I said. "Come, I want to show you something."

When we got to the door he asked, surprised: "*Hoy,* are you a karatista?" I nodded. He drew away, looked at me, and aimed a playful blow at my stomach. "*Siga—*" he said. "Are you going to show me tricks?"

"Yes," I said, "if you want to watch."

A few white and brown belts were doing the basic exercises and our best instructor, Rading, was doing his high leap and double kick at the suspended bag. He was a black belt and had won trophies at national tournaments.

Roger watched with unfeigned wonder. "Can you do that?" he asked.

"Sure," I said.

As I suspected, no one in his gang really knew karate; their theatrical postures were their imitations of what they saw in the movies, and a lot of it was, of course, phony.

"It's for self-defense," I said, "not for offense. That's very important and that is the first discipline."

I went to the locker room and took off my shoes. He did the same and watched me put on my robe.

Then I sweated through the exercises, the body bends, the jabs, then the side kicks.

The time had come. I got the practice knife; it was not sharp, but it was pointed and it could kill. "Roger," I said, "take this and stab me. Any way you like."

He demurred, his yellow buckteeth showing, his porcine, pimply face embarrassed, for now the other students were watching us.

"Take off your shirt, please," Rading, my instructor, asked him. "It might get torn."

"Do you really want me to?" he asked incredulously.

I nodded.

"And if I hurt you?"

"You can always rush me to the hospital," I said.

He wiggled off his shirt, baring the heart and dagger tattoo on his right arm, and the cobra with bared fangs on his rotund chest. Both were handsomely done. He held the knife firmly and in a half-crouch started circling me. As I suspected, with all his fat, he was clumsy and slow.

He made a wild lunge that was easy to foresee and parry. I stepped aside, grabbed his arm, then threw him down in a heap without letting go of his arm. The padded canvas mat was thick and he was not hurt. I applied just a little pressure on the arm. He was helpless under me, his other arm pinned by my leg.

"Roger," I said, "you know I could break your arm any time I want." Then I let him go. He was flustered, embarrassed, and angry at himself.

"Try again," I urged him, knowing that now, in his embarrassment and anger, he would not only try harder, but would be more reckless. This time, as I had expected, he held the knife differently. He feinted, then struck with a straight thrust. I parried the blow, tripped him in his momentum and, as he fell, twisted his hand so that the knife pointed directly at his chest. He was on his back, pinned to the floor. He gasped in surprise knowing the full impact of what could have happened.

I released him and he rose, white-faced and shaken.

"Pepe," he said in a gasp, "you are very good."

"That's really nothing," I said. "You should see what I can do if someone attacks me with a bolo."

We dressed slowly, then went down, hardly speaking, and walked over to the noodle restaurant below the karate school and ordered *mami* and *siopao*. He had no appetite and toyed with his food.

"Please, Roger, do me a favor."

He looked at me, his face expressionless.

"Don't ever tell anyone what we did just now," I said.

He was surprised.

"Not even Toto knows that I take karate," I continued, which was true. "And if Father Jess knows, I would lose my job. And I won't be able to go to school anymore. He does not like violence."

He was now grinning. "Oh, no . . . no, I will not tell anyone. But, *hoy,* you should really be a Tayo-Tayo. You will be a very useful member. You can teach us many things."

"What will the others say?" I asked. "You have been calling Toto and me *syoki** . . . maybe you should join the Brotherhood instead."

He squirmed, obviously embarrassed. "I will explain. That's what we call all sacristans anyway," he said. "As for your group, maybe I became religious. Ha! Father Jess asked me. And who can refuse Father Jess? Why don't you ask him to invite us for *merienda* at the *kumbento*?"

"*Lutong macao*," I said. "Can I ask you for other things?"

"Anything. As long as I can do it."

"You can," I said. "First, we should form a basketball team. Then we will cement the basketball court so we can play the whole year. We can also use it for meetings. For dances. Your boys should really

* *Syoki:* Not masculine; homosexual.

try to police the whole village—I mean, do the work of real policemen so that there will be no thieves, at least in our place. And our
women will be safe. Then we will cement the walks so they will not
be muddy."

He looked at me, eyes blinking.

"You will make a good president, Roger. You have organizational ability. Anyone who can organize your boys the way you have
has real talent. I can be your secretary and Toto—you know he is
very honest—can be the treasurer. And when everything is ready, we
will have a program. Perhaps a dance. But you will have to make a
speech. All presidents do. . . ."

I was going too fast, hindsight told me this; he was grinning,
then his face clouded. "But my men, you know, they are not educated."

"They will be members, but this group will be called the Brotherhood. There will be younger people—Ilocanos, Bikolanos, Pam-
pangos, not just Bisaya. And there will be girls. . . ."

He laughed. I ordered another *siopao,* which he now devoured.
When he boarded the jeepney back to Tondo, although he had not
had even a sip of gin, he was so talkative he could have been mistaken for a drunk.

BUT ROGER did not support the Brotherhood immediately, as I
had hoped he would. Looking back, I now realize I had underesti-
mated the native and intuitive wisdom that made him a leader. He
did not put it to me directly, how my book learning, my karate, and
my being a student were of no consequence, if not utterly useless, in
the treacherous and slimy world he knew and dominated through
his cunning.

In the weeks that followed I was to catch stray glimpses of it in
conversations when he dropped by the *kumbento* for a cup of coffee
and crackers with Tia Nena's blessings. I had first thought of their rituals, of their secret tattoos, as juvenile antics until I learned they
were invoked as a matter of life and death. For it was with these that
the gang was welded together in a far more stringent way than the
Brotherhood could ever unify its members.

I once told him of my escape from the maniacal drug addict
whose car I jumped from, and he had merely smiled patronizingly

and said that I had been in no real danger. We talked about how it was in Muntinlupa, what solitary confinement for a month was, the beatings, the sordid indignities; karate was useless, for when one was killed in the penitentiary for infringing on the gang taboos, he was disposed of with skill, the victim unaware. And bloodshed—had I ever seen a man who was being punished, forced to eat his own ears, which he himself had to broil before his judges? And had I ever played bowling with a decapitated head in the cell block alley during a prison riot? The perversion of Kuya Nick . . . ha! Did I know that sodomy was practiced as a matter of course in the penitentiary?

I had considered all these at first as macho drivel, but knowing that Roger did not have that kind of fetid imagination, I soon came to believe his stories and marvel at how he had lived through them without going insane.

Now, at least, his relations with me were warmer, and he was less pugnacious. Maybe Roger was always patronizing toward Toto because Toto never crossed his path, but as I see it now, he was protective of Toto. Roger could talk condescendingly to him, but only Roger did that, no one in his group had that privilege. I did not understand why until Toto told me that Roger had also come from the Hospicio, but had strayed too far. Toto was the key. But the lock was never turned until much, much later, and when it was finally done, when Roger and his group finally joined, the cost was too great.

AFTER I had set up the Brotherhood in the Barrio I had more time for Lily. She had been reluctant to join and be an auditor, for, as she said, she already had a past—an illegitimate baby that had died, fathered by an American she no longer saw. She was a salesgirl at a Chinese store in Avenida and was away all day, from early morning, when she would battle for a seat on a jeepney at Bangkusay. She attended our Sunday meetings during which we worked out athletic and social programs and even an excursion to Bataan across the bay.

She was out in the alley once, in a printed green dress that had known many washings yet was so becoming, and I wondered aloud why all that beauty was going to waste.

"She would make a good bed partner," I said more to myself than to anyone, but Toto heard and the ferocity of his reaction surprised me.

"Animal!" he screamed and I turned around to see him glaring at me, his face contorted with rage. "Can there be no other thing but filth in your mind? Don't you ever know how to show respect? Have you never learned that?"

I rose, and still in a jocular tone said, "Friend, I was just making an observation. Don't be so angry. I have not done anything to you."

Then it struck me; all through the days that I had known him, this girl often drifted into our conversation and I had missed it all. Quickly, I added, "Sorry, Toto, I had forgotten you love her."

He sat down on my cot, his voice quickly drained of anger. "Yes, yes, I love her—and there is nothing I can do."

And much, much later, I learned how he would have married her had she permitted it because he wanted to give her child a name, his name, although everyone knew the baby was not his.

I once visited her at the Avenida dry goods store where she was supposed to receive eight pesos daily, the minimum wage, but actually got only six. Her shoes and clothes were more expensive for they were all bought on installment. But even in her plain cottons, she was the prettiest in that shop, in the Barrio even, and I often wondered if her Chinese boss molested her. Her *disgracia* was brought about by a lonely Peace Corps volunteer named Paul Simpson, and it was possible that Lily may have thought that the American was the key to the good life, to America and its cornucopia of Avon cosmetics, double knits, and Detroit excesses that clotted Manila's streets. Escape from poverty was often possible only through migration to the United States, but the quotas were full, the visas were difficult to get, and thus, whether it was in the anonymity of some rural village or in Tondo itself, it was many a girl's dream to be married to an American. And those Angeles bar waitresses—dark and homely and raucous—were actually envied when, through some inexplicable alchemy, they were able to entice their American lovers into marrying them. Not so with middle- and upper-class women; while they liked American men, they often balked at the idea of getting married to them, not so much because there was no genuine emotion involved, but because they would be excoriated, mistaken for prostitutes and washerwomen with whom the Americans in the bases trucked.

"But it did not begin that way," Lily explained. "He was a teacher's aide, and after he taught school, he organized this youth dance to which we contributed. That was when we started going out."

When his term ended, Simpson returned to the United States by a circuitous route through Europe. Lily had written to him at the addresses he had left, but not once did he reply. When the baby came, someone told her to seek assistance at the American embassy, but she was too shy to do that. She had, of course, the ultimate proof in her arms—a handsome mestizo baby with brown hair and eyes that were blue "like his father's." The baby did not live long.

In spite of motherhood, Lily had not lost her girlish charm or the innocence in her eyes. If only she had better food, her skin would be much clearer and there would be no blemishes on her arms or legs. It was a minor miracle how they managed—four children, two of them in high school, with her mother making only so much by taking in washing and peddling vegetables door-to-door.

Their most intimate conversations floated across the alley to us; seldom could we hear the hiss of the frying pan to know that they were eating something more substantial than boiled vegetables and the scraps of fish that her mother could no longer sell.

Lily's mother coughed interminably and the younger kids always had skin sores. Then, one evening, Lily came home with two grocery bags and two smaller, oily ones, which, she said, contained fried chicken. Her face was flushed and happy when she passed me at the open window where I was reading, and she smiled at me before going up the stairs. Her brothers were squealing and the older ones, Boyet and Nanet, were full of questions. Her mother had started to cough again. She asked where she got the money to buy all that food and Lily was laughing and saying, "Mama, I have a new job and it pays better, much better than that store in Avenida. I am now a waitress in Makati. The tips alone! But I have to work starting at eleven until late at night."

A month later, Lily could no longer attend our programs or our Sunday meetings; she had to work on Sundays, too, and it was only on Tuesday, her day off, that she was free. For several days I had wanted to go out with her, just the two of us, before she got this Makati job. On those instances that I was free from school early, I even detoured to Avenida and went home to Bangkusay with her after the store closed. On this Tuesday afternoon, as I was starting for school, she also got out, not by coincidence, I now realize.

"I am going shopping," she said. We walked toward Bangkusay, avoiding the puddles in the alleys, and, once in the plaza where no one could hear, she said, "Pepe, I have something important to tell you. There is no one I can talk to."

"We can go see a movie now, if you wish," I said.

I had always wanted to be close to her in the dark so I could hold her, but then I remembered I had only fare money. "The devil— I don't have money. Why don't we just go to the Luneta and sit under the trees?"

She smiled, "No, too many people there. Yes, we can go to a movie—let me pay."

"I will not permit that," I said, but she won out, for I wanted to hold her.

We got off at Recto. She gave me ten pesos to buy tickets, balcony, she insisted, so that we would be up there by ourselves. "You can still attend one of your classes," she said. "I don't want you to lose your scholarship."

It was one of those kung fu movies, but no matter how well Bruce Lee fought, he could not distract me from this girl. Once settled in our seats I put an arm around her. I tried to reach down her neckline, but she held my hand firmly and said, "Now, Pepe, don't do that. What pleasure would you have holding a mother's breast?"

We laughed, then she started talking somberly, slowly, as if she were telling me her one and only secret, and perhaps it was.

"Pepe, I do not know what to do."

"I know," I said.

"Do not talk nonsense now."

"I am serious," I said.

"Don't make jokes. You know it's impossible with us. Please help me, tell me what I should do."

"Tell me your problem." I held her closer and kissed her cheek.

"Promise you will not tell anyone in the Barrio, not even Toto."

"I promise."

She paused, then said simply: "I am working in a massage parlor, Pepe . . . not in a restaurant."

For some time I did not know what to say and, noting my silence, she quickly added, a hint of irritation in her voice: "Now . . . now, don't think what you are thinking. I am not a prostitute. The money I make . . . I get it straight, not even petting. I do not let them."

"I do not believe you," I said hotly, then I was sorry I said it.

She drew away, fury in her eyes. "I made a mistake in trusting you. If I can trust you, why can't you trust me? You know that I cannot give you any proof."

I was silent.

She continued, the anger in her voice had ebbed and in its place, this sorrow. "Did you know that until I got this job, we sometimes ate only once a day? And my baby, did you know he died because I had no money for medicine? You know that Mother makes so little, that Boyet and Nanet do not earn—and those two small ones . . ."

I drew her to me, "Lily, forgive me."

Though not a sound escaped her, she was crying. I tilted her face and kissed her, saying, "Lily, I can do nothing to help you. Yet I cannot think of you in that place, with all those hands pawing you."

Her crying subsided and we were silent for some time. We even tried to watch the movie, but it was useless—we had to talk.

She said, "Mother is getting suspicious, and I do not know what to do. Once, she said she wanted to come and see the restaurant. Boyet and Nanet do not care as long as they have something to eat. But Mother— I don't know what to tell her. I never lied to her before, not even when I got pregnant."

I wanted to know the nature of her work, how much money she made, what she did with the money.

"For the first time in our lives," she said, "we are eating well. And I have saved a little. I have money in a savings bank in Makati, and I keep the bank book in my locker in the Colonial. For the job, I trained for two weeks at the Hospital Ng Maynila. That was not very difficult, and I can really give a good massage—a hard one if you wish. Someday, I will give you one, specially when you are tired."

"What else do you give?"

Without hesitation, "Sensation—no more. The management wants us to give it if the customer asks. But not if he does not want it."

I pretended ignorance and was sorry afterward, for I was degrading her by asking her to explain.

"I masturbate them," she said simply.

I was silent.

She continued evenly. "All sorts of men, with all sorts of problems and all sorts of lives. I have to be nice to each one, short and tall, fat and thin, and it is very rare that they only want a massage."

"And you give it to them?"

"No, Pepe, I swear. Just sensation."

"Shit," I said, the anger rising in me again although I had no right to be angry with her.

"Shit to you, too," she flung back.

"Look at your new clothes, that new wristwatch. Don't tell me it is the Red Cross. You got those with more than sensation, like a . . ."

"Like a whore? Is that what you want to say?"

The words were rocks in my throat. I must not spew them out.

"I am not a whore, Pepe. God sees everything, I swear to you. I don't even let them touch me."

"God," I cursed in my breath. "I want to believe you, within me I do!" And again, I embraced her, and my whole being ached.

"What will I do, Pepe? What will we do?"

She had included me. "We—" she said, and I held her hand tightly.

"You must be honest with your mother," I said. "Tell her everything. Maybe on a day that she is happy, on your day off when you can take her to Divisoria and buy her a few things."

"That's bribery, she will not like it."

"Explain to her the money you need, your brothers and sisters, their schooling, her health," I said.

"It looks so hopeless."

"It is."

"Suppose the neighbors find out?" she asked. "I cannot live in the Barrio anymore."

"How will they know? I will not tell them anything. I do not think your mother will."

"It is better that we leave the place."

"And where will you go? Some expensive place in Makati?"

"You know I will not do that. I will not be able to afford it."

"It is better in the Barrio. No one among your customers will find you there. No one among us— Shit, we don't even have money for a haircut. We will never go to the Colonial."

A salesgirl in the same shop where she clerked went to the Colonial and earned in one day what she made in a month and she did not go beyond masturbating her guests. The training, Lily said, was easy, but it was the clearances, the physical examination that she detested; she went to San Lazaro twice a month, together with the other girls, and was examined by interns from the medical schools. They took vaginal smears, looked and poked into them as if they were hogs.

"I hate it," she said vehemently.

Sometimes she had only a couple of "guests," as their customers were called, but on a busy day, she had five or six. She now had several "regulars" who waited for her or sought her and, yes, almost everyone tried to seduce her, and several even offered to put her in a "garage"—to make her a mistress at the monthly rate of two thousand pesos, plus an apartment with all the appliances and furniture.

"And it will last as long as he finds you pretty and interesting," I said.

She pinched my arm. "I humor them," she said, "but I make sure they know I would not do it. They ask me to go out with them and I always have nice excuses, about how difficult it is for me to do so. They come back."

"For sensation."

She did not speak.

"We make more than the nightclub hostesses on the boulevard, Pepe. And we don't have to spend on clothes and we are not on display in a glass booth."

"But you sensation them."

"It is hard work; sometimes, when I have six guests in a row, my back, my arms ache; sweat pours down."

"It is honest work," I said disconsolately.

"Please don't be harsh," she said.

"I love you," I said, "and I cannot make you stop working there." Her arms went around me, and she kissed me on the cheek.

When we went out, to my surprise, it was already evening—we had been inside for more than three hours and had not really done much talking or touching; it could have been forever and I would not have known.

"Your eyes," I said. "They are swollen."

"I know." She smiled.

AFTER DINNER that night I borrowed Father Jess's typewriter. He was in his khaki shorts, reading one of the new Teilhard de Chardin books that he also wanted Toto and me to read, but I had demurred for I did not like religious books. To please him, though, I did bring down *The Phenomenon of Man* only to find it unreadable.

He put his book aside, looked at me, and said, grinning, "So you are going to be a writer."

"No, Father," I said, "I just want to improve this personal essay—boyhood in a small village."

He beckoned to me to sit on the chair opposite him. We were going to have another session and I loathed it—it made me think.

"Did you have a happy boyhood?"

There was no telling him lies. The question had never been asked of me before, and without hesitation, I answered. "Yes, Father, a very happy one. I remember the fiestas, the rockets, the first rains of May, the grasshoppers and the frogs, the swimming in the irrigation ditches in the fields. Yes, I had a happy boyhood."

But what about the stigma of my being a bastard, the jokes I had to endure, the questions I could not answer? He noticed the uncertainty that had come over my face. "But?" he asked tentatively.

"It was also unhappy."

"Tell me about it."

I had gone to him for my first confession. He knew about Lucy and the fountain pen I stole when I was in high school, but he did not know of my origins.

"I am a bastard, Father. It is difficult being one, particularly when you are full of doubts, questions that no one, not even your mother, can answer."

"Remember," he said softly, "there are no illegitimate children, there are only illegitimate parents—that's not original. And sometimes it is not even their fault. Like Lily. You know that. And where is her young man now?"

I did not speak.

"There is always a reason," I said after a while. "And we cannot avoid the most important of all."

"And what is that?"

"Money, Father," I said simply.

He smiled benignly. "It is not the most important thing in the world."

"It is to me."

"I can understand that," he said. "Maybe because I come from another place. Did you not say, no priest is poor?"

I was embarrassed to hear him remember, but he kept on talking. "I must be crazy to have selected this parish, or started it anyway. I could die here of hunger and no one would be sorry—not my family, that's for sure."

"Why not?"

"You have been with me for almost a year now—that's a long time—and yet you have never bothered to ask about my family? That is unusual. People gossip and there is no shortage of that, particularly here."

"Yes, I know about your going to nightclubs and your having gotten drunk."

He roared with laughter. "Soon they will be saying I have gotten a girl pregnant. One thing I like about the priesthood is the wine. I get a drop of it every morning." He looked at me and burst out laughing again, this time so long that tears came to his eyes. "So—so, I have no more secrets, ha? You know me like you know the palm of your hand, ha? You and Toto, merely because you live with me, ha?"

I grinned.

"But you don't know about my family, where I come from."

"From Negros. I overheard you talking to an American visitor about the sugar workers."

Father Jess was silent and a smile wreathed his rotund face. He shook his head and said, "You know, Pepe, if my family had not disowned me, I would have had enough money to build a beautiful church right here. And a row of apartments, besides. And we would have the biggest freezer in any *kumbento* in the country. Do you understand?"

"We can still build a church—you have many friends, you are very good at raising money."

He sat back and said, almost in anger, "Build a church? Stone, stained glass, padded pews?"

"Why not? Look at the cathedral in Intramuros . . . the churches of the Iglesia ni Kristo."

"Those are not churches, *hijo*. Those are buildings. Don't you understand?" his voice leaped.

I shook my head.

"The church," he bellowed, beating his massive chest, "is here. In the heart. Not an air-conditioned building with wooden saints, not people kneeling and crawling to the altar—those stupid people! Not processions. The church is here!" He beat his breast again so strongly, the sounds were loud thuds. His eyes flashed and the corners of his mouth curled as he spoke, "The church that we will build is here, and it will last forever. Buildings crumble, but the church that we will build will last. So look at this humble building that some are ashamed to go to. It is here where God lives, perhaps much, much more than anywhere else, but only if I can convince you and all those around that the real church is in us, in how we live, in the sacrifices we offer to Christ who is also in each of us. Everyone, my brother. But much, much more my kin is he who has nothing and suffers. To him I will give everything I have."

Sadness touched his face, his eyes now darkened, the ape hands now folded in repose. "I sometimes feel that I am in the wrong vocation. I am so involved with the things I do, and yet I feel that I am not doing enough. Take this place for instance." He paused and looked out of the window, at the Barrio shrouded by night, at the relentless poverty that spread wherever we turned, the narrow passageways choked with refuse, cluttered with big bellied and dirty children in the daytime and, over everything, flies that never seemed to die. "I think of the place where I was born, of the houses of my relatives and of my former students—they are all comfortable and, yes, very rich . . . and here I am trying to move the world."

"You have the body for it," I said. "You can push it one inch."

"Let's make it two inches." For a moment Father Jess regained his humor, his eyes narrowing into slits, his mouth wide open, baring yellow, uneven teeth. Then he was quiet again, the wide brow furrowed. "If only I had more resources, more money."

I did not know till now of his frustrations, having presumed that, as a priest, his job was easy: he did not have to worry about food and clothing, and when he was old, there was always the Church—omnipresent, omnipotent—to take care of him.

"I hope," I said lightly, "that someday—joke only, Father—that priests like you would be allowed to marry. It must be terrible, not being able to live like a normal man."

He shook his head and replied quickly. "That is a misconception that gets said again and again. Pepe, it is not the absence of sexual life that makes the priesthood difficult. We get used to it."

"Yes, I hear they feed you papayas in the seminary morning, noon, and night till you are as limp as a squid."

"Still, it is not sex," he said. "I will tell you what is the most difficult about the priesthood. Obedience, that's what. Damn, blind obedience. We have to obey, and if we cannot, we have to learn how to obey; we have to force ourselves to obey until in our conscience we have been conditioned to do so."

"Like the army?"

"Yes," he said. "I'd like you to go into retreat this year. Not so much to study your conscience as to be alone with yourself."

"You can be alone in a crowd, Father."

"Not that. But a chance to look at what you do. Do you think you have a conscience, Pepe?"

I fumbled; the question pushed me to the wall. "Doesn't every man have one?" I asked instead.

"You are very clever," he grinned. "What you are trying to say is, as a priest, perhaps, I don't even have to bother with it. In the end, Pepe, we are all victims of circumstance. A world without injustice is not here; if it were, there would be no policemen, no courts—and yes, no priests. But there are things we do that give us happiness. That is one measure of a man." He thrust a finger at me. "What gives you happiness?"

Without hesitation, "Food."

He stood his full height, puckered his lips in mock anger, and pointed to the door.

SO WE ASPIRED, WE SWEATED to build a church here in Tondo, sought to bring light to its chicken-intestine alleys strewn with aborted hopes, slimy with crime; where no heavenly music floats above its rusting tin, and its flotsam soul drifts to the sea—not a sea of shining surf but muck and driftwood marsh awash with the turds of corruption. Look down here, those of you whose antiseptic residences will never be touched by our filthy hands, because it is not far off when the stench we breathe will give us the strength to surge beyond this dungheap into your perfumed enclaves, and with us the volcanic fires of vengeance; we will seep into each crack of your high and solid walls, flood over them like destiny, and you will not be able to hide, you will be transfixed.

Speed dreams, they have no place in my compass. I am here to survive and Tondo is just a way station, another rung in my climb from one garbage pile to another garbage pile. But we build from the past, and be it damned forever. We can never escape it so how can I now flee the old thatched house of Cabugawan, the scent of newly harvested grain, of fresh-cut grass; how can I flee the browned fields of May stirring at last to the touch of rain, the weeds thrusting up, the river finally alive, and the croak of frogs at night?

Toward the end of the schoolyear my past, which I had not told to anyone except Father Jess, finally hounded me in school; I don't know how it came about—perhaps there were those in the Brotherhood who did not like me and the attention Professor Hortenso was giving me. The national election of the Brotherhood was going to be held and I was now being groomed by him for a seat in the National Directorate.

"You are one of the most popular student leaders," he said, "and as you very well know, there will be candidates from UP who will try to get all the positions."

I balked at the prospects. In the first place, I would not have tried to run for any of the posts in school were it not for the proddings of people. But looking back, it had not been completely without benefits. There was this job that paid, the invitations to seminars—all expenses paid—and, of course, the free dinners and parties to which I was invited. Without admitting it, I had always felt inferior to those people at UP, not because they could afford to study there, but simply because they had always seemed brighter than most; they always seemed to top the board exams, in law, in medicine.

After supper that evening, I strolled onto the empty basketball court and lay on one of the cement benches we had installed. It was oppressively hot in the *kumbento* and Father Jess would be in his shorts, the electric fan on high speed. He could have had his bedroom air-conditioned but had rejected it; there was not one air conditioner in the entire Barrio, and he was not going to be the first to have one.

Above, the sky arched luminous and was dusted with stars, and the sounds of the Barrio had started to peter out. Some time back, on an equally warm evening like this, I had come here and had dozed off, then woke up with a chill. It was past midnight and I rushed back to the *kumbento*, rattling the tin siding so that Toto would let me in. I was not sleepy; I was thinking of Lucy. I had had a busy year politicking, writing essays, going over asinine manuscripts and mushy poetry. I had now very little time for myself. I did not even go home for Christmas, and I wondered how it would be with Mother now. I remembered our house, the living room and its clutter of cloth, the sewing machine in one corner, the potted begonias on the windowsill, the polished bamboo floor, shiny even in the dark; Auntie Bettina working over her lesson plan far into the night. I wondered how it would be when they were old and could no longer earn their keep. Would I still be around to care for them, to return a bit of their love? I did not even write as often as I should have, and I only sent Mother and Auntie Christmas cards—as an afterthought.

I was depressed, recalling my callousness, when footsteps crunched on the gravel and, turning, I saw that Toto was there. "I thought you were asleep," he said.

I rose and he sat beside me. "I have been wanting to tell you something since yesterday."

"Now, Toto," I said lightly, "has there been a time that you could not tell me anything?"

"This . . . this is very personal. You may not like to hear it."

"Shit," I said.

"Well, you know, the campaign for the Brotherhood Directorate is very . . . very keen, and the candidates, they are behaving like old politicians."

"Like father, like son," I said.

He was quiet again.

"Well, aren't you going to tell me?" I prodded him.

"You will not . . . you will not get angry with me?"

"Hell, Toto. Tell me!"

"It will not make any difference—no difference at all," he said, his voice lifting. "Why are people like this? They think it is dirty so they pass it around. They do not say it . . . they do not say it in the open . . . like . . . like men. They talk about it like . . . like girls. . . ."

"What are you talking about?"

"About . . . about you, Pepe. Someone does not like you . . . in the Brotherhood—he must have started it. But . . . but I want you to know . . . you have nothing to worry about. In fact . . . in fact, it is to your . . . your advantage."

"Tell me!" My chest tightened.

"Dirty politics . . . very dirty," he said. "The gossip is that you . . . you . . ." He paused and could not go on.

"Say it!" I shouted.

"A bastard . . ." almost in a whisper, then he turned away.

A great sense of relief filled me, and I laughed at the irony of it. He turned back to me and asked, "You are not angry?"

I placed an arm on his shoulder. "It is no secret, Toto," I said. "Everyone in my village knows about it. But do I have to go around shouting it? Telling everyone?"

He did not reply.

"Of course, it was difficult to bear, particularly when I was young and I asked questions, and my classmates—you know how kids are—often joked about it. There were times I wished I was not born . . . and my father, I know him now; all those years, I never knew him. He wronged my mother—" the words came easily, "and I hate him."

"Do not say that."

"I hate him," I repeated flatly.

He turned away. "It is enough that we are here. Life is good; it has problems, but it is wonderful to be here, even in this Barrio. . . ."

"This hellhole?"

"We make it the way it is."

"You are so full of hope," I said.

"What else must we have? Revolutions are not made by pessimists, and even pessimists have hope. There is no sense in their being pessimists otherwise."

"Still," I said, "there are times I wish I was not born."

It was then that Toto raised his voice. "Who do you think you are? God's loneliest man? Job? Look around you, there are hundreds of talented young people who do not go to college. They have no way of doing it. Look around us, here, in the Barrio. How many sick people do you know? With tuberculosis? Look at the children. Still, life goes on."

He was not stammering anymore because he was angry. "Look at yourself. At least you know your mother and father and you have relatives. Look at me, Pepe, look at me! Do you know where I came from? I don't know my father or my mother. No relatives! The children I grew up with were all orphans. At least my mother did not flush me down the toilet or strangle me and put me in the garbage can! They do that, you know. And you are sorry for yourself, sorry for being a bastard!"

Again, I put my arm on his shoulder, but he brushed it away brusquely. "The world is ahead of us, Pepe. We make it. Not our parents. And there is no past, just the future!"

I put an arm on his shoulder again and this time he did not push it away. "I am sorry," I said. "I am too self-centered. Everything I do I do for myself, for a reason. I have never done anything for anyone— not for my mother, for my Auntie . . . for you. Forgive me, Toto."

We went back to the *kumbento* in silence, lay in our beds and continued talking quietly. "I feel better, Toto," I said. "Thank you for talking to me."

After some time he asked: "Do you . . . do you know now what you want to be?"

"To be happy," I said simply.

He laughed softly. "No, that is not what I meant. What will you be? A writer?"

"Hell, no," I said.

"You have talent."

"But I will not be one. Maybe I will be a politician."

"The different kind," he said. "You are too honest. And when you are older . . ."

"I will not grow old. And you? Will you be a scientist with your skills in math?"

"No, no," Toto was emphatic. "I have known what I would like to be for a long time now. But it is very difficult and very expensive. I only hope Father Jess can help."

"He will help," I said. "He likes you very much."

"He has many responsibilities. And besides, he is not really healthy. He has a heart problem."

"He will not die very soon," I said. "What do you want to be really? A revolutionary like Ka Lucio? You will not get anywhere. Look at him."

Toto laughed again. "I will do it differently," he said. "I will be a doctor."

• • •

I DID NOT campaign very hard for the National Directorate at the convention in Diliman. There was not much for me to do except distribute the mimeographed handbills that Toto and I had prepared. The delegates from Mindanao were mostly Ilocanos, and I think that my being one helped. Professor Hortenso saw to it that in both the bulletin and program my "Memo to Youth," which got me the literary editorship of my college paper, was reprinted. The two-day convention was filled with blustery speeches that left me numb and reeling. I was glad when the end came, and would have been even if I had lost. That did not seem likely, and my victory—membership in the National Directorate—was not the chest-thumping kind of achievement I would have been proud of. There was something shadowy and stage-managed about the whole election, but certainly I was not one to question its outcome. Perhaps I was a bit naive to expect that young politicians were going to be different from their elders, that they would display more candor and be less concerned with meaningless argot. The first meetings of the National Directorate showed that this was not so. We would argue out the minutest point when the Brotherhood Constitution was invoked; everyone seemed anxious to show that only he saw or possessed the true light. Diliman was no longer my territory; we were not in Professor Hortenso's cramped apartment, drinking stale coffee and devouring musty cookies. Now we were meeting in a conference room while outside the musclemen of the Brotherhood kept intruders out, although I couldn't see anything secret or conspiratorial about the discussions. They were really just bloated repetitions of what was discussed in the seminars. I did not remind them of this; I did not know the members of the Directorate well, least of all the chairman—an ascetic-looking Ph.D. who certainly was not a student. I did not want to lose the privileges that came with my new post. I also wanted to feel them out, to learn what drove them and to remember, most of all, how they could be useful later.

The chairman intrigued me at first, but soon I found him quite transparent. He talked very little; instead, he was listening and guiding the discussions to where he wanted them to go: to a consensus that supported his views, some of which I did not agree with. For example, his emphasis on creating the atmosphere that would bring about armed violence, revolution, before its scheduled time—if there was even a schedule for it as evolved by social forces and events.

Then, there was his fanatical hatred of the Americans. I wondered if he really knew the poor whom he wanted to be his revolutionary fodder, if he was not indulging in book-learned fantasies. Whatever thoughts I had I kept to myself for the time being. I did not want to antagonize him, to be labeled afterward as a deviationist—his usual retort to anyone who disagreed with him.

Of all the decisions we made, what I looked forward to was the demonstration we were to mount immediately, before the schools closed. The convention was actually a preparation for it. The Brotherhood was not poor, although our dues were minimal. We had a good finance committee raising money for publications, posters, and this demonstration. I was given three hundred pesos to spend, no accounting.

The first thing I did was bring Roger and the officers of the Barrio chapter to Panciteria Asia where we had *pancit canton*, fried chicken, chop suey, and all the beer they could drink.

We also bought *cartulina*,* ink and paint at a Chinese wholesale store in Divisoria. A sign painter in the Barrio, Ka Enteng, who painted the prow of the fishing *bancas*† that plied the bay, did the posters. The slogans prepared at the convention were clichés, of course. *Ibagsak ang Imperialismo, Yankee Go Home, Close the US Bases* . . . etc. I never felt strongly about them, but Toto did, and he even improved on them, adding words like *Now!*

They were all lined up for everyone to see, and Ka Lucio saw them when he returned from that small export-import office in the Escolta where he clerked.

Toto and I were viewing our handiwork with satisfaction, but Ka Lucio just glanced at them, then shook his head.

"They will not do, Ka Lucio?" I asked.

"You want advice?"

Toto said eagerly, "Yes, you know so many things."

"Come and visit me in an hour," he said.

Ka Lucio lived in a two-room house with two nieces whom he managed to send to college. An assortment of relatives, provincemates, and old friends were constant visitors. He tried to help them find jobs or, at the very least, offer them a roof and a meal while they

---

* *Cartulina:* Cardboard, poster board.
† *Banca:* A Philippine canoe.

were in the city. He managed to look like someone's city uncle, well-bred and wise to the ways of the rich. A soft lilt to his voice camouflaged an iron will and a hardness of spirit that enabled him to endure not just years in the forest but more than a decade in army jails. Here, in the Barrio, he had not only been emasculated; here, too, was the final ignominy—to be poor and be with the poor, while many of the guerrillas of the war he had fought had become wealthy and gross and inhabited the perfumed enclaves of Makati. There is no adulation for a failed revolutionary, only a sympathy akin to pity or even contempt, not so much because he has failed but because he has lived so long.

Like most of the two-story houses in the Barrio, his was badly constructed. The living room had a cracked cement floor and a couple of sagging rattan sofas; beyond was the dingy kitchen, with its rusty kerosene stove. A transistor radio, a black-and-white TV, and a case full of books, mostly on politics, occupied a corner.

He bade us sit down while one of his nieces, who studied in the mornings, opened two bottles of Coke. They were not cold and the cookies, exposed to the air for some time, were limp.

"So, you are going to be revolutionaries," he said, a grin lighting up his face.

Neither Toto nor I replied; he sounded very patronizing.

"It is not easy," he added quickly. "But if you have set your mind to it then give it everything you have, but more than anything, give it intelligence—something I did not give. I was more passion than reason. I know otherwise now."

"What do you think of the posters, Ka Lucio?" I asked impatiently.

He stood up. Ka Lucio was tall for a Filipino. His thin lips gave him an ascetic look but his eyes, always wrinkled in laughter or a smile, put us at ease. He had surrendered, but that had not helped; he was jailed just the same and had served out his sentence without parole or lenient treatment. He walked to the shelf of books. "You are welcome to these," he said. "My library, or what is left of it."

"What is wrong with the posters, Ka Lucio?" Toto asked.

"You are engaged in propaganda," he said. "It is just as important as being out there, in the forest. No, I see nothing wrong with the posters—they are well made. Too well made, as a matter of fact. But will they be believed? To whom are you addressing yourselves?"

"They will be believed," Toto said, "because they speak the truth."

Ka Lucio shook his head. Though he was sixty-five, there was not a single gray hair on his head, and he did not wear glasses. Everything about him belied years with the Huks, the guerrilla war against the Japanese. He had lost his wife after the war in an ambush and had not remarried. Now, in his eyes, this certitude. "What is truth?" he asked. "This is not a philosophical question. It is a matter of perception. What is the truth that you know about the American bases, Toto?"

"Instruments of American imperialism, the enslavement of the Filipino people," Toto said quickly, almost by rote.

"They provide jobs for more than twenty thousand Filipinos," Ka Lucio said. "They bring millions of dollars to this country. Can you do the same, you and your revolution?"

Toto sat back; he knew the answers to such cliché questions—they had been hashed and rehashed in the seminars of the Brotherhood—and he spewed them right out. I knew them, too, but did not believe them.

"Our people do not understand such nationalism, even if it were true. It is more important, Toto," he said paternally, "that you know how the people think if you want to win them. And slogans will not do it. Do you know what this means if you cannot win the people?"

Toto was getting peeved and was no longer stammering; he began to talk in a shrill, excited squeak.

"The people do not make change, or revolution. They are conservative and they do not know how to think of the future. Look at the people here, in the Barrio. They will go anywhere, wherever they are led."

Ka Lucio shook his head. "You will learn otherwise, and when you do, it will be too late. The young are discovering politics, they are thrilled by it, they want to do something with it. And it is all very good—oh, if we only had you thirty years ago. What we could have done then!"

"But you did not have us. And you made mistakes," Toto said.

"Yes, and that is why we lost. But we did not fail. No, by God, we did not fail. We made one step . . . so that you could make the next. I hope you will make it three."

Toto sat back, his anger assuaged.

"I hope," Ka Lucio was continuing, "that you will not waste yourselves. I sometimes ask myself, what have I done with my life? It is all behind me now. And what have I to show? Twelve years in prison. No, those were not wasted years. I was able to think a lot, the mistakes we made. And more than ever, I got to know what freedom really means. Do you know what freedom is, Pepe? Again, this is not a philosophical question."

"Free speech," I said, "free elections, free assembly, free worship."

Ka Lucio shook his head. He placed his right hand over his breast. "It is here, Pepe," he said. "This is where it lives. And once it is dead here, no slogan, no demonstration, no ideology, no revolution can ever bring it back to life. And to the people, it is not free speech. It is clothing, food, shelter, medicine for the children when they are ill. Education . . . not a degree from UP or Ateneo; just the simple kind that will enable them to get jobs."

We left Ka Lucio reluctantly, Father Jess would be back, and we had to serve him dinner. We knew we would be back, if only so that I could ask how it was during the Japanese Occupation, how they fought, how it was that the Huks were defeated. Ka Lucio had opened a treasure house for me, and I coveted it.

Toto bothered me with his vaulting enthusiasms. He was much brighter than I in history; certainly, he had read a lot of Marx and Marcuse and could cite passages from Sartre and Fanon. I could only recite a few lines from Jarrell, Plath, and Thomas and relate the travel books and novels I had read. Still, I did some reading, too, not just the pamphlets Professor Hortenso prepared or had us distribute, but the esoterica at the library where I often stayed when I had time. Even if my political reading had not increased much, my conclusions were firm. There was something awry about the enthusiasms not just of Toto but of Professor Hortenso, who had a better education than all of us. We should have had more sessions with men like Ka Lucio to learn tactics, organization, and most of all, those irrevocable lessons of their failure.

"What is there to learn except consciousness?" Toto asked. "This is the most important thing. With the new consciousness, our minds are opened and we see the truth at last."

"That is a lot of messianic shit," I said.

We were in our favorite *siopao* corner and we had finished our noodles. It was one of those white-washed cubicles with waiters and waitresses in starched white. You lined up at a counter for noodles, *siopao,* and soft drinks, and then took your tray to a white Formica-topped table often soggy with the remnants of the last occupant's meal; for some reason the noodles always tasted a bit soapy, and they were dry and hard no matter how long they had been immersed in hot soup. But never mind; I was not one to complain, especially since Toto was paying.

"The Huks failed," Toto said, "because they did not have the support of the masses. They were fish caught without a sea."

"That is too glib an answer," I said, "although I will not question it. The important thing is that we should not forget it."

"We are another generation," he said stoutly.

"Yes," I said, "but we do not look back. We are a people with history but we have no sense of the past. And look at our heroes now. The movie stars who cannot act, the politicians who are crooks. We are a people without memory. Why do we rename our streets after politicians who have not done anything for the Filipinos? Why do we allow the Japanese to build monuments for their dead on *our* land—land they had ravaged?"

"I will not forget, I will always remember," Toto said.

I went back to Ka Lucio. "The Huks lost because they were betrayed."

"That was in their time," Toto said stubbornly. "This is 1970; it will not happen again."

"You are dreaming," I said. "You are blind to everything around you. Listen, our history is a history of failed revolutions. Always, in the end, someone was bought or someone turned traitor. We are a nation of traitors; we delight in seeing the downfall of others, even friends. We betray for money, for revenge, for envy, but most of the time out of sheer cussedness. So here you are in this organization. You will see me and the others claw our way to the top, over the bodies of our friends. We have the wrong memories. We remember the slightest injury to our pride, our so-called self-respect. We etch these in our hearts and wait patiently for the day when we can stick the knife in the back. But let someone do us a good deed, and we forget it easily. We are also a nation of ingrates."

He was looking at me, eyes unblinking.

"It was this way before," I said evenly. "Why should it change? Why shouldn't history be a continuity? Diego Silang, Apolinario dela Cruz, Andres Bonifacio, Antonio Luna, Gregorio del Pilar—

they were all betrayed. But the worst betrayal is when we betray ourselves for a few pesos. And sometimes we don't even know it. We are
shocked into discovering that we did it, bit by bit, until we had gone
over the brink into the cesspool. We can atone for it with knowledge.
But how about those who don't realize it or refuse to do so?"

"I will not betray anyone, and I will not betray myself," Toto
said, his lips quivering. He was beginning to stammer. "All through
our history men died for what they believed in. They were not traitors. You named only a few; the brave are more than a handful."

"But where are they now?" I asked. "It is so easy to have people
go another way. The student leaders—they can be bought. If not, all
you have to do is please them, their sense of manhood, their being
Ilocanos, or Batangueños."

"That is not true, that is not true!" Toto's voice pitched.

"The revolution against Spain—the Filipinos were bought at
Biak Na Bato. The same with the war against the Americans. And the
Japanese. Look around you now. Who are the victors? So then, why
should the young be different?"

"Because you are different and I am different!" Toto cried. I
could see people turn to our table; he was quickly aware of this, and
his voice dropped. I stood up, held his arm, and we walked out; they
went back to their noodles and *siopao,* wondering perhaps what it
was that made two friends quarrel then stop as quickly as they had
started.

Out in Recto, in the sweaty crowd and coagulating heat of afternoon, I tried to tell Toto how necessary it was to retain a certain
cynicism, a little distance from those passions that possessed us, but
he would not listen. He believed, and you cannot tell someone who
believed the sky was dark when to him it was the purest blue. Looking back, I know I could have saved him. But I was being drawn, like
the moth, into the flame that had been ignited within us.

Walking home at dusk, taking the small side streets clogged with
people and garbage, I would peer at the dimmed insides of houses,
the battered furniture of battered living rooms, and wonder about
the kind of life these people lived, how far the reality was from the
dream. Somehow, with the darkness, the hard lines of faces disappear, the dirt is hidden, and even the filth in corners no longer appears as detestable as it would in the daylight. But darkness or light,
I could see them more clearly, their riddle that is the present and

their past that should be destroyed if need be, but forgotten it must be. I see them as I see myself.

Walking home at dusk, I sort out my thoughts, try to understand how it had been, how instinctively I had drifted with the seasons. Who was it who said the bamboo survives the storm because it bends? That is what I know: to say the right things, the correct things that signify my acquiescence, my adulation, so that the wind will not break me. The storm leaves, but I stand—I stand without triumph for I have done what must be done in order to live. Is life really worth all this bending?

There are many others who will not bow, who will question belief, this course, and it is they who believe, too, that the crow will be white some day, that the skies will open up and from there, blessings will pour. They may wait forever, but forever is not time. For them, time has lost its menace. Only tomorrow matters.

TOMORROW THEN, and my first and biggest demonstration. I was quickly impressed with how an organization, working with a few dedicated members—whatever their purposes—could set up a singular machine for almost anything, to amass crowds of varying allegiances and murky origins, even the young people of the Barrio whose politics is simplified by slogans. We had planned well in the National Directorate. This demonstration was to be our show of strength; we had now aligned ourselves with other student groups—or rather they had joined us, for it was the Brotherhood that had the most chapters, the most radical slogans, articulate orators, best writers.

The delegation from our university was surprisingly large. But they came not because our cause was just but because it meant crowds, excitement, and, most of all, a good excuse not to be in class. It was perilously close to final examinations, but the dean of students granted us permission to assemble, and all classes that afternoon and evening were canceled.

We had fashioned red banners from bolts of cheap cotton and hired two dozen jeepneys, all equipped with sound systems, and these were now on the prowl, gusty with our slogans, urging on the students who had amassed in the side streets, Brotherhood activists marshaling the ranks.

Some had started to sing the Brotherhood songs in Tagalog, the "Internationale" and as Ka Lucio had said, they were as stirring as the Huk songs his comrades sang in their time.

The streets were now empty of traffic, and we had the asphalt to ourselves. Who would stand in the way of thousands of young people united for the first time? We were laughing, pleased at how we had brought ourselves together with so little money and a lot of rhetoric.

Toto was not a marshal; he did not have the build or the voice, and his eyes were bad. He was with me, and his face was aglow with the happiness that communion brought. He even had his arm on my shoulder though he was no taller than I, and it was in this manner that we marched most of the way to Plaza Miranda.

Ah, Plaza Miranda—the throbbing, malodorous heart of Manila! It is here where they all meet, the scavenging politician and his wordbound listener, the government official and his gross hypocrisies, the penitent and his worldly vows. The blooming banners, the shabby buildings loomed around us. It was four, humid and hot, and the crowd was so thick we could barely move. Not all were students—many were the poor with their plastic bags for the market, clerks with cheap vinyl portfolios, vendors in rubber slippers. The Brotherhood had arranged to have a mobile platform—actually a brokerage truck with the sidings removed—backed to the fence of the Quiapo church, and on it were our guest speaker, the aging Senator Reyes, known for his radical nationalist views, as well as orators of the Brotherhood.

All around the plaza were policemen and Metrocom troopers, armed and sullen, but they did not interrupt the meeting. We stationed marshals everywhere who knew what to do. At given signals, they led the chanting: *I-bag-sak. Marcos—Tuta. I-bag-sak!*

The marshals also led the clapping at significant pauses of the speakers. I was both fascinated and bothered. How easy it was to channel the energies, the raucous voice of the mob—for that was what we had become, how mindless, how meaningless the clichés, and how foreseeable the response.

Most of us were in blue denims and dark T-shirts, and we knew by experience then that rubber shoes gave us more speed, more comfort on the asphalt and that was where we left many of them the following morning where they were stepped upon and shucked off, together with the placards that had been ripped, the canisters of tear gas, the shards of broken bottles, and, yes, our blood—smudges of dark red on black, our signature that would describe how high we had vaulted and how we had been dashed back to earth.

Looking back, I knew then what unity meant, the sense of power it evoked from each of us as we saw our solid, swollen phalanx moving, singing, surging. But how long could such unity last? How many of us really believed in what we were doing? Well enough, deeply enough to have our blood spilled on the asphalt?

I am sure that many joined the demonstration as one would attend a fiesta—because that was what everyone was doing, because it gave a way to express resentments that could not be vented otherwise, and because being in a demonstration gave a ranking above the lethargy of the mass that was inert even in its anger. Time would tell who among us would soon react to the tragedy that hovered over us. We were no longer playing games.

But what I did not foresee was a demonstration gone wild. The last speaker had ended his piece to the usual applause. Although it was not in our plans, the demonstrators had started to move. *Malacañang! Malacañang!* was the new and electric chant.

We were marching again, intoxicated by our numbers, uncaring about the traffic jam we had created all around Quiapo. As the lead marchers reached Recto, an explosion rocked our rear. A massive surge forward separated the head of the demonstrators from the rest, but the marshals were very skillful. *Makibaka! Huwag Matakot.** They chanted, and we repeated the chant: *Makibaka! Huwag Matakot!*

It was past seven, and the neon lights along Recto were glittering, but all the shops were closed. The merchants, the people were afraid. Perhaps it was best that they should be; now they saw what massive power the young could muster if they were organized, if they were led as the Brotherhood now led them.

It did not take us long; in another thirty minutes, while we marched and formed a broader column, we reached the corner of Legarda. The repository of history, power—Malacañang—was ahead of us, across the bridge and up the broad tree-lined street. I did not know what we would do; perhaps the marshals knew. Torches of

---

* *Makibaka! Huwag Matakot!:* Join! Don't be afraid!

bamboo filled with kerosene materialized; they lighted up young faces, sweaty and happy; girls in jeans and rubber shoes. It was a euphoric binge, and we were living and enjoying every moment of it.

Toto had not left my side since the start of the march, and often he would turn to me and smile and when the chanting came, it was his squeaky voice that was loudest. We paused. Word was passed down to us that the police and the Metrocom had a barricade on the small bridge that spanned the foul-smelling *estero* between Legarda and Mendiola.

Toto and I broke from our ranks and went forward to find out what could be done, and the marshals shouted the slogans again, *I-bag-sak! I-bag-sak!*

We had gotten quickly to the front, where the marshals were waving their red banners. Across the barricades was a line of Metrocom troopers, their rifles at the ready, and with them were Manila policemen, truncheons in their hands. From our ranks, the shouts volleyed: *Sugod—sugod!** And the formation surged forward. We were lifted as if by a giant wave, and it was then, in the semidarkness, that the shots rang out, the volleys louder and different from the sounds of our exploding Molotovs. Around us were more explosions. Through the acrid haze, the Metrocom moved forward. For us, it was now each man for himself. Bullets whined above our heads, and as I started to run, Toto ahead of me staggered, then fell. As he slumped forward, his voice came clear: "Pepe, I'm hit!" God knows I wanted to go to him lying there, waiting for the oncoming flood of Metrocom and police, but by then I had jumped into the shallow ditch that led to the creek, and though I was standing and seeing everything and was conscious of the turmoil around me, I could not move. My knees, my feet had become rooted to the earth and no longer did I have control over them.

They came and pummeled everyone they could reach; then they regrouped and rushed at us again. I was now flat on my stomach. So this was what violence was, the red violence in which Toto and the Brotherhood believed, the violence that would usher an effulgent dawn, liberation, and all the boundless goodies of the earth. Around me, the thunder of explosives, tear gas, acrid smoke, the rushing and scuffling of feet. I cowered, I hugged the ground, I must live. When the

* *Sugod:* Advance!

phalanx of the demonstration was finally disbanded with tear gas, I clambered to the street and looked for Toto. He was sprawled there together with the others who had been shot; some were squatting and moaning, but Toto did not move; his left side was wet with blood and only the slight twitching of his arms told me he was still alive.

I cried for help and a Metrocom trooper came; ambulances had arrived, their sirens screaming, and we loaded Toto into one of them. I wanted to go with them, but there was no room. No jeeps were on Recto and Legarda; I had to run to the boulevard and hail the first taxi I saw; I had thought the wounded would be taken to the hospital in Avenida, which was nearest, but the ambulances were not in sight.

I boarded another taxi and rushed to Taft; they were at the hospital there, and the lobby was filled with students, policemen, and Metrocom, and everyone was tense and full of recriminations. Where are they? Is Toto alive? No one seemed to know, and they would not let any of us into the emergency rooms. Reporters were all over the place, too, asking questions, but I was too dazed, too sick with worry to talk to anyone until I realized that it was they who could get the information I wanted.

I approached one, told him I was an officer of the Brotherhood, and, yes, he was very glad to talk with me, but first I must know if Toto was alive. "I don't know," he said. "Ten are dead—they are lying in the corridor beyond the emergency room waiting to be transferred to the morgue, where they can be claimed; another twenty are on the critical list, and there are many who might have been wounded."

He was in his early thirties, and he seemed sympathetic, for all the time he was mumbling, "What a waste, what a waste." I told him how it started—we were out front; all of a sudden, the shooting, the confusion, the tear gas, the grenades.

But how is Toto? I couldn't go in, but he could; Toto had short cropped hair, white shirt, dark pants, and yes, white basketball shoes. "Please go back and tell me he is not dead; he is my best friend, my best friend."

It did not take him even five minutes. He asked me to go with him. A policeman let me through into a shabby room lighted by a single bulb. They lay on the tile floor, bathed by the yellow light, their faces, if not bloodied, ashen in death. In a corner, a girl was crumpled on the floor, crying, while a boy stood beside her, tears streaming down his cheeks. Toto was at the far corner, the blood on his shirt already dry. He did not have his glasses and, even in death, there was an ineffable quality of determination on his face, the eyes closed, the mouth slightly open. The intern who came in after me started filling out a form and at the same time asking questions. "Augusto Salcedo. Nineteen. I do not know his parents—he is an orphan. We live together. We will claim him early in the morning."

I knelt beside him and held his hand. It was already cold.

Listen, Toto, my brother, if I were an Ilocano woman, I would now fill this loathsome room with my wailing.

I will walk home tonight alone, and our room will be quiet and wide. You are dead, but memory lives. I will hear your voice, feel your presence. I will remember. How can I forget? Who will feed me now in the afternoons? No more free *siopao*, free *mami*. Who will push me on to new heights where I can see a better view?

Toto, my brother, I will miss you.

Here you are, the life snuffed out of you.

Here I am, with muscles that still move, and eyes that can still see. If it was in my power to command our fate, it should be I who is lying here, my brother, for you have done no wrong. You have always given a part of yourself away, to me, to others. Who then are the spirits you have displeased? There was a purpose to your life while there was none to mine. Is it true then that God is unkind to let the weeds grow? Is it true then that, at birth, we are already condemned? I refuse to believe this because I know, in the end, it is the good who will triumph. You were going to be a saver of lives, you were going to change the ugliness that we know. I was not going to help you. But now, what will I do so that I will at least be able to face my own conscience? You were brave, and I was a coward; if I had just a little more of your courage, a little more of your dream, you would not be here. But this is not so, and I am alive, instead. I will live for you then, Toto, my brother.

A POLICEMAN was waiting for me at the door; he saw the blood on my sleeve and said, "Ha, they missed you," then he asked me the same questions and I repeated the answers, but in between, I asked, not in anger but in sorrow, "Why did you shoot him? He did not even have a stone . . . he was unarmed."

He became angry. "Do you know," he asked, "that three policemen are dead? That many were wounded?"

"I do not know, but you are armed . . . and Toto was not."

"How do you explain those broken shop windows?" He had raised his voice and was waving his truncheon at me. "What have you against those small shopkeepers? Do you know how much damage you have caused?"

"I did not smash any window," I said.

"I did not fire at you," he said. "My hands are clean."

It is past midnight, and I am back at the *kumbento*—sick, tired, impotently angry. I hate myself; if I had not been afraid, I would have been able to rush to Toto, draw him to safety, and hurry him to the hospital even if he was already hit. But I was a coward, and so my best friend was DOA, dead on arrival. A few minutes more, God, just a few courageous minutes and he could have lived. I could have saved him with my blood. Not a drop of it had been spilled, and Toto was dead.

I woke up Father Jess; he took the news calmly, then told me to leave in a voice that cracked; he would break down, and he did not want me to see him thus.

Tia Nena, her eyes red from weeping, woke me up from a short, fitful sleep; there was hot coffee in the kitchen. Father Jess was getting ready upstairs. It was not yet three by the alarm clock on the shelf. I had slept for only an hour at the most. The Barrio was very quiet. On the way to Bangkusay, where we would get a ride—if there were any to be had at this hour—I told Father Jess what had happened.

"He would be alive, Father," I said, "if I had gone to him."

"It is not your fault, Pepe," he said softly, putting an arm on my shoulder.

"He called out my name, I heard him, but I couldn't go. I was paralyzed with fear. And I—I'm much, much older than he. He was my younger brother."

"It was not your fault, Pepe," he repeated. "You did not touch the trigger."

After a while we reached Bangkusay. We waited silently for a few minutes, but there was no jeepney or taxi, so Father Jess said we should walk on to Juan Luna. There was more traffic there.

As we walked, I could not help but cry out my shame.

"I am a coward," I repeated. "When we were at Mendiola, facing tear gas and bullets, I was in the ditch, scared. I was thinking of myself. God, there are so many days ahead of me still and I have not even slept on a bed with a mattress."

"Is this what you dream of? Is this all you can think of? It is not much of a dream, you know." There was both pity and sarcasm in his voice.

"Because you have never been poor, Father," I said. "Sometimes, when I see what is in the kitchen, I envy you."

Father Jess was silent; his being in Tondo was some sacrifice, but even in the harshest of times, as when he was working in Negros among the sugar workers, or among the dockworkers in Tondo, he always had recourse, he could always go back to the comfort of the *kumbento* or to his folks in Negros, who, I am sure, would take him back.

"Yes," Father Jess said. "It is easy for me to speak like this. I keep forgetting that I can always get away. Do not begrudge me that."

"No, Father. I am just saying what I think."

"Still, there must be some dream, some ambition particularly now. All of us have dreams, you know. We may never make them real, but they are there, prodding us on. Toto wanted very much to be a doctor."

"Yes," I said. "Maybe, my dream is to finish college and get a job. And maybe, when I have made enough, I will go back to that other Barrio, bring one whole *lechon,** a fistful of money, and the best electric sewing machine for my mother . . . yes, that is what I would like to do."

But even that was now far from reality. That morning I withdrew all my money from the bank and bought medicine and blood for our wounded, for though many stood in line to donate blood, it was not ready. In hindsight, which is the lowest form of wisdom, I realized that we had not really provided for such catastrophes as had hap-

---

* *Lechon:* A roast suckling pig.

pened in Mendiola. Our marshals were, for the most part, disorganized when the tear gas attack began. But most of all, we did not have teams to give first aid, fledgling doctors from the medical schools, who should have been organized for this. And in the hospitals, it was pure chaos just simply identifying the wounded and the dead. Only a few of our leaders, like Professor Hortenso, remained with us; the rest, like our nationalist Senator Reyes, the loud-mouthed champions of democratic nationalism and revolution, to where had they all vanished?

We brought Toto back to the Barrio before daybreak; the funeral coach could not get into the alley, so we had to carry him to the church. We set up the catafalque in the center aisle, and by the end of the six o'clock mass everyone in the Barrio knew.

Roger and his gang came and asked me to join them at one of the clapboard community centers that had long been abandoned but which they had converted into a meeting place. It was there that I realized how deeply Roger had felt about the quiet, weak-eyed sacristan whom he often badgered.

"He is dead, Roger, and no one, not even you, can push him now," I said.

His voice trembled. "You don't understand. I did not mean to hurt him at all. He was like me. He was a friend."

It is one of those inexplicable ironies that one's friends are often unknown till one is dead. "Did you know, Pepe," Roger was saying as if he were revealing a secret, "Toto and I . . . we both came from the Hospicio?"

I nodded. "Will you avenge his death?"

"We will not be still until that is done," Roger said, his oily face grim, the pugnacity wrung out of him. A murmur of assent sprang around us.

"I will help you do that," I said.

"Do you know who killed him?" They clustered around me, smelling strongly of sweat, their tattoos glistening in the light.

I nodded. "It was not a soldier nor a policeman, Roger."

"Don't make a fool of me," he raised his voice.

"I don't intend to," I said. "I am trying to tell you that avenging Toto is very difficult, and what you have in mind is futile, even childish."

I then proceeded to tell them as simply as I could about Toto's involvement with the Brotherhood—the reasons for his commitment, how our enemies wanted to discredit us, how these same enemies created this vast miasma, this Barrio, from which we would never escape if we did not do what should be done.

"You will have your revenge, and it will be sweet, but only if you don't make it personal, if you are organized, if you join us."

I wanted to give Roger what was left of the Brotherhood money so that they could buy refreshments for the wake, but Roger refused it. They would do that on their own, and it would only be the beginning. The beginning.

TWO ELDERLY NUNS came that night, their burdens imprinted on their faces, and one cried like a child. I remembered Toto's stories about his boyhood, how each of the orphans had his favorite nun and how difficult it was to get her attention, for the orphans numbered more than a hundred. He did not know then what it was to own new clothes, for with the exception of what was their "best" for church or for going out, all their clothes were hand-me-downs. But at least they ate three times a day.

We buried Toto the following morning in a small plot that belonged to the Church in La Loma. Some of our classmates and officers of the Brotherhood came. I was grateful that Professor Hortenso and his wife were present, and with them was Juan Puneta, the scholar, heir to millions, blasé and elegant, a member of the famous Puneta family of philanthropists, educators, and businessmen. He wanted us to ride in his Continental—a big, black car with a khaki-uniformed chauffeur, but Father Jess demurred, he would be with Toto's friends; so Puneta joined us in the jeepney that followed the hearse.

Lily and Roger stared at Juan Puneta in his white double-knit suit, which he did not remove although it was warm and all of us were already perspiring.

"How did it happen?" he asked no one in particular. Father Jess pointed to me. "He was there. Pepe knows, he is on the National Directorate of the Brotherhood."

Juan Puneta looked at me, his eyes noncommittal. He was in his late thirties. His Tagalog was poor, maybe because he spoke Spanish and English more. "Yes, Professor Hortenso told me about you," he said in a flat voice. "And they are all good things," he smiled. "How did it happen? Oh, damn the police, damn the Metrocom."

"He was one of the first to get hit," I said. "We were not at the head of the demonstration, we were way back, but we had gone out front when we stalled. Then the firing started—we do not know where it came from."

"The Metrocom, who else?" he said bitterly. "The police. They have guns, don't they?"

I did not speak. "The bullet hole," I said, afterward, "is just below his left breast. He died before he could get to the hospital. Loss of blood—that is what the doctor said."

"Damn the Metrocom. You should fight back. You should be armed." Puneta was gesticulating to no one in particular. He had started to perspire and the sweat glistened on his pallid forehead. He took a handkerchief from his breast pocket and daubed his forehead primly, then folded the handkerchief carefully and placed it back.

Lily wept when Toto was lowered into the grave. As Father Jess blessed the casket, tears misted my eyes. I felt this weight crushing my chest, and I could not breathe. When it was over, I decided to stay behind to watch the *cantero* smooth out the cement that marked the grave. I spelled out the inscription he would etch on it: *Augusto Salcedo. 1951–1970. The Brotherhood Honors You.*

Lily, who would not be off to her massage parlor in Makati till noon, stayed with me. It was almost eleven when the job was done and we walked to one of the greasy *lechon* restaurants in La Loma. She was silent in the cemetery. Now, she asked, "Pepe, do you like that Puneta?"

Her question startled me: "Why do you ask? It is the first time I ever saw him. But I have heard of him; he was talked about in one of the National Directorate meetings. He contributes to the Brotherhood, you know."

She was silent for a while. "It is not good money," she said. "I don't trust him."

"There is no dirty money, Lily," I said.

"I know him."

To my look of surprise, she smiled: "No, he does not know me at all. But he comes to the Colonial—almost every day. He is *syoki.*"

"He is married," I said, remembering his elegant society wedding, how his family and three children were featured in magazines, riding horses, target-shooting.

"That does not make a difference," she said. "He is *syoki*. When he goes to the Colonial, he never has a massage. He has a 'regular' and she never gives him one—or 'sensation' him. She just sits there and tells him of the men she has handled. And you know what he does? He goes to the shower, to the steam room when the traffic is heaviest, he just goes there pretending to shower when really he is enjoying himself, looking."

"You are too imaginative," I said. "You should write for *Liwayway*."

"This is the truth," she said. "A month at the Colonial and you have a lifetime, ten lifetimes, of sex education. All sorts of men and we . . . we talk about them, compare experiences, and have a good laugh now and then."

"I will never go there then."

"Good for you," she said.

I did not have any appetite and neither did she. Toto was too much on our minds.

"Toto was in love with me," Lily said.

"I love you, too."

"I did not reciprocate, and he realized that. But he was a good friend, though he seemed distant. And now he is dead and I never got to know him very well, to really thank him for the many things he had given my mother, my brothers and sisters. Did you know, Pepe, he paid Boyet's tuition fee last year?"

I was not surprised.

Lily decided not to go to the Colonial. "Let us go to a place where we can be alone and forget the Barrio."

"To a movie," I suggested. I had money and this time I would spend on her.

"No," she said. "I have never been to the zoo. Let us go there."

It was past noon. We boarded a jeepney for Quiapo. From Plaza Miranda on to Plaza Santa Cruz the sidewalks were plastered with our posters, and plywood shutters were now over all the shop windows. Garbage was piled on Plaza Miranda, and Carriedo was taken over by sidewalk vendors. In Avenida we boarded another jeepney for Mabini.

The zoo was almost deserted; we had a bench and the greenery to ourselves. Lily had looked at the giraffes and elephants with perfunctory interest. She wanted to talk.

"I did what you told me," she finally said. "I took Mother and the young ones out. We went by taxi to the Luneta. For fresh air, I said. Toward evening we went to the Aristocrat and had fried chicken. We were very happy . . . then I told Mother. The young ones were too busy eating to listen."

"What did she say?"

"She cried, right there in the restaurant, not loud, the tears just falling down her cheeks. She said I was the best person to decide, that she would pray no harm would come to me, that I would remain honorable."

"You will have difficulty doing that, Lily. You are on a precipice, just one nudge and you will keel over."

"I know," she said sadly.

"You have known how it is to be embraced by a man. What happens when you have a customer you like, and you are there . . . in the dark?"

"It has not happened yet."

"But it will happen!"

Silence, the bustle of children nearby, the tinkle of an ice cream vendor's bell.

"I wish I could have you stop, Lily."

She held my hand.

"When we are together like this, are you Number Seventeen or yourself?"

"I am myself, of course," she said, eyes flashing. "I know you are not trying to *garaje* me."

"I cannot afford it."

"It is not that. I would not let you."

"Because you do not care."

Tenderness in her eyes, she opened her mouth as if to speak, but she stopped. After a while, she asked quietly, "What is it you really want from me? Do not joke now. Everyone who has been to the Colonial wants one thing."

I wanted to assure her I was no different, that I wanted her, but I could not bring myself to tell her this although I was sure she knew.

"You will only leave me dangling," she continued.

"I am not impotent!"

"That is not what I meant," she said quickly. "You know, there will be many things on our minds, I will be thinking of my past, my job, how it will be, and it will not be enjoyable anymore."

"I try to live for now," I said.

"I have my mother, my brothers and sisters."

"I know."

"With us, nothing serious, that's all."

"I cannot be flippant with you," I said. "I am sincere. Remember that."

"But why me?" she asked. "There are so many girls in your school. They are not unwed mothers, and they do not have families to support. And most of all, they don't work in massage parlors where they give sensation to six, eight men every day—old men, teenagers, businessmen. Why me? Why can you not be clear-headed?"

"I am."

"Then keep away from me."

"Do you want me to?"

"Yes," she said, but without conviction.

I kissed her hand that had grasped a hundred penises.

"I don't understand, Pepe," she said.

"It's fate."

I was silent for a while, contemplating her face, the sad eyes, the small pert nose, the lips, and the soft line of her jaw.

"Ramona," I breathed.

"What?"

"I am dreaming again," I said. "Even with people, I sometimes forget I am here, here in Manila, here in this Barrio, here."

"What are you trying to tell me?"

"Do not laugh. Ever since I was young I have always held one girl in my heart. You know, those crushes when you are a teenager. But this one has lasted."

"Tell me about her."

"She is dark brown—very *kayumanggi*,* as they say. Usually, the girl boys dream of are fair, mestiza."

"But she is dark."

Kayumanggi: Skin color—not too dark, not too light.

"Yes, as dark as you. I will recognize her when I see her."

"You mean you have not met her?"

"Yes, I have—but here, only in my mind."

"Something like an ideal?"

"More than that. She is very real to me. I can hear her voice, and it is melodious and soft. I can see her, slim but not thin. And her breasts are small. She is slightly bowlegged. And her skin is clear and richly toned. And her eyebrows are unplucked."

"But she does not exist."

"She does, here," I gestured toward my breast.

"*Ligaw tingin, kantot hangin.** But this is worse because she does not even exist," she sighed.

"I told you, she is here."

"How did you first meet her?"

"In some melody Mother hummed when I was young. Ramona—if only she would be real someday."

"Ramona—she even has a name. But it isn't a very romantic name."

"It is to me."

"How did she get that name?"

"I don't know all the words, 'I hear the mission bells above . . . I dread the dawn when I wake to find you are gone . . .'"

"She isn't here," she said. "But I am."

"And so is the night," I said, "and it is a long, long night."

"What are you trying to say?"

How could I tell her? Describe the murk where I had been, in my mind more than in what was around us?

"The world is dark," I said, instead. Her hand tightened on mine. The sun blazed down, a boy selling ice cream came to us, but we did not want any. She had a new wristwatch, it was almost four. We had clung to words as if they were nuggets of wisdom, but the only truth was that we were together in this dismal place. How does the song go? "It's only words, and words are all I have to take your heart away . . ." And now, while I was rich with words, I could not speak the right ones to impress upon her that sitting on this edge of perdition or clinging to this razor's edge, as the old saying goes, is our only alternative.

Ligaw tingin, kantot hangin: Courting by means of just looking.

Let the People
Know

ALTHOUGH AUNTIE BETTINA said I could be a scholar if I
only tried, I was surprised to get the highest grades and to be el-
igible for free tuition in the next school year. There would be two
months of Brotherhood inactivity; we would not have any demonstrations till June or July when the universities would be full again
and most of our members had returned to Manila from the
provinces. I also found out that I had a talent for Spanish, and I studied it in the summer session, determined that after those two
months—by June—I should at least be able to understand and converse a bit in it.

My determination was wrought out of anger. When I met Betsy,
although I had already had a year of Spanish—grammar and such—
I still could not speak the language. She was born to it; her family
spoke it at home, together with English, Visayan, and Tagalog.

Now I also had a clearer image of the class against which we
were pitted. I did not have to take political science or sociology to
understand this. Instinct sufficed. Even in school, I knew my teachers, like Professor Hortenso, were different.

I tried attending to the rules, and it was not difficult, for these rules could be bent to accommodate friends, and I could, myself, assume a color to their liking. That is what we learn early. But I had been aware of what I was doing and I always had to be cautious with those I did not really know, particularly those who might be able to do me good. I was not worried about being harmed—how could anyone hurt me or drag me farther down from where I was?

But with Betsy I was never cautious; I just opened up, innards and all, as if I had known her all my life. She was a junior at Maryknoll, and like most Maryknoll girls, she talked too much.

We were invited to a seminar in Tagaytay in April. I had organized the Brotherhood in the University so well that I knew every class leader by his first name. It was difficult at first, remembering so many faces, attending meetings and working in the Barrio at the same time. But there were fringe benefits; the free seminar was one of them. By then, I was also being invited to speak before students in forums outside my university. There was nothing, however, as lavish as this seminar—a live-in and an opportunity to meet other students for one week. A Jesuit was the seminar leader, but it was Americans who financed it; perhaps they hoped to influence our thinking, although I don't see how they could possibly do that, for students usually have fixed views.

We assembled in Plaza Miranda at nine in the morning and boarded a bus. It was a sweaty drive to the other end of Manila, then through browned fields and small, scraggly towns; we went slowly up, past coconut groves, pineapple patches, and blooming fields of daisy. All the while the green heightened, the air freshened, and then, suddenly, we were up, and below was this shimmering blue lake dappled with sun and, in its middle, a green island.

Betsy was not with us in the bus; her family had taken her by car to Tagaytay. We gathered in the lobby of the lodge and registered. Afterward, as I was wandering at one end of the lodge grounds, looking at the volcano in the distance, I saw her.

I could not miss that face, those dark eyebrows, those eyes. It was Doris, the girl from the Makati Supermarket whose friend had been one of my customers. My immediate impulse was to run, to want the earth to swallow me up so that she would not see me and broadcast that I was a pusher, but how could I ignore a girl like her? Ever since I gave up the job Kuya Nick proffered, I was often nagged by this intense desire to go to the supermarket on the appointed time just to see her and perhaps talk with her, but there was no point; she was a million miles away from where I lived.

Then, gathering courage, nerve, steel, and such, I strode up to her and said, "Doris . . ." softly. She did not turn. "Doris," I said louder.

She turned around, surprised, then she broke into that smile that I always loved. "Pusher!" she cried, then pressed her hand to her mouth and looked around to see if anyone was within hearing.

"What are you doing here?" she asked.

"Selling more dope," I said. I looked at the name card on her blouse. "Liar," I said. "I always thought of you as Doris."

She looked at mine. "And I always thought of you as Toto," she said.

We both laughed and asked simultaneously: "How have you been?"

"You first," she insisted.

"Well, as you know, I did not last a week in that job. The money was very good, but not enough."

"You wanted to be the big man yourself," she said.

"Yes, and get to be a millionaire like your father. I am still trying."

"I missed you the following week," she said. "Somehow I knew you would not last. You are much too open, and therefore vulnerable."

"Spoken with wisdom. And what happened to your friend?"

"You should meet her," she said, gushing. "On my birthday, she will be there. Promise to come."

"I promise."

"She has become stout—and that is a problem, she thinks she is fat. She stopped way back. The week that you did not come, I told her mother. We took her to a doctor, to a psychiatrist. It was also a form of rebellion against her parents and a desire to get attention from them. What I suspected all along."

"What are you, a head shrinker?"

"Psychology major. But . . . what shall I call you? Jose?"

"Everyone calls me Pepe. Beatriz?"

"It sounds awful, doesn't it? Betsy. It sounds better."

"Betsy, it is wonderful seeing you."

"Same here," she said, holding my hand and pressing it.

We walked to the main building, my head light, the world aglow. She was the prettiest in the group, but I had not seen her legs in Tagaytay. She was slightly bowlegged, but her legs were not ugly; as a matter of fact, they made her look sexier.

All through the seminar, she wore two pairs of jeans, one really faded denim that had begun to break at the knees, and a brown corduroy pair that was also faded with use. Her formless *katsa* blouses were almost always buttoned up to her neck, and the only decor she wore was a touch of lipstick and that beautiful scent—Tabu, she told me later. Her shabby clothes, however, could not hide her prettiness, and once, during the meeting, she noticed me admiring the fine line of her jaw; I was embarrassed when she leaned over, a twinkle in her eyes, and whispered: "Caught you!" Much later, when I met her mother, I was quite sure that if she did not watch out, when she got married and raised children, she would be as round as a volleyball. When I told her this, she merely laughed and said she would not care, for by then she would have already bagged her man.

The fifty of us were from all over the country, and five were Muslims. About half were girls and most of them were pretty. She asked what school I came from and I said DM; that really perplexed her, so I explained, "Diploma Mill—you know, one of those downtown universities."

And she said, "Why are you so apologetic and defensive? I haven't started to work you over yet."

She said Maryknoll was an elite school, all right. Still, though you could have all the money in the world, if you did not make the grade, you would be expelled.

We listened to dull speeches every day, one in the morning and another in the afternoon, then we would break for discussions. She did not speak much at the discussions, but could put away long-winded speakers with dispatch. There was this show-off from UP who commented for more than fifteen minutes on Philippine-American relations after the guest speaker that day—a writer of considerable background and knowledge—talked about the American sugar quota and its support of the oligarchy. The UP delegate was a nice fellow, but he merely repeated what everyone already knew, and Betsy waved her hand to interrupt him. When he paused, she simply annihilated him: "We all know how much you dislike American imperialism. Will you please tell us how we can dismantle it?"

He was flabbergasted, but Betsy had summed up our feelings, and we applauded her.

At dinner that evening—we always sat together by then—I told her, "I will not permit you to dispose of me like that."

"Then," she said, "don't make stupid speeches."

I told her about Father Jess, and she was surprised that I was living with him. Yes, she knew Father Jess—her mother came from the same town as his in Negros. Father Jess's family was wealthy—in sugar like they were—but he was the black sheep, and the planters did not like him for taking the side of the seasonal workers.

"And on whose side are you?" I asked her pointedly.

"Don't generalize," she said curtly. "If not for this seminar, I would be in Negros now. I teach kindergarten for the children of our workers. They get paid very well, and they go to a hospital if they are sick."

"I don't believe you," I told her bluntly.

She was angry. "Come with me," she challenged. "I am not saying there is no injustice; all I am asking is that you not generalize."

"Behind every great fortune is a great crime," I said, remembering Balzac.

"We are not criminals," she shouted.

We parted on that, the friendship turning awry.

When I got back to the Barrio, I asked Father Jess about her family, about their hacienda. He merely grinned and, two days later, a messenger arrived with an invitation for me to attend Betsy's birthday party. In her note, she said, "Please don't fail to come. You promised. Our drug addict will be there. I will be going to Negros and won't be back till the beginning of the school year."

"You are moving up in the world," Father Jess said.

IT WAS MY FIRST visit to the Park, and I tried to make myself presentable. I had thought of cutting my hair slightly shorter—it went down past my nape—but I liked it that way; trimming it would be too much of a sacrifice for Betsy. I decided just to shampoo it instead. I now had a barong that I had worn only twice and a new pair of dark, double-knit pants. My shoes were scuffed, but I inked them black then shined them.

At the *kumbento* door Tia Nena approved and Roger said I did not look like a Barrio boy anymore. I took the bus to Makati and then a taxi to the Park.

We drove through an acacia-shaded street and, at its end, the Park gate, where a blue uniformed guard stopped us. He looked suspiciously at me, then asked where I was going. I gave him the number on Tamarind Road. He noted down the taxi plate number, asked for the driver's license, then told us to proceed. I cursed him under my breath.

Now I was here, in the gilded precinct of the oligarchy. Now it was all before me, around me—the ivy-covered walls—and through the grilled fences and opened gates, the truculent magnificence of wealth. These are the monuments to untrammeled greed, I knew, but they were lovely to look at, they were impressive in their pretension.

In one of our meetings we had talked about the Park—how convenient it was as a symbol of the oligarchy, how easily it could be taken over. Someone said it should be razed to the ground, but I had thought that was a stupid idea, all this wealth, all this comfort turning to ashes when we could, in some future time, have all of it, and these beautiful homes would then be vacation houses, the dachas of the proletariat. A demonstration against the Park was in the air; it certainly was in my mind. Such a possibility must have frightened its denizens, for, in the first big demonstration that year, they were so scared that they left their homes to be guarded by their hirelings while they trooped to the Makati hotels and waited for the demonstrations to ebb.

They need not have feared, for there was no demonstration against the Park. The demonstrations were in the crowded and poor districts of the city, in Quiapo, in Santa Cruz—places where the rich would not be. In retrospect, we missed an opportunity to confront our enemy. Were we afraid? We knew that, behind those high walls, there were guns against which we could not pit anything except our flesh and our numbers. Or if we were not scared, was it because our leaders were not really with the masses whom they said they championed? At heart, were they with our exploiters? It was so easy to demonstrate against the Americans—they were omnipresent for all to see, and they did not really fight back.

I could not explain why this was so, but I had seen it, what happened in Diliman, at the state university campus, when our cadres finally blockaded it and started manning the checkpoints. They did not stop the air-conditioned cars or demand that the passengers alight to be searched. No, they stopped the buses and the jeepneys instead, the public and dilapidated vehicles that carried the masses.

All through that tumultuous year, it was also the poor shopkeepers in Quiapo, Malate, and Ermita whose windows were stoned and whose stores were looted—not the big department stores in Makati, not the exclusive boutiques of the culture vultures of Pobres Park. I knew even then that there was something basically wrong with our demonstrations, and I would have been critical, but by then, to contest what we were doing was to confront the leadership. I was not prepared to do that, nor was I ready to be labeled a deviationist.

I got off two blocks from Betsy's house, which was easy to find. It had a low adobe wall and its wide yard was planted to palm and dwarf mango trees. A guard let me in.

The stone driveway was lined with well-trimmed santan hedges that were in bloom, and the garage at the far end, which was open, contained three fat American cars. Betsy's Volks was parked in the driveway.

It was one of those pleasant, balmy late afternoons, the sinking sun still shiny on the beige marble walls of the house, on the narra paneling and the blue-tile roof. The invitation was for five o'clock. I was thirty minutes late. I walked across the wide, red-tiled porch, and before the massive, ornately carved wooden door I was awkward and self-conscious. I pressed the doorbell.

It was Betsy in jeans as usual. "Happy birthday," I said, but she did not shake my hand; instead, she stepped back, appraised me, then exclaimed, "Pepe, you are handsome!"

My ears burned, and before I could remonstrate she grasped my hand and drew me into the wide cavern that was the de Jesus living room, refreshingly cool in the April heat. The house had central airconditioning.

It was suppose to be a birthday party, but there was no one there except a maid in white who peeped in from an open door. To my questioning look Betsy was all smiles; she guided me to an overstuffed sofa and we sat down. "My relatives will not come till after six-thirty or so. I thought that if you came early we, you know, we could talk."

"About what?"

"About imperialism," she said with a laugh.

I grunted.

She asked if I was hungry and I lied. She went to the kitchen and a maid in a white starched uniform came out immediately with two glasses of orange juice. I downed mine in a gulp.

She wanted to show me the garden, so we walked out into the last vestiges of day. The sun glinted on the palms, on the dwarf mangoes that bore fruit, bunches of luscious green that sagged to the ground. A wide, well-groomed garden with potted roses in corners. Across a small rock formation, hidden from view by jade vine pergolas and, from the street, by a screen of yellow-green Chinese bamboo, was the swimming pool. There had to be a gardener employed full-time to take care of such a spread.

"I did not like the way we parted in Tagaytay," Betsy said.

"Me neither."

"Why did you have to be mean?" She sounded disconsolate. "I did not do you any harm."

She was right, and it was gracious of her to have invited me, to have told no one that I was a pusher, and I did not even bring her anything—what could I give to someone who has everything?

"Sorry," I said. "I hope we can start a new chapter."

"Would you like to come to Negros?"

"I cannot afford it," I said. "Besides, what would I do there? I have to work in church . . . especially now that Toto is gone."

I had not told her about Toto, but now I did, and when I was through, she bit her lip and was silent. "Don't you believe me?" I asked. "It was in the papers. His name."

"Oh, Pepe," she held my hand tightly. "I believe you! I believe you! I was there!"

I wanted to embrace her then. "You fool!" I cried. "You could have been shot, too!"

She looked at me, wordless, and we could have talked more, but cars had begun to fill the driveway, and we hastened back to the house. It was now dark and the huge chandelier in the living room bloomed. I was left alone as Betsy welcomed them—mostly relatives and, just as she told me, about a dozen of her classmates, some with their boyfriends. She singled out a girl, good-looking but a little chubby, and brought her over to where I stood apart from them all, and said, "Belinda, this is Pepe; you have something in common—both of you are addicts."

She smiled, showing upper teeth in braces, and taking me by the arm, she guided me to a corner dominated by a huge Chinese vase with blue dragons. No one could hear us. "How long have you been at it?" she asked. "Betsy told me her boyfriend was on drugs."

I grinned and did not know what to say.

"We started together, you know, but she did not like it. Then she told my mama, and we had to go to a doctor. Did you have difficulty stopping?"

"Not really," I said. "Just a little willpower."

"And that is what I don't have," she said. "Now I am addicted to food. I am very fat, no?"

"You are not, Belinda," I said. "You are very pretty—even with your braces."

Her hand flew to her mouth.

"Come," she took my arm again and drew me to the dining room where the buffet table was ready; no one seemed anxious to eat except us.

They call it *merienda cena*—some fancy name for afternoon tea or snack, but it was a Rabelaisian spread, giant prawns already shelled, tenderloin strips, fresh asparagus sautéed in butter, finger sandwiches, several dip bowls of eggplant, tomato, and avocado concoctions. On one side were a variety of cheeses I had never seen before, including our own white cheese in its banana leaf wrapping.

Belinda did not bother with a plate and neither did I; we just idled around the long table, picking up pieces of fried chicken, mussels baked in butter, slices of sweet ham and turkey. And the fruit trays at the other end of the table, together with the assortment of pastries and sweets, simply overflowed with big, red apples and grapes of ebony and rose. I had never tasted grapes before, and now here they were as I had always imagined them. If I were nearer Cabugawan, I would certainly pocket a bunch for Mother.

I do not think Belinda noticed it, nor Betsy, how I ate very fast so that, in just a while, I had already tasted almost everything on that table that I had never eaten before, while close by was this gushing talk in Spanish, Visayan, and English.

Then, a tall, handsome mestizo in a gray suit, in his fifties, accompanied by a fat, waddling mestiza of about the same age came in. Betsy rushed to them, kissed them both.

"Happy birthday, *hija*," the man said, bending over and kissing

Betsy on the cheek. She came to me, took me to them, whispering, "Papa and Mama."

Betsy's father shook my hand, so did her mother.

"We met in Tagaytay during that seminar, Papa," she said.

"May I know your name, *hijo*?" Mr. de Jesus asked, his eyes wandering up from my newly shined black shoes to my mane. His wife, her diamond pendant earrings flashing, was studying me, too.

"José Samson, sir," I said.

"Samson . . . Samson. Related to Antonio Samson, the writer?"

"Yes, yes, sir," I stammered. "An uncle."

"Ah, no wonder," Betsy's mother smiled, her double chin quivered. "You reminded me of him. As a matter of fact, you looked just like him then, except for the long hair. I knew him. My husband, too. His wife—she was my best friend. I even stood as witness at their wedding. What a girl she was. You know, she died not long after the death of Tony. Did you ever know her? I don't think so."

"No, Mrs. de Jesus," I said. "I know very little about my uncle's life."

Then without warning, Mr. de Jesus talked to me in Spanish and, when he paused, I looked at him, bewildered. "I am sorry, sir, I don't speak Spanish."

"But Tony did," Mr. de Jesus said. "And he wrote in Spanish, too."

"He went to Harvard, sir," I said. "My school is in Recto."

Mrs. de Jesus looked at me again, then at Betsy, and to her she spoke in Spanish; I could not get every word, but it was obvious she was talking about me.

Betsy blushed and seemed uneasy, and when she replied, it was in English: "Mama, the educated man does not even have to go to school. Education is not Maryknoll or Ateneo—or even Harvard—"

Mr. de Jesus took it from there, and from the drift of their conversation, as he wheeled around, followed by his wife, so that they could greet the other guests, I knew that they had dismissed me, that they did not want me in Tamarind Road again.

Betsy followed them, waving her hand, her face grim as if she was on the verge of tears, then she came back to me. "*Djahe**—*djahe*," she said, "and on my birthday, too."

---

* *Djahe:* Ashamed.

"They do not like me," I said softly.

"Oh, Pepe, don't say that," she beseeched me. "This is my party, and I invited you."

"But they are your parents and they mean much to you."

"They cannot select my friends," she said angrily.

"Don't tell them, but I must leave," I said quickly and headed for the door.

"Pepe, please stay. I want you to meet my other friends."

"From La Salle, Maryknoll, and Ateneo," I said.

She held my hand tightly as we walked to the door. It would be an unlit, gloomy distance to the gate of Pobres Park and then to the bus station, and my shoes were newly shined.

"HOW WAS THE PARTY?" Father Jess wanted to know.

I did not want to rail against Betsy's parents. "Very good, Father," I said.

"Then why the hell are you back so soon?"

"I was ill at ease. I did not know anyone there except Betsy."

"You will get to know more of that class," Father Jess said. "And if you study hard, someday you will join them."

"That is not so grim a fate, Father," I said.

As I was serving him coffee after supper, I asked if he had any books in Spanish.

He was surprised at my new interest. "No, but I can teach you a bit if you want to learn." Then, as if lightning struck, "Ha, the de Jesus family impressed you! Now you must learn their language!"

I did not speak.

"It is always good, Pepe, to know what people are saying. Henceforth," he said, shaking a finger at me, "I will talk to you in Spanish."

Tia Nena came in with a piece of banana cake she had baked. And for the first time I also heard her speak in Spanish.

IN THE MORNING, as I was serving in the six o'clock daily mass— a chore I took on since the death of Toto—going out of the sacristy, I looked at the attendance, which was always small except on Sundays, when we had three masses and the church really overflowed, and there, in the front pew, was Betsy. I could not imagine how she had come at such a time when she should be asleep. When mass was over, Father Jess greeted her and asked her to join us at the *kumbento*. But Father Jess knew she did not come to Tondo to hear mass. He left us alone.

She was in her usual jeans. "I came here to see you," she said.

"Thank you," I said. "But there is really no need, Betsy. I understand everything."

"No, you don't," she said.

I did not want to talk about her party, her parents. "How did you get here?" I asked quickly.

"You gave me your address, didn't you? I simply asked the driver who came here with the invitation to give me directions."

"And you came alone and so early?"

"Yes," she said. "I parked down the vacant lot. I couldn't get in." She meant the deeply rutted main street that had yet to be asphalted.

"You can get robbed here, you know. And raped."

"I had to see you," she said simply.

I hurried with the broom as she stood by. When I was through, she said, "Let me invite you to breakfast. Please."

There was no running away from her, and I followed her to where she had parked. She drove a little recklessly, but it was her style. She was a good driver. I did not ask where we were going, I was completely in her hands. She drove up Bangkusay, alive with the riot of children, through Herbosa, then Juan Luna past the Tondo church toward the North Harbor. She drove confidently as if she had been in Tondo all her life.

"This is where the Katipunan was born," I said. "Even now, this is a radical district. Do you know that during the Huk uprising, there were gun battles here? We have a neighbor who was a Huk commander—more than twelve years he was in jail."

She turned to me and smiled patronizingly. "I read history, too, Pepe."

"Now you are castrating me," I said.

She gave my leg a playful blow then she slowed down. We were now traveling along the line of interisland ships and to our left was a monotonous huddle of shacks similar to what we had left. The smell of copra, of refuse, hung heavy in the air. We approached Del

Pan, and I wanted to point out to her the squatter huts on the left side of the bridge, their flimsy roofs held in place by rocks, but I asked instead, "Sociology, too?"

She nodded, giving my leg another playful blow. Then we crossed the bridge; but for the crumbling Intramuros walls and more squatters in the moat of Fort Santiago, we were out in the open, in another country—Rizal Park, Roxas Boulevard, the well-trimmed green, the tall whitewashed buildings.

She turned left, heading to one of the tallest buildings on the boulevard with the initials VDC on the roof, glittering at night in blue neon. Behind it was a huge shaded parking lot, and after she parked, we went to the elevator in the front. The girl who operated it greeted her. "To the restaurant, Miss de Jesus?"

"Oh, Cora," Betsy frowned. "When will you ever call me Betsy?"

We shot up to the top floor and a doorman in a black jacket over a white frilly shirt and black bow tie opened the door, bowing. "Good morning, Miss de Jesus."

It was the most luxurious place I had ever been to. The chairs were hand-carved and upholstered in deep blue. The tables had lace tablecloths and silver vases with red roses. The carpet, in paler blue, was wall to wall, and on the walls, which had fleur-de-lis designs, were Philippine paintings—part of the collection of Don Manuel Villa, which, Betsy later told me, had been started and influenced by my father. Crystal chandeliers dropped from an indigo ceiling, and though it was warm outside, I was almost freezing. Three waiters in black jackets with white gloves came forward, but Betsy ignored them; she guided me, instead, to a corner where the drapes of velvet blue were raised by blue braids, and we had an unimpeded view of the bay and the city. The building was not more than ten years old, one of the newest and the tallest, and from twenty stories up, Manila looked neat and clean. Even Tondo, beyond the dark swath of the Pasig, its houses roofed with dull red, seemed antiseptic.

This was the headquarters of the Villa Development Corporation, the giant conglomerate built by Don Manuel Villa, my father's father-in-law. He had worked here, and if he were alive, he would be here now, handing crumbs to his poor relatives. This was a haven for mestizos—they were given preference because of the lightness of their skins, their capacity for speaking Spanish. Indeed, as Professor Hortenso had said all too often, the higher up you go, the more sugary and whiter it becomes. Now I was here in the bastion of the oligarchy to which my father had attached himself. I wondered how he felt being with them, if he even remembered that he had come from an anonymous corner called Cabugawan.

I knew a little of Betsy by then, enough to realize that she did not bring me here to impress me. The waiter asked what we wanted, and though I had not had breakfast yet, I was not hungry anymore. But she was insistent.

"All right then," I said. "A cup of coffee and *pan de sal*."

The waiter looked at Betsy and smiled.

"Pepe," she spoke almost in a whisper. "This is a French-style restaurant . . . they even have a French chef from Marseilles. There is no *pan de sal*."

My ears burned.

". . . but you can have croissants."

The coffee came, black, steaming, and thick. Betsy started, "I quarreled with Papa and Mama last night, really, even before all the guests had gone. Papa was angry—oh, not at you, Pepe, please believe that—at me."

Perhaps she thought I knew her father was general manager of the corporation. "No, you don't have to worry about him coming up here and seeing us. He left early this morning for Zurich and New York." She stared at her coffee. "Pepe . . ." almost in a whisper, "I know how you feel, so please do not make it difficult for me. Perhaps one day, when you become a father, you will not be different from Papa. He does not know that I am a member of the Brotherhood, that I go out with people—"

"Like me," I added quickly.

She smiled sadly then went on, as if she was talking to herself. "But last night, we also talked about . . . about your uncle. Carmen Villa, his wife, was Mama's best friend, you know, and they shared many things, girl talk, that sort of thing." She turned to me again, her eyes bright with expectation. "You must have read *The Ilustrados*," she said.

I shook my head.

"You should—shame on you! Aren't you proud it was a relative who wrote it? How unfortunate that he is not around. I would have wanted to write a paper on his book, the ideas there. He was very right, you know, about the Filipino elite collaborating with all who are in power or those who are about to be. The last chapter—the nature of the elite—how perceptive he was, how he exposed what had been destroying us from the very beginning."

"You are making a speech," I said, unimpressed. "You said I should be wary of speeches."

She shook her head and laughed. Her omelet had come, and the croissants, which I knew were some pastry, turned out to be a kind of *pan de sal,* brown and soft.

She was undaunted. "What Antonio Samson wrote is very relevant now. Now!" she slapped the table. "If we are going to have change, there must be some purity to it. It means leadership from below, the lower classes, nothing else. Only in that way will it not be destroyed. The elite will subvert it. That is why, for all his protestations, I mistrust Juan Puneta. His grandfather was one of them."

I did not speak; the remark that was in my mind was obviously anticipated by her.

"I am *burgis,* an outsider, you know that," she said. "But my feelings are not with my crowd, Pepe. Believe me! The poor do not have a monopoly on that sense of outrage."

"Profound statement of the day," I said blithely and, looking at the antique clock at a corner, added: "Made at exactly eight forty-eight A.M."

She breathed deeply and sighed: "Now you really have devastated me."

I reached across the table and almost spilled the goblet of water, held her hand, and pressed it. She pressed my hand, too, then slowly withdrew it. The waiters were looking at us—the only people in this ritzy restaurant this early.

"How can I tell Puneta he is full of shit?" she said angrily. "I have no authority. He has a Ph.D. from Cambridge. He makes all those speeches. And he contributes generously to the Brotherhood."

"We will use him," I said.

"No, he has power, money, brains. He will use us," she said simply. "Already, he is very close to Malacañang. He wants to be ambassador to France because he speaks French and because he is also good-looking—that is what the First Lady likes. He will get the job. And he will throw lavish parties, which he likes to do, and he will spend plenty of money that his minions earn over here."

I have read how our ambassadors have so little to spend. "At least he is Filipino," I said, "and he will be spending his money for us."

She looked at me incredulously. "Oh, Pepe! You have so much to learn. Puneta is Filipino only because he holds a Philippine passport. He is Spanish, his loyalty is to Spain, where he salts his dollars. Do you know that he has a housing-development in Mallorca? And his wife is Spanish?"

I shook my head. This was something Professor Hortenso had not told me.

"All the Punetas," Betsy was saying, "since way back, have sent their children to Europe at the age of puberty so they would not intermarry with mongrels. Here, they are Spaniards, but in Spain, they call themselves Filipinos knowing that being a Filipino there opens doors. That is what Papa says. At least we— This is our home, Pepe. Even if my parents . . . they are so *burgis*. So very *burgis*!"

"They cannot do anything about that," I said, trying to sympathize with her.

She did not seem to hear. "Something in me rebels against them," she continued softly, "even against myself. Believe me. But I love them, Pepe. I really do!"

"We cannot be but what we are," I said.

The wistful, somber face, the slow shake of her head. "Please don't misunderstand. It is not guilt feelings. I like being comfortable, and I am happy that I am, as you would say, on the other side of the fence. But I also know what is on the other side. It is so easy to say that I did not make this world the way it is, that my responsibility is first to myself, and with this I would then be able to justify everything. But this also means that I have to be blind, and deaf. And these I don't want to be. But what can I do, Pepe?"

"Be true," I said. Platitudes, clichés. "I love my mother, too, but I don't like her pushing me on to college, being somebody I don't want to be." I meant every word, and at that moment, I wondered what Mother was doing, knowing how it was in Cabugawan at this time of day, the sun bright on the leaves of palms and bananas, the day alive with the grunt of hogs, the mooing of carabaos. "Still," I continued, "whatever she did, whatever she does, you don't know how much I love her!"

She bent down. "My mother wants to protect me—from you . . . something like bad luck."

"The poor are always bad luck," I said harshly.

"Pepe, please do not be angry. I would not be telling you these things if . . ." she paused, picked at her omelet. "It had something to do with Carmen Villa, with how she died. Do you know what happened to her?"

"No," I said, "and I do not care."

"She became insane and she just, well, just died slowly, not even a year after her husband died. Mama, she says Antonio Samson . . . he committed suicide—that was what Carmen Villa believed, that was what she told Mama. What a waste . . . what a waste! Do you know how he died?"

It all came rushing back. "Yes," I said, almost choking on the word. "I stayed in the room where he had lived for years, used the very bed where he had slept. And every day I would look out of the window at those infernal tracks where he was killed. And I could imagine him lying there in several pieces, I could imagine him . . ." I could not speak anymore as angry thoughts swooped into my mind.

"If only he were alive," Betsy said, "I would like to go to him, ask him for help. And explain. I want to belong, Pepe, to help. To do what is right. I would tell him that the *ilustrado* class need not be condemned. I would tell him not to generalize. And because he was such a brilliant man, he would understand, he would know."

"Betsy," I said, raising my voice so that the waiters turned to us. She was startled and I was taken aback at the vehemence of my feelings. I gripped the table's edge, bent over to her, and said calmly, "Antonio Samson, he did me, he did my mother wrong. He was not my uncle, Betsy. Antonio Samson was my father."

Down with the *Burgis*

I DECIDED NEVER to see Betsy again, to avoid her if she came to the Barrio, so I wrote her a letter, worked over it one night:

Dear Miss de Jesus—,[she would immediately get the irony of that greeting]

How I wish there were words adequate enough to express my gratitude for your kindness in inviting me to your house and to that French restaurant. I want to thank you, too, for visiting me here in the Barrio, for trying to explain things as they are. I know that there are situations [like ours] *about which we can do nothing; I know that oil and water do not mix—it is in their nature and these are what I* [not you, you really want to go against your mama and papa] *must live with. There is, therefore, no point in my wanting to see you again* [although God knows, I want to see you again, your pretty face . . . your lips, how nice you look when you pout! Hell, am I falling in love with you? It is Lily whom I love, or maybe Lucy. It is true then, men are really polygamous— bastards that we are] *but I hope, in the foreseeable future* [ha,

416

you are an optimist, after all], *under different circumstances, I will be able to meet you again. I do not want to say good- bye—there is no good-bye between friends.* [Hypocrite, you don't want to be just friends with her; you want to slip your hand up her panties!] *You know sociology so you understand what I am really trying to say. I am deeply hurt* [for once, I am saying the truth], *more than you will ever know, but it is enough that I have known you, your graciousness, your friendship.*

I kept it for some time and decided that I could do a Spanish version of it later. I was learning quickly.

By June I could converse a bit in colloquial Spanish with Tia Nena. She occupied the room next to the one Toto and I had shared and had heard us talking. I suppose there was little we had discussed that she did not know. She came with Father Jess to the Barrio and was called Tia Nena from the very beginning by everyone, and that was what I called her, too, although Lola would have been more ap- propriate, for she was in her seventies. But she was still sprightly and hardworking. Father Jess had asked her to stop washing his clothes—Lily's mother could do it—but she did it just the same, even Toto's clothes and mine, which had embarrassed me no end, so that once I changed, I washed my clothes immediately.

I never got to ask Father Jess if it was true that he salvaged Tia Nena from the Psychopathic Hospital in Mandaluyong; but if she was insane, it could not have been a serious dementia, for there was nothing in her behavior that was unusual, nothing but her reluctance to talk about herself, her mumbling before her stove about her sons. "My Luis . . . my Victor . . ." over and over again.

I went to her once and asked, "Tia, what were you saying? Vic- tor? Luis?"

She turned abruptly to me, a faraway look in her eyes. "I had two sons," she said, in a voice that was almost sepulchral. "One was white, the other was black . . ."

"I have two hands," I tried to humor her, "the left and the right." She went back to her cooking as if I were not there at all.

Toto's death had affected her. Sometimes she came into our room, looked at the things in Toto's cabinet, and shook her head. Fa- ther Jess told me to use Toto's clothes—we were, after all, about the same height—but I could not, I simply could not. So one day, Father Jess put them in a cardboard box and said he would give them away, but Tia Nena retrieved a shirt, a pair of pants, and together with Toto's pictures and notebooks, she put them in a plastic bag with naphthalene balls, then sealed everything in a milk carton, and put them atop Toto's empty cabinet.

When she was young, Tia Nena had worked for a Spanish family as a maid. Her conjugation was correct. She knew English, too, though she seldom spoke it. I was learning Spanish from her better than in school; I was sure that, by the opening of the school year, Mr. Ben de Jesus could no longer insult me to my face.

Being the new managing editor of the school paper meant an increase in pay—two hundred pesos a month. My partial scholarship was also made full; my grades had been very good, and now I started researching Philippine history, even going to original sources in Spanish. I went to see Professor Hortenso more often, not only for his books but for advice. I did not, however, tell the world that I had crammed on my Spanish. I was never a show-off. What could I be proud of? I was much, much older than most of my classmates— a sophomore at twenty-four, I should have a degree by now—and it embarrassed me no end when I thought of Betsy. She was a senior, she would be graduating at the end of the school year, and I would be there for another two years.

I did not see her for two months. I would not bring her *malas*— bad luck—like her mother had surmised, the way my father had brought *malas* to Carmen Villa. When she came back, however, we were simply fated to see each other again. I was now a member of the Educational Committee of the Brotherhood; Professor Hortenso was its chairman. We had to meet twice a month, often at Hortenso's house—just eight of us—not only to map out the information campaign for our growing membership but also to counter the now insidious propaganda of rival youth organizations that envied us, and the fact that thirty-three of our members had already succumbed to Metrocom and police guns. We kept this roster in all our publications to illustrate how committed we were.

A week after my appointment as managing editor, Professor Hortenso invited me to lunch. Mrs. Hortenso had cooked goat *caldereta* and I felt guilty, eating like a hog because it was very good;

it may have been for their supper, too. "But there is more, Pepe," she said when I hesitated after the third helping. She stood up, went to the kitchen, and brought out the pan, which was, indeed, still half full.

"It is my favorite, Mrs. Hortenso," I complimented her. "And you cook very well. The only other cook I know who can do it well is Tia Nena in the *kumbento*."

"I always knew priests ate well," she said. "Maybe you should add Juan Puneta to your list of *caldereta* cooks. He said once, didn't he, Dad," she asked her husband, "that his *caldereta* is excellent."

Professor Hortenso continued eating. "You don't have to believe everything he says," he said under his breath.

"Ha!" Mrs. Hortenso exclaimed. "Look who's talking. You believe everything he says."

Professor Hortenso looked up from his plate and glared at his wife. I did not want to witness a family quarrel, but I could not stand up and leave.

Mrs. Hortenso was undaunted. She turned to me, wanting me to be her ally. "I hope you do not misunderstand, Pepe," she said. "I believe in these things you are doing, else I would not want to live here," she cast a condescending look around her, the unpainted and grimy adobe walls, the naked lightbulb above us, the cracked cement floor, the cheap Binondo furniture. "He finished with honors, you know—the first Filipino to do so at Cambridge. He— You know, we are not poor. And he was offered a good job here with a British company—old-boy ties . . . fraternities, that is what you call them here."

"Please, honey," Professor Hortenso said, "don't talk like this."

"But he refused. He refused help from his parents. He refused to teach even in the State University where he would be getting twice what he is getting now. Teach at the diploma mill, that is where he feels he is needed. And I agree with him, of course. Over there at UP, those pampered rich, they do not need an education. . . ."

"Honey," Professor Hortenso protested again, "please, don't make us look like martyrs."

"But we are," she fairly screamed at him. "Living here; the kids not going to the best schools, you working yourself to death—and that bastard Puneta taking all the credit for the articles and speeches you write for him!"

"Please," Hortenso raised his voice, "this has gone far enough."

I was now all attention for Mrs. Hortenso, for her mobile, pretty face, the eyes flashing fire. "Pepe, do you know?"

I shook my head.

"Don't listen to my wife, Pepe," Professor Hortenso told me, a wan smile on his face. "She is tired and . . ."

"I am not tired," she hissed at him. "And I am not angry at you or at Pepe. Here," she thrust the plate of *caldereta* toward me; I took another helping.

"It was he who wrote Puneta's doctoral dissertation. And what did he get?"

Professor Hortenso flung his arms in the air in a gesture of futility.

"Nothing. Nothing! And Puneta promises and promises. And what does he give the Brotherhood? Why, my husband gives more of his own money, his time. I give more . . ."

"Don't brag, honey," Professor Hortenso said.

"I am not," she said, glaring at him again. "I am just stating the truth. How much have you spent for those pamphlets? Remember how I went to Papa and got money so that you could have the last pamphlet released from the printer? Remember?"

He had given up; he merely smiled and let his wife speak on. "A beggar who gives five centavos gives more than the millionaire who gives five hundred pesos!"

Professor Hortenso looked at his watch and rose. "Pepe, we will be late," he said. Our meeting was at three, but it was only one o'clock. I stood up reluctantly, for I wanted to hear more about Juan Puneta. I would ask Lily when I got back, and this time, I would ask for details.

Mrs. Hortenso, now calm and serene, followed us to the door and dutifully kissed her husband on the cheek. "Dad," she said as we stepped out, "it is going to rain."

A darkening sky, clouds that obscured the sun since morning. We were both optimists. We walked to the boulevard to save fifteen centavos because from there we could get a jeepney that would go directly to Taft. We had time and Professor Hortenso wanted to talk.

"I hope you will keep to yourself what my wife told you," he said.

"Is that what you want, Professor?"

He nodded. Then, after sometime, he continued wearily, "I have been bothered by people like Puneta in a very profound way. You see, he belongs to the oligarchy, but he is educated, he has liberal ideas, and is willing to help. He has helped. . . ."

Silence. We were nearing the boulevard. We would have to cross and walk a little distance to Central Market and get our jeepney there.

"I know it could be very wrong, that he is merely using us," he said pensively. "There is enough warning, enough literature on the subject. You know, the most impressive is your uncle's book, particularly the last chapter."

I knew what else he had to say, and I was no longer listening. The elite, the masses not making revolution, collaborating with those in power . . .

We crossed on the overpass. "But we have to be pragmatic," he continued firmly. "We cannot say we will reject their money because it is not pure, because it is tainted. Besides, we get to know their weaknesses so that they will not subvert the revolution as they did the last time. The important thing is that we—you and I—we know. If we are careful, we will not be fooled as they were fooled in the past!"

We got off at Taft and walked toward the bay, but as his wife had warned, it had started to drizzle, and the drizzle turned into driving rain that clattered like pebbles on the tin roofs and marquees. We ran up Herran and stopped in a souvenir shop on Mabini, where we hoped we could get a taxi to Roxas Boulevard, to the Puneta Building.

When we got there finally, we were half an hour late and dripping wet. I had not expected Betsy to be a member of the Educational Committee, and when she met us at the foyer and shook my hand, Professor Hortenso smiled. "Well, it is good to know that you know one of your committee members."

We went up in the elevator to the eighth floor, Betsy asking me in a whisper why I did not write to her; I told her I did but had not mailed it.

When we got to the office of Puneta—one of several—she whispered again. "After this I want to talk with you. Let us go some place where we can be alone."

The rest were already there, drinking coffee and eating neatly chopped sandwiches of cheese and ham. I was still full of *caldereta*, but I ate again.

Juan Puneta, tall, mestizo, always cracking his knuckles, welcomed us; he was particularly warm to Professor Hortenso, whom he called Nonong, embracing the professor as if he were a long lost brother.

The meeting did not interest me, but I was fascinated by Puneta, by his mannerisms, and I tried to find out what in his very masculine features was the clue to his homosexuality. I could not find any. He moved about with machismo and decision. In spite of his lips, there was nothing effeminate about his voice, his intonation. He dressed elegantly, but that was because he could afford it. His fingernails were not manicured. No jewelry adorned his fingers, just a simple gold wedding band. Had Lily made a mistake?

I noticed Puneta looking at me and I turned away. We were talking about reaching more people, spreading the base of the Brotherhood, even making alliances with other groups.

Betsy was taking notes and putting in a word or two, but I was soon far away, thinking of my meeting with her parents and wondering where we would go tonight. I looked at her, bent over her pad, at her finely molded face and at her full breasts under her formless *katsa* blouse.

Puneta snatched me from my reverie: "Pepito Samson—he has not contributed anything yet. I am sure he knows a lot, what with his background, where he lives."

Professor Hortenso turned to me. "Well, Pepe?"

I must have looked bewildered.

"Any suggestion you can make about broadening our base? Reaching more young people? You organized that chapter in Tondo; surely you must have ideas," Puneta pressed.

I did not have to think; I remembered Ka Lucio. For a month now he had not been working. He had tuberculosis, as Father Jess and all of us had suspected, and was at home, resting . . . on what?

"I think we can learn from the past," I said. "We have a neighbor, Ka Lucio. He was Commander Puti—he is sick now—spent twelve years in jail. He knows a lot. We can learn from him and establish links with men like him, and his followers, and the children of his followers. They are ready to join us. We have, I think, been committing mistakes, like emphasizing ideology and politics when we should be winning members, winning them on the basis of their needs. As for education, it is the leadership that needs it, but as Ka Lucio said, the Huk movement was strongest when it was facing an enemy, a real enemy, whether it was the Japanese or the Constabulary that pillaged the villages."

"We should also be able to identify those enemies who are lurking in the background, who wear the masks of friends, who steal our souls with kindness or with promises," Professor Hortenso spoke evenly. "I am, of course, referring to the Americans—just in case you have forgotten."

I recalled the Directorate sessions; I did not want to disagree openly with him, but it was best that I spoke my mind. I owed him this.

"I cannot accept this form of anti-Americanism, Professor," I said. "The Americans are not a problem as such. Just look at the hordes at the American embassy every day. Filipinos wanting to immigrate. I would rather work in an American firm than in a Filipino company. I know Americans give better pay, privileges, and I can aspire to a very high post with them. Not with the Spanish mestizo companies. I am not one of them." I was explicit. I wanted Puneta to know.

"I know what you are going to say," Professor Hortenso said. "But we have to look at our struggle in a broader perspective."

"First things first," I said. "We cannot take on the world. And besides, once you have gotten rid of the oligarchy, it should not be difficult to push the Americans out. The experience of other countries illustrates this. And even if we had a revolution and won in the end, what would we do? We would still have to produce and sell—sell, yes, to America."

"It is not just for the reason I mentioned," Professor Hortenso continued evenly. "We have to recognize our being part of Asia, our being Asian."

"But Asia means backwardness," I said. "Monuments, religious tradition—why should we worry if we don't have these? We should be able to create them ourselves. What is an ancient culture embellished with ritual if there is no freedom in that society, not enough food? We will create the new culture, and thank God we will not be shackled by the past."

"Except that the Americans have shackled us to their concepts, their megalomania." It was Betsy who spoke.

I had not intended to defend the Americans. They are such a big target and could not be avoided. They are also an overwhelming presence. Wherever one turns, they are there, with their technology, their brands, and their malaise. They are, it is true, an obstruction to legitimate nationalist aspirations, and they don't need Filipinos to defend them, least of all a self-seeking escapee from that limbo called Cabugawan. They can do that very well with their own hirelings in the elite schools, in Pobres Park—the nationalist bourgeoisie whose fortunes are entwined with theirs. Still, there are things that must be said, not in their behalf but in the interest of truth.

Puneta was very pleased. "See?" he was beaming, his white teeth gleaming, his mestizo eyes crinkling. "See? Really, Pepe, I should have a long, long talk with you. I should go over there and talk with your Ka Lucio, too."

"Isn't American imperialism real?" Betsy interrupted Puneta.

"No doubt, no doubt," I smiled at her. "But the people are pro-American, Betsy. Look at me: I have no ill feelings toward them, toward anyone. But I hate whoever was responsible for the death of Toto . . . of our thirty-three friends. Whoever killed them is the enemy."

"Go beyond that," Betsy said.

"I can. But my friends in the Barrio—their concern is food and jobs. They are not political."

"We have to be political." She was insistent.

"I don't disagree. But even in my university— I don't know about the schools of the oligarchy."

"Don't be patronizing," she said sharply. It was now she or I.

"I organize on the basis of friendships, on being Ilocano. Most of the students are not really interested in demonstrations, except that they mean no classes. Do you know what their interests really are? To pass, to be able to get a degree, and after that, a job. Politics is a luxury of the rich."

"This is reverse snobbery," Betsy countered. "Are you saying that the masses do not need political education?"

"I am the masses," I flung at her. "Do you want my credentials?"

I had pushed her into a corner, and she scowled at me. I had the floor to myself, and I did not give it away.

"Yes, everyone needs to be politicized, not just the masses. But we are talking about organizing and winning a broader base. This comes first if we are to have the sea. And we can build this sea around us first by talking the people's language—not the language of conference rooms and seminars. And this language is warm, earthy. Many of my friends in the Barrio," I continued slowly, "have not even finished grade school. When I organized the chapter there I had a broom—*ting-ting,* that I used in sweeping the church floor every day. I detached one midrib and snapped it and I said, see, alone, singly, how weak it is? Then I held out the broom to them and challenged anyone to break it. This is what unity brings, I said. Strength, usefulness. And they understood immediately. That is why we were able to get cement for the basketball court. Now we can play even in the rainy season. And we painted the multipurpose center, too. All of us. We are proud of these."

They were listening eagerly. They were all hopelessly *burgis;* what did they know about living in Tondo?

"Any day," I continued, "I can get more than fifty young people from the Barrio. Fifty! You cannot go there and make speeches and expect them to follow you. Do you know that all sorts of politicians go there and make speeches? What makes you think you're any different?"

They did not speak.

"Look, even Father Jess who has lived there seven years feels they don't really accept him. And he is right, and not because religion has become very impersonal. We all know that priests are not poor, that they are not really like us. But I—I have been there only a year and I can raise, like I said, fifty followers at any time. Not only do I live there, but I also fight with them. I give them milk, relief goods—though these are not mine. I have taken them to restaurants, got drunk with them. You don't need speeches in Tondo."

"There should really be a way for those from the villages who have gone to the cities and become other than what they were—successes, you know—they should go back to the barrios, to their roots . . ." Juan Puneta spoke to no one in particular.

I could not let it pass. "Sir, I am no success, but do you mean I should go back to my village in Pangasinan? That is unthinkable! Why should I? Life in Tondo is harsh, but life in Cabugawan is harsher. That is why I am here, this is the reason the farmer would sell his only carabao to send his son to college. If he had a chance, he would not be a farmer."

This was what Auntie Bettina and Mother had hammered into me, I wanted to tell them, for now, more than at any other time, all that I heard from them came with ringing clarity.

"You are saying then that once we industrialize, once we have a chicken in every pot, there would be no need for revolution, there would be no problem even in organizing people," Professor Hortenso concluded.

"We will organize so we will have a chicken in every pot," I said. "But we are incapable of truly uniting. It is not just the *ningas cogon*, the lightning enthusiasm that dies once the speeches are done with. Look at us. How many youth organizations are there now? It is not the Americans or the oligarchy whom we really hate most; it is those who do not belong to the Brotherhood. We call them clerico-fascists, deviationists, CIA agents. And God, we are fighting for the same cause! It is just that our names are different. How many organizations are there of lawyers, teachers, doctors? Perhaps as many as there are people who want to lead them, people who cannot go beyond their petty personal ambitions, who think they are the only true bearers of light. You find this thinking in the village, so we use the techniques that are useful in the village, but the leaders, Professor, they should be able to go beyond the psychology of our villages."

Betsy now spoke with passion: "But why do you have to look down on the village? At least, even if the people there are poor, they and the village have a certain integrity."

I did not let that pass. Briefly, there swooped into my mind the miserable lives that I have known in Tondo, the unending violence, the latent viciousness under the gloss of neighborliness that everyone seemed to exhude.

"Betsy," I faced her, shaking my head sadly. "Thank you for the kind thought, but that is a lot of bull." She turned away, and I was immediately sorry I had spoken so harshly.

"Sorry for the language," I continued contritely. "But I just want you to know there is no honor among the poor. In the Barrio, who are the thieves? Our own neighbors who take the laundry we hang outside our hovels. They steal them to sell to secondhand clothing stores. It is not the cats who get the fish we dry on our roofs; again, it is the neighbors who have nothing to eat. The Barrio is full of cheats, liars, drunks, sadists, perverts—and yes, we steal, we cheat, we lie because we don't know where the next meal will come from. We grab what we can, from anyone. I ask you not to look at the village, at the poor, with rose-colored glasses. There is nothing romantic about poverty. It is totally, absolutely degrading."

WHEN the meeting was over Professor Hortenso sought me. "Pepe, that was a revelation! We will have to rely more on you." He was complimenting me, and I was uneasy, for I did not like speeches even though they were mine, and most of all, I did not relish being a politician.

I did not want to leave with Betsy, but I had made her angry, and I wanted to tell her I was sorry; also, I was not resolute enough in my plan to avoid her. It was dusk. As we eased into the rain-drenched boulevard, she said: "I really should have kept my mouth shut, but then . . ." she laughed slightly. "If I did, you wouldn't have opened up. It is all in my notes, Pepe. You said much more than a lecture on political science."

Were we going again to that fancy restaurant? "No," she said. "We are going to Angono."

The rain had stopped, but the acacia trees still dripped and glistened in the fading light. The asphalt was as black as the thoughts that crowded my mind. Juan Puneta had drawn me out, he had made me speak against my wishes.

It was as if Betsy had divined my thoughts. "And I noticed, too, that Puneta was looking at you," she said, glancing at me.

"Do you like him?" I asked.

She was silent for a time. She shifted gears as we neared the traffic lights at Padre Faura. "I don't trust him," she said.

"How can you say that of someone who has helped the Brotherhood generously?" I asked. "We have just eaten his sandwiches."

She turned to me sullenly. "I suppose this is a personal feeling. He is very slick. There is something in his manner that is not sincere. I can feel it in his voice, in the way he conducts himself—as if he were studying everyone so that he will know how to use them. But my father— We once talked about ethical business practices. I remember Papa saying Puneta's flour company mixes cassava flour with wheat. Oh, I know that he should not be singled out. . . . I also hear he has a private army, what with all the guns he has. And that is no secret."

"He goes around without a bodyguard," I said, knowing that many wealthy Filipinos did not go to public places alone.

"He does not need protection from us," Betsy said. "It is us who need protection from him. Did not your father warn us against men like him?"

I did not speak. I wanted to banish Juan Puneta into some unreachable corner of my mind. I wanted only the nearness of this girl in this rain-washed night that now bloomed with neon lights and the last purples of sunset. The clangor of traffic was around us, and it was a long, crooked way to Angono, but nothing mattered anymore. We crossed over Nagtahan, took Santa Mesa to Cubao, then turned right to EDSA. The road to Angono was jammed; it took a full hour to reach the environs of Marikina. We did not go to Angono, however; instead, she turned left onto a private paved road and continued until we reached the golf club to which her family belonged. She asked if I was hungry. I was, so we went to the restaurant and ordered chicken and ham sandwiches, which she asked the waiter to wrap up. Back in her car, we went through a gate with a sentry and up a slope, through ascending paved roads that traversed empty lots given to weeds till we reached a promontory. She stopped. Below us was Manila spread like a vast, splendored carpet; a million lights twinkled, jewels flashing in the soft dark. Overhead a jet whined in its descent.

"It is beautiful," I said. "You don't see the dirt." I held her hand and she let me.

Then I was suddenly apprehensive; I was not armed, and though I knew a little karate it was not enough. "Isn't it dangerous here?"

She smiled. "No," she said, "this is patrolled and no car can come up here unless you pass the gate."

"I am worried just the same," I said.

"Don't be," she said. "I always come here when I am troubled and I want to think. I know this place very well—it belongs to my father."

I was immediately silent and she noticed it. "I did not mean to brag," she said quietly.

It was hopeless. What was I doing here with a girl who was beyond my reach? "Betsy," I finally said, "I am not lying; I did write to you, but thought it better not to mail it."

"And why not?"

I had to tell her. "I said good-bye to you in that letter. I was determined not to see you again. But I am a weakling, always have been. And this afternoon, when I saw you, God knows how happy I was."

"I was, too," she said simply.

Then I told her, but not about Lucy or Lily. "There is another girl."

She bolted up, turned to me quickly; her eyes were expectant.

"I suppose you may say she was my first love. I grew up with her. She is dark, not fair like you. But you have her eyes—" I looked at her, "Yes, you have the same eyes as Ramona . . . clear, dark, brooding . . . but when she smiles, it would seem like daybreak."

She turned away. "You must love her very much," she said softly. "Will I ever meet her?"

I laughed. "You will never meet her."

"Is she . . . is she dead?"

"No," I said. "She is very much alive. I can see her now." I closed my eyes and held her hand tighter. "But I can only love her in my mind. It is impossible. Like you, she is up there, and I, I am down here. Still, it is wonderful to be with you like this. Thank you for taking me along."

"Why compare me with Ramona?" There was a sharp edge to her voice.

It was then that I told her of Mother's humming the song "Ramona," how I imagined Ramona hovering over me, unreachable like her.

She leaned closer. "This place is real," she said. "The view may look unreal, but we know it is there. I have never brought anyone here or invited anyone before."

"No one would believe we are here," I said. "And it is just as well, for this is not really happening, except in my imagination."

Her breath upon my face was warm and sweet. "But I am real!" she said huskily.

I touched her face and kissed her, her hair, her eyes. Softly.

We would have tarried, but I told her, although it was not true, that Father Jess and I were going to make a house call.

On the way back she was quiet; words could build walls between us so that this would never happen again. She wanted to take me to Bangkusay, but it was late, and I did not want anything happening to her. I got off at Mandaluyong, where I could catch a bus for Divisoria, and she went on to the Park.

The Placard Is Bloody

IT WAS NOT really my desire to sit at Ka Lucio's feet and learn from him the odious truths of the past, but I had brought his name up at the meeting and I would be asked questions about him. I had not been to his house again, although it was just across the alley, since Toto and I visited him. He often smiled when I passed. He would sometimes be out in the churchyard sunning himself or talking with the older men in front of the small *sari-sari* store of Roger's father, but he had never gone to church although he did talk sometimes with Father Jess.

This morning I walked over to his house after I was through with my chores. His two nieces were out, and he was in the kitchen, cooking. He appeared paler, but not once during my visit did he cough. "Ah, my young brother," he said when he turned to the open door and saw me. "Come in and make yourself at home."

He joined me in the cramped living room and asked if I wanted to watch television, but I barely looked at the set in the *kumbento*.

"No," I said quickly. "I came here— I hope you don't mind my learning from you."

He appeared pleased; with a wave of his hand, he said, "All that I know I'll try to impart to you."

"Some of us," I said, "have decided that the time for revolution is now." And if it comes, we would not surrender—this was what we had talked about. Why did he give up? After all those years fighting the Japanese, then the Constabulary? Was he tired, was he disillusioned, and where had his surrender brought him? This shack?

He looked at me, his eyes bright with understanding. He spoke softly, as always, without bitterness. "I must tell you—if this is the only thing that I can tell you—that this is not the time."

"There would never be another time, and if you tell me now that we should wait, I tell you that we cannot. If the time is not ripe, we will help make it ripe. To believe otherwise is to have no faith."

"Big words," Ka Lucio said. His benign smile made me uneasy. "But what are the facts? I thought my time was the right one, too. But where did it get me? And how many years were wasted in remorse that I cannot express? But do not tell me that I had fought in vain, that I did not take one forward step."

"We will make it three," I said.

"No, you will be making three steps backward and only two forward. This is not the time. The people are not ready to accept violence. Do you know what they want? Just peace—peace so that we can continue our miserable lives. More than that, the Americans are here. They will interfere. The oligarchy will convince them your revolution is Communist even if it is not. And the rich . . . they are very strong, they are in power, in government. Where will you get the guns? The money? You will have to get them from the rich, and in the end, they will lead, not you. No, this is not the time."

"Rizal said that, too," I said. "Did you ask yourself when you went to the hills if it was time? Did the Huks get money from the rich?"

Ka Lucio bowed, as if in deep thought. "Everything you say, it all sounds familiar . . . very familiar."

The pot in the kitchen started to hiss and boil, and he jumped up and took off the lid. He was cooking rice; when it had simmered, he returned to me

"Yes," he said, "it is all very familiar. And I cannot argue against passion. There is no reasoning against the heart. But remember,

Pepe, we fought the Japanese, an alien enemy. You will be fighting your own people, your own brother."

"He is worse," I said, "because he is brown like me. The Japanese were foreigners."

"You are saying all that we said. So we did not fight our brothers—and we got tortured and killed. If you must do it, do not forget: the pain cannot be endured. The pain . . ." he went on as if in a reverie: "Sometimes I wish I had died long ago in those hills. Of malaria, of hunger, of bullets. It does not matter. I courted death many times. I had seen my comrades die—three of them in my arms. I know when life finally ebbs away and the body grows limp, and the heart throbs no more. Though the eyes remain open, they no longer see. I know . . ."

He turned away as his voice cracked. He breathed deeply, shuddered, and with his palm, wiped off the tears that smudged his face.

"But I loved life—no matter how bitter, no matter how harsh. I would wake up at night out there in the fields and look at the stars and listen to the sounds in the darkness. Everything would be very quiet. I could hear my heart, the voices of the dead. And when I woke up at dawn, I knew there was some reason for me to go on living, not merely because I loved life, but because I have lived through many dangers and I could, perhaps, impart some of what I have learned. Life is a learning and not much more. It is not loving because there is more hate in this world than love."

"What have you to teach us then?"

"First, stay alive."

"And live long enough to be disillusioned? Or despised?"

"Yes. And do not commit the same mistakes we made—and there were many of them."

"What are they?" I was anxious to know. I was assailed with doubts from the very beginning. I had talked too much, I realized that now, without knowing the books, relying on my own intuition as if that were enough.

"The first," he said, "is that while violence is necessary, it is not the only instrument for change. There are others just as good. But you must accept violence—you cannot begin to build until you have destroyed. You don't know love until you have hated."

I knew that and aloud, "Yes, yin-yang."

"What did you say?"

He did not know what I was talking about. "Night and day. Yes, Ka Lucio, I understand."

"No, it is more than that," he said. "You must destroy the rotten foundations to build a new edifice. You must know how to identify and hate injustice before you learn to value, above all, justice."

"I don't understand."

"Your enemy," he said coldly, "is the rich. You must be able to tell them that to their faces. And when you point the gun between their eyes, you must do it without passion—or compassion. Do it as duty, do it to survive."

I thought of Betsy, my Betsy, her *burgis* parents. I could not do what Ka Lucio was saying. But Toto— Remembering him brought the old anger back in all its primal force.

"And to survive," Ka Lucio went on, "you have to be cunning. Know human character. The evil around you. The poor are not saints, as you can see. You will see perfidy," he was emphatic. "You will see it again and again until it has become so common that you think the whole world is against you. And you will not only be confused, you will also be angry at what you consider your poor judgment. You will see an enemy behind every rock, you will suspect every smile, every gift—and this is not as it should be. For in spite of the perfidy that may surround you, there is always goodness and even sacrifice, sometimes from those you least expect it. There will be men who will give their lives not just for the purposes you believe in, but for you—for you personally—not so much in friendship but in loyalty."

"How will I recognize betrayal?"

"You cannot. Nor will you be warned, unless by some intuition you know that something is going to happen. Feelings are easy to hide. It is not like poverty, which you cannot hide. And when it happens the first time, you will be so surprised it happened at all. It will take some time for you to recover from it, that is if the treachery has not disposed of you physically."

"What makes men traitors?"

Ka Lucio shook his head. "How can I tell? A hundred reasons, as many as there are men and causes and leaders. It could be envy, money, a woman, pride, hurt feelings, or just plain human cussedness."

"Tell me about the first time it happened to you," I asked.

Ka Lucio's thin face darkened. He shook his head slowly as if wanting to dam the flood of memories that had come. Then, almost in a whisper: "It is too painful to talk about," he said. "In that ambush, if we had not been more alert, we would all have been killed. But my wife was not so fortunate." Again, silence. "How did they know we were going to take that route, on that day, at that hour? It was not luck. At least a dozen men knew we were going to pass that way and at least half of them were not with us. So, if you are to lead, lead alone. The general idea you must relay to everyone, but the details you must keep to yourself."

"But that is so basic, Ka Lucio," I said.

"Yes, but we forget the basic things. We become overconfident; we think we have done right. It is the details, the small ones, that get us."

"How did you lose your caution?"

"You live with people. You share the same dangers every day. You think you can trust everyone, you become vulnerable. You start pouring yourself out. You are flattered—oh, not the obvious kind, but small things that imply you are doing well and you are loved. You are the source of all wisdom, of all hope. Without you the whole effort crumbles. The salvation of the group—no, the whole country—depends on you. These make good wine and soon you are drunk. Not so much in believing these things, but knowing that you are esteemed. Respected, ha! That is the final accolade. We really do not look for love from people; we look for respect. Love, that is reserved for the gods. Those who are loved can expect to be hurt and be forgiven their mistakes. That is the nature of love. But those we respect—they are harsher, more demanding. We lose respect for a man and that man is dead. It is enough, I think, that we are believed."

"How do you avoid deception?"

Ka Lucio was silent again. "I do not know," he finally said. "I suppose there is no way one can avoid it. But there is one way by which one can make deception and perfidy not the end, but the beginning. I think that with our brothers we should be sincere. Love and respect everyone so they will have little cause for anger. This means looking at their problems in their minutest and protecting them from the embarrassments that come with their shortcomings.

Be a strict disciplinarian but compassionate in the dispensation of punishment."

"You cannot do that," I said. "Punishment is always harsh, or it isn't punishment."

"But one can forgive."

"And lose in the end."

"No," Ka Lucio said grimly. "That was what the Communists did, and they lost. I was against discipline without compassion, but they said no. They executed one of my commanders for being away from his post—iron discipline, they said. And do you know what he did that they knew but could not forgive? He went to his village to visit his wife who was going to have a baby—their first. It was unfortunate that in his absence there was an encounter. They also executed one of my aides. He was short of funds, it is true, but what they did not consider was that he had given the money to a brother whose wife was going to have an operation. You have to know the details and look at them with your heart, not with a book of rules."

"Still, you lost in the end," I insisted. "Like the Colorums, maybe you believed the entire country would rise with you. The same with the Sakdals*—they believed they would also have the whole nation with them merely because most of our people were poor like them."

"We did not win that particular struggle," Ka Lucio said, "but as you very well know, we have formed a continuity, a tradition. We did not really lose. We were just humiliated. And I will tell you why they were able to batter our defenses and sap our strength. They used our ideas, our words, to win the people who were our best friends. No, they did not defeat us; it is painful for me to admit and count one by one what we inflicted on ourselves. They had only to offer a little reward, the promise of some land no bigger than a man's palm. They only had to come with a few artesian wells, a few roads, and a few tins of sardines—and the people were bought. You see, we offered them less in their eyes, although in their minds they knew it was more. But what is a man's life that would be sacrificed for them? Honor, courage, loyalty—these are all very good, but they cannot buy a *ganta*† of rice, and that is what they needed. Not beautiful words for their stomachs nor beautiful thoughts for their brains. A

---

* *Sakdals:* A group of Filipino people.
† *Ganta:* A measure of capacity; one *ganta* is equal to five pints.

Mexican—Zapata, I think—once said, 'Better to die on your feet than to live on your knees.' You'd be surprised how many would rather eat gruel on their knees."

BACK at the *kumbento,* I mulled over what Ka Lucio had said. Always, Betsy came to mind, her defenselessness when I said "I am the masses." Was she the enemy? How could I ever think of her that way? She was in the same demonstration as Toto and me; she could have been killed like two other girls who were in that same demonstration. There were many questions I wanted to ask her, but I kept them to myself, flattering myself that she wanted me for what I am. She was the only one, aside from Toto, who knew Antonio Samson was my father; was she really convinced that he had committed suicide? And if she was, would she want to have a *malas* in her family, too? She would be a masochist if that was what she wanted. I had to see her again, my arms ached to hold her again. She was the dream I could never afford; if she gave herself to me, it would be charity.

Charity—then it struck me! She attended to me because she pitied me, and I could not accept that from anyone, not from Professor Hortenso, not even from Father Jess. For the first time at this old age of twenty-four, I found out that I did not want it, would never want it, that I was José Samson, strong enough to be alone, to fling damnation at everyone. I may have come from world's end—Cabugawan—immersed myself in stench, stolen, and lied, but I am me, honest with myself. That is all I had to be; when I saw her again, I would tell her. Suddenly I felt a great desire to go home.

MY DESIRE was prophetic. As I was serving Father Jess's lunch, Roger came. "There is a woman looking for you, Pepe," he said. "She was all over the Barrio, looking for the church—and you. She says she is your aunt."

Father Jess told me to prepare another plate and have her come in and lunch with us. I expected Tia Betty, maybe with a letter or an important message from home, but it was Auntie Bettina, and when she saw me, she broke down immediately.

"Pepe, your mother is dead."

It was as if someone had struck me; my stomach churned and became a bag of cold air, my feet became pillars of lead, and my breath was being choked out of me. "No, Auntie, no!" was all I could mumble. I should cry, but no tears sprang to my eyes, only this dazed feeling, this heaviness upon my chest. I am a worthless son, an ingrate—the most terrible loss—I was not my mother's son but the worthless bastard that I am, because I could not cry.

Tia Bettina did not eat. "I am sorry, Father," she said. "I have to go back. There is no one at home but the neighbors and distant relatives."

Father Jess—I will always be indebted to him—stood up without taking his dessert. "Eat quickly, Pepe," he said. "I will go to your town with you."

I was going home after two years, and in those two years, I had perhaps written only ten times, telling her what I was doing, that I already earned a little money, that she should no longer save for me. I even sent her a copy of the essay that had won me a job on the school paper. I never told her of the demonstrations that I had participated in, of Toto being killed; I never told her that I now knew who my father was.

The bus was not crowded, for it was a local run and not the express to Dagupan. Father Jess and Auntie Bettina sat together in front; I had the seat behind them to myself, listening, Father Jess telling her about the Barrio, what I did, that I had become a scholar. Her eyes became swollen from crying, but she turned to me, smiling; yes, I had not disappointed her after all, and Mother, too, if only I had told her.

"He speaks a little Spanish now," Father Jess was saying. "He is a student leader . . . and he attends parties in Pobres Park. Didn't you know all this?"

Auntie Bettina turned to me again. "You never wrote to us about these," she said. "If your mother knew, she would have been happier."

I was immersed in my own grief, going over the things I should have written to Mother, what I would have bought for her—the electric sewing machine, a gas stove such as the one Tia Nena used, and yes, a bed with a mattress, not the old rattan bed that hurt her back. A bed with a mattress.

Bits of their talk came to me. Auntie Bettina was telling Father

Jess that there were no more Samsons left in Cabugawan, just she. There were relatives—second cousins, third cousins, tenants—in the other barrios. All had gone—to Mindanao, to Palawan, and, of course, to Manila.

Father Jess was saying, "You are good-looking, why have you not married?" and she said, "No man ever proposed . . ." and Father Jess teased her, "No man is perfect, Miss Samson. If he does not have athlete's foot, he has dandruff; if not dandruff, it's bad breath. And sometimes, it is all three!"

Tia Bettina laughed, that delightful, silver laughter, then they were quiet again.

Father Jess's huge head was in the way and I could not see the road ahead. But it did not matter—the monotonous green of the rainy season, the small towns with their plazas and their main streets plastered with soft-drink signs, the pompous churches of the Iglesia ni Kristo, the battered schoolhouses. Then, in the dimming afternoon, the plains of Rosales spread to our right, and beyond, the mountain of Balungao, greenish blue in the distance. Again, memory: the edible snails, the string of green papayas I brought back and Mother reproaching me for being away all day without her knowing. I had lain under the trees in the foothills, listening to the wind in the grass, the murmur of the water over the shallows, to my heart.

I tapped Father Jess's shoulder and pointed to the town far beyond the line of trees on the horizon, its yellow water tank thrust like a knob of gold. "Cabugawan there, Father," I said. "And that mountain—I used to go there."

We stopped briefly at the Carmen junction but did not get off; the bus was headed for San Nicolas, all the way to the Caraballo foothills, and it would pass Rosales. Vendors crowded around the bus, thrusting bundles of coconut candy, rice cakes, and bunches of eggplants to us. Rosales was five kilometers away.

The town had not changed—the smallness of it, the rundown market, the plaza with its solitary kiosk and tangle of weeds, and the statue of a farmer with a plow before the unpainted *municipio* that people said was burned by Grandfather long ago. We got off at the bus station and walked.

"Our house is very small, Father," Auntie Bettina was saying. "And no real bed."

"I can sleep on the floor," Father Jess said.

It was not a long walk; we came to the wooden bridge that spanned the creek. The waters were muddy brown and sections of the bank had caved in. We walked on and the houses now were infrequent, then we turned to a small side road, really a lane, flanked by cogon-roofed houses, their yards planted to fruit trees. I knew everyone here.

Our house came into view, the split bamboo fence falling apart, the buri palm sidings now frayed and weathered, the cogon roofing disheveled where the last typhoon had messed it. We should have had the whole house roofed with tin, but there was not enough money, so only the kitchen roof was galvanized iron. The front gate was planted to hibiscus, the narrow lane graveled, flanked with purplish hedges of San Francisco. People were in the house, mostly neighbors and second cousins whom I recognized. They met us smiling wanly, and I shook their hands. Distant aunts kissed me. They smelled of betel nut and sun and I kissed their brown, gnarled hands, then went up into the house.

Mother was in the middle of the small living room, and I went to her at once, bent over her, and kissed her cold cheek. Her face was careworn and lined; a strand of hair lay on her forehead and I brushed it back into place. Her eyes were closed as if in sleep, the lips pressed together but not grimly; her hands were folded, clasping a small wooden cross—those hands that worked the sewing machine—and though I wanted to cry there was only this tightness upon my chest.

The women were cooking rice in earthen pots in the yard. One went to Auntie Bettina and told her there was not enough coffee and *pan de sal* for the night. She gestured to me, and we went back to town. We did not have time to talk before; all I knew was that Mother had had a heart attack, that she was sewing when it happened, and she fell from her stool.

There were many things I never knew and now Auntie told me—how Mother had suffered for years, how she had not gone to the doctor or bought medicine because there was no money, and the little there was she saved.

This I knew—Auntie Bettina did not have to say it. A month previous, Mother had an attack and for a week her left arm was paralyzed. Auntie Bettina wanted to write, but Mother had said, "No, don't give him worries."

"I never told her, Pepe, that you knew," she said. "If you had to know about your father, it should have been from her. And last week she felt that, perhaps, she was not going to live much longer . . . so she wrote to you. She let me read it; I wanted to mail it, but she said, no, this Christmas, when he comes home."

Father Jess was more than kind; he gave Auntie Bettina three hundred pesos—three hundred pesos!—for the wake. From Ming Tay's grocery, bags of cookies, tinned milk, and three bottles of powdered coffee.

I read Mother's letter in Auntie Bettina's room. It was on a ruled school pad. Some parts of it were in Ilocano, but most of it was in English.

My dearest son,

I am very happy that you are now doing well in Manila. I have a little money saved so that you can finish your studies. It is my dream that someday you will have a good job and will no longer know the poverty that was all I could give you. I love you very much, my son, and I am very sorry that I cannot do enough for you. Most of all, it was my fault that you had to grow up alone—and never knew your father.

You have seen the scrapbook in the chest, you have read it. I had kept it because the man who wrote it was your father. We did not sin, Pepe; it just happened that we were cousins. We loved each other and, to this day I love him, his memory. As you grow older, my darling son, you will understand. If we did not get married, if he did not come to claim you early enough, it was my fault and you must forgive me. I did not know you were coming and to tell him would have destroyed his chances—chances that would never come again. He went to the United States and, when he returned, it was too late. Do not hate him as you hated me, and I hope you will learn to love and respect his memory not because he is your father but because he is a man you must look up to. I am hoping that you will grow to be like him so that you can leave Cabugawan, too.

Let me now tell you what has bothered me all these years. When he died, I went to see his wife. I did not ask to see her; she had sent someone to look for me. I was not pre-

pared for her; she was ill, she was dying, but she was all smiles when I was admitted to her room. She motioned everyone to leave so we could be alone. She said she was deaf and that I should write everything down. There was a sadness in her voice and she spoke softly; she said she was happy that she had finally seen me. Tony, she said, had always loved me and, for that, she always envied me. Both of us were together for both of us had loved him. Tell me, she asked, what can I do for your son.

I told her I could take care of you and she smiled and said, "Yes, I knew that would be your reply." Then I told her that I did not think Tony's death was an accident, it was clear as day, and she looked at me and started to cry and she looked so frail and helpless, I went to her and held her hand to comfort her.

"I drove him to it," she said, "and now I must pay." I am not blaming her, but how could I tell you, my dear son, that your father took his own life? But I don't think he did this because he despaired, because he was wronged. I think he did it to atone for what was done, to show at least to us who knew him best that he had not changed. He left us courage, and it was with this that I have tried to live, to impart to you as well. I hope that I have succeeded, for I am troubled by many thoughts, most of all, that I have not helped you enough when you are in need. Sometimes, I wish you were here where I can cook for you and wash your clothes, but to ask you to come back to Cabugawan is to deny you the future and the promise of better days that are yours by right, because, deep in my heart, I know you are very bright like your father. If only you tried.

And that is why I am very happy to know that you are now earning some money, that you are on your school paper because I know that my expectations have not been wrong. I love you, my son.

I read the letter twice; if she loved my father, honored his memory, I must respect her wishes. But it would not do for me to regard him as I did Mother, who had sacrificed for me. What had he done for us? What had he done to deserve my respect?

Auntie Bettina had said he was a good man, but his goodness was not imprinted in my mind and heart in deeds that I would remember. Still, he was my father and I must leave this letter in the chest with all the mementos that Mother treasured.

I could not sleep, for they played blackjack and dominoes in the yard the whole night. Father Jess slept well though Auntie and I were worried, for the bed in the room that he used had no mattress. At least it was a bed, and none of our neighbors had one.

We buried Mother early the next morning; all my relatives, our neighbors, and some of the women for whom she made dresses came. They sought me out and said I should study hard; they had all known of Mother's dream, they knew I was earning my way through school. Auntie Bettina had a black shirt made for me, and she wore a black dress. We walked behind the hearse to the church and, after the prayers, we carried the plain wooden casket to the churchyard, where the town photographer took our picture, Auntie Bettina and I in front and our second and third cousins behind.

The five-piece beat-up brass band from Carmay played the Funeral March as we shuffled out of the church and headed for the cemetery in the southern end of town. It was quite a distance, past the creek, along a narrow road that had begun to muddy in places. *Cadena de amor* bloomed on fences and the *arbol de fuego* showered the road with reds, but in me was a blackness I could not hold.

At the cemetery Mother was brought first to the small chapel and the lid of her coffin was lifted. Old Bebang, a neighbor and a distant aunt, her black veil hiding her face, knelt beside the coffin and started to wail. She recalled how Mother had helped everyone, how selfless she had been in attending to her relatives, and she wailed about how Mother never failed to give her neighbors a bit if there was anything good cooking in our kitchen. Now, it would be a grim and desolate place she had left, for no one would be like her, no one could ever replace her. It was a dramatic performance, but there were no tears in her eyes when she stood up. Auntie Bettina followed after her, but she did not wail; she did not know how, I am sure. She just knelt beside the bier and wept silently. Then it was my turn; I kissed the gnarled, clasped hands for the last time, a cheek lined with wrinkles, and I looked at the dear face—how quiet, how restful Mother looked. I wanted to cry, but no tears came—nothing, nothing but this great and crushing weight upon my chest.

Before it was lowered into the pit, Father Jess blessed the coffin and said a prayer. As they eased the coffin down, Father Jess, Auntie Bettina, and I took lumps of earth and cast them on the wood. Mother, I said softly; forgive me, forgive me. . . .

We hastened back to the house where another distant aunt had prepared a basin of warm water at the foot of the stairs. We washed our feet before going up. There was coffee still and biscuits.

We were by ourselves finally.

"What will you do now, Auntie?"

"What is to be done, Pepe," she said. "I will stay here, of course, and continue teaching in San Pedro. I may ask one of our relatives to come and keep house."

"You can transfer to the city," I said, "and we can live together. You will not be alone."

"When you finish college and have a good job, I will do that. Just come here whenever you can."

She wanted me to take the album Mother treasured. A hundred and twenty pesos was all that was left of Mother's savings after everything was paid for, and Auntie had another fifty that she did not need. She thrust the money into my pocket, but I gave it back to her.

"Please tell Auntie, Father, that I am making enough."

Father Jess assured her I was doing well.

Father Jess had brought out his leather shoulder bag where he put his missal, his holy water, and extra shirt.

I turned to the old sewing machine by the window whose sound I had grown up with, whirring late into the night, and beyond it, the begonia pots, now flowering. The old narra furniture, the battered bookcase, the stacks of magazines, the novels of Willa Cather, Faulkner, Camus, all of them, the *Noli* and the *Fili* and, yes, *Don Quixote*—the glass case where Mother had the finished dresses, and beside it, the old wooden chest, its top scratched and etched with my initials, which I carved when I was in grade school and for which I was whipped. Will I come back to this old, cogon-roofed house, will I return to Cabugawan where memory has chained me no matter how much I tried to flee from it? Why did I leave the way I did? It was all too late now to explain to her, and most of all, to tell her that if I came back—and I surely will—it would be to do penance for her who had cared as no one ever did. And as I stepped down just one rung, all the grief that had been dammed finally broke loose, and I sat down at the top of the stairs, unable to move another step, and my grief became sobs that were torn from me, from my chest, my heart, like they were flesh, and tears came to my eyes, burning and like a flood. I could not stop. I was crying, and I could not stop even if I tried; Father Jess's hand was on my shoulder, Auntie Bettina whispering, "Pepe, Pepe—" but I cried on.

BACK IN TONDO two messages were waiting, and Father Jess said that I was a successful social climber because one was from Juan Puneta—he left his card with a note for me to ring him up at once. The other was from Betsy. Her letter, written on Father Jess's stationery, was sealed. She said she was very sorry to hear about Mother's death, that she would have come along, too, if she knew; that she wanted very much to talk with me about something very personal and very important, and would I please call her at this number that day or the following day and that, if she did not get the call, she would return to the Barrio.

Tia Nena said Betsy had come after nine that evening and seemed extremely distraught that I was not in. It was brave of her and risky—Tia Nena said she was alone—and I did not want her visiting us again. So at eight the following morning—she had said to call between seven and nine—I rang her up.

"I am sorry, Pepe, about your mama," she said quietly. "I never knew her, and I will never know her now. I am sorry—is there anything I can do?"

I thanked her and said life must go on.

"I must see you immediately. It is very important. I hope you understand. Can you do it? See me?"

I was calling from a drugstore in Bangkusay; there was no telephone in the Barrio, not one. "I am here in Tondo," I said. "I have work in church, you know that. And this afternoon, I have to go to school." I did not want to be involved with her further. No, no pity from her or from anyone.

"Please, I can go there, now."

"You are crazy," I said. "Coming here last night. Did you come alone?"

She did not speak.

"You could have been robbed. I warned you before."

"Shall I go there now?"

I did not want Father Jess to tease me about her. "No, I will go wherever you want," I said. "Where shall we go this time? Back to that hill?"

"No, no," she sounded aghast. "Anywhere but there." She was going to pick me up, if that was all right, downtown, perhaps in front of the Avenue Theater. We discussed it briefly, then decided that it should be at the Recto entrance of the university.

When I got there, her mustard-colored Volks was already parked before a line of cars and jeepneys. She saw me and she honked several times, anxious that I would miss her. How could I—her car was so conspicuous.

She opened the door and let me in. "Thank you," she said as we drove off.

"What is so important," I asked, "that you had to go to the Barrio late at night?" Now I was really vexed with her. "Don't you ever try that again. Do you know that I, myself, am uneasy there even in the daytime?"

She did not reply; she reached for my hand and pressed it. She asked me about Cabugawan, how it was, how Father Jess had reacted to my village. "He surely liked going home with you," she said. She had made up her mind where we would go, for when I asked her what it was that she wanted to talk about, she said, "Wait till we get there."

The bay, and I thought we would go to the French restaurant again, with its menus that I could not understand before but would now, for French is similar to Spanish, and in the back of my mind I thought I would try French the following year. But she did not drive into the compound of the Villa Development Corporation; she turned left instead, to the Malate church.

I thought we were going to hear mass, but she just parked in the churchyard, and I followed her to a nearby coffee shop in Mabini where she often went because a friend owned it.

The place was empty; the furnishings were native but elaborate, handwoven drapes, fine narra chairs, and I wondered how it could make money. The waitress in a bright green, checkered dress recognized her and took our orders—two hamburgers, two coffees.

"Neither Mama nor Papa comes here," she said. I was wondering what she was implying and afterward I knew the reason for her anxiety, for our being together. "I am going to the United States," she announced simply.

Perhaps it was best that way. "Good for you," I said, really sorry that she was leaving. I would certainly miss her in spite of my resolve not to get involved with her.

"We will miss you in the Committee," I continued. "Who will take down notes and ask those sharp, biting questions?"

"You are mean," she said bitterly. "You don't understand."

"You are going to the United States," I repeated.

"Aren't you going to ask why?"

"You can afford it," I said. "Should there be a reason? Shopping? Whatever it is."

"Mama and Papa are sending me—immediately if that were possible. But since the semester is almost over . . ."

"A month more."

"I will have just a month in Manila then. Just a month."

"I would leave immediately if I were you," I said. "Imagine, going to the United States."

She bit her lower lip. "I've been there several times," she said. Then, without looking at me, she continued quietly, "They think that by sending me there now, I will no longer see you. That is the reason."

"What have I got to do with your leaving?" I glared at her. "I am nothing in your life. I am a nobody from the Barrio studying in that Diploma Mill. Have they forgotten?"

"Oh, Pepe," she said, entreaty in her eyes.

I did not speak.

"Mama went to the club the other day. She goes there three times a week to play with friends, and the guard told her I had been there. She asked who I was with, going there at night, and he described you, long hair, wide forehead—" she smiled in spite of herself, "and good-looking. We had a nasty quarrel when I got home. She called up Papa in Zurich . . . and they decided right there."

"What do you expect me to say?"

She bowed and was silent.

"It is your life, Betsy. I am nothing to you . . . nothing!"

She looked at me, her dark eyes imploring, and when she spoke, it was almost inaudible. "Pepe, I cannot go. I—" she had difficulty saying it: "I want— I want to be with you."

The words lifted me up to the clouds, the vast, friendly sky, and joy filled me.

But this cannot be, this can never be. "Betsy," I said evenly, "I want to tell you that I have thought about you. Every day since I first saw you, and when I kissed you . . ."

She could not look at me and, again, she bowed.

"But I know who I am. What do they say? Water and oil? No, it is much, much more than that. You will have a boyfriend, someone in your own circle. You will get married, and you will forget me, your flirtation with politics, the Brotherhood."

She straightened, her eyes blazing.

"And most of all," I said, "much as I am grateful to you, for your kindness, your graciousness . . ." I remembered the letter I had written. "Please, I don't need your help, your pity, I don't want it."

"Pity! Pity!" she cried. "Pepe, it is not pity at all. No, it is not pity at all!"

I shook my head. I was determined. "It cannot be otherwise."

Our hamburgers came, but we did not touch them, nor our coffee. The waitress saw we were having a very serious talk and hastily left us.

"What do you want me to do? Prove to you that it is not pity?" Her breast was heaving, her words were a torrent. "Let us go," she said, and to the waitress she gave a ten-peso bill. She did not wait for her change nor did she take the hamburgers, which we had not touched.

I followed her to her car and we drove off, the tires screaming as she shifted gears and stepped on the gas. We tore down M. H. del Pilar, and at the end of the road, without warning, she turned right, into the entrance of the Hawaiian Motel.

I was too surprised to speak.

A boy rushed toward us as she slowed down. He pointed to an open garage door, and she drove straight to it, slammed on the brakes. In a while, the garage door went down and we were alone in the musty semi-darkness. She turned to me, her face still grim. "If it is proof you want, you will get it now. It is not pity. No, it is not pity at all."

I had never been to a motel, although I knew how they operated on a short-time basis. She was now taken aback by what she had done for she hesitated, then asked, "Pepe, what will we do? How do we . . . ?"

Our eyes locked. It was the first time for both of us, and we laughed nervously, self-consciously. A door at one side obviously led to the room upstairs. We went up the flight and opened the door to a small anteroom with a cheap, leatherette sofa, a table, and two empty glasses. Beyond was the bedroom, and, gingerly, we went in. A big double bed, music, the air conditioner turned on, and, on one side of the bed, parallel to it, a huge mirror.

Betsy and I laughed. The buzzer rang, and together we went out. The boy came up with a clean sheet, a white plastic jug of iced water, and what appeared to be a registration book. He seemed amused for Betsy and I began examining the book, the squiggles that passed for names.

"You sign your name here, sir," the boy said, but his eyes were on Betsy.

I turned to her. "What will I put down?"

"Mr. and Mrs. Pepe Samson, of course," she said emphatically.

I put it down like she said, in very legible script.

Address: Tondo, Manila. Residence Tax Number?

"I don't have any," I told the boy.

He smiled. "Any number will do, sir."

I wrote down a lot of sevens.

"How much?" I asked.

"Short time, sir?"

I looked at Betsy. "How long is short time?" she asked.

"Four hours, miss."

"Mrs.!" she corrected him.

"Mrs." the boy said sheepishly. "It is twenty-two pesos."

"I do not have that much money," I whispered to her.

"All right," she said, opening her handbag. The boy said we could pay later, but she paid at once.

ALONE BY OURSELVES, with the latch on, I watched her sit uneasily on the edge of the wide bed. When she looked at me, she blushed so beautifully I went to her, kissed her cheek, and said, "Mrs. Samson, I don't need any proof."

Her arms went around me tentatively, then tightly, and her mouth was warm and sweet. "Yes, you do," she said.

In spite of her sophistication and her liberty with words like fuck and bullshit, the truth was that she was prim, even prudish. Alone at last, she could not even undress with me before her. She went to the bathroom, and when she finally emerged, a sheet was draped around her. She had all the blinds drawn. It took us so long to begin—more than two hours, I think, and I was surprised that I was the first. And it was all there—the tiny blotches on the sheet, stark red on white. She had grimaced, but did not complain and I had thought, having read once how ecstasy and pain contorted a woman's face in the same manner, that she had been lifted to orgasmic heights, but in truth, she had suffered, and when it was over, we examined the mess. She embraced me and whispered, "We are now one."

After a while, she nudged at me, but I, too, had been hurt and could no longer respond. Also, I could only think of that silly mirror that I had forgotten to look at, and that after all these years, I had finally lain on a bed with a mattress. I remembered the two hamburgers we did not have the foresight to bring along, for by then I had become really hungry.

We were quiet most of the way back to the university. The immensity of what had happened began to worry me; it should have been the fulfillment that it was, but I was only being dragged deeper into a bog of contradiction. I wanted to escape. Still, I was grateful for her gift of love—our oneness now of spirit and being. I was humbled by this girl who would never really be mine, who had proven not her virtue but her willingness to take me as I am.

No one can explain me better than myself. How many times have I stood before the mirror of the old cabinet in Antipolo, before the cracked mirror in the cramped and narrow room I had shared with Toto and pointed the accusing finger at this face and said to him, "You sonofabitch. You screwed up everything again." And I have done this, loathing this bundle of nerves and arteries, knowing no one stands between myself and perdition. I should be grateful to Betsy, she could have everything and need not be encumbered by me. I can bring her nothing but bad luck and hardship. Who am I to covet her? Why should she breathe the same foul air that is in my lungs? I should not repeat what my father had done.

I wanted to tell her all of this and of my days in the sun, the scent of new harvest, of early evenings and December chill when smoke from morning fires was around us in a haze and the world was silvery with promise; but she came from a planet beyond my vision, and I could only mumble senselessly about the damn traffic, my having to see Professor Hortenso; I even forgot to thank her when we finally reached Recto.

Professor Hortenso was in the faculty room. I told him that I had received an urgent phone call but could not tell him about it in the presence of the other professors. He stepped out with me into the corridor.

"You must be careful now," he said. "Did you notice that there are new faces in the classrooms, students who are older than most? They are being admitted though the semester is about to draw to a close."

I did not notice them, not in our classes of sixty. Professor Hortenso said they were intelligence agents, and they may have already infiltrated the Brotherhood.

"But what can they find out?" I asked. "Everything we do is public, our publications. Surely, they know everything."

Professor Hortenso paused; the bell had rung and students had started to file out of the classrooms, transforming the sweaty corridors into rivulets of babbling, jostling humanity.

"You are wrong, Pepe," he said. "You cannot have revolution without conspiracy. You and I, we are members of that conspiracy. The leaders of the Brotherhood—and you are one—are involved."

"I am not aware," I protested.

"You will be," he assured me.

I told him about Juan Puneta, that he had gone to Tondo again, left his card at the *kumbento* and that he wanted me to ring him up.

He seemed thoughtful. "I don't know what he wants. But just the same, give him a call and tell me what happens."

He was going to his class, and he asked me to walk with him to the Education building, where he was handling a graduate seminar on Philippine culture.

"They have taken some of our boys in Diliman," he said. "We have not heard from them. We don't know what has happened to them. We have tried tracing them but without success. They just disappeared. So, be careful, Pepe. We can all be easily disposed of."

"They can arrest me any time they want," I said. "They will find nothing on me."

He shook his head. "Pepe, they will find many things. Just be careful."

I remembered Ka Lucio's warning. But what was there to betray? I knew no secrets, made no important decisions.

Professor Hortenso went on. "If I disappear, or if I leave Manila, do you know where to find me?"

I shook my head. "I don't know where many of our Directorate members live."

"I can always find you then," he said, "in the church."

"And you?"

"I am helping set up our committees in Central Luzon—Tarlac, Nueva Ecija. You were right, Pepe, the Huks, their children who are now grown up, they are important links not only to the past but to the masses—our base."

"Ka Lucio—"

"Yes," he said, "I am now sure his help is very important."

AFTER my eight-thirty class, I went to a small crummy bookshop on Recto where there was a pay phone and dialed the number Puneta left. No, he was not in—it was one of the maids who answered. But would I leave a message as to where I could be reached tomorrow? He would not be back till late that night.

I will be in school in the late afternoon, I said; and in the Barrio the whole morning.

Hortenso's warning disturbed me. I was slowly being sucked into a whirlpool, and I did not like it. Ka Lucio's warning, his lecture on betrayal, bothered me, too, but as I told Professor Hortenso, I knew no secrets and I was not about to join any armed group, much as I longed to avenge Toto's death. It is not that I was afraid of violence—I saw it every day in the Barrio, the slow, deadly violence inflicted on us, the gang fights, the knifings that were common in Tondo, the malnutrition, the stifling dreariness that deformed the body and the spirit. But I had also begun to know a woman's love, to eat not just enough but what I wanted; with a little more effort, I would not be just an acolyte; the doors that had been shut to me were finally opening and, beyond them, heroin dreams were beckoning. I was not beguiling or deluding myself merely because I had become a member of the National Directorate or a full scholar in school; after studying Spanish, I realized that if I worked hard at things I really liked, I could excel at them. And being a revolutionary was not in my compass. I could appreciate what Ka Lucio had done, what the Brotherhood was doing, and I was doing a bit if only to merit my position and to salve my conscience; but from the very beginning, politics and politicians had been a bore to me, and I was not now ready to transform myself into that slimy creature I had always loathed.

There should be ways by which I could withdraw unobtrusively from the Brotherhood's Directorate. After all, I earned nothing there. At the same time, I wanted to keep Professor Hortenso's friendship, not because it was necessary for my continued employment on the school paper, but because I had grown to respect and like him and his wife. I would still participate in the demonstrations, help in the planning, write manifestoes, things expected of me, but I would be in the shadows, then ease myself away before I finish college.

My new relationship with Betsy bothered me, not with guilt feelings but with confusion. I loved her, but at the same time I desired Lily, too, and despaired for her, wondering about her customers, and the "sensation" she gave them. I often lay awake at night, waiting for her to come home, and could only go to sleep when I heard her walk up the alley, bidding her mother good evening. She would sleep till about ten in the morning at about the same time I would be through with my cleaning, and she would talk with me from her window— nonsense things about us and the Barrio. Then she would be off by eleven after a hurried lunch, for she was expected to be at the Colonial from noon to midnight. If she was late, she would be fined, and if she was late three times in a week, she would be suspended for a week. It was only on Tuesdays that she could really talk with me, but these days were spent more on shopping, sewing, and helping her mother.

Sometimes we reminisced about Toto. Now I was working very hard in the church, and Father Jess increased my allowance. I had asked if he was going to take another fellow, but he told me flatly it was going to be my decision, because the new boy would have to share the room with me; wasn't it like that with Toto? It was he who brought me to Tondo. Roger, who lived close by, was helping a bit in the church now. Furthermore, I began to like being alone, and would find it difficult to adjust to a new roommate the way I had grown accustomed to Toto.

Yes, I missed him, his subdued and steady pushing when I flagged and, most of all, our quiet talks. I often caught myself asking questions aloud and somehow expecting them to be answered. But Toto was not there, and Roger was not bright enough to take his place.

I decided to see Ka Lucio again. I would have seen him more if only to listen to his stories about the war with the Japanese. Professor Hortenso had frightened me with his knowledge that some of our members had disappeared without any trace and that there were more who would certainly vanish.

I will not ask those asinine questions that had rankled us in the past, those impertinent questions about the validity of government, the obligations of the governed and those who govern. I had learned the answers to these early in Cabugawan.

I have also seen a bit of those forums, those university lecturers, the semantic convolutions into which they go, pondering questions that are really the pastimes of those who sit in the comfort of high offices. There is no blood to their inquiries, no dirt under their feet, the air they breathe is perfumed.

Ka Lucio had the answers, and he did not learn them in the Sierra Madre. One is this: nothing is given free. While Juan Puneta gave those niggardly "tokens" to the Brotherhood, he would someday ask for a bigger payment in kind, yet what did he need money for? He wallowed in it and would probably choke on it.

I have also asked myself what it is that I have done with my life, how has it been used? What right had I to make judgments about others without making them about myself? Indeed, I have tried to look deeply and honestly into my being—pried open the skin, fingered the nerves, the veins, and examined the blood in them. And what did I see?

Anger—and it was what has kept me alive, although I had tried to still it, keep it from flowing out, defined it in another way, and expressed it not with violence but with cynicism.

Ka Lucio had said earlier that there are two ways of looking at our lives—either as fate or as conflict. Only hogs are fated, because they cannot do anything except feed on the trough before they face the butcher's knife. But men are men; they can do something about the future, and our life is in conflict then. They—or us. Self-defense, survival. Whatever we do, we can put it simply thus. And government? Ka Lucio did not have to tell me that it was an instrument of the rich, that government committed violence on us every day by not providing us with justice. Remember, Ka Lucio had said, we are demanding justice. Here in the Barrio we live with injustice and get to know it as part of life. It is not. And it is when we learn this that the decision is made: us—or them.

There was no equivocation then about my survival; I loved myself dearly, passionately. Ka Lucio had amassed experience to live this long. He would tell me.

He was writing in longhand, on a yellow ruled pad, when I entered—the door of his house open as usual. He had just finished cooking, and the small dingy kitchen was still smoky. He bade me sit; then, putting his hands on his lap, he asked how the revolution was going.

It embarrassed me, for as it was last time, I could not quite make out whether he was making light of us or was in earnest. I decided to ignore the remark. "It won't start without you, Ka Lucio," I said.

He laughed then and asked if I wanted a cup of coffee; he had just heated water and the powdered stuff had hardened—if I did not mind it that way. He stood up; how thin he had become, and it was only a few weeks since I last saw him. I wondered if he was getting any medicine or the right kind of food—he never went inside the church, and though he often greeted Father Jess and talked with him about inanities, he never asked for help although I was sure he needed it.

"I hope you are writing your memoirs," I said.

"No, Pepe. My last conversation with you has set me thinking. I am writing a manual: how to organize the peasantry, how to raise funds, how to fight—you know, a question-and-answer handbook."

"Ka Lucio," I said, "that is perhaps the most useful thing we need right now, particularly organizational guides." I told him how I brought him up in our committee meeting as the wellspring of wisdom. In our youthful audacity, we had not considered how people like him had so much to give. He looked at me gratefully for having remembered.

"You know many of these things because you came from the village," he said.

"But you tested them all," I said, "and what I need is confirmation. Do you trust us enough? Would your former men like to help again—their children in particular?"

"Pepe, of course, they will help. Didn't you know? Once a rebel, always a rebel. It is in the blood. You don't join the Huks because you want adventure or money—and even if you did join for these reasons, afterward, the fighting, the living together, they change you."

I understood what he meant; I had joined the Brotherhood for my own reasons, but I was now, it seemed, slowly being drawn into its vortex. Though I wanted to get out, to be uninvolved in the conspiracy that Professor Hortenso had told me about, I had found myself half wanting to become part of it, maybe because the Brotherhood meant my meeting with Betsy, maybe because I was angry at what had happened to Toto.

"How did you manage to escape the Japanese? Were they really all that bad?"

He sat back, a look of shock on his face. "I keep forgetting," he said, "that the war was three decades ago, that your generation has not known what it is to live under an occupying army. Yes, Pepe, there would have been no successful guerrilla movement, we would not have been able to organize the peasantry if the people did not suffer under the Japanese. They killed many of us, but we got more of them."

He recounted how they mounted ambushes in the rivers of Pampanga, how the waters turned red. He did not go into details; it was as if he was merely recounting incidents. He melted with the people he said, and yes, he smiled in recollection, there were many times when he wore women's clothes.

I would have stayed longer, but Tia Nena was looking for me— I had a visitor—so I hurried back to the *kumbento*. It was Juan Puneta's driver asking if I would like to have lunch with Dr. Puneta? The car was out in the street, waiting.

"You are really going up—up," Father Jess said when I asked his permission.

I wanted to ride with the driver up front, but he said I should stay in the rear. It was my first ride in an air-conditioned Continental, and I was awed. I toyed with the electric knob that raised the window and then sat back. On my side was a panel, and it controlled the radio and cassette player. I turned it on and listened to a noisy announcer urging the destruction of the Marcos regime and another march of students to Malacañang. He had a stentorian voice and must have been in love with it, for he rolled his *r*'s, and made those pauses that only actors make. "We cannot tolerate any longer a man who looks with disdain at the people, who makes a mockery of democracy, who has sold this country to the Americans . . ."—clichés, so I switched to another station. The Bee Gees were beautiful—

> *How can you mend a broken heart . . .*
> *How can you stop the sun from shining . . .*

We were crossing Del Pan, into the handsome country of tall, antiseptic buildings, the Rizal Park. He slowed down on the boulevard and turned left to a Spanish-looking building.

"Please," the driver said, "Don Juan is inside—just ask the waiter."

The doorman hurried to the car and opened the door. In my jeans and T-shirt, I walked into the bastion of the mestizo elite. Puneta was in the restaurant drinking beer with a couple of mestizos in white pants—an affectation, for white pants were not worn anymore, although, as Uncle Bert once said, before the war everyone went to work in white drill suits even in the heat.

Juan Puneta came to me and squeezed my hand, saying gustily: "Well, Pepito, it is wonderful to have you accept my invitation. I have been wanting to have a long talk with you." He guided me to the table and introduced me to his companions in Spanish, adding that I was one of the brightest student leaders. I understood everything and, for a moment, I was tempted to speak in Spanish, but I held back. They shook my hand, then asked to be excused. Although I was confident of my Spanish with Tia Nena and Father Jess, I had not tried it with someone born to the language. I kept quiet and sat down as he reverted to English, asking me what I wanted to drink.

From books and magazines, I knew a bit of bar exotica, but beer or gin was all I really knew. I had never been to a place like the Casino, so I asked him to do the ordering. "Sangria," he said. "I could ask for Jerez, but there is nothing like the Sangria that the bartender here makes."

Though he was in his early forties, Juan Puneta looked more like thirty. He had obviously taken good care of his body for he did not have a paunch and his arms were muscular and wiry. He kept cracking his fingers.

Our sangria came. "*Salud*," he said, raising his glass to me, his eyes shining. Then I saw it. The eyes, cagey and shifty, gave him away—not his gait, not his mannerisms. There was in his eyes, now that he was grinning, a certain sharpness. I had never objected to homosexuals—there was no reason for me to do so. In Cabugawan, we had one for a neighbor; he lived with young boys from the other barrios and made a living frying bananas, making rice cakes, and selling them. His cakes—particularly his *cochinta* and his *puto*—were superior to any other in our town. Toto and I had a couple of classmates, too, and they were entitled to their preferences as long as they did not bother me. I like girls, always did, and I did not care to change.

I was amused by Juan Puneta because he looked so masculine, so very macho, and yet Lily had told me otherwise. He did the ordering—fried squid to start with, then bouillabaisse, which he said was excellent, and tripe, then dessert and coffee.

The squid came, deep fried and cut into small pieces, crunchy, almost like *chicharrón*. Around us was the babble of businessmen, the denizens of Pobres Park, the social elite, and I could pick up snatches of their talk, prices of minerals, saucy gossip, trips to Europe. "You know, Pepito," Puneta said, getting serious; he had exhausted all the small talk—the weather, the increasing anarchy. "You must really give attention now to organizational work. I listened to you last time, you know. You can really organize in the rural areas. How do you feel about it?"

He gave some money to the Brotherhood, so I must not antagonize him. I must be nice, polite. Meekly: "I don't really know, sir."

"Don't 'sir' me," he said in mock anger. "Really, I am not your teacher, and don't let my age and my Ph.D. intimidate you."

"Yes, sir."

He laughed. "Well, if you cannot call me by my nickname, which is Juan, then a plain Mr. will do."

"Yes, Mr. Puneta," I had no intention of calling him Dr., not after the way Mrs. Hortenso had talked against him. "I have not given it any thought, but whatever assignment will be given to me, I will do it."

"Excellent!" he enthused, cracking his knuckles again.

The bouillabaisse came. "This is the specialty of the Casino," Puneta said. I remembered reading about it as a dish from Marseilles, a thick soup with pieces of fish, clams, crab—seafood chop suey—and I liked it.

Then he asked me about the former Huk commander in the barrio.

"He is writing," I said. I held back, not sure whether I should tell him what Ka Lucio had told me, the handbook he was doing, the list of former members we should see—in Laguna, Tarlac, Pampanga, Nueva Ecija, Pangasinan, Bicol, even in far off Panay, in Mindoro, and in Mindanao. I did not know they had organized that far. I thought the Huk movement was confined to Central Luzon, particularly Tarlac and Pampanga.

"What is he writing?"

"His memoirs," I lied. "He is very sick."

"I should see him then," Juan Puneta said. He seemed thoughtful. "I am sure he needs help."

Our tripe came. I had expected us to discuss politics; I wanted to find out how well he knew Philippine communism—the subject of his Cambridge dissertation—and how intellectually sharp he was. I asked him if I could read his thesis, but he dismissed my request with an imperious wave of the hand. "Just one of those academic requirements," he demurred. "Better read the new collection of essays that I have written; it will be published soon." Then, without any warning, he asked if I had ever gone whoring.

I was caught off guard. I fumbled and could not reply. He shook a finger at me and grinned: "You seem more interested in politics than in sex."

I expected him to proposition me then, but he continued blithely: "Revolutionaries should not have emotional entanglements with women. It is bad because they will then be vulnerable. You can always go whoring for release."

I did not speak.

He suspected, perhaps, that I was not pleased. "I mean it," he said. "It is one way by which you can get release. Are you twenty already, Pepito?"

"Twenty-four going on twenty-five," I said.

"Well, you are at the height of your sexual powers. There is nothing unhealthy about whoring—if you are careful."

"I have never tried, sir," I said.

"Try it sometime," he said. "It will keep your mind away from girls who will smother you."

"I have not even—" I thought about what Lily had told me, "tried anything tamer—like the sauna and massage."

He threw his head back and laughed. "You must be a Puritan, then, working with that priest in Tondo."

"No, sir," I said, "I certainly am not."

He shook his head and went on grinning: "Well, saunas, that is one place I have never been to."

How easily he lied. "But try going to one, find out which is best, then someday"—his eyes twinkled—"we can go together."

MUCH, MUCH later I thought about the bizarre meeting and wondered why Juan Puneta had wanted to see me. He had talked about women, he was bragging about his techniques, how necessary it was to have women under male control. He had a very extensive collection of pornography, he said, which I must see some time. But more than that, I must visit him at his home, and he made a date right there—a week from Friday, at nine in the morning; I should come to his office and we would go target-shooting—no, not in a cat house, at his home, he had a shooting range there. He also collected guns and I must learn how to shoot and shoot well if I am going to be in the vanguard of the Brotherhood. As a matter of fact, he said, if I wished, we could go to his house that very moment. But I told him I had classes in the afternoon, and it was past three.

He signed the chits, asked if I wanted anything other than the small glass of *anisado**—my first drink of liqueur—I downed it in one gulp and burned my throat. The sangria had gone to work, the *anisado*, too, and I was voluble and careless. No, I did not want anything more. I should go straight to school; our finals were at hand

---

* *Anisado:* Aniseed wine.

and I did not want to lose my scholarship. If not for this I would go with him target-shooting, not only in his house.

He laughed heartily, took me to his car, and drove me off to Recto. As we neared the university and its traffic, he took some fifty-peso bills out of his wallet and handed them to me. I did not want to take them, but he thrust them into my pocket. "It's not for you," he said, grinning, "for the Brotherhood. Go to saunas—look for the best, then be my teacher. And after that the target practice."

I did not feel that I should tell Professor Hortenso what had transpired—the talk about sex techniques and target-shooting—it was too incredible to recount. But at least Puneta did not proposition me. When I got to my class, I counted the money—it was exactly five hundred pesos. It was the second time I had that much money, and for sure, within the week, Roger and the boys would have another feast in Panciteria Asia or some place fancier. And maybe, at long last, I would also be able to visit Lily where she worked.

THE COLONIAL is in a three-story boxlike building with a red neon sign in Gothic on its facade. A blue-uniformed guard stood by the ornately filigreed door. He opened it as I got out of the taxi and greeted me, "Good afternoon, sir." I stepped into a red-carpeted lobby. Giant shell lamps illumined the reception area, and though it was only half past two in the afternoon, it already seemed like dusk, for all the heavy maroon drapes were drawn.

The reception desk was crowded with business types. It was rush hour, as many of the "guests" had arrived from their lunches in nearby restaurants.

I walked up to the desk after the crowd had thinned. Two girls were manning it and one asked without smiling, "What is it, sir? Executive or VIP?" Lily had told me the Executive cubicles were more expensive, but what did I care? I had Puneta's money.

"Executive," I said. I took one fifty-peso bill and handed it to her, then asked, "Is seventeen busy?"

She looked at the listing before her and said, "No." She picked up a microphone and called: "Seventeen, ready." A boy behind the desk handed me a key with a big, white plastic holder.

"Third floor, sir," the girl said.

I went up the carpeted flight; at the landing a boy asked if I would like to shower and steam first. He guessed, I suppose, that this was my first time in the Colonial. "What is your number, sir?"

I showed my key, and he guided me to the cubicle—so dim I could not see anything. "I am blind here," I said. The boy laughed; he opened a cabinet at a corner and in a sudden flood of yellow light, they jumped up—the low platform with a foam rubber mattress, an extra towel, rubber slippers encased in plastic.

"You put your things here, sir," the boy explained, pointing to the cabinet. "Lock it and bring your key. The shower and steam bath are in front of the door where you came in."

I thanked him, then sat on the pad. I closed the cabinet with the lightbulb, and the room was thrown into darkness again. I took off my shoes but did not strip; I had no intention of taking a shower, much less a massage. The door had a small glass window, but a piece of cardboard had been taped over it so that I had some privacy. The door, however, had no latch and could be opened at any time; the panels between the cubicles did not go all the way down to the floor; there was a narrow slit between.

I lay on the pad, wondering how Lily would react when she came in. It did not take long. The door opened. "Sir," she asked tentatively. "Will it be oil? Or lotion?"

"Saliva," I whispered.

She paused, edged closer and peered down. She was used to the darkness and now so was I. Her dark eyes grew wide, then she bent down and embraced me, saying huskily; "Pepe, Pepe." She started laughing. "Now, sir, would you like your sensation first or the massage?"

I kissed her, and she responded warmly, her lips tasting of promises. Her hand wandered down.

"Hell," I said under my breath. "You do that to everyone!"

"Pepe," she said pushing me away. "It is my job, I told you!"

"Hell," I repeated.

"Are we going to quarrel? Did you come here to insult me? You paid fifty pesos for this, have you forgotten?"

"It was not my money," I said. It was senseless being sullen over something I could do nothing about. My anger left quickly. I had come here to see her; I knew what to expect. And she had kissed me. After some silence, "Two nights from now, after my last exam, I will take Roger and the rest out—we will have a wonderful dinner—and if you want to come . . ."

"I cannot leave till midnight, Pepe. You are my first guest," she said. "I don't really like teenagers, and you look like one with your long hair. The boy told me."

"What's wrong with teenagers?"

"TY, that's what. Thank you. No tips. *Gorios,* that's what we call them. We'd rather have them fat and old—they tip well, most of them anyway."

I lay down again.

"I'd really like to give you a massage," she said, holding my hand. "I am very good, you know. Hard. I have several Japanese guests; they come really for the massage, and they like me because they say I am *ichi bang.**"

"I just wanted to see you," I said. "Now that I can afford it. Juan Puneta gave me the money for this."

She drew back in surprise, then said, "You should have showered and taken a steam bath. He is there! Now!"

"He told me he has never been to a sauna."

"Shit!" she said. "You want to surprise him?" She stood up and headed for the door, but I held her back.

"I'll see Girlie," she said. "She is his regular. I told you, he just talks with her."

"Don't tell him, promise."

She laughed then went out.

In another minute, she was back. "We are in luck," she said. "They will be in the next cubicle. We can eavesdrop or even peep."

She lay beside me; we were cramped, but that was what I wanted.

"I have been thinking, Pepe," she said after a while. "Mostly about myself—what I will do. I'll go back to school and finish fine arts. But I have forgotten how to draw. I am in demand now—all of us who are young and good-looking. But how long will that be?"

"You study in the morning," I said. "Don't hurry, even if it will take six years. At least you will be prepared for a better job. I hope you have been saving."

---

*_Ichi bang:_ Number one.

"What will you finally take?" It was my turn to be questioned, but before I could answer, the door next to ours opened. The girl was saying, "I will really try my best, but very few teenagers come here."

The cracking of knuckles was enough to convince me. Puneta's voice when he replied was so low I could not understand a word.

Lily whispered, "Didn't I tell you? He has been asking Girlie to proposition teenagers for him. Five hundred pesos—as high as that!"

I shuddered; it was five hundred pesos he had given me. "What really does he do here?" I asked.

"I told you," she said. "He comes here almost every day, at this time, when we have the most number of guests, or shortly after five, rush hour. He takes time in the steam room, in the shower, looking at all those pricks. Then he comes in, but refuses a massage. He always takes Girlie, waits for her if she is busy." She got off the pad again, motioned me to peep through the slit between the rooms.

I bent over; the other cubicle was as dark as ours, but I could see the girl sitting on the pad, and the pale, handsome profile of Juan Puneta.

"Enough," I said, pulling her back to my side.

Her face was close to mine. "Even your hair smells sweet," I said.

"Wait till I have had five guests," she said. Then, seriously, "Pepe, I am worried about you. There is a general— Army officers come here, you know. This general, he is very proud of his prick. They call him a general's general. I have never serviced him, but the girls who have say it is really big. Well, he told one of the girls that the army is really going to be harsh on the demonstrators."

"They are already doing that."

"It could be worse. What will happen to you?"

"I don't know," I said. "Maybe, in the end, I will go to the mountains."

"You will be alone and you will be hungry."

"That would not be anything new," I said. "I can live on coconuts, green bananas, and papayas."

"The mosquitoes and the leeches will finish you. And you will have malaria and other fevers."

"At least I will not be getting gonorrhea. No saunas there."

"You are wrong," she raised her voice above the whisper we were conversing in.

I kissed her chin. "No nightclubs then," I said.

"And no fucking."

"I can always masturbate."

"Suppose I did that for you? Suppose I went with you?"

"Is that all you will do? You have no skills, really. You cannot take dictation and type. I don't think you can carry loads."

"You make me feel so worthless," she said.

"But you are good enough for me."

"Will you really take me if I came along?"

She sounded serious. "No," I said.

"I will wait for you then."

"Shit," I said. "You will wait forever."

The other room was now aglow; Juan Puneta was finished and was obviously dressing. I was tempted to rise and go to his room and confront him, but it was his money that I was using, and besides, I was not ready to make an enemy of him.

"We can peep through our door," Lily said, standing, and that was what we did. Puneta went out quickly, and I wondered if he had his Continental with him.

"No," Lily said, "he always comes here alone, by taxi, I think."

I had time so I tarried even after Lily had changed the sheets. She had asked me to linger—there was no one waiting for her. She would have been informed if there was.

"Your unlucky day," I said. I gave her a fifty-peso tip, which she did not want to take, but I thrust it down the pocket of her white skirt. Before we reached the reception area, she kissed me; then I stepped out into the blinding sunlight.

I went to Professor Hortenso's house the next day, for he had left word for me in the office of the school paper. Mrs. Hortenso opened the door, but before she did she peered out of the grilled window into the street.

"Come in, Pepe," she said as if she was in a hurry, then bolted the door. "Have you eaten?" She knew I had rushed from school to Dapitan and the plates were ready on the table. She was thoughtful and kind. Someday, I told myself, if and when I got married, it would be to someone like her.

Professor Hortenso sat beside me while Mrs. Hortenso came out with a plate of steaming rice, fried *bangus* and shrimp *sinigang*. I was really hungry. He watched me eat, and between gaps of silence he talked about the finals we were going through. No, I found the examinations easy, and I did not even have all the textbooks; I just listened to the lectures instead of letting my mind wander.

"You will maintain your scholarship then," he said happily. "You have to. The university will no longer accept activists who are not bona fide students, and those who are on the leadership list are under surveillance; they have to be good to stay, not only in the scholarship rolls but in the university itself. The army is applying pressure."

I was silent. "And be careful, Pepe," Mrs. Hortenso said. "Do you know that they have been watching us for the last two days? They were there—" she thrust her chin toward the street corner. "In a jeep. They had cameras. I noticed them yesterday when I went to market. I am not naturally suspicious, but I saw them; they were watching the house."

I turned to Professor Hortenso. He nodded slowly.

When I had finished, he stood up and said, "Let us go out for a walk."

Mrs. Hortenso followed us to the door. "Careful, Dad," she said, her face dark with apprehension.

We walked toward the boulevard, and once in a while, Professor Hortenso would abruptly turn around. There was no one following us. I had not seen him for almost a week. Now I told him about Juan Puneta, how he had taken me to the Casino for lunch, how he had talked about politics—just a little—nothing more, about Ka Lucio.

"He is making a list of people we should contact, and they are all over the country," I said.

"Good! Good!" Professor Hortenso exclaimed. Then he told me how worried he was; another of the Diliman boys in the Brotherhood had disappeared. That made it five student leaders without a trace. The parents had come to Manila, made inquiries with the police, the army, but there were no leads.

"They must have gone underground already," I suggested.

"No," Professor Hortenso said. "I would know. Someone in the Brotherhood would know."

We had reached the boulevard. "Pepe," he said, "I don't know, but I think you should stop seeing Puneta. It is not a question of mistrusting him—I have no evidence for that. But I think he will do us more harm than good; I reread what your uncle wrote, and he is right. We cannot afford to be misled again. Worse, misused—and know it."

It was almost midnight when I got back to Tondo. I was tempted to take a taxi—I still had three hundred pesos of Puneta's money— but I was in no hurry and I wanted to be alone to think clearly of what had transpired. I was to meet Puneta in a day at the Casino, as we had agreed, but after Professor Hortenso had warned me, I decided not to see him.

The muddied alleys of the barrio had dried, and in places they were already cemented. We had raised money for the basketball court as well. The church was lighted up, and people were there, the neighbors mostly. And in the center aisle was a coffin. When she saw me, Cora, the older of the two sisters who lived with Ka Lucio, came to me and started to cry.

"Pepe, it's uncle—"

I had greeted him that morning when I left for the university to review before my exams, and even asked him if he would care to join us at Panciteria Asia. "I will be out of place, Pepe," he had told me.

And now he was dead.

"Did he have a heart attack? Did he—"

She could not explain; it was Roger who did. Cora had already left for work and it was Nene, the younger sister, who came home from school at noon for lunch. Ka Lucio was prostrate in the living room, his head bathed in blood. Someone had come in and bashed his head. Most probably he never knew who or what hit him. In his old age, he had become so trusting that he always kept the front door open. No one had seen the killer. No noise, no scream, no struggle; it was swift and painless. He had known some peace and quiet here in the Barrio, but death stalked him here, this accursed jungle of tin and rubble and driftwood. He lived through twelve years of jail, through ambushes and travail, only to succumb to a faceless murderer.

"We told the police," Roger was saying as we went to the bier. I looked at the calm, lean face, peaceful in death. He had never been in this church while he was alive. I still had three hundred pesos, but I told Roger we would not go out anymore, the money would be for Ka Lucio.

Chain of Centuries

I T WAS BETSY who answered the phone when I took the chance and called her not at the agreed upon time. She could sense the urgency although I tried to sound flippant.

"What happened? Can you tell me?"

"Not on the phone," I said. "Between kisses, I'll tell you."

"Are they after you?"

"The way I am after you," I said.

"I will drive over as fast as I can; I should be there in twenty minutes."

From Makati, at dusk, when traffic was at its worst, it would take an hour. I walked over to the Rendezvous where my friends would be, but no one was there. I took a table in a corner where I was hidden by the evening throng, students having snacks after their afternoon classes.

The street outside was noisy with traffic, and when I walked out, the stench of garbage piled high along the gutters assailed me. Our slogans were plastered all over the stone embankment, on the walls of buildings. The new ones screamed, dark red: *Marcos Hitler Diktador.*

It had always made me feel good, waiting on the sidewalk for Betsy to come in her mustard-colored Volks. She wove out of the traffic to where she always picked me up. I darted out and got into the car, and as she shifted into first gear, I leaned over and kissed her cheek.

We got out of Quiapo quickly and onto the boulevard, hardly speaking, except for niceties, her term paper on Japan, her quarrel with her mother. Her answers were perfunctory.

We had no favorite motel; we went to what was nearest and most convenient. We rarely went to a place twice, for I did not want her to be subjected to the indignity of recognition. At M. H. del Pilar, we turned into the first motel—a prewar residence in the Malate area now converted into something tawdry but profitable. A boy standing by the row of garage doors pointed out to us an open one and we drove in. He followed us and lowered the door. Betsy went out and quickly went up the stairs. I followed her to the small anteroom and closed the door; there was the usual pair of drinking glasses, the frayed menu on the table, and beyond, the double bed with mirrors on its side; the air conditioner and the radio were on. She kissed me, the honey, the salt, the sweetness of it all, lingering in my mouth.

The buzzer rang, and she freed herself, reached into her bag for the money, but this time, I shook my head. "I have a little," I said. "Let me take care of this."

She smiled, then went to the bedroom and closed the door.

The boy came with the registry, a jug of ice-cold water, and an extra sheet. He laid the registry on the table, and I signed my real name as I always did together with a nonexistent residence certificate with lots of sevens in it. I gave him twenty-two pesos, and after he had thanked me and left, I put on the latch. We had all the time now. Betsy did not care anymore if she got pregnant, but I did not want to inconvenience her. In a few days, she would be in Bacolod for the semester break to say good-bye to relatives, friends, and her kindergarten school.

Afterward, I told her that Ka Lucio was dead, and that the list and manual he was working on could not be found. She took the news quietly. "We have enemies," she finally said, trembling.

"It's been more than a year now, Betsy," I said. "Do you think you can trust me?"

We were lying on our backs, holding hands. "Pepe, I trusted you the first time I met you. How can you ask such a question?" She sounded disconsolate.

"Though I sometimes feel I don't understand you, I trust you completely, told you things," I said.

"What things?"

"My life, for instance." I had difficulty forming the words. "You said we have enemies. We have to do something, other than those demonstrations. Suppose, after this semester, I decided to go to the mountains."

She drew back, her eyes dark with dread.

"Ka Lucio is dead. Professor Hortenso says those of us who are exposed are in danger," I said.

She lay on her back again. Her breast rose and fell; she just stared at the ceiling, at the stupid red bulb there that I had forgotten to switch off. I moved closer to her, stroked her flat stomach.

"Please, Pepe," she finally spoke, "think about it carefully. Only three more weeks, then it is America for me. I don't want to go. I'd rather be here, no matter what happens."

I touched her cheek, then raised myself on an elbow and gazed at the lustrous eyes, the full lips, the strand of hair on the smooth forehead.

She held my hand, pressed it to her breast. "What have we done? Where are we going? I am afraid."

"We must live while we can. We must not waste even a moment."

"How can you say that?" she asked. "You . . . in that place. That is not a place for people."

"You despise me then."

"No, Pepe, how can you say that? All those people crowded there— I am ashamed. The way we live. One dress—it is what one of them would earn in a month. Or even three months. That is why I wear jeans most of the time. Not because it is fashionable, but because I am ashamed."

"And I wear them to hide my poverty," I said.

I started laughing; it struck me for the first time—its triteness, its being so *bakya*. She turned to me and asked: "Is poverty funny?"

"No, sweetheart," I said, tweaking her nose. "Us—we are funny. When I was a boy, I used to see those silly Tagalog pictures. Rich boy, poor girl. Once, she was a *provinsiana*. At another time, a bus conductor. It was wonderful entertainment. Now, it is rich girl, poor boy. Can you imagine a sillier situation? It is the kind of story movies and all those radio serials that go on forever are made of. As the poor boy and the rich girl are about to marry, something happens and they break up. Wait for the next installment tomorrow, next week, next month."

"It is our life."

"It only hurts, sweetheart, when I laugh," I told her glibly.

"Stop being clever. Can you not see? I want you to be the best scholar in your university, the best leader in the Brotherhood, the best essayist . . . better than your father."

"Don't bring him into this," I said sharply. "That is what Auntie Bettina and Mother have pounded into me: be like him. I am not going to live in his shadow. I don't want to read what he has written any longer, to remember him."

"Pepe, he is your father!"

"Hell! If he committed suicide that is where he is now anyway."

"He did—because he had integrity."

"You cannot say that, you never met him."

"Reading his book, I feel I know him."

"Maybe it is him you love."

"Don't be ridiculous," she said. "You know it is you, and it will always be you. And you can be the best. But even if you are the lousiest, the meanest, the ugliest . . ."

"You wouldn't have gone out with me."

"I want you alive, I want you breathing, moving. I don't want you disappearing, or being killed in a demonstration—like Toto."

"We have to take risks. That is what we are in the Brotherhood for. You know that. We have to go beyond the demonstrations."

Slowly she put her arms around me. "I want to live, Pepe, not for myself, but for you."

I held her close, felt the thumping of her heart, the silky warmth of her legs entwined with mine.

After a long, long while she sat up, then stood before me, all the five feet two of her gleaming and tawny, regal grace, and for an instant, it seemed as if she was burdened with all the sadness in the world. She gathered her clothes on the sofa, slipped into her jeans, her faded, formless blouse.

I had not stirred from the bed. Her back turned to me, she said, "We have been leading up to this. I could see it coming." She wheeled and her face was in anguish. "But why do it? What difference would it make?"

I rose and picked up my clothes. "I was just thinking. There is a limit to words, you know that. And we cannot depend on words anymore. I did not realize how fast time had gone."

"Especially for me," she said ruefully. "Maybe because I think of nothing now but being with you." She found her shoes, sat before the dresser, and started putting on a little lipstick. She smoothed her hair with the ivory brush she always carried. In another moment, we would part.

"If you go, how will I know where you are?"

"You won't. I will see you, but it will be far between. They can trace me to you . . . and I don't want anything to happen to you. I will miss you . . . if I go."

"Oh, Pepe!" her voice broke and she rushed to me, embraced me, and sobs shook her. She would not let me tilt her face, would not let me see her face washed with tears. I hugged her, saying, "My Betsy," and got my cheeks wet, too, with her crying. She cried for a long time and, when it was over and I drew away, her eyes were swollen.

"See what you have done," I said. "Now you really need makeup."

She smiled and kissed me. "What will become of you?"

"I will die," I said, making light of everything, for I did not want our evening to be gloomier than it already was. "And there will be no grieving widow, nothing, just as it always was, for I came from nothing."

She embraced me again. "Don't talk like that!"

"All right," I said. "I will live to be a hundred. What is that Spanish saying? The weeds live long?"

Afterward, she asked: "What will become of me?"

"You will forget me like you would a bad dream."

"No. Never."

"You will," I said. "And you will fall in love with someone and you will marry him, raise children who will inherit your good looks and your brains, and none of them will ever make the same mistake you made, going around with someone like me."

"It is not a mistake," she said. "Why do you degrade yourself? You are everything—my husband." She started crying again, and I held her. "Pepe," she said, "I am so miserable."

I hugged her, a tightening in my chest, a smarting in my eyes. "I love you, Ramona," my voice sounded strange. "I cannot thank you enough for giving yourself to me."

Challenge to
the Race

I WAS FINALLY PICKED UP on the last day of the semester, just
before the two-week school break. I had just gotten off a jeepney at
Bangkusay and was walking toward the Barrio when four sunburned
men in their thirties surrounded me; they had revolvers tucked in
their waists. They could be from the rival gang of Bangkusay, but I
had not done anything to antagonize them if they were.

"*Pare*, we will not harm you if you come with us quietly."

I had no choice; we walked down the street and did not even at-
tract attention. They stopped before a van with the name "Luzon
Bakery" on the sides, and we got in—the three on the front seat and
the fourth in the back. Once inside, they frisked me; their tone of polite amiability disappeared.

"Lie down flat on your stomach," the man in the rear ordered
and when I was slow at it, he kicked me in the ribs. It hurt but I was
not frightened. I was curious about who they were, where they were
taking me.

Then, it became sunrise—they were after me because of my
work in the Brotherhood. I tried to raise my head, and it was then
that the blow came. The man sitting before me pistol-whipped me in

474

the head. For a moment I thought I would pass out as everything darkened.

"Don't raise your head," the man warned. "You are not going to find out where you are going. One more movement like that and I am really going to knock you out, tie you up, and blindfold you. You understand?" His Tagalog had an accent, perhaps Visayan, perhaps Ilocano.

"Wen, Manong," I said.*

"We are from the same region," one of the men in the front seat said.

While I could not raise my head, I could look at my tormentor's shoes. They were black army boots. The van did not smell of bread. In fact, there was no trace of flour or crumbs on the floor. It seemed to have been swept clean and was pervaded by an odor of burnt oil, of machine shops, and the tired sweaty stench of government offices.

We now bounced occasionally. We were traveling over a rutted road, and my face scraped against the steel floor and it hurt, so I rested my face on my arm. Then we were on what seemed like a good asphalt road. We drove straight and fast, perhaps for half an hour. The snort of traffic and of people talking wafted into the van.

The men out front were talking in Tagalog about how they would spend the night at some massage parlor, and one of them was openly wondering if I would be so difficult as to interrupt their evening plans.

The Directorate, I remembered, once had a seminar on how we should behave if we were arrested or taken into custody without the usual procedures. I must remember their faces, the place where they took me, their names if possible, anything I could use to identify them later on. And I must not give them cause to be violent.

The sound of traffic diminished, then disappeared. The van stopped and we got out. I was in an enclosed courtyard—probably a bodega with a bit of sky above. I did not have time to examine my surroundings, for they pushed me into an empty room walled with cement, asphalt tiles for the floor. A high window with bars was open, and there was not a single piece of furniture in the room. An old newspaper and a red plastic pail were in a corner, and when I

---

* Wen, Manong: wen—"yes" in Ilocano dialect; Manong—form of address to an older person.

looked, the pail contained toilet paper and dried excrement that still smelled.

I squatted on the dusty floor, wondering where we were. The only sounds that reached me were the distant honking of a car and the barking of a dog.

I was thirsty, but there was nothing to drink; I pounded on the door, which was locked from the outside, and asked for water, but there was no reply.

Soon it was dark and mosquitoes buzzed all around me. I switched the light on, but either the bulb was not working or there was no power. There was no way I could reach the window, which was a full two meters above me. I tried jumping to find out what was beyond, but could see only the sky.

I lay down as darkness deepened and surrendered to the anonymity, the kind and elusive peace the night had brought. Sleep would not come, and now I tried to recall what acts of conspiracy I had committed that had brought me to this room, what articles of faith I had sundered. And the more I thought, the more I was convinced that I had done no wrong.

Late in the night I was awakened by a scream—a woman in terror. There was something animal and despairing about her cry, as if she wanted help, the kind that would mean salvation. I keened for the sound, trying to figure out which part of the building it came from, but all was darkness; the barred window high above brought nothing but the muffled sound of traffic in the distance, a steady thrum lengthening into even silences, and voices indistinct and disembodied.

I pressed my ear to the wall to extract sounds I could understand, but could hear nothing. Was it really a woman's scream I had heard? I walked to the door and tried opening it, but it was locked and would not budge.

I lay again on the floor, hoping to hear a sound, a human sound, another scream that would at least show I was not alone in this building, whose breadth and height I had no knowledge of, least of all its location. I did not even know which way was east.

In the dark, I could make out the outlines of the door, the corners of the room. I closed my eyes, prayed for sleep to come, but it would not; I imagined shapes, rays of light, glowing gems of blue, fleeting and iridescent, and in between, grim, grim thoughts about what awaited me. I floated off into sleep—fitful and short.

I woke up with a sliver of sun on my face, the sound of voices beyond my door, but I could not make out the sounds. I pounded on the door and shouted, "Sir, please, if you can hear me. I am thirsty. *Paki,** please let me have some water." I waited for a reply, and when there was none, I said, this time in a shout, that I needed water.

My throat was parched and, strangely, though I had not eaten for a day now, I did not feel weak or hungry. Still no reply. It had begun to get warm so I took off my pants and shirt, folded them neatly and laid them on the floor. I lay down again and waited. I must not lose my strength, I must preserve what I could of it.

Toward afternoon the door was flung open. There was a new man—his crew cut still fresh so that the scalp was still pale. The two others were obviously enlisted men. It was the man with the crew cut, White Sidewall, who told me to put my clothes on, which I did immediately. I asked for water but they ignored me. When I had dressed, they slapped handcuffs on my wrists.

The room where I was confined adjoined another—a hall into which other doors opened. There was nothing in the hall except five iron beds that had not been made. At one end was a table with food and to it they pointed.

Although I was handcuffed, I did not have difficulty with the *pan de sal,* the cup of lukewarm coffee, and, when I finally got my drink, never before had water tasted so good.

I would be nice to them; without my handcuffs, I could fight—it would be a risk. I could kill one probably before they would be able to kill me, but I was not going to die now. I was not ready to do so.

I tried to make out the things on their beds, comic books, their guns; in a corner was an armalite and loaded magazines. They were all in civilian clothes; only their shoes showed they were military.

My interrogation started shortly after breakfast; the room adjoining the hall was bare of furniture except for a wooden chair and a long varnished table between my interrogators and me. The windows were high and they were open to let in the air, the distant sound of traffic, the whining of an air-conditioning unit.

Paki: Please.

White Sidewall could be a lieutenant or a captain. His questioning was relaxed. "You had a good breakfast, and you will continue to be fed well. I hope that you will appreciate what we are trying to do. There are snakes all over the land—very poisonous snakes—and we must seek them out and destroy them or they will kill us. It is, really, as simple as that. Now, tell us about the interesting things you saw in China when you went there last year."

The question really rocked me; he was either joking or had the wrong Samson.

"I have never been to China, sir. The closest I have been to China is Ongpin."

They scrutinized their pads, scribbled on them, then White Sidewall continued, "What campus organizations do you belong to?"

I thought it best to be honest. After all, it was public knowledge. "The Brotherhood, sir."

Smiles on their faces. White Sidewall was doing the questioning. "What is your position in The Brotherhood?"

"I am a member of the Directorate."

"As a member, what do you do?"

"I attend meetings," I said. "The Directorate lays down policy and prepares a program for the whole year."

"Did you participate in the demonstrations?"

"Yes, but not all of them."

"Were you in the demonstration at the American embassy the other day?"

I was sure there had been no demonstration at the American embassy, and while I wracked my head for an answer, a blow sent me reeling to the floor. My ear was seared by pain. I tried to rise, to get back to the chair, but now, the weakness that had eluded me came. My knees were wobbly and I could hardly stand.

"I need prompt replies," White Sidewall said, smiling. I turned to my left; there was a man in a black T-shirt and denim pants standing there—big and so well built he could have been a professional wrestler. I glanced at his powerful hands. He was no karatista; his knuckles had not hardened.

I knew then that I would be tortured. I started to think of ways by which I would be able to meet it, react to every blow, every turn of the screw as if the end had come—that would perhaps make them less violent. I decided the Brotherhood was not worth dying for; I would tell them everything I knew. After all, I was not involved in any conspiracy.

The questioning continued evenly. White Sidewall was taking his time, even joking with his companions while I sat there, listening to their ribald jokes. "I suppose you are not a virgin, Mr. Samson?"

I shook my head.

Laughter from all three. "Well," White Sidewall again, "our Berdugo"—he thrust a chin at Tarzan behind me—"has a preference for virgins, male or female." Again, peals of laughter.

They did not wear watches, so I did not know what time it was. Outside it was light, but in the room, with but one window open, it was quite dim. Someone brought in their lunches on tin trays, and they ate slowly, enjoying their fried chicken and their noodle soup. Not even out of politeness did they say, let us eat. When they were through, they smoked, lifted their feet onto the table and comported themselves as if I were not there.

The questioning, it seemed, was over. They were sleepy after the meal, so they took me back to the room. I was sure now that the building was some kind of office that had not been furnished, that we were far from houses. I lay on the floor and shut my eyes, tried to reconstruct the questions, their implications. It was obvious that they had trailed me, they knew where I often went, and they had knowledge of the organization. It was useless lying. But the direction of their questioning puzzled me. What were they really after? Were they afraid that the Brotherhood was powerful enough to start a revolution? That was Toto's fondest wish, the pinnacle of his aspirations, but it was sheer fantasy.

And the scream. Were they holding others and were they going to soften me up first before they turned on the screws? How long would it take? It was my second night. I had a very late breakfast, but there was no water, no food in the room.

My head ached where Tarzan had hit me, though there was no swelling. The blow was not intended to render me unconscious, only to instruct me in the futility of not cooperating with them. And that was what I wanted to do, if only I knew the answers to their questions!

In the beginning I had thought that hunger could be avoided or at least escaped if I went to sleep. But I couldn't do it; it was not just the mosquitoes. I did not know what to expect next, what new pain was to be inflicted on me. Perhaps this was part of the torture itself, and realizing that, I tried to think of those things I enjoyed most. Yet dark thoughts kept intruding, I remembered Betsy, my dear Betsy, her face, imagined the smell of her hair, her Tabu, the feel of her skin, her cheeks. She was in my mind when I finally fell asleep.

It was early morning when I was roused. The door was open, and Tarzan was there, looking as menacing as always.

"You will clean the toilet," he said. "So take your clothes off."

He undid my handcuffs and, for a moment I was tempted to strike at him, but there would be others outside, and they would not hesitate to use their guns.

I carried my pail with my own excrement of the day before, and went with him to the toilet at the far end of the hall. Other plastic pails were there, waiting to be emptied into the bowl.

As I bent over, emptying my pail into the bowl, something warm splashed on my head and all over me. I turned, then felt nausea; I was covered with feces, my face, my back. Tarzan had emptied one of the pails over me, and he now looked at his obscene handiwork, his eyes aglow with malice.

He laughed, and now, White Sidewall and the others came and looked at me. I was too shocked to react, and my first impulse was to rush out of the toilet and embrace them, rub the feces on their bodies, but that would only anger them and make them more severe. I knew that this was premeditated, to humiliate me, to humble me.

Tarzan threw me a mop and told me to start cleaning my mess. "You young radicals," he muttered, "you are full of shit."

I emptied the pails into the bowl, showered once, twice, thrice until there was not a trace of smell on me; I washed my jockey shorts, too, and was about to put it on, still wet, but Tarzan, who was watching all the while through the open door, said I should get out naked.

They marched me back to the room where they had interrogated me the day before. I did not try to cover my nakedness with the still wet shorts that I carried; I was weak from the work, from what had happened, and I could not endure pain.

It was the same bare cubicle, but this time a big wooden chair stood close to the wall. The windows above were shuttered, and the room was humid and warm, smelling of paint and cigarette smoke.

On the floor was a piece of machinery with handles and electric wires extending from it. They motioned for me to sit in the chair, and it was then that Tarzan became all efficiency; with canvas straps, he fastened my arms and chest to the back of the chair, spread my legs and tied them to the legs of the chair. I looked at White Sidewall, at the other two, but they seemed uninterested while Tarzan did his job.

White Sidewall examined the straps. Satisfied that they were secure, he spoke to me. "You know, Mr. Samson, we did not like your answers yesterday; you were not telling the truth. Now we have to be more careful."

"Sir," I said, looking at Tarzan, who was checking the contraption and its wires. "Will you be specific? What question did I not answer truthfully?"

White Sidewall ignored my question. "Now, please give us the correct answers. We know that a shipment of guns has landed on the Pacific coast, close to the town of Baler. These guns are for you. Can you tell us where these guns are now and who is in charge of distributing them?"

I did not know of any arms shipment, or how one would be distributed. "I don't know what you are talking about," I said.

White Sidewall nodded toward Tarzan, who returned to me with the wires; at their ends were tongs, and he attached them to my scrotum. They pinched a little. I realized then that the machine was some generator or transformer, such as what they used in the signal corps of the army. Tarzan squatted before the box his hands on the knobs.

"All right then, who is in charge of recruitment in the Northern Quezon sector?"

My legs were weightless and my throat ached. "Sir," I said, "I don't know. I really don't know. I will tell you all about the Directorate. I did that yesterday, the members, who they are, where they live—anything that I know, I will tell you. But people in Quezon Province . . . I don't know anyone."

White Sidewall nodded at Tarzan again, and slowly the man started turning a knob. It came like a sharp claw tearing at my genitals, and the pain was so severe I gasped for breath, grasped the arms of the chair. Tarzan turned the knob off. His face was wreathed with smiles. Now he stood up and took the tongs off my scrotum, then he started fingering my penis. His fingers smoothed the head caressingly, all the while his dark, pimpled face was upturned to me, grinning. I looked at the sharply burning eyes and immediately realized that he was a homosexual. He returned to his seat before the infernal machine.

"We are experts, Mr. Samson, in extracting information," White Sidewall assured me. "So please don't make it difficult for us and for yourself. You have seen how considerate we can be. You had a good breakfast yesterday, and we will return you to the Barrio, I promise you, with not a wound on your body, or with any sign that would mean we did not do our job with *delicadeza*. That is the word, right? So why don't you help us and we will do everything for you in return?"

"I will, I will," I cried. "I will tell you everything I know."

"So then," White Sidewall said, "tell us about your arms depots in Manila. Who maintains them. Surely, you know this."

I wracked my head. Was there any time that this was talked about? Had Professor Hortenso ever at any moment slipped into saying that there were such depots? I closed my eyes and tried to think; there was nothing that I knew, there was nothing I could say. I shook my head.

It did not come slowly; it was a sudden deluge of pain, so sharp and vicious and so searing, I screamed as I had never screamed before, beyond the capacity of my lungs, beyond the capacity of my body. The animal voice I heard was not mine; it belonged to some poor, tormented devil whose hour had come. It was a pain of indescribable intensity, the blackest of black, which spread faster than lightning from my loins to my entire being.

Then it stopped, and, gasping, sweating and weak, I begged my tormentors not to do it again, in the name of God, of human decency, that I did not know anything, that I would tell them anything they wanted to know if I knew it, but please, not again, not again.

"All right then," White Sidewall said, a smile lacing his lean, iron face. "Tell us slowly, very clearly, who are those in Manila who are in the shadow directorate—those who are not known to the public. You know, Mr. Samson, that you are a member of a conspiracy to overthrow by force a democratically elected government. You know that your National Directorate is just a front, that underneath is another organization. You might be a member of it."

Again, I thought hard, our meetings, our discussions, my talks with Professor Hortenso, even with Puneta. No matter how hard I tried, I could not tell him anything about a shadow directorate.

"Sir, I don't know. Please, I don't know."

That is the last I remember, for the pain came in a horrible explosion and I blacked out.

WHEN I regained consciousness, it was already dark, and I was back in the room, cold and naked. I groped for my clothes; they were nowhere. Weak and with no one outside knowing where I was, I decided that I would never be subjected to that kind of torture again, that at the first opportunity, I would attack and try to escape—die perhaps, but I would try. I remembered the scream I heard the first night and realized that there was no mercy here; if they could do what they did to me to a woman who could not fight, they would be capable of doing worse than they had already done. I was not going to find out what that would be.

I tried to reconstruct the ride. It had taken about half an hour in afternoon traffic. We must be somewhere in Caloocan, or Novaliches; the van had not taken too many turns and the ride had been smooth most of the way. Now, there was no sound of traffic, not even of habitation, of people, and in the stillness of the night I shuddered with the dread that already possessed me. There was nothing to identify them, and if I lived through this torture, I am sure that there would be no wound on my body. If I died they would most probably dispose of my body here.

I was hungry, but no longer did I crave food or water. They did not matter anymore, and I wondered if those who fasted really missed food or suffered the pangs of hunger.

I decided that if I were to get out of this, I would write about it, tell all not just to the Brotherhood, or in the school paper, but to the editors of the national papers who had been sympathetic to us. But who would believe me? What evidence would I bring? To whom would I point?

I should have gone to sleep, to conserve whatever strength I had left, but I could not, for thoughts of revenge, of escape crowded my mind. As in the first night, it was a long, long time before I dropped off into a listless sleep.

When I woke the room was already bright, and by the door was

the usual plastic cup of stale coffee, some soggy *pan de sal*, a piece
of fried meat, a plastic pitcher filled with water, and a small hand
towel.

I ate everything and then went to sleep again. I was roused in
the afternoon. Tarzan was at the door, and the very sight of him
chilled me. I had grown to hate him with all my heart, and if I ever
saw him again I would most certainly kill him. But this time, he
came with another plastic tray of food, and there was even a bottle
of ice-cold Coca-Cola on the tray. My first impulse was to knock him
down with a flying kick, but I knew that the place and the time were
not opportune.

He placed the tray on the floor without a word then slammed
the door. By the early evening I was filled with misgivings, and I
began to wonder what was behind the new and kindly treatment.
Were they softening me up for another session with the electric generator? Was this a psychological trick that would leave me wide
open and ready to admit everything and anything? I had read about
mind-conditioning in the Korean war, in the Communist countries,
and I realized how easy it was to bend the mind. Yes, I would admit
anything, the worst crimes they could ascribe to me, if only to be free
from the devil machine. I realized I was not made of steel, I was not
going to be a hero for the Brotherhood.

It all came back, too, what Ka Lucio had said: the Huks who
were captured by the Japanese, the Constabulary, or civilian guards
did not talk. He had told Toto and myself of the water cure, how slivers of bamboo were driven into their hands and, still, not a word
from them. Was it the same with us? I doubted it. Why weren't we
made of stronger stuff? Had we been weaned too late? Did we lead
such soft, pampered lives? Or did we not believe in what we said, in
the purpose for which we had banded together?

A long night, faces aglow with love, scenes of my childhood—
the brown irrigation ditches brightened with the purple of water
lilies, dew-washed mornings. What was I doing in this abysmal
place? What evil force pitched me here?

I held my penis; it was no longer numb, but was extremely tender. Even a feather touch seemed to inflame it. What had they done
to me? Had they castrated me in flesh and in spirit?

I went to sleep, now used to the mosquitoes. Sometime in the
night it drizzled and was iron cold, but there was no blanket to

warm me. I woke up late in the day, and the coffee at my door was no longer warm. Toward afternoon voices rasped outside my door, and when it opened, White Sidewall and his gang were there.

It was always White Sidewall who talked to me throughout, and now he sounded contrite: "I am very sorry, Mr. Samson. But since we have decided to free you, I hope that you will forgive us for what happened. If you were in our place, you would understand."

Shit, I said to myself.

"You will now shower. When you are ready, we will take you back to Tondo."

They took me to the toilet that I had cleaned; it was spotless, just as I had left it. The water felt delicious and I lingered under it.

My clothes were on the chair outside the bathroom and I put them on. They blindfolded me, this time tightly. They walked me outside and helped me into the van—I knew its smell by now.

But they did not take me back to Tondo; they lied to me, cheated me, for when they removed my blindfold and opened the van doors, I recognized immediately the surroundings, the atmosphere. We were in the Ermita police station.

A line of brown Metrocom buses, windows covered with wire mesh, clogged the street and were filled with young people, some of them with white headbands, some with bandages on their faces. There had been a demonstration at the American embassy and the demonstrators were being hauled to Crame.* Now the buses were pulling out and the spillover crowd of students were waiting for their ride.

"The station is full; you can see we have no more room here," the policeman at the desk was saying. "They have to go to the city jail. Why don't you take him to Crame? You have all the room there."

White Sidewall shook his head. "I have a date and I am already late. No, just do whatever you must with him."

Another policeman in civilian clothes asked me questions, which he typed, and after that, I was fingerprinted, then they hustled me off to a mosquito-infested corner where I waited for the next hour.

Should I have protested then? Should I have screamed and lashed away at the police pigs and my torturers? I thought about it

---

* *Crame:* Camp Crame; Philippine army base.

later; I did right appearing meek and submissive. I was a prisoner no matter what the law said; I did not carry a gun—they did.

A police van finally came at dusk, and together with the leftovers that could not be taken by the Metrocom buses, we were herded off to the city jail.

A brief ride, through Quiapo and its environs, the shops shuttered with plywood, the sidewalks piled with garbage, the low stone embankments in the middle of the street plastered with our slogans and posters.

We went down the underpass then made a U-turn; I had not realized that the city jail was here, beyond a cratered street and crumbling, old buildings roofed with rusting tin.

I must get in touch with someone and the first person who came to mind was Betsy. At the jail reception, I rang her number and was told by the maid that she was still in Bacolod for the semester break, which I knew but had hoped that she had not gone or had returned. Father Jess—but there was no phone in the *kumbento*. Professor Hortenso had no phone either, and at this time of the school year there would be no one in his office. I tried it nonetheless, but there was no reply. Then I thought of Puneta. But I did not want to be beholden to him, not even in this moment of need.

The policemen in civilian clothes at the reception desk were not pleased that we had to come in at night. They separated the girls and sent them to the brigade close to the entrance. We had to strip and be examined for drugs and weapons, then we were shunted off to the different brigades.

By now I had become inured to the discomfort of not having a mat or a blanket, but some of the boys were grumbling, saying they were not criminals, that they should see their lawyers. The sergeant who manned the desk and glowered at us said we could do that in the morning, that at least we had a roof over our heads.

I walked through a dimly lighted courtyard and crossed over through a barbed-wire gate that was padlocked for the night, then shown the building where I was to sleep.

It was dimly lighted, but I could make out the shapes of those asleep on the wooden bunks, stretched like carcasses, most of them half naked. Though it was already November, the heat and the humidity were still oppressive even at night, and the heat, particularly, seemed to cling like some stringent glue to the very pores of the skin.

No one stirred and there did not seem to be any place for me. I squatted on the stone floor. Clothes were strung on wires, and beyond the grilled windows I could see the rooftops of Recto, some still ablaze with neon. Mosquitoes and the sounds of the city drifted in. I thought I would never be able to sleep, but reclining against the cement wall, I dozed off only to waken in the night to a wild screaming in the next brigade—as if a man was going through what I underwent. No one was disturbed, no one stirred. I was, indeed, in another dimension.

It was still dark when the brigade started stirring, and by daybreak we were all up. A single line formed at the toilet at the end of the brigade and I joined it. A middle-aged man, perhaps forty or so, was behind me; he grinned, "So you are the one who arrived last night." I nodded.

The young inmates studied me. "You can put your clothes in that corner and sleep at the far end if you wish," the man said. "You are new here, so you must know the rules. The king is Bing-Bong over there—" he pointed to a sturdy, bald-shaved man of thirty at the gate; he was looking at me and smiling. "You do whatever he tells you. We do whatever he tells us. To disobey is to be punished. No harm will come to you if you do what you are told."

I wanted to tell him to shut up, but he seemed so friendly, and I did not really know what new ordeal I was to go through. He also had that look of having lived a long time; there was that tiredness and dumb resignation in his thin, pinched face, as if he were a chicken caught in the rain, all wet and with no shelter to go to.

I was the only one thrown into this brigade; the others were assigned to another building. Now I could see the whole jail. The battered buildings were arranged like spokes in a wheel with the main office and reception area, through which we entered, in the middle, topped by a low rusting tower. This was the Old Bilibid prison—the National Penitentiary—before it was transferred to Muntinglupa, as Chicken explained again.

The day wore on in tedious idleness, for there was nothing to do, nothing to read. We stayed in the cement courtyard, most of us in shorts, and I could see now the tattoos on arms, legs, chests, and backs, just as I had seen them in the Barrio, emblems of that other world which Roger himself wore with pride. One even kept his head perpetually shaved, for it was there that the tail of a snake was curled and the body ran down the back of his neck, coiled around his torso and down to his penis—the snake's head being the penis head itself.

Chicken was some sort of emissary or chief clerk, and it was his job to acquaint all newcomers with the rules of the brigade—rules the prisoners themselves enforced because within the jail there was another law—not the law of those who guarded us.

There were no tattoos on Chicken's skinny arms or chest. "I am too old for that," he said, laughing. Then he told me why he was in jail. A rich man's son who loved women and fast cars and was drunk most of the time had run over and killed someone. He did not stop. The people who saw the accident had taken down his license plate number and that was how he was tracked down; the victim's relatives did not want any settlement, the bastard must go to jail, and because he was a rich man's son that could not be. But justice must be done, the crime must be punished. It did not matter that Chicken did not even know how to drive—that was not important; what mattered was his confession.

"I was given five thousand pesos. Five thousand pesos!" Chicken said. "And then, of course, there is the thousand pesos every month—every month. For the duration of my being here. And my son, he comes here every week you know, together with my wife, to bring me things. You know, we don't eat enough here and one gets tired of fish and *kangkong*, fish and *kangkong*. You know."

I nodded.

"And then, of course, the best lawyers defended me. When I get out there will be another five thousand. Where else can you find something like that? Here, I can eat regularly. And when I get sick, at least there is some medicine."

"How do I get out of here?" I asked.

"If you are poor you cannot get out. There are no rich people in jail. They can afford bail, the best lawyers. They can even buy judges."

"I am poor," I said. "A self-supporting student. But I am innocent. I have not committed any crime. I swear to you . . ."

Chicken looked at me, his small sad eyes crinkling in a smile. "Who is innocent and who is guilty?" He shook his head. "The poor are always guilty and the rich are always innocent. Get some lawyer to stand for you. But while you are here, you must follow the rules—theirs and ours."

"But the law—"

"The police, what do you think they care for? Their pay, first of all—and the more they can get, through foul means if necessary, the more they will get. They are not here to help us; they are here to maintain order so that we will continue being what we are—poor."

And it came to me clearly then as it never did before, the truth that this kind of order was not for me. Look at our Barrio. What did it need? Running water, so we would not get typhoid, and toilets, simple public toilets, nothing fancy, nothing expensive, but these could not be built, not by the government, not by the civic organizations. Why should they? Everyone up there was comfortable as long as we were down here. It was as simple as that. And this jail—it was so easy to tear it down, to build cell blocks that did not leak, and toilets that did not smell. And the greatest enemy, boredom, what was there to dispel it, to defeat it? The violence, of course, was the ultimate relief. It also sustained the power of those who watched over us, of those who wanted us deeper in the bog.

My mornings were tinged with gloom and uncertainty; my thoughts concerned that most basic of needs, food, and what there was was niggardly, unfit for human beings, but we were not humans anymore. Old rice with worms and pebbles in it, and dried fish that must have lain in some dank and foul storeroom for ages. It was no different at lunch or supper, and those of us who had no money had no choice, and we devoured it while those who were able to wrangle money from visitors had the canteen to go to, where one could have coffee boiled over three times, the usual cornerstone fare, moldy pieces of pastry, some candy, a few sorry-looking bananas, and other fruit rejects from Divisoria.

I really should not complain, for in that bleak compound I had three meals a day for doing nothing, though on the first day I could barely swallow the rice—not only was it sour, but it was also half-cooked, and as it was brought to the brigade in battered tin drums, it was covered with flies.

It was either the food or the foul air, but I could recognize it at once in the harsh light of day—the inmates had that unmistakable pallor of people in Tondo, the dirty, mottled, pallid skin that hunger brought to people. Indeed, I saw it then so clearly, so implacably real. The Barrio was the far more insidious prison, for while it had no walls, the people in it were really no different from those in this jail.

Something else happened to me in the city jail that I do not want to dwell upon, because it confirms what Roger had told me— the depravity that I had refused to believe and why I was helpless in the face of the power that had defiled me.

I should have had an intimation of it when, several times that day, Bing-Bong came around saying that he had not defecated for some time. But I did not understand their language then.

I could not fight even if I had wanted to; there were four of them who pressed me down on my stomach, pinioned my legs and arms. I felt the sharp point of an ice pick, perhaps the sharpened end of a thick wire, pressed against the back of my neck, the drip of some- thing oily—cooking oil, they later told me—going down my but- tocks, Bing-Bong, the King, grunting behind me, pumping, breathing hard and finally falling on my back like an obnoxious carcass.

This, too, was what Roger had spoken about. I was now initi- ated into this dismal world peopled by those whom I thought I would call my brothers. They were not my kin, for their legs and arms were tattooed. There was this malignant odor of cuspidors and urinals about them and they had the countenance of sick rooms. Their long hair was not the long hair of youth but of necessity. What did they know of dialectics, of responsibility, of nationalism as these have been dinned into us? They were here and I loathed them, for I knew that I could be any one of them, kindred in spirit, if I did not get out as fast as I could.

I was released on the fifth day of my incarceration. Someone was killed that night in the brigade next to ours, and through the iron grills I saw the body carried out of the compound as if it were a butchered pig, the body punctured with knife wounds—faucets, they called it. Chicken told me there was a killing also in our brigade the previous week. But no one talked—and no one asked questions.

I did not even know who had been killed, it was enough that the police saw it necessary to free us, for, in truth, no charges had been filed; we had been detained—that was all.

I went through the same cubicle where we were examined and, again, I stripped to be searched, then went to the desk beyond the wooden railing. The sergeant was eating noodles from a plastic plate; he looked at me perfunctorily and then ransacked his drawer for a sheaf of papers that he brought out, meanwhile looking at me with beady eyes, his mouth bulging with food. The ballpoint pen at his desk refused to write so he stuck it between his lips, moistening its tip, then checked the papers until he found my name.

He kept me standing before his desk, but even at that distance I could smell his underarm odor, so strong and overpowering, I wondered which was stronger, the stench of the prison or that of his body.

"Here," he said finally, taking a gulp from the tall glass of water at his right, "this is your name, is it not?"

I looked at it: Samson, José.

"Sign here," he pointed to the blank bottom line.

I bent over the page and started reading. He stood up and the blow on my head made my ears ring. "I told you to sign," he shouted, "not to read it."

"Yes, sir," I said, and scrawled my name hastily.

"Now, go!"

I walked out of the reception area and into a muddy yard festooned with laundry strung on the barbed wires and on the steel girders that fenced the cell blocks from each other.

I was told I was free—and I was shown the gate, beyond the yard cluttered with jeeps and old cars, past the small pond with the image of the Virgin shielded by a canopy of leaves, the stench of prison still all around me. Then I was out into the torrid heat of Quezon, the crowds eddying around me. I was in familiar territory close to my own university.

BACK IN THE BARRIO I thought it best to tell Father Jess and Tia Nena only that I had merely gone to the province on an unexpected trip for the Brotherhood. I wanted to think about what had happened, ingest it, pummel it, conclude from it.

I wondered why it happened at all and what it had done to me. I have not accepted, and will never accept, the mindless act of Tarzan or the depravity of Bing-Bong as machinations of a supreme will, or even of fate. These men and what they did were the end products of a modern malaise that is spreading like a blob and covers, drowns, disfigures everything—the green of leaves, the fragrance of flowers, the blue of the sky. It is the evil that greed has wrought and these men were transformed; the air they breathed, the food in their stomachs, the sights that pleased them were all infected. They had died,

but they did not know it. Job is not the hero, then, but the villain—
he had known success and affluence, but it was not God who took
these away from him. It was Job himself who prepared his own
downfall. Salvation did not come in his avowal of faith but in his re-
nouncing the values that he had cherished. My torture was not punishment then, nor the humiliation that was heaped on me a
diminution of my being; these were forms of revelation—an awakening from darkness, the coming to life of ashes. If only! Yes, if only
the mind were not part of the body. This is my curse—that while I
could distort and contort the mind, it was the body that yielded, it
was the body that felt and lived and died.

I had thought of death in those nights that I could not sleep. The
young do not think of death, but I have, so I am old. And much as I
love life, I would have to bid it good-bye someday, perhaps soon,
and it was not the living now that really mattered, but the how of it.

In my room the night I was finally freed, the memory of my torture came again, bringing a black, shapeless dread to my very core. I
tried to banish my fear of having become impotent and wondered if
I would ever be a man again. In the morning, when my bladder was
full and I should have awoken with it erect and sticking up from
under the sheet, I realized with some anguish that it was limp.

I asked for fifty pesos from Father Jess, saying I needed it badly,
and then went to Makati.

It was past noon when I got to the Colonial and the after-lunch
crowd from the nearby restaurants had not yet trickled in.

Lily had already checked in. After a brief shower, I went back to
the cubicle. She was waiting at the door. "So, you are rich again," she
said as I drew her in.

She was an expert, she could do what Betsy could not, but I
could not tell either of them what had happened, the details that de-
graded and humiliated me.

"Lily," I said, "I did not come here for a massage. I have problems, emotional problems. Please help me."

She laughed, that soft easy laughter I always liked in her. "Oh,
Pepe, whatever your excuses, I like you just the same." She bent
down and kissed me, and I savored her moist lips, the saccharine recesses of her mouth.

She pulled away the towel I had draped around my waist, then
sat on the narrow shelf and ran her fingers lightly over my chest. My

skin tingled, that sharp, delicious shivering that flowed down to my navel. But it stopped there. Then her hands floated down my legs, behind my knees, my buttocks. But though I felt sensually, delightfully aroused, I was not responding in the only way I wanted to.

"It is useless, Lily," I said grimly.

I was about to rise, but she pushed me down. "You must concentrate," she said. "Think of nothing else but me, and what I'll give you."

I lay on my back again, alive to the smell of cologne, the chatter of people in the passageways. Her expert hands could do nothing.

Then she bent over. I closed my eyes and surrendered—all of me in her mouth, all of me waiting, and then, after a while, she paused and when I opened my eyes, she was gazing at me happily. "I told you I could do it," she said and rose. I had not been sure of what she was doing until she had mounted me, letting it slide neatly into place, then she gripped it, moistly, warmly, and started to gyrate.

"This is called 'the helicopter,' Pepe," she said exultantly.

Tomorrow Is
Ours

I LEFT the Colonial, grateful to Lily for restoring my manhood and at the same time saddened by the knowledge that she had fallen down the abyss. I had said earlier only a slight nudge would be her undoing. I did not blame her.

Looking back, I understood only too well how it had been with me as well, how shamefully craven I had been in my desires. I was convinced that it is the rich who should not compromise because they are strong, not we who are poor, who cannot be steadfast or unswerving when our needs cry for satisfaction.

I cursed myself then for not being made of ironwood or some such granite material so I would be able to withstand the hunger that always knotted my stomach, the gross temptations that had betrayed me. Yet I have known early enough that all of living is a compromise, this was what was pounded into me in Cabugawan, from Mother and my aunt, who never earned enough from all their labors. I knew this even after I had gone with Betsy to that fancy French restaurant, because I had to return to Tondo and to a larder that was ample only because I lived in the *kumbento*.

We compromise ourselves the day we are born. If we are looking for the original sin, there it is: our incapacity to live honestly with ourselves because we are human, because we are shackled by custom, by obligations, and we accept compromise only in the light of our individual conscience, answerable as we are only to ourselves.

This is a world not of black and white but of grays, and it is really in this huge gray geography where we act out our fates. I envy those who have chosen the black or the white, for, to them, they have simplified living. There are no more storms within them to be stilled, no more muddied choices; there is only one intractable way, clear and straight, and they cannot deviate from it.

Toto would not compromise, and if he had lived he would not have changed one bit. He would have come out of it more determined, more convinced not just of the inevitability or the necessity of his revolution, but of its righteousness. This is our hope and our curse because the righteousness exalts, and our curse because we would pursue it as Ka Lucio pursued it long after he, himself, had failed.

But I have learned from the fretfulness of older men, and what, after all, did I need in order to live? I brought back to mind those days that my stomach soured from its being filled with nothing but those abominable greens, and I knew that I could subsist on them forever, the days I saw nothing but the limits of Cabugawan, and within those confines I had wakened in the morning with wonder at the grass wet with dew, a sky swept clean. This feeling surged in me, I could do anything and God up there was smiling. Indeed, there was nothing for me to expiate in this miasma called Tondo, nothing in the world has changed but me. I had known what was beyond the stone highway and the railroad tracks. I had traversed not distance but depth, and when the discovery was over and revelation had come not as wisdom but as masochistic sorrow, there was still this me that longed not for more journeys or more sensual knowledge, but the pith, the marrow of living, why so many of us are mired in Tondo. This is, of course, no cabalistic question. I had known the answer way back, only now it must be made real.

I must no longer compromise.

Marcos, jail the young, jail all those who oppose your oligarchy and your grandiose plans. Imprison us, torture us, for by doing so you will swell our piteous ranks, you will temper us with the harshness of truth so that we will rise from the flames singed and wounded but, by God, infinitely more steadfast and strong.

THEN, November. The rains no longer lash down as frequently as in the earlier months, but the alleys of the Barrio are still murky with puddles, and from under the houses and along the shallow canals the odor of putrefaction rises like an implacable curse. But November presages Christmas, and even before the middle of the month, the radios are already noisy with carols, so that while there is darkness all around, there is, somehow, the promise of light.

The Brotherhood had been very active, and Roger and his boys had drawn up a list of the poorest of our poor. They had started making the rounds of the offices in Santa Cruz and Binondo asking for gift pledges.

Even Tia Nena, now that Toto was no longer with us, had to think far ahead; this morning, she was aglow—not that absentminded expression she had on her face sometimes, but a beatific smile that radiated warmth. She came to my room and started poking into the boxes that were piled in one corner, the Christmas lights that we would string in front of the church, the lanterns that folded that were to be dusted and hung in the lobby of the *kumbento*. She had been flitting about with this happy countenance the whole morning and it seemed as if she had gotten over the death of Toto.

She had found the colored lights, the sockets, and tested them. She sat on the stool opposite me, folding her gnarled, thin hands on her lap, her eyes squinting in the sunlight that poured down the alley into our room.

"Pepe, you have been here a long time. And you have done many things, made changes . . ."

"Not really, Tia," I said, wondering what was in her mind.

"Well, you have. Padre Jesus is happy with the Brotherhood—the young people working together, their attendance in church, their activities."

"It is nothing," I said. "I just befriended them, that's all."

"No," she said, "it is not just being friends. You know them, you understand them."

"Because I come from a village, Tia. I never really left it."

After some silence, "Pepe, there is something you do not know and I do not think Padre Jesus ever told you. I come from the same town as you."

I looked at her incredulously.

"You do not believe it?" she asked, her eyes crinkling. She was now speaking in Ilocano. "I do not speak like this often. There are many things I want to forget. Padre Jesus can tell you—he picked me up in Divisoria where I was staying, sleeping in the empty stalls, helping whoever wanted to be helped. It is not difficult for an old woman to stay alive."

"I pity you, Tia."

"There are events I don't remember now—months I was not well, that I was not myself as they would say. But everything is clearer now and I am grateful to Padre Jesus. You said you came from Cabugawan? Of course, I knew people there. I am from Sipnget. We—my father— They came from the Ilocos, too. Did you know that there was a big brick house in the town? It was burned, rebuilt, then burned again. Did you know that?"

I nodded.

"I worked there," she said, her eyes downcast. "The first house, that was where I learned Spanish—I was very young." Then she was quiet and her eyes misted.

"You don't have to tell me anything, Tia."

"I had two sons, Victor and Luis, but I lost them both. And my father, too. So I have nothing—nothing but memories. And when I lost them my mind gave way. But even now, I still carry with me their letters. And sometimes, when I want to go back to the past, I read them one by one. One by one."

She stood up and went to the open window; outside, the sun was a flood upon the Barrio.

"How is it now in Sipnget?" she asked, but did not expect a reply. "The fields must be golden, the rice as high as a man. I remember the palms, the martins there. In the dry season we used to tap them for sap that we sold as drink or boiled into sugar. You know that, don't you?"

I nodded again.

"And the tobacco fields in Carmay. I wonder if they still plant tobacco there. They used to grow so tall, their leaves so huge. We would string them and dry them below the houses. Ours were the best, good enough to be *ba-ac*. You know that?"

I nodded although I was not too sure. "This Christmas, would you like to go to Rosales again, Tia? A short visit?" I asked.

"And whom would I see there? I don't know where my sons are buried, or my father. I don't know where to go and pray for their souls."

"You can come home with me."

"Yes," she said, turning to me, her face agleam. "I should go back. I hope that day will come very soon."

With Toto gone, she was drawn closer to me as we consoled each other with our presence, our thoughts. She had asked about Betsy, how she was, and because I told her that Betsy was in the Brotherhood, that she was in the same demonstration where Toto had been killed, she now regarded her with some affection.

"How does the future look to you, Pepe?" she asked after a while. "If you go back to Rosales, will you bring Betsy with you?"

I shook my head.

"Her family, I am sure, looks down on you," she said. "But you are smart; you will flourish without help from anyone, least of all her family. When you have done that, then they will respect you."

"You are not wrong, Tia," I said. "Her parents loathe me. They are sending Betsy away, very soon, to America, so that she will no longer see me."

Tia Nena shook her head. "I hope she loves you enough to wait, maybe a long time, but you never know how steadfast women can be. You will see. And someday, I hope she will marry you."

BUT BETSY did not marry me. She came to Tondo for the last time in late November; her father had returned and her mother was going to take her to New York the next day. She had just returned from Bacolod, where she had spent the semester break.

I had gone to Divisoria with Tia Nena to help carry the food that she bought for the week, and when we got to the Barrio, Betsy's Volks was parked in the alley that led to the church. She had enough problems; I decided not to tell her about my torture and the city jail.

Father Jess was with her in the *kumbento*. She had had a long talk with him, for he looked serious and said we should be alone. She had acquired a bit of a tan and her hand, when she held mine, had roughened a little.

"What did you tell him?" I asked.

"What I came to tell you."

The receiving room of the *kumbento* was shabby—a cracked cement floor, uneven, wooden sidings, images of the Virgin and the Nazarene, a shelf of religious publications and high-backed rattan chairs that had begun to fall apart. But everything was clean, Roger and I saw to that—no mud, no dust, even the cement floor was polished. Although the cool season had started and there was a long pause in the rains, it was still gummy and warm, and beads of sweat glistened on her brow. I reached out, caressed her forehead and brought my wet fingertip to my tongue, tasting her sweat. "Very stale," I said.

She smiled, shaking her head. "I am so tense not knowing what to think, and you keep teasing me."

Though she was perspiring, her hand was cold.

"Pepe," she finally said, blushing and unable to look at me. "Please marry me."

I wanted to embrace her then—how precious little time we had! I tried to suppress the tremor in my voice. "Betsy, I do not have a job. I am not even finished with college . . ."

"I don't want to go to New York," she whispered. "And I don't want you to go to the mountains. I want you with me."

I shook my head.

"I have some savings, about twenty thousand. I have been quite frugal, you know, and I am from Negros. No new dresses the last three years unless Mama bought them. Or Papa. I have some jewelry. And the Volks is in my name—I can sell it."

I shook my head again. "Please don't be angry. I don't want it this way."

"I knew you would say that. But we can live cheaply anywhere. I will not complain . . . I promise."

I leaned over and pressed her hand. It was still cold.

"You will not mind in the beginning," I said. "Then you will be missing many things—comforts you have been used to. And I don't want you to make sacrifices for me. You . . . you caring, it is more than enough. Besides, you are very young."

"I am twenty. I do not need their permission anymore."

"Not that," I said. "You will be angry with me later. That is in the cards. You will regret what you have done. You don't know how it is to be hungry. How to live in places like this. I want you to have a good life. I want no regrets."

"I know what I am doing," she was determined.

"Did you tell Father Jess?"

She nodded.

"Everything?"

"No," she said, smiling. "But he guessed. No, Pepe, I am not pregnant, but I wish I were so I can have a hold on you"—she pinched my arm—"then you would have to make an honorable woman out of me."

I would not have shirked that responsibility, but I also did not want to appear as having taken advantage of her. Always, I could not forget Carmen Villa and my father.

"Betsy," I said, "we are one."

She looked at me gratefully and whispered, "Thank you . . . thank you."

"We must wait. You will go to New York and be there for a year, two years. You may forget me, but I will not forget you."

We were silent again.

She knew I had made up my mind. "Tell Father Jess I am leaving. And come with me. We cannot part like this."

Father Jess was in his room, waiting. "Well," he asked, "what have you decided?"

"I cannot do it, Father," I said. "What can I offer her? What kind of life would she live?"

He was silent even as we went down to the reception room. Betsy had stood up and was looking out of the window, into the alleys, the decrepit homes, the laundry flapping in the morning breeze, the bare-bottomed and skinny children playing in the multipurpose center.

They talked in Visayan, some of which I understood, then they switched to Spanish, saying good-bye, and Father Jess asked when she would be back, and she said, "If Pepe wants me back, immediately!" And I said in Spanish, "I will always want you here, but life decrees that you should be there."

It was the first time she heard me speak in Spanish and she was delighted. "Pepe, you never told me!"

Father Jess said, "He is now trying to write in Spanish, too."

He followed us to the door. "I will perform the wedding gladly, Betsy," he said. "It would be an honor. So hurry back."

WE DROVE quietly to Malate. Again, she parked at the churchyard and we walked over to the Mabini coffee shop. It was the second time we were there, and as in the first, we were again beset by this impermeable gloom. "We will miss you not only in the committee," I said, trying to cheer her up, "but when we plan the big demonstration in January."

"Write to me about it. Write to me every day if you can. I will write to you every day."

"It costs money," I said. "I will write often, but mail the letters once a week."

She settled for that. Our hamburgers and coffee came. The coffee shop wallpaper was in green, so was the upholstery.

"And my thoughts," I told her, "are also green."

We would go to our first motel again. "You will see the Golden Gate bridge in San Francisco. Write to me about it."

"With my blood," she said, and we laughed for the first time. We laughed so hard, the waitress looked at us, puzzled; the last time we were here, we had not bothered to eat. Now, we ate with ravenous appetites. I ordered two more hamburgers to take out.

I had somehow hoped that we would get the same room, but we did not. We were here in the beginning and, now, the end. We took our time; she lay beside me in that soft wide bed and we just kissed and talked, savoring our nearness. Her flight the following day would be in the late afternoon. She did not want me at the airport, but I said I would go, that I would keep to the shadows and watch her from a distance, far from her friends and her parents. Even if I did get close, they would probably not recognize me, but hell, I did not want Betsy to leave with me unable to see her.

The hamburgers came in handy before noon, but we were still hungry, so we ordered soft drinks and fried chicken. When the boy came with our order and asked us how long we would stay, I told him, till dusk. She was supposed to be out with friends, saying good-bye; it did not matter anymore if her parents found out. They would have their way anyway.

I was not going to make the day more bleak. "One day," I said, "I would like to take you to a place I used to go to. Nothing like your hilltop. But it is also isolated—on a hill with no one there."

"Your favorite spot?"

"You can call it that. An old steel bridge spans this creek and there were once rails on it. The train no longer comes so the rails were torn up, stolen and sold as scrap, but the high mound is there still. You walk on its crest, the grass thick upon it. Then you come to this black, rusting bridge and, below, the calmest, clearest pond, with reeds and lotuses. I used to swim there, gather snails, and I would sleep below the bridge, on one of the big, black girders. The whole world is quiet. Nothing but the wind rippling the water, the chirp of birds, and, above, the blue sky. Down the slope of the hill is a thatch-roofed shack with a split bamboo floor. The farmers rest in it during the harvesting or planting. I slept there once all night."

"You were not afraid?"

"Mother was angry and she scolded me when I returned the next morning. What was there to be afraid of? The crickets, the dogs howling in the distant village? The cocks crowing?"

"We could sleep there one night," she said.

"It may no longer be there," I said. She was dreaming, as I was; she had never slept on a bamboo floor.

She opened her bag. "I wonder if your father did the same thing," she said, bringing out her copy of Father's book, and she let me read her inscription: *To my dear husband—whose past, present, and future, I hope, may also be mine.*

"Be kind to his memory," she said. "I asked a lot of questions about him from Mama. That is why she is so concerned. He really did not have a chance. He committed suicide, that I now believe."

"I will never do that," I said.

"Live for me," she said.

I pressed her hand.

"Read the last chapter again. It is the most perceptive commentary on us."

"I will," I promised her.

She drew out from her bag a small packet of black velvet. It contained two rings, silvery and shiny. She brought them close so I could see the inside. The bigger one had her name and the small one had mine. "Look at the date," she said.

I had difficulty reading it.

"Remember?"

I do not have a good memory for dates but I knew.

"The first time," she said.

I kissed her as she gave me her ring to slip onto her finger. It was quite heavy and I asked why.

"Platinum," she said.

She took my left hand and slipped the ring on my finger. It fit snugly. "I was too optimistic, I guess," she said. "But we are one nonetheless."

I embraced her and promised myself I would never take it off. My chest was tightening. "There are things I will never understand," I said, my throat sandpapery. "Simple things like . . . like breathing. And these precious things I will lose not to some enemy but to my own cowardice."

"You are wrong," she said. "It is not cowardice. It is honesty."

"I am not honest. I have been selfish, and as your mother said, if I loved you, I would let you go, because with me there is no future."

"I have made the choice," she said, clinging to me.

"It is fate," I said humbly.

"Don't hide behind words."

"I wish I could still hide," I said. "But not anymore. I must face it. Here I am—unable to be with you, to have an open relationship. I must do what is right."

"And what is that?"

"It sounds so melodramatic," I said, "as if it is all lifted from those cheap Tagalog movies, the dialogues those nitwits are churning out for the housemaids. Let me tell you how and I'd like to listen to it myself, this big moment. Now really is the time for us to say good-bye—"

"You do not mean it," she said, pressing her face to my chest.

"Of course, I mean it. But how can I forget? You are now part of my life," the words were pouring out. "You are here within me, in my blood, the air in my lungs, the juices in my stomach. Listen now, what your mother wants is for you to have a good life, marry well—

even someone ugly—but someone not like me, a castaway. What future is there with me? Nothing but sorrow. Your place is there, among your kind. You are asleep now, and when you wake up, what then?"

She said simply, "I want to be with you, awake or asleep."

I disregarded her. "You will grow older and someone soon enough will come knocking on your door."

She did not speak.

"Thank you, Betsy, for everything."

She hugged me, her heart thrashing against my chest, her body shaking as she cried soundlessly. That would help ease this last sorrow I had inflicted on her.

The Dawn Is Red

I GO BACK to Tondo, my accursed present, my consecrated future. I have learned so much here and I know myself now as I never did before. My needs were so basic—a stomach, for instance, that had to be filled. Contemplation is a luxury that could waylay and lull me into forgetting that my hunger was just a symptom of a far greater need . . . all those we emblazoned in the streets, our placards crying for justice, for revolution—they had sounded so hopelessly unreal. Not anymore.

Beyond the houses the sea slammed on the seawall, bringing with it the perennial stench of oil and rotting fish and all the accumulated smells of the cesspool that the bay had become. In the late evenings when the bray of traffic had died down and the living noises had been stilled, I sometimes went out to the narrow churchyard, the night arched above me, alive with the pungencies of the swamp and above the narrow ring of rooftops, the sky—how serene and distant the stars. It brought to mind how it was in the fields of Rosales at night when I was alone in that thatched farmer's shed, surrounded by the dark that pulsed and heaved around me with the scent of grass, the crickets alive in the folds of the earth. It seemed then that I could hear my heart, my thoughts as they took shape, and it seemed, too, that there was peace—lasting and deep—only because I was alone.

Now I was alone again, surrounded by these melancholy shapes, these decrepit lives. I would always be alone, I could rely on no one but myself. A poet said that the strongest man is he who stands alone—but there was no strength in me, only this wanton disregard for time that would bring me nothing but unhappiness, a desolation of the spirit in which there would be no resurrection, no green shoot to nourish so that it would grow, as the bamboo grows. I would die, but this was no longer so horrible a fate, an abomination to be feared, for at least I would be able to do something with my life and not just breathe the foul air or fill to overflowing this pit that is my stomach.

ON THE DAY before the Misa de Gallo* started Juan Puneta came to Tondo. He had left messages everywhere, in the *kumbento,* at the office of the school paper, at Professor Hortenso's house, and once his driver came saying he wanted to see me. I had made excuses, but now there was no avoiding him. Father Jess received him as I was in the sacristy, helping Roger and the members of the Brotherhood string the colored lightbulbs for the church front.

"Ah, Pepito," he said, embracing me like a brother he had not seen in ages. He was in a khaki safari suit. He smelled of cologne.

"I have wanted to see you for some time now. Where have you been?"

"I'm sorry, sir," I said, "I have been working hard—you see, my scholarship . . ."

"I still would like very much to take you to the house. We have so many things to discuss."

"But I have work to do. We are finishing the Christmas decorations and . . ."

"It is all right, Pepe," Father Jess interrupted me. "Roger can take care of that."

I turned to Father Jess, but he could not read my urgent signals,

* *Misa de Gallo:* Midnight mass held between December 16 and Christmas Eve.

and having no more excuses, I sighed as Father Jess walked us to the door.

"He will be back before lunch, Padre," Juan Puneta said.

A blue Mercedes 280 SE was parked on the street and it was Juan Puneta who drove.

"I have so many things to tell you," he gushed. "But first, tell me how you have been. I hear that the next demonstration will really be big. Are you prepared for it—I mean for the violence that will surely come?"

"We are now prepared," I said.

He was silent. "What about the things that the Huk commander was going to write?"

"Ka Lucio?"

He nodded.

"He was murdered," I said. "Didn't you know?"

He looked surprised.

"The police came, asked questions. It was not even mentioned in the newspapers. Who would care for an ex-Huk commander in the first place?"

"I hope you learned a lot from him," Puneta said. We were going over Del Pan bridge and soon we would be in another country, the antiseptic, manicured boulevard, then the golden ghetto of Makati.

"Nothing. Nothing," I lied. I had asked Cora after Ka Lucio's funeral if there was anything he had written that I could read. But there was nothing; she knew of the ruled pad where he was writing, but it could not be found. We searched his bookcase, his desk, but it was not there.

"It is sad, very sad," Puneta kept repeating and cracking his knuckles as we paused in the traffic.

Puneta's house was at the other end of the Park, shaded by giant acacia trees on whose trunks clambered vines and orchids. At the gate he got out and unlocked the door, then we drove in. The grounds were surrounded by a tall ivy-covered wall—an expanse of green, well-trimmed grass, hedges. At the far end was a pool, and still farther, a stable.

Puneta parked in the driveway. No one was in the house, not a guard, not a maid. "The maids' day off and they will not be back till five in the afternoon. As for my wife, she has gone with the kids to visit her mother. They will not be back till this afternoon. Which is very good—we can talk without interruption. Then we can go down and shoot, have a meal. I cook, you know. You can help. And someday, you should try my *caldereta.*"

This is it. This is where I pay back the five hundred.

We went to the kitchen where he prepared two cups of coffee. It was nothing like Tia Nena's cubbyhole; it was airy and as wide as the whole *kumbento* itself; on one side, an array of stoves, ovens on the wall. On another, cabinets, a giant freezer, and a refrigerator. The breakfast nook as he called it adjoined the kitchen, actually an antiseptic-looking dining room by itself.

"I was not able to report to you on the money you gave me," I said. "I gave three hundred pesos to Cora, Ka Lucio's niece, for the funeral. I spent some of it myself—and, yes, I have found the best sauna in town." I was watching him, looking for a sign that would betray him, but his ivory mestizo face was bereft of expression. "I have been to three of them, but the best is in Makati. The Colonial."

Not even a flicker of interest.

"We should go there one day then. Now, if possible, but it does not really open till noon," I continued.

"That's interesting," he merely commented. "Yes, we should go there. But that is pretty tame, Pepito. We can go to another place where there are girls—as well as boys."

Now the proposition.

"It is quite expensive . . . but money is no problem. If you want girls. Or boys."

I smiled. "I prefer girls," I said. "As for the boys—"

"Are you willing to try?"

I was about to answer, but the phone jangled. He picked it up and said, "Hello," then he spoke in Spanish. "Yes, but wait, there is someone here with me. I will answer you in the bedroom. Call again." He hung up the phone and to me, he said in Tagalog, "A moment—"

He left and soon the phone rang again. On the second ring, when it was interrupted, I picked it up, too.

They were speaking in Spanish again: "Who is that with you?" the voice at the other end was anxious.

"Just one of those dumb village boys. But it is all right, I am here in the bedroom and he is in the kitchen. Besides, he cannot understand Spanish. What is it, *chico*?"

The man seemed frantic. "What is this I hear about another big demonstration in January? Shall we tell our men to work on the kids again? They want more money this time. After all there were more than ten killed in the last . . ."

"Of course, of course," Juan Puneta said with exasperation. "They have to be there. Always, I don't care how many get killed. They must simply make sure that the kids will blame the Metrocom, the police, for everything."

"They already do that."

"Make the fire hotter," Puneta said, "and money is of no consequence, as you know. You can pick up my share at the Casino tomorrow."

"The Army and Navy Club," the other man said, "I have a lunch there."

"All right then."

"Anything new from Tondo or from Tarlac?"

"After that Huk commander in Tondo was disposed of, nothing new," Juan Puneta said.

"Tomorrow then," the man said, and hung up. I waited till Puneta had put the phone down; then I put mine down, too.

HOW NEATLY everything was falling into place. Mrs. Hortenso was right after all, and Betsy, too—one could depend on women and their intuition. But since men depend so much on logic and verifiable data, well, here they were. Betsy had told me how Puneta had traveled in style, the same way he had come to Tondo, in his big, fat Continental. He used a helicopter to ferry his ice, his caviar, and his pâté to those distant and forgotten mountainfolds where he hunted—a reconnaissance of the battlefields of the future. His gun collection was public knowledge though few had seen it. How convenient it was for a rich man like him to have his arsenal right here, legitimate, open—all in the name of hobby.

I went to the cabinets where the saucers and cups were and started setting the table. The water had started to boil and I was taking it off the electric stove when he joined me.

"I am sorry for the interruption," he said, "an important business call." He saw what I had done and he smiled. "You really don't waste time." He brought the Nescafé. "A special European blend." He continued, "We were talking about my favorite subject, sex. What have you got against boys?"

"Nothing," I said. "Nothing really."

"That's good. We will have plenty of time. Now, I must show you my shooting range."

We left the coffee cups in the sink. I followed him across the vast, carpeted living room to a corridor lined with paintings, on to the master bedroom and beyond, a mirror with a carved gilt frame that occupied the whole end of the corridor. He pressed a button behind a small picture frame and the mirror swung open to reveal a red-carpeted stairway. It led down to a brilliantly lit cavern underneath the house.

"Surprise, surprise," he said, grinning. "Only my best friends know this place, Pepito. You are one of the anointed few. It is completely soundproof."

"Thank you, sir," I said.

"I have been collecting for a long time now," he explained. A whole wall was lined with guns, carefully oiled. At one end of the hall were target frames, ever ready for shooting. He walked to the first cabinet. "There," he said, "is one of the earliest guns used by the Spaniards in the eighteenth century. And that is a Mauser over there, used during the revolution. And yes, that blunderbuss over there. And *lantaka*—" he pointed to a Muslim brass cannon as stout as a coconut trunk.

"What is your favorite, sir?" I asked.

"Handgun or rifle?"

I didn't know the difference.

"Well, these old ones—that Krag over there, those Garands, and these Thompsons. They are all serviceable. Even that Nambu machine gun over there—" a sleek, futuristic-looking gun, mounted on a tripod; it stood on a platform with six other machine guns. "You know, it is in working order. The Japanese made it, and according to ordnance intelligence it is the best machine gun the Japanese produced. The caliber is small, but its velocity is terrific."

We walked over to a cabinet with more rifles and shotguns. About two dozen of them, and he paused before one particular long-barreled rifle. "This is the Winchester magnum," he said. "It has range, power. It can stop a charging elephant in its tracks."

"Have you shot one, sir?"

"Of course," he said expansively. "I have been on safaris in Africa. In Ceylon, we hunted leopards. And, of course, Sumatran tigers—" He pointed to three tiger skins on the floor.

We stopped before a table case, glass-topped, and, within, an array of handguns—revolvers, automatics, and small-caliber pistols that could be held in one's palm. He slid open the glass panel and picked out a revolver, its barrel a shiny blue. "This is considered the world's finest revolver," he said. "And I am partial to it. Revolvers don't jam. Unlike automatics. Remember that shoot-out in a nightclub two months ago?"

He turned to me, the revolver in his hand. "The other fellow's 45 jammed. That's how he got killed. As you can see"—he held the gun before me—"it has a ventilated rib, adjustable ramp-type front sights, and it can use both the 357 magnum and the 38 special . . . and the magnum, of course, has great power." He placed the revolver back in the case, then picked up the one beside it. He held it before me and this time, his face was really aglow. "And this . . . this is really my favorite. It's the Smith & Wesson 44-caliber magnum. It has six bullets . . . here." He let me hold the thing. It was heavy and massive. "The 8⅜-inch barrel gives it great accuracy and power. The sights are adjustable. At a hundred yards, if you are really good, you can't miss. It is the most powerful handgun in the world. I have six of them."

He brought out another. "Loaded. All of them," he warned.

We positioned ourselves at the shooting bar. After he adjusted my earmuffs his hands went down my arms and hips. I let him.

He moved away, stood at the bar, his feet planted apart, then he aimed and fired. Even with the earplugs, the roar was deafening.

He nudged at me. I aimed and fired and the gun almost jumped out of my hand. We raised our earmuffs.

"Actually," he said, "the pros will tell you to shoot with both hands. It's steadier that way." We walked over to the targets. His was off center. Mine was a bull's-eye. Beginner's luck!

"Hey," he said, squeezing my hand, "you are good!"

"The gun almost fell," I said.

"Hold it tight," he said. "And don't breathe when you fire. Your finger should be light on the trigger. And don't pull—squeeze."

We went back to the shooting bar. "I can make bullets here," he said. "I have gunpowder. So don't throw away the empty shells."

I asked what started him on this expensive and dangerous hobby.

"Fucking," he said simply. "After shooting, I get a terrific erection and I feel like fucking till I am dead."

Then I told him: "You should have done the shooting yourself at that Malacañang demonstration where so many were killed. You would have had a hundred orgasms."

He looked at me surprised, puzzled.

"What are you trying to say?" He lowered his gun on the shooting bar. I still held mine.

"When you took that call I listened on the extension," I said simply.

He drew back, the shock clear as sunlight on his face.

"What did you hear? You understand Spanish?"

"Everything, your contributions." I went into the details.

He fumbled for words then straightened up, the smile still on.

"You know," I said, my anger under complete control. "I was in the front when we were fired upon."

"More will be killed," he said finally. "What did you think it would be, a picnic?"

I repeated the cliché: "You can't make an omelet without breaking eggs."

"You may make the omelet but you won't eat it," he said patronizingly. He had regained his composure.

"Who will?"

"We will," he said, the grin plastered on his face again. "Not only because we have the money. More important, with money, we have been able to develop the brains. And if we can't have brains, we buy them."

"Like you are trying to buy me now?"

He laughed in spite of himself. "Pepito, you are very sharp," he said brightly. "Of course! This is why I brought you here. To convince you. Living in that dump, working for that priest—that is not your future, *hijo*. Your future is much brighter. The gates of Pobres Park are open to everyone, you know that. You are welcome—as long as you abide by the rules. Let the scum fight for the crumbs. Ours is the cake. And we are not going to give this cake away. No, *hijo*. We cannot lose. Can you not see? If anarchy comes, do you know what will happen? We are in the movement, too, as you already know. We are promoting it, with friends like you. As for the genuine rebels, like Ka Lucio, we will see to it that they are either discredited or destroyed. We have no room for them. And if the government—meaning the president—decides to put an end to the anarchy and declare a dictatorship, excellent!"

"I do not follow," I said, although everything was falling neatly into place; Juan Puneta was not really telling me anything new.

"Have you forgotten that we have money? We send our children to the best schools—Paris, London, Boston—well, some of them may have flirted with communism, with socialism, that is the privilege of youth. But they are ours, they know where their interests lie. They are not going to be traitors to their class. They are everywhere—in business, in government, in politics. They know what is happening. They know what is going to happen. With brains, you are always one step ahead."

"I still do not understand," I said, urging him on.

He was now the epitome of eloquence: "We—" he said with a flourish of hands, "we are going to be here for a long time. As a matter of fact, for always. We know how to change, and that is why we will always be on top. But the change comes from us, dictated by us. And as for the president, his interests are with us; he is one of us! Not with the masses—ha, the masses! That's wonderful for speeches. They could not care less for the class struggle, for ideology. Do you know, Pepito, that all they want is a roof over their heads? And three bowls of rice a day? You yourself said that. And most of all, they want a sense of order, of security. It is really that simple. Their perception of the world, of society, is dictated by their needs, and we will give them what they want, slowly, slowly. Never the pie. Just the crumbs. It has to be that way. In trade, our labor must be cheap so that we can compete. Yes, we will talk about social justice, land reform, but we will not give these in cash or in kind. We have to keep them nailed to the plow, to the machine—and we will do it deliberately because cheap labor is one of our real assets. And we will not give it up. The president— Any leader will understand it, approve of it. The president is with us. He likes to be surrounded by people who understand the impulses of power. Only the powerful know what these are. And the powerful are the rich. We will flock around him— pamper him, kowtow to him, and then suffocate him! And he won't even realize it, for this is what dictators have always been—partial to panderers. How dictators love them! Study your history books, Pepito. Have they really abolished the elite in Moscow? In Peking? They will always be with us, like death and taxes."

"Like death," I said quietly. "But why are you telling me all this?"

"Because I want you to know. So that you will work for us."

"And what will I get?"

"Anything you need. The future is not with the poor, you know that. It is always with the rich."

"How did you get that way?"

"By exploiting the poor. I love exploiting the poor." He laughed quickly, but his laughter sounded hollow.

"It was more than that." I remembered his ancestry. "You are very proud of your ancestry. But your grandfather sold out the revolution and went over to the Spaniards. Then it was the Americans, and the Japanese. Now you will subvert the revolution again and claim it as yours."

"That is the way it has always been," he grinned. "The elite always wins in the end, Pepito. How can you ever get rid of it? How can you ever run the country without the elite? And the masses don't make revolution, you know that, too."

"Have you read Antonio Samson's book?"

He nodded. "A lot of meaningless phrases strung together with hypocrisy. He married into the Villa family, you know that."

"He committed suicide," I said.

"That's a joke," he laughed again. "Not after marrying into the Villas. Why should he kill himself?"

"Some people are convinced he committed suicide," I insisted.

"Suicide, accident, does it matter? The important thing is that he married into the Villa family. And Don Manuel never tires of talking about him, particularly now in his senility! As if Samson was some genius, merely because he had a Harvard Ph.D. The doors are wide open to those who are bright, Pepito. And one of the shortcuts is marriage—if you have what it takes. You can marry Betsy—" he shook a finger at me, insinuating that he knew.

"She has left; she is in New York," I said.

"You can follow her, *hijo*," he said. "You can easily go there. Scholarships—there are so many of them floating around. Or I can send you—if you would consider the price."

"What do I have to do?" I was curious.

He clapped with enthusiasm, "Now you are really talking! First, *hijo*, there's me, my personal needs—that's not difficult for you. I am easy to please. Then help us, Pepito. We will control the Brotherhood. We'll control Malacañang, the army, surround power centers with our people, who are more pliable, more understanding of our aspirations."

The nationalist bourgeoisie—Professor Hortenso had warned us against them.

"Knowing all these now"—his chest thrust out, his eyes gleamed, and his thick lips pursed in satisfaction—"I hope you will not bargain too hard. After all, it is only money. It can easily be settled."

"Why are you so sure about my price?"

He drew away, appraised me as if I were a hunk of meat, then said in that half-mocking, half-serious tone he always affected when he wanted to stress a point, "I still cannot understand how you did it . . . well, she is very pretty, but Nick said you knew there were a dozen of us behind that mirror."

"Money," I said, not bothering to explain or deny my performance with Kuya Nick's mistress. "That is what made me do it."

He came to me, gripped my shoulder. "I meant no offense, Pepito. This is what I like about you. You know what you want. Some time soon you should consider having a male partner like me. It could be more interesting. And pleasurable. I pay much, much more. I am glad it is so easy to talk with you. Still, I couldn't understand how you could do it."

"Or how any other *toro* can do it?"

"Yes!"

I wanted to tell him of the great difference between body and spirit, that this separateness was always clear to those who knew. Puneta may have traveled widely, traversed diverse regions of the mind and wallowed in the pleasures of the body, but he had never made that crossing that would deem him more than an effete bundle of nerves; he would never understand why prostitutes would heave and moan and have their bodies possessed but would never allow their mouths to be kissed. He would never understand, and I would not now explain it to him.

"It is all a matter of will," I said.

"Will, determination, single-mindedness. You have it, Pepito. This is the single most important factor in any enterprise, whether it is playing *toro* or modernizing a country. Only those with will can achieve. And we will modernize this country," he exalted, "the way only we can do it. Go back to your Asian history. It was not the peasants who changed Japan; it was the elite—the shoguns, the samurai. And that is what we are."

So then, this is how it will be; they talk about modernization, about increases in the gross national product, and they want the bright young minds—honed in the best universities in America—to work and raise this country and these people from the garbage dump of history up to the dizzying heights of air-conditioned bedrooms, flush toilets, and paved streets. They can do this and they will do it because that is the iron compulsion of the times, and the rationale behind it is nationalism. They will use Rizal and all the bones of the illustrious dead to be the foundation of their dreams, and they will be self-righteous and self-satisfied, for they are convinced theirs is the true light, that they are acting on behalf of the people, and they know what is best for the clod, the toilers—the dumb carabaos that plow the fields. But who will talk about the dignity of men, about the living wage, the education of children, the care of the sick? Manila's hospitals are abattoirs; the districts of the poor are nightmare swamplands. The highest officials go abroad on shopping sprees with the people's money; why should their subalterns do less when the most powerful have secret bank accounts and the other accoutrements of luxury for which they have robbed the people? And we are asked to support them, to believe them—they who have drained us of our blood, who have tortured us and raped us. More than these, we are supposed to love our bondage because it is the mark of our allegiance to nation and, therefore, to God. If in the past we had done it, it was because we did not know; we had been bound to them by a mistaken sense of loyalty, by gratitude, because we felt then that we would not survive without their kindness, their patronage. But it is different now. Our eyes have been opened. Certainly not by them, but by the fact that we cannot be deceived forever. Now we will fling back to them the very sop with which they have tried to drown our protests. Nationalism means us, for we are the nation and the vengeance we seek will never be sated till we have gotten measure for measure all that was stolen from us. I live in Tondo, I came from Cabugawan. I want not just the irrevocable end to my poverty but justice as well.

I raised the magnum; the despair commingled with surprise on Juan Puneta's face was appalling, but it did not deter me. I fired and the impact was so strong, it seemed as if he was lifted off his feet then flung down. My earmuffs were not on. The explosion crashed in my ears, and for some time I could not hear.

He had died instantly and the red on his shirtfront now spread. I took my handkerchief, wiped my gun carefully and placed it in his right hand. His hand would have powder marks, too, I've read about that. I took his gun and put it in my pocket. I had difficulty moving him and removing his wallet. It had a thousand pesos, mostly in fifties. I took five hundred.

I opened the cabinets—all were without locks—and took another magnum. Boxes of the ammo were in the same cabinet as the guns; eight were enough. I went up to the ground floor and was briefly apprehensive, for the door of the shooting range was locked. I pushed and it opened.

In the master bedroom most of the rosewood cabinets were open—a hundred suits, the finery of Pobres Park, but there was really nothing of value there. I remembered his keychain. I returned to the range and removed it from his pocket. I was careful not to leave fingerprints on the cabinets as I opened them. In one was his wife's jewels lined up neatly in ivory-inlaid boxes. I did not know much about jewelry, but I did get a couple of diamond rings, a brooch—nothing more; I did not want them missed. On his writing table was a steel cash box. It contained stacks of dollar and peso bills, all in denominations of fifty and one hundred. I took half of its contents.

I returned to the range, put the keys in his pocket. Back in the kitchen, I washed the cups and saucers, placed them in the wall cabinet. The kitchen was as spotless as when I got there. When I walked out of the house, there was no one in the quiet mango-lined street. All the neighboring houses had high walls and all their massive iron gates were closed.

The paper bag I was carrying was heavy. On top of the guns and the ammo was the day's papers. I walked down the street leisurely. At the gate of the Park I had a moment of fright; the private guards were examining a taxicab and opening its trunk.

But they did not bother with me—just another houseboy going to market.

Filipinos, Wake Up!

IBOARDED the bus for Quiapo at EDSA. I must see Professor Hortenso, tell him what I had done, then leave Manila for wherever he would send me. I brought to mind our talks, the small confidences he had shared with me, and it was then that I realized with some sadness that he did not really tell me much. Perhaps because I was not trusted; perhaps because my actions were determined by animal needs and not by some unswerving ideal. This should have been clear to me when I was being tortured—and it was just as well, for I would have told my torturers everything. I had skills, I had helped, but the compulsions of my stomach and my gonads, and not the dictates of a committed mind, determined my waking hours. I was an instrument to be manipulated, and though I had the right credentials, I was naive, I was an "adventurist," not "intellectual" enough to understand and accept the ideological basis for revolution.

It all came to me, the discussions with Ka Lucio about the morality of violence. I was surprised that there was not a single qualm in me when it was my turn to do the ultimate. I had acted in passion, and now that my mind was calmer, I realized that what I had done really was nothing more than an extension of my desire to live, and that I had simply given back the violence that was inflicted on me, not so much by Puneta himself but by the instruments he created and supported. I may have acted in anger and vengeance, but also in righteousness. It is we or they, Ka Lucio had said. It was I or him, and my knowledge and acceptance of this made everything clear. The gods who manipulated the Brotherhood may mistrust me, may not include me in their councils—my friends and mentors like Professor Hortenso—but now I trusted myself, my instincts. And this, after all, was what really mattered.

But more than this new self-confidence was this feeling I could not quite describe because it was something that had never suffused me before. When I fashioned my first toy gun out of wood, I never thought I would aim and fire a real one at a man and do it without rancor or regret. I should be filled with remorse, but I was not. Instead, this overwhelming, edifying sense of freedom lifted me from the mundane. It had seemed that all my life I was imprisoned and could not break away until I had snuffed my enemy's life. Now I was being lifted to the skies. A joy that had always eluded me filled me to overflowing, bursting in my heart, gushing in my arteries, drenching me with light. I could soar and touch the clouds!

I did not have time to count the money, the thousands I would bring to my brothers. It was rightfully ours. But I was frightened when I got to Dapitan. On the door of the Hortenso apartment was a handwritten sign: FOR RENT. I knocked on the next door. Oh yes, they moved only the other day, but they did not leave a forwarding address. The other occupants had the same reply. I tried to recall what he had told me, that he would get in touch with me at the *kumbento*, but there was no message for me in Tondo. Tia Nena asked if I was hungry, for it was past one, but I was not. There would be no one in Puneta's house till five and they would not miss him till late evening, when they would start looking. I transferred the guns and the money to my tattered canvas bag; it did not look as if it could contain jewelry and all that cash.

Then I went to see Father Jess. Though it was almost Christmas, it was unusually warm. He was in his underwear and his paunch, big as a drum, drooped on his lap. He looked up from his typewriter, sweat glistening on his brow. His face, as with all those who are in deep thought when interrupted, was blank.

"Yes, Pepe," he said finally. "It must be very important for you to interrupt me like this."

"I want to confess, Father," I said.

"You know I am not dogmatic about it."

"I killed a man," I said.

Father Jess drew back and stood his full height, all six feet of him, all fat and paunch and greasy face and yellow buckteeth. The eyes that were always filled with laughter suddenly grew reptilian cold.

"You are not making up another story," he asked, half-expecting perhaps that what I told him was not true.

"I am speaking the truth," I said, unwavering before the eyes that were probing into me. "I killed a man. I drew the gun and pointed it, straight at his chest, then fired. He looked very surprised as he fell in front of me—you know, like a drunk. There was not much blood. I thought it would splatter all over the place."

"He is dead then?"

"As dead as anyone in the cemetery."

"Do I know him?"

"Yes, of course."

"God, do not make it difficult. Do not tell me things like this."

"It was difficult for me, too," I said. "But now that it is over, I knew it had to be done. From the very beginning, although I was not so sure then."

"And who—"

I did not let him finish. "Who else but Juan Puneta?"

Father Jess sank on his seat shaking his head. "No, Pepe; this is not so. This cannot be. I don't believe it!"

"It will be in the newspapers in the morning. You can go to his house right now."

Father Jess shook his head again. The fact had settled fully. "Did anyone see you?"

"I did it in the firing range under his house. All the maids were out. No one was there except us."

"Not even his wife and children?"

"I think he purposely sent them away. He wanted me alone with him."

"But why?"

"Father! Did you not know? He was *syoki*. He was propositioning me, I could perhaps earn a lot, letting those *syokis* and dressmakers— But I vomit just thinking about it."

"That was no reason, Pepe. The world is full of perverts and they ought to be pitied, not condemned. They do not mean harm. They need to be helped. Not stigmatized. Not killed."

"Shit, Father."

"Pepe, I have tried my best to show you the way, to make you forgive . . . and love."

"And that is why I killed him. I love my friends, even this god-forsaken place, and I do not want Puneta misleading us, cheating us, corrupting us!"

"It is not your right to make the final judgment, to condemn him because he is a homosexual."

I faced Father Jess squarely. "It was not a homosexual I killed. I am not opposed to *syokis*. He was a cheat, an exploiter. Yes, Father, I have finally done it. I can now look my enemy in the eye, point the gun at him. I couldn't do this before. I was enjoying his bribery."

"This is the end, Pepe."

"No, Father. The beginning. The beginning! I do not feel guilty at all. A great weight has been lifted from me. It is as if I could fly . . . and I am happy. Can you understand? Happy! I have done it. It was a great test. And I passed. I never felt like this before."

"You will be killing more, and there will be no stopping."

"Father, it is not the killing that makes me light here," I pounded my chest. I could not describe it, this lifting of the spirit, the final liberation, the freedom that we had talked about and sought. "If I should kill, I will without compunction. I am free, Father Jess. Free— as you will never imagine. They can chain me and starve me and beat me. But they cannot harm me anymore. God, how wonderful it feels!"

Then I told him what I heard on the telephone. Puneta may not have pulled the trigger, but it was his money, his orders that did it, and now Toto and Ka Lucio were dead.

"I did it for myself," I said.

"No man has any right to take another man's life. This is basic, this I have always believed."

"Am I guilty then?" I asked.

"Do not let me be the judge. I have, myself, often wanted to kill, to strangle with my hands, but I never had enough courage or hate to do that. I have asked my God, who am I to have such thoughts."

"I do not feel guilty at all."

"Why do you confess then?"

"Not to ask for absolution, but to let you know because you are someone I can confide in and for you to confirm, if you can, that I did no wrong."

"I cannot do that, Pepe. I am mortal, I commit sins, I am filled with remorse. I cannot tell you you are right. What will you do now?"

"In the back of my mind, Father," I told him, "I knew that some-day I would do something that would make me really happy. I did not know it would be this. I thought it would be something"—I had difficulty looking for the words—"something sensual. Something that would satisfy my eyes, my stomach . . ."

Father Jess nodded. "We really never know what we are capable of," he said. "That is the riddle of man, his virtue as well as his damnation."

For some time now, I had wanted to put it to him in its rawest terms, that as a priest, leader of the flock, and Christian, he must infuse his faith with life, see to it that truth is justice not in the abstract but in stone-hard reality that all can see and feel. The only way to achieve this was with the same commitment to violence with which Christ gave Himself to man. "Can you come with me?"

He bowed and was silent; when he spoke again, his words were long in coming, as if they had to be unraveled one by one from the knots into which they had all been tangled. "I asked myself this question long ago, Pepe. And I could explain my staying here by saying I am needed here, or that I am too fat to be running around with boys in the mountains, where I would be an easy target, just like an elephant is an easy target in the densest jungle. I have also told myself, each to his own vocation, that all of us have some contribution to make toward this . . . this revolution that you now seek as one would the Holy Grail. But all these are rationalizations. Yes, the priest who believes in social justice must pursue that belief to its logical action—and here, and now, it is only with violence that it can be brought about. And God, I believe this, and I should go with you. But—" his voice faltered and he turned away, mumbling in his breath, "I am not made of steel. I am human." Then abruptly, "But you must not waste your life. The young are impulsive, they do not think things out carefully and their efforts are often rendered useless."

"It is better than procrastinating, Father," I said.

A scowl spread over his face. "It is not just procrastination, Pepe, or rationalization, or cowardice—remember that. These are true if you are comfortable and you don't want to leave your comforts anymore. It is one of the most corrupting of all feelings. We get used to it."

"I'd like to be comfortable myself," I said.

"If I hold back," Father Jess continued, "it is also because I can see the risks. But more than this, I want to be sure that your blood, my blood, anyone else's blood, is not poured in the desert, and this is often done because there was not enough planning, enough studying of what is to be done, the need for organization that will bring revolution to its successful conclusion. And this is most important: that its gains are made permanent, that revolution need not degenerate into something vicious that we will all abhor. Violence breeds more violence, but if there is enough planning and commitment to ends that are not violent—"

"You are seeking the impossible, Father," I said. "You are *segurista*,* and at times like this, there is nothing sure except our readiness to risk everything."

"It need not be all that risky, if you planned more," Father Jess said. "And the first thing really is organization, a network that reaches everywhere, the farthest village, the highest mountain."

"That is what we are already doing, Father," I said.

"Build some more," he said. "Life is so precious, and you lose it only once."

I WENT DOWN to the room where I had lived for two years, the words of Father Jess like our own posters etched in my mind. Now, in this shabby room, the memory of Toto gripped me; his voice seemed to echo within these musty walls and I could imagine him as he moved about, the glow of his character, the exuberance of his si-

---

* *Segurista:* A crazy person.

lences. These came back as if to prod me on, confirming how right I had been, his redemption.

Yet I have never felt so alone as I do now, and though I could lay claim to the fealty of friends, everyone now seemed distant and far away. I had tried to seek in them—Roger, my classmates, and my comrades in the Brotherhood—those ties that would bind us so that I did not have to think or rationalize what I had done or will do. As one of them, I could withstand the punishment that circumstance would mete out. Where had I slept in the past? Where had I slaked my thirst? Will I always be alone?

I had tried to write down my innermost thoughts, but what I wrote were platitudes. I did this because it was what was expected of me, because what I had to say was like the rosary, and by invoking the heavenly phrases, I had hoped to numb my conscience.

Did I do this because I did not know? Indeed, what could I grow but my hair? Some of us could not even grow beards except a wispy broom like Uncle Ho's, nothing bushy like Fidel's.

I need not be told that it is not easy to go beyond my station no matter how capable I am; in the end, although the rules are not written down, I cannot join them up there unless I am prepared to accept the very same ends to which they have aspired, to bear the same brand or tattoo that marks them off from the common herd. The *tayo-tayo** mentality in the back alleys and the grim confines of Muntinlupa is no different from what prevails in Pobres Park.

It should not be difficult to erode the constructions of sand whereon the mighty are perched. And who am I to attempt this? I would, in all likelihood, be lost or swallowed up, a pebble in a bog, with not even a splash or a ripple. But why should I make this splash? This ripple? Each is a step forward, in the right direction, said Ka Lucio; but why was it not three steps or ten? Those who made them, those behind me, those with me, they failed, I think, because they wanted to be more than men, invulnerable, incapable of venial sin. They failed because, as Ka Lucio said, they were textbook robots who fancied themselves as the sole bringers of light, the infallible harbingers of grace, unswerving and self-righteous. As Kuya Nick said, they are not "in the compass." They lost direction because

---

* *Tayo-tayo:* We-we.

they were bloated with self-importance. If they only knew how to enjoy themselves, if they only knew how it is to love and, therefore, to forgive! I will not be like them, and even if I should die, which I surely will, even in the ennui, in the tawdry futility of it all, I will live as I have always lived, amassing memories.

Leaving this Barrio, then, is not leaving at all; it is an act of being welded deeper, stronger, with all those nameless people of my boyhood, these faceless people here who will live and die without knowing what it is to be alive.

And how about Bing-Bong, Chicken, Tarzan, White Sidewall, and all those demons of the other world that I had glimpsed? Could they be recycled from the junkyard like Roger? It had often come to me like a bad recurrent dream, and it always brought a quiet chill to my heart—my torture, how my flesh and mind were ripped apart. Was there any design to it other than to jar me, to wake me up? They were all creatures of circumstance, but this circumstance can now be changed. It should be changed! And all that pain—it was part of living after all, and it made me know the limits of experience, and the limits are yet to be enlarged.

I lay in my cot and waited for the dark; the shuffle of mah-jongg chips, *Silent Night* on someone's radio disturbed the quiet. I thought of waiting for Lily, to say good-bye to her, but she'd be back close to midnight and would be very tired; she would most probably not understand and would rather hurry to her dreamless sleep. Lily, only twenty but hardened by the Barrio and fallen down the abyss. No, I will not bother her, I will wish her sweet dreams so that in the morning she will wake up fresh and ready again to tackle the hordes at the Colonial. I hoped to God that she would make enough money in five years so that she could quit.

I thought of Betsy, my Betsy, away from all the niggling frustrations that had tormented us. I had lain awake nights after she had gone, remembering those tenuous moments we had shared. At the airport I had tried to keep away, but she had scanned the crowd and seen me behind one of the pillars. She had run to me, away from her friends, and in a final and futile gesture she kissed me, suppressing a sob as she did. "Pepe, thank you for coming!" Then she went back to her parents, her friends, as if nothing had happened, and I fled from them onto the viewing roof, lost in the crowd, and watched her trim figure in yellow go up the ramp, her eyes searching the waving crowds, searching . . .

Her letters had started to come. She wrote every day, but for how long? She wrote of her loneliness, of the ghastly and impersonal city to which she had been exiled, the nondescript course she was taking and how, after the New Year, she would return and go straight to the Barrio, not to the Park. But she would not find me and she would not know where to look.

It had become dark. Around me were familiar things—my small cabinet, the cracked cement floor that was now dry but during the rainy season was wet from the water that seeped in and was ankle-deep, and we had to walk around in rubber boots. How many times had I lain on this wooden cot, my pillow smelling of my sweat, the palm leaf mat scratching against my back where it had frayed, and listened to the sounds of the Barrio, the blare of a jukebox across the yard, the quarrel of couples, the tinkling of an ice cream cart.

The darkness had started to hide everything, the misshapen dwellings of rusting tin, driftwood, and packing crates, the alleys rank with decay. Will there ever be a good roof over my head? I turned to the strip of sky above my window now flecked with stars—how luminous, how eternal the heavens were.

On the shelf beside my bed were my old books from Father Jess, a dozen from Betsy, and at the foot of my bed, propped up by hollow blocks so that the water would not touch them, my clothes. I can count them—five undershirts, five jockey shorts, two denim pants, one khaki and olive green for ROTC, one black double knit, a barong, five shirts, the white in need of stitching where the collar had frayed. They would all fit into the old canvas bag.

I switched on the light and got a sheet of paper from my drawer; the Sheaffer pen I was going to use was Betsy's birthday gift. What can I tell her now? It was after she had gone that it came, a longing for her so intense that the ache was almost physical. Many times in a crowd, although I knew she was far away, a turn of a head, the color of green, a dash of scarf, and all would come back—the coffee shop, that night on the hill overlooking Manila, and here in Tondo. Dear Betsy, I would like to tell you now how much I need you. I have purposely held off writing this to you, and in doing so, I had turned over and over in my mind, all these past few days, why I am here and you are there—so far and so beyond my reach . . .

It had always been that way, and I have always known it,
better perhaps than you ever will. My perception of the world
is different from yours; it is not just a matter of age, or of dif-
ferent geographies. It is just that you are up there and I am
down here.

I do not want to say good-bye again, or to repeat what I
have said, that in these two years you have become a part of
my life, and I feel for you what I feel for myself, these tissues,
this skin. I have grown so familiar with you, the contour of
your body, the smell of your breath, the soft, warm crevices
of your mouth and the whole wonder of you. I know now how
difficult it is to be alone, to be here in this senseless confine
not only of my own being but of this wretched city, and to
know that you are not here where I can glory not just in your
nearness but in the thought that you did love me.

And at night I lie awake, and I speak your name as if it
were some incantation that would dispel this loneliness, for
now I am really alone. I whisper to these cold, rusting walls;
to the damp, cement floor; to the emptiness around me, Betsy,
Betsy . . . but I can only hear the echo within me and so I won-
der how you are, if you are happy as I hope you will be, and
I pray that you be not tormented as I am, that your nights are
slept and your days are bright, and if you remember, may
they be those times that we shared, the coffee shop, the tawdry
rooms and the sheet that was stained with red, the books that
had to be read, and Tondo where I had tasted your sweat; yes,
so many of these now crowd my mind, and they are all crys-
tal clear, pictures, events, places—all of them important only
because we knew them, lived them, and they have become us.

I did not want to write this letter, but it is one way by
which I can escape this bleakness that now encompasses me.
Now, too, I know how it is to be what I am and to remember
what you are, life-giver, my joy and my sorrow.

You will forget, not because you are young, but because
you are far away, and having forgotten, it will all be over
and you may, on some occasion, remember, perhaps, because
this is the way things are and we cannot change them. I don't
know if I will forget; one can never be sure, but I know that

*you are now my wife, not because God or a priest has sanc-
tified our union but because this is how I regard you. Though
I may sleep with other women, I know there will always be
you, separate from all the rest, not just because I feel that you
have given me yourself, or your faith and trust, all of which
I do not deserve, but because I have given myself to you as I
will never give myself to anyone.*

*I will be leaving Tondo now and I wish I knew my final
destination, but I do not. The compulsions that we have
talked about will take me to regions I will not recognize, but
wherever they may be, there will be a light to guide me, a talisman that will make me endure and you are all of these.*

*But above all, you are the proof I will always hold pre-
cious and true. Thank you, dear Betsy, for being with us in
thought and deed. There are a few like you, comfortable and
secure, who have chosen to be with us; I will doubt them in a
way I once doubted you and they must bear the burden of
proving themselves as you have done. Only time will tell and
time, alas, is fickle in a way I will never be, now that I know
who I am, now that I know what to do.*

*So let me go away loving you, and losing you, for, in the
end, we will lose all those we love.*

I merely signed, JS.

I folded the letter, Father Jess would have to mail it for me; he
would also be my only link with Betsy and with all the others whose
lives I have touched and who would, perhaps, surrender themselves
lightheartedly to the end that awaits us.

I unzipped the canvas bag and on top of the guns and the
money I placed my clothes, my pen knife, and a notebook. I would
have many thoughts to jot down and they will not have anything to
do with what I am and what I will be; the past is stored here in my
mind, inviolate, days when I was young, when I marveled at how the
leaves of the acacia trees close at dusk, how it would have been if
there was a father to explain to me why this was so, what was it that
closed the leaves of the *bain-bain* if I as much as breathed into them?
Where could all this wisdom be? I saw *Man's Fate*, which was
Betsy's gift, then Father's *The Ilustrados;* she had told me to read the

last chapter and reluctantly, I sat back, remembering what Professor Hortenso had also said.

"Your father committed suicide," Betsy had told me. "Mama is convinced that what Carmen Villa said is true. That is why Carmen Villa died, too—slowly, insanely."

> *The Filipino elite is flawed because the individuals who comprise it, even though they come from diverse backgrounds, do not really see themselves as leaders of a nation. They see themselves as leaders of factions, of families, of cozy coteries. Their rhetoric will deny, even attack, this assumption—but their deeds will bear their parochial, factional, and, therefore, antinationalistic loyalties.*

"—it is a great book and only a great mind is capable of writing it . . ."

> *The Filipino elite in its present composition is doomed not because of the inexorable march of history, not because the dialectic of change has condemned it. It is doomed because dinosaurs were doomed. But even the last dinosaur, in its death throes, trampled the grass.*

"Why do you hate him? You were young, Pepe; you didn't know. Please give him a chance."

> *The corruption of the* ilustrado *class was accomplished not by bribery from the Spaniards, nor by the high offices that the Americans or the Japanese gave them. Their corruption started when they started believing—with great righteousness and pride—that they were equal to their rulers. By aspiring for equality they became imbued, therefore, with the same values as their masters, values that perpetuated the very injustices they sought to avenge.*
>
> *The* ilustrados—*the intellectuals—should have no role in the revolution, in any revolution. They equivocate, they argue, they procrastinate. Writers and academics who think they have a role in revolution are flattering themselves; what they really want to do is to be part of it, to lead it, without having to raise the sword. Only those with the sword can participate in revolution, for revolution means destruction, not contemplation.*

"Even if he did not see your mother as you said, why did she love him to the end? Why did she ask you to honor and respect him? She would have been the first to hate him—because he married another. . . ."

Revolution can only succeed when men who believe in it can translate their beliefs into a conspiracy—all-embracing in its call for adherents. But to admit into the leadership of the revolution the old elite, no matter how well-intentioned they may be, would be to condemn the revolution to suspicion and even betrayal. A class war is precisely that—a class war. The revolution failed because it did not adhere to this basic requirement; a class is weakened not by the identified enemy but by the unidentified subverter who dilutes and weakens its leadership.

"He had integrity, Pepe. He saw how rotten the system and the people he had joined were; he had to cleanse himself. Carmen Villa was right: his suicide was an act of courage."

Courage, integrity—what frightening words! How many are there who can really carry them without being crushed? They had never really meant much to me, but now I understood not only what they meant but also the horrendous burden they were.

But how does one measure their weight upon the poor? Who can point with an unerring finger to those among us who have borne them?

Instinctively, I remembered Lucy and Lily, and much as I loathed thinking of what they had to go through to live, I knew deep within me that they had acted with courage and fortitude, and I can only curse myself for my incapacity to understand them.

I had been wrapped up in a fine gauze of a dream through which I could neither see nor break away. I had deluded myself without being quite aware, and, thank God, there had been an awakening.

My father's book now seemed clear to me. Reading him now, knowing the people he had to live with, I could imagine how he felt, the dilemmas he had to wrestle with so that the comforts that he knew would not blind him and bind him when, all along, memory kept shunting him back to the Antipolo that we both knew and beyond, Cabugawan, which was the beginning.

Yet it had never really occurred to me, in spite of Betsy's promise and Puneta's clever urgings, to join them no matter how I longed for the ease, the comfort of which their world had a surfeit. No matter how sincere Betsy was, I knew now that I would lose her in spite of herself, and only time would tell how soon. I could easily be lulled into thinking that she would be constant, and she would be, but I belonged to Cabugawan, not to Pobres Park, and as long as I kept that in mind, what happened to Father would never happen to me. But I did not deride him now; I had learned from him. The end that he chose for himself was not an act of pride or of despair. It was courage, which I must surpass if the son is to be better than the father, if the child is to become a man.

I could look now beyond his shoulder, to his father, my grandfather, whom I had never seen though I knew what he had done, what he and the rest whom they called Colorums had wrought in one evening of anger. Now they crowded my thoughts, not wraiths that are formless but living men who are strong, whose voices urge me on. And I believe them because I know where they came from.

And beyond them that great-grandfather, about whom Mother had spoken, who had led his clan from the Ilocos to Rosales. Who else had their blood in me? What had they dreamt of? Pepe Samson then is just a name; I had come from afar and was simply born in a corner of the world called Cabugawan. I was someone, yet no one, for I was no longer living for myself, for this bundle of nerves and flesh; I was part of those who had perished and those who were yet to come. I belonged no longer to this casement of skin, I was part of the earth, the water, the air.

THE DOOR OPENED and in the light Tia Nena, her eyes blinking. "So you are leaving," she said quietly.

"I will miss you, Tia," I said.

She came in and sat on the stool before my small reading table. There was something sprightly about her tonight.

"And you were going to leave without saying good-bye."

"I think it is better that way," I said.

After some silence, "Pepe, do not ask how I found out, but I know what is in your mind. I will soon be leaving, too, to go back to Rosales now that I can look at everything there without fear."

I turned to her, startled at what she had said.

She smiled. "Yes, I know how you feel and you may even tell yourself I am, indeed, a crazy old woman. I had nothing, too, and nothing to look forward to. Padre Jesus does not really need me to cook and do his laundry. But my home is there—the village, the hills."

"No, Tia, do not waste your life. Stay here where at least you can have food when you are hungry. And when you get sick, there will be at least some neighbors who can take you to the hospital."

"Where I will die nonetheless because I am poor."

I did not speak.

"Come to me if you need help," she said. "If you get sick, I will try and nurse you back to health. And if you get hungry, I will beg to feed you."

"And when I die?"

"Then," Tia Nena said with determination, "I will bury you and pray by your grave and put flowers there."

"I am not a patriot, Tia Nena. Please don't make it look as if I am trying to be one."

"You will never get rich," she said.

I was ready. "First, I am going back to Cabugawan, Tia Nena," I said. "That is where I will start."

"The village, that is where Victor started," she said. Her eyes were shining. "My sons, that is where they started, too. Oh, you don't know them. You never knew them. But Rosales is any town, and your village any village. We start where we know best."

I went upstairs to Father Jess. Tia Nena followed me.

"I have a letter for Betsy, Father," I said. "And if Professor Hortenso comes and looks for me, please ask him to leave his address with you. I will be going back to Cabugawan. And Betsy, if she returns, tell her . . ." I could not shape the words. "When it is over, and if I live through it, I will look for her."

Father Jess said, "I will pray for you."

He looked at Tia Nena. "There is no one now in Rosales whom you know. Your place is here."

Tia Nena merely smiled at him.

Father Jess tried again: "You must consider what will happen. You cannot run anymore."

"But I am not running, Padre," she said quickly.

Father Jess was impatient; he dismissed her remark with a wave of his hand. "I know what you are going to say, that you never ran away and you are not running away now. But where you go . . ."

Tia Nena shook her head. "They will not harm me. They cannot harm me. All the hurt was done to me long ago. I am beyond hurting now."

"I do not understand," Father Jess said.

Tia Nena turned to me. "You build a church here," she brought her closed fist to her breast.

"You are using my own words," Father Jess said.

"But they are not yours alone," Tia Nena flattered him. "The truth belongs to all who know it."

"Speeches!" I said. Time to go, and the Tondo I will leave will be brightly lit with Christmas-star lanterns, colored lights strung before windows, boisterous drinking of *cuatro cantos* and San Miguel in the *tiendas,* children with harmonicas and plaintive voices caroling. But the distance that beckoned was dark. I was afraid.

So I leave behind those who see the sword but refuse to raise it. "Bless me, Father," I said nonetheless. "I cannot leave without your blessing."

"I am mortal, Pepe," he said. As he raised his right hand, I dropped to my knees.

He helped me to my feet, and we went down. At the door, he wrapped an arm around my shoulder and hugged me briefly. Tia Nena kissed me on the cheek.

"*Hoy,* you have to cut your hair now," he said as I left them at the *kumbento* door.

I was afraid but I felt very light. I knew I could go very far without tiring.

June 30, 1976
Rue d'Echaude, Paris

AFTERWORD
NOTES ON
THE WRITING OF
A SAGA

I WAS WITH the journalists Johnny Gatbonton and Arnold Moss and my wife the other day at the Emerald on Dewey (now Roxas) Boulevard, when we got to reminiscing, marking out our past. We have known each other from way back in our student days at the University of Santo Tomas. They sometimes come to Padre Faura and we talk shop. I told them of a significant decision in my life, made after I had looked carefully into my own being.

It came in 1960, when I was putting my novel *The Pretenders* into final shape in a village called Marquina, close to the port of Bilbao in the Basque region of Spain.

Rafael Zabala, a young businessman, helped me find cheap lodging in the village which was about half an hour away by car from Bilbao. I met Rafael, or Paeng, as I called him at the Kissinger Seminar at Harvard in 1955 and asked him to help me find a hideaway where I could write. He located a small inn for which I was charged two dollars a day, including meals. I remember my breakfasts—the large pitcher of fresh milk, bread and cheese, and for lunch or dinner, merluza—fish from the Bay of Biscay.

As a journalist, I had closely kept track of our agrarian tensions, the Huk uprising from 1949 to 1953, and much earlier, had researched the Colorum peasant uprising in eastern Pangasinan in 1931. But first, I remembered my own relatives and neighbors in that small barrio where I was born, especially my grandfather, who was a tenant farmer, and how he had participated in the Revolution of 1896. My most memorable moment with that old man was when he took me to the fields beyond our village. It was harvest time, and the fields spread before us, golden with ripening grain. He had carried me on his shoulders, then he had put me down, and with one arm outstretched, he pointed to the near distance, to the land he had claimed from the forest together with his brothers, and spoke of how the land was stolen by the rich *ilustrados* with their new-fangled torrens titles. I remember most of all his crumpled face, the tears streaming down his cheeks, and his admonition: I should study, be literate so that I would not be oppressed.

Working in journalism in the fifties, I sought out Pedro Calosa, who led the Colorum uprising in eastern Pangasinan. Earlier, in 1948, I was drawn to the Huks and met their leader, Luis Taruc, when he came down from the mountains and stayed briefly at the old Quirino house in Dewey Boulevard. I was then on the staff of the Catholic weekly *The Commonweal*. Both had impressed upon me the immensity of the struggle for agrarian justice.

Now, here I was in the Basque, putting together my first novel, *The Pretenders*. I had included in it an old rebel, the father of protagonist Antonio Samson, who was in prison for being a member of the Colorum movement, and had burned the municipio of the fictional town of Rosales (Tayug).

There, far from the Philippines, I thought about the continuing poverty of our peasantry, which I knew firsthand.

In that month in Marquina, I often walked beyond the village to the hillside farms. My afternoons were punctuated by what seemed like the crack of pistol shots. The boys were playing *pelota*, the traditional Basque game that we in Manila call jai-alai. One day, a *pelotari* who had played at the fronton in Manila came in his big Ford—the only Ford in the entire region—and he drove me around the beautiful Basque country, and reminisced about the Philippines, and he made me homesick. I went to the posh resort town of San Sebastian. It was June and pleasant, and for a couple of nights I slept on the beach, the Playa dela Concha, the surf murmuring softly through the night, the laughter of vacationers lolling on the sand reaching out to me, dismembered voices from another world. I also ventured into Guernica, remembering Picasso's famous painting about the doomed town that was leveled by Hitler's planes during the Spanish Civil War.

In these meanderings I brought to mind our own revolution, its betrayal, and the continuing oppression of the Filipino masses, not so much more recently by the colonialists, but by our own mestizo elites. How did we get to be so miserable, so downtrodden? I recalled my grandfather, his careworn face, and slowly—ever so slowly—I came to realize how necessary it was for us to rebel, to overthrow the status quo, the exploiters who claimed they were Filipinos.

I had been taught to believe in the sanctity of democracy, in the use of reason, and the evil that is violence. I had read voraciously *Das Kapital* in college, and was very much impressed by it although I found it difficult reading. But it was not Marxism that made me abandon the idea of peaceful change. It was my knowledge of the poverty in that barrio where I came from and how it was almost impossible for people like us to rise from the dungheap of *internal* colonialism.

It was in that Basque village where I finally and irrevocably accepted revolution. The moment I did, I immediately felt a gladsome lifting of the spirit, as if freed from a damning burden that had weighted me down all my life.

So the main character in *The Pretenders*, Antonio Samson, kills himself. Betrayed, corrupted, his death is for him a measure of redemption.

WHERE DO you get your ideas? What inspires you? These are common enough questions often asked by readers. The imagination, of course, always helps, but the truth is that I write from my own inconsequential life. Like most egoists, I had thought of doing my autobiography but had desisted, for I know that in every story I wrote, I was in it not so much as a peacockish character, but as the fount of most of those thoughts, feelings, and the minutiae of detail and incident, I hope, that gives my fiction some semblance of throbbing reality.

For example, there is my past—our past. In conceptualizing the five-novel Rosales saga in the early fifties, I had planned on writing only four. I had not intended it to cover a hundred years of our history—perhaps, at the most, just three generations.

During the Liberation in 1945, when I was briefly in the American Army as a civilian technician, I read those free paperback editions that GIs casually threw away, among them the novels of William Faulkner. The literary geography that Faulkner created fascinated me, and I decided to try doing the same, that is, using those vivid memories of my boyhood and of my village. Too poor to buy a typewriter in those days, when my colleagues in the *Manila Times* left the office, I used to stay there and work till past midnight, writing the chapters first as short stories so that I could sell them to the weekly magazines to augment my income. As a friend, Austin Coates, said when we talked about my working habits, even if I was good at carpentry, the joints would show. And also: I should not write like this but try to get away from it all so that I could concentrate on my fiction.

Very sound advice, which I valued. Since then, I have tried writing away from my own country. The Rosales novels were mostly written abroad, with the exception of *Tree,* which I wrote in Baguio, in a modest hotel, Vallejo Inn, below the old Pines Hotel which had burned down. Vallejo, built before World War II, was for clerks, and the Pines was for the brass. I wrote *The Pretenders* in a small village in the Basque country, *Mass* in Paris, and the last to be finished, *Po-on,* in Bellagio, Italy. My favorite writing escape is Tokyo. As everyone knows, Tokyo is one of the most expensive cities in the world, but I am very fortunate to know Gaston Petit, a French-Canadian Dominican and a superb artist. His atelier is in Shibuya, just behind the Dominican church. He allows me to stay in the monastery and in his atelier. Half of the year, during the summer months, Father Petit hastens to Champlain in Canada, but when the harsh Canadian winter sets in, he returns to Japan. If his atelier, which I call the Petit Hilton, is not available, Professor Yasushi Kikuchi of Waseda, another old friend, tries to locate inexpensive lodging in his university for me.

My own generation was matured by World War II. In those three years that we were brutalized by the Japanese, we were deprived and hungry, we suffered torture and feared for our lives. War tempered and at the same time ravaged us. When we returned to school in 1945, we were fired with idealism, as young people often are. We aspired to build a free and prosperous nation. Then, through the two decades after college, I saw many of my contemporaries forsake our idealism and our consciences. I found an apt symbol for such an apostasy—the balete tree *(ficus benjamina linn)*—also known as the strangler tree. It starts as a sapling encircled by vines that fatten and eventually become the trunk of the tree itself. In their growth, they choke the young tree they have embraced. It is with such a pervasive sense of futility that I wrote *Tree*, then *My Brother, My Executioner* about the peasant Huk uprising in the early fifties. At that time, at the height of the Hukbalahap (short for Army of the Nation against the Japanese) uprising, the American writer Wallace Stegner visited the Philippines. I attended one of his lectures. Having read the fiction of the period, he said that Filipino writers were not engaged— or *engagée* as the French would call it; he had not seen anything written about that rebellion that had already cost so many lives.

A word about that peasant war. After the American liberation in 1945, the landlords who had fled during the Occupation returned to their haciendas with the blessings of the Americans and the government. The landlords demonized the peasant Huk movement as Communist and began maltreating their tenants as before—the same tenants who had joined the guerrillas fighting the Japanese. Stegner was, of course, correct: there was hardly any literature written on that period. The most moving was not fiction; it was a memoir written by the American Communist William J. Pomeroy, who had joined the Huks. It was this internecine conflict that forms the core of *My Brother, My Executioner*. Don Vicente, the landlord, who appears but briefly in *Tree*, dominates this novel. Finally, I did *The Pretenders*, which ends bleakly in the suicide of the protagonist, Antonio Samson. I intended the novel to end the saga on this note of despair.

Someone asked why. Was death the only solution to our moral conundrum? I intended Samson's demise, however, to be not just a physical death, but also a metaphor: in a revolution, the rotten structure has to be destroyed before reconstruction takes place.

Then in 1972 Marcos declared martial law and some of my contemporaries became his eager acolytes. It was then, too, that so many young people opposed Marcos and took up arms against the dictator and his minions. A glimmer of hope. I started to rethink the suicide of Tony Samson.

There was one young man, Emmanuel Lacaba, to whom I dedicated the latest edition of *Mass*. Eman used to come to my bookshop and we had several quiet talks. He was an excellent poet, like his older brother, Jose, and I published some of his poetry in my journal, *Solidarity*. He was very serious and I did not realize how passionately he felt about the rot afflicting our country. He disappeared, and months later I learned that as a cadre of the revolutionary movement, he had died in Mindanao.

Eman's death was tragic, but an even greater tragedy that has escaped most of us is the death of hundreds of our soldiers, fighting for the same cause—Filipinas. Like the cadres of the revolutionary movement, these soldiers come from the lower classes and are in the army for the simple lack of better alternatives. When can we ever resolve this horrible contradiction and promise a better future for all our young?

I was somehow heartened by the sacrifice Eman and the youth of his generation made. I also realized that they were sorely divided. The more radical fell under the influence of Communism. Although I believe in the necessity of a revolution, its righteousness and perhaps inevitability, I had hoped for a nationalist uprising, not Maoist-inspired. There is so much, after all, in our revolutionary tradition and in the writings of our own heroes of the ambrosial ideas to sustain the young.

I am not and cannot be self-righteous in my assessment of the intellectual subservience under Marcos. Many had refused to sign the appeal that I drafted in 1974, pleading with Marcos to release the writers in prison. Some of those who refused to sign were simply frightened; like most writers, they did not have an economic or social base. They depended on their government jobs and could easily be dismissed by the dictator. I understood this only too well—but what about those who had money? I recalled Virginia Woolf, who said, "Only those with independent means can have independent views." I did not persist with those who refused to sign the appeal.

I couldn't leave after Marcos declared martial law. I received many invitations to go abroad for conferences, writers meetings, and cultural festivals, but the military did not permit me.

After four years of not being allowed to travel, I finally concocted a plan. Having been interested in agrarian reform, I had supported Marcos's land reform program, particularly the first two years of it, when he outlawed tenancy in the rice and corn lands. No president had ever done this. Not even Magsaysay with his vaulting popularity could push such legislation through a landlord-dominated Congress.

An American friend, Robert Tilman, who was a college dean in North Carolina, came to Manila, and I asked him to invite me to a nonexistent conference on agrarian reform in the United States. I was to speak on the Marcos land reform decree, which I wholeheartedly supported. I showed the letter to the press secretary, Francisco Tatad, who endorsed it to the Department of Foreign Affairs. I had known the acting secretary of foreign affairs, Manuel Collantes. It was at his office where I found out why I couldn't leave. A former colleague in journalism, who was then executive secretary, had put me on the black list. I listened to their conversation when Secretary Collantes said he was taking me off the black list on his responsibility.

With my passport back, I went to Paris to attend a cultural conference, after which I decided to stay on for a month to write. I have done my best writing away from the tension and hassle in Manila—in Japan particularly, as noted, where I have enough distance from Manila but am near enough to rush back if necessary. To do the fifth novel in the saga was a compulsion I couldn't ignore, to pay homage to the courageous young people, like Eman Lacaba, who defied Marcos. Antonio Samson had an illegitimate son, Pepe, in *The Pretenders*. I made Pepe the redeemer in *Mass*, the concluding novel in the saga.

Nena Saguil, the painter who had lived most of her years in Paris, found me lodging at the Rue de Echaude, a hundred meters from the church of Saint-Germain-des-Prés on the Left Bank—seven dollars a day—no one would believe it: a tiny, spartan room, without bath, but with a washbowl, a small writing table, and a cot. Close by was the café Deux Maggots, which writers like Hemingway frequented; Jean-Paul Sartre also lived in the area.

I had little money from my small publishing cum bookshop business, which had suffered during the martial law regime.

A public market was below on the sidewalk. For the whole

month of June, I subsisted on bread and apricots, which were in season, till my stomach was sour.

I had never worked as frenziedly as I did then. *Mass* is the only novel I wrote from the beginning to the end in a month of creative spurt. I had to transfer three times from the rooms I occupied: I was disturbing the neighbors. The concierge was very understanding and finally found a corner room on the top floor so that even if I was typing the whole night with my old portable, I would not bother anyone.

When tired, I walked to the Boulevard Saint-Germain-des-Prés, idled on the sidewalk benches, and watched the girls in midsummer shorts. Sometimes I crossed the Seine to the Notre Dame cathedral and looked at the tourists.

Returning to Manila, I polished the novel in four or five drafts, after which I went to New Day. Publisher Gloria Rodriguez, who had included me on her list earlier, read the manuscript and was enthralled by it but flatly told me she couldn't use it: Marcos was mentioned in the novel by name, and she feared the consequences if it came out under her imprint.

I went next to Eggie Apostol, a college classmate and *comadre*. She was putting out *Mr. & Ms.*, a weekly magazine that, even then, was already courageously critical of Marcos. She, too, demurred. There being no publisher, and penniless as I was, I had *Mass* mimeographed and distributed to a few friends as a kind of samizdat.

Somehow, my Dutch publisher, Sjef Theunis, heard about the manuscript and asked to see it. I sent it immediately, and it turned out to be one of those flukes: it first appeared in Dutch. I asked Sjef if he might advance my royalty so I could publish it in the Philippines. With that money, I immediately put it out under my Solidaridad imprint.

Friends were apprehensive. I had been harassed by the Marcos gangsters, but the harassment was nothing compared to what had happened to the others who opposed him, those who were tortured and killed by his thugs. Now, they were specific: Colonel Abadilla, the dreaded hatchetman of the dictator, would get me.

But I knew Marcos was deliberate. In 1965, during the presidential campaign, the Macapagal government banned a movie on Marcos's life and it drew much attention instead.

At the onset of martial law in 1972, he threw Senators Jose W.

Diokno and Ninoy Aquino into prison. After two years, however, he released Diokno but kept Ninoy Aquino in jail. I asked Jose Diokno why he was released. Diokno explained: he was not in a position to really harm Marcos. He could range the world, making speeches condemning Marcos, but the dictator would still remain in power because Diokno did not have the political machine and the following to overthrow him. Ninoy did. Furthermore, Diokno did not aspire to the presidency. Why, then, should he languish in jail?

If Marcos stopped me, he would only draw attention to the book. It must be remembered that he censored newspapers and movies, but he did not censor the stage. I also knew that he believed Filipinos by and large did not read novels.

Years afterward, Alex, my son, who is an executive chef in California, told me that the apricot is the best brain food ever, which perhaps explains why *Mass* sold so well, even in Holland, where it came out in two editions. Since then, *Mass* has become my most translated novel and the one most commented on. A young Dutch teacher came to Manila only because he had read *Mass*. The novel, he said, evoked a vivid sense of place; he asked to see the setting, so I took him to Forbes Park, Manila's ritziest district, then to the massive slum of Tondo, and finally to a sleazy massage parlor in Quezon City.

Another reaction was from a myopic academic who prided himself on being Tondo-born. He dismissed *Mass* as inaccurate, saying that I did not know Tondo. How could I explain that I had known Tondo since before World War II, when I used to visit relatives there? Besides, I had also lived in a poor section in Manila, near Antipolo street in Santa Cruz.

In the late sixties, a nongovernment cooperative, SAKAP, was conceived in my bookshop by Fr. Francis Senden, Angelita Ganzon, Ramon Echevarria, former Justice Jose Feria, Jose Apostol, Tony Enchausti, and several other middle-class do-gooders. SAKAP was to work in the slums and train out-of-school youths for jobs. I elected to work in Barrio Magsaysay in Tondo where I made acquaintances through an American Peace Corps volunteer, Walter Turner. I set up a bindery shop in the slum, enlisting jobless out-of-school young people there as apprentice bookbinders. I got obsolescent equipment from printer friends, like the late Alberto Benipayo, then visited the university and college libraries soliciting bookbinding jobs. I supervised the bindery, working with the Barrio Magsaysay youth and getting to know their families. I even got the services through UNESCO of an Italian binder who worked for a while in the project. At the height of its operation it employed some twenty youths. When I had time, I showed them the sights, from my van. In Makati, at a supermarket, they found the goods there cheaper than in the stores in the Barrio. They were all so awed by the magnificence of the Manila Hotel when I took them there for *merienda*. Why was I doing so much for them? some wondered. Was I going to run for city councillor or for Congressman of the district? If I wanted votes, why did I scold them severely on occasion? Unfortunately, I soon found out that I was giving too much time to the project and neglecting my writing and my little bookshop. I started to withdraw and slowly the project fell apart. They couldn't manage it themselves—the accounting, the quality control, the collections. I asked the experts what had happened, why such a good project, backed up by the best of intentions, did not succeed. It was explained to me simply. Not only did those I left behind have no real training in management—the members of the cooperative, for that was what I intended it to be—they had no real stake, no money in it, to demand their scrutiny and loyalty. It was a stern lesson I will never forget. But with writers, no experience is ever wasted. It is all stored in the mind to be retrieved afterward. That is how I used my intimate Barrio Magsaysay slum background in *Mass*.

Some six years ago, on the occasion of the publication of a collection of my short fiction in Paris, my wife and I visited my old haunt, this time with the help of Philippe Cardenal and a generous grant from the French government. We stayed at the posh Hotel Madison across the boulevard from the church of Saint-Germain-des-Prés. With my translator, Amina Said, and her editor-husband, Ghislain Ripault, my Criterion publisher, Genevieve Perrin, and Quai d'Orsay guide Domnica Melone, we dined in fine watering holes. I revisited my old hotel, the public market below it, and was warmed with nostalgia for that June in 1976 when I wrote *Mass* and subsisted on bread and apricots. I worried that whatever I wrote would not equal *Mass* in its passionate intensity, not having a single bite of that precious fruit on this trip.

I had meant the title *Mass* to represent the Catholic mass, and the *masa*, as in EDSA in 1986. The offertory, the sacrifice—it's all there, and so is the *masa* that should usher our salvation. But, as we can see in the top officials, we had elected our damnation.

Come to think of it, on occasion I miss Marcos; he was there, the epitome of greed and moral depravity. It was so easy to mark him as the enemy who gave us—who despised him—a cause, a reason for being and unity. And listen now to the shameless arrogance of his widow and children. How could we welcome them back?

One thing is sure: Marcos defined with unerring clarity the shattered Filipino intellectual community. He clearly demarcated the line between those who pandered to him, served him, and oppressed their fellow writers, and those who remained steadfast in their integrity. Today, many of those who toadied to him are back in power, befouling media and gloating at having returned like worms that have surfaced from the woodwork. No one among them has come out to say contritely, "mea culpa, maxima mea culpa"—no, they swagger instead like untarnished paragons. This is what ails us all— we do not ostracize them, we do not punish them; we anoint these vermin instead.

How I envy some of my characters, Tia Nena and Ka Lucio in *Mass*, whom I re-created from Rizal's *Sisa* and *Cabesang Tales*, the young and old who acted with great fortitude and courage, who did not compromise as I have done. So here I am on the fringes and yet very much a part of this rotten structure I want to destroy, chained as I am to it by comfort and human frailty.

In writing my novels, I had dreamed of giving my countrymen memory, an iron sense of our heroic past that would exalt and ennoble us so that even in our poverty we could somehow hold our heads high, remembering that greatest of all Filipino writers— Rizal—who was my inspiration.

Forty years ago, in that village in the Basque country where I wrote the first novel in the Rosales saga, memory and my conscience compelled me to accept revolution; with it I also chose the pen as the instrument to help bring justice to my unhappy country.

Every so often, I bring writer friends and some of my students to that barrio where I was born. I show them the creek where as a boy I had swum, the fields where I had helped in the harvest, and my few surviving childhood friends—how shriveled and defeated they look. Through the years, I have seen my barrio become a rural slum. And so, looking around me, at the debris of our youthful dreams, the old man that I have become knows now the futility of words.

ABOUT
THE AUTHOR

F. SIONIL JOSÉ is the author of more than fifteen books—novels, stories, essays, and verse—and is one of the leading literary voices of Asia and the Pacific Rim. He is a publisher of books and of the journal *Solidarity,* a bookseller, a teacher, and a founding member of the PEN Center in the Philippines.

José studied medicine at the University of Santo Tomas, and then the liberal arts, working part-time for the U.S. Army and at newspaper jobs. Afterward, he joined the United States Information Service as an assistant editor and ultimately spent ten years with the *Manila Times.* His writings won three Palanca Awards and three from the National Press Club. In time he won the Ramon Magsaysay Award in Journalism, Literature, and Creative Communications Arts. To date, his work has been published in fifteen countries.

José (called "Frankie") and his wife, Teresita ("Tessie") have four sons and two daughters, most living in California.

A NOTE ON THE TYPE

The principal text of this Modern Library edition
was set in a digitized version of Wilke 55 Roman,
a typeface designed by Martin Wilke in 1988 for Linotype.
Wilke 55 Roman combines elements from a variety of
models, including the typeface Caslon and classical and
late-eighteenth century sources, and even the eighth-century
Book of Kells. The typeface contains virtually no straight
lines; its curves are broad and round, with playful
eccentricities in some of the letterforms and terminals.